# Victims of the Self

## THE CONFORMIST

A government official haunted by a perverse and violent act of his childhood tries to shut out its memory by becoming any face in the crowd. "An outstanding novel. . . . He brings to light the devil in the flesh and in the psyche. . . . Refreshingly adult and virile.
—Charles Rolo, *The Atlantic*

## THE FANCY DRESS PARTY

A beautiful woman plays at juggling lovers until her flamboyant sensuality brings disaster to a complicated and comic weekend party. "Tragicomedy or comic tragedy, *The Fancy Dress Party* is rewarding for the mature, and Moravia writes for no other class of reader."
—*New York Herald Tribune*

## A GHOST AT NOON

A screen-writer who adores his wife finds her love has turned to hate and searches bewilderedly for the cause—even beyond the grave. ". . . rich in substance and resonant with meaning . . . a rare achievement."
—*New York Times*

D1206116

# THREE
# NOVELS

*by Alberto Moravia*

*THE CONFORMIST*
*THE FANCY DRESS PARTY*
*A GHOST AT NOON*

**Translated by**
**Angus Davidson**

*A SIGNET BOOK*

PUBLISHED BY THE NEW AMERICAN LIBRARY

*Published as a SIGNET BOOK*
*By Arrangement with Farrar, Straus and Cudahy, Inc.*

FIRST PRINTING, SEPTEMBER, 1961

*The Conformist, The Fancy Dress Party* and *A Ghost
at Noon* were formerly published as separate Signet books.

SIGNET TRADEMARK REG. U.S. PAT. OFF. AND FOREIGN COUNTRIES
REGISTERED TRADEMARK—MARCA REGISTRADA
HECHO EN CHICAGO, U.S.A.

*SIGNET BOOKS are published by*
*The New American Library of World Literature, Inc.*
*501 Madison Avenue, New York 22, New York*

PRINTED IN THE UNITED STATES OF AMERICA

# ≫≫≫≫≫≫≫≫≫≫ *The Conformist*

## *CHAPTER 1*

Marcello, as a child, was fascinated, magpie-like, by objects. It may have been because his parents, from indifference rather than austerity, had never thought to satisfy his instinct for property; it may have been because other instincts, more profound and still vague, were, in him, masked by avidity: but he was continually assailed by furious longings for the most diverse articles. A pencil with a rubber tip, a picture book, a slingshot, a ruler, a portable ebonite inkpot— any sort of trifle served to rouse his mind to an intense and unreasoning desire for the thing he yearned for, and once it had come into his possession, to an astonished, enchanted, insatiable complacency. At home, Marcello had a room to himself where he slept and did his lessons. Here, all the objects spread about on the table or shut up in drawers had, for him, the quality of things sacred, or just slightly desecrated, according to whether they were recent or old acquisitions. They were not, in fact, objects like other objects in the house, but fragments, rather, of something already experienced or about to be experienced, something that was fraught with passion and uncertainty. He was aware, in his own way, of this singular characteristic that property possesses, and while he derived an ineffable delight from it, at the same time he suffered because of it, as he might have suffered over some fault that was continually repeated and therefore allowed no time for remorse.

Of all objects, however, those that attracted him most strongly, perhaps because they were forbidden, were weapons. Not the sham weapons that little boys play with—tin rifles, revolvers that go off with a pop, daggers made of wood—but real weapons, in which the idea of menace, of danger, of

7

death is not confined to a mere resemblance of shape but is the first and last reason of their existence. With a child's revolver you could play at death without any possibility of actually bringing it about; but with grown-ups' revolvers death was not only possible but imperative, a temptation curbed only by prudence. Marcello had, on occasion, held these real weapons in his hands—a shotgun in the country, his father's old revolver which he had shown him one day in a drawer— and each time he had felt a thrill at the contact, as though in grasping the weapon his hand had at last found its own natural extension.

Marcello had numerous friends among the small boys of the neighborhood, and he very soon realized that his taste for weapons had deeper and obscurer origins than their innocent military infatuations. They would play at soldiers with a pretence of ruthlessness and ferocity, but really their interest in the game was love of the game itself and they aped the postures of cruelty, actor-like, without any real participation of feeling. In him just the opposite occurred, it was his ruthlessness and ferocity that sought an outlet in playing at soldiers, or, when there was no game of that kind, in other pastimes falling in with his taste for destruction and death.

Marcello at that time was remorselessly, shamelessly cruel, in a manner that was perfectly natural, for it was from cruelty that he derived the only pleasures that did not seem to him insipid, and this cruelty was still childish enough to arouse no suspicions either in himself or in others. For instance, he would go out into the garden at the hottest time of day, in this time of early summer. It was a small but overgrown garden where a great number of plants and trees, abandoned for years to their own natural exuberance, grew in complete disorder. Marcello would go to the garden armed with a thin, flexible cane that he had torn from an old, broken clothes-beater he had found in the attic, and he would wander around the gravel paths, now in the cheerful shade of the trees, now in the hot sunshine, examining the plants. He felt his eyes shining, his whole body becoming receptive to a sensation of well-being that seemed to mingle with the general vitality of the exuberant, light-filled garden; he felt happy. But it was an aggressive, cruel happiness, a happiness that was, as it were, desirous of measuring itself by comparison with the unhappiness of others. When he saw, in the middle of a flower bed, a fine clump of marguerites covered with white and yellow flowers, or a tulip with its red cup erect on a green stalk, or a cluster of arums with tall, white fleshy flowers, Marcello would strike a single blow with his cane, making it whistle through the air like a sword. The cane would cut off the flowers and leaves neatly and cleanly and they would fall to the ground beside the plant, leaving the decapitated stalks standing erect. He was conscious, as he did this, of a feeling of redoubled vitality and of the delicious sort of satisfaction that results from an outlet of energy too long suppressed. He felt an indefinable sense of power and of justice. It was as though the plants had been guilty and he had punished them and had at the same time felt that it was in his power to punish them. But he was not entirely ignorant of the forbidden, reprehensible character of this pastime. Every now and then, almost in spite of himself, he would cast furtive glances at the villa, fearful that his mother might be watching him from the drawing-room window, or the cook from the kitchen. And in a confused way he was aware that it was not only the scolding he dreaded, but the mere witnessing of acts which he himself realized to be abnormal and mysteriously imbued with guilt.

The transition from flowers and plants to living creatures was imperceptible, as it is in nature. Marcello could not have said when it was that he discovered that the same pleasure he derived from smashing plants and cutting the heads off flowers could be found, even more intensely and profoundly, by inflicting the same kind of violence on living creatures. It may have been mere chance that encouraged him along this road—a stroke of his cane which, instead of maiming a shrub, smote the back of a lizard lying asleep on a branch; or it may have been incipient boredom and satiety that put into his head the idea of searching for new material on which to exercise his still unconscious cruelty. However that may be, one quiet afternoon when everyone in the house was asleep, Marcello found himself, as though smitten by a lightning flash of remorse and shame, face to face with a slaughtered mass of lizards. There were five or six of them he had managed to hunt out, by various methods, on the branches of trees or the stones of the garden wall, striking them down with a single blow of his cane just at the moment when, becoming suspicious of his motionless presence, they sought to flee for shelter. How he had reached this point he could not have said, or rather he preferred not to remind himself of it; but now it was all over, and nothing remained but the burning sunlight striking impurely upon the bleeding, dust-soiled bodies of the dead lizards. He was standing in front of the cement footpath where the lizards lay, his cane grasped firmly in his fist; and he still felt, all through his body and in his face, the excitement that had filled him during the slaughter—no longer pleasantly glowing, as it had been then, but already becoming tainted with remorse and shame. He was aware, too, that on this occasion there was not only the usual feeling of cruelty and power but an additional, special agitation that was new to him and inexplicably physical; and, as well as shame and remorse, he had a vague feeling of alarm.

He felt as though he had discovered within himself a characteristic that was completely abnormal, a characteristic that he ought to be ashamed of, that he must keep secret so as not to be ashamed of it in front of others as well as in himself, because it might result in cutting him off forever from the society of those his own age. There was no doubt of it, he was different from the boys of his own age, who for their part did not spend their time, either together or by themselves, in pursuits of this kind; and not only different, but different in a most uncompromising manner. For the lizards were dead, of that there could be no doubt; and their death, and the cruel, crazy acts he had performed in order to bring it about, were irreparable. He *was*, in fact, those acts, just as in the past he had been other, entirely innocent and normal acts.

To prove the truth of this new and painful discovery of his own abnormality, Marcello was anxious to compare notes with a little friend of his, Roberto, who lived in the house next door. In the late afternoon Roberto, having finished his lessons, used to come down into the garden, and from then until supper time, by mutual agreement of their families, the two boys used to play together, sometimes in one garden, sometimes in the other. Through all the long, silent afternoon, alone in his room, lying on the bed, Marcello waited impatiently for this moment. His parents had gone out and there was no one in the house except the cook, whom he could hear from time to time humming gently to herself in the kitchen on the ground floor. Usually in the afternoon he worked or played by himself in his own room; but on this day neither work nor play attracted him; he felt incapable of doing anything and at the same time furiously impatient of doing nothing; and he was paralyzed and irritated both by his alarm at the discovery he thought he had made and by his hope that that alarm would be dissipated by his coming meeting with Roberto. If Roberto told him that he, too, often killed lizards and that he liked killing them and saw no harm in killing them, then, it seemed to him, all feelings of abnormality would vanish and he would be able to regard his slaughter of the lizards with indifference, as an incident without significance and without consequences. He could not have said why he attributed so much authority to Roberto; vaguely he thought that if Roberto also did things like that and in the same sort of way and with the same feelings, that meant that everybody did them, and what everybody did was normal or right. These reflections were not very clear in Marcello's mind and they presented themselves more in the guise of feelings and profound impulses than as precise thoughts. But of one fact he felt he was sure: his tranquillity of mind depended on Roberto's answer.

In this state of hope and alarm he waited impatiently for the afternoon to end. He was almost falling asleep when a long, modulated whistle from the garden reached his ears: it was the agreed signal by which Roberto gave notice of his presence. Marcello rose from his bed and without turning on the light went out of the room, down the stairs and out into the garden, in the semidarkness of sunset.

The trees stood motionless and frowning in the dim summer twilight; beneath their branches the shadow was already the darkness of night. The breath of flowers, the smell of dust, waves of heat rising from the sun-soaked earth hung in the still, heavy air. The railings that divided Marcello's garden from Roberto's were completely invisible beneath an enormous blanket of ivy, thick and deep, like a superimposed wall of leaves. Marcello went straight to a corner at the far end of the garden where the ivy and the shadows were thickest, jumped up onto a big stone, and with a single, deliberate movement thrust aside a mass of the creeper. It was he who had invented this little peephole in the foliage of the ivy, and it gave him the feeling of a secret, adventurous game. When he had pushed the ivy aside, he could see the bars of the railings, and between the bars, the delicate, pale face, crowned with fair hair, of his friend Roberto. Marcello stood on tiptoe on the stone and asked, "Nobody's seen us, have they?"

It was the opening formula of this game of theirs. Roberto answered, as though reciting a lesson, "No, nobody. . . ." And then, after a moment, "Have you been working?"

He spoke in a whisper—also part of the agreed procedure. Marcello, also whispering, replied, "No, I haven't done any work this afternoon . . . I didn't feel like it . . . I shall tell my governess I felt ill."

"I wrote out my Italian exercise," Roberto murmured, "and I did one of the arithmetic problems, too . . . I've still got another one to do. Why didn't you do any work?"

This was the question Marcello had been waiting for. "I didn't do any work," he answered, "because I was hunting lizards."

He was hoping that Roberto would say, "Oh really . . . I hunt lizards too sometimes," or something of that kind. But Roberto's face displayed neither complicity nor even curiosity. So he added, with an effort, trying to conceal his own embarrassment, "I killed them all."

Roberto prudently asked, "How many?"

"Seven altogether," replied Marcello. And then, with a forced swagger of a technical, informative kind, he went on: "They were on the branches of the trees and on the stones . . . I waited till they moved and then got them on the wing— with a single stroke of this cane—one stroke each." He made a grimace of satisfaction and showed the cane to Roberto.

He saw the other boy look at it with a curiosity not un-mixed with a kind of wonder. "Why did you kill them?" he asked.

"Well. . . ." He hesitated, and was on the point of saying, "Because I enjoyed it." Then, without knowing why, he forebore, and answered, "Because they do harm . . . Didn't you know that lizards do harm?"

"No," said Roberto, "I didn't know . . . do harm to what?"

"They eat the grapes," said Marcello. "Last year, in the country, they ate up all the grapes on the pergola."

"But there aren't grapes here."

"Besides," he went on, without bothering to take up the objection, "they're vicious. One of them, when it saw me, instead of escaping, came at me with its mouth wide open . . . If I hadn't stopped it in time, it would have jumped right on to me. . . ." He was silent for a moment, and then, in a more confidential way, added, "Haven't you ever killed any?"

Roberto shook his head and answered: "No, never." Then, lowering his eyes, with a grieved look on his face: "I've been told not to hurt animals."

"Who told you?"

"Mummy did."

"People tell you all sorts of things. . . ." said Marcello, getting less and less sure of himself, "but you try, silly . . . I tell you it's fun."

"No, I shan't try."

"Why?"

"Because it's bad."

So there was nothing to be done, thought Marcello, disappointed. A surge of anger rose in him against the friend who, without knowing it, was nailing him down to his own abnormality. He managed to control himself and suggested, "Look, I'm going to have another lizard hunt tomorrow . . . If you come and hunt with me, I'll make you a present of that pack of cards for the 'Merchant at the Fair.'"

He knew that this was a tempting offer to Roberto, who had several times expressed his desire to possess that pack of cards. And indeed Roberto, as if illuminated by a sudden inspiration, replied, "I'll come and hunt with you on one condition: that we catch them alive and put them in a box and then let them go again . . . and you must give me the pack of cards."

"No, no, that won't do," said Marcello, "the best part of the game is knocking them out with this cane . . . I bet *you* couldn't do it."

The other boy said nothing. Marcello went on, "All right, come on, then . . . that's agreed . . . but you must try and find a cane for yourself."

"No," said Roberto obstinately, "I shan't come."

"But why? It's quite new, that pack of cards."

"No, it's no use," said Roberto, "I'm not going to go killing lizards . . . not even if—" he hesitated, trying to think of some object of proportionate value—"not even if you give me your pistol."

Marcello saw there was nothing to be done, and suddenly gave way to the anger which had for some moments been boiling in his breast. "You don't want to because you're a coward," he said, "because you're afraid."

"Afraid? Afraid of what? You make me laugh."

"You're afraid," repeated Marcello angrily, "you're a rabbit . . . just a rabbit." Suddenly he thrust his hand through the railing and seized his friend by the ear. Roberto's ears were prominent and red, and it was not the first time that Marcello had seized hold of them; but never had he done so with such violence and with so clear a desire to hurt. "Confess you're a rabbit."

"No, let me go," the other boy began to cry out, twisting himself about, "Ooh . . . ow."

"Confess you're a rabbit."

"No . . . let me go."

"Confess you're a rabbit."

In his hand Roberto's ear was burning hot and sweaty; tears appeared in the blue eyes of the victim. He stammered out: "Yes, all right, I'm a rabbit"; and Marcello immediately let him go. Roberto jumped down from the railing and ran away, shouting, "I'm not a rabbit. . . . While I was saying it I was thinking: I'm *not* a rabbit . . I fooled you all right." He disappeared, and his voice, tearful and derisive, was lost in the distance, beyond the shrubbery of the adjoining garden.

This conversation left Marcello with a feeling of deep discomfort. Roberto had not only refused him his support but had also denied him the absolution he was seeking and which seemed to him to be bound up with that support. Thus he was thrust back into his abnormality; but not without having first shown Roberto how important it was to him to escape from it, or without having given way—as he perfectly well realized—to both falsehood and violence. And now, to his shame and remorse at having killed the lizards was added the shame and remorse of having lied to Roberto about the reasons that had prompted him to invite his cooperation, and at having betrayed himself by that angry movement, when he had seized hold of him by the ear. To his first feeling of guilt was added a second, and he was unable to rid himself of either.

Now and then, as he reflected bitterly over these things, his memory went back to the slaughter of the lizards, in the hope, almost, that he might find it to be purged of all remorse, to be a simple fact like any other. But he realized at once that what he wanted was that the lizards should not be dead; and at the same time he was conscious again of that physical excitement and agitation he had felt while chasing them—a feeling that now came over him violently and perhaps not altogether unpleasantly, but, for that very reason, with all the more repugnance. It was so strong that he even went so far as to doubt whether, during the following days, he could resist the temptation to repeat the slaughter. This thought terrified him; not merely was he abnormal but, far from being able to suppress his abnormality, he could not even control it. He was at this moment in his own room, sitting at the table with a book in front of him, waiting for supper. He jumped up impetuously, went over to the bed and, throwing himself on his knees on the mat, as he did when saying his prayers, clasped his hands together and said aloud, in a tone of voice that seemed to him sincere, "I swear before God that never again will I touch either flowers or plants or lizards."

Nevertheless the need for absolution that had driven him to seek the support of Roberto still persisted, transformed now into its opposite, into a need for condemnation. Roberto, who could have saved him from remorse by rallying to his side, had not sufficient authority to consolidate the foundation of that remorse and, by a verdict against which there was no appeal, bring order into the confusion that reigned in his mind. He was a boy just like himself, acceptable as an accomplice but inadequate as a judge. But Roberto, in refusing his proposal, had invoked maternal authority in support of his own disgust. It occurred to Marcello to appeal to his mother. She alone could condemn or absolve him and, somehow or other, bring his deed into line with some sort of order. Marcello, who knew his mother, was reasoning from the abstract in taking this decision, which was made in reference to an ideal mother, such as she ought to have been and not such as she was. Actually, he was doubtful of the success of his appeal. But there it was; she was the only mother he had, and besides, his impulse to turn to her was stronger than any doubt.

Marcello waited for the moment when his mother came up to his room to say good night to him, after he had gone to bed. This was one of the few moments when he was able to see her alone: almost always, at meals or during his occasional walks with his parents, his father was present the whole time. Marcello, although he had not, by instinct, much confidence in his mother, loved her and felt for her—even more than love—an admiration of a perplexed and affectionate kind, an admiration such as one might feel for an elder sister of singular habits and capricious character. Marcello's mother, who had married extremely young, had remained morally and physically a mere girl. Furthermore, although she was not on intimate terms with her son, of whom she took very little notice owing to her many social engagements, she had never made any sharp division between her own life and his. Marcello therefore had grown up in a continual tumult of rushings in and out of the house, of clothes being tried on and cast aside, of telephone conversations as interminable as they were frivolous, of tiffs with dressmakers and shopkeepers, of quarrels with the maid, of ceaseless variations of humor for the most futile reasons. He was allowed to go into his mother's room at any time, an inquisitive and ignored spectator of an intimacy in which he had no place. Sometimes his mother, as though shaken out of her inertia by sudden remorse, decided to devote herself to her son and carried him off with her to a dressmaker or a hatshop. On these occasions, compelled to spend long hours sitting on a stool while his mother tried on hats and dresses, Marcello almost regretted her usual tempestous indifference.

That evening, as he saw at once, his mother was in even more of a hurry than usual; in fact, even before Marcello had time to overcome his own shyness, she turned her back upon him and was crossing the darkened room toward the half-open door. But Marcello did not mean to wait another day for the verdict of which he stood in need. Sitting up in bed, he called out loudly, "Mummy!"

She turned back from the doorway, with a gesture of annoyance. "What is it, Marcello?" she asked, and came over to the bed again.

She was standing close to him now, against the light, white and slim in her black low-necked dress. Her delicate, pale face, in its frame of black hair, was in shadow—not so much so, however, as to conceal from Marcello its discontented, fidgety, impatient expression. Carried along by his impulse to speak, he announced, "Mummy, there's something I want to tell you."

"All right, Marcello, but be quick about it . . . Mummy's got to go out, and Daddy's waiting." Meanwhile, her two hands were fumbling at the back of her neck with the clasp of her necklace.

Marcello wanted to tell his mother all about the slaughter of the lizards and ask her if he had done wrong. But his mother's haste caused him to change his mind. Or rather, it caused him to alter the sentence that he had prepared in his mind. It seemed to him all at once that lizards were creatures altogether too small and insignificant to arrest the attention of anyone so preoccupied. There and then, without himself knowing why, he invented a lie to increase the importance of his own crime. He hoped, by the enormity of his guilt, to succeed in stirring his mother's feelings, which he divined, in an obscure manner, to be obtuse and inert. He said, with a sureness that astonished him, "Mummy, I killed the cat."

Just at that moment his mother had at last managed to bring together the two clips of the clasp. With her hands joined at the back of her neck and her chin pressed firmly against her chest, she stared downward and out of impatience beat her heel against the floor. "Oh yes," she said in an uncomprehending voice, as though deprived of all power of attention by the effort she was making. Marcello clinched the matter by saying, in an uncertain tone, "I killed it with my slingshot."

He saw his mother shake her head in annoyance and then remove her hands from her neck, holding in one of them the necklace she had failed to fasten. "This wretched clasp," she burst forth angrily. "Marcello . . . be a good boy and help me with my necklace." She sat down on the bed, slantwise, her back toward the boy, and added impatiently, "But mind you make sure that the clasp catches properly . . . otherwise it'll come undone again."

As she spoke she presented her thin back to him, bare to the waist and white as paper in the light that came in through the door. Her slim hands, with their pointed, scarlet nails, held the necklace loosely at the back of her delicate neck, where the curly hair shadowed it. Marcello told himself that once the necklace was fastened she would listen to him with more patience; leaning forward, he took the two ends and clicked them firmly together in one movement. But his mother immediately rose to her feet, and bending down and kissing him lightly, said, "Thank you. Now go to sleep . . . good night." And, before Marcello could make a motion or a sound to stop her, she had vanished.

It was hot next day, and the sky was overcast. Marcello, having eaten his food in silence between his two silent parents, slipped stealthily from his seat and went out through the French window into the garden. As usual, digestion brought with it a feeling of torpid discomfort mingled with a heightened and pensive sensuality. Walking slowly, almost on tiptoe, on the crunching gravel, in the insect-humming shade of the trees, he went as far as the gate and looked out. There was the well-known street, sloping slightly, bordered on each side by pepper trees of a feathery, almost milky green. The street was deserted at this hour of the day, and strangely dark by reason of the low black clouds that overspread the sky. Opposite he could see glimpses of other gates, other gardens, other homes similar to his own. After having carefully surveyed the street, Marcello left the gate, took his slingshot from his pocket and stepped down to the ground. There were a number of large, white pebbles among the fine gravel. Marcello picked up one of these the size of a nut, inserted it in the leather pouch of his slingshot and started walking along the wall that separated his own garden from Roberto's.

His idea, or rather his feeling, was that he was in a state of war with Roberto and must keep the strictest possible watch over the ivy that covered the dividing wall and, at the slightest movement, open fire—discharge the stone that he was holding tightly in his slingshot. It was a game in which he expressed his bitterness against Roberto for not having been willing to be an accomplice in the lizard slaughter, and the brutal, cruel instinct that had spurred him on to effect the slaughter itself. Marcello knew perfectly well that Roberto, accustomed to sleeping at that time of day, would not be peeping at him from behind the leaves of the ivy; and yet, although he knew it, he acted in a serious and consequential manner, as though he was certain that Roberto really was there. The ivy, ancient and gigantic, reached right up to the very spike-tips of the railings, and its leaves, overlapping each other, big, black and dusty, like folds of lace on the calm bosom of a woman, hung still and limp in the heavy, windless air. Once or twice it seemed to him that a very faint rustle set the foliage quivering—or rather, he pretended to himself that he had seen this quivering and at once, with intense satisfaction, he discharged the stone into the mass of ivy.

The moment he had fired his shot he bent down hastily and picked up another pebble, then resumed his fighting attitude, legs wide apart, arms braced in front of him, slingshot ready to shoot. There was no knowing, Roberto might be behind the foliage, in the act of taking aim at him and with the advantage of being concealed, whereas he was completely exposed. And so, occupied with this game, he came to the bottom of the garden and to the place where he had cut out the peephole in the ivy. Here he stopped, looking carefully at the garden wall. In his imagination the house was a castle, the creeper-hidden railings its fortified walls, and the little opening a dangerous, easily passed breach. And then, suddenly, and this time without any possibility of doubt, he saw the leaves move from right to left, trembling and shaking. Yes, he was sure of it, the leaves were moving, and there must be somebody there to make them move. All in a single moment it occurred to him that it was not Roberto but was only a game, and that, seeing it was a game, he could shoot off his pebble; and at the same time that it *was* Roberto, and that he must not shoot if he did not want to kill him. Then, with sudden, unthinking determination, he stretched the elastic and discharged the stone into the thick of the foliage. Not content with this, he stooped down, inserted another stone in the slingshot with feverish haste, fired it off, seized a third one and fired that off too. By now he had put aside all scruples and fears, and it no longer mattered to him whether Roberto was there or not; his only feeling was one of hilarious, pugnacious excitement. At last, out of breath, having thoroughly riddled the ivy foliage, he dropped the slingshot and scrambled up on to the garden wall. As he had expected and hoped, Roberto was not there. But the bars of the railings were very wide apart, making it possible for him to thrust his head through into the next-door garden. Spurred on by a curiosity he did not understand, he bent forward and looked down.

On Roberto's side of the railings there was no creeper, but a flower bed full of irises running along between the wall and the graveled path. And then, right under his eyes, between the wall and the row of white and purple irises, Marcello saw a large gray cat lying on its side. A crazy terror made him hold his breath when he noticed the unnatural position in which the animal was lying—stretched flat on its side, with its paws extended and relaxed and its muzzle buried in the soil. Its fur, thick and of a bluish-gray color, looked slightly shaggy and ruffled and at the same time lifeless, like the feathers of dead birds he had sometimes seen on the marble slab in the kitchen. Now his terror increased. He jumped down to the ground, pulled up a stake from the rose bed, clambered up again, and thrusting his arm

through the railings, contrived to prod the cat's flank with
the earthy point of the stake. But the cat did not move. All
at once the irises, with their long green stalks and their white
and purple petals curling down round the motionless gray
body, seemed to be the badge of death, like flowers arranged
by some pious hand round a corpse. He threw away the stake
and, without troubling to put back the ivy in its place,
jumped to the ground.

He felt himself a prey to all sorts of terrors and his first
impulse was to run and shut himself up in a cupboard, or a
hidden recess, or anywhere, in fact, where there was darkness
and secrecy, so that he could escape from himself. He was
terrified, in the first place, because he had killed the cat,
and also, perhaps to an even greater degree, because he had
announced this killing to his mother the previous evening—
an unmistakable sign that he was predestined in some mysterious and fatal way to accomplish acts of cruelty and death.
But the terror aroused in him by the cat's death and his own
significant premonition of it was far surpassed by the terror
inspired in him by the idea that, in killing the cat, he had
really intended to kill Roberto. It was by chance alone that
the cat was dead in place of his friend. It was a chance,
however, that was not devoid of meaning; for it could not
be denied that there had been a consistent progression from
the flowers to the lizards, from the lizards to the cat, and
from the cat to the murder of Roberto which he had meditated and desired but not accomplished, but which could
nevertheless be accomplished and was, perhaps, inevitable.
And so he was an abnormal being, he could not help thinking—or rather feeling, with a lively, physical consciousness
of this abnormality—an abnormal being marked out by a
solitary, menacing fate and already launched upon a bloody
course in which no human force could arrest him.

These thoughts whirled frantically round in his head as he
crossed the brief space between the house and the gate,
raising his eyes every now and then to the windows, hoping
to catch sight there of the figure of his thoughtless, frivolous
mother. Now, however, she could no longer do anything for
him, even if she had ever been capable of doing anything.
Then, with a sudden flash of hope, he ran down again to the
bottom of the garden, climbed up on to the wall and looked
through the railings. He almost deceived himself into thinking that he would find the place empty where he had previously seen the dead cat. The cat, however, had not gone
away; it was still there, gray and motionless in the midst of
its funeral wreath of white and purple irises. And the fact of
death was affirmed, with the added, gruesome feeling of a

corpse in decay, by a black line of ants starting from the path and crossing the flower bed till it reached the muzzle, or rather the eyes, of the animal.

He watched and, all of a sudden, like a superimposed vision, it seemed to him that instead of the cat he saw Roberto, that it was he who lay among the irises, that it was he who was dead, that it was from his sightless eyes and his half-open mouth that the ants were coming and going. With a shudder of horror he tore himself away from this ghastly contemplation and jumped down. But this time he took care to pull back the mass of ivy over the peephole. For now, in addition to his remorse and his terror of himself, he began to feel a fear that he might be discovered and punished.

Nevertheless, even while he feared it, he felt that he wanted this discovery and this punishment, if only in order to be stopped in time on the slippery descent at the bottom of which murder seemed to be inevitably awaiting him. Marcello's parents, however, had never punished him, as far as he could remember, not so much because of any educational principle, excluding punishing as—and this he vaguely understood—from sheer indifference. And so, to the misery of suspecting himself of having committed a crime and, moreover, of being capable of committing other, more serious crimes, there was added the further misery of not knowing to whom to turn to get himself punished, and of being ignorant even of what the punishment might be. Marcello realized dimly that the same mechanism that had prompted him to confide his guilt to Roberto in the hope of hearing that it was not a question of guilt but of an ordinary thing that everybody did, was now suggesting to him that he should make the same revelation to his parents in the contrary hope of seeing them exclaim indignantly that he had committed a horrible crime that he must expiate with a suitable penalty. Little did it matter to him that, on the one hand, Roberto's absolution would have encouraged him to act in the precise manner which, on the other, would draw down upon him a severe condemnation. In reality—as he understood—what he wanted in both cases was to escape, at all costs and by any means, from the terrifying isolation of abnormality.

Perhaps he might have made up his mind to confess to his parents that he had killed the cat if he had not had the feeling, that same evening at supper, that they already knew everything. In fact, the moment he sat down at the table he noticed, with a mingled sense of alarm and insecure relief, that his father and mother looked hostile and ill-humored. His mother, with a self-conscious, exaggerated expression of dignity on her childish face, sat upright, with downcast eyes, in an obviously scornful silence. Opposite her, his father displayed similar feelings of ill-humor, by signs which, though different, were no less expressive. Marcello's father, many years older than his wife, often gave his son the disconcerting sensation that he coupled him and his mother together on the same childish, inferior level, as though she were not his mother but his sister. His father was thin, with a lean, furrowed face illumined but rarely by brief bursts of joyless laughter, a face in which there were two noteworthy features that undoubtedly had some intimate connection—an expressionless, almost metallic glint in the protruding eyeballs and a constant twitching of some frenetic nerve beneath the tight-drawn skin of the cheek. Perhaps by reason of the many years he had spent in the army, he had retained a taste for precise gestures, for carefully controlled attitudes. But Marcello knew that, when his father was angry, precision and control became excessive and were transformed into their very opposite, that is, into a curious sort of contained, methodical violence, aimed at charging the simplest movements with significance.

That evening, at table, Marcello noticed at once that his father was sharply emphasizing actions that were habitual and of no importance, as though to call attention to them. For instance, he took up his glass, drank a mouthful and then put it back on the table with a bang; he put out his hand for the saltcellar, helped himself to a pinch of salt and as he put it down there was another bang; he seized the bread, cut off a piece, and again banged it down on the table. Then, as though seized with a sudden craze for symmetry, he tried with the same brusque movements to place his soup plate so that it was exactly framed by the cutlery, the knife, fork and spoon meeting around it at right angles. If Marcello had been less preoccupied with his own guilty feelings, he would easily have realized that these movements, so charged with pregnant, gloomy energy, were directed not at himself but at his mother—who at each loud noise, wrapped herself up, so to speak, in her dignity, with self-satisfied sighs and long-suffering raisings of the eyebrows. But blinded by his own anxiety, he did not doubt that his parents knew everything. Roberto of course, rabbit that he was, had been playing the sneak. Marcello had wanted punishment, but now, seeing his parents so angry, he was possessed by a sudden horror of the violence of which he knew his father to be capable in such circumstances. Just as his mother's manifestations of affection were sporadic, casual, obviously dictated more by remorse than by maternal love, so his father's severities were unexpected, unjustified, excessive; inspired more by a wish to make up for lost time after long periods of inattention than by any educational intention. Without warning, after some complaint from Marcello's mother or the cook, he would remember that he had a son, would start shouting at him, getting into a rage with him and striking him. It was the blows that frightened Marcello more than anything, because his father wore on his little finger a ring with a massive setting which, during these scenes, always happened by some means or other to get turned round towards the palm of his hand, thus adding a more penetrating pain to the humiliating severity of the blow. Marcello suspected that his father turned the ring round on purpose, but he was not sure.

Nervous, frightened, he started with feverish haste to invent a plausible lie: *he* had not killed the cat, it had been Roberto, and the cat was, in fact, in Roberto's garden, and how could he possibly have killed it through the ivy and the garden wall? But he suddenly remembered that he had announced the killing of the cat to his mother the evening before, and it had then happened, in actual fact, the next day; and he saw that no sort of lie would be of any use to him. However vague she might be, his mother had certainly passed on his confession to his father, and the latter, no less certainly, had established the connection between his confession and Roberto's accusations; and so there was no possibility of contradiction. At this thought, passing from one extreme to the other, he had a renewed impulse of longing for punishment, provided it came quickly and was decisive. What kind of punishment? He remembered that Roberto had once spoken of boarding schools as places where parents sent undisciplined boys as a punishment, and he was surprised to find himself violently desiring this sort of penance. It was his unconscious weariness of a family life disorderly and lacking in affection that expressed itself in this desire, causing him not merely to long for something that his parents would consider a punishment, but also inducing him to cheat himself and his own need of that punishment by means of the rather cunning calculations that he would by this method not only allay his remorse but at the same time better his condition. This thought at once brought to his mind pictures that ought to have been disheartening but instead were pleasing to him—an austere, cold-looking, gray building with big barred windows; chilly, bare rooms with rows of beds beneath lofty, white walls; dreary halls filled with benches, with the master's desk at the far end; empty corridors, dark staircases, massive doors, impassable railings—everything, in fact, as in a prison and yet all of it preferable to the capricious, tormenting, unendurable freedom of his own home. Even the idea of wearing a uniform of striped cloth and having his head shaved, like the boys he had sometimes encountered in "crocodiles" in the streets—even this humiliating, almost repulsive idea became pleasing to him in his present desperate hankering after any kind of order and normality.

As these fantastic thoughts passed through his head he was no longer looking at his father but at the dazzling whiteness of the tablecloth, on which, from time to time, some night insect would drop down that had flown in through the open window to dash itself against the lamp shade. Then he raised his eyes and was just in time to see, right behind his father, on the window sill, the outline of a cat. But before he had been able to distinguish its color, the animal jumped down, ran across the dining room and disappeared in the direction of the kitchen. Although he could not be quite sure, his heart swelled with a joyful hope at the thought that it might be the cat he had seen a few hours before, lying motionless amongst the irises in Roberto's garden. And he was pleased at this hopeful feeling—a sign that, after all, the creature's life meant more to him than his own fate. "The cat!" he exclaimed loudly. And then, throwing down his napkin on the table and stretching out one leg at the side of his chair, he added, "Daddy, I've finished, can I get down?"

"You stay in your place," said his father in a menacing tone.

Marcello ventured nervously, "But the cat's alive. . . ."

"I've already told you to stay in your place," his father repeated decisively. And then, as though Marcello's speaking had broken the long silence for him too, he turned toward his wife and said, "Well, say something then . . . speak!"

"I've nothing to say," she answered with ostentatious dignity, her eyelids lowered, scorn on her lips. She was in evening dress, in a low-necked black gown, and Marcello noticed that she was holding tightly in her thin fingers a small handkerchief that she raised frequently to her nose, while with the other hand she kept seizing a piece of bread and then dropping it on to the table again but not with her fingers; merely with the points of her nails, like a bird.

"But say what you have to say . . . speak, for goodness' sake."

"To you I've nothing to say."

Only now did Marcello begin to understand that it was not the killing of the cat that had caused his parents' ill humor. And then everything seemed to come to a head. His father repeated once again, "Speak, for God's sake"; his mother's only reply was a shrug of the shoulders, and then his father seized the wine glass that stood beside his plate and, shouting in a loud voice, "Will you speak or will you not?" smashed it down on the table. The glass broke, his father, with a curse, raised his cut hand to his mouth, his mother rose in fright from the table and went hastily toward the door. His father was sucking the blood from his hand almost with enjoyment, arching his eyebrows above his hand as he held it to his mouth; but on seeing his wife going away, he stopped sucking and shouted at her, "I forbid you to go away . . . d'you understand?" The only answer was a tempestuous slamming of the door. His father rose from the table and rushed in the same direction. Excited by the violence of the scene, Marcello followed him.

His father had already started up the stairs, his hand on the banister, without any further bluster or, apparently, any hurry. Marcello, coming behind him, saw that he was mounting the steps two at a time, almost as though he were flying silently towards the landing above—just like, Marcello thought, just like some ogre in a fairy tale wearing the seven-league boots; and he did not for a moment doubt that this calculated, menacing ascent would get the better of the disorderly haste of his mother who, a little higher up, was scurrying up the stairs, one at a time, her legs hampered by her narrow skirt.

"Now he's going to kill her," he thought, as he followed his father. When she reached the landing his mother ran the short distance to her room, but not fast enough to prevent her husband pushing his way in behind her through the half-closed door. All this Marcello saw as he climbed up the stairs with his short, childish legs that allowed him neither to run up two steps at a time, like his father, nor to skip hastily up like his mother. As he arrived at the landing, he noticed the clatter of the pursuit had been succeeded, strangely, by a sudden silence. The door of his mother's room had been left open. Marcello, rather hesitantly, went forward and looked in.

At first all he could see was the two big, diaphanous window curtains at the other end of the almost dark room, one on each side of the wide, low bed; these curtains were streaming into the room on a strong draft, borne up and up toward the ceiling until they almost touched the lamp hanging in the middle. Silent, glimmering white in mid-air in the dark room, they gave a feeling of emptiness, as though Marcello's parents, in their swift pursuit, had vanished from sight through the wide-open windows into the summer night. Then, in the streak of light that came through the door from the passage and reached as far as the bed, he saw his parents. Or rather he saw only his father's back, for beneath him his mother was almost invisible except for her hair spread over the pillow and one arm raised toward the head of the bed. This arm and hand were seeking, feverishly, to grasp the bed rail but without success; and in the meantime his father, crushing his wife's body beneath his own, was making movements with his shoulders and hands as if he wanted to strangle her. "He *is* killing her," thought Marcello with conviction, as he stood in the doorway.

He had, at that moment, an unaccustomed sensation of cruel, pugnacious excitement and at the same time a strong desire to intervene in the struggle—though whether to give a helping hand to his father or to defend his mother he did not know. Simultaneously he saw a ray of hope that his own crime might be wiped out by means of this other, far graver crime, for what was the killing of a cat, compared with the killing of a woman? But at the very moment when, overcoming a final hesitation, he started forward from the door, fascinated and full of violent feelings, his mother's voice, in a tone that was far from strangled—that was, indeed, almost caressing—murmured gently, "Let me go"; and in direct contradiction to this request, the arm which she had been holding up in her attempt to catch hold of the bed rail moved downward and encircled her husband's neck. Astonished, almost disappointed, Marcello retreated and went out again into the passage.

Very quietly, taking care to make no noise on the stairs, he went down to the ground floor and into the kitchen. Now again he was pricked by curiosity to know whether the cat that had jumped down from the dining-room window was the one he feared he had killed. When he pushed open the kitchen door, a quiet domestic scene was visible—the elderly cook and the young maid sitting together eating at the marble-topped table that stood between the electric stove and the refrigerator, in the white-painted room. And on the floor underneath the window was the cat, its pink tongue busy lapping milk from a bowl. But—as he at once saw, to his disappointment—it was not the gray cat, it was a tabby, and entirely different.

Not knowing how to justify his presence in the kitchen, he went over to the cat, stooped down and stroked its back. The cat, without interrupting its milk-lapping, began to purr. The cook, rising, went and closed the door. Then she opened the refrigerator, took out a plate with a slice of pudding on it, put it on the table, and drawing up a chair, said to Marcello, "Would you like a piece of last night's pudding? I put it aside specially for you." Marcello, without a word, left the cat, sat down and started eating the pudding.

"Well, there are some things I can't understand," said the maid. "They have so much time all day long, and plenty of room in the house, and yet they have to start quarreling at the table, with the boy there."

The cook replied, in a sentententious tone of voice: "If you don't want to look after children, it's better not to bring them into the world."

"Why," observed the maid after a short silence, "why, he's old enough to be her father . . . Of course they can't get on together."

"If *that* was all. . . ." said the cook, with a meaning glance in the direction of Marcello.

"Besides," continued the maid, "if you ask me, that man isn't normal."

At this word Marcello pricked up his ears, though he still went on slowly eating the pudding. "And *she* thinks just the same as me," pursued the maid. "D'you know that she said to me the other night when I was helping her undress? 'Giacomina, one of these days my husband'll kill me' . . . And I answered: 'But, ma'am, why don't you leave him then? . . . and she. . . .'"

"Sh. . . ." the cook interrupted her, with a nod at Marcello. The maid understood and asked Marcello, "Where are Daddy and Mummy?"

"Upstairs in the bedroom," answered Marcello. And then, as though urged by some irresistible impulse, "It's quite true that Daddy isn't normal. D'you know what he did?"

"No, what?"

"He killed a cat," said Marcello.

"A cat? And how did he do that?"

"With my slingshot . . . I saw him in the garden, following a gray cat that was walking along the wall. Then he took a stone and shot at the cat and hit it in the eye. . . . The cat fell into Roberto's garden and then I went to have a look and I saw that it was dead." As he spoke, he became increasingly vehement, but without ever losing the tone of voice of the innocent person who tells, with candid, unknowing ingenuousness, of some misdeed at which he has been present.

"Fancy that!" said the maid, clasping her hands together, "a cat . . . and a man of that age, a gentleman, taking his son's slingshot and killing a cat! You don't have to tell me he's abnormal."

"A man who's unkind to animals is unkind to humans too," said the cook. "You begin by killing a cat and you end by killing a man."

"Why?" asked Marcello suddenly, raising his eyes from his plate.

"That's what they say," answered the cook, stroking his hair. "But you know," she went on, turning to the maid, "it's not always true . . . That man who killed all those people at Pistoia . . . I read about it in the paper . . . d'you know what he does now, in prison? He keeps a canary."

The pudding was finished. Marcello rose and went out of the kitchen.

## C H A P T E R  2

During the summer at the seaside, Marcello's dread of what fate held in store for him—so simply expressed by the cook when she said, "You begin by killing a cat and you end by killing a man"—faded graduallly from his mind. He still thought often of that inscrutable, pitiless mechanism in which his life seemed, for some days, to have become entangled, but he thought of it with a steadily diminishing fear, and more as an alarm signal than as the verdict without appeal that for some time had terrified him. The days passed happily, with their burning sunshine and their intoxicating saltiness, with their variety of amusements and discoveries; and Marcello, each day that passed, felt that he had won some kind of victory, not so much over himself—since he had never been conscious of guilt of a deliberate, direct kind—as over that obscure, malevolent, cunning, external force, darkly tinged with doom and misfortune, that had led him on, almost against his will, from destruction of the flowers to the slaughter of the lizards and thence to the attempt to kill Roberto. He felt this force to be ever-present and menacing though no longer crushing; but—as sometimes happens in nightmares when, terrified by the presence of a monster, you think you can fool it by pretending to be asleep, whereas of course the whole thing is a dream and you really are asleep—so it seemed to him that, since he could not free himself once and for all from the threat of this force, the best plan was to lull it to sleep by feigning a carefree forgetfulness he was still far from having attained.

It was one of the most unrestrained, if not the happiest, of Marcello's summer holidays, and it was certainly the last of his life in which he was a child without any distaste for childishness or any desire to escape from it. His heedlessness was partly due to the natural inclination of his age, but partly due also to his wish to escape at all costs from the evil circle of foreboding and doom. Marcello was not aware of it, but the impulse that drove him to hurl himself into the sea ten times a morning, to compete in boisterousness with the most boisterous of his playfellows, to row for hours on the scorching sea, in fact to do all the things that are done at seaside places with a kind of exaggerated enthusiasm, was exactly the same impulse that had driven him to try and make Roberto his accomplice after the slaughter of the lizards and to seek to get himself punished by his parents after the death of the cat. It was a desire for normality, a wish to conform to a recognized, general rule; a longing to be like everyone else, inasmuch as to be different meant to be guilty. But the deliberate, artificial quality of his behavior was brought to light, every now and then, by a sudden, painful recollection of the dead cat lying among the white and purple irises in Roberto's garden.

This recollection frightened him, as a debtor is frightened by the memory of his own signature at the bottom of a document acknowledging his debt. It seemed to him that, with that death, he had taken upon himself a vague but terrible obligation from which, sooner or later, he would not be able to extricate himself, even though he were to hide himself under the earth or cross the oceans so that all trace of him was lost. At such moments he consoled himself with the thought that a month, two months, three months had passed; that soon a year, two years, three years would have gone by; that, in fact, the most important things were, not to arouse the monster, and to make the time pass quickly. In any case these attacks of discouragement and fear were rare, and toward the end of summer they ceased altogether. When Marcello went back to Rome, all that he retained of the cat episode and of the other episodes that had preceded it was a hazy, almost imperceptible memory, as of something that he had perhaps experienced, but in another life with which he now had no connection whatsoever except a vague remembrance that was devoid both of responsibility and of consequences.

His forgetfulness was aided, once he had returned home, by the excitement of going to school. Marcello had hitherto had lessons at home, and this was his first year of school. The novelty of his schoolfellows; of the teachers, the classrooms, the schedules—a novelty in which an idea of order and discipline and shared occupations was always discernible, under a variety of aspects—was extremely pleasing to him after the disorder, the lack of rules, the loneliness of his own home. It was rather like the boarding school he had dreamed about that day at the table, but without constraint or servitude, with only its pleasant sides and without those unpleasant ones that made it like a prison.

Marcello very soon realized that he had a profound liking for school life. He enjoyed getting up punctually in the morning, washing and dressing in a hurry, wrapping up his textbooks and exercise-books tightly and neatly in the piece of oilcloth with elastic fastenings, and hurrying off through the streets to the school. He enjoyed rushing into the old school building with a crowd of his schoolfellows, running up the dirty staircases, through the dreary, echoing corridors, and then suddenly slowing down when he came into the classroom among the rows of benches in front of the still unoccupied teacher's desk. He enjoyed above all the ritual of the lessons—the entrance of the teacher, the roll call, the questions, the rivalry with the other boys in giving answers and the victories and defeats in that rivalry, the quiet, impersonal tone of the teacher's voice, the very manner, so eloquent in itself, in which the classroom was arranged, with the rows of boys, all sharing the same need to learn, facing the teacher as he instructed them.

Marcello, however, was a mediocre scholar, and in certain subjects he was among the very last in the class. What he loved about school was not so much the lessons as the entirely new mode of life, which suited his tastes much better than the way he had lived hitherto. Again it was normality that attracted him; and all the more in that he discovered it to be not a casual matter nor one that was dependent upon the preferences and natural inclinations of the mind, but a thing pre-established, impartial, indifferent to individual tastes, both limited and upheld by authoritative rules that were all directed toward one single purpose.

But his candor and lack of experience made him awkward and insecure before those other rules, unspoken but existent nevertheless, the rules that concerned the relationships of the boys with each other, outside of school discipline. This too was an aspect of the new normality, but one that was more difficult to master. He was made aware of it the first time he was called up to the desk to show his written exercise. When the teacher had taken the exercise-book from him and, having put it in front of him on the desk, was preparing to read it, Marcello, accustomed to the affectionate and familiar relationships he had had with the governesses who had hitherto taught him at home, instead of standing aside on the platform as he waited for the teacher's criticism, placed his arm, in a perfectly natural way, round the latter's shoulders and brought his face close to his, in order to follow him as he read the exercise. The teacher, without showing any surprise, merely removed the hand Marcello had laid on his shoulder and freed himself from his arm; but the whole class burst into noisy laughter in which Marcello seemed to detect a disapproval that was different from that of the teacher and much less indulgent and understanding. Later, as soon as he had managed to overcome his embarrassment and shame, he realized that his innocent gesture had caused him to fall short of two different standards at the same time—the scholastic standard requiring him to be disciplined and respectful toward his teacher, and the boys' standard requiring him to be crafty and to hide his feelings. And—what was even more curious—these two standards did not contradict, but actually complemented each other in some mysterious way.

Yet, as he at once realized, if it was fairly easy to become a competent scholar in quite a short time, it was much more difficult to become a shrewd, self-possessed schoolboy. This latter transformation was made difficult by his lack of experience, his family habits and even his physical appearance. Marcello had inherited from his mother a perfection of feature almost extravagant in its regularity and charm. His face was round, with brown, delicate cheeks, a small nose, a curving mouth which wore a capricious, rather sullen expression, a pronounced chin and, beneath the fringe of chestnut hair almost entirely covering his brow, eyes which were somewhere between gray and blue, slightly somber, although their expression was innocent and caressing. It was almost the face of a girl; but raw boys would probably not have noticed this had it not been that the charm and beauty of the face were stressed by certain truly feminine characteristics in Marcello that made one wonder whether he might not be a girl dressed up as a boy—an unusual facility for blushing, an irresistible tendency to display his affectionate nature by caressing gestures, a desire to please that was carried even to servility and coquettishness. These qualities were innate in Marcello though he was unconscious of them. When he became aware that they made him ridiculous in the eyes of the other boys, it was already too late. Even if he had been able, if not to eliminate, at least to control them, his reputation as a little girl in trousers was already established.

They teased him almost automatically, as though his feminine character were by now an accepted thing. They would ask him, with pretended seriousness, why in the world he did not sit at the benches where the girls sat, and what was the idea of putting on pants instead of a skirt; or how he spent his time at home, doing needlework or playing with dolls; or why hadn't he had his ears pierced for earrings. Sometimes, underneath the desk where he sat, he would find a piece of cloth and a needle and a ball of wool, put there to show him the kind of work he ought to be engaged in. Sometimes it was a box of face powder. One morning it was actually a pink brassière that one of the boys had stolen from his elder sister. And from the very beginning they had transformed his name into a feminine diminutive and called him Marcellina. These buffooneries provoked a feeling of anger mixed with a kind of flattered complacency in him, as though one part of him were not at all dissatisfied; but he could not have told whether this complacency arose from the character of the buffooneries or from the fact that his companions took notice of him, even if it was only to laugh at him.

One morning when as usual they were whispering behind his back, "Marcellina . . . Marcellina . . . is it true you wear woman's drawers?" he stood up and, having raised his arm for permission to speak, complained in a loud voice, amid the sudden silence of the class, of being called by a woman's name. The teacher, a big, bearded, coarse-looking man, listened to him with a smile that was half hidden by the hairs of his gray beard, and then said, "So they call you by a woman's name, do they? . . . And what is it?"

"Marcellina," said Marcello.

"And you don't like it?"

"No, I don't . . . because I'm a man."

"Come up here," said the teacher. Marcello obeyed and went and stood beside the desk. "Now," went on the teacher in a pleasant voice, "show the class your muscles."

Marcello obediently bent his arm, expanding his muscles. The teacher leant forward in his chair, felt his arm, shook his head in ironical approval, and then, turning to the class said, "As you can see, Clerici is a strong fellow . . . and he's prepared to show he's a man and not a woman . . . Who's going to challenge him?"

A long silence followed. The teacher looked all around the class and then concluded: "Not one . . . well, that's a sign that you're afraid of him. Then you must stop calling him Marcellina." The whole class burst out laughing. Marcello, red in the face, went back to his seat. But from that day on, instead of stopping, the teasing was redoubled, aggravated partly by the fact that Marcello had, as they told him, behaved like a sneak, breaking the unspoken law of solidarity that bound the boys together.

Marcello realized that in order to stop them from teasing him he must give his schoolfellows some proof that he was not as effeminate as he seemed; but he knew instinctively that such proof required something more than a mere showing off of his arm muscles in the way the teacher had made him do. Something more unusual was needed, something that would strike the boys' imaginations and arouse admiration. What?

He could not have said it in so many words, but in a general sense what was needed was some action or some object that would suggest the idea of force, of manliness, if not actually of brutality. He had noticed that they all had a great admiration for a boy called Avanzini because he was the possessor of a pair of big leather boxing gloves. Avanzini, a slight, fair boy, smaller than he and not as strong, did not even know how to use these boxing gloves; yet they had brought him a special sort of consideration. The same sort of admiration was also given to a boy named Pugliese because he knew—or rather claimed to know—a certain Japanese wrestling trick which, according to him, was infallible for putting your opponent on the floor. It was true that Pugliese had never been able to make the trick work, but this did not prevent the boys respecting him in the same way they respected Avanzini. Marcello was aware that as soon as possible he must show himself to be in possession of some object such as the boxing gloves, or must devise some form of prowess such as the Japanese wrestling. He was also aware that he was not so frivolous or amateurish as his companions but belonged, whether he liked it or not, to the breed of those who take life and its obligations seriously; and that, in Avanzini's place, he would have broken the noses of his enemies, and in Pugliese's, would have twisted their necks. The knowledge that he was incapable of being merely rhetorical and superficial inspired in him a vague mistrust of himself; and while he longed to furnish his companions with the proof of strength they appeared to demand from him in exchange for their respect, he was at the same time vaguely frightened of it.

One day he noticed a few of the boys, who were usually among the most determined of his tormentors, confabulating together. He thought he understood from their glances that they were devising some new joke against him. Lesson time, however, passed without incident, though looks and whispers confirmed him in his suspicions. When the class was dismissed Marcello, without looking round, went off toward home. It was early in November, the air was stormy but mild, and in it the last warmth and smell of the now dead summer seemed to mingle with the first, still hesitant harshness of autumn. Marcello felt vaguely excited by this atmosphere of natural decay and devastation; he detected a restless desire for destruction and death very similar to the desire, months before, that had urged him on to decapitate the flowers and kill the lizards. Summer had been a season of stillness, of perfection, of abundance, with clear skies and trees covered with leaves and branches full of birds. It was with delight that he now saw the autumn wind demolishing and tearing to pieces that perfection, that abundance, that stillness, driving dark, ragged clouds across the sky, snatching the leaves from the trees and whirling them on the ground, chasing away the birds that one could see, between leaves and clouds, in black, orderly bands on their migratory flight.

At the turn in the street, he noticed a group of five of his schoolmates following him, and there could be no doubt they were following *him* because two of them lived in the opposite direction; but, engrossed in his autumnal enjoyments, he paid no special attention to them. He was in a hurry now to reach the big avenue planted with plane trees from which a side road led to his home. He knew that on the pavements of this avenue the dead leaves were piled up by thousands, yellow and rustling; and he had a foretaste of the pleasure he would derive from dragging his feet through the piles of leaves, scattering them and enjoying the sound they made. In the meantime, almost for fun, he tried to make his pursuers lose track of him, going now into a doorway and now mixing with the crowd. But every time, as he soon saw, the five boys after a moment's hesitation found him again. The avenue was quite close now; and Marcello was ashamed of being seen amusing himself with the dead leaves. So he decided to face them, and, turning suddenly, asked, "Why are you following me?" One of the five, a fair boy with a sharp face and a close-cropped head, answered promptly, "We're not following you. The street belongs to everybody, doesn't it?" Marcello said nothing and walked on.

Soon he came to the avenue with its two rows of enormous, bare plane trees and the line of many-windowed houses behind the trees, and here were the dead leaves, yellow as gold, scattered over the black asphalt and piled up in the gutters. He could not see the five boys now. Perhaps they had stopped following him and he was alone in the wide avenue with its deserted pavements. Without hurrying, he thrust his feet into the leaves that lay thick on the ground and started walking slowly, enjoying the sensation of plunging up to his knees in the light, shifting mass of rustling foliage. As he stooped to pick up a handful of leaves, intending to throw them up in the air, he heard again the mocking voices, "Marcellina . . . Marcellina . . . show us your drawers." Then there came over him, all at once, a longing to fight, an almost pleasant sensation that lit up his face with pugnacious excitement. He stood up and moved in a determined fashion toward his persecutors, saying, "Will you go away—or won't you?"

Instead of answering, all five of them threw themselves upon him. Marcello had intended to behave rather like the Horatii and the Curiatii in the history books—to take them one at a time, running here and there dealing violent blows at each of them until he compelled them to abandon their undertaking. But he realized at once that this plan was impossible; the five boys had had the foresight to close in tightly upon him, and now one of them had hold of his arms, another his legs and two of them of his body. The fifth, he could see, had in the meantime hastily opened a parcel, and now approached him cautiously with a little girl's blue cotton petticoat dangling from his hands. They were all laughing as they held him, and the one with the petticoat said, "Come on, Marcellina . . . it's no use resisting . . . we're going to put this petticoat on you and then we'll let you go home to Mummy."

This was exactly the kind of joke that Marcello had foreseen—a joke that was, as usual, connected with his insufficiently masculine appearance. Furious, scarlet in the face, he started struggling as hard as he could; but the five of them were too strong for him and, although he succeeded in scratching the face of one of them and in planting a blow in the stomach of another, he felt his own movements were gradually weakening. Finally, as he was moaning, "Let me go . . . let me go," there was a cry of triumph from his tomentors; the petticoat was slipped over his head, and his protests were smothered inside a kind of bag. He went on struggling, but in vain. Skillfully the boys pulled the petticoat down to his waist, and he felt them knotting it at the back. And then, just as they were shouting. "Pull it . . . come on . . . pull it tighter!" he heard a quiet voice asking, in a tone more of curiosity than of reproof, "May one ask what you're doing?"

Immediately the five boys let him go and ran off and he found himself alone again, all untidy and out of breath, with the petticoat tied round his waist. He raised his eyes and saw standing in front of him the man whose voice he had heard. Dressed in a dark-gray uniform with a high, tight collar, pale, lean, with deep-set eyes, a large, melancholy nose, a scornful mouth and hair *en brosse,* he gave an impression at first glance of exaggerated austerity. But when you looked at him again—Marcello observed—you saw he had certain characteristics that had nothing austere about them—quite the contrary, in fact; an anxious, eager look in his eye, a certain softness, almost looseness, in his mouth, a general lack of self-confidence in his whole demeanor. He stooped down and picked up the books Marcello had dropped during his struggles, and as he handed them to him he said, "What were they trying to do to you?"

His voice too, like his face, was severe, but at the same time it was not without a certain strangled gentleness. Marcello, irritated, replied, "They're always playing tricks on me . . . they're a lot of fools." Meanwhile he was trying to undo the knot in the belt of the petticoat.

"Wait a minute," said the man, stooping down and untying it. The petticoat fell to the ground and Marcello stepped out of it, first trampling on it and then kicking it on to a heap of dead leaves. The man asked him, in a timid sort of way, "You were on your way home, were you?"

"Yes," said Marcello, raising his eyes and looking at him.

"Well," said the man, "I'll take you there in my car"; and he pointed to a motorcar standing not far off beside the pavement. Marcello looked; it was a car of a make he did not know, possibly a foreign one, long, black, old-fashioned. It came into his head that this car, standing there a few paces away from them, implied premeditation in the man's apparently casual approach. He hesitated before answering; the man insisted, "Come along . . . before I take you home I'll take you for a nice ride, shall I?"

Marcello wanted to refuse, or rather he felt he ought to refuse. But he did not have time; the man had already taken the bundle of books from him, saying, "I'll carry them," and was walking to the car. He followed, slightly surprised at his own docility but not at all displeased. The man opened the door, made Marcello get into the front, and flung the books onto the back seat. Then he took his place at the wheel, closed the door, put on his gloves and started the engine.

The car moved in a leisurely, majestic fashion, with a subdued humming, down the long tree-lined avenue. It was indeed an old-fashioned car, Marcello thought, but it had been kept in perfect condition, with all its brasswork and nickel fittings lovingly polished and shining. And now the man, holding the wheel with one hand, picked up a peaked cap and put it on his head. The cap emphasized the severity of his appearance, adding an almost military air. Marcello, embarrassed, asked him, "Is it your car?"

"No," said the man without turning his head, at the same time moving his right hand to sound the horn, which had a solemn tone and was just as old-fashioned as the car itself. "No, it's not mine . . . it belongs to my employer . . . I'm the chauffeur."

Marcello said nothing. The man, still without turning his head and driving with detached, elegant precision, went on, "D'you mind my not being the owner? Does it make you ashamed?"

Marcello eagerly protested. "No, of course not . . . Why should it?"

The man gave a faint smile of satisfaction and accelerated. "We'll go up the hill a bit now . . . up on to Monte Mario, shall we?" he said.

"I've never been there," answered Marcello.

"It's fine up there," said the man; "you can see the whole town." He was silent for a moment and then added, very gently, "What's your name?"

"Marcello."

"Yes, of course," said the man, as though talking to himself. "They were calling you Marcellina, those friends of yours . . . My name's Pasquale."

Marcello had hardly time to think that Pasquale was a ridiculous name before the man, as though he had read his thought, added, "But it's a ridiculous name . . . You call me Lino."

The car was now passing through the wide and dirty streets of a working-class quarter, between blocks of dreary tenements. Groups of urchins playing in the middle of the street scampered out of the way, bareheaded women and ragged-looking men on the pavements stared at the unusual spectacle. Marcello lowered his eyes, embarrassed at all this curiosity. "This is il Triofale here," said the man, "but we're just coming to Monte Mario." The car left the poor quarter, coming out, just behind a trolley, into a wide road that wound up the hill between two rows of houses. "What time d'you have to be home?"

"There's lots of time," said Marcello; "we never have lunch before two."

"Who is there at your home? Father and mother?"

"Yes."

"Have you any brothers and sisters?"

"No."

"And what does your father do?"

"He doesn't do anything," replied Marcello rather hesitatingly.

The car overtook the trolley at a turn, and the man, in order to take the curve as sharply as possible, merely pressed down his arms on the steering wheel, not moving his body, with a dexterity that was full of elegance. Then the car, still going uphill, passed alongside high, grassgrown walls, iron gates of villas and hedges of elder trees. Every now and then a doorway decorated with Venetian lanterns or an arch with a crimson-painted sign revealed the presence of some restaurant or rustic inn. Lino asked, "Do your father and mother give you presents?"

"Yes," answered Marcello vaguely. "Sometimes."

"Many or few?"

Marcello did not want to confess how few his presents were, or that sometimes even birthdays and similar occasions went past without any at all. So all he answered was, "Not too bad."

"D'you like getting presents?" asked Lino, opening the dashboard compartment and taking out a yellow cloth, with which he wiped the windshield.

Marcello looked at him. Lino was still looking straight ahead, his body erect, the peak of his cap well down over his eyes. "Yes, I do," said Marcello in a haphazard sort of way.

"What, for instance, would you like as a present?"

This time there could be no doubt about his meaning, and Marcello could not but think that the mysterious Lino, for some reason of his own, really intended to give him a present. He remembered in a flash the great attraction that weapons had for him, and at the same time, with the feeling of making a discovery, he said to himself that the possession of a real weapon would ensure the consideration and respect of his schoolfellows. Rather skeptically, for he was conscious of asking too much, he hazarded: "Well, a revolver, for instance. . . ."

"A revolver?" the man repeated, without showing any surprise. "What sort of revolver? A revolver with cartridges or a compressed air revolver?"

"No," said Marcello boldly; "a real revolver."

"And what would you do with a real revolver?"

Marcello preferred not to give his real reason. "I'd practice shooting at a target," he replied, "until I felt I was a crack shot."

"But why d'you want so much to be a crack shot?"

Marcello thought the man was asking all these questions more to make him talk than from real curiosity. But he answered seriously, "If you're a good shot you can defend yourself against anybody."

The man was silent for a moment. Then he said, "Put your hand in that pocket, there, in the door beside you."

Marcello, his interest aroused, did as he was told and felt, beneath his fingers, the coldness of some metal object. "Pull it out," said the man.

The car swerved suddenly to avoid a dog crossing the road. Marcello pulled out the metal object; it was a revolver, black, flat, laden with destruction and death, its barrel projecting forward as though to spit out the bullets. Almost unwittingly, his fingers trembling with satisfaction, he grasped the butt in his fist. "A revolver like that?" asked Lino.

"Yes," said Marcello.

"Well," said Lino, "if you really want it I'll give you one . . . Not that one; it belongs to the car, but another one just like it."

Marcello said nothing. He felt he was living in a fairytale world, a world quite different from the usual one, in which unknown motorists invited him to go for car rides and presented him with revolvers. Everything seemed to have become extraordinarily easy; but for some reason he could not understand he felt that this quality of easiness, appetizing as it was, might prove on further trial to have an unpleasant taste, as though some hidden difficulty, still unknown but menacing and soon to be revealed, were bound up with it. Probably, he thought quite coolly, each of them sitting there in the car had his own purpose; his was to get possession of a revolver, Lino's to obtain, in exchange for the revolver, something still mysterious and probably disagreeable. It now remained to be seen which of the two would get the best of the bargain. "Where are we going?" he asked.

Lino answered; "We're going to the house where I live . . . to fetch the revolver."

"And where is the house?"

"We're just about there," the man replied, taking the revolver from his hand and putting it in his pocket.

Marcello looked. The car had stopped in a road that looked like an ordinary country road, with trees and elder-bush hedges, and, beyond the hedges, fields and the sky. But a little farther on was an arched gateway with two pillars and a wrought-iron gate painted green. "Wait here," said Lino. He got out and went to the gateway. Marcello watched him as he threw open the two leaves of the gate and then turned back again. He was not tall, although when he was sitting down he looked it; his legs were short in proportion to his body, and he was broad in the hips. Lino got into the car again and drove it through the gateway. A graveled drive came into sight between two rows of small, scraggy cypresses which were being battered and bent by the stormy wind. At the far end of the drive, in a thin ray of sunshine, something glittered incongruously against the background of thundery sky. It was the glass of a veranda projecting from the side of a two-story building. "There's the villa," said Lino, "But there's nobody there."

"Who does it belong to?" asked Marcello.

"It belongs to a lady," said Lino, "an American lady . . . but she's away, at Florence."

The car stopped in front of the house. It was a long, low building, in which expanses of white cement and red brick alternated with the reflecting stripes of window glass, and it had a colonnade of square pillars of undressed stone. Lino opened the door of the car and jumped out, saying, "Come on, let's get out."

Marcello did not know what Lino wanted of him, nor could he succeed in guessing. But the feeling of mistrust was increasing steadily within him, the mistrust of someone who is afraid of being taken in. "How about the revolver?" he asked, without moving.

"It's in there," said Lino rather impatiently, indicating the windows of the villa; "we'll go and fetch it now."

"You're going to give it to me?"

"Yes, of course—a fine new revolver."

Without another word, Marcello got out of the car. He was at once struck by a gust of warm, dust-laden air from the intoxicating, mournful autumnal wind. He did not know why, but that gust of wind brought with it a kind of presentiment, and as he followed Lino he turned to give a last look at the graveled space in front of the house bordered with shrubs and stunted oleanders. Lino walked ahead of him, and he noticed that there was a bulge in the side pocket of his tunic: it was the revolver which he had taken out of his hand as they arrived. Suddenly he was certain that Lino had no other revolver in his possession, and he wondered why on earth he had lied to him and why he was now dragging him into the house. The feeling that he was being deceived grew stronger, and with it the determination to keep his eyes open and not to let himself be deceived. In the meantime they had come into a large sort of lounge hall in which were groups of armchairs and sofas, with a hooded fireplace of red brick in the far wall. Lino, still walking in front of Marcello, went across the room toward a blue-painted door in one corner. Marcello asked anxiously, "Where are we going?"

"We're going to my room," Lino answered lightly, without turning around.

Marcello made up his mind that, as a precaution, he would put up some preliminary resistance, so that Lino should understand that he had seen through his little game. He stayed some distance away when Lino opened the blue door, and said, "Give me the revolver at once or I'll go away."

"But I haven't got the revolver here," replied Lino, turning half around. "It's in my room."

"Yes, you have got it," said Marcello. "It's in your pocket."

"No, that's the one that belongs to the car."

"You haven't got any other one."

A slightly impatient movement on Lino's part was quickly suppressed. Marcello noticed again how the softness of his mouth and the anxious, suffering, imploring look in his eyes contrasted with the rest of his thin, severe face. "I'll give you this one," he said finally; "but come with me . . . what's the matter? . . . we might be seen here by one of the country people—with all these windows. . . ."

"And what's the harm if they do see us?" was the question Marcello would have liked to ask; but he refrained, because he was aware, in some obscure way, that there *was* harm in it, though he could not have defined it. "All right," he said in a childish sort of way; "but you'll give it to me afterward, won't you?"

"Don't worry."

They went into a small, white passage and Lino closed the door. At the other end of the passage there was another blue door. This time Lino did not walk in front of Marcello, but moved to his side and put his arm lightly round his waist. "Are you really so very keen on having your revolver?" he asked.

"Yes," said Marcello, almost incapable of speaking, so embarrassed was he by the man's arm.

Lino removed his arm, opened the door and ushered Marcello into his room. It was a small, white room, long and narrow, with a window at the far end. There was nothing in it but a bed, a table, a cupboard and a couple of chairs. All these pieces of furniture were painted a light green. Marcello noticed an ordinary bronze crucifix hanging on the wall over the head of the bed. On the bedside table lay a thick book, bound in black with red edges, that Marcello judged was a book of devotions. The room, empty of small objects and of clothes, looked extraordinarily clean, but there was a strong smell in the air, like the smell of Eau de Cologne soap. Where had he smelt it before? In the bathroom at home, perhaps, just after his mother had been there in the morning. Lino said to him, in a careless sort of way, "Sit down on the bed, won't you? . . . it's more comfortable"; and he obeyed in silence. Lino was moving around the room now. He took off his cap and put it on the window sill; he unbuttoned his collar and wiped away the sweat from around his neck with a handkerchief. Then he opened the cupboard, took out a big bottle of Eau de Cologne, wet the handkerchief and moved it with relief over his face and his forehead. "Won't you have some too?" he asked Marcello, "it's refreshing."

Marcello would have liked to refuse, for both the bottle and the handkerchief filled him with a kind of disgust. But he allowed Lino to pass the palm of his hand, in a cool caress, over his face. Lino put the Eau de Cologne back in the cupboard and came and sat down on the bed, facing Marcello.

They looked at each other. Lino's thin, austere face had now taken on a new expression, yearning, caressing, imploring. He gazed at Marcello and was silent. Marcello, losing patience— and also to put a stop to this embarrassing contemplation—at last asked, "How about the revolver?"

Lino sighed and pulled the weapon, as though unwillingly, out of his pocket. Marcello put out his hand, but Lino's expression hardened and he withdraw the revolver again, saying hurriedly, "I'll give it to you . . . but you must deserve it first."

Marcello felt almost a relief at these words. So it was as he had thought; Lino wanted something in exchange for the revolver. In an eager, falsely ingenuous tone of voice, as when at school he was swapping pens or marbles, he said, "You say what you want in exchange and then we'll come to an agreement."

He saw Lino lower his eyes and hesitate; then he said slowly, "What would you do to get this revolver?"

He noticed that Lino had avoided his question: so it was not a matter of some object to be exchanged for the revolver but of something that he had to do in order to get it. Although he did not understand what it could be, he said, still in that same falsely ingenuous tone, "I don't know; you must tell me."

There was a moment's silence. "Would you do *anything*?" Lino asked all at once, in a louder voice, grasping Marcello's hand.

Both the tone of voice and gesture alarmed Marcello. He wondered whether by any chance Lino was a thief and was trying to make him into an accomplice. However, after a moment's consideration, he decided that he could reject this possibility. Cautiously, he answered, "What is it you want me to do? Why don't you tell me?"

Lino was playing with his hand now, looking at it, turning it about, squeezing it and then relaxing his pressure. Then, almost roughly, he thrust it away from him and said slowly, looking at him, "I'm sure there are some things you wouldn't do."

"Well, tell me what you mean," Marcello insisted, a sort of good will mingling with his embarrassment.

"No, no," Lino protested.

Marcello noticed that his pale face was tinged with a curious, uneven redness on the cheekbones. It seemed to him that Lino was tempted to speak, but wanted to be sure that he himself wished him to. He then made a gesture of quite conscious, though innocent, coquettishness. He leaned forward, put out his hand and took the man's hand in his, saying, "Come on, tell me; why won't you tell me?"

A long silence followed. Lino looked now at Marcello's hand, now at his smiling face, and appeared to be hesitating. At last he thrust the boy's hand away from him again, but gently this time; then rose and took a few steps about the room. Then he sat down and again took Marcello's hand in an affectionate manner, rather like a father or mother taking the hand of a son. "Marcello," he said, "do you know who I am?"

"No."

"I'm an unfrocked priest," Lino burst out in an afflicted, heart-stricken, piteous voice, "an unfrocked priest, driven out in disgrace from the college where I was teaching . . . And you, in your innocence, don't understand what I could be asking you for in exchange for this revolver that you covet so much . . . And I was tempted to take advantage of your ignorance, your innocence, your childish greed! . . . That's who I am, Marcello." He spoke in a tone of deep sincerity; then turned toward the head of the bed and unexpectedly addressed the crucifix without raising his voice, as if in lamentation: "I have prayed to You so much . . . but You have forsaken me . . . And always, always I fall again . . . Why have You forsaken me?" These words were lost in a sort of murmur as though Lino were speaking to himself. Then he rose from the bed, went over and took up his cap from the window sill, and said to Marcello, "Come along . . . let's go . . . I'll take you home."

Marcello said nothing. He felt stunned and incapable for the moment of assessing what had happened. He followed Lino along the passage and across the hall. Outside, in front of the house, the wind was still blowing around the big black motorcar, beneath a cloudy, sunless sky. Lino got into the car and he sat beside him. The car moved down the drive and went gently out through the archway into the road. For a long time they did not speak. Lino drove as before, his body erect, the peak of his cap down over his eyes, his gloved hands resting on the wheel. They had covered a long stretch of road before Lino, without turning his head, asked, "Are you sorry you didn't get the revolver?"

These words rekindled in Marcello's mind the eager hope

that he might yet possess the coveted object. After all, he persuaded himself, there might still be a chance that all was not lost. He answered with sincerity, "Yes, of course I'm sorry."

"Well then," said Lino, "if I promised to meet you to-morrow at the same time—would you come?"

"Tomorrow's Sunday," said Marcello judiciously, "but Monday would be all right . . . We could meet in the avenue, at the same place."

The other was silent for a moment. Then, suddenly, in a loud and mournful voice, he cried, "Don't speak to me any more . . . don't look at me . . . and if on Monday you see me in the avenue at midday, don't take any notice of me, don't greet me—d'you understand?"

Whatever's wrong with him, Marcello wondered rather angrily. "I don't particularly want to see you," he answered, "it was you who made me go home with you today."

"Yes, but it mustn't happen again . . . never again," said Lino forcibly. "I know myself, and I know for certain that I shall be thinking of you all night . . . and that on Monday I shall be waiting for you in the avenue even if today I make up my mind not to . . . I know myself . . . but you're not to take any notice of me."

Marcello said nothing. Lino went on in the same violent manner: "I shall be thinking about you all night, Marcello . . . and on Monday I shall be at the avenue . . . with the revolver . . . but you're not to take any notice of me." He kept on turning the same phrase round and round and repeating it; and Marcello, with cool, innocent perspicacity, saw that Lino really did want to make an appointment with him and, with the excuse of putting him on his guard, was in fact doing so. Lino, after a moment's silence, asked him again, "Did you hear what I said?"

"Yes."

"What did I say?"

"That you'd be waiting for me at the avenue on Monday."

"That wasn't all I said," replied the other sadly.

"And that," Marcello concluded, "I'm not to take any notice of you."

"That's right," Lino confirmed, "not on any account . . . very likely I shall call out to you, beseech you, follow you in the car . . . promise you everything you want . . . but you're to go straight on and pay no attention to me."

Marcello, losing patience, answered, "All right, all right, I understand."

"But you're only a child," said Lino, passing from violence to a kind of caressing gentleness, "and you won't be able to resist me . . . of course you'll come . . you're just a child, Marcello."

Marcello was offended. "I'm not a child. I'm a boy . . . and anyhow you don't know me."

Lino suddenly stopped the car. They were still on the hill, underneath a high garden wall, and a little further on was the archway, adorned with Venetian lanterns, of a restaurant. Lino turned toward Marcello. "Truly," he said to him with a kind of painful anxiety, "truly you *will* refuse to come with me?"

"But isn't it you yourself," said Marcello, conscious, now, of what he was aiming at, "isn't it you yourself who are asking me to come?"

"Yes, it's true," said Lino despairingly, starting the car again. "Yes, it's true . . . you're right . . . madman that I am, that's just what I'm doing . . . of course I am."

After this exclamation he said no more, and there was silence. The car went down the hill and passed again through the dirty streets of the working-class quarter. Then they reached the big avenue with the tall, pale, leafless plane trees, the heaped-up yellow leaves along the deserted pavements, the high buildings with their rows upon rows of windows. Soon they were in the quarter in which Marcello's home lay. Lino, without turning his head, asked: "Where's the house?"

"You'd better stop here," said Marcello, well aware of the pleasure that this sign of complicity was giving; "otherwise they might see me getting out of the car."

The car stopped. Marcello got out and Lino handed him his packet of books through the window, saying in a decided tone: "Till Monday then, in the avenue, at the same place."

"But I," said Marcello, taking the books, "I'm to pretend not to see you—isn't that so?"

Seeing Lino hesitate, he felt a kind of cruel satisfaction. Lino's eyes, burning intensely in their deep sockets, were brooding over him now with a look of entreaty and anguish. Then he burst out passionately, "Do as you like . . . do just as you like with me." His voice trailed off in a sort of singsong, yearning lament.

"I daresay I shan't even look at you," Marcello warned him for the last time.

Lino made a gesture that Marcello did not understand but which seemed to him to indicate a despairing assent. Then the car drove off, moving slowly away in the direction of the avenue.

# CHAPTER 3

Every morning Marcello was called at a fixed time by the cook, who had a particular affection for him. She would come into the room in the dark, carrying the breakfast tray, and put it down on the marble top of the chest of drawers. Then Marcello would see her taking the cord of the shutter with both hands and pulling it up with two or three jerks of her robust body. She would put the tray on his knees and stand watching him while he ate his breakfast, ready, the moment he had finished, to throw off his bed covers and urge him to get dressed. She herself helped him, handing him his clothes, sometimes kneeling down and tying his shoes. She was a lively, cheerful woman, full of good sense; and she had retained the accent and the affectionate ways of the province where she had been born.

Marcello woke up on Monday with a confused recollection of having heard an uproar of angry voices the evening before, while he was going to sleep—voices coming either from the ground floor or from his parents' bedroom. He waited till he had finished his breakfast and then casually asked the cook, who as usual was standing beside the bed, "What was going on last night?"

The woman looked at him with feigned, exaggerated surprise. "Nothing, as far as I know," she said.

Marcello saw that she had something to tell him: the false surprise, the knowing glint in her eye, her whole attitude showed it plainly. "I heard shouts . . ." he said.

"Ah, the shouting," said the woman; "but that's quite normal . . . Don't you know that your Daddy and Mummy often shout at each other?"

"Yes," said Marcello, "but they were shouting louder than usual."

She smiled and, leaning with both hands on the head of the bed, said, "Anyhow, they must have understood each other better by shouting, don't you think?"

This was one of her little tricks—asking questions that expected no answer, questions that were really statements. Marcello asked, "But what were they shouting about?"

The woman smiled again. "Why do people shout?" she said. "Because they don't agree."

"And why don't they agree?"

"What, those two?" she cried, enjoying the boy's questions. "Oh, for hundreds of reasons . . . why, perhaps because one day your Mummy wants to sleep with the window open and your Daddy doesn't . . . another day, because *he*

wants to go to bed early and *she* wants to sit up late . .
there are always plenty of reasons, aren't there?"

All of a sudden, as though expressing a long-standing
feeling, Marcello said, with gravity and conviction, "I don't
want to stay here any longer."

"What d'you want to do then?" cried the woman, getting more and more jovial. "Why, you're a young boy, you
can't go leaving your home . . . You must wait till you're
grownup."

"I'd much rather," said Marcello, "they'd send me to a
boarding school."

The woman looked at him with tender affection and said,
"You're right . . . anyhow at a boarding school there'd be
someone to look after you . . . D'you know why they were
shouting so, last night?"

"No, why was it?"

"Wait a minute, I'll show you." She moved eagerly to
the door and disappeared. Marcello heard her rushing
downstairs and wondered again what could have been happening the night before. A moment later he heard the cook
coming upstairs again, then she came into the room with an
air of cheerful mystery. She was holding in her hand something that Marcello immediately recognized—a large photograph in a silver frame that usually stood on the piano in the
drawing room. It was an old photograph, taken when Marcello was little more than two years old. It showed Marcello's
mother, dressed in white with her little boy, also in a little
white dress, in her arms. There was a white ribbon in his
long hair. "You see this photograph?" cried the cook gaily.
"Your Mummy, yesterday evening, when she came back from
the theatre, went into the drawing room, and the first thing
she saw, on the piano, was the photograph . . . Poor thing,
she almost fainted . . . Now just have a look and see what
your Dad's done to this photograph."

Marcello, surprised, looked at the photograph. Someone, using the point of a penknife or a bodkin, had pierced
the eyes both of the mother and of the little boy, and then,
with a red pencil, had made a number of little marks underneath the eyes of both of them, as though to indicate tears
of blood gushing from the four holes. The thing was so
strange and unexpected and at the same time so mysteriously
gruesome that for a moment Marcello did not know what to
think. "It was your Dad who did that," cried the cook, "and
your Mummy did quite right to shout at him."

"But why did he do it?"

"It's witchcraft. D'you know what witchcraft is?"

"No."

"When you wish evil to somebody, you do what your Daddy's done . . . Sometimes instead of making a hole through the eyes you do it through the chest . . . through the heart . . . and soon something happens."

"What happens?"

"The person dies . . . or some misfortune happens to him . . . it depends. . . ."

"But," stammered Marcello, "I haven't done Daddy any harm."

"And your Mummy, what harm's *she* done him?" cried the cook indignantly. "But you know what's wrong with your Dad? He's crazy . . . And you know where he'll end up? At Sant' Onofrio, in the asylum . . . And now come along and get dressed; it's time you started for school . . . I'll go and put back this photograph." She ran off gaily, and Marcello was left alone.

Thinking hard, but unable to find any explanation for the incident of the photograph, he went on dressing. He had never had any special feeling for his father, and the latter's hostility, whether real or not, did not pain him; but the cook's words about the harmful powers of witchcraft gave him food for thought. Not that he was superstitious or really believed that you could do harm to someone simply by piercing the eyes of that person's photograph, but this crazy act on his father's part reawakened in him an apprehension he had deceived himself into thinking he had allayed once and for all. It was the frightening, helpless feeling of being caught in a circle of grim fatality that had obsessed him all summer and now, evoked by some malign sympathy, sprang up again in his mind, more powerful than ever, before this photograph with its stain of blood-red tears.

What was misfortune, he said to himself, what was it but a faraway speck of black in the blue of even the serenest sky, a speck that suddenly grows larger, turns into a huge, pitiless bird and dives upon its unfortunate prey like a vulture upon a carcass? Or a trap of which you have been forewarned, which you can clearly see, but into which, nevertheless, you cannot help putting your foot? Or just a curse of clumsiness, of imprudence, of blindness that creeps into your movements, your senses, your blood? This last definition seemed to him the most fitting, as the one that reduced misfortune to a want of grace and a want of grace to an intimate, obscure, inborn, inscrutable fatality—a fatality to which his attention had been again recalled by his father's act, that stood like a signboard at the opening of a sinister road. He knew this fatality implied that he would kill somebody; but what frightened him most was not so much murder as the knowledge that he was predestined to murder, no matter what he did. He was terrified, in effect, by the idea that the very consciousness of such a fatality was simply one more force that impelled him to submit to it—as though instead of consciousness there had been ignorance, but ignorance of a special kind that no one could have considered ignorance least of all himself.

But later, at school, his childish fickleness caused him suddenly to forget these presentiments. He had one of his tormentors for a desk-neighbor, a boy called Turchi, the oldest and at the same time the most ignorant boy in the class. He was the only one who, because he had had some boxing lessons, knew how to use his fists according to the rules: with his hard, angular face and close-cropped hair, his snub nose and thin lips, and the heavy, athletic looking scarf wound round his neck, he already gave the impression of a professional pugilist. Turchi understood nothing of Latin; but when in the midst of a group of boys in the street outside the school, he put up a bony hand to take a minute cigarette-stump from his mouth and, furrowing the many wrinkles in his low forehead with a look of self sufficient authority, declared, "*I* think Colucci's going to win the championship," all the boys were struck dumb, filled with respect for him. Turchi, if required, could demonstrate by taking hold of his nose between two fingers and pulling it to one side, that his nasal septum was broken just like a real boxer's; and it was not only boxing that he engaged in but football and any other popular, violent form of sport. Toward Marcello, Turchi maintained a sarcastic attitude almost solemn in its brutality. It had been he who, two days before, had held Marcello's arms while the other four slipped the petticoat over his head; and Marcello, remembering this believed that this morning he had at last found a means of winning the other boy's scornful, arrogant respect.

Taking advantage of a moment when the geography teacher had turned his back to point with his long stick at the map of Europe, Marcello wrote hastily on a copybook "Today I'm getting a real revolver," and then pushed the copybook towards Turchi. Turchi, in spite of his ignorance was, in his conduct, a model pupil. Always attentive, quiet almost somber in his heavy, expressionless gravity, his inability to answer whenever he was asked even the simplest question astonished Marcello profoundly, and the latter often wondered what on earth he thought about during lessons and why, if he was not doing his work, he pretended to be so industrious. So now, when Turchi saw the copybook, he made an impatient gesture, as much as to say, "Leave me

alone—can't you see I'm listening?" But Marcello persisted,
giving him a shove with his elbow, and then Turchi, without
moving his head, lowered his eyes and read the writing.
Marcello saw him take a pencil and write, "I don't believe
it." Stung to the quick, Marcello hastened to confirm his
former message by writing, "Word of honor." Turchi, mis-
trustful, retorted, "What make is it?" This question disconcerted Marcello; but after a moment's hesitation, he answered,
"A Wilson." He was confusing the name with Weston, a name
which he had in fact heard from Turchi himself, some time
before. Turchi immediately wrote, "Never heard of it." Marcello concluded with, "I'll bring it to school tomorrow," and
then the dialogue came suddenly to an end, for the teacher
turned round and called on Turchi to tell him which was
the biggest river in Germany. As usual Turchi rose to his
feet and, after long consideration, confessed, without embarrassment and with a kind of sporting sincerity, that he
did not know. At that moment the door opened and the
janitor put his head in to announce the end of lesson time.

At all costs, Marcello thought as he hurried through the
streets toward the avenue with the plane trees, at all costs
he must make Lino keep his promise and give him the
revolver. Marcello was aware that Lino would give him the
weapon only if he wanted to, and as he walked he wondered
what was the best line for him to take in order to be certain
of attaining his object. Although he had not divined the real
reason of Lino's odd behaviour, he guessed, with an instinctive, amost feminine coquetry, that the quickest way for him
to get possession of the revolver was the one suggested on
Saturday by Lino himself—to take no notice of Lino, to scorn
his offers, to deny his requests, in short, to make himself as
valuable as possible; and finally to refuse to get into the car
unless he was quite sure that the revolver was his. Why Lino
set so much store by him, and why he himself should be
in a position to carry on this kind of blackmail, Marcello
could not have explained. The same instinct that suggested
to him that he could blackmail Lino gave him a hint of the
presence, in the background of his relations with the chauffeur,
of an unusual type of affection, of a quality as embarrassing
as it was mysterious. But the revolver was the central point
of all his thoughts. Besides, he could not have asserted
honestly that this affection and the almost feminine role
he had to perform were really disagreeable to him. The
only thing he wanted to avoid, he thought as he came out,
hot from running, into the avenue with the plane trees,
was Lino's putting his arm around his waist, as he had
done in the corridor at the villa the first time they had met.

As on Saturday, the weather was stormy and cloudy, with
a mild wind that seemed richly laden with spoils snatched
up all along its turbulent course—dead leaves, pieces of
paper, feathers, bits of fluff, straws and dust. In the avenue,
the wind attacked a pile of dry leaves, lifting numbers of them
high up among the bare branches of the plane trees. His
attention was distracted by watching them fluttering in the air
against the gloomy background of the sky, like myriads of
yellow hands with fingers opened wide; and then, lowering
his eyes, he saw, through all these hands of gold whirling in
the wind, the long, back, shining shape of the car standing beside the pavement. His heart started beating faster, he did not
know why. Faithful to his plan, he did not hasten his step
but walked on steadily toward the vehicle. He passed the
window in a leisurely fashion and at once, as if at a signal,
the door opened and Lino, without his cap, poked his head
out and said, "Marcello, won't you get in?"

He could not help being surprised at this perfectly serious
invitation, after the solemn oaths of their first meeting. So
Lino knew himself well, Marcello reflected, and it was
positively comic to see him do a thing that he himself had
foreseen he would do in spite of every desire to the contrary.
He walked on as though he had not heard, and noticed, with
an obscure satisfaction, that the car had moved and was following him. The pavement was very wide and it was deserted
as far as the eye could reach, between the line of regular,
many-windowed buildings and the big, slanting trunks of the
plane trees.

The car followed him at a walking pace, with a subdued
humming sound caressing to the ear. After about twenty
yards it passed him and stopped a short distance ahead; then
the door opened again. He walked on without turning and
again heard that melting voice imploring him. "Marcello,
jump in . . . please do . . . forget what I said yesterday . . .
Marcello, d'you hear me?" Marcello could not help saying
to himself that the voice was rather repugnant—why should
he moan in that way? It was lucky there was no one going
along the street or he would have been ashamed. Nevertheless, he did not want to discourage the man altogether, and
as he went on past the car he half turned and looked back,
as though inviting him to persevere. He found himself
throwing him a glance almost of encouragement, and
was suddenly and unmistakably aware of the same feeling of
not unpleasant humiliation, of playing a part not entirely unnatural to him, that he had felt for a moment when the boys
had fastened the petticoat round his waist. It was as though
fundamentally he did not dislike acting the part of the coy,

disdainful woman—was, in fact, led on by nature to do so.

Meanwhile the car had started again behind him. Marcello wondered whether the moment had come to yield, and decided, on reflection, that it had not yet arrived. The car passed close to him, not stopping but merely slowing down. He heard the man's voice calling to him, "Marcello . . ." and immediately afterward, the sudden hum of the engine as the car moved forward. He was afraid that Lino had lost patience and was going away; he was assailed by a great fear of having to show himself at school next day empty-handed; and he started running, crying out, "Lino . . . Lino . . . stop, Lino." But the wind carried his words away, scattering them in the air with the dead leaves in a cheerless, noisy squall; the car was growing smaller and smaller in the distance—evidently Lino had not heard and was going away—and he would not get the revolver, and Turchi would start tormenting him again. Then he sighed with relief and walked on at a more or less normal pace. The car had gone on ahead not to avoid him but to wait for him at a crossing; and it had now stopped, blocking the whole width of the pavement.

He felt a kind of annoyance at Lino for having given him this humiliating moment of suspense, and he made an inward decision, in a sudden access of cruelty, to make him pay for it by carefully calculated harshness. Meanwhile, without hurrying, he had reached the crossing. The car was standing there, long, black, all its old brass fittings and antiquated coachwork glistening. Marcello started off as though he were going to walk round it: immediately the door opened and Lino looked out.

"Marcello," he said in a decided but despairing voice. "Forget what I said to you on Saturday . . . You've done your duty now . . . Come on, get in, Marcello."

Marcello had stopped beside the hood of the car. He turned and came back a step and said coldly, without looking at the man, "No, I'm not coming . . . but not because you told me on Saturday not to come . . . just because I don't want to."

"Why don't you want to?"

"Why should I? . . . Why should I get into the car?"

"To please me . . ."

"But I don't want to please you."

"Why? You don't like me?"

"No," said Marcello, lowering his eyes and playing with the handle of the door. He was aware that he had put on a vexed, obstinate, hostile expression, and no longer knew whether he did this as part of the game or in earnest. It was certainly a game that he was playing with Lino, but if it was only a game, why did he have such strong and complicated feelings about it—a mixture of vanity and repugnance, of humiliation and cruelty and contempt? He heard Lino laugh softly and affectionately and ask him, "Why don't you like me?"

This time he raised his eyes and looked him in the face. It was true, Lino was unattractive, he thought; but he had never asked himself why. He looked at his face, almost ascetic in its thin severity, and then he understood why he was not attracted to Lino: it was a double face, a face in which dishonesty had found, positively, a physical expression. It seemed to him as he looked at it that he could detect this dishonesty especially in the mouth—a mouth that at first sight was subtle, thin, contemptuous, chaste, but which, when the lips were parted and turned back in a smile, showed an expanse of glowing mucous membrane that glistened with the water of appetite. He hesitated, looking at Lino who was waiting for his answer with a smile, and then said with sincerity, "I don't like you because you've got a wet mouth."

Lino's smile vanished and his face darkened. "What nonsense are you inventing now?" he said. And then, quickly recovering himself, he added with easy facetiousness: "Well then, does Mister Marcello wish to get into his motorcar?"

"I'll get in," said Marcello, making up his mind at last, "only on one condition."

"And what's that?"

"That you'll really give me the revolver."

"Yes, that's understood . . . Now come on, get in."

"No, you've got to give it to me now, at once," Marcello obstinately insisted.

"But I haven't got it here, Marcello," said the man with sincerity, "it was left in my room on Saturday . . . We'll go to the house now and fetch it."

"Then I'm not coming," Marcello decided in a way that he himself had not expected. "Good-by."

He moved a step forward as if to go away; and this time Lino lost patience. "Come along, don't behave like a child," he exclaimed. Leaning out, he took hold of Marcello by the arm and pulled him into the seat beside him. "Now we'll go straight to the house," he added, "and I promise you, you shall have the revolver." Marcello, secretly delighted to have been compelled to get into the car, made no protest; all he did was to pout childishly. Lino closed the door with alacrity and started the engine; the car moved off.

For a long time they did not speak. Lino did not appear talkative—perhaps, thought Marcello, because he was too pleased to talk; and as for Marcello, he had nothing to say. Now Lino would give him the revolver and then he would go home and next day he would take the revolver to school with him and show it to Turchi. Beyond these simple and pleasing anticipations his mind did not travel. His only fear was that Lino might try in some way to defraud him. In that case, he thought, he would invent some other trick to drive Lino to desperation and force him to keep his promise.

Sitting still, with his package of books on his knee, he watched the great plane trees and the buildings slipping past, until they reached the far end of the avenue. As the car started up the hill, Lino, as though he had been thinking about it for a long time, asked, "Who taught you to be so coquettish, Marcello?"

Marcello, not quite certain of the meaning of the word, hesitated before answering. Lino seemed to become aware of his innocent ignorance, and added, "I mean so clever."

"Why?" asked Marcello.

"Well, never mind."

"It's you who are the clever one," said Marcello; "you promise me the revolver and never give it to me."

Lino laughed and put out his hand and patted Marcello's bare knee. "Yes," he said, "today I'm the clever one." Marcello, embarrassed, moved his knee; but Lino, still keeping his hand on it, added in an exultant tone, "You know, Marcello, I'm so pleased you came today . . . When I think that the other day I was begging you not to take any notice of me and not to come, I realize what a fool one can be sometimes . . . yes, an absolute fool . . . But luckily you had more sense than I did, Marcello."

Marcello said nothing. He did not altogether understand what Lino was saying to him, and besides, the hand resting on his knee irritated him. He tried more than once to move his knee away but the hand still remained. Fortunately at a bend in the road, there was a car coming in the opposite direction. Marcello pretended to be frightened, and exclaimed, "Look out, that car's coming straight at us!"—and this time Lino withdrew his hand to turn the steering-wheel. Marcello breathed again.

They reached the country road with its high walls and hedges, then the archway with its green-painted iron gate, and finally the drive, with its rows of small, scraggy cypresses on each side and the light gleaming on the glass of the veranda at the far end. Marcello noticed that the wind was tormenting the cypresses just as it had the last time, under a dark and stormy sky. The car stopped, Lino jumped out and gave a hand to Marcello, and then they went off together toward the door. Today Lino did not go on ahead but held him tightly by the arm, as though he feared he would try to escape. Marcello wanted to tell him to slacken his grip, but there was no time. Lino seemed almost to be holding him suspended in the air, as if they were flying; and in this way he hurried him through the hall and pushed him into the passage. There, quite unexpectedly, he seized him roughly by the neck, saying, "How stupid you are . . . how stupid . . . why didn't you want to come?"

His voice was no longer jovial, but hoarse and broken, tough with a mechanical sort of tenderness in it. Marcello, surprised, was on the point of raising his eyes to look into Lino's face, but at that moment he received a violent shove from behind. Just as one might thrust away a cat or a dog after seizing it by the back of the neck, so Lino had hurled him into his room. Then Marcello saw him turn the key in the lock, put it in his pocket and turn toward him with an expression of mingled joy and raging triumph. Lino cried in a loud voice, "That's enough now . . . now you've got to do what *I* want . . . that's enough, Marcello, you tyrant, you little beast, that's enough . . . come along, do as you're told and not another word."

These commanding, contemptuous, arrogant expressions were uttered with savage delight, with an almost sensual enjoyment; and Marcello, bewildered as he was, could not but notice that they were words without sense, more like fragments of some triumphal chant than expressions of conscious thought and will. Frightened and astonished, he watched Lino as he strode up and down the room pulling his cap from his head and flinging it on the window sill snatching a shirt that was hanging over a chair, rolling it up in a ball and then shutting it up in a drawer, smoothing the crumpled bedpsread, performing all sorts of practical acts with a frenzy full of obscure significance. Then, still shouting out incoherent phrases of an insolent, peremptory nature, he went over to the wall at the head of the bed, tore down the cruicifix and threw it with pretentious brutality into the cupboard drawer; and Marcello realized that by this gesture Lino intended in some way or other to make it clear that he had swept aside his last scruples. As though to confirm Marcello's fear of this, Lino took the coveted revolver from the drawer of the bedside table and showed it to him, shouting, "You see it? . . . Well, you're not going to have it—never . . . You've got to do what I want without any presents, without any revolvers . . . either for love or by force."

So it was true, thought Marcello; Lino intended to cheat

him, just as he had feared. He felt himself turn white in the face with anger; and he said, "Give me the revolver or I'll go away."

"No, no, there isn't a chance of it . . . either for love or by force." Lino was now brandishing the revolver in one hand; and with the other he seized Marcello by the arm and hurled him on to the bed. Marcello fell in a sitting position, but with such violence that he banged his head against the wall. At once, Lino, passing suddenly from violence to gentleness and from command to entreaty, knelt down in front of him. He put one arm round his legs and laid his other hand, still grasping the weapon, on the bedspread. He groaned and called upon Marcello by name; then, still groaning, flung both arms round his knees. The revolver now lay loose on the bed, black against the white coverlet. Marcello looked at Lino as he knelt there, his suppliant, tear-stained face, burning with desire, now raised toward him and now lowered again and rubbed, like the muzzle of some devoted dog, against his legs. Then he grasped the revolver and, with a violent thrust, rose to his feet. Immediately Lino, thinking possibly that the boy meant to return his embrace, opened his arms and let him go. Marcello took a step into the middle of the room and then turned round.

Later, thinking over what had happened, Marcello could not help recalling that the mere touch of the cold butt of the weapon had aroused in his mind a temptation of the most ruthless and bloodthirsty kind; but at that moment all he was aware of was a violent pain in his head where he had knocked it against the wall, and an acute sense of irritation and repugnance toward Lino. The latter had remained on his knees beside the bed; but when he saw Marcello take a step backward and point the revolver at him, he turned slightly but without getting up, and throwing out his arms with a theatrical gesture, he cried dramatically, "Shoot, Marcello . . . kill me . . . yes, kill me like a dog."

It seemed to Marcello that he had never hated him so much as at that moment, for that repulsive mixture of sensuality and austerity, of repentance and lust; and in a manner that was both terrified and deliberate—just as though he felt he had to comply with the man's request—he pressed the trigger.

The shot resounded with sudden violence in the little room; and he saw Lino fall and then raise himself again with his back towards him, clutching at the side of the bed with both hands. He pulled himself up very slowly, fell sideways onto the bed and lay still. Marcello went over to him, put down the revolver at the head of the bed, called in a low voice, "Lino," and, without waiting for an answer, went to the door. But it was locked, and he remembered that Lino had taken the key out and put it in his pocket. He hesitated, disliking intensely the idea of fumbling in the dead man's pockets; then, his eyes falling on the window, he remembered that the room was on the ground floor. Sitting astride the window sill, he turned his head hastily, casting a long, frightened, cautious look at the open space in front of the house and the car standing outside the door: he knew that if anyone happened to pass at that moment, they could not fail to see him sitting there in the window; yet there was nothing else to be done. But there was no one, and beyond the scattered trees round the house even the bare, hilly countryside appeared to be deserted as far as the eye could reach. He climbed down from the window, took his package of books from the seat of the car and walked off in a leisurely fashion toward the gate. As he walked there was reflected in his consciousness, as in a mirror, the picture of himself, a boy in shorts with some books under his arm, walking down the cypress-bordered drive, an incomprehensible figure full of gloomy foreboding.

>>>->>>->>> PART ONE >>>->>>->>>->>>->>>->>>->>>->>>->>>->>>

## CHAPTER 4

Holding his hat in one hand, Marcello took his dark glasses off his nose with the other and put them away in his jacket pocket. He entered the hall of the library and asked the attendant where he could find the files of newspapers. Then, without hurrying, he went up the broad staircase where a big window on the landing at the top blazed with the strong light of May. He felt light and almost empty, with a sense of perfect physical well-being, of intact youthful vigor. The new gray, plain-cut suit he was wearing added to this feeling another that was no less pleasant, that of a serious, precise elegance that accorded with his own tastes.

On the first floor, after filling in a slip at the entrance, he made his way to the reading room, to a desk behind which were an elderly attendant and a girl. He waited his turn and then handed in his slip, requesting the complete 1920 issues of the chief local newspaper. He waited patiently, leaning against the desk and looking at the reading room in front of him. Rows of writing tables, each with a green-shaded lamp, stretched away to the far end of the room. Marcello looked carefully at these writing tables scantily populated for the most part by students, and mentally selected his own—the last one at the back of the room on the right. The girl reappeared, her two outstretched arms supporting the big bound volume of newspapers he had asked for. Marcello took it and went to the table he had chosen.

He put down the volume on the sloping top of the writing table and then sat down, taking care to hitch up his trousers a little. He took a cigarette from a package of a cheap brand, lit it, drew in a first mouthful of smoke, and then, calmly, holding the cigarette between two fingers, opened the volume and began turning over the pages. The headings had lost their original brightness, the blackness of the print having turned almost green, the paper was yellowed and the photographs looked faded and confused, lacking light and shade. He noticed that the bigger and more extended the heading, the greater the sense of futility and absurdity it gave, announcements of events that had lost their importance and significance by the evening of the very day on which they had appeared, now, with their noisy incomprehensibility, were repugnant not only to the memory but to the imagination as well. The most absurd headings, he observed, were those that included underneath the news a comment of a more or less tendentious kind; with their mixture of graphic vivaciousness and complete absence of echo they were reminiscent of the extravant bawlings of a madman, that deafen but do not affect the feelings. Marcello compared his feelings as he looked at these headings with the feeling he imagined he would have when he looked at the heading that concerned him, and he wondered if the notice he was looking for would arouse in him the same sense of emptiness and absurdity. This, then, was the past, he thought as he went on turning the pages, this uproar now silent, this fury spent, to which the very stuff of the journal, the yellowed paper that soon would break up and fall into dust, lent a quality of shabbiness and vulgarity. The past was made up of violence, of error, of deceit, of frivolity, of falsehood, he thought as he read the news items on the various pages, and these were the only things that men had thought worthy of being published, day by day, and by which they recommended themselves to the memory of posterity. Life, in its normality and its profundity, was absent from these pages; yet what was he himself looking for, as he reflected thus, but the testimony of a crime?

He was in no hurry to find the item of news that concerned him, though he knew the precise date and could turn straight to it if he wished. He came now to the 22nd, the 23rd, the 24th of October 1920: he was drawing nearer

with each page that he turned to what he considered the
most important action of his life, but the newspaper did not
prepare him in any way for the announcement, it took no
account of preliminaries. Among all these pieces of news
that did not touch him in any way whatever, the only one
that concerned him would rise to the surface suddenly,
without warning, like a fish rising from the depths of the
sea to leap at the bait. He tried to make a joke of it,
saying to himself, "Instead of all these grand headings about
political events, they ought to have put, 'Marcello meets
Lino for the first time'; 'Marcello asks for the revolver';
'Marcello agrees to get into the car'."; but all at once the
joke died in his mind and a  sudden agitation took away
his breath. He had reached the date he was looking for.
He turned the page hastily, and there, as he had expected,
was the notice, in a column with the heading: *Fatal Accident.*

Before reading it, he felt a desire for another cigarette.
He inhaled a mouthful of smoke and then lowered his eyes
to the newspaper. The paragraph said: "Yesterday Pasquale
Seminara, chauffeur, residing at 33 Via della Camilluccia,
while cleaning a revolver, accidentally fired a shot. Help
came quickly and Seminara was at once taken to the Santo
Spirito Hospital, where he was found to have a wound in
the chest, near the heart. The case was considered critical
and during the evening, in spite of the care lavished upon
him, Seminara passed away." The notice could not have
been more concise nor more conventional, he thought as he
read it over again. And yet, even though the well-worn
formulas of this most anonymous type of journalism, two
important facts were revealed. The first was that Lino was
really dead—of which he had always been convinced but
which he had never had the courage to ascertain; the second
was that his death had been attributed—obviously on the
dying man's own evidence—to an accident. So that Marcello
himself was completely secure from any possible consequence.
Lino was dead, and that death could never be laid at his
door.

But it was not in order to reassure himself that he had
at last decided to hunt out in the library the notice of what
had occurred so many years before. His anxiety, which had
never been entirely lulled during these years, had never considered the material consequences of his act. It was, on the
contrary, in order to see what sort of feeling the confirmation
of Lino's death would arouse in him that he had that morning
crossed the library threshold. From this feeling he would
judge whether he was still the boy he had once been, obsessed
by his own fatal abnormality, or the new, completely normal

man that he had since intended to be and that he was convinced he was.

He felt a singular relief and, perhaps more than relief, astonishment, when he realized that the printed news on the yellow paper of seventeen years before aroused no appreciable echo in his mind. His reaction, he felt, was like that of a man who, having had a bandage over a deep wound for a very long time, makes up his mind at last to take it off and discovers, to his surprise, that the skin where he expected to find at least a scar, is clear and smooth without a mark of any kind. Looking for the paragraph in the paper had been like removing the bandage; and to find himself unaffected by it was to find himself cured. How this cure had been accomplished, he could not have said. But there could be no doubt that it was not merely time that had produced this result. Much was owing to himself too, to his own concious will, during all those years, to escape from abnormality and make himself like other men.

Nevertheless a kind of conscientious scruple made him take his eyes from the newspaper and gaze into space, with a feeling that he wished to visualize Lino's death clearly—a thing that until now he had always instinctively avoided doing. The paragraph in the paper was written in the conventional language of journalism, and this in itself might be a further inducement to indifference and apathy, but his own evocation of the occurrence could not fail to be vivid and moving and therefore well fitted to reawaken those ancient terrors in his mind, if they still existed. And so, following obediently in the wake of memory, which, like a pitiless, impartial guide conducted him back through time, he retrod his own childish path—his first meeting with Lino in the avenue; his longing to possess a revolver; Lino's promise; the visit to the villa; the second meeting with Lino; the man's pederastic advances; himself pointing the revolver; the man shouting theatrically, arms outstretched as he knelt beside the bed, "Kill me, Marcello . . . kill me like a dog"; himself, as if in obedience, pressing the trigger; the man falling against the bed, pulling himself up, lying there motionless on his side. He was very soon aware, as he examined all these details piece by piece, that his lack of feeling in the face of the notice in the newspaper was now being confirmed and amplified. Indeed, not merely did he feel no remorse, but the quiet surface of his conscience was unruffled even by feelings of pity, of bitterness or of repugnance for Lino—feelings that long seemed to him inseparable from his memory of that time.

He felt nothing, in fact. An impotent man lying beside

the naked, desirable body of a woman could not have been
more inert than was his mind as it contemplated that
remote occurrence of his youth. He was pleased at this indifference as a sure sign that there was now no connection
whatever, not even of a hidden, indirect, or dormant kind
between the boy that he had been and the young man that
he now was. He was really and truly a different person
he went on thinking as he gently closed the big volume and
rose from the table, and although his memory was able
in a mechanical way to recall what had happened in that
far-off October, actually his whole being, even to its most
secret fibers, had now forgotten it.

Without hurrying, he went over to the desk and gave
the volume to the librarian. Then, with the same air of
measured but energetic composure that was his favorite attitude toward the world, he left the reading room and
went down the staircase into the main hall. It was true
he could not help thinking as he came out into the strong
light of the street, it was true that the printed notice of
Lino's death and then his own evocation of it had awakened
no echo at all in his mind; and yet he no longer felt so
deeply relieved as, at the first moment, he had thought. He
recalled his sensation as he had turned the pages of the
old newspaper—like taking the bandages from a wound and
finding it completely healed; and he said to himself that
perhaps under the smooth skin the old poison was still lurk-
ing in the form of a closed, invisible abscess. He was confirmed in this suspicion not only by the transient quality
of the relief he had felt when first he had discovered that
Lino's death was a matter of indifference to him, but also
by the faint, depressing sense of melancholy, hanging like
a transparent mourning veil between him and reality. It was
as if the memory of the Lino incident, even though dissolved by the potent acids of time, had yet cast an inexplicable shadow over all his thoughts and feelings.

As he walked slowly through the crowded, sun-filled
streets he tried to establish a comparison between himself
as he had been seventeen years before and as he was now.
He remembered that at thirteen he had been a timid boy,
rather feminine, impressionable, unmethodical, imaginative,
impetuous, passionate. Now, at thirty, he was not in the
least timid but perfectly sure of himself, entirely masculine
in his tastes and in his general attitude, calm, methodical to
a fault, almost completely lacking in imagination, cool and
self-controlled. It seemed to him he could remember having
had, at that time, a certain tumultuous, indefinable richness of
character. Now his whole character was well-defined though

erhaps a little barren, and the poverty and rigidity of a few ideas and convictions had taken the place of that former enerous, confused fecundity. Lastly, he had been confiding, xpansive, sometimes positively exuberant. Now he was re-erved, always equable in temper, lacking in vivacity if not ctually gloomy, silent. The most distinctive feature, how-ver, of the radical change that had come about in those eventeen years was the disappearance of a kind of excess f vitality resulting from a ferment of unusual and perhaps ven abnormal instincts; its place seemed to have been taken y a sort of benumbed, gray normality.

It had been merely chance, he went on to think, that ad prevented his submitting to Lino's desires; and certainly is demeanor toward the chauffeur, full as it was of co-uettishness and of feminine tyranny, had been actuated not nerely by childish venality but also by a confused, un-onscious inclination of the senses. But now he was really nd truly a man just like any other man. He stopped in ront of a mirror in a shop window and looked at himself or some time, examining himself with an objective detach-nent in which there was no complacency. Yes, he was a nan just like any other man, with his gray suit, his sober ie, his tall, well-proportioned figure, his round, brown face, is well-brushed hair, his dark glasses. He remembered how, t the university, he had discovered with a kind of delight hat there were at least a thousand young men of his ge who dressed, spoke, thought and behaved like him. Now, robably, that number could be multiplied by a million. Ie was a normal man, he thought with a sharp, disdainful atisfaction, there could be no doubt about it, although he ould not say how it had come about.

He remembered suddenly that he had finished his ciga-ettes and went into a tobacco shop in the Piazza Colonna rcade. He went up to the counter and asked for his favorite rand. At that same moment three other people were asking or the same kind and the tobacconist quickly put down on he marble-topped counter, in front of the four outstretched ands holding money, four identical packs which the four ands removed with the same identical gesture. Marcello bserved that he took his pack, felt it to see that it was oft enough, and then tore open the paper in the same way s the other three. He observed also that two of the three ut the pack of cigarettes, just as he did, into a small inside ocket of their jackets. Lastly, one of the three, as soon as e got outside the shop, stopped to light a cigarette with a lver lighter exactly like Marcello's. These details gave him n almost voluptuous satisfaction. Yes, he was just like

other people, just like everyone else. Just like those wh
were buying cigarettes of the same brand and with the sam
movements as he, and just like those who, when a woma
in red walked past, turned—and he with them—to eye th
quivering solid buttocks beneath the thin stuff of her dres
Except that sometimes, as in this last case, his resemblanc
to other men was deliberate and imitative rather than
result of a conformity of inclinations.

A short, misshapen newsboy came toward him with
bundle of papers over his arm, waving one of them an
shouting at the top of his voice, his face purple with th
effort, some incomprehensible phrase in which the only rec
ognizable words were "Victory" and "Spain." Marcell
bought a paper and carefully read the heading stretche
across the top of the page; in the war in Spain the supporter
of Franco had won another victory. He was conscious o
reading this piece of news with undeniable pleasure, an
he felt this was another sign of his complete and absolut
normality. He had watched the birth of the war from th
first hypocritical heading: "What is Happening in Spain?"
and then the war had spread and become of immense impor
tance, had turned into a contest not merely of arms but c
ideas; and gradually he had noticed that he was participatin
in it with a curious feeling that was entirely detached fron
any political or moral consideration (although such consid
erations often came up in his mind), a feeling very lik
that of a sports enthusiast who takes the side of one foot
ball team against another.

From the very beginning he had wanted Franco to win—
not with any feeling of bitterness but with a profoun
tenacious desire, as though such a victory would provid
confirmation of the goodness and rightness of his own taste
and ideas not merely in the political field but in all other
as well. It was, perhaps, from a love of symmetry that h
had desired, and still desired, Franco's victory—like some
one furnishing his house who is anxious to collect in
furniture that is all of the same style. For he seemed t
read this symmetry in the events of the last few years, wit
a steady increase in its clarity and importance: first th
advent of fascism in Italy, then in Germany, then the wa
in Ethiopia, and then the war in Spain. This progress please
him for some reason—possibly because it was easy to rec
ognize in it a more than human logic, and the ability t
recognize this gave one a sense of security and infallibility
Furthermore, he thought, folding the newspaper and pu
ting it in his pocket, it could not be said that he had be
come convinced of the rightness of Franco's cause for rea

ons of politics or propaganda. This conviction had come
o him from nowhere, as it may be supposed to come to
gnorant, ordinary people—out of the air, in fact, just as
ne says an idea is "in the air." He took Franco's side just
ike innumerable other perfectly ordinary people who knew
ittle or nothing about Spain, who scarcely glanced at the
eadlines of the newspaper, who were not cultivated.

It was, in fact, out of sympathy—using that word in an
ntirely unthinking, nonlogical, irrational sense. A sympathy
hat could be said only metaphorically to come out of the
ir; for in the air there may be pollen, smoke from houses,
lust, light, but not ideas. This sympathy therefore must
ome from deeper layers of consciousness, and it provided
et another proof that his normality was neither superficial
or botched up in a deliberately arbitrary fashion, with
rguments and motives that were mere matters of opinion.
t was closely bound up with an instinctive, almost physio-
ogical condition, with a faith which he shared with millions
f other persons. Here was one single, complete thing he
ad in common with the society and the people among whom
e found himself living. He was not a solitary, an abnormal
erson, a madman, he was one of them, a brother, a fellow-
citizen, a comrade; and this, after his great fear that the
killing of Lino might separate him from the rest of humanity,
vas in the highest degree comforting.

In any case, whether it was Franco or another, it mattered
ittle, provided there was a bond, a bridge, a symbol of
ttachment and communion. But the fact that it was Franco
nd not another proved that his emotional participation in
he Spanish war, besides being an indication of unity and
ompanionship, was also a true and right thing. What else
ould truth be, if not something that was evident to all,
hat was believed and held incontestable by all? And so
here was an unbroken chain with all its links firmly joined,
rom his feeling of sympathy, prior to all thought, to the
onsciousness that this sympathy was felt in exactly the
ame way by millions of other persons; from that conscious-
ess to the conviction of being in the right; from the
onviction of being in the right, to action. For, he thought,
he possession of the truth did not merely permit, it also
mposed, action. Action was a confirmation of one's own
ormality that must be provided both for oneself and for
thers; for it was not normality at all unless it was deepened
nd reinforced and demonstrated continually.

By this time he had arrived. The big, open archway of
he Ministry was on the other side of the street, beyond
 double row of moving cars and buses. He waited a mo-

ment and then slipped in behind a large black car that was making for the same archway. He followed the car in, gave the commissionaire the name of the official he wanted to speak to, and then sat down in the waiting room, almost pleased to be waiting there like other people, among other people. He had no feeling of haste or impatience, nor of intolerance for the routine and etiquette of the Ministry. On the contrary this routine, this etiquette pleased him, as symbols of a yet vaster and more general routine and etiquette, and he adapted himself willingly to them. He felt perfectly calm and cool, even if—and this was nothing new to him—a little sad. It was a sadness of a mysterious kind he had come to consider, by now, as inseparable from his character. He had always been sad in this way, lacking in gaiety, like some lake in whose waters is reflected a very high mountain that shuts out the sunlight from it and makes it black and melancholy. One knows that if the mountain could be removed the sun would bring a smile to the face of the waters, but the mountain is always there and the lake is always sad. Like the lake, he too was sad, but what the mountain was, he could not have told.

The waiting room, a small room leading out of the porter's lodge, was filled with a heterogeneous mixture of people, quite the opposite of what one might have expected to find in the antechamber of a Ministry so famous for the elegance and social distinction of its officials. Three individuals of debauched and sinister appearance—informers, perhaps, or plain-clothes policemen—were smoking and chattering together in low voices next to a young woman with black hair and a white and red face, who was gaudily painted and dressed and was to all appearances a prostitute of the lowest kind. Next was an old man, cleanly though poorly dressed in black, with a white mustache and beard, possibly a schoolteacher. Finally, next to Marcello himself, a small, thin, gray-haired woman with a troubled, anxious expression, who looked like a housewife and mother.

He observed all these people stealthily, with a strong feeling of repugnance. This was what always happened to him. He thought he was normal and just like everyone else when he pictured the crowd to himself as an abstract whole, as a great, existing army held together by common feelings, common ideals, common aims, an army of which it was comforting to form a part. But as soon as individuals rose to the surface of this crowd, his illusion of normality broke to pieces against their diversity, since he failed completely to recognize himself in them and felt at the same time both repugnance and detachment. What was there in common between him and those three sinister, vulgar men, between him and that woman of the streets, between him and that white-haired old man, between him and that humble, worn-out mother? Nothing at all, except for the repulsion, the pity, that he felt. "Clerici," called the voice of the commissionaire. He started and rose to his feet. "First staircase on the right." Without turning, he went off in the direction he had been shown.

He walked up a very wide staircase with a narrow red carpet in the middle and found himself, after the second flight of stairs, on a vast landing with three large double doors opening from it. He went to the door in the middle, opened it and came into a big, half-dark room. In it was a long, massive table, and on the table, in the middle, a globe. Marcello walked about this room for a few moments (evidently, judging by the half-closed shutters and the covers over the settees along the walls, it was not in use), then opened one of the many doors and came out into a dark, narrow passage with glass-fronted bookshelves on each side. At the end of the passage was a partly closed door with light coming through the crack. Marcello went up to it, hesitated, and then very gently pushed the door slightly. It was not so much curiosity that urged him to do this as a desire to find an attendant to show him the way to the room he was looking for. Peeping in through the crack he realized that his suspicion that he had come to the wrong place was not unfounded. In front of him was a long, narrow room into which a suave light penetrated from a single, yellow curtained window. In front of the window was a table, and sitting at the table with his back profiled against the window was a young man with a broad, massive face and a plump figure.

Standing by the table, with her back toward him, Marcello could see a woman in a light dress with a pattern of big black flowers on a white background, and a wide black hat of gauze and lace. She was very tall and very slim in the waist, but broad in the shoulders and hips, with long legs and thin calves. She was leaning over the table and talking in a low voice to the man who sat quite still listening to her, in profile, looking not at her but at his own hand playing with a pencil on the slope of the desk in front of him. Then she moved over and stood close to the armchair, opposite the man, her back against the desk and facing the window, in a more confidential attitude; but the black hat tilted over her eye prevented Marcello from seeing her face. She hesitated, then bent over sideways and with an awkward movement, bending one leg—like someone stooping down to catch the jet of a fountain in his mouth—sought the man's lips with her own, while he allowed himself to be kissed without moving or giving the slightest visible sign that the kiss was agreeable to him. She threw herself backward again, both her own and the man's face hidden by the wide sweep of her hat, and staggered and would have lost her balance had not the man put his arm round her waist and held her up. Then she stood upright, and the man sitting in the chair was concealed by her body. It looked as if she might be stroking his head. The man's arm was still round her waist; then he appeared to relax his hold and his thick, square hand, as though pulled downward by its own weight, slid onto the woman's buttock and remained there open and with fingers spread wide, like a crab or a spider on a smooth, spherical surface that provides no foothold. Marcello closed the door again.

He went back along the passage to the room where the globe stood. What he had seen confirmed the Ministry's reputation for libertinism, for the man sitting at the desk in the room was the Minister himself and Marcello had at once recognized him; but strangely enough, in spite of his inclination to make moral judgments, this did not make any impression on the background of his convictions. Marcello was not conscious of any liking for this social, woman-chasing minister, in fact he rather disliked him; and the intrusion of his love-life into his office seemed to him highly unbecoming. But none of this affected in the slightest degree his political beliefs. It was like being told, by trust-worthy people, that other important personages were thieves or incompetent or used their political influence for personal ends. He registered these items of news with a rather gloomy feeling of indifference as things that did not concern him, inasmuch as he had made his choice once and for all and did not intend to alter it. He felt moreover that such things did not surprise him because he had, in a sense, discounted them from time immemorial owing to precocious knowledge of the less amiable characteristics of mankind. But he was above all conscious that, between his loyalty to the regime and the highly rigid moral standards that governed his own conduct, there could be no possible relation. The reasons for his loyalty had origins deeper than any moral criterion and could not be shaken by a hand feeling a woman's hip in a government office, or by a theft, or by any other crime or error. What those origins were, he could not have stated precisely; between them and his conscious thought stood the dull, opaque barrier of his obstinate melancholy.

Calmly, impassively, patiently he went to another of the

doors, glanced through it into another corridor, drew back,
tried a third door and at last found his way into the antechamber he was seeking. There were people sitting on the
settees round the walls, and gold-laced commissionaires stood
in the doorways. In a low voice he gave one of them the
name of the official he wished to see, and then went and
sat down on one of the settees. To while away the time
he opened the newspaper again. The news of the victory
in Spain was printed right across the top, and this irritated
him as an extravagance in doubtful taste. He reread the
message in heavy type announcing the victory and then
went on to a long despatch, but gave up reading it almost
at once because he was annoyed by the mannered, would-be
soldierly style of the special correspondent. He stopped a
moment to ask himself how he would have written this
article, and was surprised to find himself thinking that if
they had depended upon him, not merely the article from
Spain but all the other aspects of the regime as well, from
the least important to the most showy, would have been entirely different. In reality, he thought, there was practically nothing about the regime that he did not dislike profoundly; yet that was the path he had chosen and he must
stick to it. He opened the paper again and skimmed over
a few other news items, carefully avoiding patriotic or propagandist articles. Then at last he raised his eyes from the
paper and looked round the room.

There was no one left but one old gentleman with a
round white head and a ruddy face imprinted with an expression of mingled impudence, cupidity and cunning.
Dressed in light colors, with a youthful, sport jacket with
a slit at the back, heavy crepe-soled shoes and a gay tie,
he assumed an air of being quite at home in the Ministry,
walking up and down the room and calling out questions
in a self-possessed, joking, impatient way to the obsequious
ushers who stood at the doors. Then one of the doors opened
and out came a bald, middle-aged man, thin except for a
prominent paunch, with a drawn, yellow face, eyes buried
deep in big, dark sockets, and a brisk, skeptical, witty expression of his sharp features. The old man went straight
up to him with an exclamation of humorous protest, the
other man greeted him in a ceremonious, deferential manner,
and then the old man, with a confidential gesture, took
hold of the yellow-faced man not by the arm but actually
around the waist, as if he had been a woman, and as he
walked beside him across the room, he began speaking in
a low, urgent whisper.

Marcello had followed the scene with an indifferent eye;

then all of a sudden he realized to his surprise that he felt a crazy sort of hatred for the old man, for some reason unknown to himself. Marcello was aware that at any moment and for the most diverse reasons an excess of hatred of this kind might rise up to the dead surface of his accustomed apathy, unexpected as a monster emerging from a motionless sea; yet each time it happened he was astonished at coming face to face with an unknown aspect of his own character, which all its other aspects, so well-known and so secure, seemed to contradict. This old man, for instance— he felt he could kill him, or have him killed, with the greatest ease; in fact he wanted to kill him. And why? Perhaps it was because he saw skepticism, the fault he most hated, so plainly written upon that rubicund countenance. Or was it because his jacket had a slit at the back and the old man's hand in his pocket raised a flap of the material, thus revealing the hinder part of his too-limp and too-full pants and so gave the revolting impression of a dummy in a tailor shop window? Anyhow he hated him, and with an intensity so strong and so insufferable that he preferred, in the end, to lower his eyes and read the newspaper again. When he looked up again the old man and his companion had disappeared and the room was empty.

After a short time one of the ushers came and murmured to him that he could be received now, and Marcello rose and followed him. The usher opened one of the doors and showed him in. Marcello found himself in a spacious room with frescoed walls and ceiling, at the far end of which was a table covered with papers. Behind the table was sitting the yellow-faced man whom he had already seen in the other room; at the side sat another man whom Marcello knew well, his own immediate superior in the Secret Service. As Marcello came in the yellow-faced man, who was one of the Minister's secretaries, rose to his feet; the other man remained seated and greeted him with a nod. The latter, a thin old man of military appearance, with a scarlet, wooden-looking face and a pair of mustaches of an improbable, mask-like blackness and bristliness, formed a complete contrast with the secretary. He was a loyal, rigid, honest man, accustomed to carrying out orders without discussion, putting what he considered to be his duty above everything, even above conscience; whereas the secretary, from what Marcello remembered hearing, was a man of a more recent and entirely different type—ambitious, skeptical, of social tastes, with a passion for intrigue that was carried to the point of cruelty, beyond all professional obligation and all limit of conscience. Marcello's whole preference was, naturally, for the old man, for the added reason that he thought he could discern, in that red and ravaged face, the same obscure melancholy that so often oppressed himself. Perhaps like him Colonel Baudino was aware of the contrast between a rigid, almost bewitched loyalty with nothing rational about it and the too often deplorable aspects of every day reality. But perhaps, he thought again as he looked at the old man, perhaps it was only an illusion; perhaps he himself was, out of sympathy, endowing his superior with his own feelings in the hope of not being the only one to experience them.

The colonel, without looking either at Marcello or at the secretary, said drily, "This is Dr. Clerici about whom I spoke to you not long ago." The secretary, with a ceremonious, almost ironical promptitude, leaned across the table, held out his hand and invited him to be seated. Marcello sat down; the secretary sat down, took a box of cigarettes and offered it first to the colonel, who refused, and then to Marcello, who accepted. After he himself had also lit a cigarette, he said, "Clerici, I'm very pleased to make your acquaintance . . . the Colonel, here, never stops singing your praises . . . From all he says you seem to be an 'ace' as they call it." He underlined the words "as they call it" with a smile, and then went on: "We've gone carefully over your plan with the Minister and we judge it to be quite excellent . . . You know Quadri well?"

"Yes," said Marcello, "he was my tutor at the University."

"And you're sure Quadri knows nothing of your official position?"

"I don't think so."

"Your idea of a faked political conversion with the object of inspiring confidence and getting inside their organization and even contriving to be entrusted with a job in Italy," went on the secretary, looking down at some notes in front of him on the table, "is a good one . . . The Minister, too, agrees that something of the kind should be tried without any delay . . . When would you feel inclined to start, Clerici?"

"As soon as required."

"Excellent," said the secretary, a little surprised, nevertheless, as if he had expected the answer to be different, "admirable . . . However there's one point that must be made clear . . . You're proposing to carry out a—let us say—rather delicate, dangerous mission . . . and we were saying, with the Colonel, that in order not to be conspicuous you ought to find, to think out, to invent some plausible pretext for your presence in Paris . . . I'm not saying that they'd know who you are or would be in a position to discover . . . but, in a word, you can't be too careful—all the more so since Quadri, as you tell us in your report, was perfectly well aware at one time of your feelings of loyalty towards the regime. . . ."

"If it hadn't been for those feelings," Marcello observed drily, "there couldn't have been any conversion either . . ."

"Of course, exactly . . . But one doesn't go to Paris on purpose to call at Quadri's and say to him, 'Here I am.' No, you must give the impression of happening to be in Paris for private reasons—nonpolitical reasons—and of taking advantage of this to tell Quadri all about your spiritual crisis . . . What you must do," concluded the secretary, looking up at Marcello, "is to combine your mission with something personal, something unofficial." The secretary turned toward the colonel and added, "Don't you think so, Colonel?"

"Yes, that's my opinion," said the colonel, without raising his eyes. After a moment he went on, "But only Dr. Clerici can find the pretext that's needed."

Marcello bent his head, having no particular idea on the subject. It seemed to him that no answer could be made for the moment, since such a pretext required calm examination. He was on the point of replying, "Give me two or three days to think about it," when suddenly his tongue spoke for him almost against his will. "I'm getting married in a week's time . . . The mission could be combined with my honeymoon."

This time the secretary's surprise, though immediately covered by a prompt enthusiasm, was obvious and profound. The colonel, on the other hand, remained entirely passive, just as though Marcello had not spoken. "Excellent . . . admirable," exclaimed the secretary, looking rather disconcerted; "you're getting married . . . no better pretext could possibly be found . . . the classic Paris honeymoon."

"Yes," said Marcello without smiling, "the classic Paris honeymoon."

The secretary was afraid that he had offended him. "What I meant was that Paris is just the right place for a honeymoon . . . Of course I'm not married . . . but if I was going to be, I think I should go to Paris too."

This time Marcello did not speak. It often happened that his answer to people he did not like took this form—a complete silence. The secretary, in order to recover himself, turned to the colonel and said, "You're quite right, colonel . . . Only Dr. Clerici could have found such a pretext . . . We, even if we'd found it, couldn't have suggested it to him."

This remark, uttered in an ambiguous, half-serious tone of voice, could be taken, thought Marcello, in two ways. It could be meant as a real if slightly ironical praise, as much as to say, "Devil take it, what fanaticism!"; or it could be the expression of a feeling of amazed contempt, "What servility! He doesn't even respect his own marriage." Probably, he thought, it was both these things, since it was clear that in the case of the secretary himself the boundary between fanaticism and servility was not very precisely marked; both of them were means that he used to achieve the same ends. He noticed with satisfaction that the colonel, too, withheld from the secretary the smile which the latter's double-edged remark seemed to be asking for. A moment's silence ensued. Marcello was now looking straight into the secretary's eyes with a fixity and a lack of timidity that he both knew and wished to be disconcerting. The secretary did not return his look, but, leaning with both hands on the top of the table, rose to his feet.

"All right, then . . . Colonel, will you and Dr. Clerici make all necessary arrangements about the practical details of the mission? . . . And you," he went on, turning towards Marcello, "I want you to understand that you have the full support of the Minister as well as mine . . . In fact," he added, with an affectation of casualness, "the Minister has expressed the wish to make your personal acquaintance."

Once again Marcello did not open his mouth; all he did was to rise to his feet and make a slight, deferential bow. The secretary, who was perhaps expecting some words of gratitude, again made a movement of surprise that he quickly repressed. "Wait a moment, Clerici . . . He told me to take you straight to him now."

The colonel rose and said, "Clerici, you know where to find me." He held out his hand to the secretary, but the latter insisted on accompanying him to the door with ceremonious, obsequious zeal. Marcello saw them shake hands, and then the colonel vanished and the secretary came back to him.

"Come along, Clerici," he said. "The Minister is extremely busy, but in spite of that he insists on seeing you in order to show how pleased he is with you . . . It's the first time, isn't it, that you've been taken in to see the Minister?" These words were spoken as they were crossing a small antechamber adjoining the secretary's room. The latter went to a door, opened it and disappeared, making a sign to him to wait, and then, almost immediately reappeared and invited him to follow.

Marcello entered the same long, narrow room that he

had looked into not long before through the crack in the door, only now the room lay before him in breadth, with the table in front of him. Behind the table was sitting the man with the broad, massive face and plump figure that he had peeped in upon as the Minister was allowing himself to be kissed by the woman in the big black hat. Marcello noticed that the table was quite bare, polished like a mirror, with no papers on it, only a large bronze inkpot and a closed portfolio of dark-colored leather. "Excellency, this is Dr. Clerici," said the secretary.

The Minister rose and held out his hand to Marcello with a zealous cordiality even more conspicuous than that of the secretary, but entirely lacking in pleasantness, in fact decidedly commanding. "How are you, Clerici?" He pronounced his words slowly and with care, haughtily, as though they contained some special meaning. "I hear you spoken of in the highest terms . . . The regime has need of men like you." The Minister sat down again, took his handkerchief out of his pocket and blew his nose, at the same time examining certain papers that the secretary laid before him. Marcello retired discreetly toward the farthest corner of the room. The Minister looked at the papers while the secretary whisperd in his ear, then he looked at his handkerchief, and Marcello saw that the white linen was stained with scarlet. He remembered that as he had come into the room the Minister's mouth had looked to him unnaturally red—with lipstick from the woman in the black hat. Still examining the papers that the secretary was showing him, displaying no embarrassment, no concern at being observed, the Minister started vigorously rubbing hs mouth with his handkerchief, looking at it every now and then to see if the lipstick was still coming off. At last his examination of the papers and of the handkerchief came to a simultaneous end, and the Minister rose to his feet and again held out his hand to Marcello. "Good-bye, Clerici," he said; "as my secretary will have already told you, the mission you are undertaking has my complete and unqualified support."

Marcello bowed, grasped the thick, square hand, and followed the secretary out of the room.

They went back to the secretary's room. The latter put down on the table the papers that had been examined by the Minister and then accompanied Marcello to the door. "Well then, Clerici, into the lion's mouth!" he said with a smile, "and best wishes for your marriage." Marcello thanked him with a nod and a bow and a murmured phrase. The secretary, with a last smile, shook his hand. Then the door closed.

## CHAPTER 5

It was late now and, as soon as he came out of the Ministry, Marcello hastened his step. He took his place in the line at the bus stop, in the midst of the hungry, irritable midday crowd, and patiently awaited his turn to get on to the already crowded vehicle. He accomplished part of his journey hanging on outside, on the step, then with a great effort managed to squeeze himself onto the platform; and there he remained, hemmed in on every side by other passengers, while the bus, jolting and roaring, climbed up the steep streets running from the center of the town to the suburbs.

These discomforts did not worry him; in fact he found them helpful to him, inasmuch as they were shared with so many others and contributed, if only in a small degree, to make him like everybody else. Besides, contacts with a crowd, however disagreeable and inconvenient, pleased him and always seemed to him preferable to contacts with individuals. From a crowd, he thought, raising himself on tiptoe to breathe more freely, from a crowd he derived the comforting feeling of many-sided fellowship, whether it was a matter of cramming oneself into a bus or of patriotic enthusiasm at political meetings; whereas from individuals he derived nothing but doubts, both about himself and about others—which was what had happened that morning during his visit to the Ministry.

Why, for instance, why, the moment after he had offered to combine his mission with his honeymoon, had he experienced that painful feeling of having performed an act either of gratuitous servility or of clumsy fanaticism? Because, he told himself, the offer had been made to that skeptical, designing, corrupt man, that despicable, odious secretary. It was he who, by his mere presence, had inspired in him a sense of shame for an act which had in reality been profoundly spontaneous and disinterested. And now, while the bus rolled on from one stop to another, he excused himself by saying that he would not have had a sense of shame if he had not found himself face to face with a man like that, a man for whom neither loyalty nor devotion nor sacrifice existed, but only calculation, discretion, self-interest. His offer had not sprung from any mental speculation but from the obscure depths of his spirit—a sure proof, apart from anything else, of the authentic nature of his absorption into social and political normality. Another man—the secretary, for instance—would only have made

such an offer after long and careful calculation; he had
made it on the spur of the moment. As for the im-
propriety of combining his honeymoon with a political mission, it was not worth wasting time even in thinking about
it. He was what he was, and all that he did was right if
it was governed by what he was.

With these thoughts in his mind he got off the bus and
walked along the street of this quarter where minor officials
lived, on a pavement bordered with white and pink oleanders.
The great doorways of massive, shabby blocks of flats occupied by government officials opened on to this pavement,
and through them one could see vast, dreary courtyards.
Alternating with the doorways was a series of modest shops
that Marcello knew well—the tobacconist, the baker, the
grocer, the butcher, the druggist. It was midday and there
were many revealing signs, even in these humble concerns,
of the mild and transitory gaiety that comes with the break-
ing-off of work and the family gathering—smells of cooking
coming from half-closed windows on the ground floor; badly
dressed men hurrying into doorways, almost at a run;
voices on the radio and the sound of a phonograph. From
a little enclosed garden in a recess of one of the buildings
an espalier of climbing roses on the railings greeted him
with a wave of sharp, dusty fragrance. Marcello quickened his step and went in at the doorway marked 19, together with two or three other officials—and imitating their
haste, not without satisfaction—started to walk up the stairs.

He went slowly up the broad stairs, where dreary twilight alternated with sumptuous light from big windows on
the landings. But at the second floor he remembered that
he had forgotten something—the flowers he never failed to
bring to his fiancée each time he was invited to lunch
at her home. Glad that he remembered in time, he ran
down the stairs again, went out into the street and walked
straight to the corner of the building, where a woman squatted
on a stool with a few jars of seasonal flowers in front of
her. He hurriedly selected half a dozen roses, the best the
flower seller had, tall and straight-stalked, dark red in color,
and, holding them to his nose to breathe their perfume,
went back into the building and upstairs, this time to the
top floor. Here, there was only one door on the landing,
and a smaller staircase led up to a little rustic door, underneath which a brilliant light shone from an open terrace.
He rang the bell, thinking, "Let's hope her mother doesn't
come and open the door to me." For his future mother-in-law
displayed an almost doting love for him that embarrassed
him profoundly.

A moment later the door opened and Marcello was relieved to see in the dim light of the hall the figure of the little servant girl—almost a child—bunched up in a white apron much too big for her, her pale face crowned by a double coil of black plaits. She shut the door again, but not before she had stuck her head out for a moment to peer inquisitively onto the landing; while Marcello, breathing in the strong smell of cooking that filled the air, went through into the drawing room.

The window of this room was almost closed, to keep out the heat and light, but it was still possible in the dimness to distinguish the dark, sham-Renaissance furniture that cumbered it. They were massive pieces, severe, heavily carved, and they made a curious contrast with the ornaments scattered about the room on brackets and on the small table, all of them in a coquettish but rather out-of-date taste—a little nude woman kneeling on the edge of an ash tray, a blue pottery sailor playing the accordion, a group of white and black dogs, two or three lamps shaped like buds or flowers. There were many ash trays made of metal or china which originally, Marcello knew, had contained wedding sweetmeats from friends or relations of his fiancée. The walls were hung with red, imitation damask, and bright-colored landscaped and still-life paintings in black frames were hung upon them. Marcello sat down on the sofa, already clothed in its summer covering, and looked round with satisfaction. It was a real middle-class home, he reflected once again, the home of a middle-class family of the most conventional and most modest type, similar in every way to other homes in this same building, in this same quarter, and this was for him its most pleasing aspect—the sensation of finding himself face to face with something absolutely ordinary, almost common, and yet completely reassuring. He was aware of an almost abject feeling of complacency at the ugliness of the house. He himself had grown up in a pretty house where everything was in good taste, and he realized that everything that surrounded him at this moment was hopelessly ugly; but it was just this that he needed, this perfectly anonymous ugliness, as a further means of bringing him into line with his equals.

He remembered that for lack of money—anyhow for the first few years—the two of them, Giulia and he, would have to live in this house after they were married, and he almost blessed their poverty. By himself, following his own taste, he would never have been capable of making his home look so ugly and so ordinary. Quite soon, then, this room would be his own sitting room; just as the "art-nouveau" bedroom, in which his future mother-in-law and her late husband had slept for thirty years, would be his bedroom, and the mahogany dining room in which Giulia and her parents had eaten their meals twice a day for the whole of their lives would be his dining room. Giulia's father had been an important official in one of the ministries, and this home of his, furnished according to the taste of the period when he was young, was a kind of temple elevated in rather a touching manner in honor of the twin divinities of respectability and normality. Soon, he thought, with a joy that was almost greedy, almost lascivious yet at the same time melancholy, soon he would be absorbed rightfully into this normality and this respectability.

The door opened and Giulia came rushing in, talking to someone in the passage, perhaps the maid. When she had finished talking she closed the door and hurried over to her fiancée. Giulia, at twenty, was as handsomely developed as a woman of thirty, with a slightly coarse, almost vulgar yet fresh and solid handsomeness that showed her youthfulness and also an indefinable impression of a capacity for sensual self-deception and enjoyment. She had a very white skin, large eyes of a dark and languid clearness, thick, wavy chestnut hair and full, red lips. Marcello, as he saw her coming toward him in a light, tailormade suit through which the curves of her exuberant figure seemed to be bursting, could not help thinking with renewed satisfaction that he was marrying a really normal, ordinary girl, very similar to the drawing room that had just given him such a feeling of relief. And the same feeling of relief and comfort came over him when he heard once again her drawling, good-natured voice with its local accent saying: "What lovely roses! . . . But why? I've already told you you mustn't bother . . . It's not as if it was the first time you were coming to lunch with us." As she spoke, she walked across and put the roses into a blue vase that stood on a yellow marble column in a corner of the room.

"I like to bring you flowers," said Marcello.

Giulia gave a sigh of satisfaction and plumped down on the sofa beside him. Marcello looked at her and noticed that a sudden embarrassment—unmistakable sign of incipient excitement—had taken the place of the impulsive self-possession of a moment before. Then, all at once, she turned toward him and, throwing her arms round his neck, murmured, "Give me a kiss."

Marcello put his arm round her waist and kissed her on the mouth. Giulia was of a sensual nature, and in these kisses—which were almost always demanded by her from a reluctant Marcello—there came invariably a moment when this sensuality of hers crept in in an aggressive manner and altered the chaste, pre-ordained character of their relations as an engaged couple. This time again, just when their lips were on the point of separating, she seemed to be carried away by a violent onslaught of desire, and throwing her arm suddenly round Marcello's neck, pressed her mouth once more fiercely against his. He felt her tongue work its way between his lips and then moved rapidly round, twisting and turning inside his mouth. Meanwhile she had seized his hand and was holding it against her body, guiding it until it lay clasping her left breast. At the same time she was blowing through her nostrils and breathing hard, with an innocent, unsatisfied, animal sound.

Marcello was not in love with his future wife; but he liked Giulia and these sensual embraces never failed to excite him. But he did not feel inclined to reciprocate the transports; he wished his relations with his fiancée to be kept within the bounds of tradition, feeling that a greater intimacy would reintroduce into his life the disorder, the abnormality that he was all the time seeking to banish. After a moment he took his hand away from her breast and very gently pushed her away. "Oh, how cold you are!" said Giulia, withdrawing from him and looking at him with a smile. "Really there are times when I think you aren't fond of me at all."

"You know I'm fond of you," said Marcello.

She went on talking volubly. "I'm so pleased when you say that," she said. "I've never been so happy . . . By the way, d'you know, just this morning Mummy was insisting that we must have her bedroom . . . She'll go into that little room at the end of the passage . . . What d'you think about it? . . . Ought we to accept?"

"I think," said Marcello, "that she wouldn't like it if we refused."

"That's what I think too . . . Just fancy, when I was a little girl I used to dream of sleeping one day in a room like that . . . Now I don't know whether I like it so much . . . D'you like it?" she asked, in a doubtful and at the same time complacent tone of voice, as if she were afraid of his criticism of her taste and also anxious to have it approved.

Marcello hastened to reply: "I like it very much . . . It's a lovely room!" And he saw that these words aroused a visible satisfaction in Giulia.

Delighted, she planted a kiss on his cheek and went on. "This morning I ran into Signora Persico . . . I invited her to the reception . . . D'you know, she didn't know I was getting married? . . . She asked me such a lot of questions . . . When I told her who you were, she told me she knew your mother . . . She met her at the seaside some years ago."

Marcello said nothing. It was always highly disagreeable to him to talk about his mother, with whom he had not lived for years and whom he rarely saw. Giulia, unaware of his embarrassment, went on chattering and again changed the subject. "Now, about the reception . . . We've made out a list of people to be invited . . . Would you like to see it?"

"Yes, let me see it."

She drew a sheet of paper out of her pocket and handed it to him. Marcello took it and looked at it. It was a long list of names, grouped by families—fathers, mothers, daughters, sons. Then men were indicated not only by their Christian names and surnames but by their professional designations as well—doctors, lawyers, engineers, professors; and, if they had them, by their title too—*Commendatore, Grande Ufficiale, Cavaliere.* Beside each family Giulia, to be on the safe side, had written down the number of persons that composed it—three, five, two, four. Almost all the names were unknown to Marcello, yet he felt he had known them for a long time. They were all essentially middle-class people, in the professions or the civil service, people who had homes exactly like this one, with drawing rooms like this and furniture like this; and they had marriageable daughters very like Giulia, whom they married off to young officials with doctor's degrees very similar, he hoped, to himself. He examined the long list, pausing at some of the most characteristic, ordinary names, with a profound satisfaction tinged with his usual cold, settled melancholy. "Now who, for instance, is Arcangeli?" he could not help asking, taking a name at random. "Commendator Giuseppe Arcangeli, with his wife Iole, his daughters Cilvana and Beatrice and his son Dr. Gino?"

"Never mind, you don't know them . . . Arcangeli was a friend of poor Daddy's at the Ministry."

"Where does he live?"

"Two steps from here, in Via Porpora."

"And what's his drawing room like?"

"You do ask the funniest questions, you know," she exclaimed with a laugh. "Why, what d'you expect it to be like? It's a room just like this one and like lots of others too . . . Why does it interest you so much to know what the Arcangeli's drawing-room is like?"

"And the daughters, are they engaged to be married?"

"Yes, Beatrice is . . . But why . . . ?"

"What's her fiancé like?"

"Well really—you even want to know about him! Well, he's got an odd name, Schirinzi, and he works in a lawyer's office."

Marcello noted that no inferences of any kind as to the nature of her guests could be deduced from Giulia's answers. Probably they had no more character in her mind than they had on the piece of paper: they were simply names of respectable, indistinguishable, normal people. He ran his eye down the list again and stopped at random at another name. "And who is Dr. Cesare Spadoni, with his wife Livia and his lawyer brother Tullio?"

"He's a children's doctor . . . His wife was at school with me. You may have met her—very attractive, dark, small, pale . . . He's a good-looking young man, clever too, and well-bred . . . The brother's good-looking too . . . They're twins."

"And Cavaliere Luigi Pace and his wife Teresa and his four sons, Maurizio, Giovanni, Vittorio and Riccardo?"

"Another of poor Daddy's friends . . . The sons are all students . . . Riccardo's still at school."

Marcello saw that it was useless to go on asking for information about the people on the list. Giulia would not be able to tell him much more than could be told from the list itself. Besides, he thought, even if she gave him minute information about the characters and the lives of these people, that information would necessarily be confined within the extremely narrow limits of her own judgment and intelligence. But he was conscious of an almost voluptuous contentment—even though its voluptuous quality had no joy in it—at being able, thanks to his marriage, to enter into and become a part of this extremely ordinary society. But there was still one question on the tip of his tongue, and after a moment's hesitation he decided to put it to her: "Now tell me—am I like these guests of yours?"

"How d'you mean—physically?"

"No . . . what I want to know is whether in your opinion I have any points of resemblance with them—in manner, in look, in general appearance . . . in fact, whether I'm like them."

"For me, you're better than anyone else," she answered impetuously. "But apart from that—yes—you *are* the same sort of person . . . You're well-bred, serious-minded, clever . . . in fact, one can see that, like them, you're a good, honest person . . . But why d'you ask me that question?"

"Never mind."

"How strange you are," she said, looking at him with a kind of curiosity; "most people want to be different from everyone else . . . but you're just the opposite; anyone would think you wanted to be *like* everyone else."

Marcello said nothing, but handed the list back to her, remarking in an offhand manner, "Anyhow I don't know a single one of them."

"Well, d'you think I know them all?" said Giulia gaily. "With lots of them, it's only Mummy who knows even who they are . . . Besides, the reception is all over in a minute . . . just an hour or so, and then you'll never see them again."

"*I* don't mind seeing them," said Marcello.

"I was only talking," said Giulia. "Now listen to the menu the hotel's suggested and tell me if you approve." Giulia took another piece of paper from her pocket and read aloud:

> Consommé froid
> Filets de Sole Meunière
> Dinde au riz, sauce suprème
> Salade de saison
> Fromages assortis
> Glace diplomatique
> Fruits
> Café et liqueurs

"What d'you think of it?" she asked, in the same doubtful but complacent tone in which, a short time before, she had spoken of her mother's bedroom; "d'you think it's all right? D'you think they'll have enough to eat?"

"I think it's excellent, and plenty of it too," said Marcello.

Giulia went on: "About the champagne—we chose Italian champagne . . . It's not so good as French, but for drinking toasts it's perfectly all right." She was silent for a moment, and then went on in her usual voluble way, "You know what Father Lattanzi said? That if you want to get married you must receive communion and if you want to receive communion you must go to confession . . . otherwise he won't marry us."

For a moment Marcello, taken by surprise, did not know what to say. He was not a believer and it was perhaps ten years since he had been to church. Besides, he had always been convinced that he felt a decided antipathy toward all thing ecclesiastical. Now he realized to his astonishment that far from being annoyed by it, this idea of confession and communion was pleasing and attractive to him, in the same way that he was pleased and attracted by the wedding reception, by all those guests that he did not know, by his marriage to Giulia, and by Giulia, herself who was so ordinary and like so many other girls. It was a further link, he thought, in the chain of normality by which he was seeking to anchor himself in the shifting sands of life; and addition this link was made of a more noble a more resistant, metal than the others—religion. He was almost surprised at not having thought of it before, and attributed this forgetfulness to the obvious, easy-going character of the religion in which he had been born and to which he had always seemed to belong, even without practicing it. Curious to know how Giulia would answer, he said, "But I'm not a believer."

"Who is?" she replied calmly. "D'you think ninety per cent of the people who go to church believe in it? And the priests themselves?"

"But *you* believe?"

Giulia waved her hand in the air. "Well, well," she said, "up to a point . . . Every now and then I say to Father Lattanzi, You don't bewitch *me* with all your stories, you priests . . . I believe them and I don't believe them . . . Or rather," she added punctiliously, "let's say that I have a religion all of my own . . . different from the religion of the priests."

What does she mean by a religion of her own, wondered Marcello. But knowing by experience that Giulia often spoke without knowing very well what she was saying, he did not press the point. Instead, he said, "My case is more serious . . . I don't believe at all, and I haven't any religion."

Giulia waved her hand gaily and indifferently. "But what does it mean to you? . . . You must go . . . It means so much to them, and it doesn't cost you anything."

"I daresay, but I shall be forced to tell a lie."

"Mere words . . . Besides, it'll be a lie for a good purpose . . . You know what Father Lattanzi says?—that you must do certain things just as if you believed, even if you don't believe . . . Faith comes afterwards."

Marcello was silent for a moment, and then said; "All right . . . I'll go to confession and then have communion." And as he spoke he was again conscious of the same thrill of slightly gloomy pleasure that the list of guests had inspired in him a little earlier. "I'll go and make my confession to Father Lattanzi," he added.

"There's no necessity for you to go to him," said Giulia; "you can go to any confessor, in any church you like."

"And how about communion?"

"Father Lattanzi will administer it the same day we get married . . . we go together . . . How long is it since you confessed?"

"Well . . . I don't think I've confessed since my first communion—when I was eight," said Marcello, rather embarrassed, "never since then."

"Just think!" she exclaimed joyfully, "what a tremendous number of sins you'll have to tell them about!"

"Supposing they won't give me absolution?"

"They'll give you absolution all right," she answered affectionately, stroking his face. "In any case, what sins can *you* have to confess? You're good and kind and you've never done anyone any harm . . . They'll give you absolution at once."

"It's a complicated business, getting married," said Marcello casually.

"But I love all these complications and preparations," said Giulia. "After all, we've got to stay together all the rest of our lives, haven't we? . . . Oh, by the way, what are we going to decide about the honeymoon?"

For the first time Marcello was aware of a feeling almost of pity for Giulia, apart from his usual indulgent, straightforward affection for her. He knew that there was still time for him to draw back and, instead of going to Paris, where he had his mission to fulfill, go somewhere else for their honeymoon. He could tell them, at the Ministry, that he refused the job. But at the same time he realized that this was impossible. The mission was the most resolute, the most compromising, the most decisive step on his road toward absolute and final normality; just as his marriage with Giulia, the wedding reception, religious ceremonies, confession and communion were all steps in the same direction, although, in his eyes, of less importance.

He did not pause more than a moment to analyze this thought, whose dark, almost sinister background did not escape him, but answered hurriedly: "I thought that after all we might go to Paris."

Giulia, crazy with delight, clapped her hands and exclaimed: "Ah, how wonderful! . . . Paris . . . my dream!" she threw her arms round his neck and kissed him violently. "If you knew how pleased I am! But I didn't want to tell you how I was longing to go to Paris . . . I was afraid it might cost too much."

"One way and another, it'll cost about the same as other places," said Marcello. "But don't worry about the money . . . we'll manage all right this time."

Giulia was in transports of delight. "Oh, how pleased I am!" she repeated. She pressed herself violently against Marcello and murmured: "D'you love me? Why don't you give me a kiss?" And so, once again, Marcello found himself with her arms around his neck and her lips against his. This time the ardor of her kiss seemed redoubled by gratitude. Giulia sighed, she twisted her whole body about, she squeezed Marcello's hand against her breast, she rolled her tongue rapidly and spasmodically inside his mouth. Marcello felt himself becoming excited, and thought, now, this minute, if I wanted to, I could have her, here, on this sofa; and he seemed to be aware, once more, of the fragility of what he called normality. At last they separated, and Marcello said with a smile: "It's lucky we're getting married soon . . . otherwise I'm afraid we'd become lovers, one of these days."

Giulia, still flushed from the kiss, shrugged her shoulders and answered with a kind of exalted, ingenuous shamelessness: "I love you so much . . . I'd ask nothing better."

"Truly?" asked Marcello.

"Yes, this minute," she said boldly, "here, now . . ." She had taken Marcello's hand and was slowly kissing it, looking up at him with shining, impassioned eyes. Then the door opened and she drew back. Giulia's mother came in.

She too, thought Marcello as he watched her approaching, was one of the large number of characters introduced into his life by his quest for a redeeming normality. There could be nothing in common between him and this sentimental woman, always overflowing with melting tenderness—nothing except his desire to tie himself firmly and lastingly to a human society that was solid and well-established. Giulia's mother, Signora Delia Ginami, was a corpulent lady in whom the slackening processes of mature age appeared to manifest themselves in a sort of disintegration not only of the body but of the mind, the former being afflicted with a quivering, boneless obesity, the latter with a tendency towards the languors of a kindness that was partly natural to her and partly affected. With every step she took, beneath her shapeless clothes whole portions of her swollen body appeared to be heeling over and shifting on their own account, and the slightest trifle was enough to provoke an agonizing emotional disturbance that overcame her powers of control, filling her watery blue eyes with tears, causing her to wring her hands in attitudes of ecstasy. During this period, the imminent marriage of her only daughter had plunged Signora Delia into a condition of perpetual sensibility. She was always weeping—with contentment, as she explained—and she felt, constantly a need to embrace

Giulia or her future son-in-law, for whom, she said, she already felt as much affection as if he were her own son. Marcello, filled with embarrassment by these effusions, understood nevertheless that they were merely one aspect of the reality into which he wanted to be absorbed, and as such he endured and appreciated them with the same rather somber satisfaction as was inspired in him by the ugly furniture in the house, by Giulia's conversation, by the wedding celebrations and the ritual demands of Father Lattanzi.

At this moment, however, Signora Delia was in a state not so much of tenderness as of indignation. She was waving a sheet of paper and, after greeting Marcello who had risen to his feet, said, "An anonymous letter . . . but first let's go to the other room . . . it's ready."

"An anonymous letter?" cried Giulia, rushing after her mother.

"Yes, an anonymous letter . . . How disgusting people are!"

Marcello followed them into the dining room, trying to hide his face behind his handkerchief. The news of the anonymous letter seriously disturbed him, and he was determined not to let the two women see it. To hear Giulia's mother exclaim, "An anonymous letter," and immediately to think, "Someone has written about the Lino affair," were for him one and the same thing. The blood had left his face, he had caught his breath and had been overwhelmed by a feeling of consternation, of shame and of fear, inexplicable, unexpected, shattering, a feeling such as he had never known except in the first years of adolescence when the memory of Lino was still fresh. It had been too strong for him; and all his powers of control had been swept away in an instant, just as a thin cordon of policemen might be swept away by the panic-stricken crowd it is supposed to hold back. As he approached the table he bit his lip till it bled. He had been wrong, then, when he had looked up the notice of the crime at the library and had been convinced that the old wound was completely healed; not merely was the wound not healed, but it was far deeper than he had suspected. Luckily his place at the head of the table was against the light, with his back to the window. Stiffly and in silence he sat down, with Giulia on his right and Signora Ginami on his left.

The anonymous letter now lay on the tablecloth beside Giulia's mother's plate. The little servant girl had come in, holding in both hands a large dish of spaghetti. Marcello plunged the fork into the red, greasy tangle and lifted a small quantity of it on to his own plate. Immediately the two women began to protest. "Not nearly enough . . .

you're trying to starve yourself . . . do take some more." And Signora Ginami added, "You work hard, you must eat." And Giulia impulsively took some more of the spaghetti from the dish and put it on her fiancé's plate.

"I'm not hungry," said Marcello, in a voice that seemed to him absurdly exhausted and distressed.

"Appetite comes with eating," replied Giulia emphatically helping herself.

The maid went out, carrying away the almost empty dish, and Giulia's mother said at once, "I didn't really mean to show it . . . It didn't seem to me worth while . . . But what a world we live in!"

Marcello said nothing; he bent his face over his plate and filled his mouth with spaghetti. He still feared that the letter was concerned with the Lino affair, although his reason told him that this was impossible. But it was an uncontrollable fear, a fear more powerful than any reflection. Giulia asked, "But surely, mayn't we know what the letter's about?"

Her mother answered, "First of all I want to tell Marcello that, as far as I am concerned, even if the letter contained things a thousand times worse, he can still be sure that my affection for him remains unchanged . . . Marcello, you're a real son to me, and you know that a mother's love for a son is stronger than any insinuation." Her eyes filled with tears, she repeated, "A real son," and seizing Marcello's hand, she carried it to her heart, saying, "Dear Marcello!" Not knowing what to do or say, Marcello sat motionless and silent, waiting for the effusion to finish. Signora Ginami gazed at him with tenderness in her eyes and then added, "You must forgive an old woman like me, Marcello."

"Don't be absurd, Mummy; you're not old," said Giulia, too well accustomed to these emotional disturbances on her mother's part to attach importance to them or to be surprised.

"Yes, I'm an old woman, I've only a few more years to live," replied Signora Delia. Imminent death was one of her favorite subjects of conversation, for it was not only a moving subject to her, but she thought, perhaps, that it also had the power to move others. "I shall die soon," she went on, "and that's why I'm so very, very pleased to be leaving my daughter in the charge of such a good man, Marcello."

Marcello—who, with his hand held firmly against her heart by Signora Delia, was forced into a most uncomfortable position over the top of his plate of spaghetti—could not repress a very slight movement of impatience that did not escape the old woman. She mistook it for a protest against what he considered to be excessive praise. "Yes, it's true," she repeated; "you *are* good . . . you are *so* good . . . Sometimes I say to Giulia, 'You're a lucky girl to have found such a good young man.' I know quite well, Marcello, that goodness is out of fashion nowadays . . . but you must allow someone who's many years older than you to say it—nothing in the world matters except goodness . . . And you, luckily, you are so very, very, very good."

Marcello frowned and said nothing. "Do let the poor man have something to eat," exclaimed Giulia, "don't you see you're dirtying his sleeve in the gravy?"

Signora Ginami let go Marcello's hand, and taking up the letter, said, "It's a typewritten letter . . . with a Rome postmark . . . I shouldn't be surprised, Marcello, if one of your colleagues at the office hadn't written it."

"But, Mummy, once and for all, mayn't we know what's in it?"

"Here it is," said her mother, handing the letter to Giulia. "Read it . . . but don't read it aloud . . . There are nasty things in it that I don't want to hear . . . Then, when you've read it, give it to Marcello."

Not without some anxiety, Marcello watched his fiancée read the letter. Then, twisting her mouth in scorn, "How disgusting!" Giulia pronounced, and handed it to him. The letter, written on thin typewriter paper, contained only a few lines in the faint ink of a worn-out ribbon. "Signora, in allowing your daughter to marry Dr. Clerici, you are committing something worse than an error, you are committing a crime. Dr. Clerici's father has for years been shut up in a lunatic asylum, with a form of madness which is of syphilitic origin; and, as you know, this malady is hereditary. There is still time; stop the marriage. A friend."

"So that's all," thought Marcello, almost disappointed. He seemed to be aware that his disappointment was greater than his relief. It was as if he had been hoping that someone else might share the knowledge of the tragedy of his childhood and so might free him, in part, from the burden of that knowledge. There was one phrase, nevertheless, that struck him: "As you know, this malady is hereditary." He knew perfectly well that the origin of his father's madness was not syphilitic, and that there was no danger of his going mad, some day, in the way his father had done. And yet that phrase, in all its threatening malignity, seemed to him to allude to some other kind of madness that might really be hereditary. This idea, immediately dismissed, no more than touched the surface of his mind. Then he handed back the letter to Giulia's mother, saying calmly, "There's no truth in it."

"I know there's no truth in it," answered the good lady, almost offended. After a moment she went on, "I only know that my daughter is marrying a man who is good, intelligent, honest, serious minded . . . and good-looking too," she added coquettishly.

"Quite particularly good-looking: you needn't be shy about saying so," Giulia confirmed, "and that's why whoever wrote the letter insinuates that he's tainted . . . Seeing him so good-looking, he can't believe that there isn't some hidden worm . . . Brutes . . ."

"I wonder what they would say," Marcello could not help thinking, "if they knew that at the age of thirteen I very nearly had sexual relations with a man, and that I killed him." He noticed, now that the fear aroused by the letter had passed, the usual melancholy, speculative apathy had again come over him. "Probably," he thought looking at his fiancée and at Signora Ginami, "probably it wouldn't make much impression on them . . . Normal people have thick skins"; and he realized that he was envying the two women for their "thick skins."

All of a sudden he said, "I've got to go and see my father today."

"Are you going with your mother?"

"Yes."

The spaghetti was finished; the little servant girl came in again, changed the plates and put down a dish filled with meat and vegetables on the table. As soon as she had left the room, Giulia's mother took up the letter again and, examining it, said, "I should just like to know who wrote that letter."

"Mummy," said Giulia all at once, with a sudden, excessive seriousness, "give me that letter a minute."

She took the envelope, looked at it carefully, then extracted the thin sheet of paper, scrutinized it, frowning, and finally exclaimed in a loud, indignant voice, "I know perfectly well who wrote this letter . . there can't be any doubt about it . . . Oh, what an infamous thing!"

"Who was it then?"

"An unfortunate wretch," replied Giulia, looking down at the table.

Marcello said nothing. Giulia worked as a secretary in a lawyer's office, and probably the letter had been written by one of the clerks there. "No doubt some envious person," said her mother. "Marcello, at thirty, has a position that many older men would like to have."

Although his curiosity was not aroused, Marcello asked his fiancée, as a matter of form, "If you know the name of the person who wrote the letter, why don't you tell us?"

"I can't," she answered, more thoughtful, now, than indignant. "But I've told you, he's an unfortunate wretch." She gave the letter back to her mother and helped herself from the dish that the maid handed to her.

For a moment none of the three spoke. Then Giulia's mother began again, in a tone of sincere incredulity, "And yet I can't believe that there can be anyone so bad as to be able to write such a letter about a man like Marcello."

"Not everybody loves him as we do, Mummy," said Giulia.

"But who," her mother burst out with great emphasis, "who could help loving our dear Marcello?"

"You know what Mummy says about you?" asked Giulia, who seemed now to have returned to her usual gaiety and volubility,"—that you're not a man but an angel . . . And so I suppose one of these days, instead of coming into the house by the door, you'll fly in by the window." She suppressed a burst of laughter and went on: "It'll be a great pleasure to the priest when you go to confession, to know that you're an angel . . . It isn't every day that he listens to the confession of an angel."

"Now you're making fun of me, as usual," said her mother; "but I'm not exaggerating in the least . . . For me, Marcello *is* an angel," She looked at Marcello with intense and sugary tenderness, and her eyes began to fill with tears. She added, after a moment, "In all my life I've known only one man who was as good as Marcello— and that was your father, Giulia."

Giulia now put on a serious look, as though to devote herself to the subject, and looked down at her plate. Her mother's face was undergoing a gradual transformation: an abundance of tears overflowed from her eyes, while a pathetic grimace distorted the soft, puffy features among the stray locks of her loosened hair, so that colors and lineaments appeared confused and dimmed, as though seen through a sheet of glass streaming with water. Hurriedly she searched for her handkerchief, and holding it to her eyes, stammered: "A truly good man . . . truly an angel . . . and we were so happy together, we three . . . and now he's dead he's not here any more. . . . Marcello reminds me of your father, with his goodness, and that's why I'm so very fond of him. . . . When I think that that man who was so good is dead, my heart breaks." The last words were lost in the handkerchief.

Giulia said calmly, "Have something to eat, Mummy."

"No, no, I'm not hungry," sobbed her mother. "You must

forgive me, you two. . . . You're happy, and happiness must not be spoiled by the sorrow of an old woman." She rose hastily and went out of the room.

"Just think, it's six years ago," said Giulia, looking at the door, "and yet it's still just as if it was the first day."

Marcello said nothing. He had lit a cigarette and was smoking with bent head. Giulia put out her hand and took his. "What are you thinking about?" she asked, almost beseechingly.

Giulia often asked him what he was thinking about, for she was often filled with curiosity and even alarm by the serious, reserved expression on his face. Marcello answered, "I was thinking about your mother. . . . Her compliments embarrass me. . . . She doesn't know me well enough to say that I'm good."

Giulia squeezed his hand and replied, "She doesn't say it just as a compliment. . . . Even when you're not here, she often says to me, 'How good Marcello is!' "

"But what does *she* know about it?"

"There are some things that can be seen." Giulia rose and stood beside him, pressing her rounded hip against his shoulder and passing her hand through his hair. "But why? Don't you want people to think you're good?"

"I don't mean that," answered Marcello. "I mean that it may not be true."

She shook her head. "Your trouble is that you're too modest. . . . Now listen—I'm not like Mummy who tries to make out that everyone is good. . . . For me there are good people and bad people. . . . Well, to me, you're one of the best people I've ever met in my life . . . and I don't say that because we're engaged and because I love you . . . I say it because it's true."

"But what, exactly, does this goodness consist in?"

"I've told you. There are some things that can be seen. . . . Why does one say that a woman is beautiful? . . . Because one *sees* that she is . . . and one sees that you are good."

"Well, so be it," said Marcello, with bowed head. The conviction of the two women that he was good was not new to him, but he always found it profoundly disconcerting. In what did this goodness consist? Was he then truly good? Was it not rather that the thing which Giulia and her mother called goodness was really his abnormality, in fact his detachment, his remoteness from ordinary life? Normal men were not good, he went on to think, for normality must always be paid for, whether consciously or not, at a high price, with various sorts of complicity of a negative kind—insensibility, stupidity, cowardice if not actual criminality. He was interrupted in these reflections by the voice of Giulia, saying, "By the way, d'you know my dress has come? I want to show it to you . . . Wait here a minute."

She rushed out of the room and Marcello rose from the table, went over to the window and threw it wide open. The window looked out over the street, or rather, since it was the top-floor flat, over the jutting parapet of the building, below which one could see nothing. But beyond this emptiness lay the full extent of the attic floor of the building opposite—a row of windows with shutters open, through which the occupants of the room could be seen. It was a flat very similar to Giulia's: a bedroom, with the beds still unmade; a "good" drawing room with the usual sham, dark-colored furniture; a dining room at whose table three people, two men and a woman, could be seen sitting. These rooms opposite were very near because the street was not wide, and Marcello could distinguish the three people at the dining room table extremely clearly—a thickset, elderly man with a great mane of white hair, a younger man, thin, brown, and a blonde woman of mature, rather opulent figure. They were eating calmly at a table very like the one at which he himself had been sitting shortly before, beneath a chandelier not very different from the one in the room where he now stood. And yet, although he saw them so clearly that he had almost the illusion of being able to hear their conversation, they seemed to him—perhaps owing to the feeling created by the jutting parapet that there was a gulf between them—to be infinitely far off and remote. He could not help feeling that those rooms represented normality. He could see them. He could, by slightly raising his voice, have spoken to the three people at the table; yet in spite of that he was outside them, not only in a material but also in a moral sense. For Giulia, on the other hand, that remoteness, that foreignness did not exist. They were a purely physical fact and she was *inside* those rooms, had always been inside them; and if he had pointed them out to her she would have produced, with complete indifference, all the information she possessed on the subject of the people who lived in them—just as she had done, a little earlier, about the people invited to the wedding reception. It was an indifference that denoted not merely familiarity but actual inattentiveness. In reality she did not give any name to normality, being completely submerged in it—just as it is to be supposed that animals, if they could talk, would not give any name to the nature of which they form an integral and unconditional part. But he himself remained outside, and normality was called normality, for him, just because he was excluded from it, and because he was conscious of it as such, in contrast to his own abnormality. To be like Giulia, you had either to be born to it, or . . .

The door behind him opened, and he turned. Giulia was there in front of him in her bridal dress of white silk, holding up with both hands, for him to admire, the ample veil that flowed down from her head. She said, exultingly, "Isn't it lovely . . . look!" and, still holding out the veil with both hands, she circled about in the space between the window and the table so that her future husband might admire the wedding dress from every point of view. The wedding dress resembled every other wedding dress, but Marcello was glad that Giulia should be pleased with this perfectly ordinary dress in exactly the same way in which millions and millions of other women before her had been pleased. The rounded, exuberant curves of Giulia's figure were moulded with clumsy obviousness by the glossy white silk. All at once she came up to Marcello, and dropping the veil and holding up her face toward him, said, "Now give me a kiss . . . but don't touch me, or my dress will get crumpled." At that moment Giulia turned her back to the window and Marcello faced her. As he bent down to touch her lips with his he looked across into the dining room of the flat opposite and saw the white-haired man rise from the table and leave the room. Immediately afterward, the other two, the thin, brown young man and the blonde woman, also rose, almost automatically, and as they stood there they kissed each other. This sight pleased him, for after all he was behaving just like those two people from whom, only a short time before, he had felt himself to be divided by a wholly insuperable gulf. At the same moment Giulia exclaimed impatiently, "Never mind, my dress can go to the devil," and without letting go of Marcello, half closed the shutters with her other hand. Then, pressing her whole body against him, she threw her arms around his neck. They kissed in the darkness, hampered by the veil, and once again, as his fiancée clung tightly to him and wriggled and sighed and kissed him, it struck Marcello that she was acting in all innocence, unconscious of any contradiction between this embrace and her bridal costume; and this was yet another proof that it was permissible for normal people to take the utmost liberties with normality itself. At last they separated, breathless, and Giulia whispered, "We mustn't be impatient . . . just a few days more and then you'll be able to kiss me even in the street."

"I must go," he said, wiping his mouth with his handkerchief.

"I'll come with you."

They felt their way out of the dining room and into the

hall. "We'll see each other this evening, after dinner," Giulia said. Tenderly, lovingly she gazed at him, leaning against the doorpost. The veil, displaced by the kiss, hung untidily on one side. Marcello went up to her and straightened it, saying, "That's all right now." At that moment there was a hum of voices on the landing of the floor below. Giulia, bashful, drew back, threw him a kiss with the tips of her fingers and hurriedly shut the door.

## CHAPTER 6

The idea of confession did not please Marcello. He was not religious in the sense of formally practicing the pre-scribed rites; nor was he very sure that he had any natural inclination toward religious feeling; yet he would have been quite willing to look upon the confession demanded by Father Lattanzi as one of the many conventional acts upon which he was embarking with a view to establishing himself, once and for all, as a normal person, had it not been that this matter of confession involved the revelation of two things which for different reasons he felt it quite impossible to confess— the tragedy of his childhood and his mission to Paris. An obscure instinct told him that there was a subtle connection between these two things; and yet it would have been very difficult for him to say clearly what this con-nection was. Futhermore, he was quite aware that, among the many possible standards of behavior, he had not chosen the Christian standard that forbids man to kill, but another, entirely different one, political and of recent introduction, that had no objection to bloodshed. In Christianity, in fact, as represented by the Church with its hundreds of dignitaries, its innumerable churches, its saints and its martyrs, he did not recognize the power that was needed to bring him back into that communion with other men from which he had been debarred by the Lino affair—that power which he felt to be implicit in the plump Minister with the lipstick-stained mouth, in the cynical secretary, and in all his superiors in the Secret Service. Marcello was conscious of all this by some obscure intuition rather than by any process of thought, and his melancholy was increased by it for he was like a man who, all other ways being closed, sees but one way out, and that a distasteful one.

But he must make up his mind, he thought as he jumped on the streetcar going toward Santa Maria Maggiore, he must choose between making a complete confession, according to the rules of the Church, or confining himself to a partial, purely formal confession, simply to please Giulia. Although he was neither a practicing nor a believing Christian, he inclined to the first of these alternatives; hoping, almost, by means of his confession, if not to alter his destiny, at least to attach himself firmly to it by yet another tie. As the trolley moved through the streets he debated the problem with his usual rather dull, pedantic seriousness. As far as Lino was concerned, he felt more or less easy. He would be able to tell the story as it had really happened, and the priest, after the usual examination and the usual recommendations, could not but give him absolution. But with regard to the mission which, as he well knew, involved fraud, treachery and, in its last stage, possibly the death of a man, he realized that this was an entirely different matter. The point, in this case, was not so much to obtain approval of it as the mere fact of talking about it. He was not at all sure that he was capable of it; for to speak of it would mean abandoning one standard for another; submitting to Christian judgment something that he had hitherto considered to be entirely unrelated to it; betraying his implicit obligation of secrecy and silence; in fact, risking the whole carefully built-up edifice of his absorption into normality. All the same, he thought it was worthwhile making the attempt, if only in order to convince himself yet again, by this final certificate of official approbation of the edifice' solidity.

He was aware that he was considering these alternatives without excessive emotion, in a cool, impassive spirit like that of a detached spectator, just as if he had made his choice already and all that had to happen in the future was discounted in advance, though he could not know how or when. He was so little troubled by doubt that when he entered the vast church, filled with a comforting shade and silence and coolness after the glare and noise and heat of the street, he went so far as to forget his confession. He started to wander about over its deserted flagstones, from one aisle to another, like an idle tourist. He had always found churches pleasing to him as safe points in a fluctuating world, constructions by no means casual in which the things that he himself was seeking—order, a standard, a rule of life—had found, in other days, their massive and splendid expression. Very often he would go into a church—numerous as they are in Rome—and sit down on a bench, without praying, in the contemplation of something that might have fitted his own case if only conditions had been different. The thing that attracted him in churches was not the solutions that they offered and that it was impossible for him to accept, but rather a final result he could not but appreciate and admire. He liked all churches; but the more imposing they were, the more magnificent, the more profane, the more he liked them. In such churches, in which religion had evaporated and become a majestic, ordered worldliness, he seemed to recognize the point of transition from a primitive religious belief to a now adult society which nevertheless, without that far-off belief, could not have existed.

At this hour the church was deserted. Marcello went right up beneath the altar, and then, moving close to one of the pillars of the right-hand aisle, looked down the full length of the floor, seeking to reduce his own stature to nothing and to drop his eye to ground level. How vast the floor looked, seen thus in perspective, as an ant might see it! It seemed like a great plain and made one almost giddy. Then he looked up, and his eye, following the feeble glimmer cast by the dim light upon the rounded surfaces of the immense marble shafts, rebounded from pillar to pillar all the way down to the door where he had entered.

At that moment someone came in, lifting the heavy curtain and letting in a segment of crude white light. How small the figure in the doorway looked, far away at the other end of the church! Marcello went round behind the altar and looked at the mosaics in the apse. The figure of Christ, surrounded by four saints, arrested his attention; whoever had painted Him in that way, he thought, certainly had no doubts about what was normal and what was abnormal. He bent his head as he made his way slowly towards the confessional in the right-hand aisle. He was thinking now that it was useless to regret not having been born in other times and other conditions. He was what he was precisely because the times and conditions in which he was living were no longer the same as those that had permitted the erection of this church; and his whole moral obligation lay in the conscious recognition of this reality.

He went up to the confessional, which, made all of dark carved wood, was proportionate in size to the huge basilica, and was in time to catch a glimpse of the priest sitting inside it as he drew the curtain across and hid himself; but he did not see his face. With a habitual gesture, as he knelt down, he pulled up his trousers at the knee so that they should not get crumpled; then he said in a low voice, "I want to make my confession."

From the other side came the priest's voice, answering, in a subdued but frank, brisk tone, that he might begin at once. The voice was full and rhythmical, a deep bass, the voice of a mature man with a strong Southern accent. In spite of himself Marcello could not help conjuring up a monkish figure with a face all smothered in black beard, with thick eyebrows, a massive nose, ears and nostrils full of hairs. A man, he felt, made of the same heavy, massive material as the confessional itself, a man without suspicions, without subtleties. The priest, as he had foreseen, asked him how long it was since he had confessed, and he answered that he had never confessed except during his childhood and that he was doing it now because he was intending to get married. After a moment's silence the priest's voice on the other side of the grating said, in a somewhat indifferent tone. "You have done very wrong, my son. . . . And how old are you?"

"Thirty," said Marcello.

"You have lived for thirty years in sin," said the priest, in the tone of an accountant announcing the amount of an overdraft. He resumed after a moment's pause, "For thirty years you have lived like an animal, not like a human being."

Marcello bit his lip. The confessor's authority, as expressed in this brisk, familiar manner of judging his case before he even knew its details, was obnoxious and irritating to him. Not that the priest—probably a good man who performed his office scrupulously—displeased him, nor the place, nor the rite itself; but in contrast to the Ministry, where everything had displeased him but where authority had seemed to him obvious and unquestionable, here he felt an instinctive desire to rebel. He said, however, with an effort, "I have committed every sin . . . even the worst."

"*Every* sin?"

Now I'm going to say I killed a man, he thought, and I want to see what effect it will have upon me. He hesitated, and then, exerting himself, succeeded in pronouncing in a clear, firm voice, "Yes, every sin; I've even killed a man."

The priest immediately exclaimed in a lively manner but without either indignation or surprise, "You killed a man and yet you did not feel the need to confess."

Marcello reflected that that was exactly the right thing for the priest to have said: no horror, no surprise, merely an official reproof for not having confessed so grave a sin at the proper time. And he was grateful to the priest, just as he would have been grateful to a police inspector who, faced with the same confession, had placed him, without comment and without delay, under arrest. Everyone had to act his part, and only in that way could the world endure. In the meantime, however, he was conscious that in revealing his own tragedy he again experienced no particular feeling; and he was surprised at this indifference, which was in such strong contrast to his profound agitation of a short time before, when Giulia's mother had announced that she had had an anonymous letter. He said, in a calm voice, "I killed a man when I was thirteen . . . in self-defense . . . and almost without meaning to."

"Tell me how it happened."

He changed his position slightly as his knees were beginning to hurt him, and then began, "One morning when I came out of school a man came up to me with some excuse . . . At that time I was longing to possess a revolver . . . not a toy one but a real revolver. . . He promised to give me a revolver and so succeeded in making me get into his car. . . He was some foreign lady's chauffeur and had the use of the car all day long because she was away, traveling abroad. . . I was completely ignorant at that time, and when he made certain proposals to me I didn't even undersand what it was all about."

"What sort of proposals?"

"Sexual proposals," said Marcello soberly. "I didn't know what sexual love was, either normal or abnormal. . . I got into the car, then, and he took me to his employer's villa."

"And what happened there?"

"Nothing, or practically nothing. . . First of all he made one or two attempts, then he was sorry and made me promise that from then on I wouldn't pay any attention to him, even if he invited me again to get into the car."

"What d'you mean by 'practically nothing'? Did he kiss you?"

. "No," said Marcello, slightly surprised, "he only put his arm round my waist, for a moment, in the passage."

"Go on."

"He had foreseen, however, that he would not be able to forget me. . . And the next day he was again waiting for me when I came out of school. . . This time he again told me that he would give me the revolver, and I, longing to possess it, at first hung back a little and then agreed to get into the car."

"Where did you go?"

"As before, to the villa, to his own room. . ."

"And this time, how did he behave?"

"He was quite different," said Marcello; "he seemed quite beside himself. . . He said he wouldn't give me the revolver and that, one way or another, I had to do what he wanted. . . As he said this he was holding the revolver in his hand. . . . Then he took hold of my arm and threw me down on the bed, making me hit my head against the wall. . . The revolver meanwhile had fallen on to the bed and he was kneeling in front of me with his arms round my legs. . . I seized the revolver, jumped up from the bed and took a few steps backward, and then, throwing out his arms, he shouted, 'Kill me, kill me like a dog . . .' Then I—just as if I was obeying him—fired, and he fell back on the bed. . . And I ran away and knew nothing more about it. . . All this happened many years ago. . . Recently I went and looked up the newspapers of that time and found out that the man died that same evening, in hospital."

Marcello had told his tale without hurrying, choosing his words with care and pronouncing them with precision. He was aware, while he was speaking, that as usual he felt nothing—nothing except that cold, remote sadness that was customary with him whatever he said or did. The priest, without commenting in any way on the story, asked at once, "Are you sure you have told the whole truth?"

"Yes, I'm certain," replied Marcello, surprised.

"You know," went on the priest, suddenly arousing himself, "you know that if you keep back or distort the truth or part of it, your confession is not valid, and besides, you commit a grave sacrilege. . . What really happened between you and that man, the second time?"

"But . . . just what I've told you."

"Was there no carnal relation between you? . . . Did he not use violence?"

So murder, Marcello could not help thinking, was less important than the sin of sodomy. He confirmed what he had said, "There was nothing except what I've told you."

"It would appear," continued the priest inflexibly, "that you killed the man to avenge yourself for something that he had done to you. . ."

"He had done absolutely nothing to me."

There was a brief silence, filled, it seemed to him, with ill-disguised incredulity. "And since then," asked the priest all of a sudden, in an entirely unexpected manner, "have you ever had relations with men?"

"No . . . my sexual life has been, and still is, perfectly normal."

"What do you mean by 'normal' sexual life?"

"In that respect I am a man just like any other man. . . The first time I had a woman was in a brothel, at the age of seventeen . . . and since then I have never had any relations except with women."

"And that's what you call a normal sexual life?"

"Yes, why not?"

"But that too is abnormal," said the priest triumphantly; "that too is sin. . . Has nobody ever told you, my poor child?—the normal thing is to marry and have relations with your own wife with the object of bringing children into the world."

"That's just what I'm on the point of doing," said Marcello.

"Good, good, but it's not enough. . . You can't go to the altar with bloodstained hands."

At last we're coming to it, Marcello could not help thinking, for he had almost believed, for a moment, that the priest had forgotten the main object of his confession. He said, as humbly as he could, "Tell me what I must do."

"You must repent," said the priest; "only by a sincere and profound repentance can you expiate the evil you have done."

"I have already repented," said Marcello thoughtfully, "if repentance means a strong desire never to have done certain things, then I have indeed repented." He would have liked to add: "but this repentance has not been enough . . . it could not be enough." However, he restrained himself.

The priest said hurriedly, "It is my duty to warn you that if what you tell me now is not true, my absolution has no value. . . You know what awaits you if you deceive me?"

"What?"

"Damnation."

The priest uttered this last word with a particular satisfaction. Marcello probed his imagination to see what this word recalled, and found nothing; not even the old picture of the flames of hell. But at the same time he was aware that the word meant more than the priest had intended it to mean. And an anxious shudder ran through him, as though he knew that this damnation, whether he repented or not, was in store for him, and that it was not in the priest's power to save him from it. "I have truly repented," he repeated bitterly.

"And you have nothing else to tell me?"

Marcello was silent for a moment before replying. He realized now that the time had come for him to speak of his mission, which, he knew, would involve actions liable to be condemned—in fact already condemned beforehand —by the rules of Christianity. He had foreseen this moment and had rightly ascribed the greatest importance to his own ability to reveal the mission. And then, with a quiet, melancholy feeling of a discovery that he had expected, he found himself, almost at the moment when he was opening his mouth to speak, held back by an insuperable repugnance. It was not a moral disgust, nor was it shame, nor indeed any sense of guilt; it was something utterly different which had nothing to do with guilt. It was, so to speak, an overruling inhibition, dictated by a profound complicity and loyalty.

He *ought not* to speak about his mission, that was all, and this was intimated to him in an authoritative manner by that same conscience which had remained dumb and inert at the moment when he announced to the priest, "I have killed a man." Not entirely convinced, he tried once again to speak, but again he was conscious of that same repugnance halting his tongue and obstructing his utterance, in the automatic manner in which a lock springs open when the key is turned. Once again, therefore, and with even stronger proof, he had confirmation of the power of authority as represented at the Ministry by the contemptible Minister and his no less contemptible secretary. It was, like all other kinds of authority, a mysterious thing which, so it seemed, sank its roots down into the deepest part of his spirit, whereas the Church, apparently so much more authoritative, went no deeper than the surface. And so, for the first time being deceitful he said, "Ought I to tell my fiancée, before we get married, what I've told you today?"

"Have you never said anything about it to her?"

"No, it would be the first time."

"I don't see any necessity for it," said the priest; "you would upset her to no purpose . . . and you would be endangering your family's peace of mind."

"Yes, you're right," said Marcello.

Another silence ensued. Then the priest said, in a conclusive tone, as though he were putting his last and final question: "Tell me, my son, have you ever been a member, or are you a member now, of any subversive group or sect?"

Marcello, who had not expected this question, was disconcerted and, for a moment, silenced. Clearly, he thought, the priest was putting this question by order of his superiors, in order to ascertain the political leanings of his flock. Yet it was significant that he should ask it. He himself, who approached the rites of the Church as a matter of form, considering them as ceremonies unrelated to the society of which he desired to be a member, was in point of fact being asked by the priest not to put himself in opposition to that society. This was his request, rather than that he should not put himself in opposition to *him*. He would have liked to reply: "No, I am a member of a group that hunts down subversive elements." But he resisted this malicious temptation and simply said, "To tell the truth, I am a government official."

This answer evidently pleased the priest, for, after a short pause, he quietly resumed, "Now you must promise me that you will pray. . . And I don't mean that you must pray just for a few days, or a few months . . . or even a few years . . . but all the rest of your life. . . You must pray for your own soul and for the soul of that man. . . and you must make your wife pray too, and your children, if you have any. . . Prayer is the only thing that can draw God's attention to you and obtain His pity for you. . . Do you understand? . . . And now concentrate your thoughts and pray with me."

Marcello automatically bowed his head and listened through the grating to the subdued, hurrying voice of the priest as he recited a prayer in Latin. And then the priest, in a louder voice and still in Latin, pronounced the form of absolution; and Marcello rose from the confessional.

But, as he passed across in front of it, the curtain was drawn aside and the priest beckoned to him to stop. He saw with surprise that he was just as he had pictured him —rather fat, bald, with a big rounded forehead, thick eyebrows, round brown eyes that were serious but not intelligent, a full-lipped mouth. A country priest, he thought, a mendicant friar. The priest, in the meantime, was holding out toward him, in silence, a little booklet with a colored picture on its cover—the *Life of Saint Ignatius of Loyola* in an edition for young Catholics. "Thank you," said Marcello, examining the little book. The priest made another gesture as though to say that there was no need to thank him, and drew the curtain again. Marcello walked away to the entrance door.

Just as he was on the point of going out, however, he cast a glance round the church, with its two rows of pillars, its coffered ceiling, its deserted floor, its great altar, and it seemed to him that he was saying farewell forever to an ancient survival of a world such as he longed for and such as he knew could never exist again. It was a kind of mirage in reverse, based upon an irrevocable past from which his steps carried him further and further away. Then he lifted the heavy curtain and went out into the strong light of a clear sky, into the square with its metallic clanging of streetcars and its vulgar background of nondescript buildings and shops.

## *CHAPTER 7*

When Marcello got out of the bus in the quarter where his mother lived he became conscious, almost immediately, that he was being followed at some distance by a man. As he walked in a leisurely way down the deserted street, past the walls of gardens, he took a quick look at him. He was a man of middling height, rather stout, with a square face whose expression was honest and good-natured but not without a certain sly cunning such as is often to be seen on the faces of peasants. He was wearing a thin suit that had faded to a color between brown and purple, and a hat that was intended to be light gray was pulled well down on his head but had its brim turned up in front in the proper peasant manner. If he had seen him in the piazza of a small town on market day, Marcello would have taken him for a farm bailiff. The man had traveled up in the same bus as Marcello, had got out at the same stopping-place and now was following him on the opposite pavement without taking much trouble to conceal the fact, regulating his pace according to Marcello's and never for a moment taking his eyes off him. But this fixed stare of his seemed uncertain of itself —just as though the man were not entirely sure of Marcello's identity and wished to study his face before approaching him.

In this way they walked together the whole way up the hill, in the silence and heat of early afternoon. In the gardens, beyond the railings of the closed gates, there was no one to be seen; nor was there a sign of anyone, up the whole length of the street, beneath the green tunnel formed by the overhanging foliage of the pepper trees. Finally this solitude, this silence made Marcello suspicious, since there were conditions clearly favorable for some surprise attack, and which might have been deliberately chosen by his pursuer. Brusquely, with sudden decisiveness, he left the pavement and crossed the street to the other man. "Perhaps you were looking for me?" he asked, when he came within a few paces of him.

The man, too, had stopped at Marcello's question, with an almost timid expression on his face. "Excuse me," he said in a low voice, "I only followed you because I thought perhaps we might both be going to the same place . . . otherwise I should not have dreamed of doing so. . . Excuse me, are you by any chance Dr. Clerici?"

"Yes, I am," said Marcello, "and who are you?"

"Orlando, of the Secret Service Police," said the man, giving a kind of military salute. "I was sent by Colonel Baudino. . . He gave me two addresses for you—the boarding house where you live and this address here. . . As I didn't find you at the boarding house, I came to look for you here and it so happened that I thought you were in the same bus. . . It's an urgent matter."

"Come along, then," said Marcello, walking off without more ado toward the gate of his mother's villa. He took a key from his pocket, opened the gate and invited the man to come in. He obeyed, respectfully removing his hat and displaying a perfectly round head with sparse black hair and, at the crown, a white circular bald patch that looked exactly like a tonsure. Marcello walked in front of him down the path, making for the far end of the garden where he knew there was a pergola with a table and two iron chairs. As he went, he could not help noticing once again the neglected, overgrown look of the garden. The clean white gravel on which, as a child, he had loved to run up and down had disappeared years ago, buried under soil or scattered abroad. The outline of the path, swallowed up in rough grass, could be traced chiefly by the remains of two small myrtle hedges, uneven now, and with gaps in them, but still recognizable. The flower beds running beside the hedges were also smothered in exuberant weeds; the rose trees and other flowering plants were entangled with bristling shrubs and briars in inextricable confusion. Here and there, too, in the shade of the trees, were piles of rubbish, disintegrated packing cases, broken bottles and all sorts of similar objects which are generally consigned to attics. He averted his eyes in disgust from this sight, asking himself, as he had often done before, with a mixture of surprise and discouragement, "Why on earth can't they tidy up? So little is needed . . . Why is it?" Further on, the path ran between the wall of the villa and the garden wall, that same ivy-covered wall over which, as a child, he had been accustomed to hold communication with his neighbor Roberto. He led the Secret Service agent into the pergola and sat down on the iron chair, inviting him to do the same. But he remained respectfully standing. "There's not very much to tell, sir," he said hastily. "I am entrusted by the Colonel to inform you that you are to stop, on your way to Paris, at S." and he named a town not far from the frontier—"and to go and ask for Signor Gabrio, at 3 Via dei Glicini."

"A change of program," thought Marcello. It was characteristic of the Secret Service, as he knew, deliberately and at the last moment to make changes of plan, with the object of distributing responsibility and covering up traces. "Where is it I'm to go in Via dei Glicini?" he could not help asking, "is it a private apartment?"

"Well, actually no, Doctor," said the Secret Service man with a broad smile, half knowing and half embarrassed; "it's a bawdy house. . . The proprietress is called Enrichetta Parodi. . . But you must ask for Signor Gabrio. . . . The house, like all these places, is open till midnight. . . . But it would really be better, sir, if you went early in the morning, when there's nobody there. . . I shall be there too." He was silent for a moment. Then, unable to interpret the complete lack of expression on Marcello's face, he added in embarrassment: "That's just for the sake of security, sir."

Marcello, without saying a word, raised his eyes and considered him for a moment. It was his duty to dismiss him now, but, for some reason unknown to himself—perhaps because of the honest, homely expression on the square, broad face—he wanted to add a word or two, of an unofficial kind, to show that he felt friendly towards him. Finally he asked, at random, "How long have you been in the Service, Orlando?"

"Since 1925, sir."

"And in Italy all the time?"

"Scarcely at all, sir," answered the Secret Service man with a sigh, evidently anxious for a confidential talk; "oh, sir, if I could tell you what my life has been like since then, and what I've been through! . . . Always on the move —Turkey, France, Germany, Kenya, Tunisia . . . never still for an instant." He paused for a moment, gazing fixedly at Marcello; then with rhetorical yet sincere solemnity, he added, "And all for Family and Fatherland, sir."

Marcello again looked up at him as he stood there, hat in hand, almost at attention; then, with a gesture of dismissal, said: "All right then, Orlando. . . Tell the Colonel I'll stop at S., as he wishes."

"Yes, sir." He saluted and walked away past the wall of the villa.

Left alone, Marcello sat staring into emptiness. It was hot underneath the pergola, and the sun, filtering through the leaves and branches of the Virginia creeper, scorched his face with discs of dazzling light. The painted iron table, that once had been spotless, was now a dirty white, with black and rusty stains where the paint had flaked off. As he looked out from the pergola he could see the part of the garden wall where the opening in the ivy had been, through which he had been accustomed to communicate with Roberto. The ivy was still there, and it might still have been possible to look through into the next-door garden; but Roberto's family no longer lived there, and the villa was now occupied by a dentist who received his clients in his own home. Suddenly a lizard ran down the stem of the Virginia creeper and came fearlessly forward on to the table. It was a big lizard of the most common type, with a green back and a white belly that throbbed against the yellowish paint of the table. Rapidly, with little darting steps, it came quite close to Marcello and then stopped dead, its sharp head raised in his direction, its little black eyes staring in front of it. He looked at it with affection, and did not move for fear of frightening it. He remembered the time when as a boy he had slaughtered the lizards and then, to rid himself of his remorse, had in vain sought to involve the timid Roberto as his partner and ally. At the time he had not succeeded in finding anybody to lighten the burden of his guilt. He had been left to face the death of the lizards alone; and in that loneliness he had recognized the evidence of his crime. But now, he thought, he was not, he never again would be, alone. Even if he committed a crime—provided he committed it for certain ends—he would have the State at his back, as well as its dependent political, social and military organizations, great masses of people who thought as he did, and, outside Italy, other states, other millions of people. What he was going to do, he reflected, was a worse thing than killing a few lizards; and yet there were so many people on his side, beginning with the honest Secret Service man Orlando, a married man and the father of five children. "For Family and Fatherland"; that phrase, so ingenuous . in spite of its solemnity, was like a fine, bright-colored banner flying in a joyful breeze on a sunny day while trumpets sound and soldiers march; and it echoed in his ears, inspiring yet sad, mingling hope with melancholy. "For Family and Fatherland," he thought, "that's enough for Orlando . . . why can't it be enough for me too?"

As he sat there, he heard the sound of a car from the direction of the entrance gate, and at once rose with a brusque movement that scared the lizard away. Without hurrying, he left the pergola and walked toward the gate. An old, black motorcar was standing in the avenue, not far from the still open gate. The chauffeur, in a white livery with blue facings, was just closing it, but when he saw Marcello he stopped and raised his cap.

"Alberi," said Marcello in his quietest voice, "we're going to the clinic today, so there's no need to put the car in the garage."

"Very good, Signor Marcello," replied the chauffeur. Marcello glanced at him sideways. Alberi was a young man with olive complexion and coal-black eyes with whites like glossy white china. He had very regular features, close-set white teeth, carefully oiled black hair. He was not tall, yet he gave the effect of being built on a large scale, perhaps because of the smallness of his hands and feet. He was of the same age as Marcello, but appeared older, owing, possibly, to a kind of Oriental softness that insinuated itself into each of his features and looked as though, with time, it would inevitably turn to plumpness. As he was closing the gate Marcello looked at him again, with aversion, then he walked away toward the house.

He opened the french window and went into the drawing room, that was almost in darkness. He was immediately struck by the musty, unwholesome smell hanging in the air, comparatively slight in contrast to that of the other rooms where his mother's ten Pekinese dogs roamed freely, but all the more noticeable here where they scarcely ever penetrated. When he opened the window a little light came into the room and for a moment he saw the furniture in its gray dust covers, the rolled-up carpets standing upright in the corners, the piano muffled in sheets pinned together. He went through the drawing room and dining room and out into the hall and then started up the stairs. Half way up, on a bare marble step (the carpet, worn out, had vanished long since and never been replaced) lay a piece of dog's excrement, and he made a detour so as not to step in it. When he reached the landing he went straight to the door of his mother's room and opened it. He had barely had time to do so before all ten Pekinese, like a long-contained flood of water that suddenly overflows, surged out between his legs and rushed, barking, all over the landing and staircase. Hesitating in the doorway, he watched them irritably as they ran away, with their elegant, feathery tails and their sulky, almost catlike muzzles. Then, from the gloomy half-darkness of the room, came his mother's voice, "Is that you, Marcello?"

"Yes, Mother, it's me. . . But what about these dogs?"

"Let them go . . . poor little angels . . . they've been shut up all the morning . . . yes, yes . . . you can let them go."

Marcello frowned ill-humoredly and went into the room. The air there seemed to him quite unbreathable: the windows had been shut since the night before and a close, stuffy smell, mingled with the smell of dogs and of perfume, hung everywhere; and the heat of the sun on the outside of the shutters seemed to make all these smells ferment and turn sour. Stiffly, watchfully, as if he feared by moving to dirty himself or to become impregnated with these unpleasant odors, he went over to the bed and sat down on the edge of it, his hands resting on his knees.

As his eyes became gradually accustomed to the semidarkness, he could see the whole room. Underneath the window, in the diffused light which penetrated through the long curtains, soiled and yellow with age—that looked to him as though they were made of the same flimsy material as the many intimate garments scattered about the room—stood a long row of aluminum plates containing the dogs' food. The floor was littered with slippers and stockings. Near the bathroom door, in an almost dark corner, he caught a glimpse of a pink dressing gown hanging over a chair, just as it had been thrown there the evening before, half on the ground and with one sleeve dangling. From its survey of the room his cold, disgusted glance traveled to the bed upon which his mother lay. As usual she had not thought to cover herself when he came in, and was half naked. Lying back against the head of the bed with its worn and dingy blue silk upholstery, her hands clasped behind her head, she stared at him in silence. Beneath the mass of her hair, divided into two puffed-out, brown wings, her face showed pale and thin, almost triangular, dominated by the eyes that looked large and cadaverously dark in the dim light.

She was wearing a greenish transparent undergarment reaching barely to the top of her thighs; and once again he was forced to think of her, not as the middle-aged woman she really was, but as an elderly, dried-up little girl. The ribs in her fleshless chest stood out like a rack made of small, sharp bones; and her sunken breasts were visible through the transparent material as two round, dark patches of perfect flatness. But it was above all her thighs that aroused a feeling of disgust and of pity in Marcello: thin and puny, they were just like those of a little girl of twelve who has not yet started to develop her womanly shape. His mother's age betrayed itself by marks in her wasted skin and by the color, a frigid, sickly whiteness with mysterious bluish or livid patches. "Bruises," he thought, "or bites, from Alberi." But below the knees her legs still looked perfect, as did her very small feet with their close-set toes. Marcello would have preferred not to let his mother see his ill-humor; but once again he could not restrain himself. "How many times have I asked you not to receive me like that—almost naked?" he said scornfully, and without looking at her.

Impatiently, but without rancor, she replied: "Ugh, what a very strict son I've got!"—and drew a corner of the bed cover over herself. Her voice was hoarse; and this, too, displeased Marcello. He recalled how, when he was a child, it had been sweet and clear as a song; this hoarseness was the result of drink and other forms of excess.

After a moment he said, "Well, we're going to the clinic today."

"Very well, we'll go," said his mother, pulling herself up and groping for something behind the head of the bed; "though I feel dreadfully ill and though our going to see him makes no difference, one way or another, to him, poor man."

"Still, he's your husband and my father," said Marcello, staring at the floor with his head between his hands.

"Yes, of course he is," she said. She had now retrieved the electric cord and pressed the switch. This turned on a dim lamp on the bedside table that looked to Marcello as if it were wrapped around with a pair of women's drawers. "And yet," she went on, rising from the bed and putting her feet to the ground, "to tell you the truth, sometimes I wish he would die. . . He himself wouldn't even know it . . . and I wouldn't have to go on paying all that money for the clinic. . . I've so little. . . Just think," she added in a suddenly mournful tone, "just think, I may have to give up the car."

"Well, really, would that matter?"

"It would matter very much," she said with childish resentment and shamelessness. "As it is, with the car, I have an excuse for keeping Alberi and seeing him whenever I want to . . . If I give it up, I shan't have that excuse any more."

"My dear Mother, don't talk to me about your lovers," said Marcello calmly, digging the nails of one hand into the palm of the other.

"My lovers! . . . He's the only one I've got. . . . If you talk to me about that silly hen of a girl you're going to marry, I've a perfect right to talk about him, poor dear; he's far more attractive and intelligent than she is."

Curiously, these insults to his fiancée uttered by his mother, who could not bear Giulia, did not offend Marcello. Perhaps it's true, he said to himself, perhaps she really is rather like a hen . . . but I like her to be like that. In a softened tone, he said, "Well then, are you going to get dressed? If we're going to the clinic, it's time we went."

"All right, just a moment." Moving lightly, almost like a shadow, she crossed the room on tiptoe, picking up the pink dressing gown from the chair as she passed and throwing it over her shoulders. Then she opened the bathroom door and vanished.

As soon as his mother had gone out, Marcello went over to the window and opened it wide. The air outside was hot and still, but he felt an acute sense of relief, as though he were looking out onto a glacier instead of a stuffy garden. At the same time he seemed almost to be aware of a movement of the air in the room behind him; heavy with stale perfumes and with the stink of animals, it seemed to stir gradually, to pass slowly out through the window and then dissolve into space, like a huge aerial vomit overflowing from the throat of the polluted house. He stood there for some time, looking down at the thick foliage of the wistaria whose branches encircled the window, then turned back into the room. The disorder and the air of neglect struck him afresh, but this time they aroused in him more sadness than disgust.

In a flash he remembered his mother as she had been in her youth; and he had a strong and sickening feeling of consternation and rebellion at the decadence and corruption that had changed her from the girl she had been into the woman she was now. There was certainly something both incomprehensible and irreparable at the bottom of this transformation. It was neither age, nor passions, nor financial ruin, nor feeble intelligence, nor any other precise cause. It was something that he felt without being able to explain it, something that seemed to him to be an essential part of her life, in fact to have once constituted its chief merit, but that had since become by some mysterious transmutation, its mortal bane. He left the window and went over to the chest-of-drawers, on which, among a mass of rubbish, stood a photograph of his mother as a young woman. As he looked at the delicate face, at the innocent eyes, at the pretty mouth, he asked himself in horror why she was no longer as she had been then. As he asked himself that question there rose again to the surface of his mind the feeling of repugnance he had for any form of corruption or decadence, a repugnance now rendered even more intolerable by a bitter feeling of filial remorse and sorrow. Perhaps it was *his* fault that his mother had been reduced to this state. Perhaps if he had loved her more or in a different way she would not have gone to pieces in this squalid and hopeless manner. He felt his eyes fill with tears at this thought, so that the portrait became dim and misty, and he shook his head vigorously. At the same moment the bathroom door opened and his mother appeared on the threshold in her dressing gown. She quickly covered her eyes with her arm, exclaiming, "Shut that window . . . shut it at once. . . How can you bear that bright light?"

Marcello hastily lowered the shutter, then he moved close to his mother, and taking her by the arm, made her sit down beside him on the edge of the bed and asked her gently, "And you Mother, how can you bear this disorder?"

She looked at him, hesitating, embarrassed. "I don't know how it happens," she said, "Every time I use something I ought to put it back in its place . . . but, somehow or other, I never manage to remember."

"Mother," said Marcello, all of a sudden, "every age has its own kind of dignity. . . Why, Mother, why have you let yourself go in this way?"

He was pressing her hand; and she, with the other hand, was holding up a hanger from which dangled a dress. For one moment he thought he detected a sign of genuine grief in those huge, childishly distressed eyes, and his mother's lips trembled slightly. Then an expression of annoyance chased away all other emotions. She exclaimed, "Everything that I am, everything that I do, displeases you, I know that. . . You can't bear my dogs, or my clothes, or my habits. . . But I'm young still, my dear boy, and I want to enjoy life in my own way. . . And now leave me alone," she concluded, snatching away her hand, "otherwise, how will I ever get dressed?"

Marcello said nothing. His mother went into a corner, slipped out of her dressing gown and dropped it on the floor, then opened the wardrobe and put on her dress in front of the looking glass on its door. When she was dressed the excessive thinness of her sharp hips, of her hollow shoulders and her fleshless bosom was even more clearly revealed. She looked at herself for a moment in the mirror, turning from side to side, while with one hand she arranged her hair; then, hopping this way and that, she slipped her feet into two of the many shoes that lay scattered about the floor. "And now let's go," she said, taking up a bag from the chest-of-drawers and moving toward the door.

"Aren't you going to put on a hat?"

"Why should I? There's no need."

They started to go downstairs. "You haven't said anything to me about your wedding," she said.

"I'm getting married the day after tomorrow."

"And where are you going for your honeymoon?"

"To Paris."

"The traditional honeymoon," she said. When she reached the hall she went to the kitchen door and called to the cook. "Matilde. . . Will you be so kind—call the dogs in before it gets dark."

They went out into the garden. Beyond the trees the car was standing, black and dingy, in the drive. "Well then," she said, "it's decided that you don't want to come and live here with me? . . . Although I don't find your wife attractive, I would have made even that sacrifice . . . Besides, I've so much room."

"No, Mother," answered Marcello.

"You prefer to go to your mother-in-law's," she said lightly, "to that horrible flat: four rooms and a kitchen." She bent down as if to pick a blade of grass, but in so doing stumbled and would have fallen had not Marcello quickly seized her arm and held her up. He felt beneath his fingers the soft, meager flesh of her arm that seemed to move around the bone like a rag tied round a stick; and again he was moved with pity for her. They got into the car, Alberi, cap in hand, holding open the door. Then Alberi took his place and drove the car out through the gate. Marcello took advantage of the moment when he got out again to shut the gate behind them to say to his mother, "I would be perfectly willing to come and live with you—if you sacked Alberi and tidied up your life a bit . . . and stopped those injections."

She looked at him sideways with uncomprehending eyes. But her thin, sharp nose was trembling slightly, and finally this trembling spread to her small, faded mouth, in a pale, wry smile. "D'you know what the doctor says?" she asked. "That one of these days I might die from them."

"Why don't you stop them, then?"

"Will you tell me *why* I should stop them?"

Alberi got into the car again and put on his dark glasses. Marcello's mother leaned forward and put her hand on the chauffeur's shoulder. It was a thin, transparent hand with the skin stretched tight over the tendons and blotchy with red and bluish marks; and the scarlet of the nails was almost black. Marcello tried not to look, but could not help it. He saw her hand move along the man's shoulder until it tickled his ear in a light caress. Then she said: "Well, we're going to the clinic."

"Very good, madam," said Alberi, without turning his head.

She closed the dividing pane of glass and threw herself back on the cushions as the car moved gently away. As she fell back on the seat she looked obliquely at her son, and to the suprise of Marcello, who was not expecting such intuition on her part, she said, "You're angry because I gave Alberi a little caress, aren't you?"

As she spoke she looked at him with the childish, despairing, slightly twisted smile that was characteristic of her. Marcello tried, unsuccessfully, to alter the disgusted expression on his face. "I'm not angry," he answered. "But I'd rather not have seen."

Averting her head, she said: "You can't know what it means for a woman not to be young any more. . . . It's worse than death."

Marcello was silent. The car was moving along silently now beneath the pepper trees, whose feathery branches rustled against the glass of the windows. After a moment she went on, "There are times when I wish I was old already. . . . I shall be a thin, clean little old woman"—she smiled with pleasure, her attention already distracted by this vision of herself—"like a dried flower that's been kept between the pages of a book." She put her hand on Marcello's arm and asked him, "Wouldn't you like to have a little old woman like that for a mother—well seasoned and well preserved, as if she'd been put away in naphthalene?"

Marcello looked at her and answered with some embarrassment, "That's what you'll be like, some day."

She became serious, and, looking up at him with a dismal smile, said, "D'you really think so? . . . On the contrary, I'm convinced, myself, that you'll find me dead, one morning, in that room you so detest."

"Why, Mother?" asked Marcello; but he realized that his mother was speaking seriously and might even be right. "You're young and you must go on living."

"That doesn't prevent me from dying soon. . . . I know it; they read it in my horoscope." Suddenly she held up her hand, right under his eyes, adding without any transition, "D'you like this ring?"

It was a heavy ring with an elaborate setting around a hard stone of a milky color. "Yes," said Marcello, scarcely looking at it, "it's lovely."

"You know," went on his mother volubly, "sometimes I think you've inherited everything from your father. . . . He too, in the days when he still had his reason, didn't like anything. . . . Beautiful things meant nothing to him. . . . The only thing he thought of was politics—just like you."

This time, without knowing why, Marcello was unable to repress a strong feeling of irritation. "It seems to me," he said, "that my father and I have nothing at all in common. . . . I'm a perfectly reasonable person, normal, whereas he, even before he went to the clinic—from what I remember, and you've always confirmed it—was always . . . how shall I say? . . . rather excitable."

"Yes, but there is something in common between you. . . . You neither of you get any fun out of life and you don't want other people to do so. . . ." She looked out of the window for a moment and then added suddenly, "I shan't come to your wedding. . . . But anyhow you mustn't be offended, because I don't go anywhere nowadays. . . . But since, after all, you are my son, I think I ought to give you a present. . . . What would you like?"

"Nothing, Mother," answered Marcello indifferently.

"What a pity!" said his mother ingenuously. "If I'd known you wanted nothing, I wouldn't have spent the money. . . . But now I've bought it. . . . Look!" She fumbled in her bag and brought out a small white box with an elastic band round it. "It's a cigarette case. . . . I noticed that you always carry the pack in your pocket. . . ." She opened the box, took out a flat silver case engraved with stripes close together, flipped it open and held it out to her son. It was filled with Oriental cigarettes, and she took the opportunity of helping herself to one and making Marcello light it for her.

He was a little embarrassed, and, looking at the cigarette case lying open on his mother's knee, said, without touching it, "It's a very beautiful one and I don't know how to thank you, Mother. . . . Perhaps it's even a little too beautiful for me."

"Ugh," said his mother, "how tiresome you are!" She closed the case and, with a prettily intolerant gesture, poked it into Marcello's coat pocket. The car turned the corner of a street rather sharply, and she fell on top of him. She took advantage of this to put her two hands on his shoulders, throwing back her head slightly and looking at him. "Won't you give me a kiss," she said, "in return for the present?"

Marcello bent down and touched his mother's cheek with his lips. She threw herself back in her seat and said with a sigh, putting her hand on her breast, "How hot it is! . . . When you were little, I shouldn't have had to ask you for a kiss. . . . You were such an affectionate little boy."

"Mother," said Marcello all of a sudden, "d'you remember the winter when Father was first taken ill?"

"Indeed I do," said his mother, "it was a terrible winter. . . . He wanted a separation from me, and to carry you off with him. . . . He was mad already. . . . Lucky—I mean luckily for you—he went completely mad, and then it was obvious that I was right in wanting to keep you with me. . . . But why?"

"Well, Mother," said Marcello, taking care not to look at her, "what I dreamed of, all that winter, was not to go on living with you any more—with you and Father—but to be sent away to school. . . . Not that that prevented me from being fond of you. . . . That's why, when you say that I've changed since then, you're saying something that isn't right. . . . I was just the same then as I am now . . . and then, as now, I couldn't bear hubbub and disorder . . . that's all." He had spoken drily, almost harshly, but almost at once he repented, seeing a mortified expression darkening his mother's face. And yet he did not want to say anything that might sound as though he were retracting. He had spoken the truth, and that, indeed, was the only thing he could do. At the same time he was again conscious, more intensely than ever, of the oppression of his customary melancholy, reawakened by the unpleasant realization that he had been lacking in filial piety. His mother said in a resigned tone of voice, "Perhaps you're right." At that moment the car came to a stop.

They got out and walked to the gate of the clinic. The street lay in a quiet neighborhood, on the edge of an ancient

royal villa. It was a short street. On one side there was a row
of five or six old-fashioned suburban houses partially hidden
among trees. Along the other side ran the railings of the
clinic. At the end of the street the view was blocked by the
old gray wall and the thick vegetation of the royal park.
Marcello had been visiting his father at least once a month
for many years; yet he had never grown accustomed to these
visits, and he always experienced a mingled feeling of repugnance and discomfort. It was much the same sort of feeling that he had when he went to see his mother in the house
in which he had spent his childhood and youth. But it was
very much stronger. His mother's disorder and decay seemed
still to be curable; but for his father's madness there was no
remedy, and it seemed to point to a disorder and decay
of a more general, and utterly incurable, kind. And so,
as he came into that quiet street at his mother's side, his
heart was oppressed by a hateful sensation of wretchedness
and his knees shook. He was aware that he had turned pale,
and for a moment, as he cast a hasty glance at the black
spikes of the railings, he felt a hysterical desire to give up the
visit and make some excuse to run away. His mother, who
had not noticed his agitation, stopped in front of the small
black iron gate and pressed the clinic button saying, "D'you
know what his latest fixation is?"

"What?"

"He thinks he's one of Mussolini's ministers. . . . It began
about a month ago. . . . I suppose because they let him read
the papers."

Marcello frowned but said nothing. The gate opened and
a young male nurse appeared: he wore a white robe and was
tall and plump and fair, with a shaven head and a white,
puffy face. "Good day, Franz," said Marcello's mother
graciously. "How is he?"

"We're better today than yesterday," said the young man,
speaking with a harsh German accent. "Yesterday we were
very bad."

"Very bad?"

"We had to put on the strait jacket," explained the male
nurse, still speaking in the plural, in the affected manner
of a governess speaking of her charges.

"The strait jacket. . . How awful!" In the meantime they
had passed through the gate and were walking along a narrow
path between the surrounding wall and the wall of the clinic.
"The strait jacket, you ought to see it. . . . It's not really a
jacket, it's like two sleeves that hold the arms still. . . Before
I saw it, I used to imagine it was like a nightshirt, one of
those with a Greek key pattern at the bottom. . . It's so sad

to see him tied up like that, with his arms tight against his sides." She went on talking in a light, almost gay, tone of voice.

They went round the clinic and came out into an open space in front of the main façade. The clinic, a white, three-floored suburban villa, had the appearance of an ordinary dwelling, apart from the iron gratings over the windows. Hurrying up the stairs under the porch, the male nurse said, "The Professor's expecting you, Signora Clerici." He preceded the two visitors into a bare, rather dark entrance hall and went and knocked at a closed door, above which was an enameled plate with the word "Director" on it.

The door opened and the director of the clinic, Professor Ermini, came rushing out, his towering, massive figure bearing down upon his visitors. "Signora, I'm delighted to see you. . . Doctor Clerici, how are you?" His stentorian voice echoed like a bronze gong through the frozen silence of the clinic, between its bare walls. Marcello's mother put out a hand which the professor, bending with visible effort, his huge body enveloped in its robe, gallantly insisted on kissing; Marcello himself, on the other hand, greeted him with the utmost sobriety. The professor's face was extremely like that of a white owl, with large round eyes, a big, curved, beaklike nose, tufts of red mustache falling over a wide, clamorous mouth. Its expression, however, was not that of the melancholy night bird, but was jovial, though with a joviality that was carefully studied and shot through with a kind of cold wariness. He led Marcello and his mother up the stairs. When they were half way up, a metal object, hurled violently from the landing above, came bouncing down the stairs. At the same time a piercing scream rang out, followed by a peal of scornful laughter. The professor bent and picked up the object, an aluminum plate. "It's Signora Donegalli," he said, turning towards the two visitors. "Don't be alarmed. . . . She's just an old lady who's usually perfectly quiet but who, every now and then, gets excited and throws anything she can lay her hands on. . . ." He laughed. "Why, she'd be a champion bowls-player, if we let her. . . ." He handed the plate to the male nurse and walked on, chattering, down a long corridor between two rows of closed doors. "Why, Signora, you're still in Rome? I thought you'd gone off to the mountains or by the sea by this time."

"I'm going in about a month," she replied. "But I don't know where. . . . For once I should like *not* to go to Venice."

"You take my advice, Signora," said the professor, as he turned a corner in the corridor, "and go to Ischia. . . . I was

there just the other day on a trip. . . . It's really marvelous.
. . . We went to a restaurant kept by a certain Carminiello,
where we had a fish soup that was a positive poem." The
professor turned half around and made a vulgar but expressive gesture with two fingers at the corner of his mouth.
"A poem, I tell you—hunks of fish as big as that . . . and a
bit of everything besides—little octopuses, rascasse, dogfish,
small oysters—the latter particularly good—shrimps, small
cuttlefish . . . all combined with a delicious gravy *alla marin-
gara* . . . garlic, oil, tomato, sweet peppers. . . . Signora, words
fail me." After assuming a comic, Neopolitan accent for
his description of the fish soup, the professor fell back into
his native Roman, and added, "D'you know what I said to
my wife?—How about getting a nice little house in Ischia
before the year's out?"

"Personally, I prefer Capri," said Marcello's mother.

"But that's a place for literary people and inverts," said
the professor in a rather brutal way. At that moment a
series of piercing shrieks reached them from one of the cells.
The professor went to the door, opened the peep hole, looked
through it for a few seconds, closed it again, and turning
back, concluded, "Ischia, my dear Signora. . . . Ischia is the
place. Fish soup, sea, sun, life in the open air . . . there's nowhere like Ischia."

Franz, the male nurse, who had been walking a few steps
in front of them, now stood waiting beside one of the doors,
his massive figure clear cut against the bright light from the
window at the end of the corridor. "Has he taken up his
usual position?" asked the professor in a low voice. The young
man nodded. The professor opened the door and went in,
followed by Marcello and his mother.

It was a small, bare room, with a bed fixed to the wall
and a white wooden table facing a window with the usual
iron grating over it. Sitting at the table with his back to
the door, busily writing, Marcello, with a shudder of disgust, saw his father. A tousled mass of white hair stuck out
from his head above his thin neck, half hidden by the wide
collar of his stiff cape of striped cloth. He was sitting slightly
askew, his feet thrust into two huge felt slippers, his elbows
and knees turned outwards, his head on one side. Exactly,
thought Marcello, like a puppet with broken wires. The
entrance of his three visitors did not make him turn around;
on the contrary, he seemed to redouble his attention and
zeal over what he was writing. The professor went and stood
between the window and the table and said with false
joviality, "Well, Major, how goes it today? . . . How are
you?"

The madman did not answer; he merely raised his hand, as much as to say, "One moment, don't you see I'm busy?" The professor gave Marcello's mother an understanding look and said, "Still at that report, eh, Major? But isn't it going to be too long? . . . The Duce hasn't time to read things if they're too long. . . . He himself is always brief, concise. . . . Brevity, conciseness, Major."

The madman made the same sign as before, waving his bony hand; then, with a strange, wild craziness, he threw a sheet of paper up into the air over his own bowed head. It landed in the middle of the room, and Marcello bent and picked it up. It contained nothing but a few incomprehensible words in a writing full of flourishes and underlinings. Marcello could not be sure even that they were words. While he was examining the paper, the madman began throwing more pieces into the air, still with the same gesture as though he were furiously busy. The sheets of paper came flying up over his white head and were scattered about all over the room. As he threw them up in the air, his gestures became more and more violent, and soon the whole room was full of little sheets of square paper. "Poor dear," said Marcello's mother; "he always did have a passion for writing."

The professor bent forward slightly to speak to the madman. "Major," he said, "here are your wife and son. . . . Don't you want to see them?"

This time the madman spoke, at last, in a low, muttering, hurried, hostile voice, like someone who has been disturbed in the middle of an inportant occupation. "Let them come back tomorrow . . . unless they have any concrete proposals to make. . . . Can't you see my antechamber's filled with people that I shan't have time to receive?"

"He thinks he's a minister," Marcello's mother whispered to him.

"Minister for Foreign Affairs," the professor confirmed.

"That Hungarian affair," said the madman all of a sudden in an urgent, subdued, troubled voice, still busily writing, "that Hungarian affair. . . . And the head of the government in Prague. . . . And what are they doing in London? And the French, why can't they understand? But *why* can't they understand? Why? Why? Why?" With each "why?" the voice of the madman rose higher, until finally with the last one that he almost screamed, he leaped from his chair and turned around, facing his visitors. Marcello raised his eyes and looked at him. Beneath the white, upstanding hair, the thin, brown, wasted face, with its deeply scored, vertical wrinkles, bore imprinted upon it an expression of solemn, conscientious gravity, of anguish, almost, from the effort of rising to an imaginary occasion of speech-making and ceremony. The madman was holding one of his little sheets of paper on a level with his eyes; and without more ado he began reading, with a strange, breathless haste: "Duce, leader of heroes, king of earth and sea and sky, prince, priest, emperor, commander and soldier"—here he made a gesture of impatience, tempered however by a certain ceremoniousness, as much as to say, "et cetera, et cetera"—"Duce, in this place, which . . ."—and he made another gesture, as if to say, "I'll skip that part, it's superfluous"—then he started again: "In this place I have written a report that I beg you to read from the first"—he stopped and looked at his visitors— "to the last line. Here is my report."

After these introductory words, he threw the sheet of paper up in the air, turned toward the table, took up another and began reading the report. But this time Marcello could not catch a single word: it was true that the madman was reading clearly and distinctly, but his extraordinary haste caused him to run one word into another as if the entire speech consisted of one single word of inordinate length. The words, thought Marcello, must be melting upon his tongue even before he uttered them, as though the devouring fire of madness had dissolved their shapes like wax and fused them into a single oratorical substance, of a soft, elusive indistinctness. As he went on reading, the words seemed to enter more inextricably one into the other, becoming shorter and shorter and more and more contracted, and the madman himself began to appear overwhelmed by this verbal avalanche. With increasing frequency he took to throwing away the sheets of paper after he had read only the first line; until finally he broke off his reading altogether, leaped with surprising agility onto the bed, and there retreating into the corner at its head, standing upright against the wall, plunged into a declamatory speech.

That he thought himself to be haranguing an audience, Marcello understood more from his gestures than from his words which, as before, were disconnected and senseless. Like an orator facing a crowd from an imaginary balcony, the madman now raised both arms toward the ceiling; now bent forward with one hand outstretched, as though to introduce some subtle point; now threatened, with fist clenched; now raised his hands, palms outward, to the level of his face. At a certain point there was evidently a burst of applause from the imaginary crowd he was addressing; for the madman, holding out his hand in a characteristic gesture with palm turned downward, seemed to be demanding

silence. But the applause, clearly, did not cease, in fact it
increased in intensity; and then, having again asked for
silence with that same gesture of entreaty, the madman
jumped down from the bed, ran across to the professor and,
holding him by the sleeve, implored him in a tearful voice,
"Do please make them keep quiet. . . . What does applause
matter to me? . . . A declaration of war. . . . How can one
make a declaration of war if their applause prevents one from
speaking?"

"We'll make the declaration of war tomorrow, Major,"
said the professor, looking down at the madman from the
height of his towering figure.

"Tomorrow, tomorrow, tomorrow," yelled the madman
in a sudden excess of fury in which anger was mingled
with despair, "it's always tomorrow. . . . The declaration of war has got to be made now . . . at once."

"But why, Major? What does it matter? Now, in this
heat? Those poor soldiers, d'you want to make them fight
in this heat?" The professor slyly wriggled his shoulders.

The madman looked at him in perplexity, obviously
disconcerted by his objection. Then he cried, "The soldiers
must eat ices. . . . People eat ices in the summer, don't
they?"

"Yes," said the professor, "people eat ices in the summer."

"Well then," said the madman with a triumphant air,
"ices, lots of ices, ices for everybody," Muttering, he went
to the table, and, still standing, seized hold of his pencil
and scribbled a few words on a remaining sheet of paper
and then handed it to the doctor. "Here's the declaration
or war," he said. "I'm not going to have anything more to
do with it. . . . You must take it to the right person. . . . Oh,
these bells, oh, oh, these bells." He gave the paper to the
doctor and then went and crouched down on the floor in
the corner beside the bed, like a terrified animal, clutching
his head with his two hands and repeating in an anguished
voice: "Oh, these bells. . . . Couldn't these bells stop for a
moment?"

The doctor cast a quick glance at the sheet of paper and
then handed it to Marcello. At the top of the page was
written, "Murder and melancholy," and, lower down,
"War is declared," all of it in the same large handwriting
with elaborate flourishes. " 'Murder and melancholy' is
his motto," said the doctor. "You'll find it written on all
these sheets. . . . He has a fixation about those two words."

"The bells," whimpered the madman.

"Does he really hear them?" asked Marcello's mother, puzzled.

"Yes, probably. . . . They're hallucinations of the hearing, just as the applause was, previously. . . . People suffering from these disorders can hear different kinds of noises, even voices speaking real words . . . or the sounds made by animals . . . or the noise of an engine, a motorcycle, for instance."

"The bells!" screamed the madman in a terrible voice.

Marcello's mother retreated towards the door, murmuring, "It must be frightful. . . . Poor dear, there's no knowing what he's suffering. . . . I know that I myself, if I happen to be underneath a bell tower when they're ringing the bells, I feel I'm going mad."

"But does he suffer?" asked Marcello.

"Wouldn't you suffer if for hours and hours you heard great bronze bells ringing very close to your ear?" The professor turned to the sick man and added, "Now we'll make the bells stop ringing. . . . We'll send the bellringer to sleep. . . . We'll give you something to drink and you won't hear them any more." He made a sign to the male nurse, who immediately went out. Turning to Marcello again, he went on, "These are rather serious forms of disorder. . . . The patient passes from a state of frantic cheerfulness to one of profound depression. . . . Just now, while he was reading, he was wildly excited, now he's depressed. Do you want to say anything to him?"

Marcello looked at his father, who was still whimpering pitifully, his head in his hands, and said in a cold voice, "No, I have nothing to say to him, and besides, what's the use? . . . He wouldn't understand anyhow."

"Sometimes they understand," said the professor; "they understand more than you think, they recognize people, even we doctors are taken in. . . ." He laughed. "It's not so simple."

Marcello's mother went over to the madman and said, in an affable sort of way, "Antonio, do you recognize me? . . . Here's Marcello, your son. . . . He's getting married the day after tomorrow. . . . D'you understand? He's getting married."

The madman looked up hopefully at his wife, as an injured dog looks up at his master when the latter bends down over him and asks him, in human words, what is the matter. The doctor turned toward Marcello, exclaiming, "Getting married, getting married! Why, my dear Doctor, I knew nothing about it. . . . My warmest congratulations. My most sincere good wishes."

"Thank you," said Marcello drily.

His mother, moving toward the door, said in her ingenuous way, "Poor dear, he doesn't understand. . . . If he did, he wouldn't be pleased, any more than I am."

"Please, Mother," said Marcello shortly.

"Never mind, your wife has to please *you*, not other people," she replied in a conciliating tone. She turned back towards the madman and said to him, "Good-bye, Antonio."

"The bells," whimpered the madman.

They went out into the corridor, meeting Franz as he came in carrying a glass with the soothing mixture in it. The professor closed the door and said, "It's a curious thing, Doctor, how insane people keep up with the news, how up-to-date they are . . . and how sensitive they are to everything that interests the general public. . . . Now, for instance, there's fascism, there's the Duce, and so you'll find that a very large number of them develop fixations, like your father, with regard to fascism and the Duce. . . . During the war there was an endless number of insane people who thought they were generals and who wanted to take the place of Cadorna or Diaz. . . . And more recently, at the time of Nobile's flight to the North Pole, I had at least three patients who knew for certain exactly where the famous red tent was and who had invented a special apparatus for rescuing the shipwrecked men. . . . Mad people are always abreast of the times. . . . In spite of their madness they do not cease, fundamentally, to take part in public life, and madness itself is the means they use to take part in it— in their own character, of course, as good, but mad, citizens." The doctor laughed coldly, delighted with his own wit. And then, turning toward Marcello's mother, but with the obvious intention of flattering Marcello himself, he said, "But as far as the Duce goes, we're all just as mad as your husband, aren't we, Signora?—mad enough to need tying up, mad enough for treatment with the douche and the strait jacket. ... The whole of Italy is just one big lunatic asylum, ha, ha, ha."

"In that way my son is certainly quite mad," said Marcello's mother, naïvely reinforcing the doctor's compliments, "in fact I was saying to Marcello, on our way here, that there were certain points of resemblance between him and his poor father."

Marcello hung back in order to avoid hearing what they were saying. He saw them walk away toward the far end of the corridor, then turn the corner and disappear, still chattering. He stopped; he was still holding in his hand the sheet of paper upon which his father had written his declaration of war. He hesitated, took out his wallet and put the paper into it. Then he hastened his step and rejoined his mother and the doctor on the ground floor.

"Well then, good-bye, Professor," his mother was saying. "But that poor dear man—is there really no way of curing him?"

"For the present there is nothing science can do," answered the doctor without a hint of solemnity, as though repeating a worn-out mechnical formula.

"Good-bye, Professor," said Marcello.

"Good-bye, Doctor, and again, my warmest and sincerest good wishes."

They walked down the narrow gravel path and out into the street to the car. Alberi was there, beside the open door, cap in hand. They got in without a word and the car started. Marcello sat silent a moment and then asked his mother, "Mother, I want to ask you a question. . . . I think I can speak frankly to you, can't I?"

"What is it?" said his mother vaguely, examining her face in the little mirror of her powder-compact.

"This man that I call my father and that we've just visited—is he really my father?"

His mother started laughing. "Really," she said, "Sometimes you *are* rather strange. . . . And why shouldn't he be your father?"

"Mother . . . at that time you already had—" Marcello hesitated and then concluded "—you already had lovers. . . . Isn't it possible. . . . ?"

"Oh no, it isn't possible at all," said his mother with calm cynicism. "When I first decided to be unfaithful to your father you were already two years old. . . . The funny thing about it is," she went on, "that it was precisely with this idea of your being another man's son that your father's madness began. . . . He had a fixed idea that you were not his son. . . . And d'you know what he did one day? He took a photograph of me with you as a baby—"

"And made holes through the eyes of both of us," concluded Marcello.

"Ah, so you knew that," said his mother, rather astonished. "Well, that was really the beginning of his madness. . . . He was obsessed by the idea that you were the son of a certain man that I used to see occasionally at that time. . . . I don't need to say that it was entirely his own imagination. . . . You're *his* son, one has only to look at you. . . ."

"Surely I'm more like you than him," Marcello could not help saying.

"You're like both of us," said his mother, clinching the matter. She put her compact back in her bag, and added, "I've told you already: if there were nothing else, you've both got a fixation about politics—he like a madman, and you, thank God, like a sane person."

Marcello said nothing, but turned his face toward the window. The idea of resembling his father inspired in him an intense disgust. The reference to flesh and blood, in family relationships, had always been repellent to him as an impure, unjust definition. But the resemblance to which his mother alluded not merely disgusted, but in some obscure way frightened him. What connection existed between his father's madness and his own most secret being? He remembered the phrase he had read on the sheet of paper, "Murder and melancholy," and shuddered thoughtfully. The melancholy was already upon him, like a second skin more sensitive than his real one; and as for the murder. . . .

The car was now going through streets in the center of the town, in the false blue light of dusk. Marcello said to his mother, "I'll get out here," and he leaned forward to knock on the glass in order to warn Alberi. "Then I'll see you on your return," said his mother, giving him implicitly to understand that she would not be coming to the wedding; and he was grateful to her for her reticence. Frivolity and cynicism had at least that advantage. He got out, banged the door, and disappeared into the crowd.

# ⋙⋙⋙ PART TWO ⋙⋙⋙⋙⋙⋙⋙⋙⋙⋙⋙⋙

## CHAPTER 8

As soon as the train began to move, Marcello left the window where he was standing talking to his mother-in-law—or rather, listening to her conversation—and went back into the compartment. Giulia, on the other hand, remained at the window; and from the compartment Marcello could see her in the corridor as she leaned out and waved her handkerchief with an anxious urgency that gave a certain pathos to a gesture otherwise quite ordinary. Doubtless, he thought, she would stand there waving her handkerchief as long as she thought she could catch a glimpse of her mother's figure on the platform; and, for her, the moment when she ceased to see that figure would mark in the clearest possible way her own complete and final detachment from her life as a girl—a detachment she had both feared and longed for and which, with her own departure in the train while her mother was left behind, took on a painfully concrete character. Marcello looked a moment longer at his wife as she hung out of the window, in her light-colored dress that was ruckled up, by the movement of her arm, over the well-defined forms of her figure; then he sank back on the cushions, closing his eyes. When he opened them again his wife was no longer in the corridor and the train was already out in the open country. They were crossing an arid, treeless plain, already wrapped in twilight obscurity, beneath a green sky. Here and there the ground rose up into bald hills, and between these hills appeared wide valleys surprisingly devoid both of human habitations and of human figures. A few brick ruins, on the tops of the hills, emphasized the feeling of solitude. It was a restful landscape, thought Marcello, inviting one to reflection and fancy. And now, over the horizon at the far side of the plain, the moon had risen, round and blood-red, with a glistening white star at its right hand.

His wife had disappeared and Marcello hoped that she would not come back for a few minutes. He wanted to think, and for the last time, to feel himself alone. He went back, in memory, over the things that he had done during the last few days, and realized, as he recalled them, that they brought him a feeling of vague but profound satisfaction. This, he thought, was the only possible way in which to change one's own life and one's own personality—by action, by movement in time and in space. As usual, he was especially pleased at the things that tightened his bonds to the normal, ordinary, expected world. The wedding morning; Giulia, in her wedding dress, running joyfully from one room to another in her rustling silk; himself entering the elevator with a bunch of lilies of the valley in his gloved hand; his mother-in-law who, the moment he came in, threw herself sobbing into his arms; Giulia pulling him behind the door of a cupboard in order to kiss him at her ease; the arrival of the witnesses, two of Giulia's friends, a doctor and a lawyer, and two friends of his own from the Ministry; leaving the house for the church, with people looking out of the windows and from the pavements, as they went away in three cars—himself and Giulia in the first, the witnesses in the second, and his mother-in-law and two female friends in the third.

A curious thing had happened during the drive. The car had stopped at a traffic signal, and suddenly there had appeared at the window a red, bearded face with a bald forehead and a prominent nose. It was a beggar; but, instead of asking for alms, he had said, in a hoarse voice, "How about giving me a bridal sugar plum, you two?"—and at the same time had thrust his hand into the car. The sudden apparition of the face at the window, the indiscreet hand stretched out toward Giulia, had irritated Marcello, who with excessive severity, had answered, "Go on, get away, we've nothing for you." At which the man, who was probably drunk, had shouted out at the top of his voice, "A curse upon you!" and had disappeared. Giulia, frightened, had clung to him, murmuring, "It'll bring us bad luck"; and he, shrugging his shoulders, had replied, "Nonsense . . . he's just a drunk." Then the car had started again and the incident had slipped almost at once from his mind.

Inside the church everything had been normal, in other words quietly solemn, ritual, ceremonious. A little crowd of relations and friends sat here and there in the front pews before the high altar, the men in dark clothes, the women in light-colored, springlike frocks. The church, very rich and ornate, was dedicated to a saint of the Counter-Reformation. Behind the high altar, beneath a canopy of gilded bronze, there was, indeed a statue of this saint in gray marble, larger than life, gazing with eyes upturned to heaven and palms outstretched. Behind the statue, the apse of the church was covered with frescoes in the baroque manner, lively and full of flourishes.

Giulia and he had knelt down in front of the marble balustrade, on a red velvet cushion. The witnesses stood in order behind them, two by two. The service had been a long one, for Giulia's family had insisted on giving it the greatest possible solemnity. From the very beginning, an organ up in the balcony over the entrance door had started playing and had gone on continuously, now softly snoring, now bursting forth in a triumphant clamor beneath the echoing vaults. The priest had been extremely slow—so much so that Marcello, after observing with satisfaction that the ceremony, in all its details, was exactly as he had imagined and desired, after assuring himself that he was doing just what millions of married couples had been doing for hundreds of years before him, had allowed his attention to wander and had started examining the church. It was not a beautiful church, but it was very large, and had been conceived and built, like all Jesuit churches, in order to achieve a theatrical solemnity. The enormous statue of the saint, kneeling in a ecstatic attitude beneath his canopy, was erected over an altar painted to represent marble and crowded with commonplace silver candlesticks, vases of flowers, ornamental statuettes and bronze lamps. Behind the canopy was the curve of

the apse, with its frescoes by some painter of the period: vaporous, swelling clouds, such as might have figured on the
curtain of an opera-house, lay across a blue sky streaked
by swords of light from a hidden sun. On the clouds sat
various sacred personages, painted with a few bold strokes
and with more decorative sense than religious spirit. Prominent among the others and overtopping them all was the
figure of the Eternal Father, and suddenly Marcello, as he
looked at that bearded, haloed face, could not help seeing in
it the face of the beggar who had appeared at the window
of the car asking for a sugar plum and who had then cursed
him. At that moment the organ was playing loudly and
with an almost menacing sternness which seemed to admit
no touch of sweetness; and so it was that a resemblance
that in other circumstances would have made him smile (the
Eternal Father disguised as a beggar putting his head in at
the window of a taxi and demanding a sugar plum) recalled to his mind, for some inexplicable reason, those Biblical verses concerning Cain which his eye had happened to
fall upon when he had opened a Bible one day, a few years
after the Lino affair: *What hast thou done? The voice of thy
brother's blood crieth unto me from the ground.*

*And now art thou cursed from the earth, which hath
opened her mouth to receive thy brother's blood from thy
hand;*

*When thou tillest the ground, it shall not henceforth yield
unto thee her strength; a fugitive and a vagabond shalt thou
be in the earth.*

*And Cain said unto the Lord, My punishment is greater
than I can bear.*

*Behold, thou hast driven me out this day from the face
of the earth; and from thy face shall I be hid; and I shall
be a fugitive and a vagabond in the earth; and it shall come
to pass, that every one that findeth me shall slay me.*

*And the Lord said unto him, Therefore, whosoever slay-
eth Cain, vengeance shall be taken on him sevenfold. And the
Lord set a mark upon Cain, lest any finding him should kill
him.*

These verses had seemed to him that day to have been written especially for him, cursed as he was for his involuntary
crime, and yet, by that same curse, made sacred and un-
touchable. And then, after he had read them over several
times and meditated upon them, he had grown tired of thinking about them, and had forgotten them. But that morning
in church, as he looked at the figure in the fresco, they had
come back to him and once again they had seemed well
suited to his own case. Coldly, but not without a gloomy

conviction that he was thrusting the instrument of his thought into a soil fertile with analogy and significance, he had speculated, while the service continued, upon this point. If there was really such a thing as a curse, why had it been hurled against him? With this question his mind was again clouded over with the clinging melancholy that continually oppressed him—the melancholy of a man who is lost and who knows that there is nothing he can do to save himself —and he had told himself that by instinct, at any rate, if not by conscience, he knew that he was under a curse. Not because he had killed Lino but because he had sought and was still seeking to free himself from the burden of remorse, of corruption, of abnormality which that far-off misdeed had laid upon him, without having recourse to religion or the abodes of religion. But what could he do about it; he had gone on to think; he was like that and he could not change himself. There was indeed no ill will in him, only the honest acceptance of the condition to which he was born, of the world as he found it. It was a condition far removed from religion, a world in which the place of religion was taken by other things. He would have preferred, certainly, to have entrusted his life to the ancient, benevolent figures of the Christian faith, to God who was so just, to the Virgin so motherly, to Christ so merciful. But, at the very moment when he was conscious of this desire, he realized that his own life did not belong to him and that therefore he could not entrust it to whomsoever he wished; and that he was outside religion and could not enter into it again, even in order to purify himself and become normal. Normality, as he had thought, was now elsewhere; or perhaps it was yet to come, and had to be reconstructed through painful effort, through doubt and through blood.

As if to confirm these thoughts, he had at that moment looked at the woman beside him, at the woman who in a few minutes would be his wife. Giulia was kneeling, her hands clasped together, her face and eyes turned toward the altar, carried away by her own joyful, hopeful ecstasy. And yet, at his look—as though she had been aware of it on her body like the contact of a hand—she had at once turned and smiled at him with her eyes and her mouth, with a tender, humble, grateful smile full of an almost animal-like innocence. He had smiled back at her, though less openly; and then, as though it had sprung from that smile, he had felt—perhaps for the first time since he had known her—an impulse, if not actually of love, at least of profound affection mingled with compassion and tenderness. And then it had seemed to him that his look had undressed her, had removed both her wedding dress and her most intimate garments, and that he could see her, young and fresh and healthy with her rounded breasts and belly, kneeling there naked beside him on the red velvet cushion, clasping her hands. And he was naked too; and, irrespective of any ritual consecration, they were on the point of being truly united, as animals in the woods were united; and this union, whether or not he believed in the rite in which he was taking part, would really come about, and from it, as he wished, children would be born. With this thought it had seemed to him, for the first time, that he was placing his feet on firm ground, and he had reflected, "This woman in a short time will be my wife . . . and I shall possess her . . . and she, when she has been possessed, will conceive children . . . and this, for the present, for lack of anything better, will be my point of departure toward normality."

But at that moment he had seen Giulia moving her lips in prayer, and, as he watched that eager movement of her mouth, it had seemed to him that her nudity had suddenly been clothed again, as if by enchantment, with her wedding dress, and he had realized that, she, Giulia, believed firmly in the ritual consecration of their union; and he had not been displeased at this discovery; in fact, it had brought him a feeling almost of relief. For Giulia normality was not a thing that had to be found or reconstructed; it was there; and she was immersed in it and, whatever happened, would never forsake it.

And so, as the ceremony came to an end, there had been a sufficiency of feeling and of affection on his part. A feeling and an affection of which he had at first thought himself incapable, and that he felt to be inspired by deep impulses coming from within himself rather than suggested by the place and the marriage rite. Everything, in fact, had been carried out according to the rules of tradition, in such a way as to satisfy not only those who believed in such rules but himself also, who did not believe in them but wished to act as though he did. As he was walking out with his wife on his arm, at the moment when they stopped in the doorway at the top of the steps leading down from the church, he had heard Giulia's mother, behind him, say to a friend, "He *is* such a good, kind man. . . . You saw how deeply moved he was. . . . He loves her so much. . . . Really Giulia *couldn't* have found a better husband." And he had been pleased at having been able to inspire so satisfactory an illusion.

As he came to the end of these reflections, he was conscious of a sort of sharp, zealous impatience to reassume his

role as a husband at the point at which he had left it after
the wedding ceremony. He turned his eyes away from the
window, that now—since night had fallen—was full of
nothing but black, faintly glittering darkness, and looked
out into the corridor in search of Giulia. He was aware of a
slight feeling of irritation at her absence, and this gave him
pleasure, for it seemed to him a sign of naturalness with which
he was now playing his part. He wondered whether he ought
to possess Giulia in the inconvenient sleeping berth or wait
till they arrived at S., the end of the first stage of their
journey. At this thought he was aware of a sudden, strong
desire, and made up his mind to possess her in the train.
That was the right thing to happen in such a case, he
thought; besides, he felt strongly inclined to it, both from
carnal appetite and from a kind of self-satisfied loyalty to his
role as a husband. Giulia, however, was a virgin (a fact
he knew for certain) and to possess her would not be easy.
He realized that he would be almost pleased if, after trying
in vain to break her virginity, he was forced to wait for the
hotel at S. and the convenience of a double bed. Such things
happened to the newly wed—ridiculous though utterly
normal—and he wanted to be like the most normal of the
normal, even at the cost of appearing to be impotent.

He was on the point of going out into the corridor when
the door opened and Giulia came in. She was in a skirt
and blouse and had taken off her jacket, which she was
carrying over her arm. Her comely bosom pressed exuber-
antly against the white linen of her blouse, infusing into it a
faint, pinkish flesh-color; her face was radiant with joyous
satisfaction; only her eyes, larger, softer, more languid than
usual, seemed to reveal an amorous alarm, an almost frightened excitement. Marcello noticed all these things with complacency. Giulia was indeed the bride who prepares to surrender herself for the first time. She turned a little awkwardly (she always moved a little awkwardly, he thought,
but it was an attractive awkwardness, like that of a healthy,
innocent animal) in order to shut the door and pull down
the curtain, and then, standing in front of him, tried to
hang up her jacket on a hook beside the luggage rack. But
the train was going very fast, and as it crossed a switch at
full speed the whole car seemed to heel over and she fell on
top of him. Cunningly, she corrected her fall and sat on his
knees, putting her arms round his neck. Marcello felt the full
weight of her body rest on his own thin legs, and automatically he placed his arm round her waist. She said, in a low
voice, "D'you love me?" and at the same time lowered her
face toward his, seeking his mouth with her own. They

kissed lingeringly, while the train ran on at a high speed—the accomplice, so to speak, of their kiss, since at every jolt their teeth knocked together and Giulia's nose seemed anxious to penetrate his face. At last they separated, and Giulia, without getting off his knee, conscientiously took a handkerchief from her bag and wiped his lips, saying, "You've got about half a pound of lipstick on your mouth." Marcello, stiff in the legs, took advantage of another jolt of the train to slide her heavy body away from him on to the seat. "You naughty creature," she said, "don't you want me?"

"They still have to come and make up the beds," said Marcello, rather embarrassed.

"Just fancy," she went on without any transition, looking all around her, "it's the first time I've ever traveled in a sleeping car."

Marcello could not help smiling at the simple way in which she spoke, and asked, "D'you like it?"

"Yes, I like it very much," she said, looking around again. "When do they come to get the beds ready?"

"Soon."

They were silent; and then Marcello looked at his wife and found that she, too, was looking at him, but with a changed expression—with timidity and apprehension, almost, although the vivid, happy expression of a few minutes before still lingered in her face. She saw he was looking at her and smiled as if to excuse herself, and then, without a word, put out her hand and pressed his. From her moist and loving eyes two tears slipped down her cheeks, followed by two more. Giulia went on looking at him as she wept, trying all the time, pitifully, to smile through her tears. At last, with sudden impetuousness, she bent down and started wildly kissing his hand. Marcello was disconcerted by this weeping. Giulia was by nature cheerful and not very sentimental, and it was the first time he had seen her in tears. But she gave him no time to come to any conclusion, for she sat up and said hurriedly, "Forgive my crying like this . . . but I was thinking that you're so much better than I am and that I'm not worthy of you."

"Now you're starting to talk like your mother," said Marcello smiling.

She blew her nose and then replied calmly, "No, Mummy says these things without knowing why she says them. . . . But I have a good reason."

"What reason?"

She looked at him for some time and then explained, "I've got to tell you something, and afterwards perhaps you won't love me any more. . . . But I've got to tell you."

"What is it?"

She answered slowly, looking at him closely as though she wanted to catch the very first sign of the scornful expression she feared. "I'm not what you think I am," she said.

"What d'you mean?"

"I'm not. . . . Well, in fact, I'm not a virgin."

Marcello looked at her and suddenly understood that the normal character which he had hitherto attributed to his wife did not, in reality, exist. He did not know what was concealed behind this incipient confession, but he knew now for certain that Giulia, according to what she herself had said, was not what he had thought. There came over him a premonitory feeling of satiety at the idea of what he was going to hear, and a desire, almost, to refuse to listen to her confidences. But the first thing to do was to reassure her; and this was easy for him, because whether that famous virginity of hers existed or not did not really matter to him in the least. He replied in an affectionate voice, "Don't worry. . . . I married you because I was fond of you, not because you were a virgin."

Giulia shook her head and said: "I knew you had a modern mentality . . . and that you wouldn't make a fuss about it. . . . But I had to tell you, all the same."

"A modern mentality," Marcello could not help thinking with some amusement. The phrase was like Giulia herself, and made up for the absent virginity. It was an innocent phrase, though its innocence was not quite the kind he would have expected. Taking her hand, he said, "Come on, don't let's think about it any more," and he smiled at her.

Giulia smiled back at him. But again, while she was still smiling, tears filled her eyes and ran down her cheeeks. Marcello protested. "Come, come . . . what's the matter now? . . . I've told you I don't mind."

Giulia's response was a singular one. She threw her arms around his neck and turned away her head, holding it against his chest and looking down so that Marcello could not see her face. "I've got to tell you everything," she said.

"What d'you mean, everything?"

"Everything that happened to me."

"But it doesn't matter."

"Please let me. . . . It may be silly, but if I don't tell you I shall feel I'm hiding something from you."

"But why?" said Marcello, stroking her hair. "I supose you had a lover . . . someone you thought you were fond of . . . or that you really were fond of. . . . Why do I have to know about it?"

"No, I wasn't fond of him," she answered at once, almost

contemptuously, "and I never thought I was. . . . We were lovers more or less right up to the day when I got engaged to you. . . . But he wasn't a young man like you. . . . He was an old man of sixty—disgusting, and hard, and nasty, and exacting . . . a friend of the family—you know him."

"Who is it?"

"Fenizio, the lawyer," she said briefly.

Marcello gave a start. "But he was one of our witnesses. . . ."

"Yes, he insisted. . . . I didn't want him to be, but I couldn't refuse. . . . It was a wonder that he even allowed me to get married. . . ."

Marcello recalled that he had never cared for this lawyer Fenizio, whom he had very often met by chance at Giulia's home; he was a small, rather fair man, bald, with gold spectacles, a pointed nose that wrinkled up when he laughed, and a lipless mouth. A man, he also recalled, who was very calm and cold but who, within that same calmness and coldness, has his own unpleasant kind of aggressiveness and petulance. He was strong, too: one hot day he had taken off his coat and rolled up his shirt-sleeves, showing thick, white arms bulging with muscles. "But whatever did you see in him?" he could not help exclaiming.

"It was he who saw something in me . . . and very early, too. . . . I was his mistress, not for a month or for a year, but for six years."

Marcello made a quick mental calculation. Giulia was now twenty-one, or just over; therefore. . . . Astonished, he repeated, "Six years?"

"Yes, six years. . . . I was fifteen when .. . d'you understand?" Giulia, he noticed, although she was speaking of things which, to all appearances, still gave her pain, kept up the usual drawling, good-natured tone that she used for the most indifferent scraps of gossip. "He took advantage of me on the very day, more or less, that poor Daddy died. . . . If it wasn't the very same day, it was the same week. . . . As a matter of fact, I can tell you the exact date: just eight days after my father's funeral. . . . And remember, he was an intimate friend of my father's, and his trustee. . . ."

She paused for a moment, as if, by her silence, she wished to stress the impious behavior of the man; then she went on, "Mummy was doing nothing but weep at the time, and of course going to church a great deal. . . . He came one evening when I was alone in the flat; Mummy had gone out and the maid was in the kitchen. . . . I was sitting at the table in my room, busy doing my homework. . . . I was preparing for my exam at that time. . . . He came in on tiptoe and went around behind me, then bent over my exercise-book and asked me what I was doing. I told him, without turning around. I hadn't the slightest suspicion, in the first place because I was quite innocent—and you can believe me when I say I was innocent as a two-year-old child—and also because he was like a relation to me. . . . I used to call him 'Uncle,' just fancy! . . . Well then, I told him I was preparing my Latin exercise, and he—d'you know what he did?—he took hold of me by my hair, with one hand, but very firmly. . . . He often did that, for a joke, because I had splendid hair, long and wavy, and he said his fingers couldn't resist it. . . . When I felt him pulling, I still thought it was a joke and said to him, 'Let me go, you're hurting . . .'—but instead of letting go, he forced me to get up and holding me at arm's length steered me toward the bed, which was in the corner near the door, as it still is. . . . I—just imagine—I was so completely innocent I still didn't understand . . . and I said to him, I remember, 'Let me go, I've got to do my exercise.' At that moment he did let go of my hair . . . but no, I can't tell you. . . ."

Marcello was on the point of asking her to continue, thinking that she was ashamed; but Giulia, who had stopped merely in order to time her effects, resumed. "Although I wasn't yet fifteen, I was already very well developed, almost like a grown-up woman. . . . I didn't want to tell you because just to speak of it still hurts me. . . . He let go of my hair and squeezed me against his chest, but so hard that I couldn't even manage to scream and I almost fainted . . . perhaps I really did faint. . . . And then, after that embrace, I don't know what happened. I was lying on the bed and he was on top of me and I had understood everything, and all my strength had left me and I was just like an inanimate object in his hands, passive and inert and without any will power . . . and so he did just what he wanted with me. . . . Later I cried, and then, to comfort me, he told me he loved me, that he was mad about me—you know, the usual things. . . . But he also told me, in case I hadn't thoroughly understood, that I wasn't to say anything to Mummy unless I wanted him to ruin us. . . . Apparently Daddy, latterly, had made a mess of his affairs, and our material welfare now depended on *him*. . . . After that day he came back other times . . . but not regularly . . . always when I wasn't expecting him. . . . He used to come into my room on tiptoe, bend down over me and ask me in a severe voice: 'Have you done your exercise? No? . . . Well, come and do it with me, then.' And then, as usual, he would take me by my hair and conduct me at arm's length to the bed. . . . I tell you, he had an absolute passion for getting hold of my hair." She laughed, almost heartily, at the memory of this habit of her former lover's, as one laughs at some characteristic, amiable quality. "And so he went on for almost a year, continuing to swear that he loved me and that, if he hadn't had a wife and children, he would have married me . . . and I'm not saying he didn't mean it. . . . But if he had really been fond of me, as he said, there was only one way for him to show it—to leave me alone. . . . Anyhow, after a year, in desperation, I made an attempt to get rid of him: I told him I didn't love him and would never love him, that I couldn't go on in that way, that I couldn't get anything done and was in a bad state and hadn't passed my exam, and that if he didn't let me alone I would have to give up my studies altogether. . . . And then he—just imagine—he went and told Mummy that he understood my character and was convinced that I wasn't cut out for intellectual study and that, I was now sixteen, the best thing would be for me to get a job. . . . To start off with, he offered me a post as secretary in his office. . . . D'you see? . . . Of course I resisted as hard as I could, but poor darling Mummy said I was being ungrateful, that he had been, and still was, such a help to us, that I mustn't miss such a fine opportunity; and so, in the end, I was forced to accept. . . . Once I was in his office and with him all day long, there was no possibility of stopping, as you may imagine . . . and so I began again, and finally he got me into the habit of it, and I gave up protesting. . . . You know how it is: I felt there was no hope for me any more and became fatalistic. . . . But when, a year ago, you told me you were fond of me, I went straight to him and said to him that, this time, the whole thing was really finished. . . . He protested, vile creature that he is, and threatened to go to you and tell you the whole story. . . . So d'you know what I did? I picked up a sharp paper cutter that lay on his desk and held the point of it to his throat, and I said, 'If you do that, I'll kill you'; and then I went on, 'He shall know about our relations, it's only right that he should. . . . But *I'm* going to be the one to tell him, not you. . . . From now on you simply don't exist for me . . . and if you make the slightest attempt to come between him and me I'll kill you. . . . I'll go to prison for it but I'll kill you.' I said this in a tone that made him realize I meant it . . . and from then on he never breathed another word—except when he tried to get back at me by writing that anonymous letter in which he spoke of your father. . . ."

"Ah, so that's who it was," Marcello could not help exclaiming.

"Of course. . . . I recognized the paper at once and typing too." She was silent for a moment, and then, in sudden anxiety, took Marcello's hand and added: "Now I've told you everything and I feel better. . . . But perhaps I ought not to have told you, perhaps now you won't be able to endure me any more, perhaps you'll hate me."

Marcello did not answer, but remained silent for a long time. Giulia's tale had aroused in his mind neither hatred for the man who had abused her nor pity for her, who had endured that abuse. The very manner in which she had told her story—passionless and sensible, even when she was expressing repugnance or contempt—excluded any feelings so decided as hatred or pity. And so he himself, as it were by contagion, was inclined to regard the matter in a not dissimilar light, with a mixture of indulgence and resignation. He felt, if anything, an entirely physical amazement, unconnected with any sort of criticism—like falling into an unexpected void. And, as a reaction, he was aware of a sharpening of his habitual melancholy at being confronted with this unforeseen confirmation of a rule of decadence to which he had hoped, for a moment, that Giulia might be an exception. Yet his conviction of the profoundly normal character of Giulia's whole personality remained unaffected. Normality, he suddenly realized, did not consist so much in holding aloof from certain experiences as in the standard by which one judged them. Chance had willed that both he and Giulia had had something in their lives to conceal, and, consequently, to confess. But whereas he himself felt utterly incapable of speaking about Lino, Giulia, on the other hand, had not hesitated to reveal to him her relations with the lawyer, choosing for this revelation, the moment which, according to her ideas, was most suitable—the moment of their marriage, which she felt should wipe out the past and open up for her an entirely new way of life. This thought gave him pleasure because in spite of everything it confirmed Giulia's normality, which lay in her ability to idemnify herself by the customary, ancient methods of religion and the affections. Distracted by these reflections, he turned his eyes towards the window and did not notice how alarmed his wife was at his silence. Then he felt her trying to embrace him and heard her voice asking him, "You don't say anything? It's true, then . . . you're disgusted with me. . . . The truth is that you can't bear me any more and you're disgusted at me."

Marcello wanted to reassure her, and he made a movement to take her in his arms. But he was thwarted by a violent jerk of the train, so that, without meaning to, he struck her in the face with his elbow. Giulia interpreted this involuntary blow as a gesture of rebuff and immediately rose to her feet. The train entered a tunnel with a long mournful whistle and a thickening of the darkness at the window. Through the clatter, redoubled by the echo of the tunnel, he seemed to catch the sound of a sob from Giulia as, with arms outstretched, she swayed and stumbled towards the door of the compartment. He was suprised and, without getting up, called to her. "Giulia." Her only answer was to open the door and disappear into the corridor, still swaying and stumbling in that distressing manner.

For a moment he sat still, then suddenly alarmed, rose and followed her out. Their compartment was in the middle of the coach, and he saw his wife hurrying along the deserted corridor in the direction of the vestibule. As he saw her moving swiftly over the thick, soft carpet between the mahogany walls, the words she had spoken to her former lover flashed across his mind: "If you say anything I'll kill you!" and he thought he had perhaps been ignorant of one aspect of her character and had mistaken her good nature for sloth. At the same moment he saw her bend down and fumble with the handle of the door. Darting forward, he seized her by the arm and pulled her back.

"What on earth are you doing, Giulia?" he asked in a low voice, through the clatter of the train. "What did you think . . . ? It was the train. . . . I meant to turn round and instead I bumped into you."

She stiffened as he put his arms round her, as though she intended to struggle. But, at the quiet, sincerely surprised tone of his voice, she seemed to calm down suddenly. After a moment, bending her head, she said: "I'm sorry, perhaps I made a mistake, but I had the impression that you hated me, so I just wanted to make an end of everything . . . It wasn't a gesture; if you hadn't arrived I should have really done it."

"But why? . . . Whatever had come into your head?"

She shrugged her shoulders. "Well, to cut a long story short . . . Getting married, for me, was a far more important thing than you think. . . . When I decided you couldn't bear me any more, I thought, there's nothing else to be done. . . ." She shrugged her shoulders again and added, raising her face toward him with a smile, "Just think, you would have been left a widower almost before you were married."

Marcello looked at her for a moment without speaking. Evidently Giulia was sincere; it was perfectly true that she had attached a far greater importance to marriage than he had imagined possible. And he understood, then, with a feeling of astonishment, that her humble remark was an indication of her complete participation in the nuptial rite, which for her—unlike himself—had been what it truly ought to have been, neither more nor less. So it was not surprising that, after a self-surrender so impassioned, she should have thought, at the first disillusionment, of killing herself. He told himself that this was almost a piece of blackmail on Giulia's part: either you forgive me or I shall kill myself; and once again he was conscious of relief at finding her so like what he had wished her to be. Giulia had turned away again and appeared to be gazing at the window. He put his arm round her waist and murmured in her ear, "You know I love you."

She turned at once and kissed him with a passion so impetuous that Marcello was almost frightened. That was the way, he thought, in which pious women in churches sometimes kissed crosses, or relics, or the feet of statues. The clatter of the tunnel had meanwhile died down into the usual swift, rhythmic sound of wheels in the open air; and they separated.

They stood there side by side in front of the window, hand in hand, gazing into the darkness of the night. "Look," said Giulia at last, in her normal voice, "look over there. . . . What can it be? A house on fire?"

There was indeed a fire, like a shining red flower in the middle of the dark pane of glass. "I daresay it is," said Marcello, and lowered the window. As the mirror-like brightness of the glass was withdrawn from the outside darkness, the cool wind of the train's motion blew into his face, but the red flower remained, hanging mysteriously in the blackness of night, whether far or near, high or low, it was impossible to tell. Then, after staring for some time at the four or five petals of fire that seemed to be moving and throbbing, he turned his eyes to the bank beside the railway, along which the feeble lights of the train were running, together with his own and Giulia's shadows. Suddenly he was conscious of a sensation of acute bewilderment. Why was he in this train? And who was the woman standing beside him? And where was he going? And who indeed was he? And where had he come from? He did not suffer as a result of this bewilderment; on the contrary, it was pleasing to him as a feeling already familiar which perhaps also constituted the very background of his most intimate being. "I'm just like that fire over there in the darkness," he thought coldly. "I shall flare up and then die down again without reason and without result . . . just a little piece of destruction hanging in the blackness of night."

He started at Giulia's voice informing him, "Look, they've evidently made up our beds," and he realized that, while he himself had been lost in contemplation of that distant fire, for her there remained simply the question of their love; or rather, to be more exact, the approaching union of their two bodies. She was concerned, in fact, with what she was doing at the moment and nothing else. She had already walked off, not without a kind of repressed impatience, toward their compartment and Marcello followed some distance behind her. He paused a moment in the doorway to allow the conductor to come out, and then went in. Giulia was standing in front of the mirror and, regardless of the door being still open, was taking off her blouse, unbuttoning it from the bottom to the top. Without turning round, she said to him: "You take the top berth, and I'll have the bottom one."

Marcello closed the door, climbed up into his berth and immediately started undressing, putting his clothes in the rack as he went. Naked, he sat waiting on the bed, his arms clasping his knees. He heard Giulia moving about, the tinkling sound of a tumbler in its metal holder, the thud of a shoe falling on the carpet, and other noises. Then, with a dry click, the bright electric lights went out, leaving only the purplish glimmer of the night lamp; and Giulia's voice said, "Are you coming?" Marcello hung his legs over the edge, twisted round, put one foot on the lower berth and bent sideways to get into it. As he did this, he saw Giulia lying naked on her back, her arms across her eyes, her legs spread out. In the dim, deceptive light her body seemed of a cold, mother-of-pearl whiteness, with dark patches at the groin and under the arms and a dull pink at the breast; and she appeared lifeless, not only because of this deathly pallor but because of her relaxed and utter stillness. But as Marcello bent over her, all at once she shook herself with a violent jerk like the spring of a closing trap and pulled him to her, throwing her arms round his neck, opening her legs and clasping her feet behind his back. Later, she thrust him harshly away and curled up against the wall, all huddled up with her forehead against her knees. And Marcello, lying beside her, understood that that which she had drawn, with such frantic passion, from his body and which she had enclosed and preserved so jealousy in her own womb, no longer belonged to him, but would have its growth in her. And this, he thought, he had done in order to be able to say, once at any rate, "I have been a man like all other men . . . I have loved, I have united myself with a woman and have begotten another human being."

## CHAPTER 9

As soon as he thought Giulia had fallen asleep, Marcello got out of bed and started dressing. The room was full of a fresh, transparent half-light that gave a hint of the splendid brilliance of June over sky and sea. It was a typical Riviera hotel room, high, white, with blue plaster decorations in the form of flowers and stalks and leaves, light-colored wooden furniture in the same floral style as the plasterwork, and, in one corner, a big green palm. When he was dressed, he tiptoed to the window, pushed the shutters slightly apart and looked out. There was the wide, smiling expanse of the sea, made vaster by the perfect clearness of the violet-blue horizon that seemed, as a faint breeze passed over it, to be lit up, wave after wave, by a tiny sparkling flower of sunlight. Marcello lowered his eyes from the seat to the promenade. It was deserted; no one was sitting on the benches in the shade of the palm trees facing the sea, no one was walking along the gray, clean asphalt. He examined this view for some time, then closed the shutters again and turned to look at Giulia as she lay on the bed. She was naked and asleep. The position of her body as she lay on her side brought into prominence the pale, ample roundness of her hip, from which the upper part of her body seemed to hang limp and lifeless, like the stem of a wilting plant from a vase. The back and hips, as Marcello knew, were the only firm, solid part of that body; on the farther side of it, invisible to him now but present to his memory, was the softness of her belly, flowing over, in tender folds, on to the bed, and of her breasts, dragged down by their weight, one over the other. Her head, hidden by her shoulder, could not be seen; and Marcello, remembering that he had possessed his wife a few minutes before, had the feeling that he was looking not at a real person but at a machine made of flesh, beautiful and lovable but brutal, made for love and for nothing else. As if his pitiless stare had waked her, she suddenly stirred and sighed deeply, and then said, in a clear voice, "Marcello." He stepped quickly to her side, answering affectionately, "Here I am." She turned over, transferring from one side to the other her cumbrous weight of female flesh, lifted her arms blindly and clasped them round his hips. Then, with her hair falling over her face, she slowly, tenaciously, rubbed her nose and mouth against him, seeking his groin. She kissed him there, with a kind of humble, passionate fetishism, paused a moment, motionless, her arms still around him, then fell back on the

138

bed, overcome with sleep, her hair covering her face. And now she was asleep again, in the same position as before, except that she had changed from her right to her left side. Marcello took his coat from its peg, tiptoed to the door and went out into the passage.

He went down the wide, echoing staircase and out through the door of the hotel on to the promenade. For a moment he was dazzled by the sunlight reflected in flashing points from the surface of the sea. He closed his eyes, and then, as though his senses had been revived by darkness, he was struck by a sharp smell of horse-urine. There was a row of three or four cabs there, standing in a patch of shade behind the hotel, white covers on their seats, their drivers asleep on the box. Marcello went to the first of them and jumped in, calling out the address: "Via dei Glicini." He noticed that the driver threw him a quick, meaningful glance before, without speaking a word, he whipped up his horse.

The cab bowled along the sea front for some distance and then turned into a short street of villas and gardens. At the far end of the street rose the first of the Ligurian hills, luminous, vine-decked, with gray olive trees here and there, and a few tall red houses with green window-frames standing on the slope. The street led straight toward the flank of the hill; pavements and asphalt came to a sudden end, giving place to a sort of grassy track. The cab stopped and Marcello looked up. He saw, set back in a garden, a gray, three-floored house with a black-slated roof and mansard windows. The cabman said drily, "This is it," took his money and hurriedly turned his horse. Marcello thought that he was offended at having had to bring him to this place; but perhaps, he reflected pushing open the gate, he was attributing to him the repugnance that he himself felt.

He walked up the path between two dusty laurel hedges, toward a door set with panes of colored glass. He had always hated such places and had never entered one except for two or three times in his youth, coming away, each time, with a feeling of disgust and remorse, as though at something unworthy he ought not to have done. Feeling sick at heart, he went up the two or three steps, pushed open the glass door, letting loose a jingling mechanism of bells, and found himself in a Pompeian hall, facing a staircase with a wooden banister. He recognized the sickly smell of face powder, sweat and semen. The house was immersed in silence and summer afternoon torpor. As he was looking around, there appeared from somewhere or other a sort of maidservant, dressed in black with a white apron tied round her waist. She was small and slim, and her sharp, ferret-

like face was enlivened by two brilliant eyes. She came towards him with a shrill "Good-day" uttered in the gayest of
tones. "I want to speak to the proprietress," he said, taking
off his hat with perhaps excessive politeness. "All right,
pretty boy, you shall speak to her," replied the woman,
speaking in the local dialect; "but in the meantime you'd
better go into the drawing room. . . . The proprietress will
come to you. . . Go in there." Marcello, irritated both by her
familiar way of speaking to him and by the misunderstanding, nevertheless allowed himself to be pushed towards a
half open door. He saw, in an uneven half-light, a long,
rectangular, empty room, with a row of red-upholstered divans all round the walls. The floor was dusty, like that of a
station waiting room; the worn and dirty stuff of the divans,
too, suggested the dreariness of a public place within the
intimacy and secrecy of a private house. Marcello, uncertain
what to do, sat down on one of the divans. At the same moment—like the sudden unburdening of bowels long unmoved—he could hear through the house a sort of disintegration, a pattering sound, the precipitate rush of feet
down the wooden staircase. And then the thing that he had
feared happened. The door opened and the peevish voice of
the maid announced, "Here are the young ladies . . . all
for you."

Lazily, unwillingly they came in, some of them half-naked,
some more or less dressed, two of them dark and three
fair, three of middling height one decidedly small and one
enormous. The latter came and sat down beside Marcello,
flopping down on the divan with a sigh of exhausted satisfaction. At first he turned away his face, then, fascinated,
moved slightly round again and looked at her. She was
truly enormous, pyramidal in shape, her hips broader than
her waist, her waist broader than her shoulders and her
shoulders broader than her head, the latter being extremely
small, with a snub-nosed face and a tress of black hair
twisted round her forehead. A yellow silk brassiere supported her low, swelling breasts; below her navel a red skirt
hung wide open like the curtain of a theatre, displaying
the dark groin and the massive white thighs. Seeing that she
was being looked at, she smiled suggestively to one of her
companions who was sitting against the opposite wall,
heaved a sigh, and then passed her hand between her legs as
though to pull them apart into a less hot position. Marcello,
offended by this idle immodesty, would have liked to pull
away the hand with which she was rubbing herself underneath her belly; but he had not the energy to move. The
thing that struck him most in these female cattle was the

irreparable quality of their degradation. It was the same thing that made him shudder with horror in face of his mother's nudity and his father's madness, and was at the source of his almost hysterical love of order, quietness, tidiness, composure. The woman turned to him and said in a benevolent, jocular tone, "Well, don't you like your harem?" . . . Have you made up your mind?"—and immediately, in an impulse of frantic disgust, he got up and ran out of the room, followed by a burst of laughter and some obscene remarks in dialect. Furious, he went toward the staircase, thinking that he would go up to the floor above and search for the proprietress, but at that moment there was another peal from the front doorbell, and when he turned he saw, standing on the threshold, the astonished and—to his eyes, in his present embarrassment—almost paternal, figure of the Secret Service agent, Orlando.

"Good day, sir . . . But where are you going, sir?" the latter exclaimed quickly, "you mustn't go upstairs."

"As a matter of fact," said Marcello, pausing and becoming calm again immediately, "I think they mistook me for a client . . ."

"Stupid women," said Orlando, shaking his head. "Come with me, sir . . . I'll show you the way . . . You're expected, sir."

He preceded Marcello through the glass door and into the garden. One behind the other, they walked down the path between the hedges and turned round behind the house. The sun was scorching in this part of the garden, with a dry, sharp heat of dust and vegetation run wild. Marcello noticed that all the shutters of the villa were closed, just as though it were uninhabited; and the garden, too, was full of weeds and appeared to be abandoned. The Secret Service man was now making for a low, white building that took up the whole of the far end of the garden. Marcello remembered having noticed little houses like this, at the bottoms of gardens behind villas of this kind in other watering places. In summer the owners would let the villa and retire into them, restricting themselves to a couple of rooms in order to make money. Orlando opened the door without knocking and stuck his head in, announcing, "Here is Doctor Clerici."

Marcello walked forward and found himself in a small room fitted up, in a summary sort of way, as an office. The air was thick with smoke. A man was sitting at the table, his hands joined and his face turned toward him. The man was an albino. His face had the glowing, rosy transparency of alabaster, and was flecked with yellow freckles. His blue eyes, inflamed and almost red, with white lashes, were like those of certain wild animals that live among the polar snows. Accustomed as Marcello was to the disconcerting contrast between the dull bureaucratic style and the often ferocious tasks of many of his Secret Service colleagues, he could not help saying to himself that this man, at any rate, was perfectly suited to his position. There was more than cruelty in that spectral countenance—a kind of ruthless fury, almost, that was yet kept within bounds by the conventional rigidity of his military bearing. After a moment of embarrassing immobility, the man rose brusquely to his feet, revealing the shortness of his stature. "My name is Gabrio," he said. Then he immediately sat down and went on in an ironical tone, "So here you are, at last, Doctor Clerici."

His voice was metallic and disagreeable. Marcello, without waiting to be asked, also sat down and said, "Yes, I arrived this morning."

"I did, in fact, expect you this morning."

Marcello hesitated. Should he tell him that he was on his honeymoon? He decided not to, and concluded quietly, "It wasn't possible for me to come earlier."

"So I see," said the man. He pushed the box of cigarettes toward Marcello with an ungracious "Do you smoke?" then lowered his head and started reading a sheet of paper lying on the table. "They leave me here, in this house which may be hospitable but isn't in the least secret, without information, without directives, practically without money . . . ah, here it is." He went on reading for some time, then raised his head and added, "They told you in Rome to come and see me, didn't they?"

"Yes, the same man that brought me here just now came and notified me that I was to break my journey here and come and see you."

"Yes, exactly." Gabrio took the cigarette from his mouth and put it carefully down on the edge of the ash tray. "At the last moment, it appears, they changed their minds. . . The program is altered."

Marcello did not blink an eyelid; but a wave of indefinable relief and hope rushed over him exhilaratingly. Perhaps he would now be allowed to simplify his journey, to reduce it to its ostensible motives of Paris and a honeymoon. He said, however, in a clear voice, "What does that mean?"

"It means that the plan is modified and, consequently, your mission also," continued Gabrio. "This man Quadri was to have been watched, you were to have got in touch with him, gained his confidence, even got him to entrust you with some commission or other. . . . Now in my last communication from Rome, Quadri is specified as a troublesome person, to be suppressed." Gabrio took up his cigarette again, inhaled a mouthful of smoke, and replaced it in the ash tray. "In fact," he explained, in a more conversational tone, "your mission is reduced to practically nothing. . . . All you have to do is to get in touch with Quadri, availing yourself of the fact that you know him already, and then point him out to this man Orlando, who will also be going to Paris. . . . You can invite him, for instance, to some public place where Orlando will also be—a café, a restaurant. . . . All that's needed is for Orlando to see him with you, to make certain of his identity. . . . That's all that's asked of you now. . . . Then you can devote yourself to your honeymoon exactly as you like."

So Gabrio too knew about his honeymoon, thought Marcello, astonished. But this first thought, he at once realized, was nothing but a hastily assumed mask by means of which his mind sought to conceal from itself its own agitation. In reality Gabrio had revealed to him something more important than knowledge of his honeymoon—the decision to suppress Quadri. With a violent effort he forced himself to make an objective examination of this extraordinary, this lamentable piece of news. And he immediately established, in his own mind, one fundamental fact. In order to suppress Quadri, his own presence in Paris, his own co-operation, were not in any way necessary. Orlando could perfectly well find and identify his victim by himself. The truth of the matter was, he thought, that they wanted to involve him in an effective, though unnecessary complicity, to compromise him utterly, once and for all. As for the alteration in the plan, there was not the slightest doubt but that it was merely apparent. The plan just propounded by Gabrio had of course been already decided on and worked out in all its details at the time of his visit to the Ministry; and the apparent alteration had been due to a characteristic desire to divide and confuse responsibility. Neither he nor, probably, Gabrio, had received written orders; thus, in case of unfavorable developments, the Ministry would be able to proclaim its own innocence; and the blame for the murder would fall on him, on Gabrio, on Orlando, and on the other immediate participants.

He hesitated, and then, to gain time, objected, "I can't see that Orlando has any need of me in order to find Quadri. . . . I think he's actually in the telephone book."

"Those are the orders," said Gabrio with almost breathless haste, as if he had foreseen Marcello's objection.

Marcello lowered his head. He realized that he had been enticed into a kind of trap, and that, having put out one finger, he was now, through a subterfuge, caught by the whole arm; but, strangely, once the first shock of surprise was over, he found that he felt no real repugnance at the change of plan—nothing more, in fact, than an obstinate, melancholy resignation in the face of a duty which, though it increases in unpleasantness, yet remains unchanged and unavoidable. Probably the Secret Service agent Orlando had no knowledge of the inside mechanism of this duty, but he himself had—and that was all the difference between them. Neither he nor Orlando could evade what Gabrio called "orders," that were in fact personal situations that had now been firmly established, outside which, for both of them, lay nothing but disorder and irregularity. At last he looked up and said, "All right then. . . . And where am I to find Orlando, in Paris?"

Gabrio looked down at the same sheet of paper on the table, and replied. "You tell me where you'll be staying . . . then Orlando will come and see you."

So, they did not quite trust him, and anyhow did not consider it opportune to give him the man's address in Paris. He mentioned the name of the hotel where he would be staying, and Gabrio made a note of it at the bottom of the paper. He went on, in a more affable tone, as though to indicate that the official part of the visit was over, "Have you ever been to Paris?"

"No, this is the first time."

"I was there for two years before I ended up in this hole here," said Gabrio with characteristic bureaucratic bitterness. "Once you've been in Paris even Rome seems like a village. . . . And imagine a place like this!" He lit a cigarette from the butt of the other, and added, with empty boastfulness, "In Paris I was in clover. . . . A flat, a car, lots of friends, affairs with women. . . . As far as that goes, you know, Paris is ideal."

Marcello, though it went against the grain, felt that he ought to respond to Gabrio's affability in some way. So he said, "But with this house here, just across the way, you shouldn't be bored."

Gabrio shook his head. "Pooh, how could one think of amusing oneself with those lumps of meat fit only for conscripts, at so much a pound? . . . No," he added, "one's only resource here is the Casino. . . . D'you gamble?"

"No, never."

"It's interesting, all the same," said Gabrio, pulling himself back in his chair, as though to indicate that the interview was finished. "Fortune may smile upon anyone, on you just as much as on me. . . . It's not for nothing that she's a woman. . . . The important thing is to grab hold of her when you can." He rose, went to the door and threw it open. He was indeed very small, Marcello observed, with short legs; the upper part of his body was stiffly enclosed in a green jacket of military cut. Gabrio stood there for a moment looking at Marcello, in a ray of sunlight that seemed to accentuate the transparency of his pink, glowing skin; then he said, "I don't suppose we shall meet again. . . . On your return from Paris you'll be going straight back to Rome."

"Yes, almost certainly."

"Is there anything you need?" Gabrio asked, suddenly and unwillingly. "Have they provided you with funds? . . . I haven't much with me here . . . but if you need anything. . . ."

"No thanks, I don't need anything."

"Well, good luck, then—and into the lion's mouth!"

They shook hands and Gabrio hastily closed the door. Marcello walked away toward the gate.

But as he was going down the path, he realized that, in his hurried flight from the drawing room, he had left his hat there. He hesitated, loth to go back into that room that stank of shoes and face powder and sweat, and fearing, besides, the jests and the flattery of the women. Then he made up his mind, turned back and pushed open the door, letting loose the usual tinkle of bells.

This time nobody appeared, neither the ferret-faced maid nor any of the girls. But, through the open door of the big room, he heard the well-known, loud, good-natured voice of Orlando; and, feeling encouraged, he looked into the room.

It was empty, except for Orlando, who was sitting in the corner by the door beside a woman whom Marcello did not remember having noticed among those who had appeared at his first entry. The Secret Service man had his arm round her waist, in an awkward, confidential attitude, and he did not trouble to change his position at Marcello's appearance. Embarrassed, vaguely irritated, the latter turned away his eyes from Orlando and looked at the woman.

She was sitting in a rigid attitude, as though she wished in some way to repel her companion, or at least to keep him at a distance. She was dark, with a high, white forehead, bright eyes, a long, thin face and a large mouth enlivened by dark-colored lipstick and she wore a scornful expression. She was dressed in an almost normal manner, in a white evening dress, low at the neck and sleeveless, whose only meretricious device was that the skirt was split almost up to the waist so as to display her belly and her crossed legs, long, slim and elegant, with a chaste beauty like the legs of a dancer. She held a lighted cigarette be-

tween two fingers but she was not smoking: her hand rested
on the arm of the sofa and the smoke rose into the air.
Her other hand lay quietly on Orlando's knee. It might
as well have been lying, thought Marcello, on the faithful
head of a large dog. But what struck him most forcibly
about her was her forehead, and not so much its whiteness
as its appearance of being illumined in a mysterious way
by the intense expression of the eyes, with a purity of light
that made him think of one of those chaplets of diamonds
that women used to wear, on great occasions, at balls. Marcello continued to gaze at her for some time in astonishment,
and as he gazed he was conscious of a painful, indescribable
feeling of regret and disdain. Meanwhile Orlando, intimidated
by this persistent stare, had risen to his feet.

"My hat," said Marcello. The woman had remained
seated, and was now, in turn, gazing at him, but without
curiosity. Orlando hurried assiduously across the room to
fetch the hat from a divan on the far side. And then, suddenly, Marcello understood why it was that the sight of
the woman had aroused in him that painful feeling of regret. The truth, he realized, was that he did not want her
to do what Orlando desired, and seeing her submit to his
embrace had made him suffer as though he were witnessing some intolerable profanation. Of course she knew
nothing of the light that shone on her brow—which in
any case did not belong to her any more than beauty, in
general, is the property of a beautiful person. Yet he felt
it almost his duty to prevent her demeaning that shining
brow in order to satisfy the erotic caprices of Orlando.
For one moment it occurred to him to make use of his
authority in order to get her out of the room. He would
engage her in conversation for a short time, and then, as
soon as he could be sure that Orlando had chosen another
woman, he would go away. He also had the crazy idea of
carrying her away from the brothel and giving her the
chance of another sort of life. But, even as he had these
thoughts, he realized that they were foolish fancies. It was
impossible that she should not be like her companions,
like them irreparably and, as it were, innocently ruined
and lost. Then he felt a touch on his arm; Orlando was
in the act of handing him his hat. Automatically he took
it.

But Orlando had had time to reflect on that curious
stare of Marcello's. He stepped forward, and, pointing to
the woman in much the same way as he might have pointed out something in the way of food or drink to an hon-

ored guest, made a suggestion to him. "If you wish, sir, if you like this woman . . . I can wait."

At first Marcello did not understand. Then he saw the smile on Orlando's face, at the same time both respectful and knowing, and felt himself blushing up to the' ears. So Orlando was not retiring, he was merely yielding first place to him, from politeness as a friend as well as from discipline as an inferior—just as he might at a bar or a buffet table. Marcello said hurriedly, "You're crazy, Orlando . . . You do just as you like, I must go."

"Very well, sir," said Orlando with a smile. Marcello saw him beckon to the woman, and to his distress saw her rise at once, obedient to the signal, and—tall, erect, the diadem of light on her brow—walk over to him without hesitation or protest, with perfect professional simplicity. Orlando said to Marcello, "We shall meet again soon, sir," and he stepped aside to allow the woman to pass. Marcello, almost in spite of himself, drew back; and she walked between them, in a leisurely way, cigarette in her fingers. But when she was in front of Marcello she stopped for an instant and said: "If you want me, my name is Luisa." Her voice, as he had feared, was coarse and harsh, without any gentleness in it; and Luisa thought it necessary to follow up her words with a gesture supposed to be flattering, putting out her tongue and licking her upper lip. Marcello felt that her words and gesture relieved him, to a certain extent, of his regret at having failed to prevent her going off with Orlando. The woman, meanwhile, still leading the way, had reached the staircase. She threw her cigarette on the floor, stamped it out, and, raising her skirt with both hands, started quickly up the stairs, closely followed by Orlando. Finally they disappeared round the corner of the landing above. Somebody else—probably another of the girls and a client—was now coming downstairs. Marcello could hear their chatter. Hurriedly he left the house.

## CHAPTER 10

Having asked the hotel porter to get Quadri's number on the telephone, Marcello went and sat down in a corner of the lounge. It was a big hotel and the lounge was very spacious, with arches supported on pillars, groups of armchairs, showcases in which expensive objects were displayed, writing-desks and tables. Numbers of people were coming and going between the entrance and the elevator, the porter's desk and the manager's office, the door of the restaurant and the other public rooms beyond the pillars.

Marcello would have liked to amuse himself, as he waited, with the spectacle of this gay, swarming lounge, but
his mind, dragged down to the depths of memory by his
present distress, turned back, almost against his will, to
the first and only visit that he had paid to Quadri, many
years before. Marcello had been a student at that time,
and Quadri his tutor; and he had gone to Quadri's home
in an old red building not far from the station in Rome,
to consult him about a thesis for his doctor's degree. The
moment he entered, Marcello had been struck by the
enormous quantity of books piled up in every corner of
the flat. Even in the hall he had noticed old curtains that
appeared to conceal doors. But when he pulled them aside
he had discovered rows and rows of books in recesses in
the walls. The maid had led him down an extremely long
and tortuous passage that seemed to go round the courtyard of the building, and the passage was lined on both
sides with shelves of books and papers. When he was
shown into Quadri's study, Marcello had found himself
in a room whose four walls were closely packed with
books, from floor to ceiling. There were more books on
the desk, arranged one on top of the other in two neat
piles between which the bearded face of the professor peeped
out as though through a loophole.

Marcello had at once noticed that Quadri had a curiously flat, asymmetrical face, like a papier-mâché mask
with red-rimmed eyes and a triangular nose to the lower
part of which a beard and a pair of false mustaches have
been stuck on in a summary manner. On his forehead,
too, his hair, too black and with a look of dampness, gave
the impression of a badly fitting wig. Between his brush-
like mustache and his broomlike beard, both of them of a
suspect blackness, one caught a glimpse of a very red mouth
with lips of no particular shape. And Marcello had been
forced to the conclusion that all this badly-distributed hair
probably concealed some kind of deformity, such as a lack
of chin or a frightful scar. It was a face that had nothing
real or reliable about it, a face in which everything was
false, a veritable mask. The professor had risen to welcome
Marcello, and, in doing so, had revealed the shortness of
his stature and the hump—or rather the malformation of
the left shoulder—that added a certain distressing quality
to his excessively gentle and affectionate manners. As he
shook Marcello's hand between the piles of books, Quadri
had looked at his visitor in a short-sighted way over his
thick lenses, so that Marcello had had a momentary impression that he was being examined not by two, but by

four eyes. He had also noticed the antiquated style of Quadri's clothes—a sort of frock coat, black with silk facings, black striped trousers, a white shirt with starched collar and cuffs, a gold watchchain across his waistcoat. Marcello had no liking for Quadri: he knew him to be an anti-Fascist, and Quadri's anti-fascism, his unwarlike, unhealthy, unattractive appearance, his learning, his books, everything about him went to make up in Marcello's mind the conventional picture, continually pointed at in scorn by Party propaganda, of the negative, impotent intellectual. And, in addition, Quadri's extraordinary gentleness was repugnant to Marcello, who felt there must be something false about it: it seemed to him impossible that a man could be so gentle without deceitfulness and without ulterior motives.

Quadri had welcomed Marcello with his customary expressions of exaggerated affection. There were constant interjections of such phrases as "My boy," or "My dear boy," as he waved his little white hands about over the books; and he had begun by asking a quantity of questions about Marcello's family and about himself personally. When he heard that Marcello's father was shut up in a clinic for the insane, he had exclaimed, "Oh, my poor boy, I didn't know. . . . What a misfortune, what a terrible misfortune! . . . And can science do nothing to restore his reason?" But he had not listened to Marcello's reply and had passed straight on to another subject. He had a throaty voice, modulated and harmonious, extremely sweet and full of anxious apprehensiveness. Marcello had discerned through this languishing yet marked anxiety—like a watermark in a transparent piece of paper—a complete indifference. Quadri, far from taking any real interest in him, perhaps did not even see him. Marcello had been struck, too, by the absence of shades of meaning or variety of tone in Quadri's conversation. He continued to speak the whole time with the same uniformly affectionate, sentimental accent whether he was dealing with matters that demanded this tone or with others that did not demand it at all. Quadri, at the end of his string of questions, had inquired, finally, whether Marcello was a Fascist; and, receiving an affirmative reply, had explained in an almost casual manner, without changing his tone or showing any apparent reaction, how difficult it was for him, whose anti-Fascist feelings were so well known, to continue the teaching of such subjects as philosophy and history under a regime like that of the Fascists. At this point Marcello, in embarrassment, had tried to bring the conversation round to the object of his visit. But Quadri had immediately interrupted him. "Per-

haps you will wonder why in the world I am telling you
all these things. . . . My dear boy, I am not talking idly nor
to relieve my own personal feelings. . . . I would not
allow myself to waste the time that you ought to be de-
voting to your studies. . . . I am telling you these things
in order to justify, in some way, the fact that I am unable
to concern myself either with you or with your thesis: I
am giving up teaching."

"You're giving up teaching?" Marcello had repeated in
surprise.

"Yes," Quadri had confirmed, passing his hand with a
habitual gesture over his mouth and mustache. "Although
it is a grief, a great grief, to me, since I have devoted my
whole life to you young men, I find myself forced to resign
my position." After a moment, without emphasis, the professor had added with a sigh, "Yes, yes, I have made up
my mind to pass from thought to action. . . . The phrase,
perhaps, will not seem new to you, but it reflects my situation exactly."

Marcello had with difficulty refrained from smiling. Indeed
he seemed to him a comic figure, this Professor Quadri,
this little man in a frock coat, hunchbacked, short sighted,
bearded, peering out at him from his armchair, between
his piles of books, and declaring that he had made up his
mind to pass from thought to action. There was, however,
no doubt as to the meaning of his remark. Quadri, after
years of passive opposition, shut up in his own thoughts
and his own profession, had decided to go over to active
politics, perhaps to active plotting. Marcello, seized with a
sudden, vehement dislike for him, had not been able to
help warning him, in a cold, menacing manner, "You're
making a mistake in telling me this. . . . I am a Fascist
and I might report you."

But Quadri, speaking with extreme gentleness, in an intimate sort of way, had answered, "I know you're a dear,
good boy, a fine, honest boy, and that you'd never do a
thing like that."

"Devil take him," Marcello had thought angrily. And
he had answered, with perfect sincerity, "I might certainly
do it. . . . That's exactly what honesty means to us Fascists—reporting people like you and making it impossible
for them to do any harm."

The professor had shaken his head. "My dear boy," he
had said, "you know, even while you're speaking, that what
you say isn't true. . . . You know it, or rather, your
heart knows it. . . . And in point of fact you, honest young
man that you are, took the step of warning me. . . . An-

other—you know what he would have done, a real informer?
—he would have pretended to approve of what I said, and
then, once I had compromised myself by some thoroughly
imprudent statement, he would have reported me. . . . But
you warned me."

"I warned you," Marcello had replied harshly, "because
I don't believe you're capable of what you call action. . . .
Why can't you be satisfied with being a professor? . . .
What action are you talking about?"

"What action? . . . Never mind," Quadri had answered,
with a sly but intent look. Marcello, at these words, could
not resist looking around at the walls, at the shelves full
of books. Quadri had caught this look and, still in the
gentlest possible way, had added, "It seems strange to you,
doesn't it, that I should be talking of action? . . . Among
all these books? . . . At this moment you're thinking, 'What
sort of action is he babbling about, this little twisted, myopic,
bearded hunchback?' . . . Now, truthfully, isn't that what
you're thinking? . . . Your little Party newspapers have so
often described to you the man who is both ignorant and
incapable of taking action, the intellectual, and you can't
help smiling with pity when you recognize him in me. . . .
Isn't that so?"

Surprised at such penetration, Marcello had exclaimed,
"How did you come to guess that?"

"Oh, my dear boy," Quadri had replied, rising to his
feet, "my dear boy, I guessed it at once. . . . But, in order
to act, it doesn't mean that you have to have a gold eagle
on your cap or braid on your sleeves. . . . Well, good-bye,
anyhow, good-bye, good-bye and good luck. . . . Good-
bye." With these words, gently, implacably, he had pushed
Marcello toward the door.

And now Marcello, thinking over that meeting, realized
that there had been a strong element of youthful impatience
and inexperience in his rash contempt for the hunchbacked,
bearded, pedantic Quadri. Besides, his mistake had been
proved by what had happened. Quadri, a few months after
their interview, had fled to Paris and had soon become one
of the principal anti-Fascist leaders—perhaps the cleverest,
the most wily, the most aggressive of all. His specialty, it
seemed, was proselytism. Benefiting by his teaching experience and his knowledge of the youthful mind, he was often
successful in converting young men who were indifferent, or
even of contrary opinions, and then urging them to bold
and dangerous undertakings which were almost always dis-
astrous, if not to him, their inspirer, at any rate to their
artless executants. He did not appear, however, as he flung

these initiates into the conspiratorial struggle, to feel any of
the humane anxieties that, in view of his character, one
might have been tempted to expect of him. On the contrary,
he sacrificed them quite coolly in desperate actions that
could be justified only as part of an extremely long-term plan
and that, indeed, necessarily involved a cruel indifference
to the value of human life. Quadri, in fact, possessed some
of the rare qualities of the true politician—or at least of a
certain category of politicians; he was astute and at the
same time enthusiastic, intellectual yet active, frank yet cynical, thoughtful yet imprudent. Marcello, as part of his official
work, had often been concerned with Quadri, who was
described in police reports as an extremely dangerous element, and he had always been struck by his capacity for
combining so many contrasting qualities in one single character, profound and ambiguous as it was. And thus, gradually,
from what he had managed to learn at a distance and from
information that was not always exact, he had changed his
former contempt for an angry respect. His original dislike,
however, stood firm; for he was convinced that Quadri,
among so many qualities, lacked that of courage. This seemed
to be proved by the fact that, although he thrust his followers into mortal dangers, he never, personally, exposed
himself.

He was aroused with a start from these thoughts by the
voice of one of the hotel pages who crossed the lounge
rapidly, calling out his name. For a moment, deceived by
the page's French pronunciation, he almost thought it must
be someone else's name. But this "Monsieur Clairici" was,
of course, himself—as he realized, with a slight feeling of
nausea, when, pretending to himself that he realy thought
it was someone else, he tried to imagine what that person
was like, a person with *his* face, *his* figure, *his* clothes. In
the meantime the page was going away in the direction of
the writing room, still calling his name. Marcello got up
and went straight to the telephone booth.

He took up the receiver from the shelf and put it to his
ear. A female voice, clear and slightly singsong, asked in
French who was telephoning. Marcello answered, in the same
language, "I'm an Italian. . . . Clerici, Marcello Clerici. . . .
I should like to speak to Professor Quadri."

"He's very busy. . . . I don't know if he can come. . . .
Did you say your name was Clerici?"

"Yes, Clerici."

"Wait one moment."

He heard the sound of the receiver being put down on
the table, then footsteps receding, and finally there was

silence. Marcello waited for some time, expecting a further sound of footsteps to announce the woman's return or the arrival of the professor. Instead of which, springing without warning from the depth of that utter silence, came the echoing voice of Quadri, "Hullo, Quadri here. . . . Who's speaking?"

Marcello hastily explained: "My name is Marcello Clerici. . . . I was a student of yours, when you were teaching in Rome. . . . I should like to see you."

"Clerici," repeated Quadri doubtfully. And then, after a moment, with decision, "Clerici: I don't know the name."

"Yes, you do, Professor," Marcello insisted. "I came to see you a few days before you gave up teaching. . . . I wanted to discuss a subject for a thesis with you."

"One moment, Clerici," said Quadri. "Really I don't remember your name . . . but that doesn't mean you may not be right. . . . And you want to see me?"

"Yes."

"Why?"

"For no particular reason," replied Marcello; "but, as I was your pupil and as I've heard a good deal about you recently—I just wanted to see you, that's all."

"Well," said Quadri in a more yielding tone, "come and see me here at my flat."

"When can I come?"

"Today, if you like. . . . In the afternoon . . . after lunch. . . . Come and have some coffee . . . about three o'clock."

"I must tell you," put in Marcello, "I'm on my honeymoon. . . . May I bring my wife?"

"But of course, naturally. . . . Till later, then."

He rang off, and Marcello too, after a moment's reflection, replaced the receiver. Before he had had time to leave the telephone booth, the same page who had called out his name in the lounge reappeared and said, "You're wanted on the telephone."

"I've had my call already," said Marcello, starting to leave.

"No, someone else wants you."

He went back into the booth and took up the receiver again. A loud voice, good-natured and cheerful, immediately shouted into his ear, "Is that you, Doctor Clerici?"

Marcello recognized the voice of the Secret Service agent Orlando, and replied calmly, "Yes, it's me."

"Did you have a good journey, sir?"

"Yes, excellent."

"Is the Signora well?"

"Very well."

"And what d'you think of Paris?"

"I haven't been outside the hotel yet," answered Marcelo, slightly annoyed with this familiarity.

"Well, you'll see. . . . Paris is Paris. . . . Are we going to meet, sir?"

"Yes, of course, Orlando. . . . You say where."

"You don't know Paris, sir . . . so I suggest a place that's easy to find. . . . The café at the corner of the Place de la Madeleine. . . . Don't make a mistake—on the left as you come from the Rue Royale. . . . It has lots of tables outside, but I'll be waiting for you inside. . . . There won't be anyone inside."

"All right . . . what time?"

"I'm at the café already. . . . But I'll wait as long as you like."

"In half an hour, then."

"That's fine, sir. . . . In half an hour."

Marcello left the telephone booth and walked toward the elevator. But, just as he was going in, he heard, for the third time, the same page calling out his name. This time he was really surprised. He felt a vague hope that this might be some superhuman intervention, that, as he put his ear to the black receiver of the telephone, he might hear the voice of an oracle uttering some decisive word about his life. His heart in a flutter, he turned and went back to the telephone booth.

"Is that you, Marcello?" asked the languid, caressing voice of his wife.

"Oh, it's you!" he could not help exclaiming—whether with disappointment or relief, he could not have said.

"Yes, of course it is. . . . Who did you think it was?"

"It doesn't matter. . . . I was expecting a telephone call. . . ."

"What are you doing?" she asked, with an accent of melting tenderness.

"Nothing. . . . I was just on the point of coming up to tell you I'm going out, and that I would be back in about an hour."

"No, don't come up. . . . I'm just going to have a bath. . . . All right then, I'll expect you in an hour's time, down in the lounge."

"It might be an hour and a half, even."

"All right, an hour and a half, then. . . . But please don't be longer."

"I said that so as not to keep you waiting . . . it'll probably be an hour."

She said, hastily, as though afraid that Marcello might go away, "Do you love me?"

"Of course I do; why d'you ask me?"

"Never mind. . . . If you were with me now, would you give me a kiss?"

"Certainly I would. . . . D'you want me to come up?"

"No, no, don't come up . . . but tell me. . . ."

"What?"

"Tell me, did you like me last night?"

"What questions you ask, Giulia!" he exclaimed, a little ashamed.

"Forgive me," she went on at once. "I don't know what I'm talking about. . . . You do love me, then?"

"I've already told you I do."

"Forgive me. . . . Well then, that's understood, I'll meet you in an hour and a half. . . . Good-bye, my love."

This time, he thought, hanging up the receiver, he was not going to wait for any more telephone calls. He crossed the hall, and, pushing the glass and mahogany revolving door, went out into the street.

The hotel faced on the Seine. As he came out he stopped for a moment on the threshold, struck by the gay spectacle of the city and the brilliant weather. As far as the eye could reach, all along the parapet above the river, big leafy trees laden with the bright foliage of spring rose from the pavements. They were trees he did not know—horse chestnuts, perhaps. The clear sunlight shone on each leaf and was transmuted into a bright, luminous, smiling greenness. All along the parapets stretched the stalls of the second-hand book-sellers and the print-sellers. People were walking, in a leisurely manner, beside them, under the trees, in the playful variation of sun and shade, and the general atmosphere was strikingly like that of a quiet Sunday promenade. Marcello crossed the road and went and stood by the parapet, between two of the stalls. Beyond the river, on the other bank, rose the gray buildings with their mansard roofs. Further along were the two towers of Notre Dame; further still, the spires of other churches, the outlines of groups of houses and more roofs and gables. He noticed that the sky was paler and wider than in Italy, reflecting as it were, the invisible, swarming presence of the immense city lying beneath its vault. He looked down at the river: sunk between its sloping stone walls, with the clean quays along its sides. It looked, at this point, like a canal; the water, oily and sluggish, of a muddy green color, ringed the white piers of the nearest bridge with sparkling whirlpools. A black and yellow barge slipped swiftly, foamlessly, over the thick water, its funnel belching hasty puffs of smoke; in the bows two men were talking, one wearing a blue blouse, the other a white sleeveless vest. A fat, familiar sparrow perched on the parapet close beside his arm, chirped in a lively manner as if to tell something, then flew off again in the direction of the bridge. A thin young man who might have been a student, badly dressed, with a beret on his head and a book under his arm, attracted his attention. He was going in the direction of Notre Dame, in a leisurely way, stopping every now and then to look at the books and the prints. As he watched him, Marcello was struck by his own leisureliness. In spite of all obligations that oppressed him he might have been that young man, he thought. And then the river, the sky, the trees, the whole of Paris would have had a different meaning for him. At the same moment he saw an empty taxi coming slowly along the street and was almost surprised to find himself signaling to it to stop: one moment earlier he had not thought of such a thing. He jumped in, giving the address of the café where Orlando was awaiting him.

Leaning back on the cushions, he looked out at the streets of Paris as the taxi carried him along. He noticed the gay look of the city—gray, old, but nevertheless smiling and graceful and full of an intelligent charm that seemed to blow in at the windows together with the breeze of the taxi's motion. He liked the *gendarmes* at the crossroads, though he could not have said why. They seemed to him elegant, with their hard, round kepis, their short cloaks, their slim legs. One of them came to the window to say something to the driver. He was an energetic-looking, pale, fair young man, and he held his whistle between his teeth, while still keeping his arm, with its white baton, stretched out behind him to hold up the traffic. He liked the big horse chestnut trees that raised their branches toward the glistening windowpanes of the old gray façades. He liked the old-fashioned shop signs with their white lettering, full of flourishes, on a brown or wine-red background. He liked even the unaesthetic pattern of the taxis and buses with hoods that looked like the muzzles of dogs running along sniffing the ground. The taxi, after a short halt, passed in front of the neo-classic temple of the Chamber of Deputies, crossed the bridge, and rushed at full speed towards the obelisk in the Place de la Concorde. This, then, he thought as he looked at the immense military-looking square, enclosed at the far side of its row of arcades like regiments of soldiers drawn up on parade, this, then, was the capital of France, of that France that had to be destroyed. He felt now that he had loved this city that lay before his eyes for a long time—long before that day, when he found himself there for the first time. And yet this admiration that he felt for the majestic, kindly, joyous beauty of the town emphasized to him the somber nature of the duty he was preparing to perform. Perhaps if Paris had been less beautiful, he thought, he might have evaded that duty, he might have escaped, have freed himself from the bonds of fate. But the beauty of the city established him firmly in his hostile, negative role—as did the many repugnant aspects of the cause he was serving. He realized, as he thought over these things, that he had found a way of explaining to himself the absurdity of his own position. And he knew that he explained it in that way because there was no other way of explaining it and so of accepting it freely and consciously.

The taxi stopped and Marcello got out in front of the café appointed by Orlando. the rows of tables on the pavement were crowded, as he had warned him they would be; but when he went inside the café, he found it deserted. Orlando was sitting at a table in a recess formed by a window. As soon as he saw him, he rose and beckoned to him.

Marcello walked across without hurrying and sat down opposite him. Through the window he could see the backs of the people sitting outside in the shade of the trees, and beyond, part of the colonnade and of the triangular pediment of the church of the Madeleine. Marcello ordered coffee. Orlando waited till the waiter had gone away, and then said, "Perhaps you're thinking, sir, that you'll get an 'espresso' coffee the same as in Italy, but you're quite wrong. . . . Good coffee doesn't exist in Paris, as it does with us. . . . You'll see what sort of a brew they'll bring you, sir."

Orlando spoke in his usual respectful, good-natured, quiet tone. "An honest face," thought Marcello, eyeing the Secret Service man closely while the latter, with a sigh, poured himself out some more of the despised coffee; "the face of a bailiff or a tenant farmer or a small country landowner." He waited till Orlando had drunk his coffee and then asked, "Where do you come from, Orlando?"

"Me? From the province of Palermo, sir."

Marcello, for no particular reason, had always thought that Orlando was a native of Central Italy, of Umbria or the Marches. Now, looking at him more closely, he saw that he had been deceived by the solid, countrified look of his figure. But his face held no trace of Umdrian mildness or of the placidity of the Marches. It was, indeed, an honest, good-natured face, but the eyes, black and with a tired look in them, had a certain feminine, almost Oriental gravity about them that did not belong to those parts of the country; nor was there mildness and placidity in the smile on the wide, lipless mouth beneath the small, ill-shaped nose. "I should never have thought it," he murmured.

"Where did you think I came from?" asked Orlando, almost eagerly.

"From Central Italy."

Orlando seemed to be reflecting for a moment; then, frankly but respectfully, he said, "You too, sir—I bet you've got the usual prejudice."

"What prejudice?"

"The prejudice of the North against South Italy and in particular against Sicily. . . . You may not want to admit it, sir, but it is so." Orlando shook his head sorrowfully.

Marcello protested. "Truly I wasn't thinking about that at all. . . . I thought you came from Central Italy because of your physical appearance."

But Orlando was not listening. "I'll tell you what it is: it's like water dripping," he went on emphatically, obviously pleased with the unusual expression. "In the street, in the house, everywhere, even on duty . . . colleagues of ours from the North come and find fault even with our spaghetti. . . . My answer to them is, 'In the first place you've now taken to eating spaghetti yourselves—and even more than we do'; and then I say, 'How good your polenta is! . . .' "

Marcello said nothing. In reality he was not all displeased that Orlando should be talking about things that had nothing to do with his mission. It was a way of avoiding familiarity on a terrible subject to which it was quite unsuited. All at once Orlando burst out, "Sicily—what an amount of slander there is about Sicily! . . . The Mafia, for instance . . . You know the kind of thing they say about the Mafia. . . . For them, there's not a single Sicilian who's not a member of it. . . . Quite apart from the fact that they know absolutely nothing about the Mafia!"

"The Mafia doesn't exist any more," said Marcello.

"Of course not, it doesn't exist any more," said Orlando, with an air of not being altogether convinced. "But, sir, if it did still exist, believe me, it would be far better, infinitely better, than the same sort of affairs in the North—the Teppisti at Milan, the Barabba at Turin. . . . They're nothing but a lot of bums, people who live on women, petty thieves and bullies. . . . The Mafia was at any rate a school for courage."

"Excuse me, Orlando," said Marcello coldly, "but I must ask you to explain to me exactly how the Mafia came to be a 'school for courage.' "

Orlando appeared to be disconcerted by this question, not so much because of the almost official coldness of tone in which Marcello spoke as because of the complicated nature of the subject, that did not allow of an immediate and exhaustive reply. "Well, sir," he said with a sigh, "you ask me a question which it isn't easy to answer . . . In Sicily, courage is the first quality of a man of honor, and the Mafia considers itself an honorable society. . . . How can I explain? It's difficult for anyone who hasn't been there and seen things with his own eyes to understand. Imagine, sir, some sort of place—a bar, a café, an inn, a restaurant—in which a group of men met together, men who were armed and hostile to some member of the Mafia. . . . Well, what would he have done? He wouldn't have asked for police protection, he wouldn't have left the neighborhood. . . . No: he would have come out of his house, dressed in his best new clothes, freshly shaved, and would have made his appearance at that place, alone and unarmed, and would have spoken only the two or three words that were needed or wanted. . . . And then, what do you think? Every single person—the group of his enemies, as well as his friends, and the whole village— all had their eyes on him . . . And he knew that. . . . He also knew that it was all up with him if he showed he was afraid, either by not looking people straight in the eye, or by not speaking quite calmly, or by an expression on his face that was not completely serene . . . And so his whole attention was given to facing this examination—with a resolute look in his eye, a quiet voice, measured movements, and a normal color. . . . Easier said than done. You have to find yourself in that position to understand how difficult these things are. . . . And that's what I mean, sir—just to give you an example—by the Mafia school for courage."

Orlando, who had become excited while he was speaking, now cast a cool, inquiring glance at Marcello's face, as much as to say, "But it's not about the Mafia that we two should be talking, if I'm not mistaken." Marcello noticed his look and glanced ostentatiously at his wrist watch. "We'd better talk about our own affairs now, Orlando," he said with authority. "I'm meeting Professor Quadri today . . . According to my instructions, I am to point out the professor to you in such a way that you can make quite certain of his identity. . . . That's my part, isn't it?"

"Yes, sir."

"Well, I shall invite Professor Quadri to dine with me or meet me in a café this evening . . . I can't yet say where. . . But if you telephone me at the hotel about seven o'clock this evening I shall know the place. . . . As for Professor

Quadri, let's decide now how I'm to point him out to you.
. . . Let's say, for instance, that Professor Quadri will be the
first person whose hand I'll shake when I come into the café
or the restaurant . . . is that all right?"

"That's understood, sir."

"And now I must go," said Marcello, again looking at his
watch. He put the money for the coffee on the table, then
rose and went out, followed at some distance by the Secret
Service man.

As they stood on the pavement, Orlando's eyes scrutinized the dense traffic of the street in which two lines of cars
were moving, almost at walking pace, in opposite directions,
and he said, in an emphatic tone of voice, "Paris."

"It's not the first time you've been here, is it, Orlando?"
Marcello asked as he searched among the other cars for an
empty taxi.

"The first time?" said Orlando, with a sort of heavy vehemence. "Far from it. . . . Now just have a guess, sir, at
how many times I've been here."

"I really don't know."

"Twelve times," said the Secret Service man, "and this is
the thirteenth."

A taxi-driver caught Marcello's eye and came and stopped
in front of him. "Good-by then, Orlando," said Marcello as
he got in. "I shall expect a telephone call from you this
evening." Orlando raised his hand to show that he understood.
Marcello got into the taxi, giving the address of the hotel.

But, as the taxi bore him along, the sound of those last
words spoken by the Secret Service man, his "twelve" and
"thirteen"—"twelve times in Paris and this is the thirteenth"
—seemed to be prolonged in his ears and to wake far-off
echoes in his memory. It was as though he had put his head
into a cave and shouted, and then found that his voice came
echoing back to him from unsuspected depths. Then, all of a
sudden, reminded by those two numbers, he recalled that
he had promised to point out Quadri by shaking hands with
him and realized why it was that, instead of merely informing
Orlando that Quadri was easily recognizable by the
hump on his back, he had had recourse to this device. It was
his remote, childish memories of the sacred story that had
made him forget the professor's deformity, so much more convenient for the purpose of safe identification than a handshake. Twelve was the number of the Apostles, and he himself was the thirteenth, who, with a kiss, betrayed Christ to the
soldiers who had come to the garden to arrest Him. The
traditional figures of the Stations of the Cross, he had so
often contemplated in churches, superimposed themselves now

on the modern stage scenery of a French restaurant, with its set tables, its clients sitting at their food, himself rising and going to meet Quadri and taking his hand in his, and Orlando the Secret Service agent sitting apart and watching the pair of them. Then the figure of Judas, the thirteenth Apostle, became confused with his own, coalesced with its outlines, in fact *was* his own.

He was seized with an almost amused desire to speculate, to ponder, in face of this discovery. "Probably Judas did what he did for the same reasons that I'm doing it for," he said to himself; "and he, too, had to do it, although he did not like doing it, because, after all, it was necessary that someone should do it. . . . But why be frightened? Let's admit frankly that I have chosen the part of Judas . . . so what?"

He realized that he was, in fact, not in the least frightened. Even at the worst, he observed to himself, his customary cold melancholy coming over him, there was fundamentally nothing unpleasant about it. He went on to think—not in order to justify himself but to heighten the comparison and to recognize its limits—that Judas was, certainly, like him, but only up to a certain point. Up to the point of the handshake; or even perhaps, if you like—although he himself was not a disciple of Quadri—up to the betrayal, if understood in a widely generic sense. After that, everything was different. Judas hanged himself, or at any rate thought he could not avoid hanging himself, because the people who had suggested the betrayal and paid him for it did not then have the courage to support and justify him; but *he* would not kill himself nor give himself over to despair, because, behind him . . . he saw the crowds collected in the squares to applaud the man under whose command he served, and, implicitly, to justify him, the man who obeyed orders. His final thought was that he was receiving nothing, in the absolute sense, for what he was doing. No thirty pieces of silver for him. It was just a matter of duty, as Orlando would say. The analogy changed color and faded away, leaving behind nothing but a faint trace of proud, satisfying irony. If anything, he concluded, what mattered was that the comparison should have occurred to him, that he should have worked it out, and for a moment, found it just.

# *CHAPTER 11*

After luncheon, Giulia wanted to get back to the hotel to change her dress before they went to Quadri's. But as they got out of the elevator she put her arm around his waist and whispered, "It's not true that I wanted to change. . . . I just wanted to be alone with you for a little." As he walked down the long, deserted corridor between two rows of closed doors, with that affectionate arm around his waist, Marcello could not help saying to himself that, whereas for him this honeymoon in Paris was also, and more particularly, a mission, for Giulia it was purely and simply a honeymoon. It therefore followed, he thought, that no deviation could be permitted to him from the role of bridegroom that he had accepted when he got into the train with her—even if sometimes, as was now the case, he had a feeling of anguish that was far removed from amorous excitement. But this was the normality he had so eagerly longed for—this arm around his waist, these looks, these caresses; and the thing that he was preparing to do in company with Orlando was nothing more than the blood-money paid for such normality. In the meantime they had reached their room: Giulia, without letting go of his waist, opened the door with the other hand and went in with him.

Once inside, she let go of him, turned the key in the lock and said, "Shut the shutter, will you?" Marcello went to the window and did so. As he turned he saw that Giulia, standing by the bed, was already slipping her dress over her head; and he thought he understood what she had meant when she said, "I just wanted to be alone with you for a little." In silence he went and sat down on the edge of the bed, on the opposite side of Giulia. She was now in her underclothes and stockings. With great care she placed her dress on a chair at the head of the bed, took off her shoes, and finally, with an awkward movement, lifting first one leg and then the other, lay down behind him, flat on her back, with one arm folded at the back of her neck. For a moment she was silent, and then she said, "Marcello."

"What is it?"

"Why don't you lie down here beside me?"

Obediently Marcello bent and took off his shoes, and then lay down on the bed beside his wife. Giulia immediately moved close to him, pressing her body against his, and, full of concern, asked anxiously, "What's the matter with you?"

"With me? Nothing. . . . Why?"

"I don't know, you seem so worried."

"That's an impression you often have," he answered. "You know that my normal state of mind isn't exactly thoughtless . . . but that doesn't mean that I'm worried."

She embraced him silently. Then she went on, "It wasn't true that I asked you to come here so that I could get ready. . . . Nor was it true that I just wanted to be alone with you. . . . It's something quite different."

This time Marcello was astonished and felt almost remorseful at having suspected her of a mere erotic craving. Looking down at her, he saw that the eyes with which she gazed up at him were filled with tears. Affectionately, yet not without a touch of irritation, he said to her, "Now it's *my* turn to ask what's the matter with *you*."

"You're quite right," she replied. And immediately she began weeping, with silent sobs whose convulsions he could feel against his own body. Marcello waited a little, in the hope that this incomprehensible weeping would stop. But it appeared, on the other hand, to be redoubled in intensity. He asked then, staring up at the ceiling, "Won't you tell me what you're crying about?"

Giulia went on sobbing for a little and then answered, "For no reason at all. . . . Because I'm a fool"; and there was already a faint note of comfort in her woebegone voice.

Marcello looked towards her and repeated, "Come on . . . tell me what you're crying about."

Giulia turned her eyes to his, and though they were still filled with tears the light of hope seemed to be reflected in them; and then she smiled faintly and put out her hand and took the handkerchief from his pocket. She wiped her eyes, blew her nose, put the handkerchief back in his pocket and then, embracing him again, whispered, "If I tell you why I was crying, you'll think I'm crazy."

"Never mind," he said, caressing her, "tell me."

"Well, it was like this," she said. "At lunch time I saw you were so absent-minded—so worried-looking, even—that I thought you'd already had enough of me and were regretting you had married me. . . . I thought perhaps it was because of what I told you in the train—you know, about that lawyer —and that perhaps you'd realized you'd done a stupid thing, you, with the future you have in front of you, and with your intelligence and your goodness as well, in marrying an unfortunate girl like me. . . . And so, when I thought this, I also thought I'd take the first step . . . that I'd go away without saying anything to you, so as to save you an embarrassing good-bye. . . . So I decided, as soon as we go back to the hotel, to pack up and go . . . to go straight back to Italy and leave you in Paris."

"I can't believe you're being serious," said Marcello, astonished.

"Perfectly serious," she continued, smiling, and flattered by his surprise. "In fact, while we were downstairs in the hall and you went away for a moment to buy some cigarettes, I went to the head porter and asked him to engage me a berth in the Rome sleeping car for tonight. . . . You see, I was quite serious."

"But you're crazy," said Marcello, raising his voice in spite of himself.

"I told you," she answered, "that you'd think I was crazy. . . . But at that moment I was certain, absolutely certain, that I'd be doing the best thing for you by leaving you and going away. . . . Yes, I was as certain as I am certain now," she added, pulling herself up and touching his lips lightly with hers, "that I'm giving you this kiss."

"But why were you so certain?" asked Marcello, perturbed.

"I don't know . . . never mind. . . . There are some things one is certain of . . . without any particular reason."

"And then," he could not help exclaiming, as though he felt some remote twinge of regret, "why did you change your mind?"

"Why? Goodness knows! . . . Perhaps it was because you looked at me in the elevator in a certain way—or at any rate I had the impression that you looked at me in a certain way. . . . But then I remembered that I'd decided to go away and that I'd engaged a sleeping berth, and so, thinking that now it was too late to turn back, I started to cry. . . ."

Marcello said nothing. Guilia interpreted his silence in her own way, and asked him, "You're annoyed, aren't you? . . . You're annoyed about the sleeping berth. . . . But they'll cancel it all right. . . . One only has to pay twenty per cent."

"Don't be absurd," he answered slowly, as though he were thinking deeply.

"Well then," she said, stifling an incredulous laugh in which, however, there was still a slight tremor of fear, "then you're annoyed because I didn't really go?"

"More absurdities," he replied. But this time he felt he was not being entirely sincere. So, as if to suppress any ultimate hesitation, any last regret, he added, "If you had gone away, my whole life would have collapsed." And this time it seemed to him that he had told the truth, even if in an ambiguous manner. Would it not perhaps be a good thing if his life— that life that he had built up from the starting-point of the Lino affair—did really collapse entirely, instead of over-loading itself with more burdens and more obligations, like some ridiculous building to which an infatuated owner goes on adding towers and turrets and balconies till finally he endangers its solidity? He felt Giulia's arms enfold him even more closely, in an amorous embrace; and then heard her whisper, "Do you really mean that?"

"Yes," he answered, "I really mean it."

"But what would you have done," she insisted, with a sort of self-satisfied, almost conceited curiosity, "if I had really left you and gone away? . . . Would you have run after me?"

He hesitated before answering, and again he seemed to hear in his own voice an echo of that distant regret. "No, I don't think so. . . . Haven't I told you already that my whole life would have collapsed?"

"Would you have stayed in France?"

"Yes, possibly."

"And what about your career? Would you have let that go to pieces?"

"Without you, it wouldn't have had any meaning," he explainly calmly. "I do what I'm doing because of you."

"But what would you have done, then?" She seemed to be finding some cruel kind of pleasure in imagining him alone, without her.

"I should have done what they all do, the people who leave their own country and their own professions for reasons of this kind. I should have adapted myself to some sort of a job—as a scullion, or a sailor, or a chauffeur . . . or I should have enlisted in the Foreign Legion. . . . But why are you so anxious to know?"

"Well . . . it's interesting. . . . In the Foreign Legion. . . . Under another name?"

"Probably."

"Where is the Foreign Legion stationed?"

"In Morocco, I believe . . . and in other places too."

"In Morocco . . . However, I didn't go away," she murmured, pressing herself against him with greedy, jealous violence. Silence followed these words. Giulia did not move, and Marcello, as he looked at her, saw that she had closed her eyes. She appeared to be asleep. So he, too, closed his eyes, feeling that he would like to sleep. But he could not, although he felt prostrated with a deadly weariness and langour. He was conscious of a deep and painful feeling, as of a rebellion of his whole being; and a strange smile kept recurring in his mind. He was like a wire, simply a human wire through which flowed, ceaselessly, an electric current of terrifying energy whose refusal or acceptance did not depend on him. A wire like those high-tension cables on pylons bearing the notice: "Beware: Danger." He was simply one of those conductor-wires, and sometimes the current hummed through his body without troubling him, infusing, in fact, an increased measure of vitality into him. But at other times— as, for instance, now—seeming to be too strong, too intense; and then he longed to be, not a taut, vibrating wire, but one that had been pulled down and left to rust on a pile of rubbish in some factory yard. Why, in any case, should he have to endure this transmission of current, when so many others were not even touched by it? And again, why was there never any interruption of the current, why did it never, for one single moment, cease to flow through him? The smile diverged and branched out into questions that had no answer; and all the time his painful, aching languor increased, clouding his mind, dimming the mirror of his consciousness. At last he dozed off, and it seemed to him that sleep had in some way interrupted the current and that he was really, for once, a piece of broken-off, rusty wire thrown into a corner with other refuse. But at the same moment he felt a hand touch his arm. He jumped up into a sitting position and saw Giulia standing beside the bed, fully dressed and with her hat on. She said in a low voice, "Are you asleep? Oughtn't we to be going to Quadri's?"

Marcello raised himself with an effort and for a moment stared into the half-darkness of the room, translating her remark, in his mind, too: "Ought we not to be killing Quadri?" Then he asked, almost jokingly, "Supposing we didn't go to Quadri's? . . . Supposing, instead, we had a good sleep?"

It was an important question, he thought, looking up at Giulia; and perhaps it was still not too late to drop the whole business. He saw her looking at him doubtfully, almost as though she were displeased at his proposing to stay in the hotel now that she was all ready to go out. Then she said, "But you've been asleep already . . . for almost an hour. . . . Besides, didn't you tell me that the visit to this man Quadri was important from the point of view of your career?"

Marcello was silent for a moment; then he replied, "Yes, it's true. . . . It's very important."

"Well then," she said gaily, bending down and giving him a kiss on the brow, "what are you thinking about? Come along, get up and dress yourself and don't be lazy."

"But I don't want to go," said Marcello, pretending to yawn. "I only want to sleep," he added—and this time he felt he was being sincere—"just to sleep and sleep and sleep."

"You can sleep tonight," answered Giulia lightly, going over to the mirror and looking at herself attentively. "You made an engagement, and it's too late to change the program now." She spoke, as usual, in a good-natured, sensible way;

and it was surprising, thought Marcello, and at the same time in some obscure way significant, how she always said the right thing without knowing it. At that moment the telephone on the bedside table rang. Marcello, raising himself on his elbow, took off the receiver and put it to his ear. It was the head porter, to announce that he had taken the sleeping berth on the Rome train for that night.

"You must cancel it," said Marcello without hesitation; "Madame is not going after all." Giulia, turning from the mirror in which she was gazing at herself, threw him a look of shy gratitude. Marcello, putting down the receiver, said, "That's done, then. . . . They'll cancel it and you won't go."

"Are you angry with me?"

"Why on earth should I be?"

He got off the bed, slipped on his shoes and went into the bathroom. As he washed and combed his hair, he wondered what Giulia would have said if he had revealed the truth to her about his profession and about their honeymoon. The answer, without any doubt, seemed to him to be that, not merely would she not condemn him but would even in the long run approve of what he was doing, though she might be frightened and might go so far as to ask him whether it was really necessary for him to do it. Giulia was good—there could be no doubt of that—but not beyond the sacred limits of family affection. Beyond those limits there began, for her, a vague, confused world in which it might easily come about that a hunchbacked, bearded professor could be murdered for political reasons. And the wife of Orlando the Secret Service agent, he said to himself as he came out of the bathroom, must argue and feel in exactly the same way. Giulia, who was sitting waiting on the bed, rose to her feet saying, "Are you bored because I wouldn't let you sleep? Would you really have preferred not to go to Quadri's?"

"On the contrary, you did perfectly right," answered Marcell, preceding her into the corridor. He felt reinvigorated now, and there seemed to be nothing left in him of that sensation of rebellion against his own fate. The current of energy still flowed through his body, but without pain or difficulty, as though through a natural channel. Outside the hotel, he stood looking across the river at the gray outline of the immense city above the parapet, beneath the vast clear sky. Before him were the rows of stalls with their second-hand books, and the strollers moved slowly along, stopping to examine them. He even seemed to see again the poorly dressed young man with the book under his arm, walking slowly along the pavement beside the bookstalls in the direction of Notre Dame. Or perhaps it was another one, similar to him in his way of dressing and in his demeanor—and in his destiny as well. But he seemed to regard him without envy, though with a settled, frozen feeling of powerlessness. He was himself, and the young man was the young man, and there was nothing to be done about it. He hailed a passing taxi and gave Quadri's address as he got in behind Giulia.

## CHAPTER 12

The moment Marcello entered Quadri's flat he was struck by the difference between it and that other apartment in which he had gone to see him for the first and last time, in Rome. The building, situated in a modern quarter at the end of a narrow, winding street resembled, with its many rectangular balconies jutting out from its smooth façade a chest-of-drawers with all the drawers open; and it gave him the feeling of an obvious, anonymous way of life, governed by a kind of social mimicry—as though Quadri, when he established himself in Paris, had striven to identify himself as closely as possible with the general mass of the comfortably off French middle class. And then, inside, the difference had been accentuated: Quadri's Roman abode had been old and dark, encumbered with furniture and books and papers, dusty, neglected. This, on the other hand, was bright and new and clean, with little furniture and no signs of scholarship. They waited a few minutes in the drawing room, a spacious, bare room with nothing but a group of armchairs, all in one corner, around a glass-topped table. The only detail in less ordinary taste was a large picture hanging on one of the walls, the work of a Cubist painter—a cold but decorative combination of spheres, cubes, cylinders and parallels in various colors. Of books, of those books with which, in Rome, Marcello had been so much struck, there was not one. He felt, as he looked round at the wax-polished wooden floor, at the long, pale curtains, at the empty walls, that he was on the stage of a modern theatre, in the middle of a neat, elegant setting designed for a play with few characters and only one situation. What was the play? His own and Quadri's, no doubt; but whereas the situation was already known to him, he felt, he did not know why, that all the characters had not yet revealed themselves. Someone was still missing, and it might be that the intervention of that person would completely alter the situation itself.

As if to confirm this vague presentiment, the door at the far end of the drawing room opened and there entered not Quadri but a young woman, the same probably who had spoken to him in French on the telephone. She walked across the shining floor, tall and singularly supple and graceful in her way of walking, in a white summer dress with a bell-shaped skirt. For a moment Marcello could not refrain from looking, with a kind of furtive pleasure, at the outline of her figure visible through the transparency of her frock—a dim outline but with precise contours, elegant as that of a gymnast or a dancer. Then he looked up at her face and was certain that he had seen it before, though he could not determine where nor when. She went up to Giulia, took both her hands in hers with an almost affectionate familiarity and explained, in correct Italian but with a strong French accent, that the professor was engaged but would come in a few minutes' time. Less cordially, it seemed to Marcello, in fact somewhat hastily, she greeted him from a distance; then she invited them to sit down. While she talked with Giulia, Marcello studied her carefully, curious to account for the vague memory that had led him to suppose he had already met her. She was tall, with rather large hands and feet, broad shoulders, and a waist of incredible slimness emphasized by her big bosom and ample hips. Her long, slender neck support a pale face, innocent of make-up, which, though youthful, was not fresh in color but rather worn-looking, with a vigorous, anxious, restless, active expression.

Where had he seen her before? As though she felt herself being examined, she turned suddenly toward him; and then, from the contrast between the restless intensity of her gaze and the luminous serenity of her high, white forehead, he all at once knew where he had met her before, or rather, where he had met a person who resembled her—in the brothel at S., when, coming back into the big room to fetch his hat, he had found Orlando with the prostitute Luisa. The resemblance was entirely in the special shape, whiteness, and luminosity of the forehead. In this woman too, it was like a royal diadem. In other ways the two women differed considerably. The prostitute had a wide, thin mouth; this one's mouth was small, fleshy, tight-lipped—comparable, he thought, to a small rose with thick, slightly faded petals. Another difference was that the prostitute's hand was feminine, smooth, sensual; whereas this woman's hand was almost like the hand of a man—hard, reddish and nervous. And finally the prostitute had a horrible raucous voice such as is frequently found among women of her profession; while this woman's voice on the contrary, was thin, clear, impersonal, with the agreeable quality of reasoned and subtle music—the voice of a society woman.

Marcello noted these likenesses and these differences; and then, while the woman was carrying on a conversation with his wife, he noted also the extreme coldness of her attitude toward himself. Perhaps, he thought, she had been told by Quadri of his former political feelings, and would have preferred not to receive him. He wondered, too, who she could be. Quadri, as far as he remembered, was not married. She might, from her business-like manner, be a secretary, or, if not that, an admirer acting as a secretary. He thought again of his feeling in the house at S., when he had seen the prostitute Luisa going upstairs with Orlando—a feeling of impotent revolt, of tortured pity; and he realized that it had in reality been nothing more than sensual desire disguised as spiritual jealousy. And now this feeling was coming over him again, complete and without any disguise, for the woman who was sitting opposite him. She attracted him, in a new and upsetting manner; and he wanted to attract her; and the hostility that was visible in every one of her movements pained him bitterly. Finally he said, almost in spite of himself, thinking not of Quadri but of her, "I have an impression that our visit isn't altogether welcome to the Professor. . . . Perhaps he's too busy."

She answered quickly, without looking at him, "Not at all, my husband told me he was very pleased to see you. . . . He remembered you perfectly. . . . Anyone who comes from Italy is welcome here. . . . It's true, he is very busy— but your visit is particularly agreeable to him. . . . Wait a moment, I'll go and see if he's coming." These words were uttered with an unexpected eagerness that warmed Marcello's heart. When she had gone out, Giulia asked, without, however, showing any curiosity, "Why d'you think Professor Quadri isn't pleased to see you?"

Marcello answered calmly, "It was this lady's hostile attitude that made me think so."

"How strange," exclaimed Giulia, "she gave me quite the opposite impression. . . . She seemed to me to be so pleased to see us—just as if we knew each other already. . . . But had you met her before?"

"No," he replied, with the feeling that he was lying, "never before today. . . . I don't even know who she is."

"Isn't she the Professor's wife?"

"I don't know, I didn't think Quadri was married. . . . Perhaps she's his secretary."

"But she called him 'my husband'," exclaimed Giulia in surprise; "didn't you hear? . . . She used those words—'my husband'. . . . What were you thinking about?"

And so, Marcello, reflected, she had disturbed him to the point of making him not merely absent-minded, but actually deaf. This discovery gave him pleasure, and for a moment, strangely enough, he wanted to talk about it to Giulia, just as though she was not a person concerned but some outsider in whom he could confide freely. "I wasn't listening," he said. "His wife? He must have got married recently, then."

"Why?"

"Because when I knew him he was a bachelor."

"But didn't you and Quadri write to each other?"

"No. He was my tutor at the University; then he came to live in France and today I shall be seeing him for the first time since then."

"How odd, I though you were friends."

A long silence followed. Then the door, at which Marcello was gazing without impatience, opened, and on the threshold appeared someone whom, at first, he did not recognize as Quadri. Then his eyes traveled from the man's face to his shoulder, saw once more the deformity that raised the shoulder almost up to the ear, and realized that Quadri had merely shaved off his beard. He saw again, also, the curious, almost hexagonal shape of his face, its one-dimensional quality like that of a flat, painted mask surmounted by a black wig. He recalled, too, the eyes, staring, brilliant, red-rimmed; the triangular nose, like the clapper of a bell; the shapeless mouth, a circle of red, living flesh. The only new thing was the chin, which formerly had been hidden by the beard. It was small and crooked, curving sharply back beneath the lower lip, and of an ugliness that seemed full of meaning and possibly adumbrated some characteristic of its owner.

Instead of the frock coat in which Marcello had seen him on the first and last occasion on which he had met him, Quadri was now wearing—with the hunchback's love for light colors—a dove-gray sport coat. Beneath it he had on an American cowboy shirt with red and green checks, and a showy tie. Coming forward toward Marcello, he said, in a cordial, and at the same time utterly indifferent tone, "Clerici, isn't it? . . . Of course, I remember you perfectly well . . . particularly because you were the last student who came to see me before I left Italy. . . . I'm very pleased to see you again, Clerici."

Even his voice, thought Marcello, had remained the same —extremely sweet and at the same time casual, affectionate and yet vague. Meanwhile he was introducing his wife to Quadri, who, with a gallantry that was perhaps ostentatious, stooped to kiss the hand that Giulia held out to him. When they sat down, Marcello said, in some embarrassment, "I'm here in Paris on my honeymoon, and so I thought I would look you up . . . since you were my tutor. . . . But perhaps I've disturbed you."

"No, no, my dear boy," answered Quadri with his usual melting sweetness; "on the contrary, it gives me the greatest pleasure. . . . It was extremely nice of you to remember me. . . . Anyone who comes from Italy—if only because he talks to me in the lovely Italian language—is welcome here." He took a cigarette box from the table, looked inside it, and seeing that there was only one cigarette in it, offered it, with a sigh, to Giulia. "Take it, Signora," he said. "I don't smoke, nor does my wife, and so we always forget that other people like to. . . . Well, do you like Paris? . . . I suppose it's not the first time you've been here?"

So Quadri wants to make conventional conversation, thought Marcello. He answered for Giulia, "Yes, it *is* the first time, for us both."

"In that case," said Quadri eagerly, "I envy you. . . . Anyone who arrives for the first time in this very beautiful city is to be envied . . . and on a honeymoon, in the bargain, and at this season, which is the best of all in Paris!" He sighed again and politely asked Giulia, "And what impression do you have of Paris, Signora?"

"Me?" said Giulia, looking not at Quadri but at her husband. "Really I haven't had time to see it yet. . . . We only arrived yesterday."

"You'll see, Signora, it's a very beautiful, really an exquisitely beautiful city," said Quadri in a general sort of way, as though he were thinking of somebody else. "And the longer one lives in it the more completely is one conquered by its beauty. . . . But, Signora, you mustn't only look at the monuments, which are, no doubt, notable, but in no way superior to those of these cities of Italy. . . . You must go about, you must get your husband to take you to the different quarters of Paris. . . . The life of this city has a variety of aspects that is truly surprising."

"We haven't seen much yet," said Giulia, who did not appear to appreciate the conventional, almost ironical quality of Quadri's remarks. And then, turning to her husband, she put out her hand and touched his, caressingly, saying, "But we *will* have a good look around, won't we, Marcello?"

"Of course we will," said Marcello.

"What you must do," went on Quadri, still in the same tone of voice, "is, especially, to get to know the French people. . . . They're a charming people . . . intelligent, independent . . . and—although this partly contradicts the accepted idea of the French—good, as well. . . . That fine,

sensitive intelligence of theirs has become a kind of goodness. . . . Do you know anyone in Paris?"

"We don't know anybody," replied Marcello, "besides I'm
afraid it won't be possible. . . . We're only staying a week."

"A pity, that's really a pity. . . . One can't appreciate a
country at its true value without knowing its inhabitants . . ."

"Paris is the place for night life, isn't it?" asked Giulia,
who seemed to find herself perfectly at ease in this guide-
book conversation. "We haven't seen anything of it yet . . .
but we want to. . . . There are plenty of dance halls and
night clubs, aren't there?"

"Ah, yes, the *tabarins*, the *boîtes*—'boxes,' as they call
them here," said the professor in an absent-minded way.
"Montmartre, Montparnasse. . . . We ourselves, to tell you
the truth, have never gone in much for that kind of thing.
. . . Sometimes, when an Italian friend has been passing
through, we've taken advantage of his ignorance of such
matters to learn about them ourselves. . . . However they're
always the same . . . though it's all done with the grace
and elegance that are natural to this city. . . . But you
know, Signora, the French people are by nature serious,
very serious . . . and with pronounced family habits. . . .
Perhaps you'll be surprised when I tell you that the great
majority of Parisians have never set foot in a boîte. . .
The family, here, is very important, even more so than in
Italy. . . . And they're often good Catholics too . . . more
so than in Italy, with a less formal, more solid devotion.
. . . And so it's not surprising that they leave the *boîtes*
to us foreigners. . . . It's an excellent source of revenue,
anyhow. . . . Paris owes a good part of its prosperity to
the *boîtes* and, in general, to its night life."

"How strange," said Giulia, "I always thought that French
people themselves went in a great deal for night life." She
blushed and added, "I've been told that the *tabarins* stay
open all night and that they're always full . . . as it used
to be, once, with us, in carnival time."

"Yes," said the professor vaguely, "but the people who
go there are mostly foreigners."

"That doesn't matter," said Giulia, "I should love to see
one of them, at least . . . if only to say I'd been there."

The door opened and Signora Quadri came in carrying
a tray with a coffee pot and cups. "Excuse me," she said
gaily, closing the door with her foot, "but French maids
are not like Italian ones. . . . Today is my maid's day
out and she went off immediately after lunch. . . . We
have to do everything ourselves." She was really gay, thought

Marcello—and in a quite unforeseen manner. There was a great charm in her gaiety and in the movements of her tall figure, with its lightness and its air of self possession.

"Lina," said the professor, puzzled, "Signora Clerici wants to see a boîte. . . . Where can we recommend her to go?"

"Oh, there are so many, there's no lack of choice," she answered brightly as she poured out the coffee, supporting her whole weight on one leg while she stretched the other out sideways as if to display her large foot in its heelless shoe; "there are *boîes* for all tastes and purses." She handed a cup to Giulia and then added carelessly: "But Edmondo, why shouldn't *we* take them to a *boîte*. . . . It would be a good opportunity for you to have a little distraction."

Her husband passed his hand across his chin as if he wanted to stroke his beard, and answered, "Certainly, of course, why not?"

"D'you know what we'll do?" she went on as she handed cups of coffee to Marcello and her husband, "as we've got to dine out in any case, let's all dine together. There's a little restaurant on the right bank, which isn't expensive but which is very good. It's called *Le Coq au Vin*. Then, after dinner, we'll go and have a look at a very curious place. . . . But Signora Clerici mustn't be shocked."

Giulia, delighted with her gaiety, laughed and said, "I'm not so easily shocked."

"It's a *boîte* called *La Cravate Noire*, the Black Tie," she explained, sitting down on the sofa beside Giulia, "and it's a place where people of rather a special type go," she added, looking at Giulia and smiling.

"How d'you mean?"

"Women with special tastes. . . . You'll see. . . . The woman who runs it and the waitresses all wear dinner jackets and black ties. . . . You'll see how amusing they look."

"Ah, now I understand," said Giulia in some confusion. "But can men go there too?"

This question made the other woman laugh. "Why, of course. . . . It's a public place . . . just a small dance club, run by a woman of special tastes—highly intelligent, incidentally—but anyone can go there who wants to. . . It's not exactly a convent . . ." She gave little short laughs as she looked at Giulia, then added vivaciously, "But if you don't like the idea we can go somewhere else . . . but it won't be so original."

"No," said Giulia, "Let's go there. . . . It intrigues me."

"Unhappy creatures," said the professor, in a general way. He rose to his feet. "My dear Clerici, I must tell you that it has given me great pleasure to see you, and it'll give me even greater pleasure to dine this evening with your wife and yourself. . . . We'll have a good talk. . . . Have you still the same feelings and ideas that you used to have?"

Marcello replied calmly, "I have nothing to do with politics . . ."

"So much the better, so much the better." The professor took his hand and pressed it between both of his, adding, "Then perhaps we can hope to make a conquest of you." He spoke in a sweet, melting heartbroken tone of voice, like a priest talking to an atheist. He brought his hand up to his chest, toward his heart, and Marcello saw with astonishment that the look he gave him was dimmed and at the same time rendered more imploring by a glitter of tears in the big, round, prominent eyes. Then, as if to conceal his emotion, Quadri went over and took a hurried leave of Giulia, saying as he went out: "My wife will make arrangements with you about this evening."

The door closed, and Marcello, slightly embarrassed, sat down in an armchair facing the sofa on which were the two women. Now that Quadri had gone, the wife's hostility seemed quite obvious. She ostentatiously ignored Marcello's presence and spoke only to Giulia, "And have you seen the fashion shops, the dressmakers, the *modistes?* . . . The Rue de la Paix, the Faubourg Saint Honoré, the Avenue de Matignon?"

"To tell the truth," said Giulia, with the air of hearing these names for the first time, "to tell the truth, I haven't."

"Would you like to have a look at these streets, to go into a few shops and visit one or two dressmakers? . . . I assure you it's most interesting," continued Signora Quadri with persistent, insinuating, enfolding, protective affability.

"Oh yes, I'm sure it is." Giulia looked at her husband and then went on, "And I should like to buy something . . . a hat, for instance."

"Would you like me to take you?" proposed the other woman, at last reaching the point of all these questions. "I know some of the dressmakers' shops very well. . . . I might even be able to give you some advice."

"Would you really?" said Giulia, with somewhat hesitating gratitude.

"Shall we go today, this afternoon, in about an hour's time? You don't mind, do you, if I carry off your wife for an hour or two?" These last words were addressed to Marcello, but in a brisk, almost contemptuous tone, very different from the one used towards Giulia.

Marcello gave a start and replied, "Of course not . . . if Giulia likes . . ."

He felt that his wife would have preferred to escape from Signora Quadri's guardianship—at least, judging by the questioning glance she threw him; but he found himself answering her with a glance that ordered her to accept. Immediately afterward he wondered: do I do this because this woman attracts me and I want to see her again? Or do I do it because I am on a mission and it doesn't suit me to displease her? It suddenly seemed acutely distressing not to know whether he was doing things because he liked to do them or because they suited his plans. Meanwhile Giulia was objecting, "Really I had thought of going back to the hotel for a little—"

But the other woman did not give her time to finish. "You want to freshen up a little before we go out? To have a wash, and a rest? . . . But there's no need to go back to the hotel. . . . If you like, you can rest here, on my bed. . . . I know how tiring it is, when one's traveling, to go about all day long without a moment's pause, especially for us women. . . . Come along, come with me, my dear." Before Giulia could draw a breath she had made her rise from the sofa, and was pushing her gently but firmly toward the door. In the doorway, as though to reassure her, she said in a bitter-sweet tone, "Your husband can wait for you here. . . . Don't be afraid, you won't lose him," and then, putting her arm round Giulia's waist, she drew her into the passage and shut the door.

Left alone, Marcello jumped to his feet and took a few paces about the room. It appeared to him quite clear that this woman cherished a feeling of rooted aversion for him, and he would have liked to know the reason. But at this point his own feelings became confused. On the one hand he was distressed by the hostility of such a person, a person whom he wanted to like him; and on the other hand he was troubled by the idea that she might know the truth about him, because if that were so his mission became not merely difficult but dangerous. But the thing that caused him the greatest distress was the feeling that these two quite different anxieties were merged together and that he was no longer capable of distinguishing them from each other—the anxiety of the lover who sees himself rejected, and that of the secret agent who fears he has been discovered. In any case, he realized with a gush of his old melancholy, even if he succeeded in dissipating the woman's hostility, he would then be once again forced to place any relationship that might follow at the service of his mission. Just as when he had made the proposal, at the Ministry, to combine his honeymoon with his political function. Just as always happened.

The door opened behind him and Signora Quadri came back into the room. She went to the table, took a cigarette, lit it and then said, "Your wife was very tired and I think she's gone to sleep on my bed. . . . We'll go out together later ."

"This means," Marcello said calmly, "that you want to get rid of me."

"Oh, my goodness, no," she answered in a cold, worldly voice, "but I have a great deal to do . . . and so has the Professor. . . . You'd be left all alone here in this room. . . . There are better things for you to be doing in Paris than that."

"Forgive me," said Marcello, putting his two hands on the back of an armchair and looking at her, "but it seems to me that you're hostile to me. . . . Isn't that so?"

She answered at once, without fear or hesitation. "Does it surprise you?"

"Yes, really it does," said Marcello. "We don't know each other at all and this is the first time we've met . . ."

"I know you perfectly well," she interrupted him, "even if you don't know me."

"Now we're in for it," thought Marcello. He was conscious that her hostility—confirmed, now, without the slightest doubt —aroused in his heart a feeling of pain so sharp that it almost made him cry out. He sighed, deeply distressed, and said in a low voice, "Ah, you know me then?"

"Yes," she replied, her eyes sparkling with an aggressive light, "I know you're a police official, a spy paid by your government. . . . Are you surprised now that I am hostile to you? . . . I don't know about other people, but I've never been able to bear *mouchards*—spies," she added, translating the French word with insulting politeness.

Marcello lowered his eyes, and for a moment was silent. His suffering was acute, and the woman's contempt was like a subtle instrument pitilessly probing an open wound. At last he said, "And does your husband know this?"

"Of course he does," she answered with insulting surprise; "how could you imagine that he doesn't? It was he who told me."

"Ah, so they're well informed," Marcello could not help thinking. He went on, in a reasonable tone of voice, "Then why did you let us come here? Wouldn't it have been simpler to refuse to receive us?"

"Personally, I should have preferred not to," she said, "but my husband is different. . . . My husband is a kind of saint. . . . He still thinks that kindness is the best policy."

"A very cunning kind of saint," Marcello would have liked to reply. But it occurred to him that that was how it was: the saints must all have been very cunning people; so he refrained. Then he went on, "I'm sorry you're so hostile to me . . . because . . . I find you very attractive."

"Thank you, that doesn't interest me."

Later, Marcello asked himself what could have happened to him at that moment: it was as though a dazzling ray had darted from her luminous brow; and at the same time there had surged up in him a deep, violent, powerful impulse, a mixture of excitement and despairing love. He realized all at once that he was close to Signora Quadri, that he was throwing his arm around her waist, pulling her to him, saying in a low voice, "And also because I like you very much."

Pressed against him so tightly that Marcello could feel her tender, swelling breast throbbing against his, she looked at him for a moment in dumb amazement. "Ah, that's perfect!" she cried, in a strident, triumphant voice, "That's perfect! . . . actually on your honeymoon and yet you're ready to betray your wife . . . perfect!" She writhed furiously to free herself from Marcello's arm, and went on, "Leave me alone . . . or I'll call my husband." Marcello immediately let go of her; but she, carried away by an impulse of hostility, turned back toward him and—just as if he were still holding her—slapped him across the cheek.

She seemed at once to regret what she had done. She went to the window, looked out for a moment and then, turning round, said brusquely, "I'm sorry." But Marcello felt that she was not so much sorry as frightened at the effect the blow might produce. There was, he thought, more calculation and good intention than regret in the grudging and still ungracious tone of her voice. He said, in a decisive manner, "Now there really *is* nothing for me to do but go away. . . . Will you be so kind as to tell my wife and ask her to come here? . . . And you must make our excuses to your husband for this evening. . . . You must tell him I had forgotten I had another engagement." That was the end of everything, he thought; and his mission, as well as his love for this woman, was wrecked.

He drew back to make way for her to pass to the door. But instead she stood staring at him for a moment, then twisted her mouth into a grimace of capricious displeasure and came toward him. Marcello noticed that a dark, determined fire burned in her eye. When she was only one pace away from him, she slowly raised her arm, and, from a distance, lifted her hand to Marcello's cheek. "No," she said, "don't go away. . . . I like you too, very much. . . . If I was violent, it was just exactly because I do like you. . . . Don't go away . . . forget what happened." In the meantime she was slowly stroking his cheek, round and round, with an awkward but self-assured movement that was full of imperious determination, as if she wished to take away the sting of her recent blow.

Marcello looked at her, looked at her forehead, and beneath her gaze, under the slightly rough contact of her masculine hand, was aware, to his astonishment—for it was the first time in his life that he had felt it—of a profound excitement and agitation, full of affection and of hope, pervading his breast, harassing his breathing. She was standing in front of him, stroking him with outstretched hand, and he in one look had a full consciousness of her beauty as of something that had always been destined for him, as of his whole life's vocation; and he knew that he had always loved her, even before that day, even before he had had that presentiment of her in the woman at S. Yes, he thought, this was the feeling of love that he ought to have cherished for Giulia—if he had loved her; and that he experienced, instead, for this woman whom he did not know. He moved toward her, his arms outstretched as if to embrace her. But she disengaged herself quickly, though in a manner which seemed to him affectionate and understanding; and putting a finger to her lips, murmured, "Go away now . . . we'll meet this evening." Before Marcello had realized what was happening, she had urged him out of the room and into the hall and had opened the door. Then the door closed and he found himself alone on the landing.

## CHAPTER 13

Lina and Giulia were to take a rest and then go out and visit the dress shops. Then Giulia would come back to the hotel, and later the Quadris would come and fetch them and they would all have dinner together. It was now about four o'clock, and there were still more than four hours before dinner; but only three till the moment at which Orlando would be telephoning to the hotel to find out the address of the restaurant. Marcello therefore had three hours to himself. What had occurred at the Quadris' had made him long for solitude, if only in order to try and understand himself better. He thought as he went downstairs that Lina's behavior, with a husband so much older than herself and completely absorbed in politics, was not surprising, his own, on the other hand, a few days after his wedding and while actually on his honeymoon, both astonished and frightened and, in a vague way, flattered him. Hitherto he had believed he knew himself pretty well and was therefore able to control himself whenever he wished to. But he now realized—whether with more alarm or complacency, he did not know—that he had been mistaken.

He walked for some time through a series of small streets and then at last came out into a wide, gently sloping avenue, the Avenue de la Grande Armée, as he read on the corner of a house. And there indeed, when he raised his eyes, unexpected, enormous, rose the the great rectangular shape of the Arc de Triomphe, seen sideways at the top of the street. Massive yet almost spectral, it appeared in the blue haze of summer to be hanging in the pale sky. As he walked, his eyes fixed on the triumphal pile, Marcello was suddenly conscious of a feeling that was new to him, an intoxicating feeling of freedom and independence. It was as though some great weight that was oppressing him had been unexpectedly removed, so that his step was lighter and he seemed almost to be flying. He wondered for a moment whether he ought to attribute this powerful sense of relief to the simple fact of being in Paris, away from his usual constraints and in front of this grandiloquent monument. One sometimes mistook passing sensations of physical well-being for profound movements of the spirit. Then, thinking over it again, he realized that this sensation was, in fact, due to Lina's caress. He knew this from the flood of tumultuous, disturbing thoughts that rushed up to the surface of his mind at the memory of that caress. Automatically he passed his hand over his cheek, where the palm of her hand had rested: and he could not help closing his eyes in sheer delight; relishing again the contact of the rough, fearless hand that had moved all round his face as if it wished, affectionately, to explore its contours.

What indeed was love, he wondered, walking up the broad pavement with his eyes fixed on the Arc de Triomphe, what was this love for which, as he realized, he was now perhaps on the point of shattering his whole life, deserting the wife he had just married, betraying his political faith, hurling himself into the confusion of an adventure from which there was no turning back? He recalled that he had once, many years ago, been asked that question by a girl who was a fellow-student at the University, a girl who had obstinately rejected his wooing; and he had replied, contemptuously, that for him love was a cow standing in the middle of a field, in spring-time, and a bull rising on its hind legs to get at her.

That meadow, he now thought, was the middle-class carpet on the floor of the Quadris' drawing-room; and Lina was the cow and he the bull. Naked—in spite of the difference of place and their nonanimal limbs—they would be exactly like two beasts. And the rage of desire, vented with awkward, urgent, violence, would be the same too. But here the resemblance—so obvious yet at the same time of so little importance—ceased. For, by a mysterious spiritual alchemy, this rage of desire soon became transformed into thoughts and feelings far removed from it; and these thoughts and feelings, though they received from it the impress of necessity, could not in any way be traced to it alone. Desire, in reality, was no more than nature's decisive, powerful aid to something that existed before her and without her. It was the hand of nature, drawing from the womb of the future the child—the human, moral child—of things to come.

"To be perfectly frank," he said to himself, in an attempt to moderate and calm the extraordinary exaltation that had taken possession of his spirit, "to be perfectly frank, what I want to do is to abandon my wife during our honeymoon, to desert my post during my mission, in order to become Lina's lover and live with her in Paris. To be perfectly frank," he continued, "I shall certainly do these things if I find that Lina loves me as I love her, for the same reasons and with the same intensity."

If any doubts remained as to the seriousness of his decision, it disappeared entirely when, having reached the end of the Avenue de la Grande Armée, he raised his eyes to the Arc de Triomphe. Now, indeed, the sight of this monument raised to celebrate the victories of a glorious tyranny reminded him, by analogy, of that other tyranny he himself had hitherto served and was preparing to betray, and he felt a regret for it. Now that it was lightened and made almost innocent by the foretaste of that betrayal, the part he had been playing till that same morning seemed more comprehensible and therefore more acceptable. No longer, as hitherto, did it appear to be the fruit of a purely external wish for normality, for compensation, but to be almost a vocation, or, to say the least, an inclination that was not wholly artificial. Besides, this feeling of regret, detached and already retrospective as it was, was in fact a sure indication of the irrevocable nature of his decision.

He waited for some time for a pause in the merry-go-round of vehicles encircling the monument, and then, crossing the wide street, went straight to the Arch itself and walked, hat in

hand, under its vault, where lies the tomb of the Unknown
Soldier. There, on the walls of the Arch, were the lists of
battles won, each of which had signified, for numberless
men, a loyalty and self-sacrifice of the kind that he himself
had been bound by, to his own government, until a few
minutes ago; and there was the tomb and the perennial flame
keeping watch over it, symbol of other sacrifices no less
complete. As he read the names of the Napoleonic battles he
could not help remembering Orlando's phrase: "All for Family
and Fatherland"; and he suddenly understood that the thing
that distinguished him from the Secret Service man—who
was so convinced and at the same time so powerless to justify
his conviction by rational means—was simply his capacity
to make a choice, a capacity kept in strict control by the
melancholy that had pursued him from time immemorial. Yes,
he thought, he had made choices in the past, and now he was
again preparing to make a choice. And that melancholy of his
was, in fact, a melancholy mixed with regret, such as is aroused
by the thought of things that might have been, of things that
the act of making a choice compels one to renounce. He
came out from under the Arch, waited again for a pause in
the traffic, and then went across to the pavement of the
Avenue des Champs Elysées. The Arch spread an invisible
shadow over the rich, festive street that sloped down from
its foot; and there seemed to be some indisputable link between the warlike monument and the gay, peaceful prosperity
of the crowd that thronged the pavements. Then it occurred
to him that this too was an aspect of the thing that he was
renouncing—a bloodstained, unrighteous greatness that
changed later into a gaiety and an opulence ignorant of their
origins, a gory sacrifice that became, in time, for later generations, power, freedom and ease. So many arguments in favor
of Judas, he thought jestingly.

But his decision was now taken and he had only one desire
left—to think about Lina, and why and how he loved her.
His mind filled with this longing, he walked slowly down
the Avenue des Champs Elysées, stopping now and then to
look at the shops, at the newspapers in the kiosks, at the
people sitting in the cafés, at the cinema posters and theatre
notices. The thick crowd on the pavement pressed closely
round him on every side with a pullulating movement that
seemed to him to be that of life itself. Four lines of vehicles,
two in each direction, going up and down the wide street,
passed by him on the right; on his left luxurious shops and
gay posters alternated with swarming cafés. As he walked
he gradually hastened his step, as though he were anxious to
leave behind the Arc de Triomphe, which now, as he saw

when he turned to look at it, had become remote and insubstantial again owing to distance and the summer haze. When he reached the bottom of the street he looked for a bench in the gardens, in the shade of the trees, and sat down on it with relief, glad to devote himself in peace to the thought of Lina.

He wanted to go back in memory to the first time he had been aware of her existence—to his visit to the brothel at S. Why was it that the woman of whom he had caught a glimpse in the big room beside Orlando had aroused in him a feeling so novel and so violent? He recalled that he had been struck by the luminous quality in her forehead, and realized that the thing that had attracted him first in her and had then been brought to perfection in Lina was the purity that he had divined in both of them, in the prostitute, degraded and profaned, in Lina, triumphant. He understood now that the horror of decadence, of corruption, of impurity that had pursued him all his life and that his marriage to Giulia had not mitigated, could be dispelled only by the radiant light that encircled Lina's brow. He felt that the coincidence of the two names—Lino who had first aroused that horror in him and Lina who was setting him free from it—was an auspicious sign. In this way, naturally, spontaneously, by the force of love alone, he was finding, through Lina, the normality he had dreamed of. But this was not the rather bureaucratic type of normality that he had been pursuing all these years; it was a different normality, of an almost angelic kind. In face of this luminous, ethereal normality the burdensome trappings of his political obligations, of his marriage with Giulia, of his dull, rational life as a man of order, were revealed as nothing but a cumbersome image set up by him in unconscious expectation of a worthier destiny. Now he was setting himself free and finding himself again through those same processes of reasoning that had caused him, in spite of himself, to adopt that expedient.

As he sat on the bench with these thoughts occupying his mind, his eye fell on a large motorcar coming down toward the Place de la Concorde and gradually reducing speed; and it did in fact come to a stop beside the pavement, quite close to him. It was an old, black car, but of an expensive make, and its antiquated shape seemed to be emphasized by the almost excessive brightness and spotlessness of its nickel and brasswork. A Rolls Royce, he thought; and all at once he was assailed by a feeling of frightened apprehension, mixed, he did not know why, with a horrifying sense of familiarity. Where and when had he seen that motorcar? The chauffeur, a thin, pockmarked man in a dark blue uniform, got out quickly, as soon as the car stopped, and ran to open the door, and then, at that movement, there sprang into Marcello's memory a picture that gave him an answer to his question: the same car, of the same color and the same make, standing at the street corner in the avenue near the school, and Lino putting out his hand to open the door for him to get in beside him. In the meantime, while the chauffeur stood, cap in hand, beside the door, a male leg in a gray flannel trouser, ending in a foot with a yellow shoe as bright and spotless as the brasswork of the car, cautiously protruded itself; then the chauffeur put out his hand and the complete person became visible to Marcello as he descended laboriously on to the pavement. He was quite an old man, Marcello judged; thin and very tall, with a bright red face and hair which might still be fair; he limped as he walked, leaning on a rubber-tipped stick. And yet he was singularly youthful-looking. Marcello observed him carefully as he slowly came towards the bench, and wondered whence the old man derived that air of youthfulness. Then he understood: it was from the fashion in which his hair was arranged, with the parting at one side, and from the green bowtie he wore with a gay pink and white striped shirt. The old man walked with his eyes on the ground, but when he reached the bench he raised them and Marcello saw that they were blue and clear, with a look that was both hard and ingenuous, and that they too were youthful-looking. At last he sat down, with an effort, beside Marcello, and the chauffeur, who had followed close behind him, immediately handed him a small parcel done up in white paper. Then, with a slight bow, he went back to the car and got into it, sitting quietly in his own place behind the windshield.

Marcello, who had been following the old man's movements, now sat with downcast eyes, deep in thought. He wished he had not experienced such a sensation of horror at the mere sight of a car like Lino's; that was already enough to make him feel disturbed. But the thing that frightened him most was the sharp, confused, bitter sense of subjection, of impotence, of enslavement that accompanied his disgust. It was as though there had never been that interval of years, or worse, as though those years had been spent in vain; as though he were still the boy he had been and Lino were waiting for him in the car and he were preparing to get into it, in obedience to the man's invitation. He seemed to be once more under-going the old blackmail, only this time it was not Lino who was applying it, with a revolver as bait, but his own flesh, with its disturbing memories. Alarmed by this sudden, agitating flare-up of a fire that he had believed to be spent, he sighed and automatically fumbled in his pockets for some cigarettes. Immediately a voice said to him in French, "Cigarettes? . . . Here are some."

He turned and saw that the old man was holding out to him in his slightly shaking red hand, an untouched pack of American cigarettes. And all the time he was looking at him with a singular expression, at once kind and commanding. Marcello, highly embarrassed, took the pack without thanking him, opened it hurriedly, took out a cigarette and handed back the pack to the old man. The latter, seizing it and thrusting it with an authoritative hand into the pocket of Marcello's coat, said, in a suggestive tone of voice, "They're for you . . . you can keep them."

Marcello felt himself blush and then grow pale with some unaccountable mixture of anger and shame. His eyes, luckily, happened to fall on his own shoes, white with dust and out of shape from much walking. It dawned upon him then that the old man probably mistook him to be down-and-out or unemployed; and his anger evaporated. Quietly and unostentatiously he took the pack out of his pocket and put it on the bench between them.

But the old man did not notice this act of restitution, for he was no longer paying any attention to him. Marcello watched him open the little parcel that the chauffeur had handed to him and take out a roll. He broke it up slowly and laboriously, with his trembling hands, and threw two or three crumbs on the ground. From one of the leafy trees that overhung the bench a big, well-fed, familiar sparrow flew down. It hopped to the bread, twisted its head two or three times to look around, then seized a crumb in its beak and started devouring it. The old man threw down three or four more crumbs, and more sparrows flew down from the branches on to the pavement. With his cigarette between his lips and his eyes half closed, Marcello watched the scene. The old man, although he was bent and his hands trembled, had in truth kept something of the adolescent about him; or, to be more exact, no great effort was required to imagine him as an adolescent. Seen in profile, his red, capricious mouth, his large, straight nose, his fair hair with its almost urchin-like curl on the brow, made one think that he must have indeed been an extremely pretty youth— perhaps one of those Nordic athletes who combine the grace of a girl with the strength of a man. Bending forward, his head thoughtfully inclined on his breast, he crumbled up the whole of the roll for the sparrows; then, without moving or turning round, asked, still speaking in French, "What country d'you come from?"

"I'm Italian," Marcello replied briefly.

"Why on earth didn't I think of that?" exclaimed the old man, striking himself hard on the forehead, with a characteristic whimsical vivacity. "I was just wondering where I could have seen a face like yours—so very perfect. . . . How silly of me, in Italy, of course. . . . And what's your name?"

"Marcello Clerici," answered Marcello after a moment's hesitation.

"Marcello," repeated the old man, raising his head and looking straight in front of him. A long silence followed. The old man appeared to be meditating; or rather, Marcello thought, he appeared to be making an effort to remember something. At last, with an air of triumph, he turned towards Marcello and recited, *"Heu miserande puer, si qua fata aspera rumpas, tu Marcellus eris."*

They were lines that Marcello knew well, from having translated them at school, and also because they had drawn jests from his schoolfellows. But spoken at that moment, after the offer of the cigarettes, these famous lines gave him an unpleasant feeling of clumsy flattery. This feeling changed to irritation when the old man looked him over from head to foot, as though summing him up, and then said, "Virgil."

"Yes, Virgil," he repeated drily; "and you, what country do *you* come from?"

"I'm British," said the old man, falling strangely into a courtly, perhaps ironically intended, Italian. Then, even more strangely, mingling Neopolitan dialect with his Italian, he went on, "I lived for many years in Naples. . . . Are you a Neapolitan?"

"No," said Marcello, disconcerted by his familiar mode of address.

The sparrows, having eaten up the crumbs, had now all flown away; at a little distance the Rolls Royce stood waiting by the pavement. The old man took hold of his stick and rose painfully to his feet, saying to Marcello in a commanding tone, this time in French, "Would you kindly go with me to my car? Do you mind giving me your arm?"

Automatically Marcello held out his arm. The cigarettes had remained on the bench, in the place where he had put them. "You're forgetting the cigarettes," said the old man, pointing to them with his stick. Marcello pretended not to hear and started off toward the car. The old man did not insist further, but moved off with him.

He walked slowly—far more slowly than when he had walked by himself a short time before; and he leaned his hand on Marcello's arm. But his hand did not remain still; it moved up and down the young man's arm, caressing it in a frankly possessive manner. Marcello felt his heart fail him, and looking up, he understood why. He saw the car standing there waiting for them, and he knew he would be asked to get in, just as had happened so many years before. But what frightened him most was the knowledge that he would not be able to refuse. With Lino there had been—apart from his longing for the revolver—a kind of unconscious coquetry; with this man, he realized to his astonishment, he was conscious of a feeling of subjection that was due to memories of the past, the subjection of someone who has once given away to an obscure temptation and who, many years later, is caught by surprise in the same trap and finds no reason for resistance. It was just as though Lino had done what he wanted with him, he thought; just as though he had not, in reality, resisted Lino and had not killed him. These thoughts went through his mind with immense rapidity; they were more like flashes of light than thoughts. Then he looked up and saw that they had reached the car. The chauffeur had got out and was waiting, cap in hand, beside the open door.

The old man, without letting go of his arm, said, "Well, will you get in?"

Marcello, pleased at his own firmness, answered immediately, "Thank you, but I must go back to my hotel. . . . My wife is waiting for me."

"Poor thing," said the old man, with malicious familiarity, "let her wait a bit. . . . It'll do her good."

So there had to be an explanation, thought Marcello. "I think there's been a misunderstanding," he said. He hesitated, then, out of the tail of his eye, caught sight of a young loafer who had stopped near the bench on which the package of cigarettes was still lying. "I'm not what you think," he added; "perhaps *he* might do for you"; and he indicated the young man who, at that moment, was swiftly and furtively pocketing the cigarettes. The old man looked too, smiled, and answered with characteristic, humorous effrontery, "I can have as many of *those* as I want."

"I'm sorry," said Marcello coldly, having recovered his self-possession; and he was on the point of walking away.

But the old man detained him. "At least let me give you a lift," he said.

Marcello hesitated, looked at his watch. "All right then . . . if it gives you any pleasure."

"It gives me great pleasure."

They got into the car, Marcello first and then the old man. The chauffeur closed the door and jumped quickly into his own seat. "Where to?" asked the old man.

Marcello said the name of his hotel, and the old man

turned to the chauffeur and said something in English. The car started.

It was a silent, well-sprung car, Marcello observed, as it moved quietly and swiftly beneath the trees of the Tuileries towards the Place de la Concorde. The interior was lined with gray felt; and a glass flower case of old-fashioned shape, fixed near the door, held a few gardenias. After a moment's silence, the old man turned to Marcello and said, "I'm sorry about those cigarettes. . . . I took you for a poor man."

"It doesn't matter," replied Marcello.

The old man was silent for a short time and then went on. "It's rarely I make a mistake. . . . I could have sworn that you. . . . I was so sure of it that I was almost ashamed of making use of the pretext of the cigarettes. . . . I was convinced that a look would be enough."

He spoke with gay, cynical, well-mannered coolness; and it was clear that he still considered Marcello to be an invert. The tone of complicity in which he spoke was so assured that Marcello was almost tempted to satisfy him by answering, "Yes, you're right, perhaps I am . . . without knowing it, in spite of myself . . . and the proof of it is my agreeing to get into your car." Instead, he replied drily, "You made a mistake—that's all."

"Yes, I see."

The car was now going round the obelisk in the Place de la Concorde. Then it stopped abruptly opposite the bridge. The old man said, "D'you know what made me think so?"

"What?"

"Your eyes . . . they're so gentle, so caressing in spite of trying to look angry. . . . They give you away."

Marcello said nothing. The car, after a brief pause, went on over the bridge, but instead of turning along the river made its ways into the streets behind the Chambre des Députés. Marcello gave a start and turned toward the old man. "But my hotel is on the river."

"We're going to my house," said the old man, "won't you come and have a drink? You can stay a short time and then go back to your wife."

All at once Marcello seemed to feel again that same sense of humiliation and impotent rage that he had felt, many years before, when his schoolfellows had tied a petticoat round him and teased him by shouting "Marcellina." Like his schoolfellows, this old man did not believe in his virility; like his schoolfellows he insisted on considering him as a kind of female. He said, with clenched teeth, "Kindly take me to the hotel."

"But really! . . . What's the matter? . . . It's only for a moment."

"I got into the car simply because I was late and it was convenient that you should give me a lift. . . . Now take me to the hotel."

"How strange! I thought that what you wanted was to be carried off. . . . You're all like that, you like a little bit of violence."

"I assure you, you make a mistake in adopting that tone with me. . . . I'm not at all what you think I am. . . . I've told you so already, and I repeat it."

"How suspicious you are! . . . I don't think anything. . . . Now please, don't look at me like that."

"You've asked for it," said Marcello; and he put his hand into the inside pocket of his jacket. On leaving Rome, he had taken with him a small revolver; and, in order not to arouse Giulia's suspicions, he kept it about him all the time, instead of leaving it in his suitcase. He now pulled the weapon out of his pocket and pointed it discreetly, in such a way that the chauffeur could not see it, at the old man's coat. The latter considered him with an air of affectionate irony, then lowered his eyes. Marcello saw him become suddenly serious, with a puzzled, almost uncomprehending look on his face. "D'you see?" he said. "And now tell your chauffeur to drive me to the hotel."

The old man at once took the speaking tube and shouted the name of Marcello's hotel. The car slowed down and turned off into a side street. Marcello put the revolver back in his pocket and said, "That's better."

The old man said nothing. He appeared to have recovered from his surprise and was now looking closely at Marcello, as though studying his face. The car came out on the riverside and moved along beside the parapet. Marcello recognized the entrance of his hotel, with its revolving doors under the glass porch. The car stopped.

"Allow me to offer you this flower," said the old man, taking a gardenia from the vase and holding it out to him. Marcello hesitated and the old man added, "For your wife."

Marcello took the flower, thanked him and jumped out of the car, while the chauffeur stood bare-headed beside the open door. He thought he heard—or it may have been an hallucination—the voice of the old man taking leave of him, "Good-bye, Marcello," in Italian. He did not turn around, but, holding the gardenia tightly between his two fingers, entered the hotel.

# CHAPTER 14

He went to the porter's office and asked for the key of his room. "It's upstairs," said the porter after looking at the board. "Madame had taken it. . . . She went upstairs with a lady."

"With a lady?"

"Yes."

He was excited, and he was also immensely happy, after his encounter with the old man, to find himself so excited by the mere news that Lina was in their room with Giulia. He went to the elevator. As he entered he looked at his wristwatch and saw that it was only six o'clock. He had plenty of time to carry off Lina on some pretext or other, to take her quietly into one of the public rooms of the hotel and there decide about the future. Immediately after that he would get rid, once and for all, of Orlando, who was to telephone at seven o'clock. These contingencies seemed to him auspicious. As he went up in the elevator he looked at the gardenia that he was still holding in his fingers and was suddenly sure that the old man had given it to him not for Giulia, but for his true wife, Lina. It was now for him to hand it on to her as a pledge of their love.

He hurried along the corridor to his room and went in without knocking. It was a large room with a double bed, and it had a little vestibule that communicated also with the bathroom. Marcello pushed the door to, without making any noise, and paused a moment in the darkness of the vestibule. Then he noticed that the bedroom door was ajar, showing a crack of light; and a desire came over him to spy on Lina without being seen, as though by so doing he might ascertain whether she truly loved him. He put his eye to the crack and looked into the room.

A lamp was lit on the bed table. The rest of the room was in shadow. Sitting at the head of the bed with her back against the pillows, he could see Giulia all wrapped up in a white cloth: it was the big towel from the bathroom. She was holding the bath towel to her breast with both hands, but seemed either unable or unwilling to prevent its falling wide open at the bottom, so that her belly and her legs were visible. Crouching on the floor at Giulia's feet, her full white skirt making a circle about her, embracing Giulia's legs with both arms so that her forehead was against her knees and her breast against her shins, Marcello saw Lina. Without reproving her—in fact, to all appearances, with a kind of amused, indulgent curiosity—Giulia was stretching

190

her neck in order to observe the other woman, whom, owing to her own half-recumbent position, she could see only imperfectly. At last, without moving, Lina said in a low voice, "You don't mind my staying like this for a little?"

"No, but soon I must get dressed."

After a moment's silence Lina went on, as though resuming an earlier conversation. "How silly you are, though. . . . What would it matter to you? . . . Why, you yourself said that if you weren't married you'd have nothing against it."

"Perhaps I said that," Giulia replied almost coquettishly, "so as not to offend you. . . . Besides, I *am* married."

Marcello, watching, saw that Lina, while she was speaking, had taken one arm from around Giulia's legs and was moving her hand slowly, tenaciously upward along her thigh, pushing back the edge of the towel as it went. "Married!" she said, with intense sarcasm, and without interrupting her slow approach, "and who to, my God!"

"I like him," said Giulia. Lina's hand, hesitating, insinuating as the head of a snake, now moved from Giulia's hip to her naked groin. But Giulia took hold of it by the wrist and guided it firmly downward again, adding in an indulgent tone, like a governess scolding a restless child, "Don't imagine that I don't see you."

Lina took Giulia's hand and began slowly, thoughtfully kissing it, now and then rubbing her whole face violently against the palm, like a dog. "Little silly!" she breathed, with intense tenderness.

A long silence followed. The concentrated passion that emanated from every one of Lina's movements contrasted in a singular manner with Giulia's vagueness and indifference. The latter no longer appeared to be even curious; and though she abandoned her hand to Lina's kisses and rubbings, she was looking around the room as if searching for some excuse. At last she withdrew her hand and started to get up, saying, "Now I really must get dressed."

Lina leaped nimbly to her feet, exclaiming, "Don't move. . . . Just tell me where the things are. . . . I'll dress you."

Standing there, with her back to the door, she hid Giulia completely. Marcello heard his wife's voice say with a laugh, "You want to be my maid too, do you?"

"Why should you mind? . . . It doesn't make any difference to you . . . and it gives me so much pleasure."

"No, I'll dress myself." Out of Lina's fully-dressed figure, as though by duplication, issued Giulia, completely naked. She passed on tiptoe in front of Marcello's eyes and disappeared at the far end of the room. Then he heard her voice saying, "Please don't look at me . . . turn the other way. . . . You make me feel embarrassed."

"Embarrassed with me? . . . But I'm a woman, too."

"Yes, in a sort of way you're a woman . . . but you look at me as if you were a man."

"Well, you might as well say frankly that you'd rather I went away."

"No, stay, but don't look at me."

"I'm not looking at you . . . you silly, why d'you think I should want to look at you?"

"Don't get angry. . . . What I mean is that, if you hadn't spoken to me in that way before, I shouldn't now be embarrassed and you could look at me as much as you liked." This was said in a half-stifled voice which seemed to come from inside a dress that she was slipping over her head.

"Don't you want me to help you?"

"Oh my goodness, if you really want to so much . . ."

Determined yet lacking assurance in her movements, hesitating though aggressive, filled with fervor and at the same time humiliated, Lina moved forward, was outlined for a moment in front of Marcello, and then disappeared in the direction of that part of the room whence Giulia's voice came. There was a moment's silence and then Giulia, in an impatient but not hostile tone, exclaimed, "Ugh, how tiresome you are!" Lina said nothing. The light of the lamp fell on the empty bed, showing up the hollow place left by Giulia's hips in the damp towel. Marcello left the crack in the door and went back into the corridor.

By the time he had taken a few steps he realized that his surprise and agitation had led him, quite unconsciously, to perform a significant act: automatically he had crushed between his fingers the gardenia given him by the old man and destined by him for Lina. He dropped the flower on the carpet and made his way to the staircase.

He went down to the ground floor and out into the street, in the deceptive, hazy dimness of twilight. The lamps were already lit—white clusters on distant bridges, yellow lamps in pairs on vehicles, the red rectangles of windows; and night was rising like a somber cloud of smoke to the clear green sky from behind the black outline of roofs and spires on the opposite bank of the river. Marcello went over to the parapet and leaned his elbows on it, looking down at the darkened Seine whirling along in its black flood strings of jewels and circlets of diamonds. The feeling he was now experiencing was nearer to the deathly quiet that follows disaster than to the tumult of disaster itself. He knew that, for a few hours during that afternoon, he had believed in love; now he realized that he was revolving in a topsy-turvy, sterile world in which real love did not occur, but merely sensual relationships, from the most natural and ordinary to the most abnormal and unusual. Certainly the feeling that Lina had had for him had not been love: no more was Lina's feeling for Giulia. Love did not enter into his own relations with his wife; and perhaps even Giulia, indulgent as she was, and tempted, almost, as she had been, by Lina's advances, did not love him with a real love. In this obscure and reeling world, like a stormy twilight, these ambiguous figures of men-women and women-men whose ambiguity, when they met, was mingled and redoubled, seemed to hint at some meaning which in itself was also ambiguous, but which was bound up, nevertheless—so it appeared to him—with his own destiny and with impossibility, already proved, of escaping it. Since there was no love, and simply because of that, he would continue to be what he had hitherto been, would carry his mission to completion, would persist in his intention to create a family with Giulia—Giulia the animal, Giulia the unforeseeable. This was normality, this makeshift, this empty form. Outside it, all was confusion and caprice.

He felt himself driven to act in this way owing, also, to the light now thrown on Lina's behavior. She despised him, and probably hated him too, as she had declared she did when she was still being sincere; but in order not to sever their relationship and so preclude the possibility of seeing Giulia, to whom she had been attracted, she had contrived to simulate a feeling of love for him. Marcello realized now that from her, henceforward, he could expect neither understanding nor pity; and in face of this final, irremediable hostility, armored, as it was, with sexual abnormality, with political aversion and with moral contempt, he had a feeling of acute and helpless pain. And so that light in her eyes and on her brow, that light, so pure, so intelligent, that had fascinated him, would never be directed on him, to illuminate and soothe him with its affection. Lina would always prefer to humiliate and degrade it in flattery, in entreaty, in hellish embraces. He recalled, at this point, how when he saw her press her face against Giulia's knees, he had been smitten with the same sense of profanation that he had felt in the house at S., when he saw the prostitute Luisa submitting to the embrace of Orlando. Giulia was not Orlando, he thought; but he had desired that that brow should not be humbled before anyone; and he had been disappointed.

As he stood there thinking, night had fallen. Marcello straightened himself up and turned toward the hotel. He was just in time to catch sight of the white figure of Lina coming out of the door and hurrying to a car parked by the pavement. He was struck by her contented and almost furtive air, like that of a weasel or a stoat slinking away from a hen coop with its prey in its mouth. It was not the attitude of one who had been repulsed, he thought: quite the opposite. Perhaps Lina had managed to extract some promise from Giulia; or perhaps Giulia, out of weariness or sensual passivity, had gone so far as to permit some caress or other, valueless to herself, indulgent as she was both to herself and to others, but very precious to Lina. In the meantime Lina had opened the door of the car and had got into it, sitting down sideways and then pulling in her legs. Marcello saw her go past, holding high, in profile, her beautiful, proud, delicate face, her hands on the wheel. The car vanished in the distance and he went back into the hotel.

He went up to their room and entered without knocking. The room was all in order, and Giulia was sitting, fully dressed in front of the dressing table, finishing her hair. Without turning she asked quietly, "Is that you?"

"Yes, it's me," answered Marcello, sitting down on the bed.

He waited a moment and then asked, "Did you enjoy yourself?"

Immediately, vivaciously, his wife turned half around from the table and replied, "Yes, very much indeed. . . . We saw such a lot of lovely things and I left my heart behind in at least ten different shops."

Marcello said nothing. Giulia finished doing her hair in silence, then rose and came and sat beside him on the bed. She was wearing a black dress with a wide, ornate *décolletage* that revealed the firm, brown curves of her breasts like two fine fruits in a basket. A scarlet artificial rose was fastened at her shoulder. Her gentle, youthful face with its big smiling eyes and its full mouth wore its usual expression of sensual gaiety. In a smile that was perhaps unconscious Giulia showed, between her brightly painted lips, her regular teeth of brilliant, spotless whiteness. She took his hand affectionately, and said, "Now just imagine what happened to me."

"What?"

"This lady, Professor Quadri's wife. . . . Well, just fancy . . . she's not a normal woman."

"What d'you mean?"

"She's one of those women who love other women . . . and in fact, just imagine, she's fallen in love with me . . . just like that . . . at first sight. . . . She told me after you'd gone away. . . . That's why she insisted so much on my staying and resting at her flat. . . . She made me a regular, proper declaration of love. . . . Whoever could have thought it?"

"And you—what did you do?"

"I wasn't expecting it at all. . . . I was just dropping off to sleep, because I really was tired. . . . At first I hardly understood. . . . Then at last I did understand, and I really didn't know how to take it. . . . You see, it was real, raging passion, just like a man. . . . Tell me truthfully, would you ever have expected that, from a woman like her, so self-controlled, so very self-possessed?"

"No," answered Marcello gently, "I shouldn't have expected it . . . any more than I should expect," he added, "that you would reciprocate such effusions."

"Good heavens, are you by any chance jealous?" she exclaimed, bursting into a delighted, joyous laugh, "jealous of a woman? Even supposing I'd paid any attention to her, you oughtn't to be jealous. . . . A woman isn't a man. . . . But you can reassure yourself . . . practically nothing happened between us."

*Practically* nothing?"

"I said practically," she replied in a reticent tone, "because, when I saw she was in such despair, I did allow her to squeeze my hand while she was bringing me to the hotel in her car."

"Only just to squeeze your hand?"

"But you *are* jealous," she exclaimed again, highly delighted. "You really are jealous. . . . I've never seen you like that before. . . . Well, if you really want to know," she went on after a moment, "I also allowed her to give me a kiss . . . but only like one sister to another. . . . Then, as she went on insisting and I got bored, I sent her away. . . . That was all. . . . Now, tell me, are you still jealous?"

Marcello had prolonged the conversation about Lina mainly in order to furnish himself with yet another proof of the difference between himself and his wife—he whose whole life was upset because of a thing that had never happened, and she who was open to every sort of experience, indulgent, forgetful in the flesh even more quickly than in the spirit. He asked gently, "But you yourself, in the past, have you never had any relationship of that kind?"

"No, never," she answered with decision. This curt tone was so unusual in her that Marcello knew at once that she was lying. "Come on," he insisted; "why lie about it? . . . No one who knew nothing about these things would have behaved as you did with Signora Quadri. . . . Tell me the truth."

"But what does it matter to you?"

"It interests me to know."

Giulia sat silent for a moment, with downcast eyes, and then said slowly, "You see, the business with that man, that lawyer. . . . Until the day I met you it had given me a real horror of men. . . . Well, I had a friendship, but it didn't last long . . . with a girl, a student she was, of my own age . . . She was really fond of me, and it was mainly that affection of hers, at a moment when I needed it badly, that persuaded me. . . . Then she became possessive, exacting and jealous, and so I broke it all off. . . . I still see her occasionally in Rome, in one place or another. . . . Poor dear, she's still very fond of me." Her face, after a moment of reticence and embarrassment, had now resumed its customary placid expression. Taking his hand, she added, "Don't worry, and don't be jealous; you know I don't love anyone except you."

"Yes, I know," said Marcello. He remembered Giulia's tears in the sleeping car, and her attempt at suicide, and knew that she was sincere. From a conventional point of view she had looked on her lost virginity as a betrayal of trust, but she attached no real importance to her past errors.

"But I tell you," Giulia was saying, "that woman really is crazy. . . . D'you know what she wants us to do? She wants us all to go a few days from now to Savoy, where they have a house. . . . In fact, just fancy, she's already worked out a program."

"What program?"

"Her husband leaves tomorrow. She is staying a few days more in Paris. . . . She says it's on business of her own, but I'm convinced it's really for me she's staying. . . . Then she proposes we should all leave together and go and spend a week with them in the mountains. . . . The fact that we're on our honeymoon doesn't seem to enter her head. . . . For her, it's just as though *you* didn't exist. . . . She wrote down the address of the house in Savoy for me, and made me swear I would persuade you to accept the invitation. . . ."

"What is the address?"

"There it is," said Giulia, pointing to a piece of paper on the marble top of the bedside table, "but, good heavens, you don't really want to accept?"

"No, I don't, but perhaps you do?"

"For goodness' sake, d'you really think I take any notice of that woman? . . . I've told you already that I sent her away because she annoyed me with her persistence." Giulia had risen from the bed and, still talking, went out of the room. "By the way," she called from the bathroom, "someone telephoned for you about half an hour ago. . . . It was a man's voice, an Italian. . . . He wouldn't say who he was . . . but he left a number and said would you ring him as soon as you can. . . . I put down the number on that same piece of paper."

Marcello took up the paper, pulled out a notebook from his pocket and carefully wrote down both the address of the Quadris' house in Savoy and Orlando's telephone number. He felt he had now come to himself again after the transient exaltation of the afternoon; and he perceived this, in particular, from the mechanical nature of his actions and from the resigned melancholy that accompanied them. It was all over then, he thought, putting the notebook back in his pocket, and that fleeting appearance of love in his life had been, after all, merely the shock of his life's adjustment into its final, settled form. He thought again for a moment of Lina, and seemed to discern an unmistakable sign of fate in her sudden passion for Giulia, which, while it had allowed him to find out the address of the house in Savoy, had at the same time brought it about that, when Orlando and his men presented themselves there, she would not yet have arrived. Quadri's solitary departure and Lina's remaining in Paris fitted perfectly, in fact, into the plan of his mission. If things had gone differently, it was not clear how he and Orlando could have brought it to a satisfactory conclusion.

He got up, called to his wife that he was going down to wait for her in the hall, and went out. There was a telephone booth at the end of the corridor, and he went to it in a leisurely, almost automatic, manner. It was only the sound of the Secret Service man's voice issuing from the receiver and asking him, in a joking manner, "Well, sir, where are we going to have this little dinner of ours?" that seemed to bring him out of the cloud of his own thoughts. Quite calmly, speaking slowly but clearly, he proceeded to inform Orlando of Quadri's journey.

## CHAPTER 15

As they got out of the taxi in a narrow street in the Latin Quarter, Marcello looked up at the sign over the door. *Le Coq au Vin* was written in white letters on a brown background at the first floor level of an old gray house. They went into the restaurant. A red velvet divan ran all round the room; the tables were in a row in front of the divan; and old rectangular mirrors in gilt frames reflected in the quiet light the central chandelier and the heads of the few customers. Marcello saw Quadri sitting in a corner

beside his wife. Dressed in black, and shorter than her by a
whole head, he was looking over his spectacles at the menu.
Lina, on the other hand, in a black velvet dress that emphasized the whiteness of her arms and breast and the pallor
of her face, was sitting erect and motionless and seemed to
be anxiously watching the door. She jumped to her feet
when she saw Giulia, and behind her, almost hidden by her,
the professor also rose. The two women shook hands. Marcello raised his eyes and saw, suspended in the unostenta-
tious yellow light of one of the mirrors, an incredible apparition—the head of Orlando, gazing at them. At the same
moment the restaurant clock came to life, its metal entrails
began to writhe and moan, and finally it struck the hour.
"Eight o'clock," he heard Lina exclaim in a contented tone;
"How punctual you are!" Marcello shuddered, and, as the
clock continued to strike its mournful, solemn-sounding
notes, stretched out his hand to shake the hand that Quadri
offered him. The clock struck its last note with energy, and
then, as he pressed Quadri's palm against his own, he remembered that, according to agreement, it was this handshake that was to point out the victim to Orlando, and suddenly was almost tempted to stoop and kiss Quadri on his
left cheek, just as Judas had done, to whom he had jestingly
compared himself that afternoon. He actually seemed to feel
the rough contact of that cheek beneath his lips, and wondered at so strong a power of suggestion. Then he looked
up again at the mirror; Orlando's head was still there, hanging in the void, staring at them. At last they sat down,
Quadri and himself on chairs and the two women opposite
them, on the divan.

The wine waiter arrived with his list, and Quadri began
ordering the wines with extreme care. He seemed completely
absorbed in this occupation and had a long discussion with
the waiter about the quality of his wines, that he appeared
to know very well. Finally he ordered a dry white wine
to go with the fish, a red wine with the roast, and some
champagne on ice. The wine waiter was succeeded by the
other waiter, with whom the same scene was repeated: knowing discussions about various dishes, hesitations, reflections,
questions, answers, and finally the ordering of three dishes,
hors d'oeuvres, fish and meat. In the meantime Lina and
Giulia conversed in low tones, and Marcello, his eyes fixed
on Lina, had fallen into a kind of dream. He still seemed to
hear the frantic striking of the clock behind him while he
was shaking hands with Quadri, he seemed to see again the
decapitated head of Orlando looking at him out of the
mirror; and he knew that never, as at that moment, had he

been so clearly confronted with his destiny. He was like a stone standing in the middle of a crossroad, with two roads, different but of equally decisive importance, leading away from him, one on each side. He started when he heard Quadri asking him, in his usual indifferent tone, "Been going around Paris?"

"Yes, a little."

"Like it?"

"Very much."

"Yes, it's a likeable place," said Quadri, as though speaking on his own account and almost making a concession to Marcello, "but I wish you'd give your attention to that point that I've already alluded to today—that it isn't the vicious city, filled with corruption, that the newspapers in Italy talk about. . . . I'm certain you have that idea, and its an idea which doesn't corespond to reality."

"No, I haven't that idea," said Marcello, a little surprised.

"I'm astonished that you haven't," said the professor without looking at him, "all the young men of your generation have ideas of that kind. . . . They think you can't be strong without being austere, and in order to feel austere they invent fantastic theories of an impossible kind."

"I don't think I'm particularly austere," said Marcello.

"I'm sure you are, and I'll prove it to you," said the professor. He waited till the waiter had put down the dishes of *hors d'oeuvres* and then went on. "Now. . . . I bet that while I was ordering the wines you were secretly wondering that I could appreciate such things. . . . Isn't that so?"

How had he guessed that? Marcello unwillingly admitted, "You may be right . . . but there's no harm in it. . . . The reason why I thought so was that you yourself have what you call an austere look."

"But not like yours, my dear boy, not like yours," repeated the professor pleasantly. "But let me go on. . . . Now tell me the truth—you don't like wine and you don't understand it."

"No, to tell the truth I hardly ever drink," said Marcello; "but what does that matter?"

"It matters a great deal," said Quadri quietly. "A very great deal. . . . And I'm also willing to bet that you don't appreciate good food."

"I eat—" began Marcello.

"You eat in order to eat," finished the professor with an accent of triumph, "which is just what I meant. . . . And finally I'm sure you have a prejudice against love-making. . . . If, for instance, you see a couple kissing each

other in a public park, your first impulse is one of condemnation and disgust, and in all probability you will infer
that the city in which the park is situated is a shameless
city. . . . Isn't that so?"

Marcello understood now what Quadri was getting at.
He said, with an effort, "I don't infer anything. . . . It's
simply that I was probably not born with a taste for these
things."

"It's not only that, but for you, those that do have such
tastes are blameworthy and therefore to be despised. . . .
Admit that's what you feel."

"No, it's not that; they're different from me, that's all."

"He that is not with us is against us," said the professor,
making a sudden sortie into politics. "That's one of the
slogans that they love repeating, in Italy and in other places
too, nowadays, isn't it?" He had meanwhile started eating,
and with such gusto that his spectacles had got pushed
out of place.

"It doesn't seem to me," said Marcello drily, "that politics
have anything to do with these matters."

"Edmondo," said Lina.

"Yes, my dear?"

"You promised me we wouldn't talk about politics."

"But we're *not* talking about politics," said Quadri, "we're
talking about Paris. . . . In short," he concluded, "since
Paris is a city where people love to eat and drink, to dance
and kiss in the parks, in fact to amuse themselves—I'm
sure your opinion of Paris can only be unfavorable."

This time Marcello said nothing. Giulia, with a smile,
answered for him: "Anyhow *I* like the people of Paris very
much indeed. . . . They're so gay."

"Well said, Signora," the professor approved; "you must
try and cure your husband."

"But he's not ill."

"Yes, he is; he's ill with austerity," said the professor,
his head bent over his plate. And he added, almost between his teeth, "Or rather, austerity is just a symptom."

It now seemed obvious to Marcello that the professor—
who, according to what Lina had told him, knew all about
him—was amusing himself by playing with him like a cat
with a mouse. He could not help thinking that it was a
very innocent game compared with his own somber one,
which had been started that afternoon at the Quadris' flat
and which was destined to finish bloodily at the villa in
Savoy. With a sort of melancholy coquettishness he asked
Lina, "Do I really seem so austere . . . to you too?"

He saw her studying him with a cold, reluctant eye, in

which he discerned, to his distress, the profound aversion which she cherished for him. Then, evidently, Lina decided to resume the role of amorous woman that she had taken it upon herself to play, for she replied, with a forced smile, "I don't know you well enough. . . . You certainly give one the impression of being very serious."

"Ah, that's certainly true," said Giulia, looking affectionately at her husband. "I suppose I've seen him smile perhaps a dozen times. . . . Serious is the word."

Lina was gazing fixedly at him now, with malicious intentness. "No," she said slowly, "no, I was wrong. . . . Serious is *not* the word. . . . Worried would be more correct."

"Worried about what?"

Marcello saw her shrug her shoulders, indifferently. "That, of course, I don't know." But, at the same moment, to his great surprise, he felt her foot, under the table, slowly and deliberately first touching his own lightly and then pressing it.

Then Quadri said in a kindly manner, "Clerici, don't worry too much about looking worried. . . . It's nothing but talk, just to pass the time. . . . You're on your honeymoon—that's the only thing that ought to worry you. . . . Isn't that true, Signora?" He smiled at Giulia, with that smile of his which looked like a grimace caused by some mutilation; and Giulia smiled back at him, saying gaily, "Perhaps it's just that that's worrying him—isn't that so, Marcello?"

Lina still continued to press his foot with hers, and he experienced at this contact a sense of duplication—as though the ambiguity of his love-relationships had now been transferred to his whole life and there were two situations instead of only one: the first, in which he pointed out Quadri to Orlando and went back to Italy with Giulia, the second in which he saved Quadri, deserted Giulia, and stayed in Paris with Lina. The two situations, like two superimposed photographs, cut across each other and were confused by the varying colors of his feelings of regret and horror, of hope and of melancholy, of resignation and of revolt. He knew perfectly well that Lina was pressing his feet merely in order to deceive him and to perform faithfully her role of the woman in love; and yet, absurd though it was, he almost hoped that this was not true and that she did seriously love him. He was wondering all the time why in the world she had chosen, out of so many possible ones, this particular method—so traditional and so common —of expressing sentimental understanding, and he seemed to find in that choice another sign of her settled contempt

for him, as a person who did not require very much subtlety
or inventiveness to deceive him. Meanwhile Lina, still pressing his foot and gazing at him with intention, was saying,
"About this honeymoon of yours. . . . I've already spoken
to Giulia, but as I know Giulia won't have the courage
to speak to you about it, I'm going to make the suggestion
myself. . . . Why don't you come and spend the last part of
it in Savoy? . . . With us? . . . We shall be there the
whole summer. . . . We've got a lovely spare room. . . .
You could stay a week or ten days or as long as you like . . .
and go straight back to Italy from there."

So, Marcello said to himself, almost disappointed, so that
was the cause of the foot-pressing. It occurred to him
again, this time with a touch of spite, how extremely well
the invitation to Savoy fitted in with Orlando's plan: if
they accepted the invitation, they would keep Lina in Paris
and in the meantime Orlando would have plenty of time
to deal with Quadri down there in the mountains. He said
slowly, "Personally I've nothing against a jaunt to Savoy . . .
but not for a week or so . . . not before we've seen Paris."

"But that's perfect," cried Lina at once, triumphantly;
"You can come down there with me. . . . My husband's
going on tomorrow. . . . I've got to stay another week
in Paris too."

Marcello observed that her foot was no longer pressing
against his. As the need that had inspired it ceased, so the
flattery ceased also; and Lina had not even thought to
thank him by a glance. From Lina his eyes moved to his
wife, and he saw that she was looking displeased. Then
she said, "I'm sorry I can't agree with my husband . . .
and I'm sorry also if I seem rude to you, Signora Quadri
. . . but it's impossible for us to go to Savoy."

"Why?" Marcello could not help exclaiming. "After
Paris. . . ."

"After Paris, as you know, we've got to go to the Côte
d'Azur to join those friends of ours." This was a lie, for
they had no friends on the Côte d'Azur. Marcello saw
that Giulia was lying in order to get rid of Lina and at
the same time to demonstrate to him her indifference to
the other woman. But there was a danger that Lina, disgusted
at Giulia's refusal, might leave with Quadri. It was necessary, therefore, to guard against this and to make his re-
calcitrant wife accept the invitation without more ado. He
said hastily, "Oh, those people—we can give that up if
necessary. . . . We can see them at any time."

"The Côte d'Azur!—but how awful," exclaimed Lina,
pleased at Marcello's siding with her. And she went on, in

a gay, impetuous, singsong voice, "Whoever goes to the Côte d'Azur! . . . South American adventurers, *cocottes*. . . ."

"Yes, but we promised to go," said Giulia obstinately.

Again Marcello felt Lina's foot pressing his own. With an effort, he said, "Come on, Giulia, why shouldn't we accept?"

"Well, if you really want to. . . ." she replied, bending her head.

He saw Lina, at these words, turn toward Giulia with a disturbed, sad, irritated, surprised look on her face. "But why?" she cried, with a kind of wondering consternation in her voice, "what is it? . . . Just that you want to see that horrible Côte d'Azur? . . . That's simply being provincial. . . . Nobody but provincials wants to visit the Côte d'Azur. . . . I assure you no one in your place would hesitate for a moment. . . Why!" she went on suddenly, with desperate vivacity, "there must be some reason that you're not telling us. . . . Perhaps you've taken a dislike to my husband and me?"

Marcello could not but admire the violence of passion that permitted Lina to make what was, in effect, a lover's scene with Giulia in his own and Quadri's presence. Giulia, somewhat surprised, protested, "Please . . . really. . . . What *are* you saying?"

Quadri, who was silently eating and appeared to be enjoying his food rather than listening to the conversation, observed with his usual indifference, "Lina, you're embarrassing the lady. . . . Even if she has taken a dislike to us, as you say, she'll never tell us so."

"Yes, you've taken a dislike to us," Lina went on, taking no notice of her husband, "or rather, perhaps it's *me* you've taken a dislike to. . . . Is that so, my dear? . . . You've taken a dislike to me. . . . One imagines," she went on, turning to Marcello and still speaking with that same desperate social vivacity which hinted at things it did not say, "one imagines that somebody likes one, and sometimes, instead, it's just the people one wants to be liked by who simply can't bear one. . . . Now be truthful, my dear, and admit that you can't bear me. . . . And while I'm talking like this and stupidly insisting that you should come and stay with us in Savoy, you're thinking, 'What does this crazy woman want of me? How is it she doesn't realize that I can't endure her face, her voice, or her manners— her whole personality, in fact?' . . . Be truthful, admit that's just the kind of thing you're thinking at this very moment."

Now, thought Marcello, she had abandoned all prudence; and if it was perhaps possible for the husband to attribute no importance to these heart-wrung insinuations, he himself—for whose benefit, according to the pretence, all this insistence was being displayed—could hardly fail to realize for whom they were really intended. Giulia, mildly astonished, protested, "But what *are* you thinking about. . . . I should really like to know why you think these things."

"So it's true," exclaimed the afflicted woman, "you *have* taken a dislike to me." Then, turning to her husband, she said, with febrile, bitter complacency, "You see, Edmondo, you said she wouldn't tell me. . . . But now she *has* told me: she *has* taken a dislike to me."

"I didn't say that," said Giulia smiling; "I never even dreamed of such a thing. . . ."

"You didn't say it but you made it quite clear."

Quadri, without raising his eyes from his plate, said, "Lina, I don't understand why you go on arguing like this. . . . Why should Signora Clerici have taken a dislike to you? She's only known you for a few hours, and probably she hasn't any particular feeling about you."

Marcello saw that he would have to intervene again; Lina's eyes, angry and almost insulting in their look of scorn and imperiousness, demanded it of him. She was no longer pressing his foot now, but, with crazy imprudence, at a moment when he happened to place his hand on the table, she pretended to be taking some salt and gave his fingers a squeeze. He said, in a conciliating but decisive manner, "Giulia and I, on the contrary, both like you very much indeed . . . and we accept your invitation with pleasure. . . . We'll certainly come—won't we, Giulia?"

"Yes, of course," said Giulia, suddenly surrendering; "it was only because of that engagement of ours. . . . We really wanted to accept."

"Splendid. . . . Then that's understood. . . . We'll leave together in a week's time." Lina was radiant, and at once started to talk of the walks they would take in Savoy, of the beauty of that part of the country, of the house in which they would be staying. Marcello noticed, however, that she talked in a confused way, more in obedience, as it were, to an urge to sing—like a bird suddenly gladdened by a ray of sunshine inside its cage—than to the necessity of saying anything particular or giving any particular information. And, just as a bird gains vigor from its own singing, so did she appear to become intoxicated with the sound of her own voice, that trembled with the exultation of an imprudent, uncontrolled delight. Feeling himself excluded from the conversation between the two women, Marcello almost mechanically looked up at the mirror hanging at Quadri's back: the honest, good-natured face of Orlando was still there, suspended in the void, decapitated but alive. But it was no longer alone: beside it, in profile, no less precise and no less absurd, another head could now be seen, talking to the head of Orlando. It was the head of a bird of prey, but with nothing of the eagle about it; of a bird of prey of a poor, inferior species—with small, dull, deep-set eyes beneath a low forehead; a large, melancholy, beaky nose; hollow cheeks with the shadow of asceticism upon them; a small mouth; a shriveled chin. Marcello allowed his eyes to rest for some time upon this face, wondering if he had seen it before; and he started when Quadri's voice asked him, "By the way, Clerici. . . . If I asked a favor of you . . . would you grant it me?"

It was an unexpected question; and Marcello noticed that Quadri had waited to ask it until his wife had at last stopped talking. "Certainly," he said, "if it's in my power."

It seemed to him that Quadri looked at his wife before he spoke, as if to have her corroboration of an agreement already discussed and arranged. "It's about the following matter," Quadri then said, in a tone of voice both gentle and cynical, "You are certainly not ignorant of my activities here in Paris and of the reason why I have never gone back to Italy. . . . Now we have friends in Italy with whom we correspond as best we can. . . . One of the methods we use is to entrust letters to people who have no concern with politics, or who anyhow are not suspected of carrying on any political activities. . . . I thought perhaps you would take one of these letters to Italy for me . . . and post it at the first station you happen to come to—Turin, for instance."

There was a silence. Marcello now realized that Quadri's request had no other purpose than to put him to the test, or, at the least, to embarrass him; and he also saw that it was made by agreement with Lina. Probably Quadri, faithful to his system of persuasion, had convinced his wife of the expedience of this plan—though not to such an extent as to modify her hostility towards Marcello. The latter thought he could guess this from the cold, drawn, almost irritated look on her face. But he could not, for the moment, perceive what other purpose Quadri could have in view. To gain time, he answered, "But if they find out, I shall end up in prison."

Quadri smiled and said, jokingly, "That wouldn't do any great harm. . . . On the contrary, for us it would be quite a good thing. . . . Don't you know that political movements require martyrs and victims?"

Lina frowned but said nothing. Giulia looked at Marcello anxiously. It was obvious that she wanted her husband to refuse. Marcello resumed, slowly, "In fact, you really almost want the letter to be discovered."

"No, not that," said the professor, pouring himself some wine in a playful, careless manner which, for some reason, almost made Marcello sorry for him. "What we want is that the greatest possible number of people should compromise themselves and fight on our side. . . . Going to prison for our cause is only one of a very large number of ways of compromising oneself and joining in the struggle—certainly not the only one." He drank slowly; then went on, seriously and in an unexpected manner. "But I only asked you, so to speak, as a matter of form. . . . I know you'll refuse."

"You guessed right," said Marcello, who had been weighing the pros and cons of the proposal. "I'm sorry, but I don't think I can do you this service."

"My husband isn't concerned with politics," explained Giulia with nervous solicitude, "he's a government official . . . he's outside all that."

"Yes, of course," said Quadri, with an air of indulgence, almost of affection; "of course; he's a government official."

It seemed to Marcello that Quadri was curiously satisfied at his reply. His wife, on the other hand, looked angry. She asked Giulia, in an aggressive tone: "Why are you so afraid of your husband being concerned with politics?"

"What's the use of it?" answered Giulia, with perfect naturalness; "He's got to think of his own future, not of politics."

"That's how the women in Italy argue," said Lina, turning to her husband, "and then you're surprised that things go as they do."

Giulia was annoyed. "Really, Italy has nothing to do with it. . . . In certain circumstances the women of any country would argue in the same way. . . . If you lived in Italy, you'd think as I do."

"Now, now, don't get angry," said Lina, with a gloomy but affectionate laugh, passing her hand, in a rapid caress, around Giulia's sulky face. "I was joking. . . . You may be right. . . . Anyhow you're so charming when you defend your husband and get angry on his behalf. . . . Isn't it true, Edmondo, that she's charming?"

Quadri made a vague, slightly disgusted, sign of agreement, as much as to say, "women's talk," and then went on, seriously, "You're right, Signora. . . . A man should never be placed in the position of having to choose between truth and bread."

The subject, it seemed to Marcello, was exhausted. Nevertheless he was still curious to know the real reason of the proposal. The waiter changed the plates and put a big dish of fruit on the table. Then the wine waiter came up and asked whether he should open the bottle of champagne. "Yes, certainly, open it," said Quadri.

The waiter took the bottle out of the ice pail, wrapped its neck in a napkin, pushed the cork upwards and then, swiftly, poured the foaming wine into the champagne glasses. Quadri rose to his feet, glass in hand. "Let us drink to the Cause," he said; and turning to Marcello, "You didn't want to take the letter, but at least you won't mind drinking a toast will you?" He seemed moved, and his eyes were bright with tears; and yet Marcello noticed a certain look of cunning, even of calculation, both in the way he proposed the toast and in the expression of his face. Marcello looked at his wife, and at Lina, before he answered. Giulia, who had risen to her feet, gave him a meaning glance, as much as to say, "You can surely drink the toast." Lina was holding her glass in her hand and her eyes were downcast, and she looked cold and angry, almost bored. Marcello stood up and said, "To the Cause, then," and held out his glass to tap it against Quadri's. With an almost childish scruple he was careful to add mentally *"my* Cause," although it seemed to him now that he no longer had any cause to defend but merely a painful incomprehensible duty to perform. He noticed with displeasure that Lina avoided tapping her glass against his. Giulia, on the other hand, with exaggerated cordiality, sought each person's glass, calling their names in a touchingly eager manner. "Lina, Signor Quadri, Marcello." The sharp, melancholy tinkling sound of the glasses made him shudder again, as the striking of the clock had done previously. He looked up at the mirror and saw the head of Orlando hanging in mid-air, staring at him with bright, expressionless eyes—truly like the eyes in a severed head. Quadri held out his glass to the waiter, who filled it again; then, endowing the gesture with a characteristic, sentimental emphasis, he turned towards Marcello, raising his glass, and said, "And now to your own personal health, Clerici . . . and thank you." He stressed the word "thank you" in a meaning manner, emptied his glass at one gulp and sat down.

For some minutes they drank in silence. Giulia had twice emptied her glass, and was now looking at her husband with a tender, grateful, tipsy expression. Suddenly she exclaimed:

"How good champagne is! . . . I say, Marcello, don't you think champagne's good stuff?"

"Yes, it's a very good wine," he admitted.

"You don't appreciate it enough," said Giulia. "It's absolutely delicious. . . . I'm tight already." She laughed and shook her head and then suddenly went on, raising her glass, "Come on, Marcello, let's drink to our love."

Tipsy, laughing, she held out her glass. The professor looked on from a distance; Lina, with a cold, disgusted expression on her face, made no attempt to hide her disapproval. Suddenly Giulia changed her mind. "No," she cried, "you're too austere, it's quite true. . . . You're ashamed to drink to our love . . . so I shall drink, all by myself, to life—to life that I love and that's so beautiful . . . to life!" She drank with a joyful, awkward haste that caused part of the wine to be upset on the table; then she cried, "That brings luck!" and, wetting her fingers in the wine, made as if to touch Marcello on the temples. He could not help making a movement as though to defend himself. Then Giulia jumped up, exclaiming, "You *are* ashamed . . . well, I'm not"; and she went round the table and embraced Marcello, almost falling on top of him and kissing him hard on the mouth. "We're on our honeymoon," she said in a challenging tone as she went back to her place, breathless and laughing; "we're on our honeymoon and we're not here to engage in politics or carry back letters to Italy."

Quadri, to whom these words appeared to be addressed, said calmly, "You're quite right, Signora." Marcello, between Quadri's conscious allusions and his wife's unconscious, innocent ones, preferred to remain silent, and sat with downcast eyes. Lina allowed a moment's pause to elapse and then asked, in a casual sort of way, "What are you doing tomorrow?"

"We're going to Versailles," replied Marcello, wiping Giulia's lipstick from his mouth with his handkerchief.

"I'll come too," said Lina eagerly. "Let's go in the morning and have lunch there. . . . I'll help my husband pack and then I'll come and fetch you."

"All right," said Marcello.

Lina went on, conscientiously, "I should like to have driven you there . . . but my husband's taking the car, so we shall have to go by train. . . . It's gayer, anyhow."

Quadri did not appear to have heard. He was paying the bill, and was extracting—and emphasizing his deformity as he did so—banknotes folded in four from the pocket of his striped trousers. Marcello was on the point of handing him

some money but Quadri refused it, saying: "Some other time
. . . in Italy."

All of a sudden Giulia burst out, in a very loud, uneven
voice: "In Savoy we'll be together . . . but I want to go to
Versailles alone with my husband."

"Thank you," said Lina ironically, rising from the table;
"that's what's called plain speaking, anyhow."

"Please don't be offended," began Marcello, embarrassed,
"it's the champagne . . ."

"No it's not, it's my love for you, you stupid," cried Giulia.
Laughing, she went off with the professor toward the door.
Marcello heard her continue, "Does it seem wrong to you
that I should want to be alone with my husband during
our honeymoon?"

"No, my dear," replied Quadri gently, "it's perfectly right."

Lina, meanwhile, was commenting in an acid tone, "How
silly of me, I hadn't thought of it. . . . Of course the expedition to Versailles is part of the ritual for young married
couples."

At the door, Marcello insisted on Quadri's going out in
front of him. As he was going out, he again heard the clock
strike the hour; it was ten o'clock.


## CHAPTER 16

The professor took his seat at the wheel of the
car, leaving the door open. "Your husband can go in front
with mine," Lina said to Giulia, "and you come in the back
with me."

But Giulia answered, in a teasing, tipsy way, "Why should
I? Personally, I'd rather go in front," and she jumped in
resolutely beside Quadri. So Marcello and Lina found themselves side by side on the back seat.

Marcello now felt a desire to take Lina at her word and
behave as if he really believed that she loved him. In this
desire there was more than a mere vindictive impulse; there
was also a remnant of hope, as though in a contradictory
and involuntary way he still had illusions about Lina's feelings. The car moved off, then slowed down at a dark spot in
order to turn into a side street; and Marcello, taking advantage of the darkness, seized Lina's hand that was lying on
her knee and pulled it down on to the seat between them.
He saw her turn at his touch with an angry jerk, but this was
quickly transformed into a false gesture of complicity and of
urgent warning. The car went on, threading the narrow
streets of the Latin Quarter, and all the time Marcello was
squeezing Lina's hand. He could feel it lying tense within

his own, rejecting his caress not merely with its muscles but even, so to speak, with its skin, while the fingers wriggled impotently in what seemed to be a mixture of repugnance, indignation and rage. At a corner the car heeled over and they fell against each other. Then Marcello seized Lina by the back of the neck, just as one takes hold of a cat that might turn and scratch, and, twisting her head to one side, kissed her on the mouth. She tried to disengage herself, but Marcello took a tighter hold on the thin, shaven, boyish neck, and then Lina, with a subdued groan, gave up all resistance and submitted to the kiss. Her lips, Marcello noticed, were twisted into a grimace of disgust; and at the same time the sharp nails of the hand that he still held in his were pressed into his palm, in a gesture that might have been thought to be voluptuous but that Marcello knew was, in reality, charged with horror and loathing. He prolonged the kiss as much as he possibly could, looking now at her eyes, that were sparkling with hatred and impatient repugnance, now, at the black motionless heads of Giulia and Quadri in front. The headlights of an approaching car lit up the windshield brilliantly: Marcello let go of Lina and threw himself back in his seat.

Out of the corner of his eye he saw her fall back in her seat and then slowly raise her handkerchief to her mouth and wipe it in a thoughtful, disgusted manner. And then, noticing with what care and what distaste she cleaned those lips which, according to the pretence, should have still been palpitating and greedy for more kisses, there swept over him an obscure feeling of desperate, heart-rending pain.

"Love me!" he wanted to cry out, "love me . . . for God's sake, love me!" It suddenly seemed to him that not only his own life, but Lina's too, now depended upon her love for him—so longed-for, so impossible. Now, as though infected by Lina's steadfast loathing, he realized that he too was filled with a hatred which, though mixed with love and inseparable from it, was yet bloody and murderous. At that moment he felt he would willingly have killed her; for it seemed unbearable to him to know that she was alive and an enemy; and he felt also—though he was frightened at feeling it—that to see her die would now, possibly, give him greater pleasure than to be loved by her. Then a sudden, generous impulse of the spirit made him sorry, and he said to himself, "Thank Heaven, she won't be in Savoy when Orlando and the others get there . . . thank Heaven." And he saw that he had really wished for a moment to have her killed with her husband, in the same way and at the same time.

The car stopped and they got out. Marcello had a glimpse of a dark suburban street, with an uneven row of small houses on one side and a garden wall on the other. "You'll see," said Lina, taking Giulia by the arm, "it's not exactly a place for girls from a convent school . . . but it's interesting." They went to an illuminated doorway, above which a small rectangle of red glass bore, in blue letters, the words: *La Cravate Noire.* "The Black Tie," explained Lina to Giulia; "it means the black tie that men wear with dinner jackets and that all the women here wear, from the waitresses to the proprietress." They went into the vestibule and immediately a face with hard features and short hair, but beardless and of feminine complexion and character, appeared above the cloakroom counter, saying in a thin voice: *"Vestiare."* Giulia, amused, went up to the counter and turned around, letting her cloak fall from her bare shoulders into the hands of this attendant in a black jacket, starched shirt and bow tie. Then, in an atmosphere thick with smoke and a deafening hum of music and voices, they passed through to the dance floor.

A handsome woman, of uncertain age but no longer young, her plump, pale, smooth face rounded off under the chin by the usual black bow tie, came forward between the crowded tables to meet them. She greeted Quadri's wife with affectionate familiarity, and then, raising to her commanding eye a monocle that was fastened by a silk cord to the lapel of her masculine jacket, said, "Four people. . . . I've just the right thing for you, Madame Quadri. . . . Please come this way . . ." Lina, who appeared to have been put in a good humor by the place they were in, leaned over the shoulder of the woman with the eyeglass and made some gay, malicious remark, to which she responded, in a manly fashion, with a shrug of the shoulders and a scornful grimace. Following her, they reached an empty table at the far end of the room. *"Voilà!"* said the proprietress. Now she, in her turn, bent down over Lina who had taken her seat, murmured something into her ear with a jocular, impudent, look, and then, very upright, her small, glossy head held commandingly erect, went off among the tables.

A small, sturdy, very dark-complexioned waitress, dressed in the same fashion, came to their table, and Lina, with the gay, self-possessed sureness of someone who at last finds herself in a place that suits her tastes, ordered the drinks. Then she turned towards Giulia and said cheerfully, "You see how they're dressed? . . . Just like a convent, isn't it? . . . Don't you think it's odd?"

Giulia, it seemed to Marcello, was now looking embarrassed; and she smiled in an entirely conventional manner. In a small round space among the tables, under a kind of inverted cement mushroom that vibrated with the unreal light of neon lamps, was a throng of dancing couples, some of them women dancing together. The orchestra—also composed of women dressed as men—was banished under the stairs that led to the gallery. The professor said, in rather a vague way, "I don't care for this place. . . . These women seem to me to be more worthy of pity than of curiosity." Lina did not appear to have heard her husband's remark. She never stopped gazing at Giulia, with eyes that were filled with a devouring, infatuated, yearning light. At last, as if yielding to an irresistible longing, she suggested, with a nervous laugh: "Shall we dance together? They'll take us for two of themselves . . . it'll be amusing. . . . Let's pretend to be like them. . . . Come along, do . . ."

Laughing excitedly, she had already risen to her feet and, with one hand on Giulia's shoulder, was urging her to do the same. Giulia, irresolute, looked first at her and then at her husband. Marcello said drily, "What are you looking at me for? . . . There's no harm in it." He saw that, now again, he had to support Lina. Giulia sighed and rose slowly and unwillingly to her feet. The other woman, in the meantime, seemed to lose her head altogether, and kept repeating, "If even your husband says there's no harm in it. . . . Come along, do, come along . . ." As Giulia went off, she said, "To tell the truth, I'm not particularly anxious to be taken for one of them." But she walked off in front of Lina and, when she reached the space reserved for dancing, turned back toward her with arms outstretched so that Lina could take hold of her. Marcello watched Lina go close to her, put her arm around Giulia's waist with manly assurance and authority, and then, falling into a dance step, guide her on to the dance floor among the other couples. For a moment he gazed, in vague but painful astonishment at the two women dancing in each other's arms. Giulia was shorter than Lina, they were dancing cheek to cheek, and, at each step, Lina's arm seemed to enfold Giulia's waist more closely. To him it appeared a sad and unbelievable sight: there, he could not help thinking, was the love which, had the world been different, had life been different, would have been his, would have saved him, would have brought him joy. But he was aware of a hand on his arm. He turned and saw Quadri's red, shapeless face bending towards him. "Clerici," said Quadri in a voice full of emotion, "don't imagine that I haven't understood you."

Marcello looked at him and said slowly: "Excuse me, but now it's I who fail to understand *you*."

"Clerici," answered the other man quickly, "you know who I am . . . but I also know who *you* are." He was looking at him intently, and had now taken hold, with both hands of the lapels of Marcello's jacket. The latter, agitated, frozen with a sort of terror, stared back into his face: no, there was no hatred in Quadri's eyes, there was, rather, a look of sentimental, tearful, melting emotion which at the same time had something slightly calculating and malicious about it. Then Quadri went on, "I know who you are, and I realize that, by speaking in this way, I may give you the impression that I am under an illusion, that I am being naïve, or even downright stupid. . . . Never mind . . . Clerici, I want, in spite of everything, to be sincere with you, and I say to you: thank you."

Marcello looked at him but said nothing. Quadri's hands were still on the lapels of his coat and he felt it being pulled tightly down on his neck as though someone had seized hold of him with the object of thrusting him violently away. "I say to you: thank you," continued Quadri, "for having refused to take that letter to Italy. . . . If you had done your duty, you would have taken the letter and handed it on to your superiors . . . so as to get it deciphered and have the people it was addressed to arrested. . . . You didn't do it, Clerici, you refused to do it . . . from loyalty, from a sudden recognition of error or a sudden doubt, from honesty . . . I don't know. . . . I only know that you didn't do it and I repeat again: thank you."

Marcello was on the point of replying, but Quadri, at last letting go of his jacket, put his hand in front of his mouth. "No," he said, "don't tell me you refused to take charge of the letter in order not to arouse my suspicions, in order to act up to your own obligations as a bridegroom on his honeymoon. . . . Don't tell me that because I know it isn't true. . . . What you've really done is to take the first step towards your own redemption . . . and I thank you for having given me the opportunity of helping you to take it. . . . Go on, Clerici . . . and you may be truly reborn to a new life." Quadri fell back in his seat and made a pretence of wishing to quench his thirst, taking a long draught from his glass. "But here are the ladies," he said, rising to his feet. Marcello, bewildered, followed his example.

He noticed that Lina appeared to be in a bad temper. When she had sat down, she opened her compact in an angry, hurried sort of way, and with a series of furious dabs hastily powdered her nose and cheeks. Giulia, on the other hand, was quite placid and indifferent. She sat down beside her husband and took his hand affectionately, under the table, as if to assert clearly her feeling of repugnance for Lina. The proprietress with the eyeglass came up to them and crinkling her smooth, pale cheek into a honeyed smile, asked in an affected voice whether everything was all right.

Lina answered tartly that things couldn't be better. The proprietress bent down towards Giulia and said to her, "It's the first time you've been here. . . . May I offer you a flower?"

"Thank you," said Giulia, surprised.

"Christina," called the proprietress. Another girl in a dinner jacket came up—very different from the resplendent flower girls usually to be found at night clubs. She was pale and thin, with no make-up, and had an Oriental-looking face with a big nose, thick lips, and a bare, bony forehead beneath hair cut extremely short and unevenly, so that it looked as if it had fallen out as the result of an illness. She held out a basket of gardenias, and the proprietress, having selected one, pinned it on Giulia's bosom, with the words, "An offering from the management."

"Thank you," repeated Giulia.

"Not at all," said the proprietress. "Now, I'll bet Madame is Spanish . . . isn't that so?"

"Italian," said Lina.

"Ah, Italian. . . . I ought to have known it . . . with those black eyes. . . ." The words were lost in the noise of the crowd, as the proprietress and the thin, melancholy Christina went off together.

The band had now started to play again. Lina turned towards Marcello and said to him, almost angrily, "Why don't you ask me to dance? I should like to." Without a word he rose and followed her to the dance floor.

They began dancing. Lina held herself well away from Marcello, who could not help remembering sadly the possessive affection with which, a short time before, she had clung to Giulia. They danced in silence for a little, and then, all of a sudden, with a violence in which the fiction of their amorous collusion was curiously tinged with anger and aversion, Lina said to him, "Instead of kissing me in the car, with the risk of my husband noticing it, you might have made your wife give in about the expedition to Versailles."

Marcello was astonished at the naturalness with which she grafted her real anger on to the unreal love-relationship; and also at the cynical, brutal, familiar way in which she addressed him, which seemed typical of a woman who has no scruple in betraying her husband. For a moment he said nothing. Lina, interpreting this silence in her own way, persisted, "Why don't you say something? . . . Is this your love? You're not even capable of making that silly wife of yours obey you."

"My wife isn't silly," he replied gently, more puzzled than offended by this strange anger.

She flung herself without hesitation into the opening that this answer gave her. "What d'you mean, she's not silly?" she exclaimed, irritated and almost surprised. "My dear man, even a blind man could see it. . . . She's beautiful, certainly, but completely stupid . . . a beautiful animal. . . . How can you fail to see that?"

"I like her as she is," he hazarded.

"A goose. . . . A fool . . . the Côte d'Azur. . . . Just a little provincial miss without a crumb of brain. . . . The Côte d'Azur, indeed . . . why not Monte Carlo then, or Deauville? . . . or even just the Eiffel Tower?" She seemed beside herself with rage—which, to Marcello's mind, was a sure sign that there had been some unpleasant discussion between her and Giulia while they were dancing together.

"Don't worry about my wife," he said gently. "Just come to the hotel tomorrow morning. . . . Giulia will have to accept the fact that you're there . . . and we'll all three go to Versailles."

She threw him a look almost of hope. But then anger prevailed again and she said, "What an absurd idea! . . . Your wife said quite clearly that she did not want me to come . . . and I haven't the habit of going where I'm not wanted."

Marcello answered simply, "Well, I want you to come."

"Yes, but your wife doesn't."

"What does it matter to you about my wife? Isn't it enough that you and I love each other?"

She studied him uneasily and mistrustfully, pulling back her head, her soft, arching breast close against his. "Really," she said, "you talk of our love as if we'd been lovers for goodness knows how long. . . . But d'you think we love each other seriously?"

Marcello would have liked to say, "Why don't you love me? I could love you so much." But the words died on his lips, like echoes smothered by an impassable remotness. It seemed to him that he had never loved her so much as at this moment, when, forcing pretence to the point of parody, she insincerely asked him if he were sure he loved her. At last, sadly, he said, "You know I wish we loved each other."

"So do I," she answered vaguely; and it was clear that she was thinking of Giulia. Then, as though waking up to reality, she added with sudden rage, "In any case, please don't kiss me again in the car or anywhere like that. . . . I've never been able to bear effusions of that kind. . . . They seem to me to show not only a lack of consideration but a lack of breeding as well."

"You haven't yet told me," he said, clenching his teeth, "whether you are coming to Versailles tomorrow."

He saw her hesitate, and then, perplexed, she asked, "Do you really think your wife won't be annoyed when she sees me arriving? . . . She won't insult me as she did today at the restaurant?"

"I'm sure she won't. She may be a bit surprised, that's all. But before you come I'll be sure and bring her round."

"Will you be able to?"

"Yes."

"I have the impression that your wife can't endure me," she said in a questioning tone, as though waiting to be reassured.

"You're wrong," he replied, gratifying her half-expressed wish, "on the contrary, she likes you very much."

"Really?"

"Yes, really. . . . She was telling me so only today."

"And what did she say?"

"Oh Lord, nothing very special. . . . That you were beautiful, that you seemed intelligent . . . the truth, in fact."

"I'll come, then," she decided, "I'll come immediately after my husband leaves . . . about nine . . . so that we can catch the ten o'clock train. . . . I'll come to your hotel."

Marcello resented this haste, this relief, on her part, as yet another offence to his own feeling for her. And, kindled suddenly by an indefinable longing for a love-relationship of any kind, even a false, ambiguous one, he said, "I'm so glad you've decided to come."

"Yes?"

"Yes, because I don't think you'd have done it unless you loved me."

"I might have done it for some other reason," she replied maliciously.

"What reason?"

"We women are spiteful . . . just to be spiteful to your wife."

So she thought only of Giulia, all the time. Marcello said nothing, but, still dancing, guided her toward the entrace door. Two more turns, and they found themselves right in front of the cloakroom, one step from the door. "But where are you taking me?" she asked.

"Listen," pleaded Marcello in a low voice, so that the attendant, standing behind the counter, could not hear him, "let's go out into the street for a moment."

"What for?"

"There's no one there. . . . I want you to give me a kiss . . . of your own accord . . . to show me that you really love me."

"I shouldn't dream of such a thing," she said, her anger flaring up again suddenly.

"But why? . . . It's a deserted street, quite dark . . ."

"I've already told you that I can't bear these public displays."

"Please."

"Leave me alone," she said, in a hard, loud voice; and she disengaged herself and went quickly back to the dance floor. Marcello, as though swept away by her outburst, crossed the threshold and went out into the street.

The street, as he had told Lina, was dark and deserted, and the pavements, dimly lit by infrequent lampposts, were bare of passers-by. On the far side of the street, under the high garden wall, stood a few cars. Marcello took his handkerchief from his pocket and stood looking at the leafy tree tops above the wall as he wiped his sweating brow. He felt stunned, as if he had received a sharp, violent blow over the head. He did not remember ever having so humbly entreated a woman before, and was almost ashamed of having done so. At the same time he realized that all hope of inducing Lina not so much to love him as simply, even, to understand him, had now vanished. At that moment he heard behind him the sound of a car engine, and then the car itself slid up beside him and stopped. There was a light inside; and at the wheel Marcello saw the figure—looking just like that of a family chauffeur—of the Secret Service agent Orlando. His companion with the long, thin, bird-of-prey face sat beside him. "Sir," whispered Orlando.

Automatically Marcello went up to the car. "Sir . . . we're going now. . . . He leaves tomorrow morning by car and we shall follow him. . . . But probably we shan't wait till we get to Savoy."

"Why?" asked Marcello, hardly knowing what he was saying.

"It's a long journey and Savoy's a long way off. . . . Why wait till we get to Savoy if we can do it earlier and in better conditions? . . . Good-bye, sir. . . . See you in Italy." Orlando raised his hand in farewell and his companion gave a slight bow. The car slid away, turned the corner at the far end of the street and disappeared.

Marcello turned back into the house and re-entered the dance floor. The music had started again and he found only Quadri at the table. Lina and Giulia were dancing together;

he could see them mingling with the thick crowd on the dance floor. He sat down, took up his glass and slowly emptied it, his eyes fixed on the piece of ice at the bottom. Quadri said suddenly, "Clerici, d'you know you could be very useful to us?"

"I don't understand," said Marcello, putting down his glass.

Quadri proceeded to explain, without the slightest embarrassment. "To anyone else I would propose staying here in Paris. . . . There's plenty to do for everyone, I assure you . . . and we have a special need for young men like you. . . . But you could be even more useful to us by staying where you are now . . . in your present position."

"By giving you information," Marcello concluded, looking him in the eyes.

"Precisely."

At these words Marcello could not help recalling the sight of Quadri's eyes shining with emotion, almost tearful, sincerely affectionate, when, a little earlier, he had taken hold of him by the lapels of his coat. That emotion, he reflected, was the sentimental velvet in which were hidden the claws of cold political calculation. It was that same emotion, he reflected again, which he had noticed in the eyes of certain of his own superiors—though of different quality, patriotic instead of humanitarian. But of what use were these justificatory sentiments when, in both cases, in all cases, there grew from them no sort of consideration for *him*, for his own human personality, that was coolly regarded as a mere means, among many others, for attaining certain ends? He felt, with an indifference that was almost bureaucratic, that Quadri, in making this request, had countersigned his own death sentence. He looked up and said, "You talk as if I had the same ideas as you . . . or was on the point of acquiring them. . . . If that had been so, I should have offered my services to you myself. . . . But as things are—that is, as I neither share, nor wish to share, your ideas—what you ask of me is simply a betrayal of trust."

"Betrayal—nonsense," replied Quadri promptly. "For us, traitors don't exist. . . . There are only people who reflect upon the error of their ways and repent. . . . I was and still am convinced that you are one of those people."

"You're wrong."

"Forget I said it, then, forget I said it. . . . Mademoiselle!" Hurriedly, perhaps to hide his disappointment, Quadri called one of the waitresses and paid the bill. Then they sat silent, Quadri looking out into the room with the air of a calm spectator, Marcello with his back to the room, his eyes downcast. At last he felt a hand on his shoulder and heard Giulia's slow, quiet voice saying, "Shall we go then? I'm so tired . . ."

Marcello got up at once, saying, "Yes, I think we're all ready for bed." It appeared to him that Lina's face wore a defeated expression and was of an intense pallor; but he attributed the first to the fatigues of the evening and the second to the livid quality of the neon lights. They went out and walked to the car at the far end of the street. Marcello pretended not to hear his wife whisper "Let's sit as we were before," and got in, decisively, beside Quadri. During the whole drive none of the four spoke. The only remark made was when Marcello, about half way, said in a haphazard fashion, "How long will you take to get to Savoy?" and Quadri without turning his head, answered, "It's a fast car and as I shall be alone and have nothing to do but drive, I think I ought to get to Annecy by nightfall. . . . I shall leave at dawn next day . . ."

At the hotel they all got out of the car to say their farewells. Quadri, after hurriedly shaking hands with Marcello and Giulia, went back to the car. Lina dallied a moment to say something to Giulia, and then Giulia said good-bye to her and went into the hotel. For a moment Lina and Marcello were left alone on the pavement. He said, in an embarrassed way, "Till tomorrow, then." "Till tomorrow," she echoed, bowing and smiling in her social manner. Then she turned away from him; and he rejoined Giulia in the hall of the hotel.

## CHAPTER 17

When Marcello awoke and turned his eyes up toward the ceiling, in the dim, uncertain light of half-closed shutters, he remembered immediately that at that hour Quadri was already driving over the roads of France, followed at a short distance by Orlando and his men; and he realized that the visit to Paris was over. The visit was over, he repeated to himself, although the visit had scarcely begun. It was over because, with Quadri's death—which was already, so to speak, paid for—he had brought to a conclusion that period of his life during which he had tried by every possible means to rid himself of the burden of solitude and abnormality with which Lino's death had left him. He had succeeded in this at the price of a crime, or, rather, of what would have been a crime if he had not known how to justify it and give it a meaning. As far as he himself was concerned, he was sure that such justification would not be wanting. As a good husband, a good father, a good citizen, he would see his life slowly but steadily acquiring the completeness it had hitherto lacked; and this too was thanks to Quadri's death which, once and for all, precluded any turning back. So it was that Lino's death, that had been the first cause of his somber tragedy, would be nullified and canceled out by Quadri's, just as, once upon a time, the expiatory sacrifice of an innocent human victim nullified and canceled out the guilt of a previous crime. But it was not only he himself that was concerned. The justification of his life and of the murder of Quadri did not depend only on him. "The time has come," he argued lucidly, "when others must do their duty too . . . otherwise I shall be left alone, with this dead man on my hands, and in the end I shall have merely added nothing to nothing." The others, as he well knew, were the government he had agreed to serve by means of this murder, the social system that expressed itself in that same government, and the nation itself that accepted the guidance of that social system. It would not be enough to say: "I have done my duty. . . . I have acted in this way because I was ordered to do so." Such a justification might suffice for Orlando the Secret Service man, but not for him. What was needed, for him, was the complete success of that government, that social system, that nation; and not merely an external success but an intimate, essential success as well. Only in that way could what was normally considered an ordinary crime become, instead, a positive step in a necessary direction. In other words, there must be brought about, thanks to forces that did not depend on him, a complete transformation of values. Injustice must become justice; treachery, heroism; death, life. At this point he felt the need to express his own position in crude, sarcastic words, and said to himself coldly, "If, in fact, fascism is a failure, if all the blackguards and incompetents and imbeciles in Rome bring the Italian nation to ruin, then I'm nothing but a wretched murderer." But he immediately made a mental correction. "And yet, as things are now, I couldn't have done otherwise."

Giulia, who was still asleep beside him, stirred, and with a slow, strong, gradual movement clasped him tightly, first with her two arms, then with her legs, and laid her head on his chest. Marcello made no resistance, but he put out his arm and took up the little luminous clock on the bed table to look at the time. It was a quarter past nine. If things had gone as Orlando had led him to suppose they would, at this moment at some point or other on some French highway, Quadri's car must by lying abandoned in a ditch with a corpse at the wheel. Giulia murmured, "What time is it?"

"A quarter past nine."

"Ugh, how late it is," she said without moving. "We've slept at least nine hours."

"You see how tired we must have been."

"Aren't we going to Versailles?"

"Yes, of course. . . . In fact we ought to get dressed," he said with a sigh, "Signora Quadri will soon be here."

"I'd much rather she wasn't coming. . . . She never leaves me in peace, with her love-making."

Marcello said nothing. After a moment Giulia went on: "And what's the program for the next few days?"

Before he could prevent himself Marcello replied, "We must go home," in a voice that sounded to him positively mournful, from the melancholy he was feeling.

Giulia now roused herself and, pulling back her head and shoulders a little but not letting go of him, asked in an astonished voice, in alarm, "Go home? So soon? We've barely arrived and we've got to go back already?"

"I didn't tell you yesterday," he lied, "because I didn't want to spoil the evening for you. . . . But in the afternoon I got a telegram recalling me to Rome."

"Oh, what a pity! . . . what a dreadful pity!" said Giulia in a good-natured, already resigned tone, "just when I was beginning to enjoy Paris. . . . Besides, we haven't seen anything."

"D'you mind very much?" he asked her gently, stroking her head.

"No, but I should have liked to stay a few days at any rate . . . if only to get some idea of Paris."

"We'll come back again."

There was silence. Then Giulia, with a lively movement of her arms and her whole body, pressed up against him and said: "Well, tell me anyhow what we're going to do in the future. . . . What's our life going to be?"

"Why d'you want to know that?"

"Never mind," she answered, snuggling up against him. "Because I like so much to talk about the future . . . in bed . . . in the dark."

"Well," began Marcello in a calm, colorless voice, "we go back now to Rome and look for a place to live."

"How big a place?"

"Four or five rooms plus offices. . . . Having found it, we buy everything necessary to furnish it."

"I should like a flat on the ground floor," she said in a dreamy voice, "with a garden . . . not a big one . . . but with trees and flowers, so that one could sit out in it when it's fine."

"Nothing could be easier," Marcello agreed. "Then we'll set up house. . . . I think I'll have enough money to furnish it completely . . . not with expensive things, of course . . ."

"You must have a nice study of your own," she said.

"Why should I have a study, considering that I work in an office. . . . Better a good big living room."

"Yes, a living room, drawing room and dining room combined. And we'll have a nice bedroom too, shan't we?"

"Yes, of course."

"But none of those dreary old-fashioned beds. . . . I want a real proper bedroom, with a proper double bed. . . . And tell me . . . we'll have a nice kitchen too?"

"Certainly we'll have a nice kitchen, why not?"

"I want to have a double stove, with gas and electricity. . . . And I want a nice refrigerator too. . . . If we haven't enough money, these things can be bought by installments. That will make it easier."

"Yes, of course . . . by installments."

"And tell me, what are we going to do in this house?"

"We're going to live in it and be happy."

"I do need so much to be happy," she said, cuddling up even closer to him, "so very much. . . . If you knew. . . . It seems to me I've needed to be happy ever since I was born."

"Well, we will be happy," said Marcello with almost aggressive firmness.

"And shall we have children?"

"Of course."

"I want *lots* of them," she said with a kind of singsong intonation, "I want one every year, at least for the first four years of our marriage . . . so that then we shall have a family and I want to have a family as quickly as possible. . . . It seems to me that one oughtn't to wait, otherwise it may be too late. . . . And when one has a family, all the rest comes of itself, doesn't it?"

"Of course, all the rest comes of itself."

She was silent a moment and then asked, "D'you think I'm with child already?"

"How could I know?"

"If I am," she said with a laugh, "it would mean that our child was begotten in the train."

"Would you like that?"

"Yes, it would be a lucky sign for him. . . . You never know, he might become a great traveler. . . . The first child I want to be a boy . . . then I'd rather the second was a girl. . . . I'm sure she'd be very beautiful. . . . You're good-looking and I'm not exactly ugly. . . . We two certainly ought to have very lovely children."

Marcello said nothing and Giulia went on. "Why are you so silent? Wouldn't you like to have children by me?"

"Of course I should," he replied; and all of a sudden he felt, to his astonishment, two tears spout out of his eyes and trickle down his cheeks. And then two more, hot and scalding, like tears already wept some time long past, that had lain within his eyes to be infused with burning sorrow. He knew that what made him weep was Giulia's talk of happiness of a few minutes before, and yet he was unable to define the reason of it. Perhaps it was because this happiness had been paid for in advance at so dear a price; perhaps because he realized that he would never be able to be happy, not, anyhow, in the simple, affectionate way described by Giulia. With an effort he at last repressed his desire to weep, and, without Giulia's noticing it, wiped his eyes with the back of his hand. Giulia, meanwhile, was embracing him more and more closely, clinging to him desirously with her body, seeking to guide his listless, inattentive hands to caress and enfold her. Then he felt her bend her face toward his and begin kissing him repeatedly on his cheeks and his mouth, on his brow and on his chin, with a kind of frantic, childish eagerness. Finally she whispered to him, in an almost mournful tone, "Why won't you come to me. . . . Come and take me," and he seemed to detect in her voice of entreaty something like a reproof for having thought more of his own happiness than of hers. And then, while he was embracing her, penetrating, gently and easily, into her, and while she, beneath him, her head thrown back on the pillow, her eyes closed, was beginning to raise and lower her hips with a regular, composed, vaguely thoughtful motion, like that of a wave rising and falling with the ebb and flow of the tide—at that moment there was a loud knock on the door and a voice called: "Express Messenger!"

"What can it be?" she murmured, panting, half opening her eyes; "don't move. . . . What does it matter?" Marcello turned his head and could just see, on the floor in the brighter light near the door, a letter which had been pushed in through the crack. At the same moment Giulia became motionless and rigid beneath him, throwing back her head and breathing deeply and pressing her fingernails into his arms. She twisted her head on the pillow first one way and then the other, and murmured, "Kill me."

Irrationally, Marcello recalled Lino's cry, "Kill me like a dog!" He was conscious of a horrible anxiety sweeping over him. He waited for some time, until Giulia's hands fell back upon the bed; then he turned on the lamp, got up, fetched the letter and came and lay down again beside his wife.

Giulia had now curled up with her back to him and her eyes closed. Marcello looked at the letter before putting it down on the edge of the bed, close to her mouth which was still open and panting. The envelope was addressed to "Madame Giulia Clerici" in an obviously feminine hand. "A letter from Signora Quadri," he said.

Giulia, without opening her eyes, murmured, "Give it to me."

A long silence followed. The letter was lying level with Giulia's mouth, in the full light of the lamp. Giulia, relaxed and motionless, appeared to be asleep. Then she sighed, opened her eyes, and taking hold of the corner of the letter in one hand, tore open the envelope with her teeth, pulled out the sheet of paper and read it.

Marcello saw her smile; then she murmured, "They say that in love the one who flies is the winner. . . . Since I treated her badly yesterday evening, she informs me that she has changed her mind and has gone off this morning with her husband. . . She hopes I'll join her. . . *Bon voyage.*"

"She's gone?" repeated Marcello.

"Yes, she left at seven this morning with her husband, for Savoy. . . . And you know why she's gone? You remember yesterday evening, when I danced with her the second time? It was I who asked her to dance and she was pleased because she hoped I was at last going to take some notice of her. . . . Well, I told her, on the contrary, with the greatest frankness, that she must give up all idea of me . . . and that if she went on, I should cease to see her altogether, and that I loved no one but you, and that she must leave me in peace, and that she ought to be ashamed of herself. . . . In fact I said so many things to her she almost burst into tears. . . . That's why she's gone today. . . . You see how she calculated? —*I* go away so that *you* can join me again. . . . She'll have to wait a bit."

"Yes, she'll have to wait a bit," repeated Marcello.

"In any case I'm very glad she's gone," resumed Giulia. "She was so persistent and tiresome. . . . As for joining her again, don't let's even speak of it. . . . I don't want ever to see that woman again."

"You won't ever see her again," said Marcello.

## C H A P T E R   1 8

The room at the Ministry in which Marcello worked looked out on to a lesser courtyard. It was a very small room, unsymmetrical in shape, and contained nothing but a desk and a couple of shelves. It was at the end of a corridor that led nowhere, and was a long way from the waiting room. To get to it Marcello used a back staircase that came out at the rear of the building into an unfrequented lane. One morning, a week after his return from Paris, he was sitting at his table. In spite of the great heat he had neither taken off his jacket nor undone his tie, as many of his colleagues did. He had the punctilious habit of never altering in the office the appearance that he wore outside of it. Fully dressed, therefore, his neck enclosed in a high, tight starched collar, he started examining the Italian and foreign newspapers before getting down to work. That morning again, though six days had now passed, his first glance was for the Quadri murder. He noticed that both news and headlines were much reduced, a sure sign that the investigations had made no progress. A couple of French newspapers of the Left gave the whole story of the crime over again, punctuating their accounts with interpretations of certain odd or significant details—that Quadri had been stabbed to death in the depths of a wood; that his wife, on the other hand, had been hit by three revolver bullets at the side of the road and her body then dragged into the wood beside her husband's; that the car had also been taken into the wood and hidden among the bushes. The care with which the bodies and the car had been concealed among the trees, a long way from the road, had prevented discovery for two days.

The newspapers of the Left gave it out as a certainty that the couple had been killed by assassins specially sent from Italy. Some of the papers of the Right, on the other hand, took the risk of giving—though in a questioning manner—the official account as given in the Italian papers—that they had been murdered by anti-Fascist associates owning to divergencies of opinion about the conduct of the war in Spain. Marcello threw aside the newspapers and took up a French illustrated review. He was immediately struck by a photograph on the second page that formed part of a full journalistic account of the crime. The picture carried the title: "The Tragedy of the Forest of Gevaudan," and must have been taken at the moment of the discovery or soon afterward. It showed the undergrowth of a wood with straight tree trunks and shaggy branches, bright patches of sunlight between the tree trunks, and on the ground, half hidden in the long grass difficult to see at a first glance in the confused variation of light and shade, the two bodies. Quadri was lying on his back, and of him nothing could be seen but the shoulders and the head, and of the latter only the chin with the black line of a cut across the throat. Lina was lying half across her husband, and her whole person could be seen. Marcello calmly put down his lighted cigarette on the edge of the ash tray, took up a magnifying glass and scrutinized the photograph with care. Although it was gray and out of focus and indistinct because of the patches of sun and shade in the undergrowth, it showed Lina's body quite recognizably—at the same time both slender and fully formed, both pure and sensual, both beautiful and bizarre, with the broad shoulders below the delicate, thin neck, the full bosom above the wasplike slimness of the waist, the wide hips and the long, elegant legs. Part of her body and her widely spread skirt covered the body of her husband, and it looked as though she were trying to whisper into his ear as she lay there, twisted to one side, her face buried in the grass, her mouth against his cheek.

For a long time Marcello looked at the photograph through the magnifying glass, seeking to examine every line, every shadow, every detail of it. He felt that this picture, filled with a stillness that went beyond the mechanical stillness of the photograph had attained the last, final stillness of death, breathed an atmosphere of enviable peace. The photograph, it seemed to him, was full of the utterly profound silence that must have followed the terrible, lightning-like suddenness of the death agony. A few moments before, all had been confusion, violence, terror, hatred, hope, despair; a few moments, and all was finished, hushed. He remembered that the two bodies had lain for a long time in the undergrowth, almost two days; and he pictured to himself how the sun must have warmed them for many hours and gathered about them the humming life of insects, and how it must then have gone away, slowly leaving them to the silent darkness of the gentle summer night. The dews of night had wept upon their cheeks, the faint wind had murmured in the highest branches and in the bushes of the undergrowth. With sunrise, the lights and shadows of the day had returned, as if to an appointed meeting place, to play over the two figures as they lay there motionless. Rejoicing in the freshness and pure splendor of the morning, a bird had perched on a branch to sing its song. A bee had circled around Lina's head, a flower had opened beside Quadri's thrown-back forehead. As they lay there silent and still, the chattering waters of the brooks that wound through the forest had spoken to them, the inhabitants of the wood— stealthy squirrels, bounding rabbits—had moved about them. And all the time, beneath them, the earth on which they lay had slowly taken the impression, in its soft bed of grass and moss, of the stiff forms of their bodies, had been preparing, in answer to their mute request, to receive them into its lap.

He started at a knock on the door, threw away the review and called, "Come in!" The door opened slowly and for a moment Marcello could see no one. Then, looking cautiously through the opening, appeared the honest, peaceable, broad face of the Secret Service agent Orlando.

"May I come in, sir?"

"Of course, Orlando," said Marcello in an official tone of voice, "come in. . . . Have you something to tell me?"

Orlando came in, closed the door, and walked forward, staring hard at Marcello. And then, for the first time, Marcello noticed that everything about that florid, heated face was good-natured—everything except the eyes, which, small and deep-set below the bald forehead, glittered in a singular manner. "How odd," thought Marcello as he looked at him, "that I hadn't noticed before." He made a sign to Orlando to sit down and the latter obeyed without a word, still staring at him with those brilliant eyes. "Cigarette?" suggested Marcello, holding out his case.

"Thank you, sir," said the other man, taking a cigarette. There was silence for a moment. Then Orlando blew some smoke from his mouth, looked for an instant at the lighted end of his cigarette, and said, "D'you know, sir, what is the most curious thing about the Quadri affair?"

"No, what?"

"That it wasn't necessary."

"How d'you mean?"

"What I mean is, that on my way back, as soon as I had crossed the frontier, I went to see Gabrio, at S., to report to him. D'you know what the first thing he said to me was?— 'Did you get the counterorder?' . . . I asked him, 'What counterorder?' . . . 'The counterorder,' he said, 'canceling your mission' . . . 'And why should it be canceled?' I asked. . . . 'Because,' he said, 'they've suddenly discovered, in Rome, that at this moment an understanding with France would be useful and so they think this mission might spoil the negotiations' . . . So I said: 'I didn't receive any counterorder before I left Paris, so clearly it was sent too late. . . . Anyhow the job was done, as you'll be able to see in the papers tomorrow morning' . . . When I told him this he began shouting, 'You beasts, you've ruined me, this may upset Franco-Italian relations at a very delicate moment in international politics, you're criminals, what am I to say to Rome?' 'You must tell them the truth,' I answered quite calmly, 'that the counterorder was sent too late' . . . You see, sir? Such a lot of trouble, two people killed, and then it wasn't necessary; in fact it's done more harm than good."

Marcello said nothing. Orlando inhaled another mouthful of smoke, and then, in the naïve, self-satisfied, emphatic way of an uneducated man who likes to fill hs mouth with solemn words, he pronounced, "It was the will of Fate."

There was silence again. Orlando went on, "But that's the last time I take on a mission of this kind. . . . Next time —nothing doing. . . . Why, Gabrio was shouting: 'You're beasts' . . . and that isn't true at all. . . . We're men, not beasts. . . ."

Marcello stamped out his half-smoked cigarette and lit another. Orlando continued, "It's all very well, but there are some things I don't like. . . . Cirrincione, to mention only one of them. . . ."

"Who's Cirrincione?"

"One of the men who were with me. . . . Immediately after the job was done, I happened to turn round, in the middle of all the confusion, and what do I see?—him, licking his dagger. . . . I shouted at him, 'What are you doing? Are you mad?' And he says to me, 'Hunchback's blood brings luck' . . . D'you see what I mean? Barbarian . . . I damn near shot him."

Marcello lowered his eyes and automatically began re-arranging the papers on his desk. Orlando shook his head in a deprecatory manner and resumed, "But what I disliked most of all was the business of the lady, who had nothing to do with it and shouldn't have been killed at all. . . . But she threw herself in front of her husband, to protect him, and got two of the revolver shots that were meant for him. . . . He escaped into the wood, where that barbarian Cirrincione caught up with him. . . . She was still alive, so I had to give her another one and put an end to it. . . . She was pluckier than plenty of men I've known. . . ."

Marcello looked up at him, as though to intimate that the interview was over. Orlando understood and rose to his feet. But he did not go away at once. He put his two hands on the desk, gazed for some time at Marcello with those glittering eyes of his, and then, in the same emphatic manner in which, shortly before, he had pronounced the word "Fate," said, "All for the Family and Fatherland, sir."

Then, suddenly, Marcello knew where he had seen those peculiar, glittering eyes before. Those eyes held the same expression as the eyes of his father, shut up in the clinic for the insane. Coldly, he said, "Perhaps the Fatherland wasn't demanding all that much."

"If it wasn't demanding it," asked Orlando, leaning forward slightly toward him and raising his voice, "why did they make us do it?"

Marcello hesitated, and then said, "You've done your duty, Orlando, and that should be enough." He saw the Secret Service agent, half mortified, half approving, give a slight, deferential bow. Then, after a moment's silence, for a reason that he could not have explained—possibly to relieve, in some way, that distress which was so like his own—he added gently, "Have you any children, Orlando?"

"Why, of course I have, sir . . . five of them." Orlando drew out a big, tattered billfold, took from it a photograph that he handed to Marcello, who took it and looked at it. It showed five children between thirteen and six years old, standing in a row in order of size, three girls and two boys, all in their best clothes, the girls in white, the boys in sailor suits. All five of them, Marcello observed, had round, peaceable sensible faces very like their father's. "They're in the country with their mother," said Orlando, taking back the photograph Marcello handed to him; "the biggest girl's already working as a dressmaker."

"They're fine children, and very like you," said Marcello.

"Thank you, sir. . . . Well, good-bye then, sir." Orlando, cheerful again, bowed twice as he retreated backward. At that moment the door opened and Giulia appeared, "Thank you again, sir, thank you again." Orlando stood aside to let Giulia pass, and then disappeared.

Giulia came in and said immediately, "I was passing this way and I thought I'd pay you a visit. . . . How are you?"

"I'm all right," said Marcello.

Standing in front of the desk she looked at him, hesitating, full of doubt and apprehension. Finally she said, "Don't you think you're working too hard?"

"No," answered Marcello, throwing a quick glance at the open window. "Why?"

"You look tired." Giulia walked round the desk and then stood still for a little, leaning against the arm of the chair and looking at the newspapers scattered over the table. Then she asked, "No news?"

"About what?"

"In the papers, about the Quadri affair."

"No, nothing."

After a moment's silence, she said, "I feel more and more certain that it was men of his own party who killed him. What d'you think about it?"

It was the official version of the crime, handed out to the Italian newspapers from the propaganda offices the same morning that the news had arrived from Paris. Giulia, Marcello noticed, had mentioned it with a kind of determined good will, as though she were hoping to convince herself. He replied drily, "I don't know. . . . It might be so."

"I'm convinced of it," she repeated resolutely. And then, after a moment of hesitation, she went on ingenuously: "Sometimes I think that if I hadn't treated Quadri's wife so badly that evening, at the night club she would have stayed in Paris and she wouldn't be dead. . . . And then I have a feeling of remorse. . . . But what could I do? It was her fault, because she wouldn't give me a moment's peace."

Marcello wondered whether Giulia had any suspicion of the part he had taken in the killing of Quadri. After thinking it over, he decided against the possibility. No love, he felt, could have stood up to such a discovery. Giulia was telling the truth: she felt remorse for Lina's death, because—though in a perfectly innocent manner—she had been the indirect cause of it. He wanted to reassure her, but could find no better word than the one already pronounced, with such emphasis, by Orlando. "You mustn't feel remorse," he said, putting his arm round her waist and drawing her toward him, "it was the will of Fate."

Lightly stroking his head, she answered, "I don't believe in Fate. . . . The real reason was that I love you. . . . If I didn't love you—who knows?—I might not have treated her so badly, and she wouldn't have gone away and she wouldn't be dead. . . . What is there fatal about that?"

Marcello remembered Lino, first cause of all the troubles of his life, and explained to her, thoughtfully, "When one says Fate it's exactly those things that one means, love and all the rest. . . . You couldn't help acting as you did, nor could she, indeed, help going away with her husband."

"So we're not really able to do anything?" asked Giulia in a dreamy voice, looking at the papers scattered over the desk.

Marcello hesitated, and then replied, with profound bitterness, "Yes, we're able to know that we're not able to do anything."

"And what's the use of that?"

"It's useful to ourselves, the next time. . . . Or for others who come after us."

She walked away from him with a sigh and went to the door. "Don't forget to be in good time today," she said as she stood in the doorway; "Mummy's got a specially good lunch for us. . . . And remember you mustn't make any appointments for the afternoon. . . . We've got to go and look at those flats." She waved to him and vanished.

Left alone, Marcello took a pair of scissors, carefully cut

out the photograph from the French review, put it in a drawer with some other papers and locked the drawer. At that same moment the piercing wail of the noonday siren came down into the courtyard from the burning sky above. Immediately afterward church bells, near and far, began to ring.

## CHAPTER 19

Evening had fallen, and Marcello, who had spent the day lying on the bed smoking and meditating, rose and went to the window. Black in the greenish light of the summer dusk rose the surrounding blocks of flats, each with its bare cement courtyard adorned with small green flower beds and hedges of clipped myrtle. Here and there a window shone red, and in pantries and kitchens one could see menservants in striped working jackets and cooks in white aprons attending to their household duties among painted cupboards or electric stoves. Marcello looked up above the flat roofs of the buildings to where the last purple vapors of sunset were vanishing in the darkening sky; then he looked down again, and saw a car coming into a courtyard and stopping, and the driver getting out, together with a big white dog which at once started running about the flower beds, whining and barking with joy. This was a wealthy quarter, newly arisen in the last few years, and, looking at those courtyards and windows, nobody would have thought that a war had been going on for four years and that, on that very day, a government that had lasted for twenty years had fallen. Nobody except himself, thought Marcello, and those who found themselves in the same position as he. There flashed upon him, for a moment, the image of a divine rod hanging over the great city as it lay peacefully beneath the clear sky, striking a family here, a family there, bringing terror and dismay and affliction upon them; while their neighbors remained unharmed. His own family was among those smitten, as he knew and as he had foreseen ever since the beginning of the war: a family just like other families, with the same affections and the same intimate ways, a perfectly normal family, possessing the normality that he had sought after with such tenacity for so many years and which was now revealed as a purely external thing entirely made up of abnormalities.

He remembered how he had said to his wife, on the day war broke out in Europe, "If I was logical, I ought to commit suicide today"; and he remembered also the terror that those words had aroused in her. It was as though she had known what they concealed, not merely that she foresaw an unfavorable outcome to the conflict. Once again he had wondered whether Giulia knew the truth about him and about the part he had taken in Quadri's death; and once again it seemed to him impossible that she could know, although, from certain indications, one might well suppose the contrary.

He realized now, with perfect clarity, that he had, as they say, backed the wrong horse; but why he had backed it in that way, and why the horse had not won—this, apart from the most obviously established facts, was not clear to him. He would have liked to be certain that all that had happened had had to happen; that, in fact, he could not have backed any other horse nor arrived at any different result: and he had a greater need of this certainty than of any liberation from a remorse that he did not feel. For him, the only remorse possible was for his mistake—that is, for having done what he had done without any absolute and fatal necessity. For having, in fact—either deliberately or involuntarily—ignored the possibility of doing things that were entirely different. But if he could have the certainty that this was not true— well, then it seemed to him that he could be at peace with himself, even if only in his usual dim, colorless manner. In other words, he thought, he must be sure of having recognized his own destiny and of having accepted it as it was, as a thing useful to others and to himself perhaps in a merely negative way, but useful nevertheless.

He was comforted, meanwhile, in the midst of his doubts by the idea that, even if he had been wrong—a possibility that could not be excluded—he had yet staked more than anyone else, more than all those who found themselves in the same position as himself. This was a comfort to his pride, the only comfort now left him. Others would be able, tomorrow, to change their ideas, their party, their lives, their very characters. For him, however, this was impossible—not merely with respect to others, but to his own self as well. He had done what he had done for reasons entirely of his own, regardless of any communion with other people. To change now, even if it had been permitted him, would mean annihilation of himself. And that, of all the many methods of extinction, was the one he most wished to avoid.

At this point it occurred to him that, if he had been wrong, his first and greatest mistake had been in wishing to escape from his own abnormality and in seeking some kind of normality through which to communicate with other people. This mistake had had its origin in a powerful instinct. Unfortunately the normality that this instinct had happened to light upon was nothing more than an empty shell, inside which everything was abnormal and motiveless. At the first knock, this shell had been broken to pieces; and the instinct, so well justified and so human, had turned him from a victim into an executioner. His mistake had been not so much that he had killed Quadri, as that he had attempted, with inadequate means, to obliterate the original flaw in his own life. But, he wondered again, might it perhaps have been possible for things to have gone differently?

No, it would not have been possible, he thought, answering his own question. Lino had had to set a trap for his innocence, and he, to defend himself, had had to kill him, and afterward, in order to rid himself, of his resulting sense of abnormality had had to seek after normality in the way he had done; and in order to obtain this normality had had to pay a price equivalent to the burden of abnormality of which he intended to rid himself; and that price had been the death of Quadri. Everything, therefore, though freely accepted, had been ordained by fate, just as everything had been at the same time both right and wrong.

All these things were not so much thoughts as feelings, of which he was acutely and painfully conscious, with a sensation of anguish he rejected and defied. He wanted to be calm and detached in face of the disaster to his own life, as though he were watching some gloomy but remote spectacle. His sensation of anguish made him suspect the existence of a panic relationship between himself and outside events, in spite of the clearness with which he forced himself to examine them. In any case it was not easy, at this moment, to distinguish between clearness and fear; and perhaps the best course was to maintain, as always, a decorous, impassive attitude. After all, he said to himself, almost without irony and as though adding up the total of his own modest ambitions, he had nothing to lose—provided that loss was understood to mean the sacrifice of his mediocre position as a government official, of this home that had to be paid for by installments in twenty-five years, of the car, which also had to be paid for within two years, and of a few other oddments of comfort that he had felt Giulia must be allowed to have. He had really nothing to lose. And if they had come at that moment to arrest him, the scantiness of the material advantages he had derived from his position would have astonished even his enemies.

He left the window and turned back into the room. It contained, as Giulia had wished, a large double bed, and the furniture was of shining, dark mahogany with bronze handles and ornaments, in a more or less "Empire" style. It occurred to him that this furniture had been bought on the installment plan too, and that he had finished paying for it only the year before. "The whole of our life," he said to himself sarcastically, taking his jacket from the chair and putting it on, "is on the installment plan . . . but the last ones are the biggest and we shall never manage to pay them." He pushed back the rumpled bedside rug with his foot and went out of the room.

He went along the passage to a half-closed door at the other end, through which a little light was visible. It was his daughter's bedroom, and he paused a moment as he went in at the door and saw, with incredulity, the familiar, everyday scene that faced him. It was a small room, done up in the pretty, gaily colored style suitable to rooms in which children sleep and live. The furniture was painted pink, the curtains were pale blue, and the walls were covered with a paper that had a design of little baskets of flowers. On the carpet, also pink, were scattered untidily a number of dolls of varying sizes, as well as other toys. His wife was sitting beside the bed, in which lay Lucilla, their child. Giulia, who was talking to the child, turned slightly as he came in and cast a lingering glance at him, without, however, saying anything. Marcello took one of the little painted chairs and sat down beside the bed. "Good evening, Daddy," said the little girl.

"Good evening, Lucilla," replied Marcello, looking at her. She was a dark, delicate-looking child with a round face, enormous, melting eyes, and very fine features—features so excessively dainty that they looked almost affected. He did not know why, but at that moment she seemed to him to be too pretty and also too conscious of her own prettiness, in a manner that might well be a first sign of innocent coquettishness and that reminded him, unpleasingly, of his mother, whom the child strongly resembled. This coquettishness was noticeable in the way she rolled her big, velvety eyes when speaking to him or to her mother—an effect that was indeed odd in a child of six; and also in the extreme, almost unbelievable assurance of her conversation. In her blue nightgown, all lace and puffed sleeves, she was sitting up in bed with hands clasped, in the midst of her evening prayers which were interrupted by the entrance of her father. "Come on, Lucilla, don't sit there dreaming," said her mother in a good-natured way. "Come on, say your prayers after me."

"I'm not dreaming," said the child, turning her eyes up to the ceiling with an impatient, prim grimace. "It was you who stopped when Daddy came in . . . so I stopped too."

"You're quite right," said Giulia, unmoved, "but you know the prayer perfectly well. . . . You could have gone on by yourself. . . . When you're bigger, I won't always be there to help you. . . . But you'll still have to say it."

"Look what a lot of time you make me waste . . . and I'm

so tired," said the child, raising her shoulders slightly but keeping her hands clasped. "You start arguing, and I could have finished saying my prayers by now."

"Come along," repeated Giulia, smiling now in spite of herself, "let's begin again from the beginning: 'Hail Mary, full of grace.'"

The little girl repeated in a drawling voice, "Hail Mary, full of grace."

"The Lord is with thee, blessed art thou amongst women."

"The Lord is with thee, blessed art thou amongst women."

"And blessed is the fruit of thy womb, Jesus."

"And blessed is the fruit of thy womb, Jesus."

"Can I rest a moment?" asked the child at this point.

"Why?" asked Giulia. "Are you tired already?"

"You've kept me like this for an hour, with my hands clasped," said the child, pulling her hands apart and looking at her father. "When Daddy came in we'd already said half the prayer." She rubbed her arms with her hands, making a disdainful, flirtatious display of her own weariness. Then she clasped her hands again, and said, "I'm ready now."

"Holy Mary, mother of God;" Giulia resumed quietly.

"Holy Mary, mother of God," repeated the child.

"Pray for us sinners."

"Pray for us sinners."

"Now and at the hour of our death."

"Now and at the hour of our death."

"So be it."

"So be it."

"But, you, Daddy, don't you ever say your prayers?" asked the child, without any transition.

"We say them in the evening before we go to bed," replied Giulia hurriedly. The child, however, was looking at Marcello with a questioning and incredulous air. He hastened to confirm what Giulia had said. "Of course, every evening before we go to bed."

"Now lie down and go to sleep," said Giulia, rising and trying to make the child lie flat. She managed to do this, but not without some difficulty, for Lucilla did not seem at all disposed to go to sleep; then she pulled up to the child's chin the single sheet which was the only covering on the bed.

"I'm hot," said the child, kicking at the sheet. "I'm so hot."

"Tomorrow we're going to Granny's and you won't be hot any more," answered Giulia.

"Where's Granny?"

"Up in the hills. . . . It's cool there."

"But where?"

"I've told you dozens of times—Tagliacozzo. . . . It's a cool place and we're going to stay there all the summer."

"But won't the airplanes come there?"

"The airplanes won't come any more."

"Why?"

"Because the war's over."

"And why is the war over?"

"Because two and two don't make three," said Giulia brusuely but not ill-humoredly. "Now that's enough questions. . . . Go to sleep, because we're leaving early tomorrow morning. . . . I'm just going to fetch your medicine." She went out, leaving father and daughter alone together.

"Daddy," asked the little girl immediately, sitting up in bed again, "d'you remember the cat belonging to the people who live underneath?"

"Yes," replied Marcello, rising from his chair and coming across to sit on the edge of the bed.

"It's had four kittens."

"Well?"

"The little girls' governess told me that they can give me one of the kittens. . . . Can I have it? I could take it to Tagliacozzo."

"But when were these kittens born?" asked Marcello.

"The day before yesterday."

"Then it's impossible," said Marcello, stroking his daughter's head. "The kittens must stay with their mother until they can take milk. . . . You can have it when you come back from Tagliacozzo."

"Supposing we don't come back from Tagliacozzo?"

"Why shouldn't we come back? We're coming back at the end of the summer," replied Marcello, twisting his fingers in his daughter's soft brown hair.

"Ooo, you're hurting me," wailed the child instantly, at the first touch.

Marcello let go of her hair and said, with a smile, "Why d'you say I hurt you? . . . You know it's not true."

"But you *did* hurt me," she replied emphatically. She put her hands up to her forehead, in a willful, feminine sort of way. "Now I shall have a terrible headache."

"Then I shall pull your ears," said Marcello jokingly. Delicately he lifted the hair over the little round, pink ear and gave it the faintest pull, shaking it like a bell. "Ooo, ooo, ooo," cried the child in a shrill voice, pretending to be hurt, a slight blush spreading over her face, "you're hurting me."

"You see what a little liar you are," said Marcello reprovingly, letting go of her ear. "You know, you oughtn't to tell lies."

"That time," she said sagaciously, "I promise you did really hurt me."

"D'you want me to give you one of your dolls for the night?" asked Marcello, looking down at the carpet where the toys lay scattered.

She cast a quietly scornful glance at the dolls and answered in a self-possessed manner, "If you like."

"If *I* like?" asked Marcello, smiling. "You talk as if it was *you* who were giving *me* a pleasure. . . . Don't you like having a doll to sleep with?"

"Yes I do," she conceded. "Give me—" she hesitated, looking down at the carpet, "give me that one with the pink dress."

Marcello also looked down. "They've all got pink dresses," he said.

"There's pink and pink," said the child, in an impatient, know-all kind of way. "The pink of the doll I want is exactly the same as the pink of the pink roses on the balcony."

"Is this the one?" asked Marcello, taking up from the floor the finest and largest of the dolls.

"You see, you don't know anything about it," she said severely. She jumped out of bed, ran barefoot to one corner of the carpet, and picking up an extremely ugly rag doll with a squashed and blackened face, hurried back to bed again, saying, "There you are!" This time she lay down quietly under the sheet, on her back, her rosy, placid face pressed affectionately against the dirty, surprised-looking face of the doll. Giulia came in again with a bottle and a spoon.

"Come along," she said, going up to the bed, "take your medicine." The little girl obeyed promptly. She sat half up in the bed, stretching out her face with her mouth open, like a little bird about to be fed. Giulia put the spoon into her mouth, then tilted it quickly to let the liquid run out. The child lay down again, saying, "How nasty it is!"

"Well, good night," said Giulia stooping to kiss her daughter.

"Good night, Mummy, good night, Daddy," said the child in her shrill voice. Marcello kissed her on the cheek and then followed his wife. Giulia turned out the light and closed the door.

In the passage, she half turned toward her husband and said, "I think it's ready." Marcello then noticed, for the first time, in that revealing dimness, that Giulia's eyes were swollen as if with weeping. His visit to the child had cheered him; but when he saw his wife's eyes, he began to be afraid again that he would not be able to appear as calm and firm as he wished. Giulia had gone on in front of him into the dining room, an extremely small room with a little round table and a sideboard. The table was laid, the central light was burning, and through the open window came a radio voice describing, in the breathless, triumphal style of a football commentator, the fall of the Fascist government. The maid came in, served the soup, and went out again. They started eating, slowly and with measured movements. The radio suddenly became frantic. The announcer was now describing, in exalted terms and a feverish tone of voice, how a huge crowd was gathering throughout the streets of the city, acclaiming the King. "How disgusting!" said Giulia, putting down her spoon and looking towards the window.

"Why disgusting?"

"Until yesterday they were clapping their hands at Mussolini. . . . A few days ago they were applauding the Pope because they hoped he would save them from air raids. . . . Today they acclaim the King, who threw Mussolini out."

Marcello said nothing. Giulia's opinions and reactions in the matter of public affairs were so well known to him that he could always mentally anticipate them. They were the opinions and reactions of an extremely simple person, entirely devoid of curiosity as to the deeper causes from which public events originate, and guided mainly by personal and emotional standards. They finished their soup without speaking while the radio continued to blare out a torrent of words. Then, after the maid had brought in the second course, it ceased, and there was silence, and with the silence came back the suffocating, sultry feeling of the airless summer night. They looked at each other and then Giulia asked, "What will you do now?"

Marcello replied briefly, "I shall do the same as all the other people who find themselves in my position. . . . There are quite a lot of us in Italy who believed in it."

Giulia hesitated before speaking. Then she went on, slowly, "No, I mean, what will you do about the Quadri business?"

So she knew, then; perhaps she had always known, after all. Marcello felt his heart fail him at her words, just as it would have failed him ten years earlier if someone had asked him, "What will you do now about the Lino business?" His answer, at that time—if he had the gift of prophecy—would have been, "Kill Quadri." But now? He put down the fork at the side of his plate, and as soon as he could be sure that his voice would not tremble, answered, "I don't understand what you're talking about."

He saw her lower her eyes, with a grimace as though she were weeping. Then she said, in a slow, sad voice, "Lina told me in Paris—perhaps because she wanted to get me away from you—that you were in the Secret Police."

"And what did you answer her?"

"That it didn't matter to me if you were . . . that I was your wife and that I loved you, whatever you did . . . that if you were doing that, it meant you thought it was the right thing to do."

Marcello said nothing, deeply moved, in spite of himself, by this obtuse, unshakable loyalty. Giulia continued, in a hesitating voice, "But then, when Quadri and Lina were killed, I was terrified that you had something to do with it . . . and I've never been able to stop thinking about it. . . . But I never said anything to you because, as you'd never told me anything about your profession, I thought there was all the more reason why I couldn't speak about *this*."

"And what d'you think now?" asked Marcello after a moment's silence.

"What do I think?" said Giulia, raising her eyes and looking at him. Marcello saw that her eyes were shining, and he knew that those tears already gave him his answer. She added, however, with an effort, "You yourself told me in Paris that the visit to Quadri was very important for your career. . . . So I think it may be true."

He answered at once, "It *is* true."

He realized, simultaneously, that Giulia had been hoping, up to the very last moment, that he would contradict her. And indeed, at his words, as though they had been a signal, she threw her head down on the table, buried her face in her arm and started sobbing. Marcello got up, went over to the door and turned the key. Then he went up to her, and without bending down placed his hand on her hair and said, "If you like, we'll separate, from tomorrow on. . . . I'll take you and the child to Tagliacozzo and then I'll go away and you needn't see me any more. . . . D'you think that would be the best thing?"

Giulia at once stopped sobbing—just as though, it seemed to him, she had not been able to believe her own ears. Then, from the hollow of her arm, where her face was hidden, came her voice, sad and surprised, "Whatever do you mean? Separate? . . . It's not that . . . but I'm so frightened for you. . . . What will they do to you now?"

So Giulia, he said to himself, felt no horror of him, nor did she feel regret for the deaths of Quadri and Lina; it was merely fear on his behalf, fear for his life, for his future. Such insensibility, coupled with such love, affected him strangely; it was like going upstairs in the dark and lifting your foot, thinking to find another step, and instead finding only emptiness because you have reached a landing. He had, in reality, foreseen and even hoped for a feeling of

horror and a severe verdict from her. Instead of which, he
found only the usual blind, loyal love. Somewhat impatiently, he said, "They won't do anything to me. . . . There
are no proofs . . . and in any case I was only carrying out
orders." He hesitated a moment, feeling a kind· of bashful-
ness, mixed with repugnance, for the commonplace remark;
then, with an effort, concluded, "I only did my duty, just
as a soldier would."

Giulia quickly snatched at this worn and hackneyed
phrase which, not so long ago, had not sufficed to tran-
quillize even Orlando, the Secret Service man. "Yes, I
thought of that," she said, lifting her head and then seizing
his hand and kissing it frantically, "I always said to myself,
'Marcello, after all, is just like a soldier. . . . Soldiers, also,
kill because they're ordered to do so. . . . It's no fault of
his if they make him do certain things. . . .' But don't you
really think they'll come and take you away? . . . I'm sure
the people who gave you the orders will escape . . . and that
you, on the other hand, you who have nothing to do with it
and who only did your duty, will be the one to suffer. . . ."
After having kissed the back of his hand she turned it over
and started kissing the palm with equal fury.

"Don't worry," said Marcello, stroking her head, "for
the present they'll have other things to do besides looking
for me."

"But people are so dreadful. . . . If there's even just one
person who hates you . . . they'll denounce you. . . . Besides, it's always like that. The big people, the ones who
give orders and who've made millions, get away; while the
little ones like you, who have done their duty and haven't
saved a penny, are the ones who suffer. . . . Oh Marcello,
I'm so frightened."

"You mustn't be frightened, everything will come right."

"Ah, but I know it won't come right. I feel it. . . . And
I'm so tired." Giulia spoke now with her face pressed against
his hand, but no longer kissing it. "After Lucilla arrived,
although I knew what your profession was, I used to think:
now I'm properly established, I've got a baby, a husband
that I love, I've got a home and a family, I'm happy, truly
happy. . . . It was the first time in my life that I'd been
happy and it seemed too good to be true. . . . I could hardly
believe it . . , and I was always so much afraid that everything would come to an end and that the happiness wouldn't
last. . . . And indeed it hasn't lasted, and now we've got to
run away. . . . And you'll lose your job and goodness knows
what they'll do to you. . . . And that poor little creature
will be worse off than if she was an orphan. . . . And every-

thing will have to be started all over again. . . . And perhaps it won't even be possible to start again and our family life will be broken up." She burst into tears and buried her face in her arm again.

All of a sudden Marcello recalled the image that had flashed across his mind earlier—the divine rod pitilessly smiting his whole family, himself, the guilty one, and his wife, and child who were innocent, and he shuddered at the thought. There was a knock at the door and he shouted to the servant that they had finished and didn't need her any more. Then, bending down towards Giulia, he said gently, "Please don't go on crying, and don't worry. . . . Our family life won't be broken up. . . . We'll go away to America, or to Argentina, and make a new life for ourselves. . . . We'll have a home there, and I'll be there, and Lucilla. . . . Be brave, and you'll see everything will be all right."

Giulia now raised her tear-stained face toward him, and, filled with sudden hope, said, "We'll go to Argentina. . . . But when can we go?"

"As soon as possible. . . . As soon as the war's really over."

"And in the meantime?"

"In the meantime we'll get away from Rome and go and stay at Tagliacozzo. . . . No one will look for us there. . . You'll see, everything will be all right."

Giulia seemed cheered by these words, and particularly, Marcello thought, as he saw her rise and blow her nose, by the firm tone in which they had been pronounced. "I'm sorry," she said, "it's silly of me. . . . I ought to be helping you, and all I can do is to cry like a fool." She began clearing the table, taking the dishes and stacking them on the sideboard.

Marcello walked over to the window and, leaning on the sill, looked out. Through the opaque glass panes in the building opposite, floor after floor, right up to the sky, the staircase lights shone silently. In the deep cement courtyards the shadows thickened, black as coal. The night was still and hot, and even if one listened carefully the only sound to be heard was the hissing of a garden hose with which, down in the darkness of the courtyard, someone was watering the flower beds. Marcello turned and said, "Shall we take the car and drive into town?"

"Why?" she asked. "What's the point of it? . . . Goodness knows what the crowds must be like. . . ."

"You could witness," he replied almost lightly, "the fall of a dictatorship."

"There's Lucilla. . . . I can't leave her alone. . . . Supposing the airplanes come?"

"Don't worry, they won't come tonight."

"But why go into town?" she suddenly protested. "Really I don't understand you. . . . D'you want to *make* yourself suffer? . . . What pleasure is there in it?"

"You stay, then," he said. "I'll go alone."

"No, then I'll come too," she said at once. "If anything happens to you, I'd rather be there. . . . After all, the maid can see to the child."

"But don't be afraid . . . the planes won't come tonight."

"I'm going to change," she said, leaving the room.

Left alone, Marcello crossed over to the window again. There was somebody going down the stairs in the opposite building,—a man. The dark outline of his figure could be seen through the opaque window panes, descending slowly from floor to floor. He walked down in a self-possessed sort of way, to judge by the slenderness of his outline. He must be a young man thought Marcello enviously, he was whistling. Then the radio started to blare again Marcello heard the usual voice winding up, as if at the end of a speech, with the words, ". . . the war continues." It was the message of the new government, that he had already heard shortly before. He took out his case and lit a cigarette.

## CHAPTER 20

The suburban streets were deserted, silent, dark, as though dead, like the extremities of some large body whose blood has suddenly collected all in one spot. But as the car drew nearer to the center of the city Marcello and Giulia saw more and more groups of people gesticulating and shouting. At a crossroad Marcello slowed down and stopped while a line of trucks went past, packed with boys and young women waving flags and placards with slogans on them. These overloaded, flag-decked trucks with people clinging to the mudguards and the footboards were greeted with confused applause by the crowds thronging the pavements. Someone stuck his head in at the window of Marcello's car and shouted ."Long live Freedom!" in Giulia's face, disappearing immediately afterward as though sucked back into the multitude that swarmed all around. Giulia said, "Wouldn't it be better to go back home?"

"Why?" replied Marcello, surveying the street through the glass of the windshield. "They're all so pleased. . . . They're certainly not thinking of doing any harm to anyone. . . . We'll leave the car somewhere and then walk about and see what's going on."

"Won't they steal the car?"

"Don't be absurd."

Marcello drove the car through the crowded streets in the center of the town in his usual thoughtful, composed, patient manner. In spite of the gloom of the black-out it was possible to distinguish quite clearly the movements of the crowd, with groups of people forming and groups encountering each other and then scattering and running here and there—all the movements shifting and varying, yet all animated by the same single, sincere exultation at the fall of the dictatorship. People who did not know each other embraced in the middle of the street. Here someone, after standing still for a long time, dumb and attentive, as a flag-decked truck drove past, suddenly took off his hat and yelled applause; there someone was running like a dispatch-bearer, from group to group, repeating phrases of encouragement and rejoicing; someone else, seized with a sudden fury of hatred, lifted a threatening fist at a dark, closed building that had been the seat of some public office. Marcello noticed there were large numbers of women on their husbands' arms, sometimes with their children too—a thing that had not happened for a long time, in the forced public manifestations of the fallen regime. Columns of determined-looking men, united, apparently, by some secret party bond, formed and marched past for a moment or two amid applause, and then seemed to be lost in the crowd; large, roving groups surrounded an impromptu orator; others gathered to sing hymns of freedom at the top of their voices. Marcello drove gently and patiently respecting each concourse of people and advancing very slowly. "How pleased they all are!" said Giulia, in a good-natured, companionable tone, forgetting both her fears and her own interests.

"In their place I should be too."

They went some distance up the Corso, through the crowd, following two or three other slowly moving cars; then, at a narrow side street, Marcello turned, and, after waiting for a column of demonstrators to pass, managed to drive into it. He drove on quickly into another completely deserted lane behind the side street, stopped, switched off the engine, and turning to his wife, said, "Let's get out."

Giulia got out without a word, and Marcello, having carefully locked the doors of the car, walked with her toward the street they had recently left. He felt completely calm now, completely detached and master of himself, just as he had desired to be during the whole of that day. He kept a careful watch on himself, however; and as he came out again into the crowded street and the joy of the throng exploded in his face its tumultuous rush of aggressive sin-

cerity, he immediately asked, not without anxiety, whether
this joy did not arouse in his mind some feeling that was
far from serene. No, he thought, after a moment of careful
self-examination, he felt neither regret, nor scorn, nor fear.
He was truly calm, apathetic, dead, and he was ready to
contemplate other people's joy without sharing in it but also
without resenting it as a threat or an affront.

They started wandering about aimlessly among the crowd,
from one group to another, from one side of the street to
the other. Giulia was no longer frightened now, and appeared, like him, to be quite calm and self-possessed; but
this, he knew, was because of her good-natured capacity for
identifying herself with other people's feelings. The crowd
instead of diminishing, seemed to increase each moment.
It was a crowd, Marcello noticed, almost wholly joyful, with
a joy that was amazed and incredulous and awkward at expressing itself, and not yet quite sure that it would do so
with impunity. More trucks, forcing their way with difficulty
through the multitude, moved past laden with working-class
people, both men and women, waving flags, some of them
tricolor, some red. A small German open car went past
with two officers lolling quietly back in their seats and a
soldier in battle dress sitting on the edge of the door holding
a Tommy gun: whistles and sneering cries rose from the
pavements. Marcello noticed that there were numbers of soldiers about, very much at their ease and carrying no arms,
but embracing each other, their stolid peasant faces lit up
with a kind of inebriate hopefulness. The first time he saw
two of these soldiers walking along with their arms round
each other's waists like two lovers, their bayonets bouncing up
and down against their unbuttoned tunics, Marcello found
they produced in him a feeling very much like scorn: they
were men in uniform, and for him uniform meant, inexorably,
decorum and dignity, whatever the feelings of its wearer
might be. Giulia, as though guessing his thoughts, pointed
at two affectionate, untidy soldiers and asked him, "Didn't
they say the war was to continue?"

"They said so," answered Marcello, admitting himself suddenly, and with a painful effort of comprehension, to
be in the wrong, "but it isn't true. . . . Those poor fellows
are quite right to be pleased: for them the war really is
over."

In front of the great door of the Ministry to which Marcello had gone for his orders the day before he left for
Paris, there was a great crowd of people protesting and
shouting and waving their fists in the air. Those nearest
the door were beating upon it with their hands and d

manding that it should be opened. The name of the now
fallen Minister was being loudly repeated, in a tone of
particular loathing and disgust, by many of those in the
crowd. Marcello watched this concourse of people for some
time without understanding what the demonstrators wanted.
At last the door was very slightly opened and in the crack
appeared a pale, imploring commissionaire in a braided uniform. He said something to those nearest to him, somebody
went in the door that was immediately closed again, the
crowd yelled again for a little and then dispersed, but not
entirely, for a few obstinate people remained, still knocking
at the closed door and still shouting.

They left the Ministry and went on into the adjoining
square. A shout of "Make way, make way!" caused the
crowd to fall back and them with it. Stretching his head
forward, Marcello saw three or four rough youths coming
along, pulling behind them by a rope a large bust of the
Dictator. The bust was bronze in color but was really of
painted plaster, as one saw from a number of white chips
caused by the violent way in which they bounced it over
the paving stones. A little dark man, his face, almost hidden behind a huge pair of tortoise-shell spectacles, looked
at the bust and then turned toward Marcello and said, laughing, in a sententious voice, "It looked like bronze but really
it was just vulgar chalk." Marcello did not answer, and for
a moment, craning his neck, he stared intently at the bust
while it went bouncing heavily along in front of him. It
was a bust like hundreds of others placed here and there
in ministries and public offices—coarsely stylized, with jaw
thrust out, eyes round and hollow, smooth, swollen cranium.
He could not but reflect how that mouth of sham bronze,
image of another, living mouth once so arrogant, was now
trailing in the dust amid the sneers and whistles of the
same crowd that had once so warmly acclaimed it. Again
Giulia seemed to guess his thoughts, for she murmured,
"Just think, once upon a time a bust like that in a waiting
room was all that was needed to make people lower their
voices!"

He answered drily, "If they had him here now, in the
flesh, they'd do the same to him as they're doing to that
bust."

"D'you think they'll kill him?"

"Certainly, if they can."

They walked on a little farther, through the crowd that
jostled and swirled in the darkness like turbulent, unstable
flood-water. At one street corner a group of people had
put up a long ladder at the corner of a building, and a

man who had climbed to the top of the ladder was hammering vigorously at a stone that bore the name of the regime. Someone said with a laugh to Marcello, "There are Fascist signs everywhere . . . it'll take years to efface them all."

"It certainly will," said Marcello.

They crossed the square and made their way through the crowd to the arcade. It was almost in darkness, but by the dim light of the blacked-out lamps they came upon a group of people at the point where the two arms of the arcade meet, standing in a circle around something that could not be seen. Marcello went closer to look, and found there was a boy dancing in the middle of the circle: he was giving a comic parody of the gestures and contortions of a woman performing the *danse du ventre;* and he had a portrait of the Dictator, a colored oleograph, fixed over his head by means of a hole made in the paper, like a collar, so that he looked like someone who has been put in the pillory and is dancing with the contraption still hanging round his neck. As they were going back towards the square, a young officer with a little black beard and frenzied eyes, with a dark, excited, bareheaded girl on his arm, leaned over toward Marcello and shouted to him in a tone that was both exalted and didactic, "Long live freedom . . . but even more, long live the King!"

Giulia looked at her husband. "Long live the King!" said Marcello, without blinking an eyelid. They walked away and then Marcello remarked, "There are plenty of Monarchists who are trying to turn the thing to the advantage of the monarchy. . . . Let's go and see what's going on in the Piazza del Quirinale."

They went back, not without some difficulty, to the turning, and thence to the lane where they had left the car. As Marcello was switching on the engine, Giulia said to him, "D'you really want to? . . . I'm so tired of all this screeching."

"Well, we've nothing better to do."

He drove the car quickly by side streets to the Piazza del Quirinale. When they reached the square, they saw that it was not completely full of people. The crowd, at its thickest underneath the balcony on which members of the Royal Family usually showed themselves, grew more and more scattered toward the edges of the square, so that there was plenty of empty space. Even here there was little light; the big iron lamp-standards, with their clusters of feeble, dreary, yellowish lights, scarcely relieved the dull blackness of the throng. There was little applause, nor were there frequent calls from the crowd for anyone to appear on the balcony. Here in the square, more than elsewhere, the crowd did not seem to know very clearly what it wanted. There was more curiosity than enthusiasm: just as people had previously assembled, as though to watch some spectacle, in order to see and hear the Dictator, so now they wanted to see and hear whoever it was who had overthrown the Dictator. As the car moved gently round the square, Giulia asked in a low voice, "Will the King really come out on the balcony?"

Before answering, Marcello twisted his head round to take a look at the balcony through the glass of the windshield. It was feebly illuminated by the reddish light of a couple of torches, and in between them they saw the closed window shutter. Then he replied, "I don't suppose so. . . . Why should he?"

"Then what are all these people waiting for?"

"Nothing at all. . . . It's just the habit of going into a piazza and calling for somebody."

Marcello circled very slowly round the square; it was as though he were politely pushing the reluctant groups of people out of his way with the fenders. Giulia said, quite unexpectedly, "D'you know, I feel almost disappointed?"

"Why?"

"I thought they'd be doing something or other—burning houses, killing people. . . . When we came out I was afraid for you, and that was why I came. . . . But there's nothing —nothing but yelling and clapping, Long live this and down with that, and singing and marching. . . ."

Marcello could not refrain from answering, "The worst is yet to come."

"What d'you mean?" she demanded in a frightened voice. "For us, or for the others?"

"For us *and* for the others."

He immediately regretted having spoken when he felt Giulia seize his arm violently, in distress. "I knew all the time," she said, "that what you were telling me wasn't true—when you said that everything would come right. . . . And now you're saying the same yourself."

"Don't be frightened. . . . I was only just talking."

Giulia said no more; but she held tightly to his arm with both hands and pressed herself against him. Embarrassed, but unwilling to repel her, Marcello drove the car back through side streets toward the Corso. Once there, he continued to follow the less frequented streets and at last reached the Piazza del Popolo, and from there continued his way up the steep slope of the Pincio towards Villa Borghese. Crossing the Pincio, dark and peopled only by marble busts,

they followed the riding-track in the direction of Via Veneto.
When they came to the entrance at Porta Pinciana, Giulia
said suddenly, in a sad and languishing voice, "I don't want to
go home."

"Why?" asked Marcello, slowing down.

"I don't know why," she replied, looking straight in front
of her, "but my heart sinks at the very thought of it. . . . It
seems to me like a place that we're going to leave forever
. . . I don't mean anything terrible, though," she hastened to
add, "just a place we've got to move out of."

"Where d'you want to go, then?"

"Anywhere you like."

"Shall we drive round Villa Borghese?"

"Yes, let's do that."

Marcello took the car down a long, dark avenue at the
far end of which was the pale glimmer of the Borghese
Museum building. When they reached the open space in front
of it, he stopped, switched off the engine and said, "Shall we
go for a little walk?"

"Yes, if you like."

They got out and walked off arm in arm toward the
gardens at the back of the Museum. The park was deserted,
political events having depopulated it even of loving couples.
The marble statues, with their mournful or heroic gestures,
gleamed dully white in the dim light, against the dark, leafy
background trees. They walked as far as the fountain and
lingered there for a moment, in silence, looking down into its
still, black water. Giulia was clinging tightly now to her
husband's hand, pushing her fingers vigorously between his
in a sort of miniature embrace. They walked on, turning into
a very dark avenue leading through a grove of oak trees.
After a few steps Giulia suddenly stopped, and, turning, put
her arm around Marcello's neck and kissed him on the mouth.
They stood like that, embracing and kissing in the middle of
the avenue, for some time. Then they separated, and Giulia,
taking her husband by the hand and drawing him in among
the trees, whispered, "Come and let's make love here . . . on
the ground."

"No, really," Marcello could not help exclaiming, "here?"

"Yes, here," she said. "Why not? . . . Come, I want it
so as to feel reassured."

"Reassured about what?"

"Everyone thinks about war, and politics, and air raids
—when they could really be so happy. . . . Come on
. . . Why, I'd do it right in the middle of one of their public
squares," she added with sudden exasperation, "if only to

show that I, at least, am capable of thinking about something else. . . . Come on."

She seemed now to be in a state of exaltation, and went in front of him into the thick darkness among the tree-trunks. "You see what a lovely bedroom," he heard her murmur. "Soon we shan't have a home at all . . . but this is a bedroom they can't ever take away from us. . . . We can sleep and make love here as often as we like." All of a sudden she vanished, as though she had sunk into the earth. Marcello looked about and then caught sight of her in the darkness, lying on the ground at the foot of a tree, one arm pillowing her head, the other raised toward him in silent invitation to lie down beside her. He did so, and no sooner was he there than Giulia twined her arms and legs tightly round him, kissing him all over his face with a blind, slow energy, as though she were seeking, on his brow and cheeks, other mouths through which she might penetrate into him. But almost at once her embrace slackened, and Marcello saw her half raise herself above him, gazing into the darkness. "Someone's coming," she said.

Marcello, too, sat up and looked. Through the trees, still some way off, the light of a pocket lamp swayed as it advanced and threw a feeble circular glimmer on the ground in front of it. There was no sound, for the thick carpet of dead leaves dulled the footsteps of the unknown person. The lamp advanced in their direction, and Giulia quickly composed herself and sat up, throwing her arms round her knees. Sitting side by side with their backs to the tree, they watched the light approach. "It must be a park-keeper," murmured Giulia.

The lamp was now shining on the ground at a short distance from them; then it was raised and its rays fell full upon them. Dazzled, they gazed at the dim, shadowy face of the man from whose fist the white light issued. The light, thought Marcello, would surely be lowered, once the park-keeper had taken a good look at them. But no, the light continued to shine full in their faces as the man stared at them in a silence that seemed, to Marcello, to be fraught with astonishment and speculation. "May I ask what you want with us?" he then demanded in a resentful tone.

"I don't want anything, Marcello," replied a gentle voice at once. At the same time the light was lowered and began to move away from them.

"Who is it?" murmured Giulia. "He seems to know you."

Marcello sat motionless, not daring to breathe, profoundly disturbed. Then he said to his wife, "Forgive me, one moment. . . . I'll be back at once." He jumped to his feet and pursued the unknown man.

He caught up with him at the edge of the garden, beside the pedestal of one of the white marble statues. There was a lamppost not far off, and as the man turned at the sound of his footsteps he recognized him immediately, even after all those years, by the smooth, ascetic face beneath his brush-like hair. He had seen him before in a close-fitting chauffeur's tunic; and now, too, he was wearing a uniform—black, buttoned up to the neck, with wide breeches and black leather gaiters. He held his cap under his arm and grasped the pocket lamp in his hand. He said at once, with a smile, "People who don't die always reappear."

The remark seemed to Marcello to be altogether too well suited to the circumstances, although it was meant as a joke and was perhaps unconscious. Breathless with agitation and with running, he said, "But I thought I'd . . . I thought I'd killed you."

"I hoped you knew that they'd saved me, Marcello," answered Lino quietly. "It's true that one paper announced that I was dead, but it was a mistake. . . . Somebody else died in the hospital, in the bed next to mine. . . . And so you thought I was dead. . . . I said rightly, then: people who don't die always reappear."

It was not so much the rediscovery of Lino that now filled Marcello with horror as the familiar, conventional, although somber, tone that had at once been established between them. He said, unhappily, "My having believed you dead has had all sorts of consequences. And you weren't dead after all. . . ."

"For me too, Marcello, there were all sorts of consequences," said Lino, looking at him with a kind of compassion. "I thought it was a warning, and I got married. . . . Then my wife died. . . . And then," he added more slowly, "it all began over again. . . . Now I do night duty as a park-keeper. . . . These gardens are full of good-looking boys like you." He spoke these words with gentle, quiet effrontery, but without the slightest suggestion of a compliment. Marcello noticed, for the first time, that his hair was graying and that his face had become a little fatter. "And you're married," he went on. "That was your wife, wasn't it?"

Suddenly Marcello was unable to bear this subdued, dreary chatter any longer. Seizing hold of the man by the shoulders and shaking him, he said, "You talk to me as if nothing had happened. . . . D'you realize that you ruined my whole life?"

Without attempting to free himself, Lino replied, "Why d'you say that to me, Marcello? You're married, I dare say you've got children, you look as if you were comfortably off—what are you complaining of? It would have been worse if you had really killed me."

"But I," Marcello could not help exclaiming, "I, when I met you, was innocent . . . and since then I haven't been, ever again."

He saw Lino look at him in surprise. "But all of us, Marcello," he said, "all of us have been innocent. . . . Wasn't I innocent myself once? And we all lose our innocence, one way or another; it's the normal thing." He freed himself without difficulty from Marcello's already relaxed grip, and added, in a knowing sort of way, "Look, here's your wife. . . . We'd better leave each other."

"Marcello," called Giulia's voice in the darkness.

He turned and saw Giulia approaching in a hesitating manner. At the same moment Lino put on his cap, raised his hand in salute and hurried away in the direction of the museum. "Well, who was it?" asked Giulia.

"A schoolfriend of mine," replied Marcello, "who's ended up as a park-keeper."

"Let's go home," said she, taking his arm again.

"Don't you want to walk any more?"

"No. . . . I'd rather go home."

They went to the car, drove away, and did not speak until they reached home. As he drove, Marcello thought again of Lino's words, so unconsciously significant, "We all lose our innocence, one way or another; it's the normal thing." Those words, he thought, held a concentrated judgment on his life. He had done what he had done in order to redeem himself from an imaginary crime; yet Lino's words had made him see, for the first time, that, even if he had not met him and had not fired at him and had not been convinced that he had killed him, even if, in fact, nothing had happened, he would still have done what he had done simply because, in any case, he would have had to lose his innocence and, consequently, would have desired to regain it. Normality was precisely this desire—as wearisome as it was vain—to justify a life trapped in its own original guilt, and it was not the deceptive mirage that he had pursued ever since the day of his meeting with Lino.

He heard Giulia's voice asking, "What time shall we leave tomorrow morning?" and he dismissed these thoughts as so many troublesome and now useless witnesses of his own error.

"As early as possible," he answered.

## CHAPTER 21

Marcello woke at dawn and saw, or thought he saw, his wife standing in the corner of the room near the window, looking out in the gray light of the first moment of daybreak. She was completely naked. With one hand she held aside the curtain and with the other she covered her breast, but whether her gesture was one of modesty or of apprehension, it was impossible to say. A long lock of loose hair hung down her cheek; her face, bent forward, was pale and colorless and wore an expression of desolate thoughtfulness, of pensive dismay. Her body seemed during that night to have lost its look of robust, eager exuberance; her breasts, slightly flattened and relaxed by maternity showed in profile a flabby, tired crease that he had never noticed before; her belly seemed not so much rounded as swollen-looking, and gave an impression of clumsy, helpless heaviness, accentuated by the attitude of her thighs that were pressed together, as though trembling, to hide her groin. The cold light of awakening day, like an indiscreet but apathetic eye, fell dismally on this nudity. As he looked at her, Marcello wondered what was passing through her mind as she gazed, motionless in that shaft of pale dawn light, at the deserted courtyard. And he said to himself, with a sharp feeling of compassion, that he could very well imagine what those thoughts might be. "Here am I," she was no doubt thinking, "here am I, driven out of my home before half my life is over, with a young child and a ruined husband who has nothing to hope from the future, whose fate is uncertain, whose very life may be in danger. This is what has come of all our efforts, of all our passion, of all our hopes." Truly, he thought, she was Eve driven out of Eden; and Eden was this home of theirs with all the modest things that it contained—the cupboards filled with their belongings, the cooking utensils, the drawing room for receiving friends, the plated spoons and forks, the sham Persian carpets, the china that her mother had given her, the refrigerator, the vase of flowers in the hall, this double bedroom with its false Empire furniture bought by installments—and he himself, lying in the bed watching her. Her Eden also consisted, without doubt, in the pleasure of sitting at table twice a day with her family, of sleeping at night in the arms of her husband, of attending her household, of making plans for the future for herself, for her daughter and for him. And finally, Eden meant peace of soul, harmony with herself and with the world, the serenity of a heart composed and satisfied. From this Eden she was now driven out, forever, by a raging, pitiless angel armed with a flaming sword, who was thrusting her, naked and defenseless, into the hostile outer world.

Marcello watched her for some time, while she stood there motionless, absorbed in her melancholy contemplation; then, as sleep weighed heavy on his eyelids, he saw her leave the window, move on tiptoe to the hanging cupboard, take down a dressing gown, put it on and noiselessly leave the room. She was probably going to sit beside the bed of the sleeping child, for further painful contemplation, or perhaps to finish her preparations for departure. For a moment he thought of joining her, to comfort her in some way or other. But he was still heavy with sleep and he soon dropped off again.

Later, in the pure light of the summer morning, while they were driving towards Tagliacozzo, he thought again of that mournful vision, wondering whether he had dreamed it or had really seen it. His wife was sitting beside him, pressed close against him in order to make room for Lucilla, who was kneeling on the seat with her head out of the window, enjoying the drive. Giulia sat upright, her jacket unbuttoned over her white blouse, her face raised and shaded by the traveling hat she wore. Marcello noticed that she held on her knees an object of oblong shape done up in brown paper and tied with string. "What have you got in that parcel?" he asked in surprise.

"It'll make you laugh," she answered, "but I couldn't bear to leave that crystal vase that stood in the hall. . . . I'm fond of it first of all because it's beautiful and then because it was you who gave it to me—d'you remember?—a short time after the child was born. . . . It's a weakness of mine, I know, but never mind. . . . I'll put some flowers in it when we get to Tagliacozzo."

So it was really true, he thought; he hadn't dreamt it, it was really Giulia, in flesh and blood, not a dream figure, that he had seen that morning standing by the window. He said, after a moment, "If you wanted to bring it away, you did quite right. . . . But I assure you, we'll go home again at the proper time, as soon as the summer's over. . . . You really mustn't be alarmed."

"I'm not alarmed."

"Everything will turn out for the best," went on Marcello, changing gear as the car started up a hill, "and then you'll be just as happy as you've been during these last years, or even more."

Giulia said nothing but did not appear convinced. Marcello,

as he drove, glanced at her for a moment. With one hand she held the vase on her knee, while her other arm was round the waist of the child looking out of the window. All her affections, all her possessions, her attitude seemed to declare, were now here, in this car: her husband on one side of her, her child on the other, and—symbol of family life—the crystal vase on her knee. He recalled how at the moment of leaving she had cast a last look at the front of the building and had said, "I wonder who will come and occupy our flat"; and he realized that he would never be able to persuade her because there was no reasoned conviction in her mind, merely the frightened presentiment of instinct. He asked her, however, in a calm voice, "Tell me what you're thinking now?"

"Nothing special," she replied, "I wasn't really thinking about anything. . . . I was looking at the landscape."

"No, I mean, what do you think in general?"

"In general? I think things are going badly for us . . . but that it's nobody's fault."

"Perhaps it's my fault."

"Why your fault? It's never anybody's fault. . . . Everybody's right and wrong at the same time. . . . Things go badly because they go badly, that's all." She spoke these words in an uncompromising tone, as if to show that she did not wish to talk any more. Marcello said nothing, and from that moment silence fell between them for some time.

It was still early, but there were already signs that the day would be hot. Already, in front of the car, between the hedges, dust-covered and shimmering with light, the air was quivering and the midsummer sun, beating down on the asphalt, made mirror-like reflections. The road wound through undulating country, among yellow hills of dry, shaggy stubble, with brown and gray farm buildings hidden here and there at the bottom of lonely, treeless valleys. Every now and then they met a horse-drawn cart or an old-fashioned car. It was an unfrequented road and not used by military traffic. Everything looked calm, normal, indifferent, thought Marcello as he drove along; one would never have thought oneself in the heart of a country that was both at war and in the middle of a revolution. The faces of the few peasants they saw, leaning against fences or digging in the fields, expressed nothing more than the usual feelings of stolid, quiet attention to the normal, everyday, obvious things of life. These people's thoughts were of harvests, of sun and rain, of food prices, or, indeed, of nothing at all. Giulia had been for years like these peasants, he said to himself; and now she was grieved at her peace being torn away from her. The thought even came into his mind: so much the worse for her. Living, for human beings, did not mean abandoning oneself to the peaceful torpor provided by the indulgence of nature; it meant, rather, a state of continuous struggle and agitation, it meant the solving, every moment, of some tiny problem within the limits of larger problems that were contained, in turn, in the all-embracing problem of life itself. This thought restored his self-confidence; and now the road was leaving the monotonous, desolate country and climbing up among the high red rocks of a chain of hills.

Owing, perhaps, to his feeling, as he drove the car, that his body was part and parcel of the machine that so resolutely and tirelessly faced and overcame the difficulties of the winding, hilly road, he became aware of a current of cold, adventurous optimism, the first he had known for many years, like a gust of rushing wind at last sweeping away the clouds from the stormy sky of his spirit. Now indeed, he felt, he could consider a whole period of his life as finished and buried, now he could begin all over again, on a different plan and with different methods. His meeting with Lino, he felt, had been most valuable; not so much because it had freed him from remorse for a crime he had not committed as because Lino, with those few words he had happened to say about the inevitability and normality of the loss of innocence, had made him realize that for twenty years his feet had been obstinately set on a wrong road that he must now unhesitatingly abandon. This time there would be no need for justification or for other people's support; and he was determined not to allow the crime he had really committed—the killing of Quadri—to poison his life with the torments of a vain search for purification and normality. What had happened had happened. Quadri was dead; and over that corpse he had lowered the stone slab of complete and final forgetfulness, heavier than any tombstone.

The landscape had changed now from the sultry desert they had passed through earlier, and an abundance of invisible water had brought into being, at the edges of the road, a profusion of grass and flowers and ferns and, higher up, along the tufa rock-ledges, the thick, exuberant foliage of small trees. This was the reason, perhaps, why Marcello felt that from now on for good and all, he would know how to avoid the desolation of those deserts in which man follows his own shadow and feels himself pursued and guilty; and would seek instead, freely and adventurously, places like the one he was now passing through, places that were rocky and pathless, fit for brigands and wild animals. He had bound himself, voluntarily, obstinately, stupidly, with unworthy ties and with obligations even more unworthy; all this he had done for the mirage of a normality that did not exist; but now those ties were broken, those obligations dissolved, and he was free again and would know how to make use of freedom. At that moment the landscape appeared at its most picturesque: on one side of the road the plantation of young trees covered the hillside; on the other a grassy slope, with a few huge, leafy oaks, fell away to a ravine filled with bushes through which glinted the foaming waters of a stream. On the far side of the ravine rose a wall of rock down which plunged a waterfall like a shining ribbon. Suddenly Marcello stopped the car and said, "What a lovely place! . . . Let's stop for a moment."

The little girl turned round from the window and asked, "Have we arrived?"

"No," said Giulia, "we haven't arrived yet, we're going to stop for a moment," and she took her in her arms and lifted her out of the car.

When they had all got out, Giulia said she would take the opportunity of their halt to let the child fulfill the needs of nature, and Marcello stayed near the car while she took Lucilla by the hand and led her a little distance away. She walked slowly, not stooping down toward the child, who, in her little white, short dress, with a big bow on the top of her hair that hung loose on her shoulders, chattered away with her usual animation, looking up every now and then towards her mother, no doubt to ask a question. Marcello wondered what place his daughter would have in the new, free future that his sudden fit of elation had depicted, and he told himself, with a rush of affection, that he would anyhow be able to put her on her way toward a life inspired by motives entirely different from those that until now had guided his own. In his daughter's life, he felt, all must be liveliness, caprice, grace, lightness, clarity, freshness, adventure; it must all be like a landscape that knows neither mist nor sultriness but only those quick, purifying storms that clear the air and make colors look brighter. There must be nothing in it of the savage pedantry which, until the day before, had shaped his own destiny. Yes, he said to himself, she must live in the fullest freedom.

With these thoughts in his mind, he left the edge of the road and went toward the shady wood on the other side. The trees here were tall and leafy, there were briars and other bushes beneath them, and beneath them again, in the sylvan shade, grass and flowers grew on a bed of moss. Marcello put his hand through the tangle of branches and picked one of these flowers, a campanula of an almost violet blue.

It was a single campanula with white-streaked petals, and when he held it to his nose it had a bitter grassy smell. He reflected that this flower, that had grown amid the shady tangle of the undergrowth, on the thin layer of earth that clung to the infertile tufa, had not sought to imitate taller, stronger plants nor to examine its own fate for the purpose of accepting or rejecting it. In full unconsciousness and freedom, it had grown where its seed had chanced to fall, until the day when his hand had gathered it. To be like that solitary flower, on a patch of moss in the dark undergrowth—that, he thought, was a truly humble and natural fate. On the other hand, the deliberate humility of seeking an impossible relationship with a normality which was in any case fallacious was merely a mask for inverted pride and self-esteem.

He started when he heard his wife's voice saying, "Come along, let's go on," and went back to his place at the wheel. The car moved swiftly along the curving road, skirting the slope where the scattered oak trees grew, and then, after passing through a thick wood, came out through a deep cleft in the hillside at a point where there was a view over an immense plain. The distant horizon, with its rim of blue mountains, was indistinct in the July sultriness. In the golden light, through the faint haze, Marcello could see, in the middle of the plain, a solitary, precipitous crag, and on its top, like an acropolis, a little town consisting of a few houses clustering beneath the towers and walls of a castle. He could see distinctly the gray sides of the houses hanging sheer above the road that ran round the walls and continued, spirally, round and down the mountain; the castle was square in shape, with a squat, cylindrical tower at one side; the town was rose pink in color, and the blazing sunlight struck murderous sparks from the windows. At the foot of the crag the road ran in a white line, dead straight, towards the farthest limits of the plain; and opposite, on the farther side of the road, lay the wide, level, yellowish-green expanse of an airfield. In contrast with the ancient houses in the town, everything about the airfield looked new and modern—the three long hangers camouflaged in green and blue and brown, the mast at the top of which fluttered a red and white pennant, the numbers of silvery aircraft placed as though at random round the edges of the field.

Marcello looked carefully at this landscape as the car, twisting and turning down the steep road, descended rapidly toward the plain. The contrast between the ancient crag and the utterly modern airfield seemed to him significant, but his mind was suddenly distracted and he did not succeed in defining where, precisely, the significance lay. For at the same

moment he became conscious of a strange feeling of familiarity, as though he had seen this landscape before. And yet
he recollected that this was the first time he had ever traveled
by that road.

They reached the bottom of the hill and started along the
straight road that appeared so interminable. Marcello accelerated, and the pointer of the speedometer rose gradually
to forty-five, then to fifty miles an hour. The road now ran
between two wide expanses of mown fields, of a metallic
yellow color and without a tree or a house. Evidently, thought
Marcello, the local people all lived in the town and came
down in the morning to work in the fields. In the evening
they went back into the town again. . . .

His attention was drawn away from these reflections by
his wife's voice. "Look," she said, pointing to the airfield.
"What's happening?"

Marcello looked and saw a number of people running over
the great flat field, waving their arms. At the same time, looking all the more strange in the dazzling light of the summer
sun, a tongue of flame—red, pointed, almost smokeless—
blazed from the roof of one of the three hangers. Then another
flame darted from the second roof and yet another from the
third. Now the three flames seemed to be united in one single
flame that moved violently, while clouds of black smoke
rolled downward to the ground, hiding the hangers, spreading
everywhere. All sign of life had meanwhile vanished and the
airfield looked utterly deserted.

Marcello said calmly, "An air raid."

"Is there any danger?"

"No, they must have gone past already."

He accelerated, and the speedometer rose to sixty, to
seventy-five miles an hour. They were right below the town
now, and could see the road running round the walls, the
sides of the house, the castle. At the same moment, Marcello heard behind him the clamorous, furious roar of an airplane coming down low. In the midst of the noise he could
distinguish the hail-like patter of machine-gun fire, and he
realized that the plane was behind him and would soon be
over him. He could tell from the sound of its engine
that it  was  following the    line  of  the  road,  straight
and inflexible as the road itself. Soon the metallic roar was
right overhead, deafening, just for one moment; and then it
was further away again. He felt a violent blow on his shoulder, like a blow from a fist, and then a deathly languor came
over him. He managed, desperately to summon all his
strength and to steer the car to the side of the road and stop

there. "Let's get out," he said faintly, putting his hand to the door and opening it.

The door flew open and Marcello fell out; then, his face and hands in the grass at the side of the road, he dragged his legs free of the car and lay on the ground near the ditch. But no one spoke, and no one appeared at the still open door of the car. At that moment, from far away, the roar of the airplane as it turned became loudly audible again. He said to himself, "Oh God, let them not be hit . . . they are innocent," and then he waited, resigned, face downward in the grass, for the plane to come back. The car, with its open door, was silent, and he had time to realize, with a sharp pang of pain, that no one would now get out of it. Then at last the plane was right above him; and it drew after it, as it receded into the burning sky, a curtain of silence and darkness.

# The Fancy Dress Party

>>>->>>->>>->>>->>>->>>->>>->>>->>>->>>->>>->>>->>>->>>->>>->>> *Party*

>>>->>>->>>->>>->>>->>>->>>->>>->>>->>>->>>->>>->>>->>>->>>->>>->>>->>>

## CHAPTER 1

The fortunes of a certain country on the other side of the ocean, whose population had been decimated, ruined and exhausted by almost ten years of violent civil war, were finally entrusted to the guiding hand of General Tereso Arango.

Tereso, a cautious man as well as a brave one, was the survivor and conqueror of half a dozen generals who, at the head of their various armies, had competed for power during those ten long years of internal strife. His tastes were simple, soldierly, not to say crude. The brilliant society of his capital could scarcely claim to have come into contact with him at all except on occasions of patriotic celebration or military review. Not for Tereso were the *salons* and receptions of the aristocracy; he preferred an intimate dinner with his old companions-in-arms, a cockfight, a bullfight, a popular theater—or even some good history book, or the facile music of a small orchestra of guitars.

In this simplicity and waywardness may be found the explanation why Tereso, for many years, had firmly declined the invitations of the Duchess Gorina, who was by far the most illustrious, the richest, the most hospitable lady of title in the whole country. But the Duchess had sworn to herself that she would overcome Tereso's misanthropy; and so, seeing that fawning and flattery had no effect, she determined to find out the General's vulnerable point. With all his valor Tereso, she argued, was but a man, and therefore must surely have one. The Duchess, under an appearance of the proudest, stiffest reserve, concealed a slyness of character that was good-natured as well as penetrating. It did not take her long to discover that Tereso, so courageous in war, could be disarmed by a single look from a woman who attracted him; and that, in particular, he was at this moment enamored of a certain Fausta Sanchez, a very young widow and one of the loveliest ladies in high society. The Duchess invited Fausta to her house and shut herself up for a couple of hours with her in her own private sitting room. The result of this conversation was that a few days later, at a diplomatic reception, Tereso found himself once again invited to the Duchess's house.

Tereso hated the Duchess, whom he regarded as the incarnation of all the pride, ignorance, corruption and vanity of the country's ancient nobility. And so he gave his customary reply: that he was sorry, but affairs of State absolutely prevented him from taking part in entertainments of the kind she suggested. The Duchess, stiff and unmoved, remarked casually that his refusal would certainly be a great disappointment to the Countess Sanchez, who had much hoped to see him at the party.

At the mention of this name, Tereso, who for months had been in vain pursuit of Fausta, felt his heart begin to pound, notwithstanding his age and experience, in a youthful fashion. "Who told you," he asked imprudently, "that my presence would please her?"

"Who would *not* be pleased at Your Excellency's presence?" replied the Duchess, with an air not so much of flattering him as of teaching him a lesson.

Tereso bit his lip and retorted drily that, if Fausta was so desirous of seeing him, she had only to come to the palace during audience hours and she would be immediately received. The Duchess replied that, though it was true that Fausta had lost her husband, she still had a brother; and how could Tereso imagine that this brother would allow his sister to cross a threshold that had already proved fatal to the reputations of so many women? Tereso's success with women, she said, was too well known for Fausta's brother to take such a risk. "I understand," thought Tereso, "Fausta's price, in the first place, is my presence at the party." So he told the Duchess that he accepted her invitation, and would come to the ball. It so happened, he added, that he had to go to Antigua (a small town not far from the villa where the Duchess's party was to be given) and would take the opportunity to run out and visit her. In saying this he thought to deceive the Duchess as to the real motives which led him to accept her invitation. But the Duchess meanwhile was saying to herself that at last the fish was hooked.

Actually Fausta, with her brother's agreement, had already made up her mind to become Tereso's mistress. She knew, however, that men—especially men in positions of power —reckon the value of things they ardently desire in exact accordance with the difficulty they experience in obtaining them. To consent to a meeting with Tereso at the palace, or in some hunting lodge, would mean cheapening their relationship from the very beginning, and making it extremely brief and exactly like all the other relationships that had preceded it. Fausta had been quite ready to take counsel with the Duchess, and the latter had advised her to wait until the party she gave each year at her country villa. During the course of the party, and after a great deal of fuss, Fausta would give Tereso to understand that she was not entirely indifferent to him. After that the two women would play their cards in such a way as to keep Tereso perpetually in suspense and perpetually unsatisfied; and so would get as much out of him as they possibly could.

The party was thus becoming a network of self-interest. The Duchess, in persuading the General to come to her house, was at last satisfying her longstanding and hitherto unfulfilled ambition as a hostess. Fausta would be enabled to cast her net. Her brother, Manuele, hoped to obtain from the General certain favors which so far had always been resolutely refused him. Tereso counted on achieving, at last, the conquest of Fausta. And at the last moment there was added to all these intrigues yet another one, more complicated than any of them, on the part of the Chief of Police, Osvaldo Cinco.

The Chief of Police was a small, hunchbacked man, with a hunchback's characteristically large, sickly sweet face, and was celebrated throughout the land for his stud of pedigree bulls and for his cream-colored silk shirt cuffs that stuck out, dingy and crumpled, several inches over his long hairy hands, and which he was continually pushing back. For some years he had been observing with consternation that his influence with Tereso was visibly diminishing. He had been very useful to Tereso in the first period of his rule, when it had been necessary, for the peace of the country, to alternate mildness with stronger measures. But with the years Tereso's popularity had become firmly established; and the General had had less and less recourse to Cinco's methods, which were, to tell the truth, of a rather shady kind. Quietly, and one by one, Tereso had replaced all the former delegates of his authority. His government was tending to become more and more benignant and fatherly; as times changed the old, violent companions of his early struggles were no longer needed. He had not yet got rid of the Chief of Police, merely because he realized that all hatred for his government—if indeed there was any left—fell upon the head of Cinco, while he himself remained immune. Now, however, Tereso, beloved by all, no longer required even this kind of lightning conductor. He was thinking of replacing Cinco by some new man, some ordinary bureaucrat, a reliable underling with an unsullied record and clean hands. This intention on the part of Tereso showed itself in an ever increasing coldness toward Cinco. And Cinco, who regarded the control of the national police as his own personal life work and foresaw that he would soon be compelled to hand it over to one of his subalterns, was miserable.

He realized that the main causes of his impending removal from the post of Chief of Police were the tranquility of the country and the unparalleled popularity which Tereso now enjoyed. He discovered that Tereso was going to the Duchess's party; and he suddenly had the idea that if, during the party, he could succeed in staging a faked attempt on the General's life the latter would be frightened and would postpone his dismissal. Cinco did not fail to see that it was a dangerous game and that by it he might lose not only his job but his life. But he was a gambler, and he knew that the most hazardous throw is often the most successful. He obtained an audience with Tereso and, without fuss or preamble, told him plainly it had come to his knowledge that an attempt on his life had been planned to take place during the Duchess's party.

"This is a very serious matter," concluded Cinco. "We are up against people who are desperate and ready for anything. I advise Your Excellency to make an excuse and not go to the party. . . . It is true that in that way we should not be able to lay hands on the conspirators—but at any rate all danger would be avoided."

These words were designed to provoke Tereso's courage and vanity and to make him decide, without more ado, upon a course of action exactly contrary to that which the cunning Chief of Police recommended. Fausta and a love intrigue were mixed up in this affair; and Tereso, entirely indifferent to danger, was afraid that his plan of seduction might be frustrated.

"You tell me you have the names of all the conspirators," he said sharply. "Well—arrest them . . . and don't let me hear any more about it."

"But how can I do that, Excellency?" said the other, pushing back over his wrists the silk cuffs which, even at that early hour, were all crumpled. "We must have proof—even a minimum of proof. Otherwise we shall find ourselves arresting, not conspirators, but peaceful citizens."

This conversation took place in the "Hall of Battles," so called because Tereso had had pictures of the most important of the encounters in which he had taken part painted on the walls. Tereso rose from his desk and began to walk up and down the great room.

"This is the result of your much-vaunted system," he grumbled. "An attempt on my life. . . . Just because for once I come out of my lair they make plans to kill me. It's all your fault and the fault of your cursed police, who don't know their job. But I'll get rid of you. I'll smash you. . . . I'll be done with the whole pack of you."

Cinco, not in the least frightened, smiled. He knew by experience that these outbursts meant nothing at all. It was in fact Tereso's habit to cover up moments of doubt and reflection by means of such tantrums; and when conscious of insecurity he would exaggerate his air of self-assurance and aggressiveness. At this moment Tereso was thinking of Fausta and wondering what he should do. Cinco, he admitted, was right: the conspirators must be caught in the act. On the other hand, there was the danger that his own little adventure might, in all the confusion of the discovery and the arrests, be completely thwarted. Women were so fickle; their ideas and feelings were so easily affected. Tereso, clearly, was laboring under several illusions about Fausta, and he did not realize that her feelings would certainly not be changed in any way by the discovery of the plot. At last he inquired sharply whether Cinco felt certain of being able to carry out his operation without in any way disturbing the party. Cinco readily guaranteed that he could do this and that no one would notice anything. After one or two more outbursts of ill humor, Tereso began to think that if things really went as Cinco promised—and, in view of Cinco's proved ability, there was no reason to doubt it—the plot, instead of spoiling his adventure, might give it a certain piquancy.

Women, reflected Tereso, love brave men. To Fausta he would appear, not merely as the head of the government, but also as a man whose life had been in danger and who, notwithstanding this danger, had had the courage to think only of love. It must be mentioned at this point that Tereso really was a brave man; and that nine out of ten men in his situation would have listened to Cinco's hypocritical advice and given up both the party and the adventure. But Tereso happened to be in that special state of mind, at the same time passionate and melancholy, that afflicts old men who are in love; to them death itself, far from being an impediment to their passion, seems almost to be a stimulus to it. He was reflecting that even if the plot were successful he could not come to a nobler end—at the height of his glory and power, weltering in his own blood in the arms of the woman he loved. Tereso felt in his heart the passion of greatness; and this passion, which had raised him from the lowest rank to the heights of supreme power, gave him an immeasurable superiority over his ministers and the whole of his entourage.

It was decided, therefore, that Tereso should go to the party as he had intended, and that Cinco, on that same occasion, should exercise all his virtuosity as a policeman, making a clean sweep both of plot and plotters without anything being noticed. Tereso, reassured, dismissed Cinco. The latter went off to prepare his *coup de main,* for only a few days now remained before the party.

## CHAPTER 2

Among his many collaborators there was one whom Cinco trusted absolutely—a man called Perro, who was at once the subtlest and the strangest character of all his numerous *agents provocateurs.* Perro, in reality, had less of the spy in his composition than of the kind of actor who, as occasion demands, can turn himself into a perfect incarnation of many quite dissimilar roles. Above normal height, with a strong, well-proportioned figure, he had a face like a mask of colored wax, a mask with an absolute regularity of feature, without the slightest defect. His high, narrow forehead, his well-shaped eyes, wide open and with an ironical fixed gaze like the eyes of ancient statues that have stones for pupils, his long sagacious nose, his wide mouth that turned up at the corners, always smiling and ceremonious beneath a neat mustache—all these were reminiscent of the face of some actor who, even off the stage, retains an unreal, fixed, dazed look, as though its owner were possessed by a spirit. Perro's face wore the expression of easy, alert detachment of the man who is acting a part, the dazzled look of an actor at the front of the stage who sees nothing but a black chasm beyond the row of lights that illuminate him.

It was as a result of this unrecognized theatrical vocation that Perro took to playing the spy. Another man in his place would have tried, with no less success, to charm the stalls. Actors also love applause; Perro, on the contrary, had a passion for mystery, concealment, secrecy. Apart from his taste for disguise, he had an innate love of intrigue, deceit and stratagem. With his ability to make men speak from the depths of their most secret and dangerous passions, he felt himself to be more truly powerful than Tereso, who made them march in columns of fours, rifle on shoulder. Perro was conscious of exercising a creative power over those whom he deceived; he was the showman of a complicated farce acted by puppets. To him the consequences of his ceaseless treachery, whether the prison cell or the firing squad, were not of great importance. He felt justified by his sense of duty; yet even without this justification he would have acted in the same way. He was, however, ambitious, and aspired to occupy, some day, the position now filled by Cinco. He considered that, given certain circumstances, it was not the ministers but the police who ruled. He aspired to the post of Chief of Police so that he might become a sort of indispensable Gray Eminence to a Tereso grown old and tired, so that he might transform the whole country into a theater of intrigue, the scene of a positive orgy of duplicity. It was only this ambition that prevented him from playing a double game with Cinco too, by acting as his spy and at the same time giving his services to some secret political organization. But in any case political parties, whether secret or not, had for some time now entirely vanished from the country.

Cinco therefore summoned Perro and explained what he wanted. What was required was to unearth some deluded idiot, some madman or simpleton, and force him to make the attempt, providing him with all that was necessary in the way of arms and accomplices, of place and opportunity. Discovered in the nick of time, the plot would procure honors, promotion and rewards for Cinco and for all the others who took part in it—except, of course, for the one man who really believed in it. Cinco did not tell Perro of his own reasons for this piece of trickery—not from shame, but because he knew there was no need of it, since Perro, from the first word, at once understood what it was all about.

Having listened to Cinco's exposition, Perro said that he could lay his hand on exactly the right man—a kind of madman, in fact, whom he had been, so to speak, keeping warm for several years for just this kind of affair. Let Cinco, he said, leave it to him, and everything would go perfectly. Cinco asked him to explain his idea. Perro calmly and complacently expounded his plan of action with the precision of an instructor dismantling a machine piece by piece in order to demonstrate it to his pupils. Cinco, who loved this mathematical lucidity of Perro's, was entirely convinced. Without any further instructions he dismissed him, making an appointment to meet him in three days at the Duchess's party.

So Perro left for Antigua. For a day and a night, dressed as an unemployed manservant, in black trousers, a light jacket and a stiff shirt, he sat in a third-class carriage, behaving in a ceremonious, obliging, gentlemanly manner suitable to the part he was playing. His traveling companions, peasants and working people for the most part, were fully convinced, after much conversation and explanation, that they were talking to a nice young footman who was going into the service of the famous Duchess Gorina. Perro, acting the simpleton, went so far as to ask for a description of the Duchess's villa from one of them who had worked there as a gardener.

"From what I understand," said Perro when the man had completed his catalogue of the splendors of the Duchess's estate, "it's just the place for me. I've always wanted to get a job in one of these grand houses. There's less work and you make more money."

"And besides," observed another man, a prosperous farmer, "we all know that you fellows don't waste your time in places of that sort . . . you get a little bit here, and a little bit there," and winking one eye in his broad, fat face, he made a gesture as of someone stealing things.

Perro, offended, protested that he was an honest man; if they did not believe him he could show them references from half a dozen places where he had been employed, among them one from the Countess of Villahermosa, who had been particularly pleased with him. A discussion followed, in which other passengers took part; and the farmer had finally to admit, in the face of Perro's lively indignation, that he had spoken in general, without reference to present company. Perro might easily have spared himself this complication of hypocrisy, just as there was no real necessity for him to travel third class. But he did not care to do things by halves; besides, it pleased him to mix with working-class people in order to gauge their humors and opinions.

He arrived at Antigua toward sunset; and after helping an old peasant woman lift down her bundles and baskets, he crammed a cyclist's cap of rough cloth on to his head, grasped his ugly fiber suitcase and walked out of the station. Antigua, once a wealthy and populous town supported by its neighboring silver mines, is now no longer of any importance. But from its past there survive some hundred churches and smaller chapels, scattered throughout the maze of its narrow streets among hovels and baroque palaces. Coming out of the station, Perro boarded a small dilapidated streetcar full of workmen and peasants and went on it as far as the main square. He knew that around this square—a large rectangle surrounded by gigantic plane trees—were all the new, pretentious public buildings of the town: the governor's palace, the municipal offices, the bank, the principal hotel, the two cafés where politics were discussed. Outside the square there was nothing but narrow streets, darkness, empty churches, hovels and squalor.

Negligently carrying his big suitcase, he started to stroll round the square; and it did not take him long to find out, from listening here and there to the groups of people walking under the plane trees or sitting on the benches, that the sole subject of conversation in the square, and therefore in the town, was the forthcoming visit of Tereso and the Duchess's party. But, while preparations for the General's arrival were limited to the usual proclamations stuck on the walls, the usual illuminations, the usual triumphal arches of flowers, the Duchess seemed to have turned the whole place upside down. From what Perro gathered, she had reserved the whole of the two largest hotels in Antigua so as to place their old-fashioned, smelly, provincial rooms at the disposal of her too numerous guests. For days past tailors had been working for her on fancy dresses, provision dealers and caterers had been busy assembling the vast amount of supplies she required, nursery gardeners and building contractors had been making preparations for the illumination of the park and the decorations. Tereso, in comparison, gave them far less trouble and the purely military design of the ceremony of welcome that the town was preparing for him had not even the charms of novelty.

In the square itself, parked around the equestrian monument of Simon Bolivar, Perro saw at least twenty enormous, luxurious motorcars. Idlers and street urchins were loitering around them, commenting on the strange shapes of their hoods and the richness of their shining metal bodies. Pursuing his researches, he went on to the two cafés; and here, too, while he casually sipped a foul drink made of synthetic alcohol, the only subject of conversation he heard was the Duchess Gorina's party. People were talking of not merely hundreds, but thousands, of guests, of fancy dresses and of orchestras, of cooks and of food. But he noticed that their remarks were more admiring than ill-natured—a sure sign, he said to himself, that there was not too great a degree of poverty among the populace and that this extraordinary outburst of extravagance was not therefore resented as an act of defiance. After resting for a little on a seat occupied by three or four old men who were discussing the probable prices of the Duchess's guests' motorcars, he went into each of the two hotels to ascertain from porters beaming with satisfaction that all the rooms were taken; he then went off toward the lower part of the square, where a street less winding and narrow than the others led out of it—the Alameda Dos de Mayo.

Near the beginning of this street was a smart confectioner's shop at which he wanted also to take a look; it was the only one in the town, and its windows were overflowing with pastries and sweets. Flattening his nose against the glass, he could see that the shop was full of odd people, dressed in clothes that were, at any rate in those parts, unusual—the men in short, full breeches and leather jackets, with colored scarves around their necks, yellow cowhide riding boots, and wide-brimmed hats; the women in leather trousers, checked shirts, high boots and big felt hats. These were so-called "ranchers' " costumes—though there was nothing in the whole province in the way of a ranch; and in this small ecclesiastical town, in this very urban confectioner's shop, they looked more like an anticipation of the Duchess's fancy dress ball than like people in everyday clothes. The Duchess's guests (for it was indeed they) filled the little tables inside the shop and sat in a tight row round the zinc bar, raising their glasses and jokingly imitating the uncouth, exaggerated gestures of cowboys. It was like peeping into an opera house during a dress rehearsal.

After gazing attentively at this curious scene, Perro went on down the Alameda. He went down its whole length, pausing every now and then in front of shop windows, till he came out into a deserted, grass-grown square over which a church dedicated to the Madonna de Los Remedios raised its dark and crumbling façade. He immediately noticed —though twilight had fallen—a figure dressed in a faded suit of a color somewhere between lilac and brown, with a very light, almost milk-white, hat on its head, black pointed shoes whose shape was distorted by large bunions on the feet inside them, and an umbrella, notwithstanding the fine weather, hooked over its arm. Perro went straight to this man and put a hand on his shoulder. The other turned toward him a brown, sharp-featured face with a long, pointed, shiny nose.

"Inspector!" said Perro fiercely, "what on earth are you doing here in this square with an umbrella in this fine weather? Is it to protect you from the swallows?"

"Excuse me," said the detective, "but when I came out I thought it was going to rain."

"Also," continued Perro, "do you allow yourself to be held up like that by anybody who shouts 'Inspector!' at you? What if I had been leading you on?"

"I had already recognized you," said the other with an awkward laugh.

Perro administered a few more reprimands, asked the man whether he had noticed anything ususual, and when informed that the town was as quiet as it could possibly be, left him to his duty.

## CHAPTER 3

With the assurance of one who knows the place well, Perro turned left out of the square through a network of winding lanes. Night had fallen, and in these narrow streets only an occasional lamp post illuminated faintly the huge solemn gates of palaces and the little doors of hovels, the flights of steps, the alleys, the iron bars over windows, the cross roads. Every now and then some irregular square opened out around the high, dark façade of a church. Relying on the darkness to reach his destination unobserved, Perro finally entered the hall of a large, handsome building. After ascending two flights of a dignified but dirty staircase, he went through some swinging doors lined with green baize and came to a series of small rooms used as offices. He went straight to a room at the end of a corridor, where a light shone through glass doors, and entered it unhesitatingly and without knocking, finding himself immediately in front of a desk in an office filled with shelves and files. A newspaper was spread out on the desk, and above the open sheets glistened the bald rotundity of a bent head. At the sound of the door closing the head raised itself, showing the bespectacled face, spotted with large, pale warts, of the local police commissioner. The moment he saw Perro he rose to greet him, reluctantly, and with an expression of obvious irritation.

Perro carefully closed the door, put down his suitcase in a corner and, seating himself without ceremony in front of the commissioner, started asking him a series of questions in a sharp, peremptory voice. It was quite clear that the commissioner did not care for Perro's tone. He was an old-fashioned sort of man who liked his comforts and was faithful to police methods Perro considered antiquated; and Perro, of whom he had heard much, seemed to him not merely an innovator but downright destructive. Another reason for his antipathy was that Perro, though so much younger, had already risen so high that he was in a position to order him about. Perro's career might be said to be just beginning, while he, after thirty years of service, saw himself approaching the time when he would be dismissed with a pension. Perro did not give him a moment's respite from questioning; and the commissioner, chafing with rage, tried to hide his ill-humor behind clouds of smoke from a half-finished cigar gripped between his teeth. He answered slowly and unwillingly, sometimes even with an evasive sarcasm that he vainly imagined might pass unobserved. Perro, however, was immediately aware of this hostility, of this attitude that seemed to say: "We got on so well here without you; what have you come for?"—and he decided at the first favorable opportunity to teach the man a lesson.

After informing himself exactly of the measures taken by the local police for the protection of Tereso on his arrival, Perro asked the commissioner to show him the list of people who had been placed under precautionary arrest. The commissioner, without getting up, stretched out a short arm among the files on the desk and, puffing smoke from his cigar, proffered a sheet of paper containing the list. Perro examined it eagerly, knowing that he would find in it the pretext he was looking for. He did in fact discover the name of a person who, in his opinion, should not have been arrested; and he immediately began to abuse the commissioner unmercifully. At first his tone of voice remained level, though it was more intense than before; then, seeing that the commissioner was unmoved and answered phlegmatically and with indifference, he suddenly raised his voice and started shouting, relentlessly, that everything was going wrong, that everyone was asleep in this town, that it was high time to finish with these antiquated methods—and so on.

This time the commissioner turned pale, put his cigar on the edge of the ash tray and took off his glasses, showing two deep-set eyes, black and dim like those of a blinded bird. But Perro, who wanted to see him really terrified, did not let him speak, and began to walk up and down the room, shouting that it was a disgrace, that he would send a report to headquarters, that he would have him sacked and the whole of his staff with him. The commissioner was now really frightened, as Perro had intended; and, rising from his seat as hurriedly as his stout body would permit, he started running up and down behind the enraged Perro, trying to justify himself and at the same time to admit that his tormentor was right—a difficult task because the two views were mutually exclusive. Finally, in desperation, not knowing what to do to calm Perro's transports of anger (by which he was quite taken in), he declared that he would go himself and give orders for the release of the individual in question; and he left the room.

The moment he had gone Perro, as though by enchantment, became perfectly calm and, sitting on the edge of the desk, began to read the newspaper. In a short time the commissioner came in again, creeping forward now in a most respectful manner. The poor man did not dare sit down, but took care to assure Perro that the prisoner would be released at once.

"If I did wrong," he said finally, easing his sweat-soaked collar with two fingers, "it was because I was overzealous."

But Perro would not make any acknowledgment of this, though he craved it so humbly; he merely asked him, angrily, for the list of the Duchess's guests. With a servile haste very different from the unconcern with which he had shortly before handed him the list of arrests, the commissioner ran to a bookshelf, pulled out some sheets of paper, and placed them right under the nose of Perro, who, in the meantime, had usurped his own chair behind the desk.

Standing beside him, the commissioner pointed to the first line. "If you like, we can go through it together," he proposed.

But Perro replied rudely that he preferred to do his work without help and to be left alone. The commissioner, afraid that he would pry into his papers and find the pretext for another scene, then suggested that he might prefer to go to the reception room, which was so much more spacious and clean, and where, also, he would be in no danger of being disturbed. But Perro, still in a rude tone, replied that the room suited him perfectly; the commissioner could go himself, if he liked, to the reception room. The latter, with a sigh, started toward the door, requesting, however, that Perro call him whenever he needed him. Perro, already absorbed in the papers, pretended not to hear; but, just as the wretched man was going out on tiptoe, he called him back and told him to have a complete dinner sent up from some nearby restaurant. It pleased him to inflict this final humiliation on the commissioner by treating him just as if he were a waiter. The commissioner hastily promised that the meal should be sent up at once.

Left alone, Perro worked for about two hours, comparing the list of the Duchess's guests with the list made by the Central Police, which had notes written beside each name, some long, some short, concerning the type, character, history and importance of the person in question. Perro, who was entirely devoted to his profession as a police spy, had no social ambitions or jealousies and was completely lacking in that vindictive, carping spirit particularly characteristic of people who, for some professional reason, are mixed up in the affairs of a class higher than their own. But, with all his impassiveness, he could not help raising his eyebrows when he saw the type of person that was to be found among the Duchess's guests. There was a sample of everything: secret vice, illicit passion, dishonesty, violence, crime, suppressed scandal, obscure abnormality, intrigue, treachery, corruptness, venality. These were the people dressed as cowboys, the sleek, well-fed men, the beautiful women, that he had seen through the window of the confectioner's shop; but here each was reduced to a mere brief summing-up, a mere name in a plain list of delinquents. There was no lack, it is true, of normal or simply insignificant people; they were indeed in the majority. But the vicious minority seemed to infect the rest, its moral defects being more conspicuous than the lack of character of the others and coloring the whole mass with a sinister hue. So true is it that one rotten apple spoils a whole basketful.

Except for that raising of the eyebrows, however, Perro skimmed quickly over the names; these people were too effete to be a serious nuisance. His interest was more particularly concentrated on certain people, of varying importance, who in the past had displayed some political activity or who had recently been in trouble. But it did not appear to him that even these could be called dangerous. Most of them were people who for one reason or another, either because they were compromised in some way or because of that last and final compromise, advancing age—were no longer in a position to do anything.

Perro worked without smoking, without even sipping the water that the commissioner had placed in a carafe in front of him. Occasionally, coming upon a name that seemed familiar, he would raise his head and, gazing at the ceiling, search his memory for a face grown pale and dim. When he was halfway through his work the commissioner entered, followed by a waiter carrying a tray of food. The commissioner himself lifted the covers to show Perro the dishes; he hoped to be praised at any rate for his zeal as a flunkey. But Perro did not even raise his head from the papers, merely saying that he was all right, and would they put the tray on the desk? Working continuously, he slowly ate his dinner. Then, finishing simultaneously his meal and his business, he called the commissioner and gave him back his files. The commissioner was still hoping for one look, one word, if not of praise, at least of sympathy. But Perro, pulling down his cap on his head and picking up his suitcase, advised him not to make any more mistakes of the kind that he had been obliged to rectify.

"May I hope that His Excellency Cinco will know how I—?" began the commissioner. But he paused, astonished, staring at the empty doorway. Perro had vanished.

## CHAPTER 4

So far Perro had struck only a few preliminary chords on that instrument of falsehood of which he was so consummate a master. But now, his footstep light, his mind filled with the joy of adventure, he prepared to embark upon his principal theme. Quite apart from his profession he derived a truly profound pleasure from deceiving his neighbor. He himself could not have explained the reasons for this quite genuine satisfaction. Perhaps it came from a delight in power, increased and multiplied by virtue of the deceit he practiced; perhaps from a feeling that his duplicity gave him the advantage of being able to keep a watch, as though through the crack of a door, over throbbing human lives unaware of his presence.

The intrigue on which he was now embarking was of a type after his own heart. He took a particular delight in assuming a nobility of sentiment and manner. In such cases his hypocrisy acquired a refinement of cruelty, developing a style brilliant, lucid, and sharp as a razor. The counterpoint of word and deed was dominated by an urgent, regular rhythm that intoxicated him until his acting took on a positively lyrical quality. Apart from his own job Perro really believed in nothing but the most elementary material necessities. Everything else seemed to him mere froth and fog and wind. In contrast to those whom he called idealists he found himself in the detached, superior state of mind of a professor explaining to his pupils that lightning is not an expression of heavenly anger but simply electrical energy released by storms. Perro would have sold Jesus Christ, not for money nor from malice, but just to show Him that He was wrong to speak as He did.

When he came out of the police station Perro walked straight on, carrying his suitcase and wearing his cap pulled down over his eyes, in the manner of an out-of-work footman. After making his way through several narrow streets he came out at last under the town walls. He followed the wall for some distance till he came to the gate he was making for, and then, passing through it, found himself in a great bare space interspersed with holes and scattered mounds of rubble—more like a piece of waste ground than a public square. This space was plunged in darkness, but at its further edge glittered the irregular lights of a shabby fair ground. People were walking in the open space in the dark, and beyond, around the lighted booths, one could see little groups of idlers. The noise of shots rang out from the shooting

274

galleries, and there were sounds of laughter and whistling. A flagstaff stood in the middle of the open space with some sort of flag hanging from it, flapping heavily in the occasional gusts of wind.

Perro had an appointment in this open space—immediately under the flagstaff, in fact. But he knew the person he was looking for only too well and, noticing a brawl near one of the fair booths, went off in that direction, certain that he would find his man in the middle of it.

The booth in question was the shooting gallery, a kind of box hung in red material, with two acetylene flares giving a brilliant white light. Inside it a sad-looking, black-haired girl, dressed in mourning, stood beside a counter against a background of targets punctured with holes, and bottles of fizzy drinks. She was reloading the rifles, bending back their steel barrels as she did so with a thin white arm that looked too feeble for the job. She did it all without ever speaking a word. An underfed little urchin, with big bright eyes and a twisted, pinched mouth, handed her the cartridges.

The brawl, however, had been caused by four or five youths who wore trousers clipped at the ankles and cycling shirts. They had formed a ring around a squat, misshapen individual and, with many gibes, were bouncing him backward and forward between them like a ball. The man who was providing all this fun had a large head with curly hair like wool. He wore the very strong glasses of extreme short sight, and had a crooked, curving nose—like some kind of fish—in the middle of a broad, pale face covered with freckles. His big, shapeless mouth, with its entire lack of expression, reminded one of the mouth of a deaf mute. He wore a black jacket with silk facings—like a notary—but his trousers were light colored and tightly stretched over an enormous behind which stuck out clumsily below the austere jacket and forced up the hem.

The boys were pushing and tossing him about, with gibes and taunts that seemed lacking in novelty both for the man who was their butt and for the jesters themselves. It was evidently a time-honored custom to surround and torment him in this way whenever he appeared. But, not unnaturally, the victim had never become accustomed to it. He was pulled about, pinched, shoved here and there, but he was never able to tell where the pinch or the squeeze or the push came from.

"Let me alone," he begged, struggling to get away. "Mind your own business. What harm have I done you? I was here and I didn't even look at you." The final touch of monstrosity was that the voice issuing from his spluttering mouth was shrill, feminine and stammering.

"Go away, leave him alone," suddenly exclaimed a fair-haired youth, whose cheeks were flushed with savage joy, and who seemed to be the chief of the band, "let him alone. I'll take him under my own protection. . . ." As he said this he caught the big head under his arm with the neat, dexterous movement with which a man grips a wine flask to pour it out, and with the other hand pretending to protect him, he pulled his hair.

But the "protected" man was suffocating. "Let me go," he yelled.

The other at last released his hold, and his victim, scarlet in the face, rose to his feet panting. The smallest of the group, a little thin boy with an enormous bicycle cap pulled down to his projecting ears, possibly encouraged by the passive attitude of the sufferer, took a leap and seized him by the hair, hoping, perhaps, to drag him to the ground. But the other, maddened with pain, completely lost his temper, and seizing the boy by the neck, squeezed with all the strength of his large hands. The myopic, freckled face was merciless, and the boy's companions realized that unless they rescued him he might actually be strangled. All four of them threw themselves upon the tightly clasped pair, and for a moment there was a struggling heap of bodies on the ground in front of the booth. Then, one after another, the youths got up, panting but satisfied; and finally their victim rose also. His starched collar was hanging loosely outside his black jacket which was all dirty and dusty. A trickle of blood came from one of his nostrils. He had lost his spectacles and was groping in the void.

"Blackguards!" he stammered. "Murderers! You'll see if I don't get my revenge."

To which the fair-haired youth, stepping in front of him and shaking his forefinger under his nose, replied threateningly: "You meant to hurt him, didn't you? But remember, this was only a sample. . . . Next time we'll break your arms —both of them—d'you understand?"

Perro had looked on motionless at this scene. To tell the truth, he was not sorry to see Saverio, the boys' victim, treated in this way. He felt that if he had been forced to intervene he would have liked to take the part, not of the sufferer, but of his tormentors, and to give the former a good kick in those pale, inflated pants of his. But the moment came when he felt he must make his presence known. His tall, erect figure moved resolutely from the edge of the light cast by the acetylene flares of the shooting gallery and forced its way through the group. He put down his suitcase on the counter, took a rifle from the girl's hand, raised it to his shoulder, and with speed and precision fired off a dozen shots, hitting the bull's eye every time. A cry of admiration rose from the group of boys. Saverio, in the meantime, had recognized him and, after making a very expressive face at him, found his glasses on the ground and limped away. Perro threw down a silver coin, waited for the girl to count out his change, and then with a "Keep the rest," left his admirers open-mouthed, took up his suitcase and went off across the open space.

## CHAPTER 5

Perro had not been boasting when he had declared to the Chief of Police that he could lay his hand on just the man that was needed. He had known Saverio for a couple of years and had been able during all that time to "keep him warm," as he himself expressed it, until he should be required—so that all he now had to do was to serve him up, without even putting him back on the fire, since he was cooked to a turn. To speak plainly, Perro, in the course of his professional reconnoiterings, had had the idea of creating a secret revolutionary party of the most violent type and of enrolling in it a number of discontented fanatics. By this ingenious method he served the double purpose of keeping a good many dangerous characters quiet and at the same time of placing a revolutionary party under the direct orders of the police. He had made Saverio, in common with all the others, believe that there existed in the capital a mysterious central committee from which he himself took orders as an inspector-general; and that this committee, in its turn, was in contact with another, much larger, international organization.

In this party of his Perro had enlisted only simple-minded, unrealistic people of the type of Saverio, for he knew that a professional agitator would not have found much difficulty in seeing through it. In this undertaking, besides amusing himself in his own way with his collection of simpletons and fools, Perro was also acting in obedience to an obscure apprehension that slumbered in the depth of his police-spy consciousness. Who knew whether, some day or other, a revolution might not really break out in the country? There had already been so many of them. On that day he, Perro, would throw aside his policeman's cloak and save his own skin by displaying his activity as a conspirator. Cinco was not ignorant of his acolyte's prowess in this matter; but, apart from his Chief, Perro had not confided the existence of his party to anyone. This was also because he felt that the Party was a

creation exclusively his own: if others meddled with it, its
whole charm and inspiration would vanish.

Perro caught up with Saverio beyond the open space,
on the main road. It was a night of full moon; trees
bending out over the hedges cast here and there dark, broken,
motionless shadows across the road, which was white in the
cold light. Saverio, hobbling along clumsily at Perro's side,
suddenly took hold of his arm and, in a low voice, started
abusing the youths at the shooting gallery. As he spoke
he would be caught up by his stammer, and then he would
stop and gaze fixedly at Perro for a moment through his thick
glasses while he struggled with the rebellious syllables.
Finally the word would come bursting out violently, as
though he were spitting it forth. He said that, as soon as certain things came to pass of which Perro knew, he would take
his revenge upon them, as upon all the other people in the
town who mocked at him.

"What will you do to them?" asked Perro, concealing
his amusement at this extraordinary mixture of clumsiness
and rage.

Saverio, stuttering wildly over his words, answered that
he would have them all shot as counter-revolutionaries, for
that was what they were. They were the people who formed
the idle, pleasure-loving mass upon which reactionary gov-
ernments are usually founded; people far more dangerous
than the bourgeoisie themselves, since the latter at least
minded their own business, whereas these people corrupted
the healthy, revolutionary populace among whom they lived.
Perro said that in that case he would have to shoot half
the population of the country, for half the population thought
of nothing but bullfights and cockfights, of *pelota* and wom-
en, of singing and dancing. Saverio replied that if it proved
necessary he would do so. Revolutions were forged in blood.
Perro slyly inquired whether he did not think that, when
they saw him slaughtering his personal enemies, his rivals
would accuse him of using the revolution to pay off his own
private grudges. Saverio was much struck by this observation,
for he was always very careful not to let himself be surprised
in any position that was in the least unorthodox.

"Yes," he objected, with a knowing solemnity, "but would
it not perhaps be an equally great tactical error to spare
counter-revolutionary elements like these?"

Perro replied that there is nothing worse than to give the impression of mixing private with public life. Saverio, uncertain,
was silent. Perro chuckled. This was the Saverio that he loved.

They walked at a good pace; and Saverio, his anger having
now evaporated, began to ask Perro a number of questions

about the activities of the Party. Stammering all the time and avoiding such freedom of expression as he considered dangerous, he made certain criticisms he had been meditating for a long time. He said he certainly did not wish to give the Committee the impression that he was insubordinate; in fact, as far as that went, they ought to know that nowhere in the whole country could they count upon any initiate more obedient or more zealous than himself. And yet, if he might be permitted, he would like to make one or two remarks—quite confidentially, of course—to Perro, whom he now thought of not merely as a superior, but as a friend. Besides, had it not been expressly recommended by the Committee that any member of the Party should make such criticisms as he thought most opportune—always, of course, within the limits of strict orthodoxy?

Perro admitted the truth of Saverio's remark. The latter, encouraged, began by saying that the various members of the Party were too much left to themselves. Apart from Perro's own rare visits, he himself had had no contact, either direct or indirect, with the Committee during these two first years of his militant membership. There was a risk, he added, obviously alluding to his own case, of their finding that their most valuable instruments had become rusty with idleness or uncertainty. For instance, there was much, very much, to be done among the workers and peasants in this particularly poor and oppressed province. All these people were waiting impatiently for a new call to faith and action. Why did the Party not allow a carefully prepared underground agitation? And, on the other hand, why did the Party keep him so short of its own publications? Except a small handbook (printed under the auspices of the police, thought Perro, who could not help smiling), and one or two insignificant leaflets, he had never received anything. Perhaps they had forgotten all about him far away in this remote place? Did the gentlemen of the Committee realize that in a revolution the rural masses are sometimes more valuable than the town masses? Perhaps they did not know that seventy per cent of the best propagandists are usually recruited from casual laborers, that is, from people who, thanks to their wandering life, are in a better position than anyone to develop a widespread, ramifying activity? Again, why was he not permitted to do the same thing with other people here as Perro had done with him? He was a "cell," so far, so good, but what about other cells?

Perro, who was inwardly highly amused, replied vaguely that other cells existed—perhaps more of them than he imagined—but that it was not his business to worry about them.

Saverio seemed slightly comforted by this answer, that appeared to him quite in accordance with revolutionary practice. But he insisted that it was a mistake to leave him with nothing to do, so completely idle and inactive. Perro replied gravely that the Committee would soon be making use of him. But he must first arm himself with a thorough study of theory, and for this purpose, it seemed to Perro, he had plenty of books. This time Saverio admitted that he had derived very great profit from his latest reading and in particular from the book called *The Civilization of the Future,* by the celebrated Francisco Segoviano—a splendid work, a work of purest gold, overwhelming in its dialectic, perfect in its practical logic, a work as valuable as a battle won, a work which by itself had done more to further the cause of the proletariat than the whole of the social literature of the last twenty years. Perro approved this enthusiasm, but he advised him to be on his guard against certain Utopian complacencies in Segoviano, whose greatest weakness, he must not forget, lay precisely in that dialectic which he so much admired, for he lacked the empiricism without which true revolutionary action was not possible. Saverio answered that that was true; and he did, in fact, vary his reading of Segoviano with the perusal of the manual of revolutionary tactics by the no less incomparable Henrique which was also an extremely good and valuable book and which seemed exactly suited to fill the gaps and repair the omissions of Segoviano. Segoviano, in short, might be termed the brain; Henrique the arm of the revolution.

But Saverio, in the midst of all this enthusiasm, did not forget his own personal position; and he again began asking Perro to put his case before the Committee. He prudently added, however, that he would not wish his observations, in the exact terms in which he had made them, to become known in the highest circles of the Party. They were only confidential criticisms, and he hoped that they would go no further. The Committee, on the other hand, should know that he was always at its service, now as ever, and ready for anything. Perro, with some solemnity, praised his fine discipline and told him that soon, very soon, much sooner than he expected, the Committee would be making use of him.

"Really?" stammered the other, considerably cheered, "really?"

"Yes," answered Perro.

Saverio then declared that he also had certain plans to propose to Perro. But Perro reduced him to silence by saying that it was not his business to make plans, but merely to carry out blindly the plans of the Party. He must be careful not to fall into the very grave error of an excessively bourgeois individualism. His criticisms had already been a bad sign, and they had not always been kept within the bounds of official orthodoxy. Saverio was so frightened by this warning that he at once held his tongue. They continued on their way in silence.

## CHAPTER 6

At a turn in the road, between two tall, leafy trees, a winding, stony lane became palely visible against the darkness of the earth. "This way," stammered Saverio. But at the same moment a tall, slim figure, whose face could not be distinguished in the shadow of the trees, almost ran into him.

"What are you doing, Saverio?" asked a clear voice. "Hunting glow worms?"

"I—I—I was going for a walk," answered Saverio.

"Be careful you don't let Ludra out; shut the gate properly," said the voice again, and then a soft whistling and a sound of footsteps becoming gradually fainter showed that the person was getting further away.

"Who was that?" asked Perro.

"Se—Se—Se—" Saverio began, stammering; then, circumventing the difficulty, he exploded: "My half-brother Sebastiano."

"Ah, Sebastiano," repeated Perro indifferently, turning round to look. Perro knew of the existence of this half-brother, but he had only seen him a couple of times and then from a distance. He knew that Saverio was the irregular offspring of a rich landowner called Rivas and a peasant girl of the humblest type. When Rivas died, Saverio was left in an anomalous position, somewhere between that of servant and relation. He and his half-brother lived their own lives, in the same villa, but sometimes not seeing each other for weeks at a time. Saverio lived in a kind of cabin outside; Sebastiano had a small room in the villa, the only room that had remained furnished. For Rivas, a man of extremely dissolute life, had left Sebastiano nothing but the villa—and that was mortgaged. Everything else—land, motorcars, horses, dogs, even the furniture of the house—had been gradually sold off to pay his debts. Perro had often reproved Saverio for feeling an affection unworthy of a revolutionary for this half-brother who was a gentleman and a landed proprietor—to which jocular accusations Saverio, who took them quite seriously, had replied that his father, by ruining him in this way, had made Sebastiano into a proletarian

like himself. In any case, he had added, he was entirely
lacking in class consciousness.

They had now arrived at the villa. Behind the white bars
of the gate could be seen the graceful dark shadow of a
dog jumping nimbly up and down and wagging its tail, at
every leap making a new pattern against the wrought-iron
grille. This was Ludra, and Saverio, entering first, quickly
grasped her by the collar for fear she should run after her
master. A short road between two rows of aloes led to the
house, which was white, rectangular and plain, with three
rows of green-painted windows. Against one side of it was
a low building, the cabin where Saverio lived. The latter led
his guest toward it, observing that it was the best place for
a talk. In the town, he said, they might have been overheard. And he added that for some time now he had felt himself to be continually spied upon, although, to tell the truth,
he was unable to tell precisely how and by whom. His remark made Perro smile.

The cabin had one window and a small door. When
they had entered Perro found himself in a very large room
with perfectly bare whitewashed walls. There was no furniture except a couple of chairs, a rough bed tousled and unmade, with the sheets trailing on the floor, and a small
table upon which, among a confusion of papers, was an ancient typewriter. Otherwise the room was encumbered on all
sides with books. There were rows of them on the floor
against the walls, they were piled in the corners and heaped
on the chairs. There were more books underneath the couch,
and also on the table and on a cast-iron stove that stood in
one corner of the room. One glance from Perro's expert
eye was enough to show him the nature of these books—refuse from the warehouses of old anarchist and socialist pub-
lishers, discarded rubbish from libraries of "popular culture,"
floods of propaganda leaflets, masses of publicity material on
political and social questions; books badly bound and worse
printed, with squalid, provincial-looking jackets whose
"clandestine" origin could be smelled a mile off, or with
symbolic designs on them in the fashion of thirty years
before. It formed a library which was valuable, in its own
way, for its completeness, and Perro could not help thinking
how many handcarts, attics and out-of-the-way corners Saverio must have searched in order to amass this collection of
a class of literature now immensely rare and almost all of
it forbidden.

"What a lot of books!" he could not help exclaiming as his
astonished glance swept the room.

Saverio, with affected indifference, replied that, without

wishing to boast, he could certainly claim to be the owner of an extremely rich library on the subjects that interested him. Then, carried away with the enthusiasm of the true collector, he added that he even possessed a copy of such-and-such a book which it was quite impossible to find, of such-and-such a publication that was now extremely rare. And, pulling them out from their hiding place under the bed, he showed Perro two or three anti-Tereso pamphlets which had been suppressed with particular severity. On the cover of one of them was portrayed the gigantic figure of a workman breaking his chains, while a tiny Tereso, dressed as a lion-tamer, recoiled in terror, letting his whip fall from his hand.

"If they knew I had these," concluded Saverio awkwardly, "who knows what they would do to me? But luckily everyone in this part of the country takes me for a sort of idiot."

And so you are, thought the pitiless Perro. He sat down on a low stool, put his suitcase beside him, took off his cap and stroked his thick, shining black hair. Then he started to speak in a cold, serious voice to Saverio, who for lack of a chair squatted on the bed, his head between his hands and his elbows on his knees. He began by saying that the Central Committee had kept him inactive for all that long time, first in order to test his loyalty, and second, because the moment for action had not yet come. Now, however, the members of the Committee knew that they could count upon him as one of their best and most trusted servants (here Saverio shook his head with a gesture of perfectly sincere modesty, as though to say: "Please don't mention it"), and besides, the moment for action had arrived. At these words Perro paused and gave Saverio a significant glance. The latter made a twisted grimace as if to say: "I am ready."

"No one is listening?" Perro asked, this time genuinely anxious. Saverio reassured him. Nobody, he said, could possibly be listening.

Then Perro, lowering his voice a little, said that perhaps he knew that the Duchess Gorina was giving a big fancy dress party at her villa next day. Saverio replied that of course he knew it, and added the propagandist cliché that there was great indignation among the poor at this silly, wicked outburst of luxury and frivolity.

But perhaps he didn't know, pursued Perro, that General Tereso, in person, would be present at this party? Saverio opened his eyes wide behind his glasses and made a gesture of astonishment. Yes, continued Perro, Tereso would be there, that was all arranged; and the Central Committee, considering the time to be now ripe, had decided to strike the decisive blow. For this they were relying upon him, Saverio. It was he who would have the honor of being, if not the prime mover, at any rate the instrument by which the detested regime should be finally overthrown.

These words raised Saverio into a state of exaltation that astonished even Perro, accustomed as he was to dealing with people in that state of mind. Saverio leaped to his feet and, stuttering more violently than ever, rushed to shake Perro by the hand, saying that this was the happiest day of his life, that he was absolutely ready for action and that, if necessary, he would joyfully lay down his life. At that moment all the spitefulness of the freak and the underdog, all the bookish pedantry of the propagandist, vanished; Saverio, in a trembling, ineffective manner peculiarly his own, was quite transfigured. If Perro had not been what he was, he might well have been moved—not, perhaps, at the excellence of the ideas with which Saverio was infatuated, but at his sincere and vigorous offering of his own life for the cause in which he believed. But Perro was anxious to get his business concluded, and these outbursts on Saverio's part appeared to him in excess of what was required. There was no need for all this embarrassing enthusiasm; the usual blind credulity was quite enough. He therefore received Saverio's display of emotion in a condescending manner and, after asking whether he was prepared to listen and receiving a stammering affirmative reply, went on with his explanation.

Briefly, the position was this. They would both present themselves on the following day at the Duchess's villa, and would dress themselves in her footmen's livery. He already had an understanding with the Duchess's butler, who was himself affiliated with the Party. They would thus find themselves in the midst of the entertainment and would be able to do what they wanted in regard to the General. But prudence would be necessary, for it was just in cases like this, when everything seemed to go easily, that one slip might upset the most perfectly arranged plans. He had brought with him, in his suitcase, a time-bomb. He would hand over this bomb to Saverio, as being the most energetic and resolute among them. Saverio, under the pretense of bringing in a tray of food, would enter Tereso's rooms and hide the bomb in the bathroom. The bomb was an extremely powerful one and the General had little hope of escape. It would destroy not only Tereso's rooms but the whole, or nearly the whole, of the villa. It had been set to explode half an hour after it was placed in position. They would thus have time to make their escape; reaching the station, they would take the first train to the capital, where in the meantime their friends of the Committee would have started a rising. Everything was therefore organized to perfection. So much so that he, Saverio, who was now sitting there in front of him, would find himself, before three days were past, a member of the new government the revolution would place in power.

Perro expected that when confronted with this extraordinary proposal Saverio would be frightened, or would at least show some hesitation. But here he was wrong. Saverio again jumped to his feet, saying that he was quite ready; then, deeply moved, he asked Perro if he might embrace him. What was going to happen, he said, was of so great an importance that their pact must be sealed with a brotherly kiss. And so Perro, though filled with repugnance at this unexpected consequence of his treachery, was forced to rise to his feet and allow himself to be kissed by Saverio, and even to return his embraces. This embrace between himself and his victim might perhaps, at another moment, have amused him; but now, after two days of traveling and nervous strain, he was extremely sleepy and simply wanted to go to bed. Saverio, however, did not look at things at all in the same light.

He sat down again on the bed and took off his thick glasses, showing two beautiful blue eyes with a faraway look in them such as is often to be seen in the short-sighted. For Saverio, despised and ill-used by his neighbors, his head filled with dreams of social regeneration, alone always with his books, was conscious of a great desire to confide in his companion. Perro, he felt, was the only person to whom he could speak with perfect sincerity. Besides, Perro inspired in him a profound, almost envious, admiration. Saverio, clumsy, enthusiastic, muddle-headed, admired above all things Perro's methodical, reflective calm, his slightly ironical decorum in the fact of action. It was almost as though he were engaged in some complicated, graceful dance, a minuet, for instance, instead of a revolutionary plot, and the supremely important thing was not to get his steps wrong. He himself, thought Saverio, was too emotional, too passionate; he could never attain such complete self-control. The poor wretch attributed Perro's impassiveness to conscious courage, whereas in reality it was due to the security and insensibility of the professional deceiver.

Having agreed to take part in the plot, Saverio was conscious of a sincere and profound emotion. The imminence of the danger he was preparing to face had swept away all the confusion and pedantry that had been mixed up with his ideals, and there now remained nothing but the ideals themselves, tested and purified, together with the naked emotion of a man who, for the sake of his ideals, is about to place his own life in jeopardy. He felt that Perro, at such a mo-

ment, must be experiencing a similar feeling; and this was a
rare encouragement to the making of confidences. Now that
the fatal decision had been taken, he said to himself, they
were no longer two agitators, two conspirators, but two men
bound together by the same fate, two brothers.

He began by telling Perro that he must not think he was
afraid. Not only had he no fear, but he was grateful to Perro
for having at last procured him the honor to which he had
so long aspired. And since he had started to speak, and
there was no knowing how long it would be before they
found themselves alone again, he felt he would like not
merely to express his intense gratitude but also to explain
the reason for it. Was Perro willing to hear him out? Perro,
who was dropping with sleep, told him, nevertheless, to continue. Then Saverio, beginning from the very beginning,
started to describe his state of mind at the time when he was
not yet a member of the Party in which he now served. He
was then, he said, merely an isolated individual, indescrib-
ably lonely and lost, tormented, helpless, vindictive, muddle-
headed, and quite incapable of forming judgments either
about himself or about world affairs. He had no standard of
true values, no guide to help him in his way. He felt himself
a pariah; and yet at times he was carried away by a vast
enthusiasm, and at such moments seemed capable of great
things—if only he had been granted an opportunity for
action. He felt, above all things, that egoism was not enough;
that it was not enough to be what is commonly called a man
of honor, or a man at peace with himself and with others,
caring for nothing but his own interests; that, in fact, one
could not live only for oneself, with no other justification
than one's own personal advantage. Instead, one must have
faith in something that transcends the wretched, sterile individual, one must be obedient to some superior authority.
One must practice idealism, not the low cunning of those
who have no ambition except to succeed in a career. But all
of a sudden, from the very day he met Perro, his whole life
was changed. No more doubt, no more disgust, no more resentment, no more grievances against himself and against
the world. Like a rushing wind that sweeps the clouds from
the sky, leaving it cleansed and shining, so had the act of
enrolling himself as a member of the Party cleared his spirit
of all impurity. Whereas before he had not known the meaning of the word "action," and had felt himself sinking deeper
every day into the poisonous bog of indecision and aimless
caprice, now he was urged on by an irresistible force, now
he was aware of an absolute justification behind his every
word and deed. Before, there had been many roads and

one seemed as good as another; now there was only one: the road along which Perro had directed him.

Saverio was particularly anxious to explain the feeling inspired in him by his membership in the Party. It was a feeling of trustful abandonment, of perilous security, as though one were lifted up in the arms of a giant and carried by him wherever he wished, trusting him utterly, though without knowing where he was going. He realized that his whole life had been yearning toward this one thing—to serve blindly and with absolute loyalty, to move by command of a superior authority, to have faith in a transcendent idea. And what idea could be more exalted than that in which they believed? The world was rotten through and through and they wanted to restore it—not superficially, but right to its foundations —even if they had to destroy it and rebuild it all over again. He understand now what might have been the feeling of the first Christians who met together in the catacombs—the sweet, deep pleasure of sacrificing themselves for the greater good of humanity, the paradox of despising all that was of importance to others and of valuing highly what was generally held in contempt, and, finally, that perfect sureness of being, once and for all, beyond all possible error. All this he owned to Perro. So far he had kept silent, but now that he was preparing himself for so serious an act he felt it his duty to tell him of it. Afterward he would return to a completely unquestioning obedience and would become merely one of the many soldiers in the Party ranks.

This singular speech interested Perro in spite of himself. He could not help reflecting that these were almost the same feelings that he himself had experienced when as a very young man he had joined the secret police. He, too, had tasted the sweetness of a service that demanded absolute devotion and blind loyalty. He, too, the first time a somewhat delicate mission had been entrusted to him, had felt the thrill of initiation. Perro, of course, was considering only the act of service; he was not concerned with examining the difference between the greater good of humanity in which Saverio believed and the efficiency of the police to which he himself was so zealously dedicated. Following the thread of his own thoughts, Perro ended by saying to himself that with such proclivities Saverio might have made a very good secret agent. It was a pity that, instead, he had wasted such excellent qualities on becoming a revolutionary. But in any case his fate was sealed and there was nothing to be done.

Meanwhile Saverio, whose eyes were moist with emotion, had replaced his thick glasses and retired again into himself after his outburst of feeling. He asked at what time they were to present themselves at the Duchess's villa to put on their livery; and Perro, yawning, answered that they must get there very early the following morning. In the meantime he would like to stay with Saverio—perhaps he could improvise some sort of a bed for him? To have Perro staying with him seemed to Saverio too good to be true, and he told him that he must take his own bed, saying that he himself would manage somehow. Perro objected to this. Saverio's bed, with its sheets of doubtful whiteness still disarranged from the previous night, did not attract him; so he insisted on Saverio finding him a blanket and a couple of pillows. Saverio, without replying, went out of the room to fetch them.

## C H A P T E R   7

If he had been less blinded by his enthusiasm, Saverio would have noticed, as he went out, that somebody was standing just behind the door, peering through the window between the leaves of the closed shutters. Sebastiano, Saverio's half-brother, had been intrigued by the presence of Perro, whom he had never seen before. He thought of Saverio as a kind of uncouth, stuttering monster; and Perro, with his tall, elegant figure, was the most surprising companion for him that could be imagined. It was enough to make Sebastiano follow them at a distance and peep in at the window of the cabin.

The conversation between the two in Saverio's room had astonished Sebastiano to an extraordinary degree. "Who could have imagined it?" he said to himself. "I thought I had a sort of idiot in the house, and instead I find a Brutus. . . ."

Sebastiano waited for Saverio to return with his load of pillows and blankets; then, seeing that the two of them were getting ready for bed, he felt there was no further reason for spying upon them and went back into the villa.

On a rustic straw-seated chair, which had replaced the vanished furniture of the hall, he threw down his cap and whip (Sebastiano loved riding but having no horse had to content himself with going about in riding dress) and went up a bare and unadorned staircase to the floor above. In order to get to his bedroom, situated in a corner of the second floor, he had to go through two or three rooms, one of which was a large drawing room, once filled with furniture but now empty. Sebastiano went through these rooms in the dark, although there were still some electric light bulbs hanging from wires which in the past had held sparkling chandeliers of Bohemian crystal. He had had this ability to end his way in the dark ever since his childhood, when, to prove to his mother that he was not afraid, he had taught himself to go about all over the house without turning on the lights, and—what was more difficult, since the rooms were crowded with old-fashioned furniture—without bumping into anything. Sebastiano, who believed himself to be made in a different way from other people, had come to mistake this habit of his for a special quality: he was honestly convinced that he could see in the dark like a cat.

This walking in the dark, however, spared him, above all, the sight of the squalor produced all over the house by the sale of the furniture. It made him almost believe that nothing had happened, that the house was still furnished, that his mother was still alive and he himself still a little boy. During his childhood, whenever he came out of his room at night, he had had to pass through not only the drawing room and two other smaller rooms but also a very solemn bedroom where his mother slept in a great four-poster bed. Little Sebastiano, hurrying with bare feet over the cold floors and coming into the thick darkness of this last room, filled with the presence of his sleeping mother and with the sound of her breathing, used to say "Good-night, Mamma," in a trembling, ecstatic voice. But only in a whisper, so as not to awaken her. Then he would wriggle his way like a cat to his own room and plunge with a joyous shudder under the sheets. Now his mother was dead, and the furniture, even the four-poster bed, had all gone to a second-hand dealer, but Sebastiano still continued to behave in exactly the same way as when he was a child. He would cross the drawing room on tiptoe, thinking: "I mustn't run into the console-table . . . nor the grand piano . . . and here's the red sofa," then, holding his breath, would enter his mother's bedroom, say good-night to her in a whisper, and, in great haste and still in the dark, go and undress in his own bedroom.

Sebastiano had remained an adolescent. He liked to play the game of pretending to himself that he was a completely different person from his real self. He feared boredom more than anything, and among all the things that produce it he had a special horror of the pedantic point of view. He liked to imagine that life was a kind of adventure in which nothing happened that was final or irreparable. He therefore preferred to think, when he went to bed and wished his mother good-night, that she, who had died while still young and beautiful, was still alive. He had never—not even once—been to the cemetery where she was buried in the family tomb. And, in the same way in which he chose to ignore his mother's death, he refused to believe in the wreck of his inheritance. This attitude of incredulity permitted him never to think of it and to behave as though it had never happened.

This evening, after his usual good-night to his mother, Sebastiano, instead of taking off his clothes, sat down fully dressed on the edge of the bed in the white brilliance of the moonlight that flooded in through the curtainless windows. "Here I am in a fine mess," he began thinking. "I have discovered a plot—and, what is worse, a plot that has every chance of succeeding. . . ."

Sebastiano's "mess" was due to his being desperately in love with Fausta Sanchez, the woman on whose account Tereso was going to the party. And he believed that she returned his love. For Fausta, however, Sebastiano's love was merely a passing adventure; and now, fearing that her relations with him might hinder the development of her ambitious projects, she had invented an elaborate story in order to get rid of him. According to Fausta, she had a brother called Manuele (which was true), who was now in prison for political reasons (which was untrue); and Tereso had insisted on her yielding herself to him as a condition of Manuele's release; therefore she saw herself forced to accept these hard terms; and that, in consequence, it was better that their love affair—which was too exalted in any case to lead to any satisfactory result—should come to an end. Sebastiano, of course, had believed every syllable of this tale. He therefore had now a double purpose in view—to secure Manuele's release, and at the same time to save Fausta from having to pay for it by a surrender to the General's desires.

One might think that to attain his purpose Sebastiano had only to allow the conspiracy to follow its course. Tereso dead, Manuele would come out of prison and there would be nothing to prevent Sebastiano from living in peace with his beloved Fausta.

But, in the first place, there was the danger that Fausta might perish in the ruins of the villa, and, secondly, that Tereso might be killed after, rather than before, he had gained what he desired of her. Besides, Sebastiano, who did not share the enthusiasm of his half-brother, was of a generous enough nature not to wish to be the accomplice of a crime simply for his own advantage. Also he had not the slightest wish that Tereso should be assassinated.

Sebastiano was profoundly bored except when he was with Fausta. His boredom came from a complete skepticism about the destiny of humanity in general and of his country in particular. He had had no political experience. But he belonged to a generation wnich had been, as it were, inoculated in a prenatal state by the recent appalling upheavals, and believed in nothing—neither in the State nor in revolution, neither in liberty nor authority. The vast majority of his contemporaries were therefore prepared to embark, without either scruples or illusions, upon some career or other. But in a few cases, like that of Sebastiano, this skepticism had led to dreaminess and boredom, to idleness and dilettantism.

Sebastiano was capable of seeing that Tereso's government was in many respects arbitrary and was founded wholly on force. But the idea of a government composed of people like Saverio was utterly horrifying to him. Tereso, he said to himself, at least knew how to sit a horse. In concluding thus he was following the dictates of taste, which seemed to him more reliable than any reasoning. To Sebastiano, who was very serious in his frivolity, there was no greater sin than lack of elegance and no greater inelegance than a belief in something. Saverio was ugly, misshapen and badly dressed, and believed in too many things. This was quite enough to make Sebastiano prefer Tereso to him and to people of his sort.

To Sebastiano skepticism was not simply a mode of thought but in a certain sense actually a duty. He believed that, just as he had to empty his body every day so that it would not become poisoned, so must he preserve his mind from becoming obstructed and burdened with beliefs. He hated beliefs because he scented in them a weakness of which he wished to purge himself at all costs. It seemed to him that true strength should be incredulous of everything —but always graceful and easy in its gestures, like a dancer.

Sebastiano heartily detested the masses, to whose limitless imbecility he attributed the tediousness of the present period. It seemed to him that the General had already shown himself far too easygoing with them. As to what would happen under a government of the kind that Saverio wanted to set up, Sebastiano preferred not to think of it. The masses, in all their fanatical stupidity, would then rule the roost. At this thought he felt suddenly tempted to rush off to the police and denounce the conspiracy.

Apart, however, from his repugnance to acting in any way as an informer, another consideration, a more personal and deliberate one, held him back. Though he far preferred one Tereso to a hundred Saverios, the fact remained that Tereso was laying siege to his mistress, and also that Fausta seemed to have made up her mind to yield to his blackmailing proposition in order to save her brother.

"There are several different points to be reconciled," thought Sebastiano. "I must frustrate the plot and at the same time prevent the horrible possibility of Fausta falling into the arms of Tereso. Again, in order to frustrate it I cannot descend to becoming an informer, which would be altogether too base and ignoble. Also I must only *half*-frustrate it, otherwise I cannot make use of it as a means of forcing Tereso to give up Fausta."

At this point in his reflections Sebastiano began to be amused. As we have already shown, he had remained a boy. And he was strongly attracted by what he already knew of fun and adventure.

"I've somehow got to have it both ways," he thought again. "It's difficult; that's a thing that always is difficult. Besides, I have very little time. The Duchess's party takes place tomorrow evening. And during the party, unless I do something about it, Tereso will be killed, but not before Fausta has vainly sacrificed her honor to save her brother. . . .

"I must prevent Tereso being killed. But this I must do without turning informer; in such a way that he releases Manuele and does not touch Fausta; and without Saverio coming to any harm."

Sebastiano felt that there must be a solution, as in every problem rationally expounded, but he did not succeed in finding it. A merely approximate solution, in which a great deal would be left to chance or good luck, would be useless; it must be precise, geometrical. Two and two must make four, thought Sebastiano, otherwise Manuele remains in prison and Fausta is lost.

He thought for a long time, sitting on his bed, his elbows on his knees and his head in his hands. Finally he struck his hand against his forehead, asking himself out loud why he had not thought of this before.

He had suddenly realized that there was one way of frustrating the plot without giving information, a way by which he could get at Tereso, obtain Manuele's pardon from him, and rescue Fausta from his clutches. And that was to take part himself in the conspiracy. By so doing he could present himself to Tereso and dictate his terms when the fuse of the bomb was, so to speak, already alight. If Tereso accepted, he would simply cut away the fuse, without revealing the names of his accomplices. If Tereso rejected his terms, Sebastiano, who had no interest in life apart from his love for Fausta, accepted the fact that he must die in company with her and the General.

He was pleased with this plan because it was bold and almost impossible. Sebastiano, beneath his frivolous attitude, was desperate. It seemed to him sweet to die with Fausta; in comparison with that all risks became negligible. But at the same time there came to him the afterthought that it was no uncommon thing, for a general who had pledged himself to death, both to save his own skin and to win the battle. His deep, hopeless desire to die with Fausta might possibly be powerful enough to convince Tereso and so to save his own life and that of his mistress as well.

He rose from the bed, went in the darkness through the second floor rooms, down the stairs and out on to the open space in front of the villa.

## CHAPTER 8

The bright moonlight made the space in front of the house look smaller than it was in reality, because of the long, motionless shadows cast across its blank surface by an irregular line of tree tops. The night was calm, soft and windless. Attracted by the crunch of Sebastiano's footsteps on the gravel, the dog Ludra came up to her master, whining and jumping lightly up and down beside him. Sebastiano patted her to keep her quiet. He did not wish to wake the two men who were asleep in the cabin.

He walked down the road and, pushing the dog back into the garden, went out of the gate. The lane was bright in the moonlight. Sebastiano followed it for some distance, but shortly before he came to the main road he turned off to the left by a side path. He went through a wood and crossed a little bridge over a deep ditch. Beyond the bridge the path ran between the wood and a high wall with branches hanging over it. This was the wall that encircled the great park belonging to the Duchess Gorina.

Sebastiano knew every inch of this path. For about three weeks he had walked along it every night at the same time to meet his mistress. He had already been to his customary appointment with her that evening. But it had been agreed between them that, if ever Sebastiano wanted for some reason to see her a second time, he was to come back and attract her attention by a special whistle. She would then come out into the park.

That night Sebastiano had left Fausta after a violent argument, at the termination of which they had decided by agreement that this was the last time they would see each other. Fausta had in fact announced that she intended to accept Tereso's conditions for her brother's release. Sebastiano, who would willingly have sacrificed Manuele (whom he did not know), seeing that all his suggestions and all his protestations were in vain, had declared in that case he would rather not see her again. This was, as we know, just what Fausta wanted, since she feared that Sebastiano's love for her might create obstacles in the way of her coveted career as the General's mistress.

So they had embraced for the last time, Sebastiano with a mind distracted and eyes full of tears, Fausta feigning an equal grief and—in the absence of those tears that cannot be simulated—saying she intended to kill herself as soon as she had obtained her brother's pardon.

These farewells had left Sebastiano profoundly depressed. Virtue did not exist, or, if it did exist, could avail nothing: of this, in his skepticism, he was convinced. But he believed, and had always believed, in luck. Now, however, even luck had deserted him. He saw before him nothing but a wretched life full of despairing memories, far from the woman he loved and whom he knew to have been defiled. If Fausta really killed herself as she threatened, he had firmly decided to put an end to his own life too.

But the luck in which Sebastiano believed and which had always come to his help in the worst moments of his life was now becoming friendly again, through the secret he had overhead at the cabin window. He was now going to see Fausta and tell her that he had once again found his ancient protectress.

He followed the encircling wall for some distance until he came to one of the many entrances into the park. This gate was never used and was almost completely covered by the heavy foliage of wistaria. Its branches were twisted round the bars of the gate, and Sebastiano made use of them every night to climb over into the park.

Once inside, he took his way along a white gravel path beside a high, black wall which, in the brilliant moonlight, could be seen to consist of a hedge of boxwood of extraordinary size and thickness, cut into square blocks and placed close together in line following the curve of a driveway. On the further side the box hedges framed a wide meadow that sloped down in front of the villa. Passing between two blocks of the thick hedge he came out into this meadow. It was flooded in moonlight from end to end, and the grass, bathed in the night dew, shone like silver. On the far side rose another hedge, black and tall. The meadow lay spread out over the slope like an enormous shaggy carpet. At the top stood the Duchess's villa, reddish in color and, in its regularity and simplicity, with its four floors and forty windows, a little like a military barracks. At the opposite end of the meadow, at the bottom of the slope, the dark waters of an artificial pond gleamed in the moonlight. Sebastiano, raising his eyes toward the villa, saw that among the few windows still illuminated was that of Fausta.

He had made Fausta's acquaintance by chance one day during the summer when she had lost her way on a walk and had come to his house to ask for directions. Sebastiano, with the blissful, easy alacrity of a young man of twenty who, never having had an adventure, is afraid of nothing except being thought shy, had put his arm around her waist just at the moment when she, having received the information she needed, was turning away, slowly and somewhat reluctantly, toward the door. He had expected a slap in the face, or at any rate a rebuff of some kind. Instead he suddenly found the lady lying in his arms, with blank, upturned eyes and parted lips. It was brought home to him at that moment how deeply his father had injured him by selling all the furniture. Here he was, clasping this lovely woman in his arms and not knowing where to put her down. Then he had suddenly remembered that his one remaining farm laborer had put some sacks full of flour in a corner of one of the empty rooms on the ground floor. To this room, adjoining the vestibule where they were, he had accordingly dragged Fausta, like a young lion dragging his still-living prey into his den to devour it at his leisure. In the dark room, that smelled like a granary, he had laid her gently down upon the sacks. He had feared that this makeshift arrangement, betraying his poverty, might bring the adventure to its expected end. But Sebastiano did not know how handsome he was, with his fair hair and dark eyes and smooth skin; nor had he any idea how delicious his rough way—and his flour sacks—seemed to her.

From that day onward they had met every night in the park. Sebastiano had fallen madly in love with Fausta, and attributed similar feelings to her. If he had been less infatuated, he would have realized that the very facility with which she had yielded to him denoted a character entirely different from the one he imagined. But he was at the age at which every act of desire seems a surrender of true love, every sensual woman an angel.

Sebastiano was neither an aristocrat, a rich man, a leader of society, nor a celebrity. And so, without his being conscious of it, the subtle pride of knowing himself the lover of a woman who was courted by so many, of knowing, too, that the most powerful man in the country was his rival, played a considerable part in the process of his mad infatuation. He liked to think that no one knew of his love, that the world was very far from imagining that he, the lonely disinherited young man, was master of this difficult, exquisite being. Combined with this feeling was a certain sense that it was a jest, a comedy. There were moments when Sebastiano acted his love affair instead of living it.

He had no idea that, to Fausta, he was simply a new, unaccustomed taste to a spoiled and jaded palate. Fausta collected love affairs, and it seemed to her that she had now tried everything except what she called "romantic" love. The poor young man living near the rich villa, the moonlight, the subterfuges and secrets, the solemn oaths and passionate phrases—all these were new to Fausta, who was accustomed to intrigues as rapid as they were brutal. Yet at the same time this love of Sebastiano's, just because it was romantic love, as she called it—or because, in fact, it might be true love—frightened her. She did not want to be under obligation; and so Tereso's passion had come just at the right moment. She would be able simultaneously to get rid of Sebastiano, become Tereso's mistress, and procure for her brother Manuele a certain very lucrative government contract he had been sighing after for years. So the tale she had told Sebastiano had had enough truth in it to justify, to some extent, the almost sincere tone of voice in which she had told it. But privately she had sworn that she would never again allow herself to be entrapped in a love like Sebastiano's. There were, she thought, too many dangers in it, not the least of which was the danger of having to remain faithful.

Sebastiano was so absorbed in his thoughts that he scarcely knew himself to be walking; he felt almost that he was flying lightly over the dew-drenched grass as he took his way up the great meadow toward the villa. The splendor of the moonlight, silent and intense between the high, black walls of the boxwood hedges, inspired him with a bold, crazy exaltation. He fancied himself admitting Fausta into his secret and, with her help, building up within Saverio's plot another smaller, personal plot—within the political conspiracy a love-conspiracy. He felt quite capable of himself murdering Tereso out of jealousy as a rival. After that he would either fly with Fausta or die with her. Sebastiano, as he reasoned in this way, had no idea that he was quite crazy, utterly out of touch with reality, living in a world of fantasy though at the same time moving in a world of action.

## CHAPTER 9

When he reached the villa, Sebastiano leaned against the wall and for a moment gazed dreamily at the meadow in front of him. He became aware then of a slight rustling sound, and looked down. A number of large toads were leaping about silently and nimbly in the moonlight on the grass and on the cement footpath. They were jumping here and there in a casual, thoughtful manner, with their muzzles thrust forward, their four feet seeming never to be in agreement, landing on their pale, plump bellies with their dumpy shadows following close behind. Sebastiano bent down and picked up one of them, a very large, heavy one, by its hind foot, just at the moment when it was preparing to leap. The toad struggled, dangling in the air, then became motionless, pretending to be dead but showing plenty of life in its little, wide-open eyes. Sebastiano, with his other hand, took hold of it by the back like a crab. The toad started kicking wildly with its four feet. And now its eyes, two glassy blobs among the bumps and warts of its flat head, looked as though they would swell till they burst like two soap bubbles; and its white paunch twitched convulsively.

Still holding the toad in his hand, Sebastiano stopped under Fausta's window and gave a low melancholy whistle like the call of a hunter. Almost immediately a shadow appeared in the window through the slats of the closed shutters, and a hand was thrust forth, the fingers making a sign as though telling him to wait.

He did not wait long. In a moment one of the ground floor windows opened slowly, first one shutter and then the other, and Fausta appeared on the threshold. She was dressed in a long black silk gown with a low neck and silvery trimmings that gleamed in the moonlight, as did the diamonds on the hand with which she opened the shutter.

Fausta's face was like that of a very dark boy. The same almost invisible down that is on the cheeks of young boys softened its round outline. But her eyes, black and widely opened, curiously opaque and with no light in them—blind, one might almost say—were characteristic of a woman of her type, far removed from all innocence; and the thin eyebrows, raised and pointed like two circumflex accents—the kind of eyebrows that form part of an actor's make-up for the role of Mephistopheles—added a touch of cruelty, of ruthlessness, to the dull inexpressiveness of the eyes. She had a short, sensual, blunt nose, a small, tight, fleshy mouth in which the sharp white eyeteeth became visible even at the slightest smile, and a broad, rounded jaw rather like that of a cat. She wore her hair very short, like a boy's; but it was set in a crisp, uneven style that was purely feminine, and arranged so as to suggest almost that it had been roughly and forcibly clipped. She was spare and slenderly built, and her brown skin had an almost burnt look. All softness seemed to have deserted her thin limbs and to have concentrated itself in her heavy, rounded breasts, large but delicate and tender—the only feminine feature of her masculine figure, yet enough to be a vivid reminder to anyone who looked at her that she was, after all, a woman, and not merely a woman but more of a woman than most. She seemed aware of this, for she carried these splendid charms with ostentatious vanity, throwing back her head and shoulders as she moved.

Fausta had come down from her room with reluctance. She was afraid lest her lover had already repented of his uncompromising attitude and had come back to announce that he would continue to love her even if she gave herself to Tereso. She knew by experience that love, so justly called blind, would sometimes submit to the deepest humiliations, the most abject compromises, rather than release its prey. "But this time," she thought as she came downstairs, "this time I shall tell him the truth, and then at last he will leave me in peace." Fausta was spurred to this resolve by the sort of cruel obstinacy that animates a housewife who sees a chicken still struggling after she has wrung its neck, and decides to give it the *coup de grâce* by cutting its throat into the bargain.

She appeared on the doorstep with a frowning, anxious face and eyes full of ill will under their arched eyebrows. But Sebastiano, convinced that he had found the thread to lead him out of the labyrinth in which he was entrapped, was now in jovial mood and not in the least anxious to enter at once upon the disagreeable subject of their future relations. He showed her the toad, which he was still grasping by its back, and told her that on his way home the creature had stopped him and prayed to be taken to the lovely Fausta, about whom all the toads in the neighborhood were talking. This whimsical remark pleased Fausta, who had been expecting a jealous scene, and, without displaying any of the repugnance that women usually feel for these warty amphibians, she put out her long, thin, brown hand with its sparkling diamonds and poked the closed mouth of the toad with the scarlet tip of her nail.

"He wants to give you a kiss," said the infatuated Sebastiano, full of inventiveness.

"A kiss?" she repeated, arching her brows agreeably, "a kiss—where?"

"Here," said Sebastiano, pointing to her ear, half hidden by her hair.

Fausta had small, perfectly shaped ears, which Sebastiano never tired of praising whenever he saw her. Intrigued, she said that the toad was a bold fellow, but she already felt an interest in this new, monstrous sensation, and inquired cautiously whether the toad would bite her and whether it was poisonous. When Sebastiano replied that there was nothing to fear, she threw away the cigarette she held between her fingers and languidly brushed aside her short hair, uncovering her small round ear. Sebastiano held the toad's mouth close to it.

"He is talking to me!" she exclaimed after a moment, with a shrill laugh; and indeed the toad had moved its mouth as if it wanted to whisper something to her. But the toad had also kissed the lobe of her ear, she added, and it was a curious sensation; its lips were cold as crystal, like the night itself.

Sebastiano then put the toad down on the ground, telling it to go and announce its extraordinary good fortune to its friends. Then, rising, he asked Fausta what the toad had said to her.

"It told me that you and I must part," she said, looking at him seriously.

This interlude with the toad had sufficed to cool Sebastiano's excitement and to make him change his mind again. It was true, he was sure, that Fausta loved him; but the fact that she had resigned herself to accept Tereso's condition in order to save her brother did not show an excessive strength of mind, and such a person certainly had not the makings of a conspirator. He suddenly thought it would be better to tell her nothing and to act without her knowledge. Once again fortune favored Sebastiano. For if Fausta had known of the plot she would not have hesitated to denounce the whole lot of them without exception, including Sebastiano himself. Sebastiano first of all, in fact, for she would have been delighted to be rid of him and at the same time to get into Tereso's good graces, and would have felt that she was protecting not only Tereso but her own personal plans and Manuele's future as well.

Sebastiano therefore, after coming back to the villa and bringing Fausta down from her room, had nothing to say to her. But the words that she had put into the mouth of the toad went to his heart like the stab of a dagger. He answered her by asking sadly whether she disliked the idea of their relationship continuing as much as she seemed to. But, he added, she need not worry, for he had only come back in order to say a last, final farewell. Fausta laughed, reassured, and put out her mouth for him to kiss.

"So it is really decided?" Sebastiano asked timidly after he had kissed her. He still hoped that she might sacrifice her brother for his sake, not so much because he now thought this sacrifice necessary as because it would have given him a proof of her love. But Fausta, glad of an opportunity to reiterate the necessity of their parting, replied that there was nothing to be done. He must not try to insist, nor must he embitter their last moments together. If she wanted to save her brother

she must yield. It was hateful, not only to do so, but even to
think of it, but she could see no way out. She spoke in a sorrowful tone that suggested she was going to her death rather
than setting out upon a new love affair.

"Perhaps we might meet again tomorrow—during the day,
I mean—for the last time?" Sebastiano asked. And though
he knew he was trying to deceive himself his eyes suddenly
filled with tears.

"I don't think so," Fausta answered, kindly but firmly.

Sebastiano loved Fausta so passionately that, although he
knew it was not really the last time he would see her, he
nevertheless had all the feelings common to a final farewell.
He experienced a mingled sweetness and bitterness, and at
the same time was possessed by a furious, insatiable desire
to gaze closely at those beloved features, to stamp them
deeply upon his memory. Their farewells were long pro-
tracted. He could never weary of kissing those lips, that neck,
those eyes; and Fausta accepted his desperate hunger as the
final thrill of a love affair that had already given her many
thrills. More than once Sebastiano, instead of pressing a
final kiss upon the hand she gave him, seized the hand and
drew her to him again for another mad, sweet embrace. At
last they separated, and Fausta ran off along the wall of the
villa, dark in the brilliant moonlight. Sebastiano knew that
the moment had now come when he must occupy himself
actively with Saverio's plot.

In great haste he went back over the way he had come,
and as he went he thought over everything he had decided to
do and say. In any case it was merely a question of making a
choice, for—quite apart from having overheard the conversation of the two conspirators through the window and thus
obtaining a pretty exact idea of their motives in the attempt
on Tereso's life—it would certainly not be difficult for him to
produce arguments against the General's government, considering the incessant chatter and discussion that had gone
on for years throughout the country; even a child brought up
among such political murmurings could have recited them
by heart. Furthermore, Sebastiano felt himself inspired with
the providential, lightning-quick lucidity that usually comes to
the aid of rash men in their most risky undertakings. He felt
capable not merely of improvising the language and spirit of a
plotter but of behaving, that night, as though in all his life he
had had no thought but of overthrowing Tereso's government.

There were two ways by which he might get himself admitted into the conspiracy: either he might rouse Saverio
gently and confide first in him; or he might burst into the

cabin and make an immediate proclamation of his intentions. He chose the second method as being the more expeditious; also he rather liked the theatrical quality of this sudden declaration of faith, because he felt it might disguise his real lack of sincerity.

And so, all of a sudden, there appeared to the two sleepy, dazed conspirators Sebastiano, terrible and beautiful as an announcing archangel in the brilliant, startling illumination.

"I am here to join you," he said. "I heard all you said, I agree with all your ideas, I beg you to make use of me and to let me share in your plan of action."

Before the pair could recover from their surprise (Saverio's hand had reached for the pistol that he kept always under his pillow) there poured from Sebastiano a flood of words proving his good faith, a torrent of fraudulent arguments, of disingenuous requests, of loftily-expressed blackmail. The idea of saving Fausta from Tereso's clutches made him eloquent and perfectly sincere, so that in a very short time Saverio—who, as we have seen, cherished a curious sort of affection for his half-brother—was fully convinced of the genuineness of his proposal. As for Perro, he neither believed nor disbelieved. However the affair went, his own position was not affected. What could it matter to him if there were one conspirator more or less? Now that the machine had been set in motion, it merely meant that Sebastiano, for reasons known only to himself, would share the fate of Saverio; that was all. So while a sort of recognition scene was going on between Saverio and Sebastiano—just as though the latter had that moment arrived back from a long journey to a distant land and Saverio were recollecting his appearance gradually, bit by bit—Perro, leaning his elbow on the pillow, waited sleepily for their affecting conversation to end.

Saverio jumped right out of bed in his enthusiasm, showing his naked body sinewy and gnarled like the trunk of a tree, and embraced Sebastiano. Then he turned toward Perro and asked what task should be assigned to his half-brother. "I will answer for him," he kept repeating, "I will answer for him."

Perro, speaking slowly and with studied coldness, said that he could come and put on a footman's livery too, provided he kept his mouth shut. At these words Sebastiano, taking his cue from Saverio's excited demonstrations, felt it advisable to go and shake Perro warmly by the hand. The latter, however, told him to think the matter over carefully, because there was quite a chance that he might not come out of it with a whole skin. But Sebastiano, in perfect sincerity and thinking of Fausta, answered that he had made up his mind. Perro then explained that he must come back again early next morning and they would all go together to the Duchess's villa. Perro thought he was deceiving Sebastiano, and Sebastiano thought he was deceiving Perro; but the only one who was really deceived was Saverio.

Finally Perro turned his face to the wall and went to sleep again, while Saverio, crazed with enthusiasm, made Sebastiano sit on the bed close beside him while he explained the workings of the plot and how they intended to put it into effect. Again and again during his explanations he came back to the theme of how they were fighting, and would perhaps give their lives, to bring freedom and a better future to mankind and to inaugurate a new world—a distressing and profound subject which lay deep in Saverio's mind and to which he kept returning with real emotion, like a musician coming back again to the main theme of his composition. But Sebastiano saw Saverio merely as a deluded fool, and thought only of Fausta. As for Perro, he thought him a more serious, and therefore more dangerous, type than Saverio. But he did not despair of being able to fool him as well. He was a little suprised at the readiness with which Perro, who seemed so much more cautious than Saverio, had accepted his proposal. But he was reassured by the thought that all these conspirators, even when they appeared, like Perro, to be prudent and to know what they were doing, were fundamentally fanatics.

At last, at a very late hour, Sebastiano and Saverio separated.

"Let us embrace," Saverio suggested again as he accompanied Sebastiano from the cabin. "From today onward we are truly brothers."

Sebastiano was quite unable to understand all this enthusiasm for the future of the world. He himself would not have lifted a finger to save and redeem mankind. But he was quite willing to let his half-brother embrace him. As for Saverio, he was in such a state of confusion and exaltation that, before finally leaving Sebastiano, he felt he must make a short speech in praise of Perro, who had remained asleep in the cabin.

"He is a leader of men," said Saverio, "so much stronger, so much wiser, so much more resolute than we are. We must all imitate him, we must take him as our model. . . . What can *we* do? We are just private soldiers, and we know it . . . but he—he is born to command. And a proof of that is that he can sleep so quietly on the eve of a fateful day like tomorrow.

Sebastiano, who had not found Perro particularly agreeable and who did not feel in the least inferior or like a "private soldier," as Saverio had tried to make out, made no reply. Saverio went back into the cabin; and Sebastiano, passing as usual through the dark, empty rooms of the house, at last retired to bed.

# CHAPTER 10

The three men got up next morning in states of mind that varied considerably according to the private preoccupations of each. Perro, refreshed by sleep and extremely calm, was now feeling completely self-confident, and therefore free in his mind and more coldly calculating than ever. Saverio, who had not closed an eye during the whole night, was in a state of even greater exaltation and excitement than the evening before. Sebastiano, aware of the risks he was running between the police on the one hand and the conspirators on the other, was watchful and intent on playing his part. He and Perro instinctively felt themselves superior to Saverio and in a way were spying upon each other. Perro did this more from professional habit than from mistrust; accustomed to divide men into only two categories—the guardians, and the breakers, of the law—he said to himself that Sebastiano, who was certainly not an agent of the police, must therefore be a criminal. And what did one conspirator more or less matter to him? His net was capacious enough to catch not one but ten fish as big as that. Nevertheless, the manner in which Sebastiano had presented himself, the odd fact that he had been an eavesdropper to their conversation, caused him instinctively to mistrust him. Had he not been so completely sure of never having seen him in police circles, he might almost have suspected him of being another *agent provocateur*. Sebastiano, on his side, found Perro altogether too calm and self-controlled. Even in a man born, as Saverio said, to command, such serenity appeared to him excessive. On the other hand he was afraid lest Perro might discover that he neither was, nor desired to be, a real conspirator, but that he had in fact decided to frustrate the plot simply for his own ends. He also feared some underhand trick. He had heard of the summary executions of disloyal conspirators and *agents provocateurs* at the hands of their comrades, executions described as secret, brutal and pitiless; and he felt that to end with a rope round his neck or a bullet through his head at the hand of Saverio would be, in the general absurdity of life, altogether too absurd a death.

That morning, therefore, all the way from Sebastiano's house to the Duchess's villa, while Saverio, as usual, wandered from one subject to another, preaching and declaiming, there was a continual skirmishing between the other two, with questions and answers, with cautious investigations and no less cautious dissimulations. Perro was trying to find out why in the world a young man of the upper classes, scarcely grown up, handsome, frivolous, had taken it into his head to overthrow the government and initiate a new order; while Sebastiano was cautiously seeking to discover how in the world Perro could remain so cold and formal at a moment like this.

In answer to Perro's questions, Sebastiano replied that for some time now he had been aware of the inadequacy of his selfish, pleasure-seeking life; that he had felt the need to put his faith in some transcendent cause, to serve that cause and fight for its ultimate victory; that he was ready even, if necessary, to die, since he saw clearly that life was not worth living if one lived entirely for oneself. In fact he repeated, in a slightly modified form, all the things he had heard from Saverio.

"The devil take it!" Perro said to himself, observing Sebastiano's handsome face, so strangely lit up as he recited these phrases; "all these fellows are dying to serve and believe in something!"

In reality Sebastiano was all the time thinking of Fausta; and the fervor that so astonished Perro was produced by a mere substitution of words. Love of mankind was love of Fausta. "The cause" was Fausta. The obstacles in the path of the revolution were Tereso and Manuele, who obliged him to part from Fausta. Finally, the selfish, epicurean life that he now despised was his own life before he met Fausta. After answering Perro's questions, however, he went over to the counteroffensive and in a friendly manner declared that he very much admired him for retaining so much self-control in the present circumstances. He himself, for instance, however hard he tried to control himself, could not quite succeed in repressing a certain agitation.

"Devil take it!" thought Perro again, "our friend is observant. . . ." Then assuming an incisive, terse manner, firm and at the same time full of latent significance, and looking Sebastiano straight in the eyes, he replied that he was accustomed to this sort of thing, and that was why he remained so calm. But he, too, at the beginning of his career as a revolutionary, had often felt he was on the point of losing his head. Besides, it was essential that somebody should keep calm. Saverio certainly was not calm and never would be, and as he had not yet seen him put to the test he must himself take full responsibility. And he smiled in Saverio's direction with a look of sympathetic complicity which Sebastiano could not help returning.

In truth, the nearer they came to the Duchess's villa the more elated and the more uncontrolled did Saverio become.

He was walking in front of the others, whirling with a whistling sound in the air a stick that he had pulled from a hedge. The freshness of the morning, still cold and misty, intoxicated him, till he seemed to himself to be no longer the old, stuttering Saverio, but a ruthless executioner, preordained by fate, an adventurous, fearless conspirator, a man of action on the march toward a shining goal.

"It may seem to you strange," he began, just as they crossed the little bridge over the ditch, "it may seem to you absurd—but we three, at this moment, are making history. . . . Who would think so, to look at us? We look simply like three men who have got up very early and are walking through a wood, whereas perhaps in reality, as a result of this morning walk of ours, there will arise a whole new world, a new mode of feeling, a new civilization, a new period of history. . . . Here one can see the force of the spirit, its superiority over brute matter. If this thing that we have decided to do is successful, in centuries to come people will still be talking of this walk of ours which seems like so many other walks. They will speak of it with wonder and with gratitude, as of something legendary, mythical, prophetic. They will say that we three, on that far-off distant morning, had faith in the destiny of man and of human society against all the obscure forces that sought to keep them in brutishness and barbarism. . . . Do you not believe me? I tell you that people will come here on pilgrimages . . . and yet we are just three men who are simply going to do what we consider our duty. . . . Don't you see? That is how history is made—on mornings like this—on woodland paths like this—by people with faces like ours. . . ."

"Be careful, don't shout so loud," said Perro, to whom all this meant nothing—except that Saverio was making mountains out of molehills. "We're behind a wall which is probably guarded by police officers every hundred yards."

"What do I care?" answered Saverio, shrugging his shoulders. Then he went on. "Look over there, how the sun shines as it rises behind the white trunks of the birch trees! How fresh the air is, how pure, as it comes up from the hoar frost on the grass! How sweet the flowers smell as they open their petals! Listen to the birds singing in the trees as they awake and salute the sun! Ah, this is nature, always the same whether man is free or in bondage. What is there to prevent us from enjoying life? In a moment the sun will be high in the heavens and everywhere will be heard the murmuring of insects among the flowers. We might abandon everything and, instead of going to the Duchess's villa, turn off here to the right and take a morning's ramble through the

countryside, content to dream instead of to act. But we shall
turn to the left. We shall go where danger threatens, where
perhaps death awaits us. . . . Who will then have the courage
to deny the existence of the spirit, to deny that it is a more
concrete, a more palpable, a more powerful thing than all
visible reality? Who will deny the existence of the soul, of
the liberty of man?"

With such words Saverio, flushed with optimism and energy,
sought to express the fervor and passion of his spirit. To
Perro, enclosed in the impenetrable armor of his falseness,
his words seemed merely comic and distasteful. But upon Sebastiano, who, being young and in love, was more suscepti-
ble to expressions of idealism, they had quite a different effect. Though he did not share his half-brother's enthusiasm,
he nevertheless felt that it was genuine, and recognized in his
words a sincerity and originality that Saverio's uncouth
appearance would never have led one to suspect.

"Come, my friends," concluded Saverio when he had finished his harangue, "let us sing in chorus like soldiers
marching to battle." And without troubling to see whether
the others joined in he began, in his shrill voice, to chant
the *Marseillaise*. The other two, for reasons of their own, had
not the courage to sing with him. But Saverio did not notice
this; he walked in front, his stick whistling through the
air as he cut off the heads of imaginary enemies of the people; and his voice, stammering and out of tune, rose high in
the numbed stillness of the misty morning, painfully exultant and with distressing mistakes in French pronunciation
that caused shivers to run down Sebastiano's back.

And so, with Saverio singing and making speeches, Perro
trying to keep him quiet, and Sebastiano thinking sometimes
of Fausta and sometimes forced into listening to his half-
brother's strange rhapsodies, they took their way along the
path in the pure, joyful light of the serene morning. Every
now and then a ray of sunshine shot, like a sudden exclamation, through the trunks of the birch trees, lighting up the
three men, the path, the old wall. In the wood they could
hear the chatter of little streams running over the rocks,
and there was a smell of damp earth and moss in the air,
still sharp after the night frost. Saverio was all wrong, Sebastiano could not help thinking; this was a morning to go
out shooting, or to walk through the woods picking mush-
rooms and cyclamen, not to weave plots against an elderly
general, over tiresome questions that were not worth a single
one of the flowers that grew along the edge of the path. And
yet, he considered, he was the only one of the three who
had valid reasons for giving up these pleasures. Fausta was

fresher and more thrilling than all the purity and fragrance of the morning, sweeter than the sunshine when it shone upon them, more beautiful than all the beauties of nature.

They reached the gate that Sebastiano had climbed over the evening before, on the way to his meeting with Fausta, and pulling themselves up by the wistaria branches, jumped down on the other side of the wall. Then they followed the drive beneath the austere green wall of the box hedge. Here and there between the box trees were gaps through which they caught a glimpse of a little white marble temple, of a pool in which swans slowly sailed, of a secret enclosure with a mossy, weather-stained seat around it, enlivened by a circle of gesturing statues. The sun was rapidly mounting the sky and brilliant shafts of light infiltrated to every point, bringing a smile to the face of this combed and civilized nature. The attitudes of the sculptured figures assumed a discreet playfulness in spite of the grime clothing their rounded limbs. The green water in the marble basins reflected sky and trees and the graceful, faintly trembling inverted images of the swans. The great peacocks emerged tottering onto the grass, stretched their legs wide, and began to unfold their fans of gilded plumage in the early sunshine.

Perro, immersed in his plans, observed these beauties with a distracted eye. Sebastiano, as he drew nearer to Fausta, could not help remembering the many nights on which he had strolled, closely entwined with his beloved, among the pools and the simpering statues. But Saverio, after his distressing burst of inspiration, succumbed again to his habitual political propagandism. Certainly this park was extremely beautiful, he said, there was no doubt about it; the form of civilization now on its deathbed would at least be able to leave behind it these monuments of its taste. But it was scandalous that a few privileged people should enjoy all these delights; scandalous that an unwarlike, corrupt oligarchy should have the sole right to such a place for its own private amusements; scandalous, in fact, that so much beauty should be forbidden to the majority who were the most deserving of it. Tomorrow this park would be open to all; all would be permitted to improve their minds with the sight of these beauties; all would be able to enjoy this peaceful solitude. Besides, if the dying civilization had been capable of creating ten such places, the new civilization, the one which they were perhaps inaugurating with this morning walk of theirs, would create a hundred of them. Greater liberty would produce greater beauty, and more of it. . . . And so on.

Perro, now that they were approaching the villa, no longer

found him even comic, and fearing a premature arrest that would have sent the whole of his intrigue sky-high, told him to be quiet. And Sebastiano went on thinking about Fausta. Passing by a seat upon which he and she had sat together for a long time the night before, he caught sight of her handkerchief on the ground and picked it up. It was soaked with dew, but still had a perfume about it like that of the grass itself. Sebastiano, in a dream of delight, allowed the other two to go on ahead, and so his discovery was not noticed. Walking behind the taciturn Perro and the chattering Saverio, he clutched the handkerchief in his fist and pressed it against his lips.

As they came out into the open, the villa became suddenly visible, looking very cold and solid with all its windows shut. The guests were not yet awake. Saverio observed sarcastically that all these refined gentlefolk, fatigued with doing nothing, slept heavily; at this hour the peasants had already been busy for some time at their work in the fields. But Perro, thoroughly sincere for once, said he envied them; after his short disturbed night, in spite of a deceptive clear-headedness when he awoke, he could feel the desire for sleep going to his brain like strong wine. Sebastiano's eyes traveled at once to the closed shutters of Fausta's room. For a moment her figure was superimposed upon them, faint and melancholy as a ghost in its diaphanous black dress, smiling at him, it seemed, and making ghostly signs with its head. A great deserted silence enveloped the house. The sun, although it was already sending long swords of light across the sloping meadow, lit up only one corner of the villa; all the rest of the façade was still veiled in deep shadow.

## CHAPTER 11

Perro, who apparently already knew the place, went straight behind the house to a small, unimportant looking door, and telling his companions that they must now, in effect, put on their masks, rang the bell. With a promptness that astonished Sebastiano, the door opened and the butler appeared. He was a thickset, broad-shouldered man, with a round, bald head and a pale face like an unhealthy moon, and was dressed in a striped working jacket and black trousers. This man, who was also in the pay of the police as an informer and spy of minor rank, had been told of the fake conspiracy by Perro some time before. Like the police commissioner of Antigua, he did not approve of these dangerous methods, but he had to obey.

The butler, speaking in a low voice and looking, not at

the faces of the three men, but at the sky, said that they had arrived just in time, and led them into the basement of the villa. One single passage, narrow, bare and gloomy, wound about like a maze in this part of the house, and endless rooms, large and small, led off it. Just as though they were important guests he showed them the vast, complicated kitchen, like a laboratory with its many stoves and pipes rising to the ceiling; two or three rooms in which men and women were cleaning and putting in order the shoes and clothes of the guests; and—after passing numbers of small servants' bedrooms, still untidy and smelling heavy and musty after the night—he even showed them the woodshed, the pantry and the storerooms. Saverio said nothing, having been forbidden to speak; but he relieved his feelings by exchanging significant glances with his two companions as if to say: this is where the poor labor in order to keep the rich happy and well fed. Finally the butler led them into a kind of dressing room where a row of green-painted iron lockers stood facing a row of gray cement showerbaths and wash basins. He opened one of the lockers and showed them their liveries hanging all ready on hooks inside. Then, telling them to get dressed and join him in the kitchen, he left them.

They dressed in the dismal, icy, underground room, that smelled like a soldiers' latrine and a hospital combined. Perro, when he was ready, looked a very questionable sort of footman, with an appearance altogether too elegant and formal—so much the footman, in fact, that it seemed doubtful whether he could be a footman at all. Sebastiano looked more like an impersonation than either of the others—almost as though he were one of the Duchess's guests trying on an eighteenth-century cavalier's costume for the fancy-dress ball that evening. The most convincing looking flunkey of the three was Saverio, whose livery seemed to show off all his most essentially ill-bred points, his squat figure, his general uncouthness and shapelessness. He looked as though in all his life he had never worn anything but a braided tail-coat, knee breeches and white stockings. The stockings displayed his disproportionately large, plebeian calves, just as the coat, of heavy material and plastered with gold braids, seemed to show off the thick, slightly humped shape of his shoulders—the shoulders of one who is used to carrying burdens. Perro remarked that spectacles looked a bit odd on a footman, but that, on the whole, he had seen worse. Then they held a short council of war. It was decided that Perro should see to the concealment of the bomb for the moment and that the other two were to take their orders from him. Then they left the dressing room and went to the kitchen.

The butler, as soon as he saw them come in, left a group of menservants whom he was instructing and came forward quickly to meet them. This was not so much out of deference to Perro as from a desire not to create confusion among the staff for which he was responsible. These three intruders, as well as Perro's numerous other agents who had arrived the evening before, must not be allowed to mix with the regular household staff but must be kept apart on unimportant tasks, in out-of-the-way corners. The butler, fearing some catastrophe, was cursing the day he had been forced to take part in these intrigues. He cursed the police and cursed General Tereso. "I would give a whole year's tips and still think myself lucky," he thought, "if I could get through till tomorrow morning without any disasters." But none of these thoughts was visible in his face, round as a ball, on which the long mustaches faded into the dirty shadow of the unshaven beard (he usually shaved just before lunch, at midday, so as to appear before his employers with a fresh, clean face; and he had a second shave in the evening, just before dinner). He told the three men he had three separate jobs for them and they must be careful to do exactly as they were told, otherwise there would be a muddle.

Leading the way, the butler took them up a small winding stair cut in the thickness of the wall, till they came to a little door which, when opened, proved to be simply one of the frescoed panels of a vast hall from which the stately main staircase led to the rooms above. From this hall he led them through various rooms to the right wing of the villa. The windows of the reception rooms at this hour were still closed and the air was full of the smoke and stuffiness of the evening before. Everywhere in these great white and gold rooms they saw traces of the Duchess's house party— ash trays full of cigarette butts, seats and armchairs disarranged by groups of talkers, piles of counters and scattered packs of cards on little green tables, ruffled carpets, half-empty bottles, dirty glasses, vases full of faded flowers whose petals were scattered over marble table tops. Saverio looked at all these things with the eye of a political agitator and decided to test the reactions of the butler. He remarked that all this waste and disorder made one think by contrast of the poor homes of the Antigua workmen, and that in fact such injustice, such disparity of lot were intolerable and ought to be abolished. The butler, who had been for some time secretly studying the faces of Sebastiano and Saverio and wondering whether they were the hare or the hounds, replied with ill-concealed embarrassment that he was quite right; it was certainly so. But inwardly he thought: "You d—d scoundrel . . . If there were no more rich people what should I do? Be a policeman, eh? What would my wife and children do? But, luckily, tomorrow you'll be in the lockup, and a very good thing too. . . . You've certainly asked for it."

His eye, however, doubly trained by his avowed duties as a butler and his secret duties as an informer, had perceived in Sebastiano's face something rather unusual, the expression, of a man who is accustomed to give orders and not to serve—not even to serve the police. It seemed to him odd that a person of that kind should have got himself mixed up, in company with a bumpkin like Saverio, in a plot staged by the police. "You would think he was one of Her Excellency's guests," thought the butler, "not a police agent like Perro or a lout like the other fellow. . . . What's his idea in this intrigue? Is he just amusing himself or trying a new sensation?" By which it can be seen that the butler, long accustomed to service with people of Sebastiano's kind, had come very near the truth. But it must also be observed that the butler, though he had taken a profound dislike for different reasons both to Perro and Saverio, did not therefore look with any greater sympathy upon Sebastiano, though he had placed him at the first glance as belonging to the class which provided him and his children with a living. The butler was essentially of the servant class, neither patrician nor plebeian, wavering always between envy and respect, between sarcasm and flattery. He was incapable of loving anyone, even himself, for by dint of always wearing livery and bowing and obeying orders he no longer even knew whether he liked or hated his own profession. However, these feelings were fugitive and vague. His dominant sensation at the moment was one of disgust and fear at being forced to participate in an intrigue which he instinctively felt to be pregnant with troubles and dangers and which disturbed his sense of order.

Perro had already spoken to the butler about Saverio, describing him as an idiot and a fanatic and advising that he should be given some entirely unimportant job so that he would have no chance of attracting attention by his usual indiscreet manner. The butler took the three men by another small staircase to the second floor and led them down a long corridor, flanked with many doors, right to its farthest end where, beneath a large indicator-board full of numbers, sat a girl all alone. Saverio, said the butler, was also to sit under the indicator, and every time one of the numbers jumped up and the girl went to take orders from the various rooms he was to give notice of it by telephone to the kitchens. The girl did not think Saverio worth even a glance when he sat down, extremely embarrassed, on the other side of the table. She was reading a novel with a brightly colored cover on which Sebastiano, always curious about women of whatever walk in life, managed to read, slantwise: *Forsaken on Her Wedding-Day*.

Having disposed of Saverio, the butler took Perro and Sebastiano to the other end of the corridor and thence, through a couple of anterooms, into a short gallery, vaulted and highly decorated, with only three doors opening out of it, all of them surmounted with marble coats of arms and friezes. This, he announced, was known as "The Gallery of Busts." He told them that this gallery, so called because of the busts of Pizarro, Cortez and other conquistadors which stood all along one side between the windows, was the most luxurious and imposing part of the house and was usually kept for distinguished guests. At the end of the gallery was a fourth door, loftier and more ornate than the others, and this, he explained, was the door of the chapel. Of the other three doors, the first led into the Duchess's own apartments, the second into the suite reserved for Tereso, and the third into that of the Countess Sanchez—at which name Sebastiano's heart at once began to beat faster. The butler ended by saying that they were to remain in this gallery and be ready to attend upon these three important personages.

Still with an air of stiff and surly deference, he then took a bunch of keys from his pocket and unlocked the door of Tereso's suite. This suite consisted of a small vestibule, a bedroom, a bathroom and a study. The butler went to the two windows of the bedroom and threw open the shutters. Then, leaning against the window sill, he pointed to the great white and gold bed and related how the heads of many illustrious guests—princes, ambassadors, politicians, generals—had rested upon its pillows. He knew very well that these two were not much interested in learning of such things, about which most visitors to the villa were so inquisitive. In relating them he was merely yielding to the almost unconscious vanity of a sevant in a great house. Perro, guessing his uneasiness and wishing to frighten him, said jokingly that he was forgetting the best story of all—that in that same bed Venustiano Valdez, the president who had been in power immediately before Tereso, had slept the last sleep of his life before being taken away under escort to Antigua and there shot against a wall—by order of his successor. "A strange coincidence," concluded Perro, winking at Sebastiano. The butler gave him a quick glance, his eyes large and round with fright. Then he said he had things to do and went out hurriedly.

After he had gone Perro took an expensive cigar from a box on the bedside table, lit it, and sat down in an armchair at the foot of the bed, crossing his legs. He had not yet given up his attempt to find out what Sebastiano was really like, and with this purpose in view, began with a wealth of detail to describe the means by which the assassination would be carried out. Saverio would bring up the bomb on a tray, concealing it with one of these metal dish covers that are used for keeping food hot. He would go into the General's bathroom and place the bomb in the little cupboard where the towels were kept. In the meantime Perro and some of his assistants would be on guard in the gallery. Saverio, after depositing the bomb, would come back into the gallery, having locked both the cupboard and the bathroom door. They would all make their escape together; half an hour later the bomb would go off, blowing up the villa and burying Tereso and everyone else in the ruins.

Perro spoke slowly, mouthing his words beneath his neat mustache and pausing every now and then to inhale the smoke of his cigar and to look with a sly, sardonic glance at his companion. Sebastiano, standing in front of him, listened with horror—not so much at the brutality of the intended murder as at the thought of his beloved Fausta's danger. "If I hadn't listened at Saverio's window," he thought, "not only would Fausta have had to yield to Tereso's demands, but she would have perished with him into the bargain, in his arms, beneath the ruins of the villa." In the coincidence that allowed him not only to save Fausta but at the same time to preserve his love for her unsullied, he recognized yet another manifestation of the good luck in which he so firmly believed.

Hoping to discern some sign of fear in Sebastiano, Perro emphasized the tremendous power of the bomb and the many dangers involved. But Fausta alone occupied Sebastiano's mind; and he, in turn, was puzzled and surprised at Perro's polite and elegant intrepidity. "My goodness, Saverio is right, he's a real professional terrorist," he thought, astonished. Perro, on his side, was thinking: "This fellow is certainly a tough nut; he doesn't blink an eyelid."

Sebastiano, who now had a plan of his own, suddenly asked Perro what he was to do while they were mounting guard in the gallery and while Saverio was hiding the bomb. Perro, whose aim was to catch the two half-brothers in the very act, replied after a moment's reflection that he had better help Saverio to place the bomb in position, since two were always better than one. But Sebastiano said that Saverio could quite well manage it by himself and that he would merely get in his way. He thought it would be better for him to take up his position in one of the two rooms adjoining Tereso's—the Countess Sanchez' for instance—and there, armed, he could keep watch in case anyone tried to spy upon their preparations. This ingenuous proposal, which was suggested to Sebastiano not by the real requirements of the plot but by a desire to be able to enter Tereso's room without warning and interrupt his interview with Fausta in the nick of time, was almost his undoing. "Why take up a position in an adjoining room?" thought Perro; "what's the use of that?" But good luck again befriended Sebastiano, and suggested to Perro that after all it might be more convenient to arrest the two half-brothers separately than together. Being both of them strong and energetic, they might try to defend themselves; and Cinco had expressly desired that there should not be any kind of disturbance.

So Perro for the moment gave up trying to guess the hidden purpose in Sebastiano's mysterious proposal, though instinct made him certain that in it somehow lay the explanation of his extraordinary calm; all he did was to inqure whether he was armed. When Sebastinao replied that he was not, Perro took his own pistol from his pocket and gave it to him. It was only an *agent provocateur's* pistol, the kind that such men slip into the pockets of unarmed participators in riots and demonstrations, so that when arrested they can be charged with the illegal carrying of firearms, and it could only fire a single round; but it would be more than sufficient to prove Sebastiano's guilt. Perro, who was dropping with fatigue, gave Sebastiano one or two further instructions, then, throwing away his half-smoked cigar, went off to sleep in the servants' quarters.

## CHAPTER 12

Left alone, Sebastiano in his turn sat down at the foot of the bed and thought over the situation. What he now longed for was clearly impossible. He wanted to see Fausta —whose breathing he imagined he could hear in the next room—without her recognizing him or at any rate without his having to reveal the reason for his disguise. Thus thinking, he rose from the armchair and began to walk up and down. He put his eye to the keyhole of the door that led to her room, but could see nothing. Then he went to the window and leaned out, assuring himself that Fausta's shutters were still closed. The window looked out to the east across one end of the villa, and the sun, now risen above the great box hedge, shone on part of the open space in front of the house. Farther away, down the drive, a young gardener was raking the gravel with a monotonous, remote sound; from this height it was possible to see exactly which part of the gravel had been raked and which had not. Sebastiano, after watching the gardener for a while, decided to remain at the window until the shutters of Fausta's window opened and Fausta herself appeared. This seemed the only way of seeing her without being seen. Fausta, only half awake, would certainly not look at him, whereas he would be able to enjoy for a moment the charming sight of his beloved while she was still all relaxed and rumpled from her bed.

He waited; and the gardener with his wooden rake methodically combed the gravel, still crossed here and there by the tire marks of cars. At last the sound of an opening window made his heart beat wildly. A vigorous hand pushed out the shutters, flinging them wide open. Sebastiano, in his confused state of mind, had forgotten that a lady in Fausta's position does not get up to open her own window. It is her maid who lets in the light of morning upon her while she herself remains comfortably warm and drowsy in bed. And so when, holding his breath and with his heart in a tumult, he leaned forward a little to catch a glimpse of Fausta, it was quite a different face that met his eye.

It was the face of a young but atrociously ugly woman, a face resembling in every respect that of a Pekinese dog, with goggle eyes under a projecting brow, snub nose, wide red mouth shadowed with black down, and round, dark cheeks. So great was Sebastiano's astonishment that he could think of no way of hiding it except by wishing the ugly creature good morning. The staring eyes received his greeting with composure, as though it were quite the proper thing. "Good morning," she answered, and vanished. Sebastiano could not help thinking that here was a woman with whom he could do anything he wanted.

But what did he want? That was the problem. After spending nearly an hour trying to puzzle it out, wandering restlessly around the room and listening intently to the sounds next door, he went out, still undecided, into the gallery. Almost immediately Fausta's door opened as if by chance and out came the snub-nosed maid. She was of medium height, but behind her coquettish little apron was a firm, vigorous, slim, well-proportioned figure which partly mitigated the unfortunate impression created by her face. Sebastiano went up to her and with a spontaneity that surprised even himself, asked if he could do anything to help her.

"Ah, you're one of the new ones," she said, smiling and displaying very white teeth, her dark cheeks furrowed by two curiosly unattractive dimples. But she thanked him for his offer, explaining that her own particular jobs could not be done by a man. And yet, she said, to tell the truth, the Duchess would not at all mind seeing a handsome young man like him coming into her room instead of herself. Thus Sebastiano learned at the same moment that the Duchess Gorina was partial to good-looking menservants and that the ugly maid liked him.

"I'm not a handsome young man," he protested, but as he said these words there must have been such a charming look of shyness in his eyes that the ugly creature could not help smiling with pleasure.

"Oh, go on, you know very well you are," she said gaily. She was quite excited already; and those round, staring dog's eyes of hers seemed now, instead of merely looking at, to be positively caressing the young man's face.

"And who is in there?" asked Sebastiano, affecting complete indifference as he pointed toward Fausta's door.

"No poaching allowed *there*," she replied crudely. And she explained that General Arango's mistress-to-be lived there; there was nothing for him in *that* quarter. She said this with such virulence that Sebastiano trembled with instinctive jealousy. But he quickly consoled himself with the thought that, after all, it was both delightful and flattering to be the possessor of Fausta's favors without anyone suspecting it.

"Well," she said, half irresolute, half coy, "I must go . . . See you later."

But she did not move; and Sebastiano, knowing what was expected of him, without delay put his arm round her waist. She at once let herself fall against him with a gentle sigh of happiness, her moist lips pressed convulsively, violently against his.

"Is that what you do with all the girls?" she asked a moment later when they had separated; and her unlovely eyes sparkled with an excitement so intense that Sebastiano felt his cheeks burning with shame. He realized, however, that she might be extremely useful to him later, when he wanted to take up his position in Fausta's bedroom.

"You *are* a good-looking boy," she whispered to him meanwhile, and with a rough hand slowly and tremblingly caressed his face. "What beautiful eyes you have . . . My name is Giustina—what's yours?"

Sebastiano picked a name at random. "Ricardo," he said.

"Ricardito," she repeated, caressingly, "Ricardito," and adding that she must go and take the Duchess her breakfast, she ran away.

In a few moments she reappeared, breathless, carrying

a tray. "Please," she said hurriedly, "will you take this to Her Excellency for me?" She explained that she had to rush off to somebody else who had called her. But he must be careful, she said facetiously, not to go too near the mistress's bed; the Duchess was quite capable, if she liked the look of him, of making a grab and pulling him down beside her with her arms around his neck. That had been known to happen. With these words she ran off, leaving Sebastiano in great discomfort.

It was the first time in his life that he had carried a tray, and he was terrified that some clumsy movement might cause him to drop the whole thing on the floor. The wide tray was spread with a little lace tablecloth, and on it were a coffee pot and milk jug, a butter dish, a jam pot, a cup and saucer, two egg cups with eggs in them, and there was a great dome-shaped cover over the top. It was made of heavy antique silver, with the Duchess's arms engraved on each piece. Holding the tray balanced on an unsteady hand, his eyes lowered, Sebastiano went to the Duchess's door and knocked. He immediately heard a shrill voice bidding him enter, in a sustained, ringing tone; and pushing open the door he went in, his eyes still fixed on the tray. When he raised them he saw a room very like the one prepared for Tereso, except for a great many feminine garments scattered untidily about on the chairs. In the middle, in a vast bed whose canopy was adorned with an enormous carved and gilded coat of arms surmounted by a no less gorgeous golden coronet, sat the Duchess, propped on a pile of pillows. With her lofty crest of dyed hair, her little bleary eyes, her big red nose and her haughty mouth, she was looking even more than usual like a great parrot, frowning and full of a sort of crazy arrogance. Her figure, though small, was generously formed, and the foaming, lacy edges of her elaborate nightgown allowed a glimpse of a voluminous bosom, flabby, wrinkled, red, upon which hung a great cross of purple gems. From other lacy frills issued her thick, freckled arms, reddish in color, and having the appearance of meat that has been finely minced and tied up tightly in a fine, smooth membrane. Her hands, with their knots of bluish veins, their heavily beringed fingers wide apart, were joined in front of her on the bedclothes.

But the stately, absurd ugliness of the Duchess did not hold Sebastiano's embarrassed glance for more than a moment. For suddenly, with a sinking of the heart, he had seen Fausta, lying across the foot of the Duchess's bed. She was wearing a light woolen dress that he knew well. He recognized her at once from the back of her neck, narrow and delicate, where her short hair ended in a number of little pointed curls. Fausta, who had just finished dressing, had come to pay a morning visit to her protectress, and at the moment when Sebastiano entered she was speaking of the imminent arrival of Tereso.

Sebastiano was violently agitated at the sight of the back of Fausta's neck, and he very nearly dropped the tray he was carrying. But Fausta, whose back was turned to him and who did not move, could not see him. The Duchess, on the other hand, had immediately turned her small, imperious eyes upon him and could see him very well indeed. Beneath her proud haughtiness of manner the Duchess concealed a great deal of good sense and a great deal of penetration—in everything, that is to say, except in affairs of the heart, as is so often the case. She certainly did not consider herself beautiful; neither did she consider herself ugly: or rather, she did perhaps consider herself to be ugly and at the same time somehow seductive because of the youthful ardor of her senses, the importance of her position as a rich and titled woman, and her long and liberal experience of love. The facetious warning given to Sebastiano by Giustina was not merely the gibe of a jealous woman, for it was true that the Duchess now and then deigned to grant her favors to one or the other of the most attractive of her menservants. She was so young in heart that she believed, or at least she tried to believe, that these young men loved her for herself. She behaved toward them in every possible respect as a beautiful woman toward her lover; scenes of jealousy or coquettishness, affectations, rebuffs, flatteries, even tears—she spared them nothing. But afterward she had enough sense to reward their long-suffering patience with extravagantly generous presents.

Neither Sebastiano's charm nor his obvious agitation escaped the Duchess's notice. She immediately thought he was excited on her account; and she in her turn became conscious of the sharp sting of desire. So convinced was she of having completely captivated him that in her heart she cursed the presence of Fausta, for had it not been for her intrusion what might not have happened? The Duchess gazed at Sebastiano with a frown as overpowering as his own agitation, and then asked: "You are one of the new footmen?"

"Yes, Your Excellency," answered Sebastiano.

"Put down the tray on that table."

"Yes, Your Excellency."

"Not that one—what are you doing? On the wheeled table over there."

"Yes, Your Excellency."

"Now bring it here—do you have to be told everything!"

"Yes, Your Excellency."

"Can't you say anything except yes or no? . . . What is your name?"

"Ricardo, Your Excellency."

"Ricardo . . . Where were you before Ricardo?"

"In a hotel, Your Excellency."

"Pour out the coffee, then, Ricardo—half coffee and half milk."

"Yes, Your Excellency."

"But what are you doing? You've upset the coffee."

"Just a drop, Your Excellency."

"Just a drop! Just a hundred drops . . . Are you engaged to be married, Ricardo?"

"No, Your Excellency."

"Well, then, leave the maids alone. . . . Very well, you may go now, Ricardo."

"Yes, Your Excellency."

Sebastiano retired toward the door followed by the burning glances of the Duchess; but he had time to hear Fausta ask, as though resuming an interrupted conversation: "But will it really be necessary for me to put lampblack on my face?"—obviously referring to the fancy dress she had chosen for the party that evening. Then he found himself outside the room again, in the gallery, with a tumult in his breast and his body damp with sweat under the hard heavy livery.


## CHAPTER 13

Giustina was waiting for him in one of the window recesses and at once asked him how he had got on. But Sebastiano was thinking of Fausta, and did not at first understand her question. Then Giustina, with a knowing laugh, told him that he looked completely bewildered—a sure sign that the Duchess had made a conquest of him. She did not seem at all convinced by the embarrassed account that Sebastiano hastened to give her as soon as he understood to whom she was alluding; and as at that moment the Duchess's bell rang again, she told him peevishly that she would go herself this time. She was absent only a few minutes; but when she returned, with the tray almost untouched, she informed Sebastiano that he must have made a great impression on the old woman, since, apart from the fact that she had hardly touched her breakfast—a thing that happened very rarely—she had also asked a great many questions about him, showing clearly that she was annoyed at his not having come back again instead of her.

"Before two days are out she'll promote you to be her personal servant—and then you're for it," concluded the maid.

There was jealousy and also a kind of envy in the tone in which she pronounced these words. Sebastiano could not help smiling when it occurred to him that he ought, of course, to regard it as another piece of good luck that the Duchess's amorous fancy should have fixed itself upon him.

Giustina angrily seized a broom and thrust it roughly into his hand, saying that in the meantime, until he became the Duchess's lover, he had better do some work. He had better come and help her sweep out and tidy up the Countess Sanchez' room. At this name all Sebastiano's agitation returned. Automatically he took the broom and followed her.

"How terribly unfair this is!" thought Sebastiano, as Giustina moved about the bedroom; "here am I for the first time in this room I have longed to be in and dreamed about—and instead of kissing, one by one, these delicate garments that Fausta has worn on her lovely body, instead of burying my face in the pillow on which she has laid her cheek or in the sheets whose folds still preserve her precious warmth, instead of breathing at my ease the air already breathed by her, I have to stand by while all these delicious things are destroyed; while this rude servant girl throws the clothes that Fausta has worn into a corner; while she tears the bed to pieces, and with it the impression that Fausta's limbs have left; while in place of this warm air, still perfumed and throbbing with Fausta's presence, she lets in the brutal, insipid freshness of the morning. . . ." Sebastiano, with these thoughts in his mind, looked eagerly around the room, as though to fix carefully in his memory every detail of its beloved disorder. His gaze was drawn especially to the hollow that Fausta's body had left in the tumbled bed. He longed to throw himself upon this sweet imprint and cover it with kisses.

Giustina put the broom and bucket in a corner and started to tidy the room. She was not envious of her surroundings, as a middle-class woman might have been; she was too familiar with the intimacies of her mistress's life not to feel that Fausta's luxuries were almost her own property, but her remarks were not without a certain unconscious cruelty which made Sebastiano wince.

"Look at these dresses," she said, pointing to the cupboard in which Fausta's innumerable garments were hung in a tightly packed row. "She doesn't even know how many she's got. But they cost her plenty. She has to put up with old men's kisses in order to get them . . . They say the

General's quite old, too—Ugh! I wouldn't have anything to do with old men, not even if they made me a Duchess." Then she took one of the diaphanous pink garments that had been tossed on a chair and handed it to Sebastiano, saying: "Throw it on the floor; it's got to be washed."

To Sebastiano it seemed a sin to cast into the dust this wisp of gauze that had embraced Fausta's naked body. Taking advantage of a moment when Giustina turned her back upon him he raised it to his lips and kissed it, breathing in its perfume. But Giustina was watching him in the wardrobe mirror.

"Ha," she laughed scornfully, "you like perfumes and women's clothes, do you? You're a pretty vicious one, it seems to me . . . Smell it, smell it, my boy. *You'll* never get a chance of touching these clothes—except maybe when they're being sent to the laundry."

Sebastino, who remembered that not many hours before he had fumbled with impatient fingers between these very folds of silk and the sweet, yielding flesh of his mistress, smiled at Giustina, almost grateful to her for her mistake; then he threw the garment into a corner.

Giustina was not content with tidying the room. She was also, as Sebastiano was quick to see, indiscreet and a bit of a thief. Standing in front of the dressing table, twisting her head conceitedly before the mirror with an atomizer in her hand, she covered herself with perfume. Then she took up something from among the bottles and boxes and slipped it into her pocket.

"Hey, what are you taking?" Sebastiano could not help asking.

She showed him what it was—a lipstick. "She must have about a hundred of them," she said casually.

After the lipstick came an almost untouched box of exotic cigarettes she insisted on Sebastiano's accepting, saying that the countess would never miss them. Sebastiano, embarrassed, had to hide the cigarettes in his pocket.

Giustina's real reason in inviting Sebastiano to help her was simply in order to be alone with him—for she knew that Fausta would not come back to her room. She hoped he would embrace her and that after much coyness and resistance and many kisses he would finally push her on to that large, convenient and comfortable bed. But Sebastiano avoided her passionate glances and kept his head bent, feverishly dusting objects that had no need of being dusted and remaining as far away from her as possible. In the end, after tidying the dressing table, Giustina lost all constraint and let herself drop, with a great sigh, flat on her back on the bed, her head on the pillow and her legs spread out, declaring that she felt tired and must have a little rest. The invitation was so obvious that Sebastiano shuddered. He was shocked at the idea of betraying Fausta, even from necessity, actually on her own bed. He sat down in the armchair at the foot of the bed and lit a cigarette.

"You come and lie down, too," Giustina said brazenly. "What are you doing there in that armchair?"

Sebastiano, with an embarrassed cough, objected that the Countess might come in at any moment. And to avoid any more insistence on the subject he hurriedly proposed that they meet after lunch in some other part of the villa, in Giustina's own room, for instance.

"You're so nervous," said the girl contemptuously, rising from the bed. "Anyhow, what did you think? I was only asking you to come and lie down. . . . After lunch I don't know if I shall be able to . . ." She seemed highly annoyed, and Sebastiano, to drive away her ill humor, had to steel himself to beg for another of her long, honeyed kisses.

In order to avoid talking about this new love affair, which Giustina already seemed to regard as an established fact, Sebastiano started asking her questions about Fausta. Giustina, who had returned to her sweeping, told him, as she wielded the broom, that Fausta was beyond comparison the most beautiful of all the ladies staying in the villa at the moment.

"But she's bad," added the maid, "and a liar. If I were a man I certainly shouldn't trust her."

Sebastiano asked her whether Fausta had any other lover besides the General. Giustina replied that there certainly must be another one, for she had proof, having found a man's linen handkerchief with the initials S.R. embroidered on it in her mistress's bag one morning. But who this lover might be, concluded Giustina, she had not been able to find out, though she had done her best to spy upon them. It was one of the other guests, no doubt. Sebastiano, who one night recently had lent Fausta his handkerchief, smiled with satisfaction. Of course she loved nobody but him. Giustina's words provided another proof of it—if indeed there was still any need of proof.

Sebastiano had not, like Perro, a confirmed habit of dissimulation; besides, during the last few weeks his hours of sleep had been short. At the present moment, as a result both of the nervous strain of playing a part and of the fatigue of many sleepless nights, he was conscious of a pleasant but irresistible torpor creeping over him. His eyelids closed as he stood talking to Giustina, and when he looked at Fausta's bed he was tempted by the sudden, impossible idea of throwing himself down on the coverlet and going to sleep. When Giustina disappeared in order to fetch the vacuum cleaner, he too left the room. From the gallery he went through the reception rooms into the great hall. He tried to find the panel that opened on to the service staircase, but however much he searched he could not discover it. So, keeping close against the wall and moving with the leisureliness and composure proper to menservants, he started going down the great wide steps of the main staircase.

He had descended the first flight in the silence of the still sleeping villa, and was just starting on the second when, from one of the reception rooms, an imperious voice called out: "I say . . . you there." He hoped that the order was intended for some other servant and continued downstairs. But the voice repeated: "I say, you—are you deaf? Yes, you . . . I am speaking to you. . . ."

Sebastiano did not know what a profound effect a livery can have on its wearer's behavior. He tried to go on down the stairs as though he had not heard, but the livery pulled him back. "Now I really *am* a footman," he said to himself, amused; and he obeyed the voice.

Standing in the middle of the room beside a table was a young man dressed in riding clothes who was impatiently tapping his whip against his yellow calf riding boot.

"Will you please go—?" he began; but as he raised his eyes to Sebastiano an immense astonishment made him pause. "Sebastiano! What on earth are you doing here?"

"Be quiet, for goodness' sake," whispered Sebastiano, hastening forward.

The young man was a certain S., a wealthy landowner in the neighborhood. Sebastiano had been out shooting with him less than a month before. He began hurriedly to explain that he was dressed up like this in order to—in order to . . . The other suddenly gave a wink and did not let him finish.

"Ah, I understand. . . . Women again, eh? But you're crazy, all the same. If that old witch of a Duchess got to know about it . . . But, I say, you do look nice in your livery, you know."

Sebastiano, relieved at the turn things had taken, confirmed his friend in his supposition—which was, after all, perfectly true—and begged him not to betray him. The other promised he would keep his mouth shut, swearing on his word of honor as a gentleman that he could be trusted.

"All the same, you're crazy," he repeated, "quite crazy. Turn round, I want to see how your calves look."

Sebastiano had to stand and be admired while the other man went into fits of ill-suppressed laughter. At last, after a final injunction to him to say nothing, and a renewed assurance from his friend that there was no cause for anxiety, Sebastiano was able to make his escape.

This time, however, he was determined not to run the risk of being given any more orders or of being recognized again. Sleep he must, and as soon as possible, otherwise he was afraid he might find himself dozing off in one of the great solemn armchairs that adorned the staircase landing. So, without bothering any more to behave like a trained servant, he rushed headlong down the second flight and out into the park. He was afraid that if he went and rested in one of the small staff rooms in the basement he would be courting the possibility of an amorous visit from Giustina—not to mention Perro and Saverio and their accursed, abominable plot. He remembered that he and Fausta, during their nights of love-making, had often taken refuge in a sort of sham Alpine hut on the top of a little hill in a solitary corner of the park. That was just the hiding place for him now, and he almost ran as he went toward it.

Leaving the drive he went behind the box hedges and followed a narrow path, carpeted with dead leaves, which ran between the wood and the encircling wall. He passed the black, lily-starred waters of the artificial lake, the water clock, the swans, he crossed the little bridge over the stream beside the tiny cascade, and came at last to the mossy steps and rustic balustrade that wound corkscrew-fashion through a thick grove of laurels and ilexes, and on up the hill. He started to walk up the steps, leaning on the balustrade. In the silence he could hear birds twittering and fluttering their wings in the undergrowth; and a pleasant damp, woody smell came to his nostrils, reminding him of the times he had mounted the steps at night with his arm around Fausta, eager to reach the top yet at the same time so impatient that he had to pause every now and then for a kiss or two. At the top of the steps, on the highest point, in a clearing among the trees, was the cabin. It was made of tree trunks whose bark had been left untouched and which bristled with points where boughs had been sawn off, and was a careful imitation of a certain type of hut to be found in the Alps.

Sebastiano pushed the door open and went in. It was dark inside, except for the threads of light which crept in between the joints of the tree trunks. But when the eyes grew accustomed to the gloom it could be seen that the hut was divided horizontally in two, halfway up to the roof, by a plank flooring. This upper level could be reached by means of a wooden ladder leaning against it. Sebastiano thought how often he had mounted that ladder with his eyes on his mistress's garter and his nostrils entranced by her perfume, and was almost surprised to see that it was such an ordinary ladder, made of plain wood; on those wonderful nights it had seemed more splendid and dazzling than if it had been of gold or some other shining metal. He climbed now into the loft, gently drew up the ladder and laid it down on the planks. Up there, there was light and air from a number of little doors under the eaves, and at night a few pigeons which inhabited the trees on the hill came in to roost. But since Sebastiano had taken to coming there with Fausta the place had been closed to the pigeons, who found one evening that their little doors had been stuffed up with newspapers. Sebastiano had cleaned the birds' droppings from the planks so that Fausta should not spoil her exquisite clothes, and had brought from home a camp mattress and a couple of cushions. The loft had thus become a regular bedroom. There was even a collection of candles and matches in one corner.

Sebastiano now crept to the bed in the dark and lay down upon it with a sigh of satisfaction. But before settling down to his much-needed sleep he took the ball of newspaper from one of the little doors and looked out. Through the hole thus made he could see out over the treetops to the great sloping meadow and, beyond the meadow and one or two small hedges, could command a view of the swimming pool, a long rectangle of green water sparkling gaily in the sun, together with the red-tiled roof of its bath house and its shining nickel-plated diving board. Small figures, red, blue, green, yellow, were moving about in the liquid golden sunlight round the white marble rim of the pool, figures of men and women in bathing suits. Now he saw one of the figures slowly climb the springboard ladder to the highest platform, join its hands above its head, bend its knees and launch itself into space. There was a great spurt of water, and then another little figure climbed on the diving board and raised its arms. "That's Fausta," thought Sebastiano, who was sure he had recognized her red bathing suit. And then, head foremost, she plunged, and with her—into deep sleep—plunged Sebastiano.

## CHAPTER 14

The distant figure that Sebastiano had seen diving from the high springboard was indeed that of Fausta. As she came up from beneath the water, shaking her head and blowing through her nostrils, she saw an unusual commotion

under the bath pavilion veranda. All the bathers were hastily
rising from the rubber cushions on which they had been lying
motionless and corpselike in the sun, and others who had
been splashing in the water were clambering out onto the
edges of the pool. The Duchess herself, her squat, plump
figure swathed in some red, flowered material and a huge
stray sugarloaf hat on her head, was hurrying from the
veranda. All this turmoil was caused by a little man in a
smart, tight-fitting uniform of brownish green, who was advancing slowly, followed at a distance by other personages
also in uniform, all of them taller than he, but looking as
if they were trying to bend down and make themselves small
as they walked so as not to insult him by their superior
stature. He, on the other hand, strutted along with his chest
thrown out, his uniform stretched tight over the hard
muscles of his broad, square shoulders and of his short,
bowed legs, which seemed ill at ease, as though they longed
to be astride a horse. His big head was close-cropped and
bristling with grizzled hair, his cheeks so close shaven that
they looked as if the blood had come to them; his forehead
was large, round and prominent, his nose small and hooked,
like the beak of an owl. His face had a firm, hard look, like
a profile on a medal—except for his eyebrows, which were of
an extraordinary thickness and blackness and which he
now wrinkled up in the September sunshine with an expression of great condescension and good nature. He was
wearing trousers with riding straps and enormous silver
spurs—a real little fighting cock, thought Fausta as she
looked at him; and one sleeve of his jacket, bearing the braid
and stars of a general, hung empty from his shoulder.

It was Tereso. But instead of climbing out of the pool and
running to make her bow to him all dripping with water
like the other bathers, Fausta remained where she was. She
had enough experience to know that given certain circumstances all men, whether generals or flunkeys, are much
alike. She knew also that it was for her that Tereso had come.
It was up to her, therefore, not to lose her head, but to pull
in her line with extreme caution, for the fish was too big
to risk its getting away through carelessness on her part.
"Strut about like a peacock if you want to," thought Fausta,
"I'm certainly not coming to meet you; it's you who must
come and look for me." This decision was the result of a
plan fully discussed by Fausta and the Duchess. They had
come to the conclusion that Tereso, in spite of the power
he wielded, in spite of his valor in war and his wisdom in
peace, was, in affairs of love, a simpleton, far more innocent
and defenceless than all the frivolous young men who were

now advancing to meet him. Fausta knew she must take full advantage of this naïveté. So she took one more look at the group formed by the General, his suite and the bathers, and then, as if nothing had happened, struck out with energy and determination through the deserted waters of the swimming pool.

The two women had not erred in their calculations. Tereso was not merely a simpleton where love is concerned but—which is worse—refused to resign himself to that role; he made the illogical but perfectly natural mistake of thinking that success ought to attend him in love as it had in all other spheres, and that to achieve this success he had merely to apply, in a slightly modified form, the methods that had brought him victory in the civil war. These methods consisted either of plain, carefully calculated brutality or of unscrupulous duplicity; but though they worked well with mobs and armies they proved too crude when applied to the more delicate encounters of love. Moreover, every time he tried them, Tereso was disappointed to find that he had again become involved in the same illusions, the same incorrect valuations, the same blunders that he had so often sworn to avoid.

He had a profound and long-standing contempt for men of all sorts, a contempt perhaps derived from his own secret but fundamental modesty; for he had conquered and subdued them all, without ever ceasing on that account to consider himself, in his own heart, a perfectly ordinary man. But he extended this contempt to women as well; and here he was guilty of a too hasty judgment, for at their hands he had never known anything but defeat. In all his life he had never found anything but venality and unfaithfulness in the women with whom he had had to do. The women who, when he was young and obscure, had decieved him with the most unworthy of his rivals, now, since he had become powerful, pursued him with sweetness and flattery to obtain his favors. With men he could tell at a glance what their designs and ambitions were; with regard to women, on the other hand—that is, until he had satisfied his desire and then thrown them aside—he always suffered under the most naïve illusions. When confronted by a woman who attracted him, Tereso became as inexpert as he had been at twenty, he was terrified of a rebuff, he was unable to conduct his wooing with that straightforwardness which in peace as in war had never failed to throw his adversaries into confusion; and he always imagined, at the slightest sign of virtuous behavior on the part of the lady, that he was in love and that his love was returned. But these moments of exaltation were

invariably followed by the same disillusionment; and then he
felt no wish to approach any but purchasable women,
whom he could treat with perfectly safe contempt even before
his desire was satisfied. Soon, however, the unsatisfactory
quality of these casual affairs would drive him to make
another bid for a less facile kind of love, with the result
that he would be involved in more blunders and more disap-
pointments. And so, between his attitude of contempt on the
one hand and his naïveté on the other, he had arrived at
the age of fifty in a state of frustration.

The same thing happened with Fausta as with so many
other women. Tereso knew perfectly well that she was
mercenary and was merely serving her own ends in her
relations with him. Yet though he despised her, he could
not help falling madly in love with her, hoping vaguely that
her notorious venality might perhaps, in his case, be put aside
and that she might love him for himself. From the moment
of his first advances he realized that she intended to make
use of him; but although her plan was quite obvious to him
he was naïvely surprised and annoyed when he found himself experiencing all the feelings that she had set out to
arouse by her artful evasiveness. Tereso, who often felt
skeptical about his own power and fame—more from a wish
to weigh their significance than from true humility—suddenly discovered, under the ordeal of his passion for Fausta,
that he really believed in his own importance. It was almost
as though the disappointment and vexation of unrequited
love had at last furnished him with a touchstone which the
flattery of his followers and the admiration of the populace
had denied him.

"So this is what I have come to," he sometimes said to
himself quite candidly. "I am the most powerful man in the
country. I have the applause of the crowd. I am at the height
of my strength and my glory. Yet a hussy with a few specious
tricks causes me more anxiety than all the machinations of
my enemies and of rival nations." He did not realize that
his political and military successes were a direct result of
his unimpaired youthful faculty for self-delusion and infatuation, of that same violence of feeling that took his
breath away whenever he thought of Fausta's lips, of her eyes,
of her body.

Today Tereso, though always so self-controlled and calculating, had committed the initial error of allowing Fausta
to see his impatience. He should not in fact have arrived
at the villa until the evening, after attending some patriotic
parade or other and the opening of a bridge at Antigua.
Under the pretext of obviating any possible attempt at assas-

sination, the whole of this program had been put off until the following day. A prudent postponement of this kind was not unusual during the General's tours in the provinces. But this time there was no question of an attempt on his life; what had really happened was that Tereso had been unable to contain his impatience at the prospect of meeting Fausta.

As he advanced slowly, erect, his chest thrown out, acknowledging the bows of the Duchess and her guests with precise, stiff salutes, his heart was beating very fast beneath his tunic; and his eyes, half hidden under his thick eyebrows, were darting swiftly over the little crowd of people in search of Fausta. The dissimulation of feeling was so habitual with Tereso that even the Duchess, cunning as an old fox, was not sure of the exact significance of his facial expression. "He is looking for Fausta, obviously," she thought, "but he is not showing all the impatience I should wish to see."

Tereso was so worried at not seeing Fausta among the guests that he answered the Duchess rudely when, after making her curtsy, she hinted that she had been taken by surprise and that she certainly had not expected the honor of his presence so early, otherwise she would have made all preparations for receiving him in a worthy manner. Yes, he had arrived before the time appointed, Tereso replied drily, and what was there strange about that? Perhaps she would like him to go back again, so as to give her time to make her preparations? His violent and unconcealed ill humor did not particularly frighten the Duchess, but it provided her with the clue she was looking for. There could be no doubt that he was thus inordinately upset because he had failed to discern Fausta among the crowd of women that swarmed about him—a sure sign that the fish was hooked and all that now remained was to pull in the line. But the old woman carefully refrained from calling Fausta, who went on calmly swimming about the pool.

When greetings and introductions were over, Tereso sat down in a wicker armchair in the shade of the veranda, crossing his legs and placing his cap on his knee. His mind was filled with disappointment and annoyance—disappointment at not having found Fausta as he had hoped, annoyance because, as always and in spite of the many lessons he had received, he had yielded to the urgency of his passion and, by his early arrival, had betrayed how important she was to him. Soon, tired of looking at the Duchess, who was pouring forth a flood of polite questions about his journey and his visit, he lowered his eyes to the pool, where each wavelet glittered with the reflected midday sun; and, as soon as he became accustomed to the glare he saw Fausta, whose beautiful brown arms rose and fell as they cleft the tumbled waters.

At the sight of her his whole body gave a start, like a horse suddenly shying at some unexpected object; but it would have been impossible to detect, in the dry and casual tone in which he asked the Duchess who it was swimming in the pool, how deeply the discovery had affected him. The old woman hastened to reply that it was Fausta, without adding title or surname—a little piece of cunning that made Tereso jump with surprise.

"Fausta who?" he asked, quickly recovering himself.

"The Countess Fausta Sanchez," said the Duchess.

"The Countess doesn't seem particularly impatient to see me," remarked Tereso gently, with a faint melancholy equally suitable to a disappointed lover or a skeptical but indulgent autocrat.

The Duchess, alarmed, started to explain that Fausta had no doubt been too deeply absorbed in her swimming to notice his arrival; otherwise she would certainly have hurried to welcome him. But if he liked, she added, with a tempting look in her eye, she could call her.

"Why?" said Tereso, brusquely, but without ill humor. "I came early on purpose, so as not to be bothered with ceremony. The Countess has done quite right not to worry about me: let her go on with her swimming."

Tereso intended this remark to imply that it was not, as it might appear, out of impatience to see Fausta that he had arrived early. The Duchess, however, was not taken in.

In the meantime Fausta, who, as she swam, had followed this whole scene out of the corner of her eye, came up very slowly out of the pool. The bottom of the pool was an inclined plane which decreased in depth toward the end opposite from the diving board. It was by slow degrees, therefore, that the lovely Fausta rose up out of the waters —first her brown boyish head and her magnificent bosom, whose curves, adorned with pearly drops, seemed to rebel against the tightness of the scanty bathing suit; then her slim waist and narrow, straight sides like those of an adolescent; and finally her long, smooth, shapely legs. Slowly, beneath the frowning eyes of Tereso, she stepped out of the pool, shaking off the water from her. Standing on the marble rim, she pulled off her rubber cap with a fine indolent gesture and shook out her hair. Then, walking on the tips of her toes and gracefully moving her hips, she went to greet the General and the Duchess. Tereso had not missed a single one of her movements, and his heart was beating faster than ever.

He was hoping that after they had exchanged greetings the lovely creature would come and crouch on the floor at his feet, humbly and obsequiously. He was already preparing something to say to her, something that should begin with a slight reproof and end with a pardon. But Fausta, after a deep bow and a few flattering but entirely conventional words which left Tereso searching for a reply, excused herself on the ground that she must dry herself and disappeared behind one of the doors of the bath house.

## CHAPTER 15

Other women, in the meantime—all those, in fact, who were present—had seated themselves on the floor round Tereso's feet, forming a graceful circle of young, scantily clad figures with lovely curving backs browned by the sun and dark or golden heads. The Duchess took the opportunity of rising and going to look for Fausta. She did not find her in her dressing room, but on the lawn behind the bath house. She was wearing dry clothes and walking about slowly in the sun, smoking and looking at her nails, her feet bare on the cool mown grass. The Duchess anxiously observed that it was high time she made a pretense of some sort of interest in Tereso; actually she was afraid that Tereso, annoyed at Fausta's coldness, might leave them all in the lurch and go back to Antigua. The situation was already strained, she said, and disaster must be avoided. But Fausta shrugged her shoulders with indifference.

"He's going to be kept waiting for a bit the ugly brute," she said in her warm, harsh voice. "Perhaps he thinks he has to do with another Carlota or Maruja?"—naming two of Tereso's recent easy conquests. "If he's had enough already, he'd better go back to Antigua; he can get what he wants there for five *scudi*."

"Yes, but I don't want him to," said the Duchess; and she explained how she was afraid that there was some likelihood that the General really might go off to Antigua in a huff.

"Ah, you're afraid he'll spoil your party, are you?" said Fausta with a loud laugh. "Don't worry. . . . I've got him at my mercy now. You can be quite sure he won't budge from here."

But the Duchess was still so nervous that Fausta promised that she would come in a moment without fail. The Duchess, reassured, returned to the swimming pool.

Fausta walked about in the sun again for a little, smoking, apparently in meditation but in reality thinking of nothing. Then she threw away her cigarette and strolled back in a

leisurely, lazy fashion onto the veranda. In one corner stood
a little wheeled table laden with drinks and *hors d'oeuvres*.

Fausta had an idea. Taking hold of the handle she pushed
the table toward the group of women squatting at Tereso's
feet, asking in an obsequious, sing-song voice like a waiter's
whether anybody wanted a drink or a sandwich. Tereso, bored
by his circle of silly, fawning women, answered promptly
that he was thirsty and longed for a drink. Tereso was an
obstemious man, but he gulped down at one draught the
extremely strong mixture that Fausta, fancifully imitating
the gestures of a barman, prepared and handed to him. Then,
under the pretext of wanting to watch a young man, a very
fine diver, who was standing on the highest springboard,
Tereso rose from his armchair and the group of fawning
women were scattered.

The diver, who was short and muscular and wore scanty
trunks that emphasized the powerful build of his body, raised
his arms and bent his legs as if to test their strength, then,
taking a spring, hurled himself head foremost, neat and
compact as a fish, piercing the surface of the water with
hardly a splash.

"Bravo! . . . good," exclaimed Tereso loudly.

"A beautiful dive, wasn't it?" said Fausta, approaching
with a glass in each hand.

Tereso turned and took the glass she held out to him. He
raised it till it touched Fausta's glass and drank her health,
looking her full in the eyes. After they had drunk they stood
for a moment side by side without saying a word, looking at
the pool. Suddenly Tereso had what he thought was a supremely brilliant idea for getting away alone with Fausta;
actually it was no more than the artless device of any amorous youth. He said he had heard so much about the park
and was very curious to see it. But he did not want any
guide except her.

Fausta was anxious to see how much more strain the situation would bear before it reached the breaking point dreaded
by the Duchess. So after replying with a slight bow that his
request was a very flattering one, she said she was sorry but
at that moment was not in a position to grant it; she was soak-
ing wet and by the time she had dried herself and dressed
it would be lunch time. The lie was a flagrant one, since not
a single drop of water remained on the whole of Fausta's
perfectly dry body. After lunch, however, she added, she
would have great pleasure in accompanying him around the
park—although, to tell the truth, there was nothing much to see.

This time Tereso saw that she was merely trying to play
with him, and the thing that the Duchess had been so afraid

of happened. He decided all at once that he would leave. He would wash his hands of Fausta and go back to Antigua, where at least he would find the crowd ready to do him honor. Without a word he put down his glass on the table and went off determinedly toward the gate. The officers of his suite ran up from all over the place and hurried after him, while the Duchess and her guests, realizing confusedly that something had happened, rose to their feet in surprise. But Fausta knew there was no question of her losing her hold over Tereso. She remained standing where she was, glass in hand, talking in an affable voice that became suddenly audible in the silence that followed Tereso's departure, to the diver who, up to his neck in the water, clung to the edge of the pool at her feet.

The distance between the pool and the red-painted iron gate was not more than thirty yards. In the space of those thirty yards a bitter conflict raged in Tereso's mind. He longed to abandon Fausta once and for all to her sterile, mercenary tricks, yet this longing made him unspeakably miserable; and, at the same time, he wished exactly the opposite. The prospect of having to spend the day amid the applause of enthusiastic crowds at Antigua, which at another time might have pleased him, now appeared inexpressibly depressing. But after walking away with such an air of determination, he could not possibly retrace his steps. His agony did not last long. When he was three yards from the gate he had a sudden inspiration and decided that he would neither go away nor turn back, but that, under the pretext of business that had to be disposed of with his secretary, he would go and shut himself up in his own rooms at the villa. He turned toward the Duchess who, with a frightened expression on her face, was asking the secretary what had happened, and brusquely invited her to show him to his room. Then, advancing between two ranks of bowing bathers with his usual slow, firm, heavy step—the same step with which he walked when reviewing the ranks of his soldiers—and followed at a distance by the Duchess and the officers, he took his way toward the villa. "Now I am going to keep *you* in suspense for a bit," he thought angrily. "We shall see who is the stronger." It was thus that Tereso disguised to himself that, during those thirty yards between the pool and the gate, he had suffered a crushing initial defeat.

Alone in his room, having dismissed his suite and the dismayed Duchess, instead of examining the papers that the secretary had put ready for him on the desk, Tereso took off his tunic and cap, and in his white undershirt, his left arm bare and the stump of the other protruding nakedly, started walking up and down the room in the shuttered half light. "What is the point," he thought, "of having vanquished all my enemies, of being the most powerful man in the country, of having defied twenty attempts on my life and won a hundred battles, of never having trembled or faltered in face of danger—if a stupid, mercenary slut, hardly even pretty (here he admitted to himself that he was being spiteful), a perfectly ordinary little strumpet, can keep me dangling like this at the mercy of her caprices? . . . As soon as I've had what I want of her she's going to pay heavily for all these silly tricks. I'll teach her to make a fool of Tereso." Thus the General reflected as he paced up and down the room. But even as he marched up and down, cursing Fausta and her mercenary coquetries, he could not help pricking up his ears in case a discreet knock should be heard above the splashing of the fountain in the courtyard, and the sound of a beloved voice, warm and husky, craving admittance.

He was listening so intently that, in the midst of his own furious comings and goings, he clearly heard someone quietly enter the next room and shut the door. He knew, having been told by the Duchess herself as she accompanied him, that the room next door was Fausta's. "But if she thinks I am going to knock at her door," thought this fiery man, whose heart began to beat twice as fast, "if she thinks I am going to call her, she's wrong; oh, how wrong she is! . . ." And to give a semblance of reality to these stern decisions, Tereso sat down at the desk, opened the portfolio, and with a deep frown on his face started to go through the papers it contained. Every now and then, as he always did when his mind was deeply engrossed, he started gently scratching the swollen ridges on the stump of his missing arm with his one hand. He found the tickling sensation pleasant, and it seemed in some way to ease his nervous tension. But this time neither the industrious effort at concentration nor the tickling of the stump succeeded in distracting him from the thought that dominated his mind.

The lines on the sheets of paper in front of him wriggled like snakes in the first warmth of spring, twisting themselves into knots and swaying up and down before his bemused eyes. His overexcited body was intimately conscious of the vibrations of Fausta's light footsteps in the next room; they stirred him with an effect more powerful and more profound than his own weighty affairs of state. She was moving to and fro and did not appear to be making more than an ordinary amount of noise, he thought. She was not humming, or dropping things, or sighing. In fact, she did not seem to be trying in any way to make her presence known or to attract his attention. The realization of this was very painful to him; at the same time it made him furious both at her triumphant self-possession and at his own incorrigible simplicity.

In the end, unable to endure it any longer, Tereso jumped up from the desk, went to the communicating door and raised his hand to knock. At the last moment he became conscious of his appearance in trousers and undershirt, his stump exposed, his arm and neck bare, and said to himself that it would be more fitting to appear before Fausta in his general's tunic. He took the tunic from the chair upon which he had thrown it and contrived, with the aid of his one arm, to put it on. Tereso had a strong instinct for formal dignity, and this, apart from his ability to calculate his own advantage, was the only quality he possessed to act as a brake on his passions.

The mere act of putting on his tunic, however, had had the effect of cooling his mad impatience for a moment. "What am I doing?" he asked himself. "Am I starting to knock at women's doors like a panting school-boy in search of adventures? Am I forgetting who I am? Am I losing my head altogether?" He sat down again at the desk, calmly and methodically opened the portfolio he had angrily closed when he had got up to knock at Fausta's door, separated the papers into various piles of unequal thickness and, taking up one of them, held it up to study it. As he looked Tereso believed he had at last found the best solution of the problem of seeing Fausta without at the same time compromising his dignity. The document he was looking at concerned her brother; it was a request for the contract of a government monopoly. Tereso knew that Fausta's brother was a swindler, and that he was asking for the contract with the express purpose of enriching himself at the expense of the State. After a pretense of reading the document that he already knew by heart, he pressed the bell four times—the signal for his secretary.

"Contreras," said Tereso as the secretary entered, without turning round or taking his eyes off the document, "go to the Countess Sanchez' room next door and tell her that I will consent to see her about that affair of her brother's." Tereso, in order to give greater verisimilitude to the pretense that he was very busy, had stuck a showy tortoise-shell-rimmed monocle, attached to his tunic by a ribbon, into his eye. His sight was excellent, and the monocle a piece of clear glass; but it was a sign to his subordinates that the matter in hand was of a really serious nature. The secretary clicked his heels and went out.

Tereso had sat down purposely with his back to the door. As soon as Contreras had gone out he took a chair that stood in front of him and placed it beside him. On the chair he arranged his gloves, his cap and his whip. Then he took up the document and again pretended to examine it.

In less than two minutes the secretary presented himself again and said that the Countess Sanchez was outside and asked to be received. Tereso replied that she was to wait, and as soon as the secretary had again gone out he put his arm on the table, uncovered his wrist and began to follow the movement of the second hand of his big gold wrist-watch. The hand went around with a hitherto unknown and agonizing slowness, but Tereso clenched his teeth and re-sisted the longing to call Contreras back again and tell him to show Fausta in. He decided to keep her waiting for ten minutes, though he considered that this was little enough and that a good half hour would hardly have been too much. He knew that there is nothing like a long wait in an ante-room to induce awe and respect. But at the third minute he could not bear it any longer. He realized that it was not Fausta but he himself who was being kept waiting, and each tiny fragment of the dial, as his eye measured it, became iden-tified with the weight of physical discomfort and feverish desire with which the passage of each second was burdened. He seemed to see Fausta's brown, boyish face mocking at him in the bright convex glass, while the busy, petulant hand of the watch went calmly round with tiny regular jerks across her smiling mouth. Then he could not longer see her face but only her figure from neck to waist, the curves be-sprinkled with pearly drops of water, the breasts firm and pointed under the tight silk of the bathing suit—just as he had seen her at the pool; and the hand of the watch continued on its way, from one breast to the other, from throat to belly. Finally the complete Fausta, naked, remote, small, made him a mocking bow, throwing him a kiss with both hands as she retreated further and further into the shining convexity of the glass; and still the hand went around. It was now the fifty-eighth second of the fifth minute. Tereso, dazed and be-wildered, shook his head violently and then rang the bell. The secretary entered with his usual military salute and his usual click of the heels—so irritating at that particular mo-ment. And then a moment later he was discreetly retiring and Fausta was walking forward across the carpet.

## CHAPTER 16

Fausta had guessed at once what was hidden be-hind the pretext of her brother's petition: Tereso wanted to see her and had taken recourse to this stratagem to save his own face. So while Tereso deluded himself that he was misleading her, Fausta was simply amused. She came in wearing black jacket and trousers, with a sky-blue handkerchief round her neck. The first thing she saw was Tereso's back, slightly stooping, and the sheet of paper he held in his hand. The shutters were closed and the room was filled with a subdued light.

"Ah, it's you," said Tereso without turning around. "Come in." Now he could scarcely breathe, and he was so intensely excited that he had to put down the document on the table so as not to show how his hand was trembling.

After greeting him with all the signs of the most profound deference, Fausta replied that it was indeed she. The secretary, she said, had told her that he wished to speak about her brother; and she dared to hope that his request had at least been granted.

Tereso, furious with himself for feeling so agitated and at the same time so completely incapable of controlling his agitation, instinctively looked for some channel into which he could pour out his feelings of compressed rage. A few moments passed. Fausta, standing in front of him, made a quiet show of casually looking at herself in the mirror of the cupboard opposite, putting up her hand to arrange the hair above her ear, while Tereso, burning from head to foot with intolerable excitement, his head lowered, fixed unseeing eyes on the document spread upon the table. Finally he looked up and said violently: "Your brother is a swindler!"

Fausta, who had been expecting anything rather than this abuse, was struck dumb. But Tereso, who had spoken on the spur of the moment and had only by chance hit upon this particular outlet for his anger, did not even give her time to protest.

"Yes," he went on, with a fury surprising even to himself, "I called you here expressly to tell you that your brother is one of the most confirmed and shameless robbers that ever infested this country. You are asking me for a government contract for him. I am tempted to give him a contract once and for all for six by three feet of consecrated ground. . . . Yes, shot—that's what he ought to be—he and all those that behave as he does. Against a wall—against a wall, I say—once and for all—and then a common grave. . . ."

Tereso was now shouting like a lunatic, overcome with delight at having recovered the metallic voice, with its controlled range and carefully calculated effect, that he habitually used to terrify his subordinates. But after her first moment of alarm, Fausta realized that he was making this scene entirely in order to conceal his true reason for sending for her and so as to strengthen his own position in her eyes. She began to feel quite sure of her brother's request being granted.

"He's a swindler—I have the proof of it," continued Tereso, and he started wildly rummaging among the papers, and took out a few sheets and shook them under Fausta's nose. "A whole mountain of proofs. . . . He's a swindler— has been for years. . . . Look at this, there's not a single post that he's occupied in which he hasn't committed the most brazen robberies."

Tereso got up from his chair and started to walk up and down the room. "It's a disgrace that cannot be allowed to go on any longer. This hard-working people—honest, poor, patriotic, devoted"—and in speaking thus Tereso, who came from the people, was genuinely moved—"this people that has entrusted its fortunes into my hands with such absolute freedom and confidence must be protected from swindlers like your brother. They deserve something better. They have been asking for years for such robbers to be hounded out and punished, for justice to be done. . . . Do you think I don't know? Do you think I don't know all about it? I know everything; and nobody can say that my patience is inexhaustible. . . . I love this people, from whom I came. I know the burdens and sufferings they have to bear in order to earn a meager living. Before I became a general I was a peasant among peasants, a miner among miners, a workman among workmen. I know their splendid virtues, their simplicity of heart, their sobriety. The thought of there being swindlers like your brother who make fools of them, who take shameless advantage of them, providing themselves with a safeguard of patriotic rhetoric by which this poor but great people is honestly deceived—this thought rouses me to indignation and cuts me to the heart. The time has come to put an end to all this. The time has come to make an example, to execute justice."

Carried away by his own eloquence—which was, indeed, quite sincere—Tereso nevertheless began to feel that his first violent flush of indignation was gradually cooling. Not that he did not believe what he wasy saying; but he knew by experience that it was impossible, by the mere force of the law, to stop men swindling; that only conscience could make them honest; and that the populace, with all its virtues, was capable of excesses far more harmful than the malpractice of a few dishonest officials. A Manuele who steals, thought Tereso even as he went on shouting, may still be a clever and wise administrator provided he does not steal too much; but a populace that breaks loose fills the country with slaughter and ruin.

By this time, however—like a man who has gone up to a great height in a balloon and then loses control of it and does not know how to come back to earth—by this time Tereso began to see that it was going to be extremely difficult to descend from the airy heights of his indignation to the lower levels he had previously contemplated, that is, to the granting of Fausta's brother's request. Fausta herself had not failed to notice the growing embarrassment in Tereso's tone underneath his angry, threatening words. Realizing that unless she came to the rescue there was no knowing how much longer he would go on floundering between abuse and threats, she promptly provided him with the excuse he was seeking.

She chose a moment when Tereso had paused, silent, between one shout and the next, and declared with sorrowful humility that she had never known of her brother's misdeeds; that, since he made this affirmation, there could be no doubt of its truth; and that, this being the case, she took it upon herself to withdraw the petition, since she would not wish to do anything for an unworthy person, even though it was her own brother. In the meantime, if the General permitted, she would like to leave the room. And she started to do so.

Tereso had made use of Manuele's petition in order to get Fausta into his room, but he had not foreseen that she would make use of this same petition in order to again evade his attentions. There was no time to think out a new plan. He must act quickly, for she was near the door. Forgetting all restraint he threw himself between the door and Fausta.

"What the devil is the matter?" he began confusedly. "What is it? Wait a moment. . . ." And then recovering something of his usual commanding tone: "Remember that you are in audience and that you cannot leave until I dismiss you."

"That is true," said Fausta penitently.

But this time, as if to make it clear that she had won the first round, she went, without speaking and without waiting to be invited, and sat down on the bed. Tereso meanwhile had started walking up and down the room again.

"What the devil—?" he began again. "You needn't try to show greater solicitude for the fate of the country than I do. . . . What I told you about your brother is true—at least, if I can trust my police reports, which may possibly have been exaggerated. But it is also true—and this I have always known—that your brother has rendered signal services to the country and to my cause, and that he was one of my best officers at the time of the civil war. I know, in fact, both his bad and his good side. . . . Also, as I said before, there may be exaggerations or inaccuracies in the police reports: you know of course that the police lay it on rather thick. . . . Our officials, both low grade and high grade, and even those of the highest rank, are badly paid. It sometimes happens that they are tempted to take an interest in business or financial deals, and in return use is made of their political influence. They should not do it, but it's only human. . . . In fact," concluded Tereso, stopping suddenly in front of Fausta, "you needn't worry. Just this once more I'll give your brother the benefit of the doubt. He shall have his contract. . . . Are you pleased now?"

"Your Excellency is too kind," said Fausta coldly, "but if my brother is a swindler he ought not to have this contract. And if he is not a swindler, you ought to tear up the report which accuses him and punish the official who drew it up."

"That is not possible," said Tereso without hesitation.

"Then it is better for me to go away," began Fausta. "The Sanchez family has never allowed its honor . . ." She did not finish the sentence and remained seated. She wished to see just how much Tereso would put up with from her. Such knowledge might come in useful for the future, she thought, on occasions when she might make other requests and put forward other claims.

But now again, as at the swimming pool, the situation reached a breaking point. Tereso suddenly understood what Fausta was aiming at, and he lost patience.

"The Sanchez family," he said, with a very disagreeable, sarcastic laugh, "the Sanchez family honor. . . . The Sanchez family," concluded Tereso all at once in an awe-inspiring voice, "is a family of robbers. I shall institute an inquiry and compel you to pay back everything you have stolen."

"Now I've gone too far," thought Fausta. And immediately, in self-defense, she took a handkerchief from the pocket of her jacket and began sobbing into it. And Tereso, when he had stopped shouting, realized that he also had gone too far. "Another of these outbursts," he thought unhappily, "and I shall lose her for good."

He sat down on the bed near Fausta and, in quite a different voice, began imploring her not to weep, saying he would do all he could to please her. Fausta, as though she had not understood, continued to sob into her handkerchief, but at the same time, languidly and as though by accident, she put out one hand behind her and allowed Tereso to imprison it in his. She expected him to take advantage of the situation and kiss her. But she had not taken the General's shyness into account; all he did was to stroke her hand and go on telling her that she must not cry.

"I wasn't crying because I was hurt," said Fausta, taking the handkerchief from her eyes and turning toward Tereso a face that was penitent but quite dry, "but because I was frightened. I think you must have imagined that I was one of your soldiers. You scared me with your anger and with that voice of yours. You were terrifying. Feel how my heart is beating." And taking Tereso's hand she guided it to the region of her ribs under her left breast. She intended this gesture to serve a double purpose—to flatter Tereso's vanity by making him think that he had been really terrifying, and at the same time to trouble his senses by a very intimate contact. And this time instinct was more powerful than natural diffidence. Tereso, with his arm around Fausta's soft, yielding waist, drew her to him and kissed her on the mouth.

But Fausta knew her Tereso. She knew that if she gave herself to him then and there, on that very bed, her brother would get nothing. Such cases of double-dealing on the part of Tereso were frequent, and were on everybody's lips. Nor was Fausta unaware that Tereso, though quite straightforward in all decisions regarding the exercise of authority, would do anything, even after that kiss, to avoid keeping his promise. So she pretended to be flustered to an unforeseen extent by this impetuous and inescapable embrace and, as soon as they had separated, leaped to her feet, exclaiming that it was late and that she must go to the Duchess. Tereso also rose, disappointed, biting his lips, and asked when they would meet again. Fausta, in a vague, uncertain manner, answered that she did not know: today, perhaps, or perhaps the next day. She feigned the nervousness of a woman who has yielded to a passing weakness and then regrets it. And Tereso, who was anxious to kiss her again and made a move as though to put his arm around her waist, found himself immediately rebuffed with a gesture of confusion and dismay.

"Forgive me," said Fausta, seeing his face darken, "but I feel quite upset. . . . This is the first time since my husband's death. . . ."

It was such a preposterous lie that even Fausta herself, who had invented it on the spur of the moment for lack of anything better, had not the courage to continue; and Tereso felt all his former contempt rise and mingle with his desire, making it bitter and distasteful. "A woman like this," he could not help thinking, as he looked at Fausta standing in front of the mirror very carefully re-doing the color on her lips, "should be thrown down on that bed, made use of, and then—just kicked out. Instead of which I treat her with respect and even swallow lies of that magnitude." But he understood what was wanted of him; and, without looking at her again, he went and sat down at the desk, saying: "What you really want is for your brother to get his contract. . . . Of course that's only fair."

These words were intended by Tereso to convince Fausta, and himself too, that sentiment no longer entered into the matter; it was merely a question of a bargain, and the sheet of paper on the desk was the price; nothing else, neither love nor respect, counted. But his tone was sad rather than scornful, for he was really hurt by Fausta's coldness and even now was ready to deceive himself, if only she would give him the desired opportunity by some little caress or a rather less outrageous lie. Still troubled, he looked for a moment with unseeing eyes at the already drawn-up document that gave the desired contract to Fausta's brother. Then, suddenly making up his mind, he took a pen, dipped it in the ink, signed his name and handed the paper to Fausta, telling her that she must pass it to his secretary for registration. Fausta, who had watched the act of signature over his shoulder, took the paper, folded it and thrust it into her coat pocket.

"Now you will be content," said Tereso, looking at her with an expression of mingled bitterness and expectancy.

Fausta did not say yes or no, she merely answered that she had never doubted his generosity. She knew that Tereso had set his heart upon her conquest, and she had already thought of an indirect method of fanning the flame of his desire and making it, if possible, even fiercer and more impatient.

"Have you a chimney here?" she inquired suddenly, her eyes sparkling with mischief.

"A chimney?" repeated Tereso in surprise, half turning to look round the room. "No—that is, yes . . . but why?"

"Your chimney," said Fausta airily, "must certainly need cleaning; who can tell how much soot there is in it? So if a poor little chimney sweep comes in here this evening with his brush and bucket and rags, don't send him away, and tell your officers not to send him away. He will come this evening after dinner before the party begins."

"Ah! I see what you mean," said Tereso, understanding at last, his whole face lighting up. "A little chimney sweep . . . well, he will be very welcome."

"A poor little chimney sweep," repeated Fausta, with a radiant smile, and giving her hand to Tereso who could not refrain from kissing it devotedly, she went hastily out of the room.


From Tereso's room Fausta went straight to the Duchess's.

She found her sitting in front of her dressing table in a flowered house gown, vehemently scolding Giustina, who was combing her hair, for not having been able to find any trace of Ricardo, the new footman who had brought in her breakfast that morning. Giustina, disentangling the Duchess's thick, black-tinted locks, was explaining how the young man had mysteriously vanished during the brief moment when she had gone to fetch the vacuum cleaner. But the Duchess, abusing her like a pickpocket, answered that she did not believe a single word of such an absurd story. A man does not vanish in that way like a cloud of smoke.

"And yet, Your Excellency," said Giustina, who was amused at the discovery of her mistress's anxiety, "we have looked for him all over the house."

"But you know quite well where he is," said the Duchess in a tone of deep suspicion.

To this Giustina, with the weightiest oaths, protested an ignorance as complete as the Duchess's.

Angry, jealous, alarmed, the Duchess, after a moment's silence, said that she did not believe her since she knew quite well that she had a habit of telling lies and swearing false oaths. She had better not start trying to hatch intrigues, said the Duchess; otherwise she would find herself thrown out, neck and crop, and her lover with her.

"Besides," concluded the Duchess, not bothering to control her silly jealousy, "besides, my poor girl, there's no use in your thinking that you, with your puppy face, can be attractive to a young man like that. Yes—since perhaps no one has ever told you—you have a face just exactly like a dog's."

This childish, angry frankness made Giustina smile, for she was convinced that she had made a conquest of Sebastiano and was not in the least sorry, considering the Duchess's passion, that he had disappeared. But the Duchess, who was watching her maid's face in the cheval glass, saw the smile, and suddenly, just at the moment when Fausta sat down beside her and told her in a low voice that she had obtained from Tereso the favor "that she knew of"— suddenly the stout little woman leaped to her feet, upsetting a stool and everything on it, and planted two smart slaps on the girl's face. Giustina ran off sobbing, and the Duchess, panting, sat down again and immediately asked Fausta, in a hasty, agitated manner, how her interview with Tereso had gone; adding, by way of excuse, that she must not take any notice, the maid was an insolent girl, and if she did not treat her like that there was no knowing what familiarities she might not take upon herself.

"It went extremely well," said Fausta, who had observed the

scene between the Duchess and her maid without any particular emotion. She described in a mischievous and lively manner her meeting with Tereso, laying special stress upon her own cleverness and the naïveté of the General. But the Duchess was hardly listening, she was still panting and scarlet in the face, and held one hand pressed against her bosom to restrain it's indignant heavings. She turned occasionally toward the door, muttering words of scorn and casting furious glances; only at moments did she appear to remember that Fausta was speaking to her, and then, pulling herself together, she would give a little forced laugh of comprehension, or an agitated nod of approval. Her passion and jealousy had reached a culminating point, and between her rage at Giustina's smile and her anxiety at Sebastiano's disappearance, she was no longer capable of thinking or speaking to the purpose. Finally, she mustered enough self-control to say, with an air of mingled confusion and authority, that Fausta had done very well to get the paper signed before yielding to Tereso. With all his simplicity, she said, Tereso was cunning in his own way; and if Fausta had given herself to him her brother would have waited a very long time for his contract. Tereso was a man of the people, concluded the Duchess tartly, and one must never forget it; one knew what the lower classes were. The Duchess, thinking of Giustina and her handsome footman, twisted her mouth into a grimace of bitter disgust, like someone spitting. She calmed down slightly, picked up a big silver bell from the dressing table and shook it violently several times. Giustina came in again, with eyes still tear-stained, and the Duchess ordered her to finish combing her hair—but without breathing a word or she would be instantly thrown out.

"Above all," resumed the Duchess, regaining her normal self-possession and gazing at herself in the mirror, "above all, remember you must flatter him. He's very vain."

"As vain as a peacock," said Fausta, and she described how she had taken Tereso's hand and placed it on her heart so as to make him feel how terrified she had been at his threats. "And the best of it was," she added with a laugh, "my heart has never beaten with such absolute calm as it did at that moment . . . but he didn't notice that; he was much too occupied with his own, which certainly *was* going pretty fast—just like an alarm bell."

The Duchess smiled at this. Her return to her usual serenity was encouraged by the thought that, after all, as long as Giustina remained in her room, she could not be with Ricardo. She was so pleased at this simple idea that, with a rush of generosity as sudden and irresistible as her recent outburst of rage, she took a large box of powder from the dressing table and gave it to Giustina, telling her to keep it. It would be very useful to her, she added—yielding to a last impulse of jealous spite—to brighten up that ugly black skin of hers a little. Then turning to Fausta, who was wandering about the room, she advised her sharply not to be too pleased with herself, since everything still remained to be done and everything depended on how she behaved that evening. Fausta shrugged her shoulders and went out, saying she was going to the swimming pool.

## CHAPTER 17

Apart from her love affairs with Sebastiano and Tereso, Fausta had found means of embarking on yet another affair, stranger and more novel than the first two. She was one of those women who like complete freedom of conduct, and unable to achieve this ideal through virtue, seek it in a multiplication of intrigues and subterfuges. To her way of thinking, one love affair canceled out another; and so, by juggling with several at a time, she succeeded in giving only the minutest fraction of herself to each of the many men who so crazily desired her. For this third intrigue, which she intended as a release from the other two, Fausta had not hesitated to select someone of the servant class. Doroteo— for that was his name—was a short, strongly built youth with curly red hair and a profile a little like a goat, whose job was caddying at the golf course. Fausta had spoken to him first, and had been delighted at his unbelievably rough, crude way of speaking. Then one afternoon, while everyone in the villa was asleep, she had called him to go with her— for a little golf practice, she said; and the two of them had gone off together over the hills and meadows. They had not come back till the evening. That day Fausta had at last experienced a genuinely new sensation—that of having to submit to a male assault for fear of being forcibly ravished or even murdered. Doroteo, who was just eighteen, had a cold, pitiless brutality that fascinated her. He was one of those who strike a blow looking straight into the eyes of their victim—the sort of person who, in the kitchen, is always given the job of wringing the chickens' necks or crushing the heads of half-dead birds. Between Sebastiano's devoted and delicate love on the one hand and Tereso's flattering attentions on the other, this red-haired, brutal Doroteo provided Fausta with an entirely new thrill.

With the same light step with which she had hurried

from Tereso's room to the Duchess's, she now tripped down the staircase and across the courtyard to the great sloping meadow. It was late, and she almost ran. She had to find Doroteo at the hut where golf clubs and other gear were kept and tell him of the change in the day's program, for she had originally arranged to meet him that afternoon, and afterward, having promised Tereso to show him the park, had had to run and put off the engagement. But now, having got what she wanted out of Tereso and made an appointment with him for the evening, she again felt the desire to spend the afternoon with Doroteo. On her way to find him Fausta's little feet, always swift upon the path of pleasure, sped far more rapidly than when they went to meet the true love of Sebastiano or the promises and gifts of Tereso. She ran down across the great grassy meadow, the sun now high above her, her chest thrown forward, her legs embarrassed by the steepness of the slope, her mouth half open and panting for breath, excited by her own speed and by the thought of all her various intrigues. Not Doroteo but freedom seemed to be awaiting her at the end of her race—freedom from Sebastiano's love and from Tereso's attempts to bind her in chains with his favors.

At that hour Doroteo was always to be found in the little pavilion at the golf course, a round, hutlike building made of tree trunks, with a conical thatched roof, copied from the rude habitations of the natives of Australia. When she arrived, breathless with running, Fausta stopped for a moment at the door of the hut, pressing her hand against her breast, and then went in. Bare-armed and wearing a sweatshirt with horizontal red and blue strips, a black scarf tied tightly round his waist, and a pair of blue cotton trousers, Doroteo was squatting in a corner, whittling a forked stick of pine wood. Stacked all around against the rustic walls were rows of leather bags containing golf clubs. A big round table of rough wood occupied almost the whole of the hut. Doroteo's back was turned toward the door. At each stroke of the knife blade the big, slightly soft muscles of his white-skinned arms swelled and tightened. His head, with its copper-colored curls, was bent to one side. Below his hair the skin of his neck and shoulders was covered with freckles.

Fausta, though not in the least affected in her manner with Tereso or Sebastiano, was quite unable to talk to Doroteo except in an artificial, snobbish, overrefined tone of voice, interlarding her conversation with frivolous epithets and foreign expressions. Never for a moment, in fact, did she cease to be Countess Sanchez, assuming all the pride, the capriciousness, the self-sufficiency that she considered suitable

to her title and position. The whole significance of this intrigue with Doroteo was, indeed, based on their differences
of rank which, instead of dividing them as usually happens,
had for them been the main source of attraction. Always in
search of new flavors, Fausta had found pleasure in the debasement of her quality as a fine lady; the greater the difference in rank the greater the thrill. If possible she would
have liked to meet Doroteo at night when she was dressed
in a low-necked gown, adorned with jewels, and all aglow
with a sort of queenly dignity. The contrast with the boy's
rough manners would have then been even more piquant.
Though she was capable of riding for hours on end and was
impervious to fatigue, with Doroteo she assumed the languors
of a fragile and exquisite being; and she took pleasure in
complaining, in her most shocked and affected tone, that he
was a "monster" and that he would certainly be the death
of her. In her relations with him she went so far as to invent for herself a new character, quite different from her
true one, a character at once languishing, delicate, frivolous,
sentimental, modest, and perpetually surprised and bewildered. She thought that Doroteo, in his boorishness, would
despise all these qualities.

But Fausta was deceived in supposing that Doroteo was
flattered by her favors, that he was like the slave to whom
the queen secretly gives herself. She was entirely wrong. This
was not his first adventure with guests from the villa; two
other ladies of rank had already preceded Fausta along the
road she imagined she walked alone. Hence Doroteo, with
his modest intelligence, had come to believe that it was quite
the normal thing for grand ladies to choose their lovers
from among the servants—a curious thing, mysterious perhaps, but too convenient to worry about. Moreover, Fausta
quite honestly believed that it was she who had chosen
Doroteo for her lover; whereas it had been Doroteo, encouraged by the successes of former seasons, who had ogled
and seduced her. And so, after all her intrigues, and at the
very moment when she thought she had found her freedom,
she was falling into an even more abject slavery.

She went up to him and, in a low and still rather breathless voice, asked him what he was making. Doroteo, without
turning round, answered that she could see for herself—a
slingshot.

"A slingshot? What for?" asked Fausta, already intimidated by his manner.

Doroteo replied in a sarcastic voice that he was making a
slingshot to go and fish in the river.

"In the river? I don't understand," said Fausta.

"Yes, in the river," answered the boy. "To fish for fish in the river."

"For fish?"

"Yes, for fish."

He had now finished stripping the bark from the forked stick; he took up from the floor two long rubber straps joined by a small circle of leather and tied them to the two ends of the stick. Then, in a contemptuous tone, he explained that slingshots were used for shooting at birds in trees.

"Monster!" exclaimed Fausta. "Poor little birds . . ."

She would certainly not have spoken in this tone or used such words if one of the guests at the villa had shown her a double-barreled gun and explained that it was used for killing thrushes and partridges. In any case she herself was a good shot.

Still without saying a word and as though determined to ignore Fausta's presence, Doroteo got up, went outside the hut and, picking up a stone, put it in his slingshot. Fausta looked around just in time to see a pigeon, which was perched, cooing, on the edge of the roof, beat its wings and fall to the ground dead, its head broken and bloody. She gave a cry of horror and repeated again that Doroteo was a monster. Why had he killed that innocent little creature? Doroteo picked up the bird and threw it into a clump of shrubs; then replied that he had just wanted to try the slingshot.

What chiefly discomforted Fausta, however, was that Doroteo should be pretending to ignore her presence—his rustic way of showing ill humor. She complained of this with an air of giving him a lesson in manners. But he answered roughly that he was busy and had no time to attend to her. Such were the relations of these lovers—which will seem strange only to those who think that love must be all sweetness. Doroteo behaved in this rude way because he believed that it was pleasing to the refined Fausta—in the same way that Fausta pretended to be refined because she thought that Doroteo despised refinement. Both were playing a part, each attributing to the other tastes that did not exist.

She loved to insult and provoke him. And when she saw him re-enter the hut and squat down again on the ground she said to him playfully that he was a boor: when a lady came in he ought to rise to his feet. Doroteo, intent on tightening the knots of his slingshot, shrugged his shoulders and said that if she did not like him she was at liberty to go away: there were other caddies, anyhow. Fausta, to whom this contemptuous manner was sweeter than a caress, sighed that he was a villain and that he offended her. Then she came

and stood behind him as he remained seated on the floor and
thrust her long, thin fingers into his red curls. She liked his
dirty, tangled hair, that looked like thick tow plastered
with dust and salt. But Doroteo shook his head and told her
to leave him alone as he had no time to waste. She was worried by this determined rudeness and asked him coyly why he
treated his little Fausta in this way. He replied that she knew
very well why. And there was an accent of genuine sincerity
in his voice as he said this.

But Fausta insisted on knowing why he was angry with
her. She liked to put herself in a position of inferiority with
this boy. She apologized again for having put off their appointment for that afternoon, but this had been due, she
explained, to that important person General Tereso, and
although he bored her very much she had not been able to
help it.

"No, no," said Doroteo, testing the slingshot, his head bent
and one eye half shut, "that's not the trouble."

Fausta replied in an alarmed tone that she did not understand. Besides, she said, she had come to tell him that in
spite of what she had previously said they could, after all,
go out that afternoon on the hills for their usual practice.
She would wait for him on the mound, in front of the Swiss
hut, after lunch. That was all right, said Doroteo, and wished
her a good appetite.

"And you must tell me then what is the matter," said Fausta
tenderly, poking her fingers into his hair again, "you *must* tell
tell me, you ruffian." But when he threw back his head she
saw in his glassy blue eyes a look of such sheer malevolence
that she trembled and quickly released her hold.

"Go on, go away," said Doroteo, returning to his slingshot.

"Don't kill all those poor little birds, you monster," repeated Fausta, and she went out of the hut on tiptoe.

## CHAPTER 18

Slowly, and with all the dignity she could muster,
Fausta now took her way toward another point in the park
where she knew that luncheon was to be served. Besides the
Alpine hut in which Sebastiano was sleeping, besides the
Australian cabin where Fausta had met Doroteo, there were
in the park many other fantastic constructions—artificial
grottoes, Swiss chalets, Chinese pagodas, classical ruins; and
to these the Duchess's carefree guests betook themselves for
meals on different days. Today the tables had been laid in a
shell-lined cavern dripping with stalactites. Its entrance, like
the entrance to a real cave, was through a narrow, irregular

cleft; but inside, beneath a vault covered with incrustations and bats with wings made of velvet, in a coolness produced by rills of water gushing discreetly in the hollows of artificial rocks amongst moss and maidenhair ferns, hidden lamps diffused a greenish cavern-like light upon seven or eight sumptuously arranged tables. The guests, their faces tinged with an emerald luster, were seated in their places; and Fausta, the last to arrive, was greeted with a joyful clamor. Smiling and eager, she went and sat down at the principal table, already occupied by the Duchess in her great conical straw hat, by Tereso in his tight-fitting uniform, and by Tereso's secretary.

Fausta had promised Tereso to conduct him around the park that afternoon; but afterward, having obtained what she wanted from him, she imagined he would be content with the appointment she had made with him for the evening and would disregard their former arrangement. She was therefore much annoyed when he reminded her of it. A new complication arose: how was she at the same time to accommodate both Tereso and Doroteo? This problem occupied Fausta's mind all through luncheon, while Tereso made labored efforts at conversation, the Duchess supporting him with approbation and flattery and the secretary eating steadily and in silence. What could she do to get rid of Tereso? For there could be no shadow of doubt in Fausta's mind: between Doroteo and Tereso it was Tereso whom she preferred to sacrifice—and this for three good reasons. The first was that Doroteo's ill humor troubled her and she wanted to know the cause of it as soon as possible; the second, that she found his company, rude and boorish as he was, more attractive than that of the gallant Tereso; and the third, that if she wished to attach Tereso it was better not to make too many concessions. But it was also true that the situation was strained, as the Duchess had already intimated to her, and that she must be careful not to alienate Tereso altogether by showing him that having obtained the favor she desired she no longer had any use for him.

When luncheon was over all the guests left the grotto together, some going to rest, others dispersing about the park; and in a short time Fausta and Tereso were left alone. Fausta was quite unable to think of a way of getting rid of him. They were standing under a low pergola, from the green leaves of which hung large, heavy bunches of black grapes, and Fausta, while talking, now and then picked a single grape and put it into the General's mouth. Tereso, on his side, was in a confidential mood. He still thought that Fausta had a mercenary object in her relations with him; but owing to his usual fatal sentimentality this thought did not in any way modify his feelings, and he felt himself drawn toward this beautiful woman with tender, if misguided, abandonment. No matter what Fausta really was, for him, at that moment, she was the woman he loved, the woman who loved him. Thus Tereso's simple nature triumphed once again over his long experience of human worth. But this time, contrary to his usual habit, he did not mind—in fact he asked nothing more than to be allowed to deceive himself.

Tereso was in a state of mingled exaltation and melancholy. He reflected that he had saved the nation from civil war and that he was the most powerful man in the country and one of the most powerful in the world. Yet, in spite of that, here he was at the feet of a worthless woman. He was thinking, too, of the emptiness and sterility of everything—of power as well as of love. And yet both of these things were so sweet, so irresistible. Such thoughts embellished, in his own eyes, the image that he made of himself. And, carried away by his love of Fausta, he wanted her to see him in the same light. He began to tell her, after much laborious preamble, that she must not look at him as the head of the State but simply as a man.

"Ah, yes," said Fausta, intent on gathering a grape from a bunch that hung higher than the rest.

Tereso, whose political utterances were always of a concrete nature, instinctively attempted the same concreteness of expression in his declarations of love. He wanted Fausta to love him as, for twenty years, the crowds had loved him. All at once he remembered the wave of indignation against the criminals, the wave of fanatical love for himself, that the rare attempts on his life had never failed to awaken among the populace. On those occasions he had felt himself truly close to the heart of the people, and those had been the best moments of his long career—moments when he had been conscious of being newly confirmed, by the affection of the entire nation, in the benevolence of his ideas and of his government. It seemed to him that the same thing ought to happen in the case of Fausta. It seemed to him that in her, too, the news of the danger that he was facing for love of her, of the plot that he was defying in order to see her, ought to release a gush of love and of gratitude. In making these calculations he failed to see that there was not the same distance between himself and Fausta as between himself and the populace, who perceived him only from afar, surrounded with glory; and he forgot that, in order to acquaint Fausta with the danger that threatened him and so affect her emotions as he wished, he was not able to employ the expert pens of countless journalists but only his own single human voice.

Fausta, her face and arms raised to the vines above her, continued to pick the big, sun-warmed grapes, and Tereso began to tell her that she did not know how much he had already done for her sake. In an absent-minded way she asked him what he meant. She thought Tereso wished to speak to her again about her brother's contract.

"I am exposing myself to a conspiracy on your account," said Tereso, suddenly swelling with anger at the very thought of it; "here, in this very house, there are people who are plotting an attempt on my life. They want to kill me, to destroy my work. . . ."

He expected, at these words, to see her stop her grape-picking and open her eyes wide with terror; but Fausta, who had scarcely been listening and imagined that he was revealing mere suspicions, simply asked in an indifferent tone how that could be possible, since he was so much loved.

"Oh, yes, I am loved," replied Tereso bitterly, already disappointed by her lack of interest, "but that does not prevent some blind fanatic, imbecile, or criminal from taking it into his head to make an attempt on my life."

He went on to say that this would prove to her how his power, though so bitterly envied and coveted, though so brilliant and so glorious, was in reality beset with dangers and continually haunted by treachery and death. But, he said, he had performed this act of rash courage joyfully because he was conscious of doing it out of love for her. Besides, he felt exaltation rather than fear at the idea of danger; he preferred to go and face it in the open rather than fly from it like a coward. He was still that same Tereso who, at the battle of Escalona, alone and with one arm torn by a jagged shell splinter, had led the famous cavalry charge that had given him victory.

"People think I have grown old," concluded the General, "but they shall see." Tereso, as he said this, was transfigured. His sincere and still unsatisfied yearning for greatness filled him with emotion. It seemed to him that he was truly in love with Fausta, and it pleased him to place his life in jeopardy for her sake. At the same time his breast swelled with a savage tumult at the thought of having to fight once more, once more to defy danger—at the thought, indeed, that he was still the courageous, unsubdued Tereso of twenty years before.

Tereso expected that this harangue would have the effect he had calculated upon Fausta, but he soon saw how mistaken he was. Fausta's first feeling at hearing him insist in this way upon the imminence and reality of the danger that threatened him was not, as he had hoped, one of grateful affection toward him for facing the danger for her sake, but simply one of fear. It was not a very urgent or violent fear, it is true, for Fausta was no coward, but it was a quite genuine fear of being involved in Tereso's fate and killed at his side. All at once she stopped picking grapes and asked, in an unexpectedly anxious voice, why Tereso, knowing all this, remained one moment longer at the villa. He replied, simply, that he remained because of his love for her. Besides, he added, with swift disappointment at seeing on Fausta's face a look of surprise and dismay as though she did not much appreciate the regard shown for her—besides, the police had exactly identified the conspirators, and they would be arrested and taken away before they had the chance of putting their plan into execution. Nobody in the villa would notice anything—not even she; there was no need for her to worry, for she was in no danger. Fausta, when he said this, saw that she ought in some way to try and mitigate the bad impression that her own selfish solicitude had evidently made upon Tereso, so she quickly went on to say that since she saw he had no fear she was not afraid either. She concluded gaily that it might even add a spice of variety to the party—which otherwise would be extremely boring.

But her tone was cold; and as she spoke Tereso felt the enthusiasm and emotion of a few minutes before gradually evaporating. He saw that he had failed to kindle in the heart of a woman the love he had so often excited in the hearts of multitudes. But at this point Fausta had an inspiration which revived Tereso's already half-extinguished illusion.

"I want to remain beside you," she said suddenly, "as much as I can. Instead of having dinner with all the others this evening, why shouldn't we dine alone, just the two of us, in your room? In that way," she concluded with her loveliest smile, "if the attempt comes off we shall die together."

These words had a pleasant sound in the ear of the General, and his feelings were again stirred. He was touched, and would have liked to ask Fausta if it were really true that she loved him enough to be willing to die with him. But his usual shyness would allow him only to thank her and to bend down and hiss her hand.

"I will come in my fancy dress," added Fausta. "Do you remember? The poor little chimney sweep with his brush and pail."

Tereso answered that he would await the chimney sweep with impatience. He had forgot the coldness of Fausta's previous words and was now deceiving himself afresh over this hopeless and improbable love affair.

Fausta, in spite of Tereso's disclosure of the conspiracy, in spite, too, of his proffered love, had not given up her plan of spending the rest of the day with Doroteo. She had made the suggestion of dining together not, as Tereso supposed, out of a sudden access of affection, but in order that she might be able, without too much difficulty, to disengage herself for the afternoon. As Tereso's heart was blossoming anew with the craziest of hopes, Fausta, who considered she had already made too many concessions, was preparing to drown those hopes in a fresh flood of bitterness. Of course, she went on after a moment, in a casual manner, if they were to meet in the evening so much earlier than arranged it would be better to put off their walk round the park till the next day. She must go and sleep for at least a couple of hours, for she still felt tired, she said, after the reception of the night before. And then she must also try on her costume.

These words, notwithstanding the light, casual tone in which they were uttered, chilled Tereso. He had counted on the walk in the park as a certainty and, just at the moment of Fausta's retracting her promise, had been on the point of suggesting that they should start at once. "It is obvious," he thought, "that this woman is laughing at me." And at this thought all his love was turned to hate. For a moment he was tempted to tell her what he thought of her and, having finally shamed her, to wash his hands of her altogether. But there had been an odd, faint tone of embarrassment in Fausta's voice as she was excusing herself from her engagement. Tereso thought that it would perhaps be more profitable to have her watched; and in the evening, with the proofs in his possession, to take a just and well-planned revenge. The proofs of what? Tereso did not know, but, with a flair sharpened by thirty years of public life, he could smell an ordor of deceit and treachery in the air. No sign of these reflections appeared in his face. He too, he said quickly, as though remembering something, had some business to transact with his secretary that ought not to be postponed. They would meet in the evening, then. Fausta, well pleased at having solved the problem of the afternoon without either sacrificing Doroteo or arousing the General's suspicions, assented with genuine enthusiasm. Then taking leave of Tereso with a smile and a slight, confidential pressure of the fingers, she went off hurriedly in the speckled autumn sunshine, beneath the grape-hung pergola.

When she had gone Tereso felt a further uncertainty. Was it possible, he asked himself, that that sweet smile, that sweet caress, were false? But the graceful figure of Fausta, erect in the golden sunlight, was receding further and further from the green sprays and dark grape clusters of the pergola; and now, if ever, was the time to discover whether she was lying. He called his secretary, who was waiting near by, and ordered him to have Fausta shadowed during the whole afternoon. In taking these precautions he still flattered himself that they were superfluous and that Fausta had really gone to rest as she had said.

When she came out of the pergola Fausta gradually quickened her step until by the time she was in the middle of the meadow she was actually running. She was conscious of an approaching storm, and she rushed to meet it with a feeling of almost sensual pleasure that frightened her a little. She could foresee that she and Doroteo would come to blows that day. What else, after all, had she expected when she gave herself to this boy? "I shall end up by being murdered," she thought with conviction as she began, panting, to climb the steps that led to the hut, "murdered by some tough like Doroteo— that's how I shall end up. But it's stronger than I am . . ."

She expected to meet Doroteo inside the hut. Instead, she found him lying on the ground outside, flat on his back, his arms behind his head, his eyes fixed on the sky and a blade of grass between his teeth. She hovered around him in hesitating silence for a moment, then called him by name, telling him to get up as she was ready. But Doroteo did not move. She knelt down beside him and, putting her hand in his hair, shook him. At last he turned his eyes toward her and, still without moving, announced in a drawling voice that he did not want to come with her that day; he wanted to stay where he was and sleep for a couple of hours, and she could do what she liked. This tone of cool detachment was something entirely new on the part of Doroteo, whose sensuality, beneath his rough manners, was always easily aroused; and Fausta, frowning and tenderly calling him a "brute," asked him what he meant by all this strange behavior. Doroteo's only reply was to tell her to let him sleep in peace.

"Well, tell me what has happened, then," said Fausta.

Doroteo, still looking with eyes half-closed at the sky, promptly asked her what she was doing in the park the evening before, near the pool where the swans were. Up till now he had never been jealous, because he foolishly believed that when women gave themselves to him it meant that they did not love anyone else. But the sight of Fausta and Sebastiano, the previous evening, embracing on a bench in the park, had made him feel the sting of jealousy for the first time in his life. Now Fausta was certainly no stranger to this kind of accusation on the part of her lovers, but with Doroteo she realized that there would be neither use nor advantage in telling a lie—a thing she never felt with Tereso or Sebastiano. She liked Doroteo for his brutality; to lie to him would imply a desire to avoid the delicious violence she both feared and longed for. She replied, therefore, with the insolent, calculated coldness of a high-born lady, that she did not have to account to him for her actions; that if he really wished to know there was no reason why she should not tell him: the man she had been with was her lover.

At these words Doroteo leaped to his feet, seized Fausta by the arms and started forcing her backward into the hut. There, pressing her back with her shoulders against the wall, he commanded her to repeat what she had just said. In the darkness of the hut Fausta could not see his face, but, conscious of the fury that expressed itself in the grip of his powerful hands on her arms, she was both attracted and afraid. Nevertheless, she found strength to give a contemptuous, insulting laugh, and to reply that she did not intend to repeat anything and that if he was deaf she, for her part, would not waste her breath.

"Oh, so I'm deaf, am I?" said Doroteo, blind with rage, and struck her a violent blow across the cheek, insisting breathlessly that she should repeat what she had said.

Fausta, dazed by the blow, stared at him open-mouthed, and then Doroteo struck her again, on the other cheek this time. But, even though bewildered and hurt, Fausta was all the time coldly wondering whether she should go on provoking Doroteo, for, in spite of the terror it inspired in her, she felt an irresistible desire to foment his violence with fresh insults. She was afraid he might black her eye with his fist, or break one of her teeth; otherwise she did not shrink from his blows. She admitted to herself that her relations with Doroteo had up till now been merely a necessary preliminary to this outburst, and all at once she saw that its dangers were worth facing.

Accordingly, as soon as she could regain her breath, and with Doroteo still gripping her arms, she poured forth a flood of insulting abuse interspersed with screams of contemptuous, forced laughter.

"Perhaps you thought I was in love with you, did you? But after all you're only a caddie . . . Perhaps you were forgetting that? Just a servant, among a pack of other servants. . . . A mere menial, do you understand? And really I have no obligation at all to be faithful to anyone of your sort. I was just amusing myself with you . . . and I shall go on amusing myself. But when I get tired of you

I shall dismiss you, like the menial that you are . . . and if you make a fuss I shall get the Duchess to give you the sack, to throw you out like a dog. I shall say that you were wanting in respect. I shall have you beaten like a slave . . ."

Fausta screamed these words at him in as cutting and cruel a voice as she could, all the time studying Doroteo's fixed, stony expression, which she could distinguish quite well now that her eyes had become accustomed to the darkness of the hut. When she felt she had abused him to her satisfaction she began to struggle, crying out to him to let her go as she had had enough of him. She calculated that, coupled with her insults, the wild, strenuous movements with which she now strove to break away from him would infuriate Doroteo till he finally and completely lost his temper. She knew that there is nothing like violence to attract violence; and she was not mistaken. Doroteo's face appeared to undergo a kind of painful, frenzied contraction; and Fausta, before she realized what was happening, found herself seized, crushed, jostled, smothered with blows. She took care to protect her face with her arm; but otherwise she abandoned herself completely to this delicious violation. Finally they fell together on to a pile of hay in one corner of the hut. There, in the darkness, blows quickly turned to rough caresses, cries to sighs, fury to desire, and hate to love.

Outside the hut, Tereso's agent, who had watched the scene with an attentive eye, saw that he now had more than enough material for the report he had to draw up, and went off in the direction of the villa.

## CHAPTER 19

But another person besides the agent had been a witness, though an involuntary one, of the quarrel between Fausta and Doroteo—Sebastiano. Awakened suddenly by the harsh, scornful voice of Fausta as she railed at the youth, Sebastiano thought for a moment that he was still dreaming of the voice of his mistress, as those who are in love sometimes do; though the angry tone and harsh words had nothing of the subdued, vague quality suitable to dreams. Then, after an interval of silence, the voice began again; and he was shocked into realizing that he was no longer asleep and that it was really Fausta who was speaking. Sebastino was so overcome with horror that for a moment he was not aware of any pain; but in reality—as sometimes after a very bad fall—the pain was there, but was so deep-seated that all sensation was numbed. Breathless, with a horrible sinking of the heart, he sat up and listened, leaning against the wall, his eyes wide open in the darkness. The voice was now insistent, and the abuse, violent, vulgar, cruel, came thick and fast, leaving no doubt of its absolute, full-blown reality. Like a dying man who, though mortally wounded, can barely muster the strength to drag himself to a stream and expires before he is able to wet his lips, Sebastiano threw himself face downward on the floor and was just able, through a crack between two of the planks, to watch what was happening below. He watched the pair as they quarreled; Doroteo slapping those cheeks that he himself had so often caressed with a trembling hand, and he watched as Doroteo pushed Fausta toward the pile of hay. They fell together outside his range of vision and he remained where he was, face downward, his eye glued to the crack through which he could no longer see anything, his cheek pressed against the rough wood, his whole body chilled, exhausted, inert. From the pile of hay, sounds came to him whose meaning was only too painfully clear, and then Sebastiano wished he might lose his senses altogether and neither see nor hear any more. It was not jealousy that he felt, but rather the sense of an appalling catastrophe that was beyond tears or cries; and, hidden inside this dim feeling like a needle in a ball of wool, he could feel every now and then the sharp stab of an agonizing thought: "Fausta is there, just underneath me . . . with another man . . . Fausta is betraying me."

Sebastiano could not have told how long he remained lying on the planks of the floor. The silences that alternated with the sighs and murmurs of the pair on the pile of hay beneath sometimes almost made him hope he had been dreaming; but then a voice, a sound of creaking, told him that he was wrong. At last they were quite quiet and still, and Sebastiano tried to forget his pain by thinking of something else; but the pain had an irresistible attraction for him, and just when he thought he had succeeded in thrusting it from his mind, back it came again, in the train of the most unlikely reflections. Every argument, every subject that his mind touched upon led by unforeseen paths to Fausta; everything was transformed into her image, everything bore her reflection, everything became converted into a symbol of her. Sebastiano did not know that it was possible to suffer so much; and the quality of his pain and the continuance of its cause precluded the possibility of any relief from an impatience so agonizing.

At last he heard Fausta and Doroteo leave the hut, and their voices grew fainter and fainter in the distance and were lost in the silence of the park. Then, without using the ladder, he jumped down from the loft and went out. He saw that the light of day was already dimmed, and the sky streaked with trailing clouds, red from the setting sun. Almost eight hours had passed in sleeping and in the time spent in his hateful vigil.

He did not know what to do or what to think. Stunned and miserable, it seemed to him that not only all life, but each separate moment of it, had lost all aim and reason. He was very hungry, and this aggravated his misery, for it was a sign of continued life and vigor despite the mortal anguish that oppressed his heart. With these confused thoughts in his mind he descended the hill, skirted the lake—in which everything, water, swans, and water clock, was now deep in shadow—went through a thicket of magnolias and came out into the great meadow. It was now the moment of sunset. The whole sky seemed to be converging toward the west, in a vast drift of long, trailing clouds darkly fringed with red; and against their movement the villa, as it looked down across the meadow, appeared black, squat and square, like a stationary mass in the middle of a stream. Sebastiano looked at the evening sky and at the clouds moving with the wind and felt a sudden desire to sing. But when he started stammering out the words of a popular song that had been in fashion some years before, the sound stuck in his throat and he began weeping. The clouds were traveling in the opposite direction to the one in which he was going; and he kept his eyes turned to the heavens, faltering out the foolish, bitter words of the song as he ran, weeping, across the meadow. Now and then he stumbled in the thick grass, and then the sound of his voice swelled to an even more plaintive lament; now and then he remembered he was hungry, and his tears flowed faster.

When he came near the swimming pool he felt he must find something to eat and went into the bathing pavilion. The pool was deserted; the yellowish water had a thick, tepid look like the water of a pond; underneath the diving board floated an enormous, tightly inflated green-and-white india-rubber frog. Sebastiano went straight to the bar and found what he was looking for—a plate of sandwiches wrapped in a napkin. But as he ate he continued to weep, and his pain grew so much sharper that all at once, after the second mouthful, he found he was no longer hungry. Leaving the half-eaten sandwich on the bar, he went out and started toward the villa.

Sebastiano had an exact knowledge of every part of the park, of every seat and shrubbery and nook, from having frequented it at night with Fausta. But now, in the gathering darkness, through the veil of tears that dimmed his sight, all these places, though perfectly intact and undamaged, had, in his eyes, a look of sinister devastation. The ghost of Fausta seemed still to hover about them, sullied with the dark, livid colors of treachery; and it was worse then if she were dead. Sebastiano, fumbling absent-mindedly in his pocket, came across her handkerchief which he had picked up that morning, and, obeying a sudden impulse, hurled it away into a clump of bushes.

This gesture brought him back to reality—or at least to a consideration of how he must behave; and for the first time the voice of self-respect, hitherto silent, made itself heard through his grief. His tears dried quickly and he began to think of what was to be done. It was true that he had a prompt and safe means of revenge at hand; he had merely to return home and allow the plot to take its course. If he did this Fausta would be punished without his intervention, meeting the end she deserved in the arms of Tereso. For a moment it seemed to Sebastiano that there was something providential in this neat chain of circumstances and that it only remained for him to accept the vengeance that chance offered him. Then, thinking it over, it appeared to him that the best kind of vengeance would be, on the contrary, to save Fausta, as he had already planned. By doing so he would be able to show her, after the plot had been frustrated, that he was capable of rising above her and her treachery, proving to her his own conscious magnanimity and his final resolution to have nothing more to do with her. In pursuance of this train of thought Sebastiano's imagination dallied for some minutes with the various possibilities that suggested themselves—whether to save Fausta's life and then tell her of it and take leave of her; or to save her and then take leave of her without telling her he had saved her; or again, to save her and then neither say anything nor even see her, but vanish out of her life forever.

Sebastiano, whose innate delicacy of mind always ultimately prevailed, would have liked to adopt the last of these three courses, but he realized that for technical reasons he must choose the second. He felt that having once set forth upon the path of generosity he ought to have gone the whole way. But in that case Fausta would not have been left punished, nor would she ever know why he had left her. Sebastiano was still in too emotional a state to see that this last resolution was not dictated, as he believed, by offended pride, but by love pure and simple, by a love that was stronger than any disillusionment or any betrayal, that could find its satisfaction in sacrifice and silence, and that was not con cerned with revenge, even of the kind that wears a mask of disdainful magnanimity or high-toned forgiveness.

It was quite dark when he reached the villa. He went by the servants' entrance into the basement, where he found preparations for dinner already in full swing. Footmen were running back and forth, orders were being shouted, bells were ringing, and from the kitchen came a clatter of dishes and pots and pans. Sebastiano had only one desire now—to get it over as quickly as possible with Fausta and then escape to his own home. He saw now that his first, complicated plan to save her before Tereso laid hands on her, at the same time without either denouncing his half-brother or allowing the plot to be put into execution, was no longer feasible. So he decided to do nothing beyond warning her of the danger she was in and, apart from that, to leave Tereso, Saverio and Perro to their fate. If the attempt were successful, so much the worse for Tereso; if it were unsuccessful, so much the worse for Perro and Saverio. Sebastiano, who had always been indifferent to political affairs, had now, since his recent disillusionment, lost interest in human affairs too. It seemed to him that human beings were a mass of corruption and imbecility; that human destinies were controlled by chance alone; and that, between the wickedness and folly of humanity on the one hand and the frantic absurdity of chance on the other, there was only one thing to be hoped for—the early destruction of the entire human race. At that moment he had a feeling of real and positive disgust for every creature that walked upright and wore clothes. And more than once, in that basement corridor, as he watched the footmen scurrying busily about, he was surpised to find himself thinking that if all went well they at any rate would soon be wiped off the face of the earth by Saverio's and Perro's infernal machine.

Sebastiano looked for the service staircase that led to the upper floors. But after wandering for some time through the low-ceilinged passages he found he had forgotten where it was. He was on the point of stopping one of the menservants and asking him when, as he passed in front of a half-closed door, he distinctly heard the voice of Saverio. He pushed open the door and went in.

In the middle of the room, which was low and very large, was a big rectangular table covered with a red felt cloth. Round this table a number of women in white aprons were vigorously wielding hot irons, pressing trousers and other garments belonging to the Duchess's guests; other sat sewing; yet others were polishing shoes, holding them up under the light of three great green-shaded lamps that hung from the vaulted ceiling. The numerous wires from the electric irons and the steam rising from the garments as they were pressed gave the room the appearance of a sort of domestic laboratory. There were all women in the room, and the air was heavy with the kind of smell that hangs about a copying office or a tailor's workshop. All women, that is, except one solitary man standing at the far end near an area window, cleaning a pair of black dancing shoes. The man was Saverio.

Saverio had vowed to himself, on entering the villa, that he would behave like a proper conspirator—like Perro, in fact, who never made a superfluous movement nor spoke a word too much. However, what with the enthusiasm that seethed in his heart and the ideas whirling in his brain, he had soon forgotten his good intentions. He had begun by talking to the girl at the indicator board; then he had started conversations with any of the menservants who had come within range; finally, in pursuit of the indicator girl, he had plunged into this room. Any crowd is tempting to a propagandist, even if it be only a collection of housemaids and kitchen-maids. And so Saverio, at first more or less in jest and then more and more in earnest, had let himself go, and had started to hold forth in front of all these women as though he were addressing a gathering of well-informed and already convinced comrades.

He told them, as he carefully polished the dancing shoe, that they were oppressed, that they were the servants of other women exactly like themselves, that in the new social order there would no longer be either masters or servants. The women, vigorously handling their irons, laughed at him and did not appear to take him seriously.

"What good will it do me if there are no more masters and mistresses?" suddenly remarked a young woman with a round, massive face and a big bosom; "what I want is to become a mistress myself."

Savario replied that that was not possible; the time of masters and mistresses was coming to an end; and then everyone would have the advantage of the things that were now enjoyed by a restricted and privileged class.

"Rubbish!" exclaimed a thin, faded woman, in a distrustful voice; "there will always be masters and mistresses—and we shall always have to slave for them."

But an old woman who was busy sewing, all huddled up on a stool, and who, at each stroke of her needle, wrinkled up her face like one of the Three Fates, suddenly burst out fiercely: "Keep your ideas to yourself. We don't want any trouble. You ugly fool, don't you know that the police arrest people who talk like that? If they put us in prison you certainly won't be able to get us out with *your* silly chatter."

Saverio, the pedantic agitator, answered that if they were all arrested, so much the better, for the cause had need of martyrs and victims.

This reply, straight from the revolutionary handbook, was received with a chorus of protests. "Go to prison yourself," "Idiot," "Blackguard," "If you don't stop, we'll report you," and other similar remarks were hurled at him from all sides. One woman, for lack of any more effective missile, threw at him the horsehair-stuffed pot holder with which she was grasping her iron. All the others immediately followed her example, and the poor wretch was deluged with a hail of pot holders. He shielded his face with his arm and went on shouting that they were just blind slaves, that he was trying to save them and this was the way they treated him. In the end, as the missiles came ever thicker and more accurate, he ran around the table and arrived beside Sebastiano, who had been watching this scene from the doorway. "You hags," screamed Saverio.

But the butler, who was passing along the corridor at that moment, hearing the din, put his face in at the door and demanded, with a scowl, to know what was happening. There was an immediate silence, in which suddenly was heard the caustic voice of the old woman who had already abused Saverio.

"He's a shameless one," she cried, turning a fierce face toward the wretched Saverio. "He came in here with the excuse of helping to clean the shoes, but all he's done is to put his hands on the girls. If he was even good-looking—but he looks like a toad."

This accusation was received with screams of laughter from the younger women, and with indignant protests from Saverio, who saw himself suddenly degraded from the rank of political agitator to that of a servants' hall Don Juan. But the butler silenced the tumult with a gesture and bade the women get on with their work. Then he sternly ordered Saverio to take the shoes up to their owner.

"That'll teach you to leave the girls alone," the old woman shouted after him. She had evidently enjoyed the scene.

The younger women started to sing a song in chorus; and Saverio and Sebastiano went off toward the service staircase.

"There's nothing to be done with servants," panted Saverio as they climbed the narrow, winding stair. He went on to explain that among servants, unlike peasants and workmen, class consciousness was completely lacking. Servants, he added, were in a position very like that of intellectuals—that is, they were attached to, and parasites of, the bourgeois class. There was, in fact, nothing much to be expected either from a poet or a lackey—from the former because art is always profoundly reactionary and conservative, from the latter because to serve is to betray. But in a revolution some use can be made of intellectuals to do the work of propaganda; whereas servants are not merely useless but actually harmful and must therefore be ruthlessly liquidated. In revolutions it is the servant class that, by committing atrocities and taking infamous reprisals upon its former masters, brings dishonor to the cause it claims to be fighting for. From its ranks may come executioners, but never apostles. This was Saverio's way of avenging himself for the pot holders he had been pelted with by the girls in the room below.

Sebastiano listened absent-mindly to Saverio's outbursts. After his first agony of grief, after the later promptings of self-respect, he now felt quite calm and apathetic; his decision to save Fausta's life had become little more than a matter of duty. This calm, it is true, was ruffled now and then by memories of the past, and by recollections of recent rebuffs which made him tremble with indignation; but he was easily able to subdue these onslaughts of his old passionate spirit. "I had only that one illusion left," he concluded by thinking, as he came out behind Saverio into the Gallery of Busts, "the illusion about love; and now I have lost that too. Now the boredom will be complete." He felt he had aged by twenty years in the space of a few hours.

## CHAPTER 20

In the gallery Perro came forward to meet them. He was dog-tired, and the consummate actor's ceremonious calm was almost played out. Although he was certain that the organization of the plot left nothing to be desired, he still could not help being afraid of a possible hitch, and then his career as an *agent provocateur* would be ruined. He asked Sebastiano in a peremptory manner where the devil he had been hiding all day, to which Sebastiano, gloomy and indifferent, gave the perfectly truthful reply that he had been asleep.

"Asleep?" repeated Perro, opening his eyes wide.

"Yes, asleep," repeated Sebastiano drily without looking at him.

Perro saw that he was not lying and was once again astonished at a self-control that surpassed even his own. "Either he's a half-wit—which he does not seem to be . . . or he's a police agent, which is not possible . . . or he's the most ruthless, hardened terrorist I have ever met in my life," he thought. To be able to sleep within an hour of the assassination . . . Perro was amazed, and looking at Sebastiano's sad but tranquil countenance, could not believe his own eyes.

This dialogue took place in the gallery, beneath the forbidding faces of the Spanish conquistadors, while from every direction came insistent sounds of the Duchess's impatient guests ringing their bells. Perro announced that the decisive moment was at hand. In a short time the Countess Sanchez would be going to dinner in Tereso's room, and the bathroom would be empty. Then Saverio would carry up the tray with the bomb on it. Meanwhile he himself would take up his position in one of the window recesses in the gallery. Sebastiano, to be ready for anything that might occur, was to hide in the adjoining room—which was Fausta's. Perro wanted to suggest an excuse to Sebastiano to enable him to get into this room; but Sebastiano cut him short, saying, in a joyless tone, that there was no need to worry about an excuse as he had already, that morning, found means of ingratiating himself with the maid. Perro was again astonished. He was counting on having Sebastiano arrested at his appointed post with the pistol in his possession, and Saverio at the moment when he was placing the bomb. Caught in the act, they would be handcuffed and carried straight off, bodily to the car that was waiting at the park gate. Nobody would notice anything, not even Tereso, who would receive his report much later, when all was over.

After a few more explanations, Saverio and Perro went off to fetch the bomb which Perro had previously concealed, and Sebastiano was left alone in the gallery. He had been waiting impatiently to go and warn Fausta before she went to the General's room, and was on the point of knocking at her door when that of the Duchess was half opened and the face of the Duchess appeared, wearing an expression of mingled imperiousness and embarrassment. She beckoned to him and in a low voice called him by name: "Ricardo."

Sebastiano was so distracted by his own troubles and plans that he did not notice the Duchess's embarrassment nor her subdued, confidential tone. But the moment he was inside her room he realized his mistake. The Duchess, whose short, corpulent figure was clothed in an undergarment of pink weighted silk stretched to bursting point over her massive, flaccid sides, had already taken up her position in front of a great cheval glass, whose three mirrors reflected, as though in some grotesque triptych, three different images—full face and two profiles—of her squat, ill-formed person. Stretching a languid arm toward Sebastiano she ordered him to help her

dress, saying that for some reason or other her maid had
vanished. But the Duchess's face was suffused with a red,
fiery glow to the very tip of her prominent nose, and wore an
expression of visible excitement beneath its usual exalted
arrogance, showing clearly not only the truth of the pretext
but also the nature of the feelings that had led her to summon Sebastiano.

For a moment he felt inclined to burst out laughing. It
was thus, he thought, that Fate wished to cure him once
and for all of the sweet illusion of love, first revealing Fausta's
treachery and then adding jest to injury by presenting him
with a flamboyant, repulsive caricature of amorous passion,
the Duchess's senile infatuation. But there was no time to be
lost even in wondering at the ironical lessons of Fate. With the
same mechanical resoluteness with which that same morning he had brought himself to put his arm around Giustina's
waist, Sebastiano now went up behind the old woman and
repeated the gesture. He then remained motionless, his arm
and his whole body dragged to one side by the weight of his
massive burden, his eyes fixed sadly and dreamily on the
mirror that reflected with painful exactness the image of the
two interlaced figures.

The Duchess, who had not hoped to be understood quite
so promptly, grew even more purple in the face—if that
were possible—but did not blink an eyelid. All she did was
to move one plump, ring-laden hand to her side and grasp
Sebastiano's hand tightly, at the same time asking him in a
slow, confused way whether she should dress up as a *vivandière* or as a gypsy—which would he advise? She added
that the gypsy fancy dress was certainly very becoming to her
type, but that the *vivandière* costume, on the other hand,
was much prettier and more youthful. Besides, with so
many dark women, there would certainly be a great number
of gypsies at the party; whereas very few would think of
dressing up as *vivandières*. As she said these things, in a
voice that with every syllable seemed about to succumb beneath the weight of its own excitement, the Duchess continued to look at herself with a stern expression in the cheval
glass, crudely illuminated by three unshaded lamps. And
with her hand she grasped the inert fingers of the so-called
Ricardo more tightly than ever.

The Duchess's question had suddenly reminded Sebastiano
that no more than two days before Fausta had expressed
similar doubts, asking him in the same faraway, meditative
voice and with the same dreamy expression whether she
should dress up as a pierrot or a chimney sweep. He had advised the latter as being more suitable to her brown boyish

face. "Some day," he could not help saying to himself, "Fausta, old and ugly like this woman here, will also fall into the arms of some footman or other, and she too will fondly imagine that the passing years have made no difference." This thought saddened him, for he still had in his heart a grateful admiration for Fausta's beauty; and it took away all bitterness and all desire to laugh at the Duchess. So instead of answering with some expression of veiled sarcasm, as he was at first tempted to do, he took his arm from the Duchess's waist and replied kindly, with the sort of indulgence shown toward the whims of a child, that he himself really did not know much about it, but that perhaps, on the whole, the *vivandière* costume was to be preferred.

"Yes, I agree," said the Duchess, delighted. "It is so much prettier. I shall have a flowered dress, a big hat with a feather, and a little cask at my side. I shall put some good wine into the cask and I shall go round saying 'Who wants some wine?' "

The Duchess was so pleased with this prospect that she did not notice until a moment had passed that she was speaking to herself. When she did notice it she was quite frightened. Who was this handsome footman and why was he continually disappearing in this way? The Duchess, who had been expecting a renewal of Sebastiano's embrace, instinctively crossed herself in a most devout manner.

Sebastiano went straight from the Duchess's room to Fausta's and entered it without knocking. All the lamps were lit, and there was a warm, pink glow. Fausta, sitting entirely nude on the edge of the bed, was stretching out her smooth, well-shaped leg toward Giustina who, kneeling on one knee, was preparing to slip a rolled-up stocking over the small foot. Fausta, seen from behind, was so lovely and so pure of form, with her long bare back slightly curved, her neat head bent to one side above her shapely neck, her rounded brown arms stretched forward, that for a moment Sebastiano felt himself completely in love with her again. Then the two women screamed and jumped to their feet, terrified, and Sebastiano once more thought of nothing except saving Fausta's life.

"Don't scream," he said urgently. "I have simply come to tell you that you are in danger. Get away from the villa while there is still time."

The more bewildered of the two was now Giustina, who was smitten with profound amazement at seeing the footman who had made advances to her speaking with such familiarity to her mistress. But Fausta, who had immediately recognized Sebastiano, was struggling, with violent, wilful movements to put on a dressing gown, at the same time telling him in an irritated voice to go away.

"I shall not go," said Sebastiano, "unless you come with me." His tone was firm, and he avoided looking at Fausta for fear of falling under her fascination again.

"But what is the danger?" said Fausta, annoyed, and speaking in a low voice. "It's you who must get out. . . . Are you crazy? Get out before they find you here."

Sebastiano knew Fausta well enough to see that his abrupt entrance had made her completely furious. Those frowning eyebrows, that somber brow, that trembling voice, were indicative of nothing but fear, selfishness, hatred. Of love there was none behind that angry mask—nor indeed had there ever been. This realization brought a great relief to Sebastiano and took away all hesitation. He sprang toward her and seized her by the arm.

"Don't be a fool," he said with stubborn insistence. "If you won't come I shall force you to come." And, so saying, he drew from his pocket the revolver that Perro had given him.

Fausta realized that Sebastiano was in earnest. She had suddenly perceived that the danger to which he was alluding was the plot of which Tereso had already told her. But the General's assurances made her skeptical of the imminence and the reality of the danger, and with feminine mistrust she saw in Sebastiano's intervention merely the act of a jealous lover. There could be no doubt of it; he was making a last attempt to prevent her going to Tereso. All at once a plan took shape in her mind and she decided to put it into effect immediately.

With a change of tone she said to the young man that it was all right, she would do as he wished, but at least he must give her time to dress. In the meantime he had better go and wait for her in the park, by the main entrance. She would dress and in five minutes, or ten at the most, would be with him. Fausta, ignorant of Sebastiano's new feeling about her, thought it necessary to add a touch of flattery to her lying words; so she explained that she was asking him to go entirely for his own good because somebody might come in at any moment and discover him. These propositions were accompanied by a caress of the hand on Sebastiano's sulky face. He had not the courage to turn away his cheek from the fingers he had once loved so dearly.

Sebastiano hesitated whether he should accept her suggestion or not, and Fausta tried to overcome this hesitation by an appearance of haste and efficiency. "Go on—go on—hurry up," she said, pushing him toward the door. And turning to the maid: "Quick Giustina, my black silk dress."

But this haste had an effect contrary to her expectation. Sebastiano, becoming suspicious, stopped at the door and said he would prefer to wait there, inside the room. He would have liked to add sarcastically that Fausta certainly need not claim to be shy in front of him, but he modestly restrained himself. His tone was again firm and cold, and Fausta saw that she must find some new method of persuasion.

"You don't trust me . . . all right," she said, still in the same hurried manner. "Well then, instead of waiting for me in the park, wait outside in the gallery. If you still don't trust me, here is the key. Take it—and now go." She took the key from the lock, thrust it into Sebastiano's hand, and pushed him outside. This time he did not resist, and went out into the gallery.

When Sebastiano had gone Fausta still maintained her feverish haste, but for a purpose quite different from the one she had professed.

"Quick, Giustina," she said, "put on the black dress yourself." And, before the astonished servant had time to draw breath, Fausta was taking off the maid's apron and unbuttoning her dress. And while Giustina, all bashful in her ugly white cotton undergarment, stood covering her half-bare breast with her arm, Fausta explained that she was to go and meet Sebastiano in her place. They were both of the same height, and if she hid her face with a mask and drew a shawl over her head he would never notice the difference. She must leave the house with the young man by a side door and lead him as far away as possible, wearing her mask all the time and taking care not to give away the trick. She could, indeed, keep up the pretense as long as she liked, not taking off her mask at all and allowing the young man to make love to her and kiss her. These last words made Giustina start, for in spite of her recent disillusionment she still preserved all her partiality for Sebastiano.

But Fausta thought that her start of surprise was due to modesty. "You silly," she said, "when will you ever find such a handsome young man again? Don't worry, and have some fun while you can. If you're worrying on my account, you needn't be afraid. I pass him on to you with pleasure—body and soul."

Fausta, pleased with her intrigue, was laughing now, showing her sharp white teeth; and meanwhile she was moving eagerly around the embarrassed Giustina, putting the last touches to her disguise.

"You *must* keep your face covered," she said, adjusting the little black silk mask on Giustina's snub nose, "not only

because he mustn't see who you really are but also because
you've got such an ugly mug that you'd frighten him, poor
boy. But not your chest; you've got a well-formed one, like
mine, so let him see a little bit of it and he'll be all the more
willing to follow you."

When she had finished dressing Giustina, Fausta clapped
her hands with delight at seeing her standing so erect and
stiff in her low-necked gown—almost intimidated, as it were,
by her own splendor. With a sudden generous impulse she
took from a box an old necklace of lapis lazuli and gold and
placed it round her neck, saying she would trust her with it,
and the disguise would be all the more complete. The necklace had been a present from Sebastiano; it had belonged to
his mother and had been the sole object that he had been
able to save from the wreck of his inheritance. Fausta, however, gave no thought to the added pain she would be inflicting upon him; she was taken up with her inventions. She liked
the idea of making Giustina a present of Sebastiano and his
love—just as she sometimes made her a present of cast-off
clothes. She liked to imagine Sebastiano's surprise when, after
many kisses and declarations of love, he finally took off the
mask and discovered that he was holding not Fausta but this
hideous monster in his arms. She liked the idea of disencum-
bering herself of Sebastiano's passion once and for all by
means of this low comedy trick.

Finally she muffled up Giustina in a magnificent cashmere
shawl and, advising her once more not to be silly but to
make the most of her opportunity, pushed her out of the
room.

## *CHAPTER 21*

Tereso, in the meantime, had had the report of the
spy he had sent to watch Fausta. The report, in spite of its
bureaucratic dryness, omitted no detail: Fausta and Doroteo,
the slaps, the blows, the final embrace—nothing was lacking.
It appeared to Tereso as he read it that the whole world was
growing dark before his eyes, and he instantly felt a savage
desire to rush into the adjoining room and kill Fausta with
his own hands. But this seemed too feeble a revenge, and,
swallowing his anger, he started to pace up and down the
room. He heaped the most atrocious insults upon the head of
Fausta, and one after the other rejected as being too gentle
the various methods of avenging himself that his indignant
imagination suggested. To kill her was a small thing, he
argued: she must go on living so that she might suffer and so
that he might gloat over her suffering. He thought of having

er disfigured in some unsightly manner by one of his hired hugs, so that her beauty would be ruined; or of shutting her up as a madwoman in an asylum; or, again, of confiscating all her property and sending her to ply the trade she was born for in a brothel. Tereso, since he had risen to power, had never used that power for his own personal feuds. But his career as a rebel general—almost a brigand—before his rise to the presidency was filled with bloodthirsty deeds which were the common knowledge of all. And at that moment it was those early years, fraught with blood and cruelty, that rose up in his mind.

He spent a few more minutes meditating tortures and barbarities as he walked up and down the room, then all at once he stopped and burst into a roar of laughter. Anyone who had seen him would certainly have taken him for a madman; but Tereso had hit upon a mode of revenge that satisfied him. He would not hurt a hair of Fausta's head, he said to himself; but all her property and all her brother's property—the fruit of robberies old and new—should be confiscated. And, under pain of death, he would force her to marry Doroteo—her beloved Doroteo, Doroteo the illiterate caddie. He himself would be one of the sponsors of this splendid marriage; he and the Duchess, that excellent Duchess who had plotted and planned so busily to bring him and Fausta together. The wedding should take place that very night, in the chapel at the end of the gallery. Fausta was a widow, and the successor of the late lamented Count Sanchez should be—Doroteo the caddie. Afterward he would send the happy couple for their honeymoon to the islands of Los Ladrones, the penal settlement, which were damned with a tropical climate and infested with mosquitoes; and there he would leave them, the dear young pair, to rot for a few years.

Tereso was delighted with this plan, for with the years there had come to him a certain contempt for violence—which is always stupid and in the end not very efficacious. It was a cruel but intelligent plan, a good joke in fact. He was especially delighted with his idea that the wedding should take place instantly, that very night, in the chapel of the villa. But it must not take place without anyone knowing of it, thought Tereso. A secret marriage would be altogether too convenient from Fausta's point of view. Everybody must know both of her infamous conduct and of her downfall, and he would send to inform all the guests at the villa so that they might come, just as they were in their fancy dresses, to the ceremony. Without any further delay he called his secretary and gave him his strange orders. He told him to go at once and summon the chaplain of the villa (if he were

asleep he must wake him) and tell him to get ready to celebrate a wedding; at the same time he was to send someone
to find and arrest a young, red-haired caddie at the golf
course by name Doroteo, who was to be brought along under
escort. Finally he was to go to all the rooms in the villa and
inform the guests that they were to be present at a wedding
before dinner. At this last order the secretary opened his
eyes wide in astonishment and asked how this was to be
done: since there were more than a hundred guests how could
he possibly inform them all? But Tereso replied peremptorily
that he must find a way somehow. The house was full of
police agents and servants. In any case, he must act quickly
and do everything as he had been ordered. The secretary,
completely bewildered, clicked his heels and went out.

The discovery of Fausta's crowning infidelity and—perhaps
even more—the neat perfection of his plan of revenge had
killed all desire in Tereso. It was therefore without the slightest agitation that a little later he heard a knock at the communicating door. The dinner table, shining with crystal and
silver, had been placed between the bed and a sofa. Tereso
sat down on the sofa, crossed his legs, and called to Fausta to
come in. But the door did not open wide; at first it was merely unlatched and a small sooty hand was laid upon the white-
and-gold paint of the doorpost. Then a brush became visible,
its worn straw bristles also soot-stained; then an iron pail;
and finally Fausta herself in her sweep's costume. She was
wearing a light shirt and a pair of patched, tattered trousers,
and on her feet were a huge pair of men's shoes, torn and
falling to pieces. Both shirt and trousers were dark and dirty
with soot, but one or two cunningly arranged holes allowed a
glimpse of the pale curve of her breast and of her well-turned
calf. Fausta's round face was plastered over with smudges
and fingermarks of lamp black, and her short hair, under a
peaked cap, was arranged with careful untidiness. She looked
absurdly small in her disguise—just like a boy—thought Tereso wistfully. The pail, filled with rags, hung on her arm,
and under her arm, like an umbrella, she carried the brush.
Shutting the door behind her she came forward, trailing her
feet in her enormous shoes with the lazy, thoughtless air of
a chimney sweep, the peak of her cap pulled down low. Her
eyes were sparkling with mischievous gaiety, and her mouth
pursed as though she were whistling softly.

"I'm a poor little chimney sweep," she said in a singsong
voice as she wandered round the room without looking at
Tereso. "A poor little chimney sweep out of a job. I was told
there was a chimney here full of soot, overflowing with it.

. . . Do I disturb you? I see you are expecting someone to dinner. If I am disturbing you, please say so at once and I will go away."

Tereso, looking at Fausta with quite other eyes than those of a lover, could not help thinking her extraordinarily charming dressed up thus like an urchin, with those holes in her clothes through which one caught glimpses of her lovely body. But he felt sure of himself and of his decision to take revenge, and more remorseless than he had ever been, even on the eve of those battles of which the issue was most secure. So he answered quite calmly that the chimney sweep did not disturb him at all; moreover, if he would like it he could offer him a glass of sherry before he set to work. In a ceremonious manner he rose and filled two glasses. He wanted to play with Fausta a little as she had played with him. But Fausta, who had already grown tired of acting her part, suddenly declared in her natural voice that she could endure the dirt on her face no longer and would go and wash it off in the bathroom. So saying, and before Tereso had time to open his mouth, she put down her pail and brush on the floor and went out, passing through the vestibule and into the bathroom.

Now, at almost exactly the moment when Fausta had gone into Tereso's room, Perro had handed over to Saverio the tray holding the imitation bomb hidden by a dish cover. Saverio, after fervently shaking the hand of the police spy, took the tray, went straight to Tereso's door and entered it without knocking. He found himself in the vestibule, facing three doors, the middle one leading to the General's room—from which at that moment came the sound of voices—the one on the left leading to the bathroom, and the one on the right into the study. Saverio went into the bathroom.

He acted with a precision and calmness; the direct result of his absolute faith in the righteousness of his cause and of his consequent readiness to die for it if that should prove necessary. He turned on the light, closed the door, and put down the tray on a painted stool near the bath. Then he went to the little towel cupboard, opened it, returned to the stool, lifted the dish cover and taking out the bomb placed it in the cupboard between two piles of folded linen. At that moment the door opened and Fausta came in.

Saverio had not yet shut the door of the cupboard, in which the black box containing the bomb showed conspicuously amongst the white towels; and it was this fact that sealed Fausta's fate. If the cupboard door had been closed Saverio might have had enough presence of mind to pass himself off as a real footman and find some excuse for being there. But with the cupboard door wide open and the black object in full view nestled in the white linen, it did not seem to Saverio that he could take any risks. In any case he lost his head the moment Fausta appeared. Before he realized what he was doing he leaped at her, clapped his hand over her mouth and dragged her inside the bathroom, shutting the door again. Then, during the brief moment of their struggle between the narrow walls of the little room, he wondered what he ought to do—according to the rules of revolutionary procedure, of course. He decided there could be no doubt. Fausta must be liquidated. It was a question of murder, but Saverio knew that for the sake of the cause one could— or rather, if necessary, one should—commit murder; and that was enough for him. So he took away the hand he had placed over Fausta's mouth to prevent her screaming and with both hands seized her by the throat, squeezing with all his might. She had just time to utter one brief cry which was immediately strangled, and to wave her hands in the air with a gesture by which she attempted to offer Saverio, in exchange for her life, the big solitaire diamond that sparkled on her sooty forefinger; then her strength gave out. Saverio knew she was dead because suddenly, as he was still frantically squeezing her throat, he almost fell forward, dragged down by the weight of the lifeless body as it collapsed.

Having killed Fausta, Saverio saw that in trying to avoid one danger he had fallen into another. Fausta alive would have denounced him; but Fausta dead would by her absence arouse the suspicions of the General, who would certainly come or send someone to look for her, and that would be the end of the plot. Not knowing what to do, Saverio had the idea of putting Fausta's body in the bath and turning on the taps. The sound of running water would make the General think that Fausta was having a bath and so would delay the discovery of the crime. To carry out this fanciful plan Saverio immediately lifted the body, with a great effort, from the floor, slid it into the bath and turned on both taps. The bottom of the bath began to fill with a rush of water that swelled out the trousers and shirt of the dead woman, who was resting almost in a sitting position, with her head and shoulders over the edge of the bath. At this point Saverio, who had so far acted simply as a conspirator, for the first time did something which was essentially the act of a murderer. Fausta's head was dangling backward, the hair ruffled, the tongue between the lips, the eyes blank and turned up—a horrible sight. Saverio, in a sudden panic, took a towel from the wash basin and wrapped it right round the dead woman's head. He was just going to close the cupboard when there was a crash as the door was forced open, and Tereso appeared on the threshold.

The bathroom, which was next to the bedroom, was separated from it only by a rather thin wall, so that the one short cry uttered by Fausta before she died had been heard by Tereso. For a moment he was struck dumb; then, remembering the plot, he seized his revolver and rushed to the bathroom. The door was locked. Tereso took a step back and hurled himself against it with his shoulder, snapping the little chain with which Saverio imagined he had secured it. One glance was enough for Tereso, as he stood in the doorway, to understand what had happened—Fausta lying back over the edge of the bath in the foaming water, her head a bundle of white, Saverio turning toward him, on the point of rushing at him. Tereso took a step backward into the vestibule and waited till Saverio's onrush should bring him as far as the door. Then he fired, aiming carefully at his chest. Saverio, who had realized who Tereso was, and who, in a last attempt to save the tottering edifice of the conspiracy, intended to throw himself on the General, disarm him and then kill him, bent down to seize his hand and received the bullet in the arm. He lurched forward, but, instead of falling against the door that led to the gallery, crashed right into Perro, who was just coming in to arrest him, followed by several police officers and Cinco himself.

"There must be a bomb in the little room," said Cinco breathlessly, while two of the men dragged Saverio away. "But you, Excellency, you are still alive—thank God. . . . Your Excellency, please go back into your own room as though nothing had happened and leave things to us. . . . Arrest that man," he added, turning to Perro, "and the rest of you search the bathroom—but don't make a noise. No one must notice anything."

Cinco, in evening dress, revolver in hand, spoke in an excited but subdued voice meant to convince Tereso of the timeliness of his interference. He was still anxious to do everything in a discreet and refined manner, as he had promised his superior. But the General's demeanor, and still more the look in his eyes, suddenly paralyzed him. Raising his hand to stop the two policemen as they were rushing into the bathroom to carry out Cinco's orders, Tereso himself entered first, went to the bath and, with his one hand, bit by bit without hurrying, unwrapped the cloth that enfolded Fausta's head.

"She is dead," he said coldly, looking at the Chief of Police. "My congratulations, Cinco. . . . You two—carry her out of here and lay her on my bed."

In the meantime Perro, in a final attempt to justify the calamity, went to the cupboard, took out the bomb and showed it to his chief, intending that Tereso also should see it, and said: "Here it is." But Tereso did not deign to glance at this demonstration of police efficiency. The two men lifted Fausta out of the bath and carried her, dripping, into the bedroom. Tereso, turning his back on Cinco and his acolyte, went out.

## CHAPTER 22

After Fausta's body had been laid on the bed the room soon filled with people—a couple of footmen and a maid attracted by the noise of the shooting; a number of plain-clothes policemen, including the two who had carried in the body; Cinco and Perro, who, terrified by Tereso's silence, kept near the door; and finally the Duchess herself. She had waited a while for Sebastiano's return. Then, thinking that one of her guests must have called him, she had dressed herself up in her *vivandière* costume as he had advised. She was putting on her make-up when she heard the commotion, and ran out with only one cheek rouged. Bewildered, uncomprehending, in her red frogged *vivandière* jacket with a small bright-colored wooden cask at her side and a big plumed hat on her head, she went from one person to another asking what had happened. But no one took any notice of her. They were all frightened by the sight of the dead body lying on the bed and even more by the presence of Tereso, erect and motionless before the window at the far end of the room.

Tereso was furious, with a bitter, empty fury that hurt him more than any direct pain. Fausta was dead and her death seemed, in some degree, an act of justice. But there had been a flaw—nay, worse, a definite, irreparable break—in the supreme, orderly, uncompromising rhythm of his day as a statesman. It was this that infuriated him. This corpse, this commotion, this invasion of his room were so many assaults upon his dignity and authority. Not even death, not even the danger to which he had been exposed, could justify this irritating, ridiculous pandemonium. Tereso decided that mere dismissal would be too light a punishment for Cinco, with whom rested the prime responsibility for all the confusion.

At last Cinco and Perro, cowed by the General's ominous silence, left the room, followed by the police officers. But in the door of the vestibule they passed more people who were arriving in ignorance of what had happened. First came Tereso's secretary, in a state of exhaustion, on his way to report the execution of the General's orders, and he was followed by a police officer holding an untidy and bewildered Doroteo tightly by the arm.

At first the secretary noticed no one except Tereso standing erect by the window. He clicked his heels as he entered and saluted stiffly, and then announced that all the General's orders had been carried out. The boy Doroteo was here; the priest had been notified, also the guests. . . . But then he caught sight of the corpse lying on the bed, and he was silent.

At last Tereso spoke. The jest had been turned into tragedy, but there was no reason why the secretary should know it. Besides, Tereso was grateful to him for his arrival. Here at least was someone who carried out his orders faithfully, when everyone else, from Cinco to Fausta herself—whose death seemed to him, in his rage, to be a final and extreme act of disobedience—appeared to be in league to evade his wishes. Tereso decided to turn the wedding into a funeral; it would at least be an occasion for ceremony, and after so much confusion he felt a great need for some sort of formality, even that of a funeral. Speaking slowly, he answered the secretary. He had done very well, he told him, and now he must go and inform the priest that it was not a wedding but a funeral at which he was to officiate. He was then to come back bringing some of the footmen to carry the body into the chapel. The secretary said he would do so and went out. Tereso, still standing in the window, stared at the door with a fixed, stern look which all the people present quickly interpreted as a command. One by one they retreated, noiselessly, to the door. Tereso was left alone.

When the door finally closed on the last of the intruders Tereso, freed from all startling, unseemly disturbance, felt that he could breathe again. This was his own room, his own bed, his own desk with its papers, his own table laid for dinner. Had it not been for the dead woman lying on the coverlet he might even have imagined that nothing had happened, so quiet and intimate was the light shed over the room by the two candelabra on the table. And, in the silence that followed the recent disturbance, he was relieved to discover in himself the serene, concentrated quality that he always liked. Refreshed by this quietness his fury at last left him. He slowly approached the bed, and after a moment's hesitation, sat down on the edge.

As he looked at Fausta's lifeless body, he found—now that his longing for order and ceremony had been appeased —that the bitterness of her death rose up again in his mind more sharply than ever. It was upon that very bed that he had hoped to embrace this woman, but Fate had willed

·that she should lie upon it only in death. Fausta, who had tricked him so many times, had now eluded him forever. Tereso, musing over this thought, experienced once again that sense of impotence which vain strivings after love had so often awakened in him. But now it was mingled with a new kind of rage that rebelled against this macabre form of frustration, against the finality of this irremediable loneliness.

Tereso had lowered his eyes in the effort to thrust back within himself the emotion that stunned him; now he raised them and looked at Fausta. She was lying stretched out on the bed, but in their haste the police officers had not troubled to put her down so that her head lay upon the pillow. It was resting flat on the coverlet and was turned slightly toward her shoulder, showing her face in profile, in a light that was softened by the shadow of the curtains. Her body lay peacefully at full length and there was no outward sign of death except the position of the mouth. It remained half open, like the beak of some tiny dead bird that looks as though it had lived on air. Her short, ruffled hair fell over her cheeks and little pointed curls stood out all around her head. But though the serene expression of her face seemed to belie death, death was clearly visible in the folds of the soaked shirt and trousers. These folds had fallen in lines different from those of the recumbent body; wrinkled, clinging to the breast, the belly, the legs, the form they had taken seemed to suggest that they had been produced by some living impulse—the impulse of a life which, in those limbs, no longer existed. Tereso had seen innumerable dead bodies in every attitude in his fighting days, and he tried to remain, as then, indifferent. But this final disillusionment, sterile and apathetic in itself, and affecting as it did both passion and power, forced him against his will to continue in a kind of inert, miserable contemplation.

And so, it seemed, there was nothing to be done but to give in and admit defeat, and at best try to adjust this mysterious, lamentable disorder to some kind of human order. Tereso got up, walked round the bed, and with the thumb of his one hand closed the lids over the dead woman's eyes. Then, without haste and in an almost casual, negligent manner, he lifted the heavy, lifeless arms one after the other by the wrists and placed them together on the breast, crossing the hands. A small ebony and ivory crucifix hung on the wall above the bed. He took it down and put it between the hands.

At this moment there was a discreet knock at the door. Tereso stepped quickly back from the bed, went to the wardrobe, took down his belt and fastened it round his waist, and called: "Come in." It was the secretary, with four footmen who were carrying a kind of camp bed by the bars of its bright metal frame. During the summer Fausta had often lain on this camp bed, naked in the sun, to acquire the tan that suited her complexion so well. The four men placed her body on it and spread over it the coverlet from the bed.

The secretary had not had time to cancel the wedding invitations that his emissaries had delivered to each room in the villa. As the four men came out of Tereso's room carrying the camp bed they found a crowd gathered at the end of the gallery on the opposite side to the chapel. Four or five police officers with hands linked formed a barrier across this part of the gallery, and behind them the people in the crowd stretched their necks and poked their heads forward to see what was happening. All the guests were in their fancy dresses, and in the dusk of the dimly lit gallery could be seen an assemblage of painted faces, brightly colored costumes, gay silks and feathers. It was not too dark to distinguish some of these costumes: here an enormous cardboard nose, scarlet and warty, there a gigantic Punch's head, here a yellow-faced Chinaman, there a monstrous red and white mask with features fixed in a drunken laugh. When they saw the four men appear carrying the body all the guests could do was to take off their hats—those that were wearing them; others took off their false noses, their masks, their beards. And so the four footmen carried the dead woman to the chapel under the curious eyes of the masquerading crowd. The Duchess, in tears, her little cask swinging at her side, for once unable to maintain her air of haughtiness, followed behind with the secretary, melancholy, bespectacled, very tall and thin. Then came the police officer and Doroteo. And last of all Tereso, upright and stiff in his neat, tight uniform, his thumb thrust into his belt. The little procession slowly, hesitatingly traversed the whole length of the gallery, beneath the saturnine gaze of the Spanish conquistadors. Beyond the barrier formed by the police officers the grotesque crowd stretched their necks for a last look. Then the chapel door closed behind Tereso.

The chapel was small but high-ceilinged. A black-and-gilt balcony with a curving balustrade circled the whitewashed walls; and along the walls, close to each other in a line, were the baroque tombs of the Duchess Gorina's ancestors. Tortuous coats of arms, skulls of glossy yellow marble, tables with ornamental bronze inscriptions, plump cherubs— nothing was missing of the funereal trappings of former times. The altar at the far end was a blaze of golden swords. Above it was a big, dark picture, without a frame, of a livid Christ crowned with great blood-dripping thorns, the feet transfixed by a rough nail and entwined in the coils of a black serpent.

The priest, a big man laden with rich vestments, was standing before the altar. He had felt no great surprise at receiving an order first to celebrate a wedding and secondly to change the wedding into a funeral. Baptisms, weddings, funerals: after the many years he had been performing his functions, he had long ceased to see any essential difference between these very different ceremonies. Not that he was a skeptic; but human life, reduced to these three events, had become too wretched and insignificant for him still to be able, after so long, to make any emotional distinctions between them. In the present case, it was true, there was the strangeness of the hour and of the sudden alteration, and the unusual element of a violent death. But the authority of Tereso was enough to counterbalance these oddities.

When he saw the little funeral procession enter the chapel the priest raised his arm and, without betraying the slightest curiosity in his plump, doleful face, told them in a low, distinct voice to come forward and put down the bier at the foot of the altar. Then, turning to his acolyte, he whispered to him to be quick and find the Office for the Dead in the Missal. The organist, however, who in the confusion had been told nothing, was unable to see from his closed box that there had been an alteration in the ceremony; and so, as the four men carefully put down their burden before the altar, the silence was suddenly broken by the triumphant, exultant music of a wedding march. The priest could not refrain from a gesture of annoyance and made a sign to the acolyte, who was then seen to run down the aisle as fast as his red and white cassock would permit, and disappear into the covered staircase leading to the organ. Abruptly, on its most joyful note, the music stopped.

The priest, after looking about for a moment to see that nothing was missing, turned his back on the chapel, walked to the Missal and began to intone the prayers. The acolyte crossed himself and knelt on the lowest step of the altar. The sonorous, hurried voice of the priest was suddenly drowned by the organ playing the opening phrases of the *Requiem*.

The Duchess had seated herself on the bench nearest the altar on the left, Tereso on the corresponding bench on the right. The Duchess was thinking chiefly of her party and of her social position, both of them now sadly prejudiced. But she could not help wondering, almost in spite of herself, what had become of Sebastiano. She crossed herself devoutly and began to move her lips in prayer. The little wine cask was still dangling at her side, but she had exchanged her plumed hat, which she had left in Tereso's room, for a handkerchief.

Tereso, too, was kneeling, his forehead pressed against his hand. In his own way, and in a very formal manner, Tereso was a religious man. With a feeling of humility, both bitter and touching to him on account of his own high position, he was thinking as he prayed, not of the murdered Fausta, but of himself and of death. He had been, till that moment, a disappointed lover. As he knelt before the Crucifix he felt himself a statesman again; to him it seemed that he was not only rediscovering the dignity of his own power but also a sense of his own nullity before God.

Doroteo, standing at one side of the door, understood nothing of what had happened, not even that Fausta was dead. On the opposite side stood the police officer who had arrested him and whose only thought now was to keep him under strict observation in the hope that the General would notice his zeal. The secretary, kneeling at a bench in the background, speculated vainly, as he bowed his bald head, upon the cause of this mysterious affair, of this wedding turned at the last minute into a funeral.

At the same moment, at the far end of the park, on a seat in the shade of a magnolia, Giustina, after much artifice and coquettishness, had just taken off her mask, and Sebastiano was making the mortifying, hateful discovery that he had once again been deceived. Fausta was now lost to him finally and forever—and by a contemptible trick in which there was nothing lacking, not even the moon rising behind the woods, to make it appear a parody of his former rapturous nights.

At the same moment also Saverio, in the agony of death, with three mortal wounds in different parts of his body, was being jolted up and down in a car carrying him at full speed along the Antigua road for burial in the cemetery there. It was Cinco's favorite method of getting rid of embarrassing prisoners—the so-called *ley-fuga,* or "escape law." The prisoner was killed, and it was then given out that he had tried to escape. Cinco, certain of dismissal, was no longer interested in staging the grand trial that he had formerly planned. But the man who had given Saverio the death blow, by shooting him in the back of the neck, had been Perro.

# A Ghost at Noon

>>>>>>>>>>>>>>>>>>>>>>>>>>>>>>>>>>>>>>>>>>>>>>>>>>>>>>>>>

## C H A P T E R  1

During the first two years of our married life my relations with my wife were, I can now assert, perfect. By which I mean to say that, in those two years, a complete, profound harmony of the senses was accompanied by a kind of numbness—or should I say silence?—of the mind which, in such circumstances, causes an entire suspension of judgment and looks only to love for an estimate of the beloved person. Emilia, in fact, seemed to me wholly without defects, and so also, I believe, I appeared to her. Or perhaps I saw her defects and she saw mine, but, through some mysterious transformation produced by the feeling of love, such defects appeared to us both not merely forgivable but even lovable, as though instead of defects they had been positive qualities, if of a rather special kind. Anyhow, we did not judge: we loved each other. This story sets out to relate how, while I continued to love her and not to judge her, Emilia, on the other hand, discovered, or thought she discovered, certain defects in me, and judged me and in consequence ceased to love me.

The less one notices happiness, the greater it is. It may seem strange, but in those two years I sometimes thought I was actually bored. Certainly, at the time, I did not realize that I was happy. It seemed to me that I was doing what everyone did—loving my wife and being loved by her; and this love of ours seemed to me an ordinary, normal fact, or rather, to be in no way precious—just like the air one breathes, and there's plenty of it and it becomes precious only when it begins to run short. If anyone had told me, at that time, that I was happy, I should even have been surprised; in all probability I should have answered that I was not happy because, although I loved my wife and she loved me, I felt a lack of security for the immediate future. This was true: we barely managed to grub along on what I earned, with great difficulty, as film critic on a daily paper of secondary importance, combined with other similar journalistic activities; we lived in a furnished room in a lodging-house; we often had no money for extras, sometimes not even for necessities. How could I be happy? Thus I never had so much to complain of as I did during the time when in truth—as I came to realize later—I was completely and profoundly happy.

At the end of those two first years of married life our situation at last improved: I got to know Battista, a film producer, and for him I wrote my first film-script—a job which, at the time, I considered to be merely a stopgap, particularly in relation to my more exalted literary ambitions, but which was fated, on the other hand, to become my profession. At the same time, however, my relations with Emilia began to change for the worse. My story, in fact, begins with my own first beginnings as a professional script-writer and with the deterioration of my relations with my wife—two occurrences that were almost simultaneous and, as will be seen, directly linked together.

Looking back, I am aware of having preserved a confused memory of an incident which appeared at the time to be irrelevant but to which, afterwards, I was forced to attribute a decisive importance. I see myself standing on the pavement of a street in the center of the town. Emilia, Battista and I had dined at a restaurant and Battista had suggested finishing the evening at his house and we had accepted. Now we were all three in front of Battista's car, a very expensive red car, but with a narrow body and only two seats. Battista, who was already sitting at the wheel, leaned over and opened the door, saying: "I'm sorry, but there's only room for one. You'll have to find your own way, Molteni . . . Unless you'd rather wait for me here: in that case I'll come back and fetch you." Emilia was beside me, in her black silk evening dress, the only one she had, a low-necked, sleeveless dress; and over her arm she was holding her fur cape: it was October and still warm. I looked at her, and for some reason noticed that her beauty, usually so serene and placid, had in it, that evening, a new kind of restlessness, almost a disturbed look. I said gaily: "Emilia, you go on with Battista . . . I'll follow in a taxi." Emilia looked at me and then answered slowly, in a reluctant tone of voice: "Wouldn't it be better for Battista to go on, and for us two to go together in the taxi?" Then Battista put his head out of the window of the car and exclaimed in a joking way: "You're a nice sort of person, you want me to go all alone." "It's not that," began

Emilia, "but . . ." and then I suddenly noticed that her beautiful face, usually so calm and harmonious, was now darkened and, one might say, distorted by an almost painful perplexity. But in the meantime I had already said: "You're right, Battista; come on, Emilia, you go with him and I'll take a taxi." This time Emilia yielded, or rather, obeyed, and got into the car. But—a further sensation that comes back to me only now, as I write about it—once she was seated beside Battista, with the door of the car still open, she looked at me with a hesitating glance, a glance of mingled pleading and repugnance. I took no notice of my own sensation, however, and, with the decided gesture of one who closes the door of a safe, I slammed the heavy door. The car moved away, and I, feeling very cheerful and whistling to myself, started off towards the nearby taxi stand.

The producer's house was not far from the restaurant, and normally I should have reached it in a taxi, if not quite at the same time as Battista, at any rate very shortly afterwards. But what should happen, when we were half way there, but a mishap at a crossroads: the taxi ran into a private car, and both sustained some damage; the taxi had a fender scratched and bent, and the side of the other car was dented. At once the two drivers got out and faced each other, arguing and swearing, people collected, a policeman intervened and with some difficulty separated them, and finally names and addresses were taken. All this time I sat waiting inside the taxi, without impatience, in fact with a sensation almost of happiness, because I had had plenty of good food and drink and at the end of dinner Battista had proposed that I should take a share in the script of one of his films. But the collision and the subsequent explanations had lasted perhaps ten, perhaps fifteen minutes, and so I arrived late at Battista's. As I came into the sitting-room I saw Emilia sitting in an armchair, her legs crossed, and Battista standing in one corner in front of a bar on wheels. Battista greeted me gaily: Emilia, on the other hand, asked me, in a plaintive, almost melting, tone, where I had been all that time. I answered lightly that I had had an accident, realizing at the same time that I was adopting a tone of evasiveness, as if I had something to conceal: in reality it was simply the tone of one who attributes no importance to what he is saying. But Emilia persisted, still in that strange tone of voice: "An accident . . . what do you mean, an accident?"—and then I, surprised and perhaps even a little alarmed, gave an account of what had happened. This time, however, it seemed to me that I went into too many details, as though I were afraid of not being believed; and I was, in fact, aware of having made a slight mistake, first by being reticent and now by being over precise. Emilia, however, did not insist further; and Battista, full of laughter and affability, put down three glasses on the table and invited me to drink. I sat down; and so, chattering and making jokes —especially Battista and I—we passed a couple of hours. Battista was so exuberant and gay that I hardly noticed Emilia was not so, at all. In any case she was always rather silent and retiring, because she was shy, and so her reserve did not astonish me. I was only slightly surprised that she did not take part in the conversation at least with glances and smiles, as she usually did: but she did not smile or look at us; all she did was to smoke and drink in silence, as though she were alone. At the end of the evening, Battista talked to me seriously about the film in which I was to collaborate, telling me the story, giving me information about the director and about my fellow scrip-writer, and finally inviting me to come to his office next day in order to sign the contract. Emilia took the opportunity of a moment's silence, after this invitation, to rise to her feet and say that she was tired and wanted to go home. We said good night to Battista, we left the room and went downstairs to the ground floor and out into the street, and we walked along the street to a taxi stand, without speaking a word. We got in and the taxi moved off. I was wild with delight at Battista's unhoped-for proposal, and I could not help saying to Emilia: "This film-script comes just at the right moment. I don't know how we should have got along without it. I should have had to borrow money." Emilia's only reply was to ask: "How much do they pay for a script?" I told her the amount and added: "So our problems are solved, anyhow for next winter"; and as I spoke I put out my hand and took Emilia's. She allowed her hand to be pressed and did not say any more until we arrived home.

## CHAPTER 2

After that evening, everything went, as far as my work was concerned, in the best possible way. I went next morning to see Battista, signed the contract for the script, and received my first advance of money. It was, I remember, a film of little importance, of the comic-sentimental type for which, serious-minded as I was, I did not imagine myself to be cut out, but which in fact showed me, as I worked on it, that I had an unsuspected vocation. That same day I had a first meeting with the director and also with my fellow script-writer.

While it is possible for me to indicate exactly the starting-point of my career as a script-writer, which was that evening at Battista's, it is very difficult for me to say with the same precision when my relations with my wife began to deteriorate. I could of course point to that same evening as the beginning of this deterioration; but that would be what is called being wise after the event; and all the more so because Emilia gave no sign, for some time afterwards, of any change in her demeanor towards me. The change certainly took place during the month which followed that evening, but I really could not say at what moment, in Emilia's mind, the decisive turn of the scale occurred, nor what caused this to happen. At that time we were seeing Battista almost every day, and I could relate, with an abundance of detail, many other episodes similar to that of the first evening in his house; episodes, that is, which were then in no way to be distinguished—to my eyes, anyhow—from the general color of my life, but which later acquired some special prominence or meaning. There is just one fact I wish to note: every time Battista invited us, which now happened very often, Emilia always showed, at first, a certain reluctance to go with me, not a strong nor a very decided reluctance, it is true, but curiously persistent in its expression and in its justifications. She always adduced some pretext or other that had nothing to do with Battista in order not to come with us; always, in the same way, I proved to her without any difficulty that the pretext did not hold good, and insisted on trying to find out whether she disliked Battista, or what her reason was; always, in the end, her answer to my question, given with a slight touch of perplexity, was that she did not in the least dislike Battista, that she had no fault to find with him, and that she did not want to go out with us simply because these evenings tired her and, really and truly, bored her. I was not content with these vague explanations and returned to my point, hinting that something must have happened between her and Battista, even though Battista himself was not conscious of it, or had not intended it. But, the more I tried to prove to her that she did not like Battista, the more she seemed to persevere in her denial: her perplexity, in the end, disappeared altogether, and its place was taken by a wilful obstinacy and determination. Then, completely reassured with regard to her feelings towards Battista and Battista's demeanor towards her, I went on to point out to her the reasons that told so strongly in favor of her giving us her company on these occasions: how hitherto I had never gone out without her, and Battista knew it; how her presence gave pleasure to Battista, as was shown by his urging, every time he invited us: "Of course, bring your wife"; how her absence, unexpected and difficult to justify as it was, might appear ill-natured, or, even worse, insulting to Battista, upon whom our living now depended; how, when all was said and done, since she was unable to show any valid reason for her absence whereas I was in a position to give many excellent reasons for her presence, it was preferable that she should put up with the fatigue and boredom required of her. Emilia usually listened to these arguments of mine with a dreamy and contemplative attention: it might have been thought that it was not so much the reasons themselves as my face and my gestures while expounding them that interested her; then, in the end, she would invariably give in and start silently dressing to go out. At the last moment, when she was ready to go, I would ask her, once more and for the last time, if she really disliked coming with me—not so much because by now I was doubtful of her answer, as in order to leave her no doubts about her freedom of decision. She would answer, in a categorical manner, that she did not dislike going, and then, out we would go.

All this, however, I reconstructed later, as I have already mentioned, patiently retracing in memory a number of occurrences which—at least at the time—had seemed insignificant, and which had passed almost unobserved by me at the moment when they took place. At that time I had been aware merely of a change for the worse in Emilia's demeanor towards me, but without explaining or defining it to myself in any way; in the same way one becomes conscious, through a change and a heaviness in the air, of the approach of a thunderstorm though the sky is still serene. I began to think she loved me less than in the past, because I noticed that she was no longer so anxious to be near me as in the first times after our marriage. In those days I would say: "Look, I've got to go out; I'll be out for a couple of hours but I'll come back as soon as I can"; and she would not protest, but she showed, by her expression of mingled sadness and resignation, that she did not like my being away. So much so, indeed, that often I either gave up going out, excusing myself somehow from my engagement; or, if possible, took her with me. Her attachment to me then was so strong that one day, when she had gone with me to the station from which I was to leave for a very brief trip to North Italy, I saw her, as we were saying good-bye, turn her face to hide the tears that filled her eyes. That time I pretended not to notice her grief; but during the whole journey I was haunted by remorse for that shamefaced but uncontrollable weeping; and from then onwards I ceased completely to travel without her.

But now, instead of assuming the usual, beloved expression with its slight suggestion of mortification and sadness, all she would do, if I announced that I was going out, was to answer calmly, often without even looking up from the book she was reading: "All right, I understand; then we'll see each other at dinner. Don't be late." Sometimes she seemed actually to want my absence to last longer than I myself intended. I would say to her, for instance: "I've got to go out. I'll be back at five"; and she would answer: "Stay out as long as you like . . . I've got things to do." One day I remarked in a light tone of voice that she seemed almost to prefer that I shouldn't be there; but she made no direct answer, merely saying that, since I was busy, one way and another, almost all day, it was just as well that we shouldn't meet except at mealtimes, and so she would be able to get through her own jobs in peace. This was only partly true: my work as a script-writer obliged me to be out of the house only in the after-noons; and hitherto I had always arranged matters so that I could spend the rest of the day with her. From that day onwards, however, I took to going out in the morning as well.

In the days when Emilia gave me to understand that my absences were displeasing to her, I used to leave the house with a light heart, well content, in reality, at her displeasure, as being yet another proof of the great love she felt for me. But as soon as I became aware that not merely did she show no disappointment, but even seemed to prefer to be left alone, I began to experience an obscure feeling of distress, as if I had felt the ground give way beneath my feet. I went out now not only in the afternoons to go and work at the film-script, but in the mornings too, as I said, and often without any other purpose than to test Emilia's indifference, so utterly new and, to me, so bitter; and yet she did not show the slightest displeasure, in fact she accepted my ab-sences with placidity if not actually—so it seemed to me— with ill-disguised relief. At first I tried to console myself for this coldness by arguing that, after two years of marriage, habit, even though it may be an affectionate habit, creeps into love with fatal effect, and the assurance of being loved takes away all character of passion from a married couple's relationship. Yet I felt that this was not true: I felt it rather than thought it, for thought is always more fallible, even in its apparent preciseness, than obscure, confused feeling. I felt, in fact, that Emilia had ceased to be displeased at my absences, not because she considered them inevitable and without consequence to our relationship, but because she loved me less, or indeed not at all. I also felt that something, without doubt, must have happened to change her feeling, which had once been so tender and so possessive.

## CHAPTER 3

At the time when I first met Battista, I found myself in an extremely difficult situation, and I did not know how to escape from it. My difficulty consisted in my having at that time acquired the lease of a flat, although I had not the money to complete my payment for it and did not know how I should be able to get the money. We had lived, Emilia and I, during our first two years, in a large furnished room in a lodging-house. Any other woman but Emilia would perhaps not have put up with this provisional arrangement; but, in the case of Emilia, I think that, by accepting it, she gave me the greatest proof of love that a devoted wife can give to a husband. Emilia was, indeed, what is called a born housewife; but in her love of home there was more than the natural inclination common to all women; I mean that there was something that resembled a deep, jealous passion, almost a hunger, which went beyond her own self and seemed to derive its origin from some ancestral situation. She came of a poor family; she herself, when I first came to know her, was working as a typist; and I think that her love of home was an unconscious means of expression for the frustrated aspirations of generations of disinherited people who were chronically incapable of setting up an abode of their own, however modest. I do not know whether she was under the illusion that, with our marriage, her dreams of domesticity would come true; but I remember that one of the few times I ever saw her weep was when I was forced to confess, shortly after we became engaged, that I was not yet in a position to provide her with a home of her own, even a rented one, and that we must be content, at first, with a furnished room. It seemed to me that those tears, quickly suppressed as they were, were an outward expression not only of bitter disappointment at seeing her cherished dream thrust away into the future, but also of the actual power of that dream, which for her was, as it were, more a reason for living than just a dream.

And so we lived, those first two years, in a furnished room; but how meticulously tidy and bright and clean Emilia always kept it! It was obvious that, as far as possible—and in a furnished room it is possible only to a limited degree— she wanted to deceive herself into believing that she had a home of her own; and that, lacking her own household furni-

ture, she wanted at least to infuse her own concentrated domestic spirit into the lodging-house keeper's shabby utensils.
There were always flowers in a vase on my desk; my papers
were always arranged with loving, inviting orderliness, as
though to encourage me to work and guarantee me the
greatest possible privacy and quietness; the tea service always
stood ready on a small table, with napkins and a box of
crackers; never was an undergarment or other intimate object to be found where it should not be, on the floor or the
chairs, as so often happens in similar cramped, temporary
abodes. After the first hurried cleaning by the servant-girl,
Emilia would subject the whole room to a second, more
scrupulous, personal cleaning, so that everything which could
shine and reflect *did* shine and reflect, even the smallest brass
knob on the window-frame or the least visible strip of wood
on the floor; at night, she insisted on preparing the bed herself, without the help of the maid, laying out her own muslin
nightgown on one side and my pyjamas on the other and
carefully turning down the sheets and arranging the twin
pillows; in the morning she would get up before me, and,
going to the lodging-house keeper's kitchen, would prepare
the breakfast and bring it to me herself, on a tray. She did
all these things in silence, discreetly, without drawing attention to herself, but with an intensity, a concentration, an
eager, absorbed solicitude that betrayed a passion too deep
to be openly proclaimed. Nevertheless, in spite of these pathetic efforts on her part, the furnished room remained just
a furnished room; and the illusion that she sought to create
for herself and for me was never complete. And then, from
time to time, in moments of excessive weariness or discouragement, she would complain—gently, it is true, and almost
placidly, in accordance with her character, but not without
evident bitterness—asking me how long this provisional, this
inferior, way of living would have to continue. I was aware
that it was a real sorrow that lay behind this very moderate
expression of displeasure; and I worried myself with the
thought that, sooner or later, I would somehow have to satisfy her.

In the end I decided, as I said, to buy the lease of a flat:
not because I had the means to do so, for such means were
still lacking, but because I understood how she was suffering
and how her suffering would perhaps some day overcome
her powers of endurance. I had put aside a small sum of
money during those two years; to this sum I added some
more money which I had obtained on loan; and so I was able
to pay the first instalment. In doing this I did not, however,
experience the joyful feelings of a man preparing a home for

his bride; on the contrary, I was anxious and seriously distressed, because I did not know in the least how I would manage when, a few months later, the time came to pay the second instalment. At that time, in fact, I was so desperate that I had almost a feeling of rancor against Emilia, who, by the tenacity of her passion, had in a way forced me to take this imprudent and dangerous step.

However, the profound joy of Emilia when I announced that the matter was settled, and later the unaccustomed feelings—strange, to me, both in their quality and their intensity—which she displayed on the day we went for the first time into the still unfurnished flat, made me for some time forget my troubles. I have said that, with Emilia, love of home had all the characteristics of a passion; and I must add that, on this occasion, that same passion appeared to me to be bound up with, and mingled with, sensuality, as though the fact of having at last acquired a flat for her had made me, in her eyes, not merely more lovable but also, in a wholly physical sense, closer and more intimate. We had gone to inspect the place, and Emilia, to begin with, walked round all the cold, empty rooms with me while I explained the purpose of each of them and the way in which I thought to arrange the furniture. But, at the end of our visit, as I was walking over to a window with the intention of opening it and showing her the view to be enjoyed from it, she came close up to me and, pressing her whole body against me, whispered to me to give her a kiss. This was quite a new thing for her, usually so discreet, so almost shy, in any expression of love. Excited by this novelty and by the tone of her voice, I kissed her as she wanted; and all the time the kiss lasted—certainly one of the most violent and most abandoned we ever exchanged—I felt her clinging more and more closely with her body against mine, as though inviting me to greater intimacy; and then, wildly, she tore off her skirt, unbuttoned her chemise, and thrust her belly against mine. The kiss over, in a very low voice that was like an inarticulate breath and yet was melodious, melting, she murmured in my ear—or at least so it seemed to me—that I should take her; and meanwhile, with all the weight of her body, she was pulling me down towards the floor. We made love on the floor, on the dusty tiles, under the sill of the window I had meant to open. Yet in the ardor of that embrace, so unrestrained and so unusual, I was conscious not only of the love she felt for me at that time, but more particularly of the outpouring of her repressed passion for a home, which in her expressed itself quite naturally through the channel of unforeseen sensuality. In that embrace, in fact, consummated on that dirty floor, in the chilly gloom of the empty flat, she was giving herself, so I felt, to the giver of the home, not the husband. And those bare, echoing rooms, still smelling of paint and fresh plaster, had stirred something in the innermost recesses of her heart that no caress of mine, hitherto, had ever had the power to awaken.

Between our visit to the empty flat and the day of our entry into it a couple of months went by, during which the necessary contracts were drawn up, all in Emilia's name, because I knew that this gave her pleasure; while we also collected together the small amount of furniture that, with my very limited means, I could afford to buy. Meanwhile, when the first feeling of satisfaction was over, I felt, as I have mentioned, extremely anxious about the future, and, at moments, positively desperate. I was earning enough by now, it is true, for us to live in a modest manner and even put aside a few pennies; but these savings were certainly not sufficient to pay the next instalment on the flat. My desperation was all the more acute inasmuch as I could not even have the relief of talking about it to Emilia: I did not wish to spoil her pleasure. But I recall that time as a period of great anxiety and, in a way, of diminished love for Emilia. Indeed I could not help realizing that she was not in the least worried to know how I had managed to come by so much money, although she knew our real position perfectly well. This thought was vaguely surprising to me, and there were moments when it inspired me almost with irritation against her—she who now, all busy and cheerful, thought of nothing but going round the shops looking for things to furnish the flat, and who every day, in her most placid tone of voice, announced some new acquisition. I wondered how it came about that she, who loved me so much, failed to guess at the cruel anxieties that oppressed me; but I realized that, probably, she thought that if I had bought the lease of the flat I had no doubt also taken steps to procure the necessary money. Nevertheless her serenity and satisfaction seemed to me, in contrast to my own wretched worries, to be a sign of selfishness, or, at the least, of insensibility.

I was so troubled at that period that even the image I had hitherto made of myself in my own mind had changed. Up till then I had looked upon myself as an intellectual, a man of culture, a writer for the theater—the "art" theater, I mean —for which I had always had a great passion and to which I felt I was drawn by a natural vocation. This *moral* image, as many call it, also had an influence on the *physical* image; I saw myself as a young man whose thinness, short sight, nervousness, pallor and carelessness in dress all bore witness, in anticipation, of the literary glory for which I was

destined. But at that time, under the pressure of my cruel
anxieties, this very promising and flattering picture had given
place to an entirely different one, that of a poor devil who
had been caught in a shabby, pathetic trap, who had not
been able to resist his love for his wife and had over-reached
himself and would be forced to struggle, for goodness knows
how much longer, in the mortifying toils of poverty. I saw
myself changed in my physical aspect as well: I was no longer
the young and still unknown theatrical genius, I was the starving journalist, the contributor to cheap reviews and second-
rate newspapers; or perhaps—even worse—the scraggy employee of some private company or government office. This
man hid his anxieties from his wife, so as not to worry her;
he ran about the town all day long, looking for work and
often not finding any; he would wake up in the night with a
start, thinking of the debts that had to be paid; in fact, he no
longer thought of, or saw, anything but money. It was a
touching picture, perhaps, but lacking in luster and dignity,
the picture of a wretched, conventional literary figure, and I
hated it because I thought that, slowly and insensibly, with
the years, I should end by resembling it, in spite of myself.
But there it was: I had not married a woman who could understand and share my ideas, tastes and ambitions; instead I
had married, for her beauty, an uncultivated, simple typist,
full, it seemed to me, of all the prejudices and ambitions
of the class from which she came. With the first I could have
faced the discomforts of a poverty stricken, disorganized life,
in a studio or a furnished room, in expectation of the theatrical successes that were bound to come; but for the second
I had had to provide the home of her dreams. And at the
cost, I thought in desperation, of having to renounce, perhaps for ever, my precious literary ambitions.

There was another factor which contributed at that time
to increase my feeling of anguish and impotence in face of
material difficulties. I felt that the metal of my spirit, like
a bar of iron that is softened and bent by a persistent flame,
was being gradually softened and bent by the troubles that
oppressed it. In spite of myself, I was conscious of a feeling
of envy for those who did not suffer from such troubles, for
the wealthy and the privileged; and this envy, I observed,
was accompanied—still against my will—by a feeling of
bitterness towards them, which, in turn, did not limit its aim
to particular persons or situations, but, as if by an uncontrollable bias, tended to assume the general, abstract character of a whole conception of life. In fact, during those difficult days, I came very gradually to feel that my irritation
and my intolerance of poverty were turning into a revolt

against injustice, and not only against the injustice which struck at me personally but the injustice from which so many others like me suffered. I was quite aware of this almost imperceptible transformation of my subjective resentments into objective reflections and states of mind, owing to the bent of my thoughts which led always and irresistibly in the same direction: owing also to my conversation, which, without my intending it, always harped upon the same subject. I also noticed in myself a growing sympathy for those political parties which proclaimed their struggle against the evils and infamies of the society to which, in the end, I had attributed the troubles that beset me—a society which, as I thought, in reference to myself, allowed its best sons to languish and protected its worst ones. Usually, and in simpler, less cultivated people, this process occurs without their knowing it, in the dark depths of consciousness where, by a kind of mysterious alchemy, egoism is transmuted into altruism, hatred into love, fear into courage; but to me, accustomed as I was to observing and studying myself, the whole thing was clear and visible, as though I were watching it happen in someone else; and yet I was aware the whole time that I was being swayed by material, subjective factors, that I was transforming purely personal motives into universal reasons. I had never wished to become a member of any political party, as almost everyone did during that uneasy period after the war, just because it seemed to me that I could not take part in politics, as so many did, for personal motives, but only from intellectual conviction, which, however, I had so far lacked; and I was therefore very angry when I felt my ideas, my conversation, my whole demeanor going very gradually adrift on the current of my own interests, slowly changing color according to the difficulties of the moment. "So I'm really just like everyone else," I thought furiously; "does it only need an empty purse to make me dream, like so many other people, of the rebirth of humanity?" But it was an impotent fury; and one day when I felt more deseperate or less firm than usual, I let myself be convinced by a friend who had been hovering around me for some time, and became a member of the Communist party. Immediately afterwards I reflected that, once again, I had behaved, not like the young, unrecognized genius, but like the starving journalist or the scraggy employee into which I was so terrified that time would transform me. But the thing was done now, I was inside the party and I could not draw back again. Emilia's reception of the news of the step I had taken was characteristic: "But now only the Communists will give you work . . . the others will boycott you." I had not the courage to tell her what I was thinking—which was that, in all probability, I should never have become a Communist if I had not bought the lease of that over-expensive flat, in order to give her pleasure. And that was the end of it.

At last we moved in, and the very next day, by a coincidence that seemed to me providential, I met Battista, and, as I have already related, was at once invited by him to work on the script of one of his films. For some time I felt relieved and more cheerful than I had been for many weeks: I thought I would do four or five film-scripts to pay off the lease of the flat, and then devote myself again to journalism and my beloved theater. Meanwhile my love for Emilia had come back to me stronger than ever, and sometimes I went so far as to reproach myself, with the bitterest remorse, for having been capable of thinking ill of her and judging her to be selfish and insensitive. This brief bright interval, however, lasted only a very short time. Almost immediately the sky of my life clouded over again. But at first it was only an exceedingly small cloud, though of a decidedly gloomy color.

## CHAPTER 4

My meeting with Battista took place on the first Monday in October. The day before, we had moved into the flat, which was now completely furnished. This flat, the cause, to me, of so many anxieties, was in truth neither large nor luxurious. It had only two rooms—a big living-room, of greater length than width, and a bedroom, also of good proportions. The bathroom, the kitchen and the maid's room were all three very small—reduced, as always in modern buildings, to the smallest possible size. Besides this there was a little windowless box which Emilia intended to make into a dressing-room. The flat was on the top floor of a newly built block, as smooth and white as if it had been all made of plaster, in a narrow, slightly sloping street. The whole of one side of the street was occupied by a row of buildings similar to ours, while along the other side ran the boundary wall of the garden of a private villa, with branches of great leafy trees hanging over it. It was a beautiful view, as I pointed out to Emilia, and we could almost delude ourselves into thinking that this garden, in which we could catch glimpses of winding paths and fountains and open spaces, was not cut off from us by a street and a wall, and that we could go down and walked about in it as often as we liked.

We moved in during the afternoon. I was busy the whole day, and I do not remember where we dined, nor with whom; I only remember that, towards midnight, I was standing in

the middle of the bedroom in front of the triple looking-
glass, looking at myself and slowly undoing my tie. All at
once, in the mirror, I saw Emilia take a pillow from the double bed and go off towards the door of the living-room. Surprised, I asked: "What are you doing?"

I had spoken without moving. Still in the mirror, I saw her
stop in the doorway and turn, as she said in a casual tone:
"You won't mind, will you, if I sleep on the divan bed, in the
other room?"

"Just for tonight, you mean?" I inquired, puzzled and still
uncomprehending.

"No, for always," she replied hurriedly. "To tell you the
truth, that was one of the reasons why I wanted a new home.
I really can't go on sleeping with the shutters open, as you
like to do. I wake up every morning at the crack of dawn and
then I can't go to sleep again, and I go about all day long
with a sleepy feeling in my head. You don't mind, do you? I
do think it's really better for us to sleep separate."

I still failed to understand, and at first I felt no more than
vaguely irritated at an innovation so completely unexpected.
Walking across to her, I said: "But this can't go on. We've
only two rooms; in one there's the bed, and in the other, the
armchairs and divans. Why . . . ? Besides, sleeping on a divan,
even if it can be turned into a bed, is not very comfortable!"

"I never dared tell you, before," she answered, lowering
her eyes without looking at me.

"During these two years," I persisted, "you've never once
complained . . . I thought you'd got accustomed to it."

She raised her head, pleased, it seemed to me, that I had
taken up the point of the excuse she had made. "I've never
got accustomed to it . . . I've always slept badly . . . recently,
in fact, perhaps because my nerves are bad nowadays, I've
hardly been sleeping at all . . . If we could only go to bed
early; but, one way or another, we're always late . . . and
then . . ." She did not finish her sentence and made as if to
move away towards the living-room. I went after her and said
hastily: "Wait a minute. If you like, we can perfectly well
give up sleeping with the shutters open. It's all right—from
now on we'll sleep with them shut."

I realized, as I spoke, that this proposal was not merely a
demonstration of affectionate compliance; in reality, as I knew,
I wanted to put her to the test. I saw her shake her head, and
she answered, with a faint smile: "No, no . . .why should you
sacrifice yourself? You've always said you feel suffocated with
the shutters closed. It's better for us to sleep apart."

"I assure you, for me it will be a very slight sacrifice . . .
I shall soon get used to it."

She appeared to hesitate and then said, with unexpected firmness: "No, I don't want any sacrifices—either great or small . . . I shall sleep in the other room."

"And what if I say I don't like it, and that I want you to sleep with me?"

She hesitated again. Then, in the good-natured tone which was usual to her: "Riccardo, that's just like you. You didn't want to make this sacrifice two years ago, when we got married; and now you want to make it, at all costs. What's the matter with you? Plenty of married people sleep apart and are fond of each other just the same. And you'll be freer in the mornings, too, when you have to go to work; you won't wake me up any more."

"But you've just said you always woke at dawn . . . I don't leave the house at dawn! . . ."

"Oh, how pig-headed you are!" she exclaimed impatiently. And this time, without paying any more attention to me, she left the room.

Left alone, I sat down on the bed, which, despoiled of one of its pillows, already had about it a suggestion of separation and desertion, and so I remained for some moments in bewilderment, looking at the open door through which Emilia had disappeared. One question came into my mind: did Emilia not want to sleep with me any longer because the daylight really annoyed her, or simply because she did not want to go on sleeping with me? I was inclined to believe in the second of these alternatives, although I longed with all my heart to believe in the first. I felt, however, that if I had accepted Emilia's explanation, there would always have been a doubt in my mind. I did not admit it to myself, but the final question, in reality, was, "Has Emilia perhaps ceased to love me?"

In the meantime, while, absorbed in these thoughts, I sat looking about the room, Emilia was coming and going, carrying into the living-room, after the pillow, a pair of folded sheets that she took from the cupboard, a blanket, a dressing-gown. It was the beginning of October, and the weather was still mild, and she was going about the flat in a gauzy, transparent chemise. I have not yet described Emilia, but I should like to do so now, if only in order to explain my feelings that night. She was perhaps not really a tall woman, but to me, owing to the feeling that I had for her, she seemed taller and, above all, more majestic than any woman I had ever known. I could not say whether this look of majesty was innate in her or whether it was my own ravished glances that attributed it to her; I only remember that, on the first night after our wedding, when she had taken off her high-heeled shoes, I went up to her in the middle of the room and embraced her, and was vaguely surprised when I noticed that her forehead barely came up to the top of my chest and that I was taller than her by a head and shoulders. But later, when she was lying beside me on the bed, there was a further surprise: her naked body now looked to me big, ample, powerful, although I knew that, in reality, she was not in the least massive. She had the most beautiful shoulders, the most beautiful arms, the most beautiful neck I had ever seen, full and rounded, shapely in form and languid in movement. Her complexion was dark, her nose pronounced and in form severe; her mouth full and fresh and laughing, with two rows of teeth of a luminous whiteness which seemed always to be wet and gleaming with saliva; her eyes very large, of a fine golden brown, sensual in expression, and sometimes, in moments of abandon, strangely relaxed and dazed-looking. She had not, as I have already said, a really beautiful figure; and yet she appeared to have—for some reason that I cannot explain; perhaps because of the supple slenderness of her waist which emphasized the form of her hips and breast; perhaps because of her erect, dignified carriage; perhaps because of the youthful boldness and vigour of her long, straight, well-shaped legs. She had, in fact, an air of grace and of placid, unconscious, spontaneous majesty such as comes from nature alone, and which, on that account, appears all the more mysterious and indefinable.

And so that evening, as she went backwards and forwards between the bedroom and the living-room, and as I followed her with my eyes, not knowing what to say, and feeling at the same time both displeased and embarrassed, my glance traveled from her serene face to her body, which was more or less visible through the thin stuff of her chemise, its colors and contours being veiled and broken up by its folds; and suddenly, the suspicion that she no longer loved me sprang into my mind again, in an abrupt, haunting sort of way, as a feeling of the impossibility of contact and communion between my body and hers. It was a sensation I had never felt before, and for a moment I was stunned and at the same time incredulous. Love is certainly, and before all else, a matter of feeling; but it is also, in an ineffable, almost spiritual manner, a communion of bodies—that communion, indeed, which up till then I had enjoyed without being conscious of it, as something obvious and completely natural. And now, as if my eyes had been at last opened to a fact which was clear and yet, till that moment, invisible, I was conscious that this communion might no longer exist between us, in fact, no longer did exist. And I, like a person who suddenly realizes he is hanging over an abyss, felt a kind of painful nausea at the thought that our intimacy had turned, for no reason at all, into estrangement, absence, separation.

I came to a pause at this staggering notion; meanwhile Emilia, who had gone into the bathroom, was washing, as I could tell from the sounds of water flowing from taps. I had an acute feeling of impotence and, at the same time, a violent desire to overcome it as quickly as possible. So far I had loved Emilia both easily and ignorantly; and my love had always manifested itself as if by enchantment, with a thoughtless, impetuous, inspired impulse which hitherto had seemed to me to spring from myself and from myself alone. Now, for the first time, I realized that this impulse depended upon, and nourished itself upon, a similar impulse in Emilia, and, seeing her so changed, I feared that I should no longer be capable of loving her with the same ease and spontaneity and naturalness. I feared, in fact, that that admirable communion, of which I had only now become aware, would be succeeded by, on my side, an act of cold imposition, and on hers . . . I did not know what her attitude would be, but I felt intuitively that if, on my side there was imposition, on hers there could only be a non-participating passivity, if not worse.

At that moment Emilia passed close to me as she came and went about the room. I leant forward with an almost involuntary lunge and seized her by the arm, saying: "Come here . . . I want to talk to you."

Her immediate reaction was to draw away from me, then, next moment, she yielded and came and sat down on the bed, though at some distance from me. "Talk to me? What do you want to talk to me about?"

For some reason or other, my throat now felt choked by sudden anxiety. Or perhaps it was shyness—a feeling which had hitherto been absent from our relationship and which more than anything else, seemed to confirm the change that had taken place in it. "Yes," I said, "I want to talk to you; I have an impression that something has changed between us."

She threw me a rapid, sideways glance and answered with decision: "I don't understand you . . . what do you mean changed? Nothing's changed."

"I haven't changed, but you have!"

"I haven't changed in the least. I'm still just the same."

"You used to love me more. You used to be sorry if I left you alone when I went out. You used not to mind sleeping with me than . . . on the contrary."

"Ah, that's what it's all about," she exclaimed, but I
noticed that her tone was less assured; "I knew you would
think something like that . . . But why don't you stop tormenting yourself like this? I don't want to sleep with you,
merely because I want to sleep, and with you I can never
manage to—that's all."

Now, strangely, I felt that arguments and ill-humor were
melting quickly away and dissolving into nothingness, like
wax at the fire: she was sitting beside me, in that vaporous,
crumpled chemise through which it seemed that only the
most intimate and secret colors and forms of her body were
visible; and I desired her and felt it strange that she should
not be aware of it and should not stop talking and embrace
me, as had always happened in the past at the mere meeting
of our disturbed glances. On the other hand, this feeling of
desire made me hope not only that I should be drawn with
the old, irresistible force towards her, but also that I should
arouse in her a similar impulse towards me. I said, in a
very low voice: "If nothing's changed, prove it to me."

"But I prove it to you every day, every hour!"

"No, now."

As I said this, I leant forward and took hold of her almost
violently by the hair and tried to bend her head back to kiss
her. Obediently she allowed herself to be drawn towards
me, but at the last moment she avoided my kiss by a slight
movement of her head, so that my lips could only reach her
neck. Letting her go, I said: "Don't you want me to kiss you?"

"It's not that," she murmured, rearranging her hair with
characteristically wayward indolence; "if it was just one
kiss, I would willingly give it you. But then you go on . . .
and it's late already . . ."

I felt hurt by these prudent, discouraging words. "It's
never too late for such things," I said.

Meanwhile I was trying to kiss her again, pulling her towards me by the arm. "Ow," she cried out, "you're hurting
me!"

Now I had scarcely touched her, and I remembered how,
at the time when we loved each other, I had sometimes clasped
her violently in my arms without drawing so much as a
sigh from her. Irritated, I said: "In the old days it didn't hurt
you!"

"You've got hands like iron," she replied; "you don't realize . . . You must have left marks on me now!" All this was
said in an indolent sort of way, but without the slightest
coquettishness.

"Come on," I insisted sharply, "are you going to give me
that kiss, or not?"

"Here you are"; and she leant forward and, in a motherly way, flicked me a light kiss on the brow. "And now let me go to bed; it's late."

I did not intend to put up with that; and I took hold of her again, with both hands, just below the waist. "Emilia," I said, leaning towards her as she drew herself away, "that's not the kiss I wanted from you."

She thrust me away, saying once again, but now in a distinctly rough tone of voice; "Oh, let me alone . . . you hurt me!"

"It's not true, it can't be true," I muttered between my clenched teeth, throwing myself upon her.

This time she disengaged herself with two or three energetic, simple movements; then rose to her feet and, as if suddenly making up her mind, said, without any show of modesty: "If you want to make love, all right then . . . But don't hurt me; I can't bear to feel myself squeezed like that!"

I was left breathless. Her tone was now utterly cold, I could not help noticing, and practical, without the faintest touch of feeling in it. For a moment I sat quite still on the bed, my hands clasped, my head bent. Then her voice reached me again: "Well then, if you really want to, let's get on with it . . . shall we?"

Without raising my head, I said in a low voice: "Yes, I want to." It was not true, for by this time I no longer desired her, but I wished to endure this new, curious sense of estrangement to the bitter end. I heard her say "all right," and then I heard her walking about the room and moving around the bed behind me. All she had to do was to take off her chemise, I thought, and I recalled how in the past I had watched this simple act with enchanted eyes, like the brigand in the fairy-tale who, when the magic word had been uttered, saw the door of the cave slowly open, revealing the splendor of the marvelous treasures within. But this time I was unwilling to look, knowing that I should be looking with different eyes, eyes that were no longer childish and pure, even if desirous, but that had been, by her indifference, made cruel and unworthy both of her and of myself. I remained as I was, leaning forward, my hands in my lap, my head bowed. After a little I heard the springs of the bed creak gently; she had got on to the bed and was lying on top of the bed-clothes. There was again a slight rustling as though she were changing position, and then she said, still in that horrible new voice: "Well, come along then . . . what are you waiting for?"

I neither turned nor moved; but all of a sudden I wondered

whether it had always been like that, in our relationship. Yes, I said to myself at once, it had always been like that, more or less; she had always undressed and lain down on the bed: how else could it have been? And yet, at the same time, everything had been different. Never until now had there been this mechanical docility, cold and detached, such as was apparent from the tone of her voice and even from the creaking of the bed-springs and the rustling of the pressed-down bed-covers. Formerly everything, on the contrary, had happened in a cloud of inspired haste, of intoxicated unconsciousness, of ravished complicity. It happens sometimes, when one's mind is absorbed by some profound thought, that one puts down an object of some kind—a book, a brush, a shoe—somewhere or other, and then, when the fit of absorption is over, one looks for it in vain for hours and, in the end, finds it in some strange, almost unbelievable place, so that a physical effort is required to reach it—on top of a cupboard, in a hidden corner, inside a drawer. That is what had happened to me, hitherto, in relation to love-making. Everything had always run its course in a mood of swift, feverish, enchanted absorption, and I had always come to myself again in Emilia's arms almost without being able to recollect how it had all happened and what I had done between the moment when we were sitting opposite each other, quiet and without desire, and that other moment in which we were joined together in the final embrace. This absorption was now entirely lacking in her and therefore in me also. Now, I could have observed her movements with a cold, even if excited, eye, just as she, no doubt, could have observed mine. All of a sudden, the feeling which was becoming clearer and clearer in my furious, disgusted mind took on the character of a precise image: I was no longer face to face with the wife I loved and who loved me, but with a rather impatient and inexpert prostitute who was preparing to submit passively to my embraces hoping only that they would be brief and not too tiring. I had this image right before my eyes for a moment, like an apparition, and then I felt that it went, so to speak, around behind my back and became one with Emilia lying behind me on the bed. At the same moment I rose to my feet, still without turning around, and said: "Never mind . . . I don't want to, now . . . I'll go and sleep in the other room; you stay here"; then, on tiptoe, I went to the door of the living-room.

The divan bed was ready, with the sheet turned down and Emilia's nightdress laid out on top with the sleeves spread wide. I took this nightdress, the slippers she had placed on the floor, and the dressing-gown she had arranged

on an armchair, went back into the bedroom and put them
all down on one of the chairs there. But this time I could
not help raising my eyes and looking at her. She was still
in the attitude she had taken up when she lay down on the
bed and called to me: "Come along then." She was lying
quite naked, with one arm behind her neck and her head
turned towards me, her eyes wide open but indifferent and
as it were unseeing, and the other arm lying across her body
so that her sex was covered by her hand. But now, it seemed
to me, she was no longer the prostitute; she had now become
a semblance in a mirage, with a haze of impossibility, of nos-
talgia, about her, and infinitely remote, as though she were
not only a few paces away from me but in some far-off region,
outside reality and outside my personal feelings.

## CHAPTER 5

I certainly had a presentiment that evening that a
period full of difficulties was beginning for me, but, strange to
say, I did not infer from Emilia's behavior the results that
might have been expected. There was no doubt that she had
shown herself cold and indifferent, and it was perfectly true
that I should rather have renounced love altogether than
obtain it in that way. But I loved her, and love has a great
capacity not only for illusion but also for forgetfulness.
Next day—I don't know how—the incident of the previous
evening, which later on was to appear so full of significance
to me, had already lost, in my eyes, much of its importance,
losing its burden of hostility and reducing itself to an insignificant divergence of opinion. The truth is that one easily
forgets what one does not want to remember; and furthermore
I think that Emilia herself contributed to my forgetfulness,
for a few days later, though she still insisted on sleeping
alone, she did not refuse my love. It is true that on this
occasion she again behaved in the cold, passive manner
which had previously roused me to revolt; but, as often
happens, what had seemed intolerable to me on that first
evening seemed, a few days later, to be not only tolerable
but even flattering. I was already, in fact, without being
aware of it, in the slippery region where the coldness of the
day before becomes, a day later—thanks to false arguments
and the goodwill of a mind in need of illusion—warm-hearted
love. I had thought that Emilia, that first evening, had behaved like a prostitute; but less than a week afterwards I
consented to love her and be loved by her in exactly that
way; and since, in the obscure depths of my mind, I had
perhaps feared that she really did not want me any more,

I was grateful to her for her cold, impatient passivity just as though it had been the normal attitude in our sexual relations.

But, if I continued to delude myself that Emilia still loved me as in the past, or rather, if I preferred not to put the question of our love to myself, there was one thing which betrayed the state of my heart towards the change that had come about between us. That was my work. I had, for the time being, given up my theatrical ambitions and devoted myself to the cinema, simply in order to satisfy Emilia's longing to possess a home of her own. As long as I had been sure that Emilia loved me, the work of script-writer did not seem to me too onerous; but after the incident of that evening it seemed to me that a subtle feeling of discouragement, of restlessness, of repugnance had crept into it. In reality—as I have already said—I had accepted this job just as I would have accepted any other, even more uncongenial and even farther removed from my own interests, merely out of love for Emilia. Now that this love was on the point of failing me, the work lost its meaning and justification and acquired, in my eyes, the absurd character of sheer slavery.

I want to say a few words about the job of script-writer, if only to give a better understanding of my feelings at that time. As everyone knows, the script-writer is the one who —generally in collaboration with another script-writer and with the director—writes the script or scenario, that is, the canvas from which the film will later be taken. In this script, and according to the development of the action, the gestures and words of the actors and the various movements of the camera are minutely indicated, one by one. The script is, therefore, drama, mime, cinematographic technique, *mise-en-scène* and direction, all at the same time. Now, although the script-writer's part in the film is of the first importance and comes immediately below that of the director, it remains always, for reasons inherent in the fashion in which the art of the cinema has hitherto developed, hopelessly subordinate and obscure. If, in fact, the arts are to be judged from the point of view of direct expression—and one does not really see how else they can be judged—the script-writer is an artist who, although he gives his best to the film, never has the comfort of knowing that he has expressed himself. And so, with all his creative work, he can be nothing more than a provider of suggestions and inventions, of technical, psychological and literary ideas; it is then the director's task to make use of this material according to his own genius and, in fact, to express himself. The script-writer, in short, is the man who remains always in the background; who expends the best of his blood, for the success of others; and who, although two thirds of the film's fortune depends upon him, will never see his own name on the posters where the names of the director, of the actors and of the producer are printed. He may, it is true—and as often happens—achieve excellence in his inferior trade, and be very well paid; but he can never say: "It was *I* who made this film . . . in this film *I* expressed myself . . . this film is *me*." This can only be said by the director, who is, in effect, the only one to sign the film. The script-writer, on the other hand, has to content himself with working for the money he receives, which, whether he likes it or not, ends by becoming the real and only purpose of his job. Thus all that is left for the script-writer is to enjoy life, if he is capable of it, on the money that is the sole result of his toil—passing from one script to another, from a comedy to a drama, from an adventure film to a sentimental film, without interruption, without pause, rather like a governess who goes from one child to another and never has time to grow fond of one before she leaves it and starts again with another; and in the end the fruit of her labors is enjoyed entirely by the mother who is the only one with the right to call the child her own.

But, apart from these disadvantages, which we may call fundamental and immutable, there are others also, in the job of the script-writer, which, though varying according to the quality and type of the film and of his collaborators, are no less annoying on that account. Unlike the director, who enjoys a considerable measure of independence and freedom in his dealings with the producer, the script-writer can only accept or refuse the task offered to him; but, once he has accepted it, he has no choice whatever in the matter of his collaborators: he is himself chosen, he does not choose. And so it comes about that, as a result of the personal likes and dislikes, the convenience, or the caprice of the producer, or simply as a result of chance, the script-writer finds himself forced to work with people he does not care for, people who are his inferiors in culture and breeding, who irritate him by features of character or behavior that are offensive to him. Now working together on a script is not like working together in an office, let us say, or a factory, where each man has his own job to do independently of his neighbor and where personal relations can be reduced to very little or even abolished altogether. Working together on a script means living together from morning to night, it means the marriage and fusion of one's own intelligence, one's own sensibility, one's own spirit, with those of the other collaborators; it means, in short, the creation, during the two or three months that the work lasts, of a fictitious, artificial intimacy whose only purpose is the making of the film, and thereby, in a last analysis (as I have already mentioned), the making of money. This intimacy, moreover, is of the worst possible kind, that is, the most fatiguing, the most unnerving and the most cloying that can be imagined, since it is founded not on work that is done in silence, as might be that of scientists engaged together on some experiment, but on the spoken word. The director usually calls his collaborators together early in the morning, for this is necessitated by the shortness of the time allowed for the completion of the script; and from early morning until night-time the script-writers do nothing but talk, keeping to the work in hand most of the time but often talking from sheer volubility or fatigue, wandering away together on the most varied subjects. One will tell dirty stories, one will expound his political ideas, one will psychologize about some common acquaintance, another talk about actors and actresses, another relieve his feelings by telling of his own personal circumstances; and in the meantime, in the room where they are working, the air is filled with cigarette-smoke, coffee-cups pile up on the tables amongst the pages of the script, and the script-writers themselves, who had come in in the morning well-groomed, tidy and with neatly brushed hair, are to be seen in the evening rumpled and sweaty and untidy, in their shirt-sleeves, looking worse than if they had been trying to ravish a frigid, restive woman. And indeed the mechanical, stereotyped way in which scripts are fabricated strongly resembles a kind of rape of the intelligence, having its origin in determination and interest rather than in any sort of attraction or sympathy. Of course it can also happen that the film is of superior quality, that the director and his collaborators were already, beforehand, bound together by mutual esteem and friendship, and that, in fact, the work is carried out in the ideal conditions that may occur in any human activity, however disagreeable; but these favorable combinations are rare—as, indeed, good films are rare.

It was after I had signed the contract for a second film-script—this time not with Battista but with another producer—that courage and determination suddenly abandoned me and I began, with increasing repugnance and annoyance, to resent all the disadvantages of which I have already spoken. Each day, from the time when I got up in the morning, seemed like an arid desert, with no oasis of meditation or leisure, dominated by the merciless sun of forced cinema inspiration. As soon as I entered the director's house and he welcomed me in his study with some remark such as: "Well, did you think about it last night? Did you find a solution?"—I had a feeling of boredom and rebellion. Then, during our work, everything seemed to be infected with impatience and disgust —the divagations of every kind by which the director and the script-writers, as I have already mentioned, seek to alleviate the long hours of discussion; the incomprehension or obtuseness or simple divergence of opinion amongst my collaborators as the script was gradually written; even the director's praises for each of my inventions or decisions, praises which tasted bitter to me because I felt, as I have said, that I was giving the best of myself for something which did not fundamentally concern me and in which I was not participating willingly. This last disadvantage, in fact, appeared to me at that time to be the most intolerable of all; and, each time that the director, speaking in the demagogic, vulgar way that is common to so many of them, jumped up in his chair and exclaimed: "Bravo! You're a wow!"—I could not help thinking, contemptuously: "I might have put that idea into some drama or comedy of my own." Furthermore, by some strange and bitter contradiction, I could never manage, in spite of my repugnance, to fail in my duty as a script-writer. Film-scripts are rather like the old-fashioned four-in-hands, in which there were some horses, stronger or more willing, who did the pulling, and others who pretended to pull while really they allowed themselves to be dragged along by their companions. Well, in spite of all my impatience and disgust, I was always the horse who did the pulling; the other two, the director and my script-writer colleague, when faced with any difficulty always waited—as I very soon noticed—for me to come forward with my solution. And I, though inwardly cursing both my conscientiousness and my facility, did not hesitate but, with some sudden inspiration, provided the solution required. I was not driven to do this from any spirit of rivalry, but merely from a sense of honesty stronger than any contrary desire: I was paid, therefore I had to work. But each time I was ashamed of myself and had a feeling both of avarice and of regret, as though, for a little money, I had ruined something beyond price, something of which I could, somehow or other, have made an infinitely better use.

As I said, I did not become aware of all these disadvantages until two months after I had signed the first contract with Battista. And at first I did not understand why they had not been obvious to me from the beginning and why I had taken such a long time to notice them. But, when the feeling of repugnance and failure aroused in my mind by the work

I had once so ardently desired still persisted, I could not
help—very gradually, as often happens—coming to connect
it in some way with my relations with Emilia. And at last I
realized that the work disgusted me because Emilia no longer
loved me, or at least gave an appearance of no longer loving
me. And that I had faced the work with courage and confidence as long as I had been sure of Emilia's love. Now that
I was no longer sure of it, courage and confidence had deserted me and the work seemed to me nothing better than
slavery, waste of talent, and loss of time.

## CHAPTER 6

I began therefore to live like one who carries within
him the infirmity of an impending disease but cannot make up
his mind to go to the doctor; in other words, I tried not to reflect too much either upon Emilia's demeanor towards me, or
upon my work. I knew that some day I should have to face
this kind of reflection; but, just because I was aware that it
was unavoidable, I sought to put it off for as long as possible:
the little I had already suspected made me shy away from
it, and also, albeit unconsciously, fear it. And so I went on
having those relations with Emilia which at the beginning had
seemed to me intolerable, and which now, when I feared the
worst, I tried to persuade myself—without any success—
were normal: during the day indifferent, casual, evasive conversations; at night, from time to time, love-making with
much embarrassment and a hint of cruelty on my side, and
no real participation on hers. In the meantime I continued to
work diligently, even furiously, though more and more unwillingly and with a more and more decided repugnance. If
I had had the courage to acknowledge the situation to myself, at that moment, I should certainly have renounced my
work and renounced love as well, for I should have been
convinced, as I was later, that all life had gone out of both.
But I did not have that courage; and perhaps I deluded myself
into believing that time would take it upon itself to solve my
problems, without any effort on my part. Time, in fact, did
solve them, but not in the way I should have wished. And so
the days passed, in a dull, dim atmosphere of expectancy,
with Emilia denying herself to me and myself denying myself
to my work.

The script I was writing for Battista meanwhile was near-
ing its end; and at the same time Battista mentioned a new
undertaking to me, of much more serious importance than the
first, in which he wanted me to have a share. Battista was a
hurried, evasive sort of man, like all producers; and the very

fleeting hints he gave me never went beyond such remarks as: "Molteni, as soon as you've finished this script, we're going to start at once on another . . . a really important one"; or: "Molteni, be prepared, one of these days . . . there's a proposal I've got to make to you"; or again, rather more explicitly: "Don't sign any contracts, Molteni, because in a fortnight's time you're going to sign one with me." So I knew that, after this first, comparatively unimportant script, Battista was preparing to give me another, more important one to do, for which, naturally, I should be far better paid. I must confess that, in spite of my growing distaste for this type of work, the first thing I thought of, instinctively, was the flat and the money that still had to be paid on it; and I was delighted at Battista's proposal. In any case, that is what film work is like: even when, as in my case, one is not in love with it, every new offer is agreeable, and if offers do not arrive, one becomes suspicious and fears that one is being excluded.

But I said nothing to Emilia of this new offer of Battista's, and that for two reasons: in the first place because I did not yet know whether I should accept it; and also because I had by now realized that my work did not interest her and I preferred not to speak of it, so as not to provoke some further confirmation of her coldness and indifference, to which, however, I persisted in paying no importance. These two things, furthermore, were linked together in a manner of which I was vaguely conscious: I was not sure about accepting the job precisely because I felt Emilia no longer loved me; whereas if she had loved me I should have talked about it to her, and talking about it to her meant, really and truly, accepting it.

I went out one morning in order to go and see the director with whom I was working on a script No. 1 for Battista. I knew it was the last time I should be going there, because there were now only a few pages left before the end, and this thought cheered me: at last this toil was on the point of finishing and I should again be my own master for at least half the day. Besides, as always happens with film-scripts, two months of work had sufficed to imbue me with a profound dislike for the characters and the story of the film. I knew that I should very soon find myself at grips with a set of characters and a story destined quickly to become, in their turn, no less intolerable; but in the meantime I was escaping from the first set, and the prospect of this was enough to bring me considerable relief.

My hope of approaching freedom caused me to work, that morning, with unusual facility and inventiveness. In order to complete the script, not more than two or three points, of little importance, required touching up; upon these, however, we had been hesitating for some days. But, carried away by my inspiration, I succeeded, from the very beginning, in guiding the discussion along the right lines and solving, one after the other, all the outstanding difficulties, so that, after barely a couple of hours, we realized that the script was really finished, this time beyond question. In the end—just as happens with a certain kind of interminable, unnerving mountain excursion, when the goal, by now despaired of, appears suddenly at a bend in the path—I wrote down a sentence of dialogue and then exclaimed in surprise: "Why, it can finish here!" The director, who was walking up and down his study while I was writing at the desk, came across to me; he looked over my shoulder at the page and then he too said, in a surprised, almost incredulous voice: "You're right, it can finish there." So I wrote the words THE END at the bottom of the page, closed the copybook and rose to my feet.

For a moment we said nothing, both of us looking at the desk upon which lay the portfolio, now closed, containing the completed script—indeed rather like two almost exhausted mountain-climbers looking at the little lake or rock which it has cost them so much toil to reach. Then the director said: "We've done it."

"Yes," I repeated, "we've done it!"

This director was called Pasetti and was a fairish young man, angular, thin, precise and clean-looking, with the appearance of a meticulous geometrician or accountant rather than of an artist. He was about the same age as myself; but, as always happens with script-writing, the relations between him and me were those of superior and inferior, for the director always has greater authority than any other of the collaborators. After a moment he resumed, with his characteristically cold, awkward pleasantness: "I must say, Riccardo, I must say, you're just like a horse that smells its own stable. I was certain we'd have to work for at least four more days . . . and now we've polished it off in two hours. It was the prospect of the cash, was it?—that inspired you!"

I did not dislike Pasetti, in spite of his mediocrity and his almost unbelievable psychological obtuseness; and there had grown up between us a relationship that was in a way well-balanced, he being a man without imagination and without nerves, but conscious of his limitations and fundamentally modest, while I was all nerves and imagination, morbidly sensitive and complex. Adopting his facetious tone and joining in the joke, I answered: "Of course, what you say is quite true—it was the prospect of the cash."

Lighting a cigarette, he went on: "But don't imagine the game is finished. All we've done is the main part of the job;

we've got to revise the whole of the dialogue . . . You can't rest on your laurels yet."

I could not help noticing, yet again, how he expressed himself almost entirely in commonplaces and ready-made phrases; and I looked discreetly at the clock. It was almost one. "Don't worry," I said; "I shall be at your service for any touching-up that's needed."

Shaking his head, he replied: "I know my own chickens. I shall tell Battista to hold up the last instalment of your pay until you can't hold out any longer."

He had his own way, facetious yet authoritative, and surprising in one so young, of spurring on his collaborators by alternating praise with blame, flattery with reserve, entreaty with command; and in this sense he might even have been called a good director, since directing—two thirds of it, anyhow—consists in having a shrewd knowledge of how to get others to do one's bidding. I answered, drawing him out, as usual: "No, you get him to pay me the whole instalment and I promise you I'll be at your service for any touching-up that's needed."

"But what do you do with all this money?" he asked, awkwardly jocose; "it's never enough for you . . . and yet you haven't any mistresses, you don't gamble, you haven't any children. . . ."

"I have to pay the instalments on the flat," I replied seriously, lowering my eyes, slightly annoyed at his indiscreetness.

"Have you much to pay still?"

"Almost the whole amount."

"I bet it's your wife who bullies you until you get yourself paid what's owing to you. I can hear her saying, 'Now, Riccardo, remember to make them pay you that last instalment!' "

"Yes, it's my wife," I lied, "but you know what women are. Their homes are immensely important to them."

"You're telling me!" He started talking about his wife, who very much resembled him and whom he, nevertheless—or so I gathered—considered to be a bizarre creature, full of caprices and all sorts of unexpected things—in fact, a woman. I listened with an attentive expression, though in point of fact I was thinking about something else. He concluded in an unforeseen manner: "That's all very well . . . but I know what you script-writers are: you're all the same, the whole lot of you. After you once get your money, one's lucky to see you again. No, no, I shall tell Battista to keep back the last instalment!"

"Come on, Pasetti, do what I ask!"

"Well, well, I'll see. But don't count on it."

I glanced stealthily at the clock again. Now I had given him the chance to flaunt his authority and he had taken it: so I could go away. I began: "Well, well, I'm pleased to have finished the job—or rather, as you say, the main part of it. But now I think it's time for me to go."

He exclaimed, in his blundering, vivacious way: "Not at all, not at all; we've got to drink to the success of the film. My goodness, of course we have. You're not going away like that, after finishing the script!"

I answered resignedly: "If it's a question of a drink, I'm all for it."

"Come this way, then. I think my wife would be pleased to have a drink with us."

I followed him out of the study, and along a narrow passage, bare and white and smelling strongly of cooking and baby's garments. He preceded me into the sitting-room, calling out: "Luisa, Molteni and I have finished the script. Now we're going to drink to the success of the film."

Signora Pasetti rose from her armchair and came forward to meet us. She was a small woman with a large head and two bands of smooth black hair framing her long, oval, very pale face. Her eyes were large but light in color and inexpressive, and they became animated only when her husband was present: and then she never took them off his face for one single moment, like an affectionate dog with its master. But when her husband was not there she kept them lowered, with an almost stubbornly modest air. Fragile and minute in figure, she had brought four children into the world in four years of matrimony. With his usual embarrassing cheerfulness, Pasetti now said: "Today we have a drink. I'm going to make a cocktail."

"Not for me, Gino," Signora Pasetti warned him; "you know I don't drink."

"*We'll* drink, then."

I sat down in an armchair of sand-papered wood with a flowered cover, in front of a red-brick chimney-place; and Signora Pasetti sat down on the other side of the fireplace, on another identical chair. The sitting-room, I noticed, when I looked round, was an accurate copy of its master: furnished with a "suite" in sham rustic style, it was bright and clean and orderly but at the same time rather bleak—like the house of a meticulous accountant or bank clerk. I had nothing to do but look, for Signora Pasetti did not appear to feel any need to speak to me. She sat opposite me with eyes lowered, her hands in her lap, quite motionless. Meanwhile Pasetti went over to the other end of the room, to an extremely ugly composite piece of furniture, a radio containing a bar; then he stooped down twice, on his thin legs, and, with precise, angular movements, took out two bottles, one of vermouth and one of gin, three glasses and a shaker. He placed them all on a tray and carried the tray over to a small table in front of the fireplace. I noticed that the bottles were both of them sealed and intact: it did not look as if Pasetti often allowed himself the drink he was now about to prepare for us. The shaker, too, was bright and shining and appeared quite new. He announced that he was going to fetch some ice and went out.

We sat a long time in silence, and then, in order to say something, I said: "We've finished the script, at last!"

Without raising her eyes, Signora Pasetti replied: "Yes, so Gino said."

"I'm sure it will make a fine film."

"I'm sure it will too; otherwise Gino would not have agreed to do it."

"Do you know the story?"

"Yes, Gino told it to me."

"Do you like it?"

"Gino likes it, so I like it too."

"Do you always agree, you two?"

"Gino and I? Yes, always."

"Which of the two of you is in command?"

"Gino, of course."

I noticed that she had contrived to repeat the name of Gino each time she had opened her mouth. I had spoken lightly and almost jokingly; she had answered me all the time with the utmost seriousness. Then Pasetti came in again with the ice-pail and called out to me: "Your wife's on the telephone, Riccardo."

For some unaccountable reason I felt my heart sink, with a sudden return of my usual unhappiness. Mechanically I rose and started towards the door. Pasetti added: "The telephone's in the kitchen—but if you like you can answer it here . . . I've switched it through."

The telephone was, in fact, on a cabinet beside the fireplace. I took off the receiver and heard Emilia's voice say to me: "I'm sorry, but today you'll have to go out to lunch somewhere . . . I'm going to my mother's."

"But why didn't you tell me before?"

"I didn't want to disturb you at your work."

"All right," I said, "I'll go and eat at a restaurant."

"We'll meet later; good-by."

She rang off and I turned towards Pasetti. "Riccardo," he asked at once, "are you not lunching at home?"

"No, I'm going to a restaurant."

"Well, stay and have lunch with us . . . pot-luck, of course . . . but we'd be very pleased."

An inexplicable feeling of despondency had come over me at the thought of having lunch alone at a restaurant, probably because I had been looking forward with pleasure to announcing to Emilia that the script was finished. Perhaps I should not have done this after all, knowing, as I have said, that she was no longer interested in what I did; but at first I had yielded to the old habit of our past relationship. Pasetti's invitation gave me pleasure; and I accepted it with almost excessive gratitude. He, in the meantime, had uncorked the two bottles, and now, with gestures more like those of a chemist calculating a dose of medicine rather than of a drinker, he was pouring the gin and the vermouth into a measure and then transferring them into the shaker. Signora Pasetti, as usual, never took her eyes off her husband. At last, when Pasetti had thoroughly shaken the cocktail and was about to pour it out into the glasses, she said: "Only just a drop for me, please. And you too, Gino, don't drink much; it might do you harm."

"It isn't every day that one finishes a script!"

He filled our two glasses, and in the third put only a little of the cocktail, as his wife had requested. We all three took our glasses and raised them in a toast. "To a hundred more scripts like this one!" said Pasetti, just wetting his lips and putting his glass down again on the table. I emptied mine at one draught. Signora Pasetti drank with little sips and then got up, saying: "I'm going to the kitchen to see what the cook is doing . . . if you'll allow me."

She went out. Pasetti took her place in the flowered armchair, and we started chattering. Or rather, *he* chattered, talking mostly about the script, and I listened, showing my approval by muttered words and nods of the head, and drinking. Pasetti's glass was always at the same point, not even half emptied; but I had already emptied mine three times. I now, for some reason, had an acute feeling of unhappiness, and I drank in the hope that tipsiness would drive it away. But I can stand a lot of alcohol and Pasetti's cocktails were light and watered down. And so those three or four little glasses served no purpose except to increase my obscure sense of wretchedness. All at once I asked myself: "Why do I feel so unhappy?"; and then I remembered that the first stab of pain had come when, shortly before, I had heard Emilia's voice on the telephone, so cold, so reasonable, so indifferent; and above all so different from that of Signora Pasetti, whenever she pronounced the magic name of Gino. But I was unable to analyze my thoughts more closely, because, shortly afterwards, Signora Pasetti appeared in the door and told us we could come through into the dining-room.

Pasetti's dining-room resembled his study and sitting-room: neat, cheap, coquettish furniture of sand-papered wood; colored earthenware crockery; glasses and bottles of thick green glass; tablecloth and napkins of unbleached hemp. We sat down in this tiny room which was almost entirely taken up by the table, so that the maid, when handing round the dishes, could not help disturbing first one, then another of the party; and then started eating apologetically and in silence. Soon the maid changed the plates, and I, to get the conversation going, asked Pasetti some question or other as to his plans for the future. He answered me in his usual cold, precise, undistinguished voice, in which modesty and lack of imagination seemed to be responsible not merely for the choice of words but even for the slightest variation in tone. I was silent, finding nothing to say, for Pasetti's plans did not interest me and, even if they had, that monotonous, colorless voice of his would have made them tedious. But, as my bored glances wandered from one object to another without managing to find anything to detain them, they came to rest at last upon the face of Pasetti's wife who was also listening, her chin supported on her hand and her eyes fixed, as usual, upon her husband. Then, as I looked at her face, I was struck by the expression in her eyes—amorous, melting, a mixture of humble admiration, unlimited gratitude, physical infatuation and a sort of melancholy timidity. This expression astonished me, partly because the feeling behind it was, to me, utterly mysterious: Pasetti, so colorless, so thin, so mediocre, so obviously lacking in qualities that might please a woman, seemed an incredible object for attention of that kind. Then I said to myself that every man always ends by finding the woman who appreciates and loves him, and that to judge of other people's feelings on the basis of one's own is a mistake; and I had a feeling of sympathy for her, in her devotion to her man, and of satisfaction on Pasetti's behalf, for whom, as I have already said, I cherished, in spite of his mediocrity, a sort of ironical friendship. But, suddenly, just as I was losing interest and turning my eyes elsewhere, I was transfixed by a thought from I know not where, or rather, by a sudden perception: "In those eyes is the whole love of this woman for her husband . . . he is content with himself and with his own work because she loves him. But it is a long time since that feeling showed itself in Emilia's eyes. Emilia does not love me, she will never love me again."

At this thought, which revived in me a deep-seated pain,

I had a sense almost of physical shock; so much so that I made a grimace, and Signora Pasetti asked me anxiously if by any chance the meat I was eating was tough. I reassured her: the meat was not tough. Meanwhile, though I still pretended to listen to Pasetti who went on talking about his plans for the future, I tried to analyze that first sensation of pain, so acute and at the same time so obscure. Then I understood that, during the last month, I had been seeking all the time to accustom myself to an intolerable situation, but that I had not, in reality, succeeded: I could not endure to go on living in that way, what with Emilia who did not love me and my work which, owing to her not loving me, I could not love. And suddenly I said to myself: "I can't go on like this. I must have an explanation with Emilia, once and for all . . . and, if necessary, part from her and give up my work as well."

Nevertheless, although I thought of these things with despairing resolution, I realized that I could not bring myself wholly to believe in them: in reality I was not yet altogether convinced that Emilia no longer loved me, nor that I should find the strength to part from her, give up my film work and go back to living alone. In other words I had a feeling almost of incredulity, of a painful kind quite new to me, at finding myself faced with a fact that in my mind I now held to be indubitable. Why did Emilia no longer love me, and how had she arrived at this state of indifference? With a feeling of anguish in my heart, I foresaw that this first general conclusion, already so painful, would demand an infinite number of further, minor proofs before I became completely convinced—proofs which, just because they were of lesser importance, would be more concrete and, if possible, still more painful. I was, in fact, now convinced that Emilia could no longer love me; but I did not know either why or how this had come about; and in order to be entirely persuaded of it I must have an explanation with her, I must seek out and examine, I must plunge the thin, ruthless blade of investigation into the wound which, hitherto, I had exerted myself to ignore. This thought frightened me; and yet I realized that only after carrying my investigation through to the bitter end should I have the courage to part from Emilia, as, at the first moment, the desperate impulse of my mind had suggested.

In the meantime I went on eating and drinking and listening to Pasetti, but almost without noticing what I was doing. In due time, however, lunch came to an end. We went back to the sitting-room, and there I had to submit to all the various formalities of the bourgeois guest—coffee with one, or two, lumps of sugar; the offer of a liqueur, sweet or dry, received with the customary refusal; idle conversation to pass the time. Finally, when it seemed to me that I could take my leave without giving an impression of haste, I rose from my chair. But, just at that moment, the Pasettis' eldest little girl was brought into the room by her nurse, to be displayed to her parents before her daily walk. She was a dark-haired, pale child with very large eyes, of a very ordinary type, insignificant, in fact, like her parents. I remember that, as I watched her letting herself be kissed and embraced by her mother, this thought crossed my mind: "I shall never be happy like them. Emilia and I will never have a child"; and immediately afterwards, as a result of this first thought, a second one, even more bitter: "How shabby all this is, how ordinary, how unoriginal. I am following in the footsteps of all husbands who are not loved by their wives—envying a perfectly ordinary couple while they kiss and hug their off-spring . . . exactly, indeed, like any ordinary husband who finds himself in my position." This mortifying idea aroused in me a feeling of impatience at the affectionate scene I was witnessing. I declared, brusquely, that I must go. Pasetti accompanied me to the door, his pipe between his teeth. I had a feeling that my leave-taking had astonished and shocked his wife, who was perhaps expecting me to be touched at the edifying sight of her maternal love.

## CHAPTER 7

I had no engagement until four o'clock, so that I had an hour and a half to spare; and when I was in the street, I started off, more or less instinctively, towards home. I knew that Emilia could not be there, since she had gone to lunch with her mother; but, filled as I was with distress and bewilderment, I almost hoped that this might not be true and that I should find her there after all: in which case, I said to myself, I would pluck up courage to speak to her frankly, to insist on a decisive explanation. I was aware that upon this explanation depended not only my relations with Emilia, but also my work; but now, after so many pitiful shilly-shallyings and hypocrisies, I felt I preferred any kind of disaster to the prolongation of a situation that was becoming only too painfully clear and less and less tolerable. Perhaps I should be compelled to part from Emilia, to refuse Battista's second script; so much the better. The truth, whatever it might be, seemed to me now to be infinitely more desirable than my present obscure, degraded position, with falsehood on the one hand and self-pity on the other.

As I came into my own street, I was again seized with perplexity: Emilia was certainly not at home, and I, in that new flat which now seemed to me not so much strange as actively hostile, should feel more lost and miserable than I should in a public place. For a moment I was almost tempted to turn back and to go and spend that hour and a half in a café. Then, with a sudden, providential reawakening of memory, I recalled that I had promised Battista, the previous day, to be at home at that time, so that he could telephone me and arrange an appointment. This would be an important appointment, because Battista was to speak to me at last about the new script, and to make concrete proposals and introduce me to the director; and so I had assured him that I would be at home at that time—as, indeed, I always was. It is true that I myself could have telephoned to Battista from a café; but, to begin with, I was not entirely sure of finding him at home, because Battista often lunched at a restaurant; and, in addition, as I said to myself, I needed some pretext, in my acute state of bewilderment, to go back home; and Battista's telephone call exactly provided me with such a pretext.

So I entered the hall, crossed to the elevator, closed the doors and pressed the button for the top floor on which I lived. But, while the car was going up, it suddenly came into my head that in reality I had no right to fix this appointment, inasmuch as I was not at all sure that I should accept Battista's new proposition. Everything depended upon my explanation with Emilia, and I knew that, if Emilia declared explicitly that she no longer loved me, not merely should I not write this new script but I should never write any more film-scripts for the rest of my life. Emilia, however, would not be at home; and when Battista telephoned, I should not be in a position, honestly, to tell him whether I agreed to discuss his proposition or not. Now, amongst all the many absurd things in my life, one of the most absurd would be, I felt, to negotiate a deal and then back out of it. At this thought I was assailed by an almost hysterical impulse of rage and repugnance, and all at once I stopped the elevator and then pressed the button to go down again to the ground floor. It was better, I said to myself, far better not to let Battista find me at home when he telephoned. Later on, that same evening, I would have my explanation with Emilia; and next day I would give the producer an answer in accordance with its result. In the meantime the elevator was going down and I was looking at all those floors going past one after another, behind the ground glass doors, with the desperate eye of a fish seeing the level of the water rapidly descending inside the tank in which it lives. At last the car stopped and I was on the point of opening the doors. But then, suddenly, a new idea made me pause: it was true that my decision about the new job with Battista depended upon my explanation with Emilia; but if it should happen that Emilia, that same evening, made me a fresh avowal of her love, should I not be taking the risk of annoying Battista by not being at home when he telephoned, and thereby losing the job? Producers, as I knew from experience, were as capricious as so many petty tyrants; a hitch of this kind might be enough to make Battista change his mind, and might induce him to choose another script-writer. These reflections pursued one another swiftly through my aching head, producing in me an obscure feeling of acute wretchedness: truly I was an unfortunate creature, I said to myself, torn between egotism and affection, incapable of choice or decision. And I do not know how much longer I should have stayed there, hesitating and bewildered, inside the lift, if a young lady, her arms laden with parcels, had not suddenly thrown open the doors. She uttered a cry of fright on discovering me standing there, stock still, in front of her; then, recovering herself, she too came into the car and asked me which floor I wanted to go to. I told her. "I go to the second," she announced, and pressed the button. The elevator started to ascend again.

Once on my own landing, I had a sense of profound relief; and at the same time it occurred to me: "What sort of a state am I in, to be behaving like this? How can I have descended so low? What point have I reached?" With these thoughts in my head I went into the flat, closed the door and went through into the living-room. And there, lying on the sofa, in a dressing-gown, reading a magazine, I saw Emilia. Beside the sofa was a small table upon which could be seen plates and the remains of lunch: Emila had not gone out, she had not lunched with her mother; in short, she had lied to me.

I must have had a troubled expression on my face, for she, after looking at me, asked: "What's the matter? What's happened to you?"

"Weren't you going to have lunch with your mother?" I said in a stifled voice; "how on earth do you come to be at home? You told me you were out for lunch!"

"My mother telephoned afterwards to say that she couldn't," she replied placidly.

"But why didn't you let me know?"

"My mother rang up at the last moment. I thought you'd have left the Pasettis'."

Suddenly—why, I could not tell—I was certain she was

lying. But, being incapable of producing any proof of it, not
merely to her but even to myself, I was silent, and I too sat
down on the sofa. After a moment, turning over the pages of
the magazine, she asked without looking at me: "And you—
what did you do?"

"The Pasettis asked me to stay."

At that moment the telephone rang. I thought: "It's Battista. Now I shall tell him I'm not going to do any more
scripts. To hell with everything. It's perfectly clear that this
woman doesn't feel the smallest crumb of affection for me."
Meanwhile Emilia, with her usual indolence, was saying: "Do
just go and see who it is . . . it's sure to be for you." I rose
and went out.

The telephone was in the adjoining room, on the bedside
table. Before picking up the receiver, I looked towards the
bed, saw the solitary pillow lying at the head of it, in the
middle, and felt my resolution harden: all was finished, I
should refuse the script and then leave Emilia. I took off the
receiver, but then, instead of Battista's voice, I heard that of
my mother-in-law, who asked: "Riccardo, is Emilia there?"

Almost without thinking, I answered: "No, she's not here.
She said she was lunching with you. She's out. I thought you
were together."

"Why, I telephoned her to say I couldn't manage it because
my maid has her day off today!" she began in astonishment.
At that moment I looked up from the telephone and saw,
through the door which had been left open, Emilia lying on
the divan looking at me; and I noticed that her eyes, which
were fixed upon me, were full not so much of wonder as of
quiet aversion and cold contempt. I realized that between the
two of us, now, it was I who had lied, and that she knew why
I had lied. So I mumbled a few words of farewell and then,
suddenly, as though correcting myself, I cried: "No . . . wait
. . . Here's Emilia just coming in. I'll send her to you." At
the same time I beckoned to Emilia to come to the telephone.

She got up from the sofa, crossed the room with her head
bent and took the receiver from my hand without thanking or looking at me. I walked away towards the living-room,
and she made an impatient gesture as if to tell me to shut
the door. I did so; and then, my mind filled with confusion,
I sat down on the divan and waited.

Emilia was a long time at the telephone, and I, in my painful, apprehensive impatience, almost felt that she was doing
it on purpose. But of course, I kept saying to myself, her
telephone conversations with her mother were always very
long: she had remained deeply attached to her mother, who
was a widow and all alone, and she had no one but her;

and she seemed to have made her her confidante. At last the door opened and Emilia reappeared. I sat silent and still, fully conscious, from her unwontedly hard expression, that she was angry with me.

And indeed she said at once, as she started collecting the plates and forks on the little table: "Are you crazy? Why on earth did you go and tell Mother I was out?"

Hurt by her tone, I did not open my mouth. "To see if I had told the truth?" she went on; "to see if it was true that Mother had really told me she couldn't have me to lunch?"

I answered at last, with an effort: "That may have been the reason."

"Well, please never do such a thing again. I speak the truth, and I've nothing to hide from you, and I just can't endure that kind of thing."

She spoke these words in a tone of finality and then took up the tray on which she had put together the plates and glasses and went out of the room.

Left alone, I had, for a moment, a bitter feeling of victory. It was true, then: Emilia no longer loved me. In the old days she certainly would not have spoken to me like that. She would have said to me, with a mixture of gentleness and amused surprise: "Perhaps you really thought I had told you a lie?" and then she would have laughed, as if at some childish, easily forgivable error, and finally—yes, finally she would have even shown herself flattered: "My goodness, you don't mean to say you're really jealous? And don't you know I love nobody except you?" It would all have ended in an almost motherly kiss, and a caress of her long, large hands on my brow, as though to chase away all thought and anxiety. But it was also true that in the old days I should never have thought of watching her, still less of doubting her word. Everything was changed: she in her love, I in mine. And everything seemed set for a steady change for the worse.

But man is always ready to hope, even when convinced that there is no hope. I had had a clear proof that Emilia no longer loved me, and yet there was still a doubt in my mind—or rather, a hope—that I might have placed a rash interpretation upon an incident which, fundamentally, was devoid of importance. All at once I said to myself that I must not be precipitate; that I must make her tell me herself that she no longer loved me; that only she could provide me with the proofs that I still lacked . . . These thoughts pursued each other swiftly through my mind as I sat on the divan staring into vacancy. Then the door opened and Emilia came in again. She came over to the sofa and lay down again, behind me, and took up the magazine. Then, without turning, I said: "In a few moments Battista is going to telephone and make a proposal for me to do another script . . . a very important script."

"Well, you must be pleased, aren't you?" she said in her calm voice.

"With this script," I went on, "I shall be able to earn a lot of money . . . anyhow, enough to pay two instalments on the lease."

This time she said nothing. I continued: "This script, moreover, is important for me because, if I do it, I shall have others to do afterwards . . . this is to be a big film."

At last, in the detached voice of a person who is reading and who speaks without looking up from the page, she asked: "What film is it?"

"I don't know," I replied. I was silent for a moment, and then, in a rather emphatic tone, I added: "But I've decided to refuse this job."

"And why?" Her voice was still quiet, indifferent.

I rose, walked round the sofa, and came and sat down in front of Emilia. She was holding the magazine in her hand, but when she saw me sit down opposite her, she lowered it and looked at me. "Because," I said with full sincerity, "I, as you know, hate this work and do it only for love of you . . . in order to pay the instalments on this flat, which means so much to you or seems to mean so much to you. But now I know for certain that you no longer love me . . . and so all this is useless."

She was looking at me with her eyes wide open, but she said nothing. "You don't love me any longer," I went on, "and I shall not go on doing these jobs. As for the flat . . . well, I shall mortgage it or sell the lease. The fact is, I can't go on like this any longer and I feel that the moment has come to tell you so. So now you know. In a short time Battista will telephone and I shall tell him to go to the devil."

Now I had said it, and the moment had therefore arrived for the explanation I had so long both feared and desired. At this thought I felt almost relieved, and I looked at Emilia with a new frankness as I awaited her reply. She was silent for a little time before she answered me. Obviously my forthright declaration had surprised her. In the end, indeed, rather cautiously and precisely as if she wanted to gain time, she asked: "What makes you think I don't love you any more?"

"Everything," I answered with passionate vehemence.

"For instance?"

"Tell me first of all whether it's true or not."

She insisted, obstinately: "No, you tell me what makes you think that."

"Everything," I repeated; "your way of talking to me, of looking at me, the way you behave to me. Everything. A month ago you even insisted on our sleeping apart. You wouldn't have wanted that, once upon a time!"

She looked at me, irresolute; and then, suddenly, I saw her eyes light up with rapid decision. She had, in that precise moment, I thought, determined upon the attitude to be taken with me, and now would not deviate from her decision, whatever I might say or do. At last she replied, quite gently: "But I assure you, I swear to you. I cannot sleep with the shutters open. I need darkness and silence. I swear it."

"But I offered to sleep with the shutters closed."

"Well," she hesitated, "must I also tell you, then, that when you're asleep you're not silent?"

"What do you mean?"

"You snore." She smiled faintly and then went on: "You used to wake me up every night . . . That's why I decided to sleep by myself."

I was somewhat disconcerted at this detail of my snoring, of which I was ignorant and which, furthermore, I found it difficult to believe: I had slept with other women and none of them had ever told me that I snored. "And then," I said, "I know you don't love me because a wife who loves"—I hesitated, slightly shamefaced—"does not make love in the way you've been doing, for some time past, with me."

She immediately protested, irritably and roughly: "Really I don't know what it is you want. We make love every time you wish to. And have I ever refused you?"

I knew that of the two of us, in this kind of confidential talk, it was always I who was the modest, the shamefaced, the embarrassed one. Emilia, usually so reserved and proper, seemed, in intimacy, to lose all idea of modesty or embarrassment: in fact, in a way that vaguely astonished me every time and that I found attractive for some quality it had of natural innocence, she used to talk, before, during, and after our love-making, of that love-making itself, without the slightest veil of tenderness or reticence and with a disconcerting crudeness and freedom. "No, not refused," I muttered; "no . . . but . . ."

She resumed, in a conclusive tone of voice: "Every single time you've wanted to make love, we've done so. And you're not one to be contented with just the simple act . . . you're good at making love, you know."

"Do you think so?" I asked, almost flattered.

"Yes," she said drily, without looking at me, "but if I

didn't love you, the very fact of your being good at making love would irritate me, and I should try to avoid it . . . and a woman can always find excuses for refusing, can't she?"

"All right," I said, "you do it, you've never refused me . . . but the way in which you do it is not the way of a person who loves."

"Why, in what way do I do it?"

I ought to have answered her: "You do it like a prostitute who submits to her client and wants only that the thing shall be quickly over . . . that's how you do it!" But, out of respect for her and for myself too, I preferred to remain silent. And in any case, what would have been the use of it? She would have replied that it was not true, and—quite probably—she would have reminded me, with crude technical precision, of certain transports of sensuality on her own side, in which everything was included—skill, pursuit of pleasure, violent excitement, erotic fury—everything except tenderness and the indescribable abandonment of true surrender; and I should not have known what to say to this; and, into the bargain, I should have offended her with that insulting comparison and thus have put myself in the wrong. And so, in despair, realizing that the explanation I had wanted to bring about had now dissolved into thin air, I said: "Well anyhow, whatever the reason, I'm convinced you don't love me any more—that's all."

Again, before either answering or moving, she looked at me as if to calculate, from the expression of my face, what would be the most suitable attitude for her to take towards me. I noticed then a peculiarity which I already knew: her beautiful, dark, serene face, so harmonious, so symmetrical, so compact, underwent, through the irresolution that cleft her mind, a process almost, as it were, of decay: one cheek seemed to have grown thinner (but not the other), her mouth was no longer exactly in the middle of her face, her eyes, bewildered and dim, seemed to be disintegrating within their sockets as though within a circle of dark wax. I said that I already knew this peculiarity of hers: this same thing did in fact happen every time she had to face a decision which she disliked or towards which she did not feel herself naturally drawn. And then, with a sudden impulse of her whole body, she threw her arms round my neck, saying in a voice that sounded to me false: "But Riccardo, why do you say that? . . . I do love you . . . just as much as I did in the past." Her breath was warm in my ear, and I felt her pass her hand over my forehead, my temples, my hair, and pull my head down against her breast, clasping it tightly between her arms.

But the idea came into my mind that she was embracing me like that so as not to show me the expression on her face, which was perhaps merely bored and at the same time diligent, the expression of a person who does something in which his spirit has no share, purely from volition; and as I pressed my face, in a desperate longing for love, against her breast, half-bared and rising and falling with her calm breathing, I could not help thinking: "These are only gestures . . . but she is bound to give herself away by some remark or some intonation in her voice." I waited a little, and then she ventured to say, cautiously: "What would you do if I really had ceased to love you?"

So I was right, I thought in bitter triumph; she had betrayed herself. She wished to know what I would do if she had ceased to love me, so as to weigh up and estimate all the risks of complete frankness. Without moving, speaking into her soft, warm breast, I said: "I've already told you . . . the first thing I'd do would be to refuse Battista's new job." I should have liked to add: "And I should part from you"; but I had not the courage to say it at that moment, with my cheek against her breast and her hand on my forehead. In reality I still hoped that she might love me, and I was afraid that this separation, even by the admission of its mere possibility, might really come to pass. Finally I heard her say, while she still went on embracing me closely: "But I do love you . . . and all this is absurd. Now, you know what you're going to do? As soon as Battista telephones, you must make an appointment with him and then you must go and accept the job."

"But why should I do that, seeing that you've ceased to love me?" I cried in exasperation.

Her answer, this time, was given in a tone of reasonable reproof. "I love you, but don't go on making me repeat it . . . and it means a lot to me to stay in this flat. If it doesn't suit you to take this job, I shall not make any objection . . . but if you don't want to take it because you think I've ceased to love you or because you think the flat doesn't mean anything to me, let me tell you you're quite wrong."

I began almost to hope that she was not lying; and at the same time I realized that, at least for the moment, she had persuaded me. And yet, in desperation, I now wanted to know more, to be utterly sure, to have incontestable proofs. Then, as though she had an intuition of my desire, she loosened her hold of me all of a sudden and whispered: "Kiss me—won't you?"

I raised myself up and looked at her for a moment before kissing her; I was struck by the air of fatigue, almost of exhaustion, that was visible in her face, now more disintegrated, more irresolute than ever. It was as though she had undergone a superhuman strain while she had been speaking to me and caressing and embracing me; and as though she were preparing to undergo another, even more painful, during the kiss. Nevertheless I took her chin in my hand and was on the point of bringing my lips close to hers. At that moment the telephone rang. "It's Battista," she said, disengaging herself with obvious relief and running into the next room. From the sofa, where I remained seated, I saw her, through the open door, take off the receiver and say: "Yes . . . yes, he's here, I'll get him at once . . . How are you?"

A few words followed, from the other end of the line. Then, with a gesture of understanding towards me from where she stood, she said: "We were just talking about you and your new film. . . ."

A few more mysterious remarks. In a calm voice she said: "Yes, we must meet as soon as possible. Now I'll get Riccardo for you."

I got up, went into the other room and took the receiver. Battista told me, as I had foreseen, that he was expecting me next day, in the afternoon, at his office. I said I would come and exchanged a few more words with him, then replaced the receiver. Only then did I become aware that Emilia had left the room while I was speaking. And I could not help thinking that she had gone away because she had succeeded in persuading me to agree to the appointment with Battista; there was now no further need either of her presence or of her caresses.

## CHAPTER 8

I went to my appointment next day, at the time arranged. Battista's offices occupied the entire first floor of an ancient palace, once the abode of a patrician family and now—as so often happens—the business premises of a number of commercial concerns. The great reception-rooms, with their frescoed, vaulted ceilings and stuccoed walls, had been divided by him, with simple wooden partitions, into a number of little rooms with utilitarian furniture; where once old paintings with mythological or sacred subjects had hung, there were now large, brightly colored posters; pinned up everywhere were photographs of actors and actresses, pages torn out of picture papers, framed certificates of festival awards, and other similiar adornments generally to be found in the offices of film companies. In the anteroom, against a background of faded sylvan frescoes, rose, thronelike, an enormous counter of green-painted metal, from behind which three or four female secretaries welcomed visitors. Battista, as a producer, was still young, and he had made good progress in recent years with films inferior in quality but commercially successful. His company, modestly called "Triumph Films," was, at the moment, regarded as one of the best.

At that hour the anteroom was already thronged, and, with the experience of film types I had now acquired, I could classify all the visitors with certainty at the first glance: two or three script-writers, recognizable by their look of mingled fatigue and industriousness, by the copy-books they held under their arms, and by the style of their clothes, at the same time both smart and careless; one or two elderly cinema organizers or managers, looking exactly like country estate-agents or cattle-brokers; two or three girls, aspiring actresses or rather walkers-on, young and pretty perhaps, but as it were spoiled in advance by their ambitions, with their studied expressions, their excessive make-up, and their way of dressing from which all simplicity was banished; and finally a few nondescript individuals such as are always to be found in producers' anterooms—out-of-work actors, suggestion-mongers, cadgers of various kinds. All these people were walking up and down on the dirty mosaic floor, or lounging on the high-backed, gilt chairs round the walls, yawning, smoking and chattering in low voices. The secretaries, when they were not speaking on one of the numerous telephones, remained motionless behind the counter, staring into vacancy with eyes that, from sheer boredom and absence of thought, looked glassy and almost squinting. From time to time a bell rang with violent and unpleasant shrillness; and then the secretaries would rouse themselves, call out a name, and one of the visitors would jump up hastily and disappear through a white-and-gold double door.

I gave in my name and then went and sat down at the far end of the room. I was now in a state of mind just as desperate as the day before, but much calmer. Immediately after my conversation with Emilia, and on thinking it over, I had convinced myself once and for all that she had lied to me in saying that she loved me; but for the moment, partly from discouragement, partly from a punctilious wish to force her into the complete and sincere explanation which I had not yet obtained, I gave up the idea, provisionally at least, of acting in accordance with my conviction. I had therefore decided not to refuse Battista's new job, although

I knew, for certain, that—like all the rest of my life, indeed—it now served no purpose. Later on, I thought, as soon as I had managed to wrest the truth from Emilia, there would always be time to break off the job and throw up everything. In some ways, in fact, I preferred this second and more clamorous solution to the first. The scandal and loss would to some extent emphasize my desperation and, simultaneously, my absolute determination to be done with all hesitation and compromise.

As I say, I felt calm; but it was the calm of apathy and listlessness. An uncertain evil causes anxiety because, at the bottom of one's heart, one goes on hoping till the last moment that it may not be true; a certain evil, on the other hand, instils, for a time, a kind of dreary tranquillity. I felt tranquil, but I knew that soon I should no longer be so: the first phase, the phase of suspicion, was over—or so I thought; soon would begin the phase of pain and revolt and remorse. All this I knew, but I knew also that between these two phases there could be an interlude of deathly calm, just like the false, stifling calm that precedes the second and worse period of a thunderstorm.

Then, as I waited to be shown into Battista's room, it flashed across my mind that so far I had restricted myself to making certain of the existence, or non-existence, of Emilia's love. But now, it seemed to me, I knew for certain that she no longer loved me. Therefore, I thought, almost surprised at my new discovery, I could now turn my mind to a new problem—that of the reason why she had ceased to love me. Also, once I had divined the reason, it would be easier for me to force her to an explanation.

I must admit that, as soon as I had put the question to myself, I was struck by a sense of incredulity, almost of extravagance. It was too unlikely, too absurd: it was quite impossible that Emilia could have a reason for ceasing to love me. From what source I derived this assurance, I could not have said; just as, on the other hand, I could not have said why—since according to me she could have no reason for ceasing to love me—it was quite obvious that she did *not* love me. I reflected for a few moments, bewildered by this contradiction between my head and my heart. Finally, as one does with certain problems in geometry, I said to myself: "Let us grant it absurd that there should be a reason, although there cannot but be a reason. And let us see what it can possibly be."

I have noticed that the more doubtful one feels the more one clings to a false lucidity of mind, as though hoping to clarify by reason that which is darkened and obscured by feeling. It gave me pleasure, at that moment when instinct produced such contradictory replies, to have recourse to a reasoned investigation, like a detective in a crime story. Someone has been killed; the motive for which he may have been killed must be sought out; if the motive is discovered it will be easy to trace the criminal . . . I argued, then, that the motives might be of two kinds: the first depending upon Emilia, the second upon me. And the first, as I immediately realized, were all summed up in a single one: Emilia no longer loved me because she loved someone else.

It appeared to me, on first thinking about it, that this supposition could be rejected without more ado. Not merely had there been nothing in Emilia's behavior in recent times to lead one to suspect the presence of another man in her life, but there had been actually the opposite—an increase both in the amount of time spent alone and in her dependence upon me. Emilia, I knew, was almost always at home, where she spent her time reading a little or telephoning to her mother or attending to her household chores; and for her distractions, whether going to the cinema, or taking a walk, or dining at a restaurant, she depended almost entirely upon me. Certainly her life had been more varied, and, in its modest way, more sociable, immediately after our marriage, when she still retained a few friendships from the time when she was a girl. But the bonds of such friendships had very soon been loosened; and she had clung ever more tightly to me, depending upon me, as I have already mentioned, more and more, to an extent that was sometimes, for me, positively embarrassing. This dependence, moreover, had not weakened in the least, with the weakening of her feeling for me; she had not sought, even in the most innocent way, to find a substitute for me nor in the slightest degree to prepare for such an eventuality: in the same way as before—except that the love had gone out of it—she would sit at home waiting for my return from work, and she still depended on me for her few amusements. There was, in fact, something pathetic and unhappy about this loveless dependence of hers; it was as if somebody, by nature faithful, went on being faithful even when the reasons for faithfulness had disappeared. In a word, although she no longer loved me, it was almost certain that she had no one but me in her life.

Furthermore, another observation I had made caused me to exclude the possibility that Emilia might be in love with some other man. I knew her, or thought I knew her, very well. And I knew that she was incapable of telling lies, in the first place because of a certain rough and intolerant frankness in her, owing to which all falsehood appeared to her, not so much repugnant, as tedious and laborious; and secondly because of her almost complete lack of imagination, which did not permit of her grasping anything that had not really happened or that did not exist in concrete form. In view of this characteristic I was sure that, in the event of her having fallen in love with another man, she would have found it best to tell me at once; and, into the bargain, with all the brutality and unconscious cruelty of the more or less uneducated class to which she belonged. Of reticence and silence she was perhaps capable, as indeed she was now proving herself to be with regard to her change of feeling towards me; but it would have been very difficult, if not impossible, for her to invent a double life in order to conceal adultery—I mean, the appointments with dressmakers and milliners, the visits to relations or friends, the delays at entertainments or the traffic hold-ups to which women usually have recourse in similar circumstances. No, her coldness towards me did not mean warmth towards another. And if there was a reason, as indeed there must be, it was to be sought, not in her life, but in mine.

I was so deeply absorbed in these reflections that I did not notice that one of the secretaries was standing in front of me, smiling and repeating: "Signor Molteni . . . Dr. Battista is waiting for you." Finally I pulled myself together, and, interrupting my investigations for the time being, hurried off to the producer's office.

He was sitting at the far end of a spacious room with a frescoed ceiling and walls adorned with gilt plasterwork, behind a desk of green-painted metal, exactly like the secretaries' counter that encumbered the anteroom. I realize at this point that, though I have often spoken of him, I have not yet described him, and I think it may be expedient to do so. Battista, then, was the kind of man to whom his collaborators and dependents, as soon as his back was turned, referred to with charming names such as "the brute," "the big ape," "the great beast," "the gorilla." I cannot say that these epithets were undeserved, at least as regards Battista's physical appearance; however, partly owing to my dislike of calling anyone by a nickname, I had never succeeded in adopting them. This was also because these nicknames erred, in my opinion, in not taking into account one of Battista's highly important qualities, I mean his most unusual artfulness, not to stay subtlety, which was always present, though concealed under an apparent brutishness. Certainly he was a coarse, animal-like man, endowed with a tenacious, exuberant vitality; but this vitality expressed itself not only in his many and various appetites but also in an acuteness that was sometimes extremely delicate and calculating, especially in relation to the satisfaction of those appetites.

Battista was of medium height, but with very broad shoulders, a long body and short legs; whence the similarity to a large ape which had earned him the nicknames I have mentioned. His face, too, was a little like that of an ape: his hair, leaving the two sides of his forehead bare, came down rather low in the middle; thick eyebrows, with a sort of pensive mobility of their own; small eyes; a short, broad nose; and a large but lipless mouth, thin as a slit made by a knife and slightly protruding. Battista's figure was characterized by a stomach rather than a paunch; by which I mean that he habitually thrust out his chest and the upper part of his abdomen. His hands were short and thick and covered with black hair which continued upwards beyond his wrists into his sleeves: once when we had been at the sea together I had noticed that this hair bristled on his shoulders and chest and came right down to his belly. This man who looked so brutish expressed himself in a gentle, insinuating, conciliatory voice, with a polished, almost foreign accent, for Battista was not a Roman. It was in this unforeseeable, surprising voice that I detected an indication of the astuteness and subtlety of which I have spoken.

Battista was not alone. In front of the desk was sitting someone whom he introduced to me by the name of Rheingold. I knew very well who he was, although this was the first time I had met him. Rheingold was a German director who, in the pre-Nazi film era, had directed, in Germany, various films of the "colossal" type, which had had a considerable success at the time. He was certainly not in the same class as the Pabsts and Langs; but, as a director, he was worthy of respect, not in the least commercial, and with ambitions with which one might not perhaps agree but which were nevertheless serious. After the advent of Hitler, nothing had been heard of him. It was said that he was working in Hollywood, but no film under his signature had been shown in recent years in Italy. And now here he was, popping up strangely in Battista's office. While the latter was talking to us, I looked at Rheingold with curiosity. Have you ever, in some old print, seen the face of Goethe? Just so, just as noble, as regular, as Olympian, was the face of Rheingold; and, like that of Goethe, it was framed in a fringe of clean and shining silver hair. It was, in fact, the head of a great man; except that, on closer examination, I became aware that its majesty and nobility were lacking in substance: the features were slightly coarse and at the same time spongy, flimsy, as though made of cardboard, like those of a mask; giving, in fact, the impression that there was nothing behind them, like the faces of the enormous heads that are carried round by tiny little men at carnival-times. Rheingold rose to shake me by the hand, giving a little bow with his head only, and a slight click of the heels, in the stiff German manner; and then I realized that he was quite a small man, although his shoulders, as if to match the majesty of his face, were very wide. I noticed also that, as he greeted me, he smiled at me in an extremely affable manner, with a broad smile like a half-moon, showing two rows of very regular and altogether too-white teeth which I at once imagined, I don't know why, to be false. But immediately afterwards, when he sat down again, the smile disappeared in a flash, leaving no traces—just as the moon is obliterated in the sky by a cloud passing in front of it—giving place to a very hard, unpleasant expression, both dictatorial and exacting.

Battista, following his usual method, started off in a roundabout way. Nodding towards Rheingold, he said: "Rheingold and I were just talking about Capri . . . do you know Capri, Molteni?"

"Yes, a little," I answered.

"I have a villa in Capri," went on Battista, "and I was just saying to Rheingold what an enchanting place Capri is. It's a place where even a man like me, taken up as I am with business affairs, feels himself becoming a bit of a poet." It was one of Battista's favorite habits to profess an enthusiasm for fine and beautiful things, for the things, in fact, that belong to the sphere of the ideal; but what disconcerted me most was that this enthusiasm, to which he called attention in so sure a manner, was perfectly sincere, though always, somehow or other, connected with purposes that were not at all disinterested. After a moment, as though moved by his own words, he resumed: "Luxuriant nature, a marvellous sky, a sea that is always blue . . . and flowers, flowers everywhere. I think that if I were like you, Molteni, a writer, I should like to live in Capri and take my inspiration from it. It's strange that painters, instead of painting the Capri landscape, should give us all these ugly pictures that no one can understand. In Capri, pictures are ready made, so to speak. . . . All you have to do is to put yourself in front of the landscape and copy it . . ."

I said nothing; I looked at Rheingold out of the corner of my eye and saw him nod his approval, his smile hanging in the middle of his face like a sickle moon in a cloudless sky. Battista went on: "I'm always intending to spend a few months there, away from business, without doing anything, but I never manage it. We in the city here lead a life that is altogether against nature. Man isn't made to live amongst files of papers, in an office . . . and the people of Capri do, in fact, look far happier than we do. You ought to see them in the evening, when they come out to take a walk—young men and girls, smiling, serene, attractive, gay. It's because they have a life made up of small things, with small ambitions, small interests, small troubles. My goodness, how lucky they are!"

There was silence again. Then Battista resumed: "As I was saying, I have a villa in Capri and I'm never there, worse luck. I must have stayed there just about a couple of months altogether, since I acquired it. I was just saying to Rheingold that the villa would be the best possible place for writing the script of the film. The landscape would inspire you . . . especially because, as I was pointing out to Rheingold, the landscape is in harmony with the subject of the film."

"One can work anywhere, Signor Battista," said Rheingold; "certainly Capri might be useful . . . especially if, as I think, we take the exterior shots of the film in the Bay of Naples."

"Exactly. . . . Rheingold, however, says he would rather go to a hotel, because he has his own habits and, besides, he likes to be alone at certain times and to think over the work by himself. But I think that you, Molteni, might stay at the villa, together with your wife. It would be a pleasure for me, if at last there was someone living there. . . . The villa has every convenience, and you would have no difficulty in finding a woman to look after you . . ."

At once I thought of Emilia, as always; and I felt that a stay in a lovely villa in Capri might perhaps solve many difficulties. What I am saying is true: all of a sudden, for no reason, I was absolutely certain that it would indeed solve them. It was therefore with genuine warmth that I thanked Battista. "Thank you," I said. "I also think that Capri would be the best possible place for writing the script . . . and my wife and I would be delighted to stay at your villa."

"Excellent; that's understood, then," said Battista, holding up his hand, with a gesture that vaguely offended me, as if to check a flood of gratitude which I really had no intention of letting loose. "That's understood; you'll go to Capri and I'll come and join you there. And now let us talk a little about the film."

"High time too!" I thought, and looked closely at Battista. I had, now, an obscure feeling of remorse at having accepted his invitation so promptly. I did not know why, but I guessed instinctively that Emilia would have disapproved of my hastiness. "I ought to have told him I must think it over," I said to myself with some irritation, "that I must first consult my wife." And the warmth with which I had accepted the invitation seemed to me misplaced, a thing to be almost ashamed of. Battista, meanwhile, was saying: "We're all agreed that something new in the way of films has got to be found. The after-the-war period is now over, and people are feeling the need of a new formula. Everyone—just to give an example—is a little tired of neo-realism. Now, by analyzing the reasons for which we have grown tired of the neo-realistic film, we may perhaps arrive at an understanding of what the new formula might be."

I knew, as I have already mentioned, that Battista's favorite way of attacking a subject was always an indirect one. He was not a cynical type of man, or at any rate he was determined not to appear so. Thus it was very difficult for him to speak openly, as did many other producers franker than he, about financial matters: the question of profit, no less important to him than to the others—in fact, perhaps even more important—remained always shrouded in a discreet obscurity; and if—let us suppose—the subject of a film did not seem to him sufficiently profitable, he would never say, like the others: "This subject won't put a penny into the cash-box," but rather: "I don't like this subject for such and such a reason"; and the reasons were always of an aesthetic or moral order. Nevertheless, the question of profit was always the final touchstone; and the proof of this was to be seen when, after many discussions upon the beautiful and the good in the art of the film, after a good many of what I called Battista's smoke-screens, the choice fell, invariably, upon the solution that held the best commercial possibilities. Owing to this, I had for some time now lost all interest in the considerations, often extremely long and complicated, put forward by Battista on films beautiful or ugly, moral or immoral; and I waited patiently for him to reach the point where, always and inevitably, he came to a halt—the question of economic advantage. And this time I thought: "He certainly won't say that the producers are tired of the neo-realistic film because it isn't profitable . . . let's see what he will say." Battista, in fact, went on, after a moment's reflection: "In my opinion, everyone is rather tired of the neo-realistic film mainly because it's not a healthy type of film."

He stopped and I looked sideways at Rheingold: he did not blink an eyelid. Battista, who had intended, by pausing, to stress the word "healthy," now went on to explain it. "When I say that the neo-realistic film is not healthy, I mean that it is not a film that inspires people with courage to live, that increases their confidence in life. The neo-realistic film is depressing, pessimistic, gloomy. Apart from the fact that it represents Italy as a country of ragamuffins—to the great joy of foreigners who have every sort of interest in believing that our country really *is* a country of ragamuffins—apart from this fact which, after all, is of considerable importance, it insists too much on the negative sides of life, on all that is ugliest, dirtiest, most abnormal in human existence. It is, in short, a pessimistic, unhealthy type of film, a film which reminds people of their difficulties instead of helping them to overcome them."

I looked at Battista and once again I remained uncertain as to whether he really believed the things he was saying or only pretended to believe them. There was sincerity of a kind in what he said; perhaps it was only the sincerity of a man who easily convinces himself of the things that are useful to him; nevertheless, sincerity there was. Battista went on speaking, in that voice of strangely inhuman timbre, almost metallic even in its sweetness. "Rheingold has made a suggestion which interested me . . . He has noticed that in recent times films with subjects taken from the Bible have been highly successful. They have been, in fact, the best money-makers," he observed at this point, almost pensively, but as though opening a parenthesis to which he himself wished no importance to be paid. "And why? In my opinion, because the Bible remains always the *healthiest* book that has ever been written in this world . . . And so Rheingold said to me, the Anglo-Saxon races have the Bible, and you Mediterranean peoples, on the other hand, have Homer. Isn't that so?" He interrupted himself and turned towards Rheingold, as if uncertain that he was quoting him correctly.

"That's it, exactly," confirmed Rheingold, not without an expression of slight anxiety on his smiling face.

"To you Mediterranean peoples," continued Battista, still quoting Rheingold, "Homer is what the Bible is to the Anglo-Saxons. . . . And so why shouldn't we make a film from, for instance, the *Odyssey?*"

There was silence. Astonished, I wanted to gain time, and so I asked, with an effort: "The whole *Odyssey*, or an episode from the *Odyssey?*"

"We've discussed the matter," Battista answered promptly, "and we've come to the conclusion that it will be best to take into consideration the *Odyssey* as a whole. But that doesn't matter. What matters most," he went on, raising his voice, "is that, in re-reading the *Odyssey*, I've at last understood what I've been looking for for so long without realizing it . . .

something that I felt could not be found in neo-realistic films
. . . something, for instance, that I've never found in the
subjects that you, Molteni, have suggested to me from time
to time recently . . . something that I, in fact, have been
feeling—without being able to explain it to myself—have
been feeling was needed in the cinema as it is needed in
life—poetry."

I looked again at Rheingold: he was still smiling, perhaps
a little more broadly than before, and was nodding his approval. I hazarded, rather drily: "In the *Odyssey*, as one
knows, there is plenty of poetry. The difficulty is to get it
over into the film."

"Quite right," said Battista, taking up a ruler from the
desk and pointing it at me; "quite right . . . but to do that,
there are you two, you and Rheingold. I know there's poetry
in it . . . it's up to you to pull it out."

I replied: "The *Odyssey* is a world in itself . . . one can
get out of it what one wants. It depends what point of view
one brings to it."

Battista seemed now to be disconcerted by my lack of
enthusiasm, and was examining me with ponderous intentness as though trying to guess what purposes I was concealing behind my coldness. At last he appeared to be postponing
his scrutiny to a later occasion, for he rose to his feet and,
making his way around the table, started walking up and
down the room, his head held high, his hands thrust into
the hip pockets of his trousers. We turned to look at him;
and, still walking up and down, he resumed: "What struck
me above all in the *Odyssey* is that Homer's poetry is always
spectacular . . . and when I say spectacular, I mean it has
something in it that infallibly pleases the public. Take for
example the Nausicaa episode. All those lovely girls dressed
in nothing at all, splashing about in the water under the eyes
of Ulysses who is hiding behind a bush. There, with slight
variations, you have a complete Bathing Beauties scene. Or
take Polyphemus: a monster with only one eye, a giant, an
ogre . . . why, it's King Kong, one of the greatest pre-war
successes. Or take again Circe, in her castle . . . why, she's
Antinea, in *Atlantis*. That's what I call spectacle. And this
spectacle, as I said, is not merely spectacle but poetry too . . ."
Much excited, Battista stopped in front of us and said sol-
emnly: "That's how I see a film of the *Odyssey* produced
by Triumph Films."

I said nothing. I realized that, to Battista, poetry meant
something very different from what I understood by it; and
that, according to his conception of it, the *Odyssey* of Triumph Films would be a film based upon the big Biblical and

costume films of Hollywood, with monsters, naked women, seduction scenes, eroticism and grandiloquence. Fundamentally, I told myself, Battista's taste was still that of the Italian producers of the time of D'Annunzio; how indeed could it have been otherwise? In the meantime he had made his way back around the desk and sat down again, and was saying to me: "Well, Molteni, what do you say to it?"

Anyone who knows the world of the cinema knows that there are films of which one can be certain, even before a single word of the script has been written, that they will be brought to a final conclusion; while there are others which, even after the contract has been signed and hundreds of pages of the screen-play completed, will equally surely never be finished. So now I, with the experience of the professional script-writer, recognized immediately, even while Battista was speaking, that this *Odyssey* film was, precisely, one of those which are much discussed but, in the end, never made. Why should this be so? I could not have said; perhaps it was because of the inordinate ambitiousness of the work, perhaps it was Rheingold's physical appearance, so majestic when he was seated, so meager when he stood up. I felt that, like Rheingold, the film would have an imposing beginning and a paltry conclusion, thus justifying the well-known remark about the Siren: *desinit in piscem*, she ends up in a fish. And then, why did Battista want to make such a film? I knew that he was fundamentally very prudent, and determined to make money without taking risks. Probably, I thought, beneath his desire there lay the hope of obtaining solid financial support, perhaps even American support, by playing upon the great name of Homer—the Bible, as Rheingold had remarked, of the Mediterranean peoples. But on the other hand I knew that Battista, no different from other producers in this respect, would find some pretext, supposing the film were never made, for refusing to give me any remuneration for my hard work. It always happened like that: if the film failed to come off, payments also failed to come off, and the producer, generally, suggested transferring the emolument for the already completed script to other work to be done in the future; and the poor script-writer, forced by necessity, did not dare to refuse. I said to myself, therefore, that I must in any case forearm myself by asking for a contract and, above all, an advance; and that to achieve this goal there was only one method: to place difficulties in the way, to set a high price upon my collaboration. So I answered, tartly: "I think it's a very good idea."

"You don't seem, however, to be very enthusiastic."

I replied, with a sufficient show of sincerity: "I am afraid it may not be my kind of film . . . it may be beyond my powers."

"Why?" Battista seemed irritated now. "You've always said you wanted to work at a film of quality . . . and now that I give you the chance, you draw back."

I tried to explain what I meant. "You see, Battista, I feel myself to be cut out chiefly for psychological films . . . whereas this one, as far as I understand, is to be a purely spectacular film . . . of the type, in fact, of the American films taken from Biblical subjects."

This time Battista had no time to answer me, for Rheingold, in a wholly unexpected manner, broke in. "Signor Molteni," he said, summoning back his usual half-moon smile on to his face, rather like an actor suddenly sticking on a pair of false mustaches; and leaning forward slightly, with an obsequious, almost fawning expression. "Signor Battista has expressed himself very well and has given a perfect picture of the film I intend to realize with his help. Signor Battista, however, was speaking as a producer, and was taking into account, more especially, the spectacular elements. But if you feel yourself cut out for psychological subjects, you ought, without any possible doubt, to do this film . . . because this film is neither more nor less than a film on the psychological relationship between Ulysses and Penelope. . . . I intend to make a film about a man who loves his wife and is not loved in return."

I was disconcerted by this, all the more so because Rheingold's face, illuminated by his usual artificial smile, was very close to me and seemed to cut me off from any possible loophole of escape: I had to reply, and at once. And then, just as I was about to protest: "But it's not true that Penelope does not love Ulysses," the director's phrase "a man who loves his wife and is not loved in return" brought me suddenly back to the problem of my relations with Emilia—the relations, precisely, of a man who loved his wife and was not loved in return; and, at the same time, through some mysterious association of ideas, it brought to the surface of my memory a recollection which—as I immediately became aware—seemed to provide an answer to the question I had put to myself in the anteroom, while I was waiting to see Battista: why did Emilia no longer love me?

The story I am now going to tell may seem lengthy: in reality, owing to the almost vision-like speed of the recollection, the whole thing lasted only an instant. Well then, as Rheingold bent his smiling face towards me, I saw myself, in a flash, in my study at home, in the act of dictating a

script. I had just reached the end of a dictation which had
lasted several days, yet I still could not have said whether
the typist was pretty or not; and then a minute incident
opened my eyes, so to speak. She was typing out some sentence or other when, bending down to look at the sheet of
paper over her shoulder, I realized that I had made a mistake. I leaned forward and tried to correct the error myself
by tapping out the word with my finger on the keys. But,
as I did so, without meaning to I lightly touched her hand
which, I noticed, was very large and strong and strangely in
contrast with the slightness of her figure. As I touched her
hand, I was conscious that she did not withdraw it; I composed a second word, and again, this time perhaps not without intention, touched her fingers. Then I looked into her face
and saw that she was looking straight back at me, with an
expression of expectation, almost of invitation. I also noticed with surprise, as if for the first time, that she was
pretty, with her little full mouth, her capricious nose, her
big black eyes and her thick, curly, brushed-back hair. But
her pale, delicate face wore a discontented, scornful, angry
expression. One last detail: when she spoke, saying with a
grimace: "I'm sorry, I wasn't thinking," I was struck by the
dry, precise, decidedly disagreeable tone of her voice. I
looked at her then, and saw that she sustained my regard
perfectly well—in fact, she returned it in a manner that was
positively aggressive. I must then have shown some sign of
emotion and indeed have given a mute response, for from
that moment, for several days, we never stopped looking at
each other. Or rather, it was she who never stopped looking
at me, impudently, with deliberate effrontery, at every opportunity, pursuing my eyes when they avoided hers, seeking
to hold them when our eyes met, delving into them when
they came to a halt. As always happens, these glances, at
first, were few and far between; then they became more and
more frequent; finally, not knowing how to escape them I
was reduced to walking up and down behind her as I dictated. But the tenacious coquette found a means of circumventing this obstacle by staring at me in a big mirror hanging
on the wall opposite, so that, each time I raised my eyes, I
found hers waiting there to meet them. In the end, the thing
that she wanted to happen, happened: one day when, as
usual, I was leaning over from behind her to correct a mistake, I looked up at her, our eyes met, and our mouths
were joined for one moment in a swift kiss. The first thing
she said, after the kiss, was characteristic: "Oh, at last! . . . I
was really beginning to think you'd never make up your
mind." Indeed she now seemed sure that she held me in her

clutches, so sure that, immediately after the kiss, she did not trouble to demand any more but went back to her work. I was left with a feeling of confusion and remorse: I found the girl attractive, certainly, otherwise I should not have kissed her; but it was also certain that I was not in love with her and that the truth of the matter was that she had forced the kiss from me by working upon my male vanity with her petulant and, to me, flattering persistence. Now she went on typing without looking at me, her eyes lowered, prettier than ever with her round, pale face and her big mop of black hair. Then she made—on purpose, perhaps—another mistake, and I again leaned over her, seeking to correct it. But she was watching my movements, and, as soon as my face was close to hers, she turned in a flash and threw her arm round my neck, seizing hold of me by one ear and pulling my mouth sideways against hers. At that moment the door opened and Emilia came in.

What happened then, I think it is hardly necessary to relate in detail. Emilia withdrew at once, and I, after saying very hurriedly to the girl, "Signorina, that's enough for today, you can go home now," almost ran out of the study and joined Emilia in the living-room. I expected a scene of jealousy, but all Emilia said was: "You might at least wipe the red off your lips." I did so, and then sat down beside her and tried to justify myself, telling her the truth. She listened to me with an indefinable expression of suspicious, but fundamentally indulgent, mistrust, and at last remarked that, if I was truly in love with the typist, I had only to say so and she would agree to a separation forthwith. But she spoke these words without harshness and with a kind of melancholy gentleness, as though tacitly inviting me to contradict them. Finally, after many explanations and much desperation on my part (I was positively terrified at the thought of Emilia leaving me), she appeared to be convinced and, with some show of resistance and reluctance, consented to forgive me. That same afternoon, in the presence of Emilia, I telephoned to the typist to inform her that I should not need her again. The girl tried to wrest an appointment from me at some outside meeting-place; but I gave her an evasive answer, and have never seen her since.

This recapitulation, as I said, may seem lengthy, whereas in reality the scene flashed across my memory in the form of a lightning-like image: Emilia opening the door at the moment when I was kissing the typist. And I was at once surprised at not having thought of it before. There could be no doubt, I now felt, that things had taken the following course. Emilia, at the time, had shown that she paid no importance to the incident, whereas in reality, perhaps unconsciously, she had been profoundly disturbed by it. Afterwards she had thought about it again, weaving round that first memory an ever-thicker, ever-tighter cocoon of increasing disillusionment; so that that kiss, which for me had been nothing more than a passing weakness, had produced in her mind a trauma (to use a psychiatrist's term), that is, a wound which time, instead of healing, had increasingly exacerbated. While I was pondering these things there must no doubt have been a very dreamy expression on my face, for all at once, through the kind of thick mist that enveloped me, I heard Rheingold's voice asking in alarm: "But do you hear what I am saying, Signor Molteni?"

The mist dissolved in an instant, and I shook myself and saw the director's smiling face stretching out towards me. "I'm sorry," I said. "My mind was wandering. I was thinking of what Rheingold said: a man who loves his wife and is not loved in return . . . but . . . but . . ." Not knowing what to say, I made the objection that had come into my mind in the first place, "But Ulysses in the poem *is* loved in return by Penelope . . . in fact, in a sense, the whole of the *Odyssey* hinges on this love of Penelope's for Ulysses."

Rheingold, I saw, swept aside my objection with a smile. "Loyalty, Signor Molteni, not love. Penelope is loyal to Ulysses but we do not know how far she loved him . . . and as you know, people can sometimes be absolutely loyal without loving. In certain cases, in fact, loyalty is a form of vengeance, of blackmail, of recovering one's self-respect. Loyalty, not love."

I was struck once again, by what Rheingold said; and again I could not help thinking of Emilia, wondering whether, in place of loyalty and indifference, I would not perhaps have preferred betrayal and the consequent remorse. Yes, undoubtedly I should: if Emilia had betrayed me and had felt guilty towards me, it would have been possible for me to face her with assurance. But I had now demonstrated to myself that Emilia was not betraying me; that it had been I myself, in fact, who had betrayed her. As my mind was wandering in this new direction I was aroused by the voice of Battista saying: "Well then, Molteni, it's agreed that you'll work with Rheingold."

"Yes," I answered with an effort, "yes, it's agreed."

"Excellent," declared Battista with satisfaction. "Then let us arrange it like this. Rheingold has to go to Paris tomorrow morning and will be there for a week. You, Molteni, during that week, will make me a summary of the *Odyssey* and bring it to me . . . and as soon as Rheingold comes back from Paris, you'll go together to Capri and start on the work at once."

After this conclusive remark, Rheingold rose to his feet, and mechanically I rose also. I realized that I ought to speak about the contract and the advance, and that, if I did not do so, Battista would have got the better of me; but the thought of Emilia upset me and, even more, the strange resemblance between Rheingold's interpretation of Homer and my own personal affairs. I managed nevertheless to murmur, as we went off towards the door: "And how about the contract?"

"The contract is ready," said Battista in an entirely unexpected manner and in a casual, magnanimous tone of voice, "and the advance is also ready, together with the contract. All you have to do, Molteni, is to go to my secretary, and to sign the one and take away the other."

Surprise almost stunned me. I had expected, as had happened in the case of other film-scripts, that there would be the usual maneuvers on the part of Battista to cut down my remuneration or delay its payment; yet here he was paying me at once, without any discussion. As we all three passed into the adjoining room, which was the manager's office, I could not help murmuring: "Thank you, Battista. You know I need it."

I bit my lip: in the first place it was not altogether true that I needed it—not urgently, anyhow, as my remark implied; and besides, I felt that I ought not to have spoken those words, though I did not quite know why. Battista's reply confirmed my regret. "So I guessed, my dear boy," he said, clapping me on the back with a protective, fatherly gesture, "and I saw that you had what you wanted." Then, to a secretary who was sitting at a desk, he added: "This is Signor Molteni . . . for that contract and the advance."

The secretary rose to his feet and at once opened a portfolio and took from it an already drawn-up contract to which was pinned a check. Battista, after shaking Rheingold by by the hand, clapped me on the shoulder again, wishing me good luck with my new job, and then went back into his office. "Signor Molteni," said Rheingold, coming up to me in his turn and holding out his hand, "we shall meet again on my return from Paris. In the meantime you'll be making that summary of the *Odyssey* . . . and then taking it to Signor Battista and discussing it with him."

"Very well," I said, looking at him in some surprise because I thought I had seen him give me a sort of understanding wink.

Rheingold noticed my look and, all of a sudden, took me by the arm and put his mouth close to my ear. "Don't worry," he whispered to me hurriedly; "don't be afraid. Let Battista say what he likes. We'll make a psychological film, a purely psychological film." I noticed that he pronounced the word "psychological" in the German way—*"püschologhical"*; then he smiled at me, shook my hand with a brisk nod of the head and a click of the heels, and walked away. Watching him go, I started when I heard the secretary's voice saying to me: "Signor Molteni . . . will you be so good as to sign here?"

## CHAPTER 9

It was only seven o'clock, and when I reached home, I called in vain to Emilia through the deserted flat: but she had gone out and would not be back till dinnertime. I was disappointed and in a way felt positively bitter. I had counted on finding her in and talking to her at once about the incident of the typist; I was sure that that kiss had been at the bottom of our differences, and, feeling myself full of a new boldness, was confident that I could dispel the misunderstanding with a few words and then tell her the good news of the afternoon—my contract for the *Odyssey*, the advance I had received, our departure to Capri. It is true that my explanation was postponed only for a couple of hours, yet, all the same, I had an irritating feeling of disappointment and almost of foreboding. At that moment I felt sure of my own case; but I wondered whether, in two hours' time, I should have the power to be equally convincing. It will be seen that, although I pretended to myself that I had at last found the key to the difficulty, that is, the true reason why Emilia had ceased to love me, fundamentally I was not at all sure of it. And this unfortunate absence on her part was quite enough to fill me with apprehension and ill-humor.

Listless, demoralized and perplexed, I went into my study and looked mechanically in the bookshelf for the translation of the *Odyssey*. Then I sat down at the desk, put a sheet of paper into my typewriter and, having lit a cigarette, prepared to write the summary. I thought that the work would soothe my anxiety or at least make me forget it: I had tried this remedy on other occasions. So I opened the book and read, slowly, the whole of the first canto. Then at the top of the page I typed the title: *Synopsis of the Odyssey*, and, underneath it, began: "The Trojan War has been over for some time. All the Greek heroes who took part in it have now gone home. All except Ulysses, who is still far from his own island and his dear ones." At this point, however, a

doubt as to whether or not it was suitable to introduce into
my summary the Council of the Gods in the course of which
this same return of Ulysses to Ithaca was discussed, caused
me to interrupt my work. The council was important, it
seemed to me, because it introduced into the poem the notion of Fate, and of the vanity and, at the same time, the
nobility and heroism of human effort. Cutting out the council meant cutting out the whole supramundane aspect of the
poem, eliminating all divine intervention, suppressing the
figures of the various divinities, so charming and poetical in
themselves. But there was no doubt that Battista would not
want to have anything to do with the gods, who would seem
to him nothing more than incompetent chatterboxes who
made a great fuss about deciding things that could perfectly
well be decided by the protagonists. As for Rheingold, the
ambiguous hint he had given of a "psychological" film pre-
saged no good towards the divinities: psychology obviously
excludes Fate and divine intervention; at most, it discovers
Fate in the depths of the human spirit, in the dark intricacies
of the so-called subconscious. The gods, therefore, would be
superfluous, because neither spectacular nor psychological.
. . . I thought about these things with ever-growing confusion
and weariness; every now and then I looked at the typewriter and said to myself that I must get on with my work,
but I could not bring myself to it and sat without moving a
finger; and finally I fell into a profound but blank meditation, sitting there at the desk, my eyes staring into vacancy.
In reality I was not so much meditating as stirring together
in my mind the cold, acid flavors of the various feelings, all
of them disagreeable, that agitated me; but, in my bewildered, weary, vaguely irritable state, I did not succeed in
defining them to myself in any precise manner. Then, like an
air-bubble that rises suddenly to the still surface of a pond
after remaining for who knows how long under water, this
reflection forced its way into my mind: "Now I shall have
to submit the *Odyssey* to the usual massacre, to reduce it to a
film, and once the script is finished, this book will go back
into its shelf along with all the others that have served me
for other screen-plays. And in a few years' time, when I am
looking for another book to cut to pieces for another film,
I shall come upon it and say: 'Ah, yes, of course, that was
when I was doing the script of the *Odyssey* with Rheingold.
And then nothing was done about it . . . nothing was done,
after talking for months, morning and evening, day in and
day out, about Ulysses and Penelope and the Cyclops and
Circe and the Sirens. Nothing was done because . . . because
there wasn't enough money.' " At this thought I was con-

scious, yet again, of a feeling of profound disgust with the trade I was forced to follow. And again I was conscious, with acute pain, that this disgust was born of the certainty that Emilia no longer loved me. Hitherto I had worked for Emilia, and for Emilia only; since her love had failed me, my work had no further object.

I do not know how long I remained like that, hunched up motionless in my chair in front of the typewriter, with my eyes turned towards the window. At last I heard the front door bang, at the other end of the flat, and then the sound of footsteps in the living-room, and I knew that Emilia had returned. I did not move, but remained where I was. Finally I heard the door of the study open behind me and Emilia's voice asking: "Are you in here? What are you doing? Are you working?" Then I turned around.

She was standing in the doorway with her hat still on her head and a parcel in her hand. I said at once, with a spontaneity which astonished me after so many doubts and apprehensions: "No, I'm not working. . . . I was just wondering whether I ought or ought not to accept this new script of Battista's."

She closed the door and came and stood beside me, near the desk. "Have you been to see Battista?"

"Yes."

"But you haven't come to an agreement. . . . Doesn't he offer you enough?"

"Yes, he offers enough . . . and we have come to an agreement."

"Well, then. . . . But perhaps you don't like the subject?"

"No, it's a good subject."

"What is the subject?"

I looked at her for a moment before replying: as usual she appeared absent-minded and indifferent, and one could see she was only speaking from duty. "It's the *Odyssey*," I answered briefly.

She put down the parcel on the desk, lifted her hand to her head and slowly took off her hat, shaking out her pressed-down hair. But her face was blank and inattentive: either she had not understood that I was speaking of the famous poem, or—which was more probable—the title, though not entirely unknown, conveyed nothing to her. "Well," she remarked at last, almost impatiently, "don't you like it?"

"Yes, I told you I did!"

"Isn't the *Odyssey* the thing one learns at school? Why don't you want to do it?"

"Because I don't feel like doing it, now."

"But surely, only this morning, you had decided to accept the job?"

All of a sudden I realized that the moment had come for another, and this time really decisive, explanation. I jumped to my feet, took hold of her by the arm and said: "Let's go in there, into the living-room; I must talk to you."

She was frightened, more, perhaps, by the almost frenzied force with which I gripped her arm than by the tone of my voice. "What's the matter with you? are you mad?"

"No, I'm not mad. . . . Let's go in there and talk."

Meanwhile I was dragging her, forcibly, across the study. I opened the door and thrust her into the other room, in the direction of an armchair. "Sit down there!" I myself sat down facing her, and said: "Now let's talk."

She looked at me dubiously, and still a little frightened. "Well, talk then, I'm listening."

I began in a cold and colorless voice. "Yesterday—do you remember?—I told you that I had no desire to do this script because I was not sure that you loved me . . . and you answered that you did love me and that I ought to do it. Isn't that so?"

"Yes, that's so."

"Well," I declared resolutely, "I believe you were telling me a lie. . . . I don't know why—perhaps because you were sorry for me, perhaps in order to serve your own interests—"

"But what interests?" she interrupted me harshly.

"The interest you may have," I explained, "in remaining in this flat which you like so much."

Her reaction was such that I was struck by its violence. She sat up straight in her chair and said, in a louder voice than usual: "Who told you that? This flat doesn't matter to me in the least, not in the very least. I'm perfectly ready to go back and live in a furnished room. . . . It's quite obvious you don't know me. . . . It means nothing to me."

These words gave me a feeling of acute pain, pain such as a man might feel who sees some gift, for which he has faced bitter sacrifices, despised and insultingly spurned. After all, this home of ours, of which she spoke with such contempt, represented my life for the last two years; for this home I had abandoned the work I most wished to do, I had renounced my dearest ambitions. I asked, in a thin, almost incredulous voice: "It means nothing to you?"

"Nothing, absolutely nothing." Her voice sounded flat and unmusical, from some unexplained passion of contempt. "Nothing . . . do you understand? nothing!"

"But yesterday you said you cared very much about staying in this flat."

"I only said it to please you . . . because I thought it was you who cared."

I was inwardly amazed: so it was I, I who had sacrificed my theatrical ambitions, I who had never held such things to be of great importance, it was I who cared about the flat! I saw that she had now entered, for some reason unknown to me, upon the path of deceit, and I told myself that it would serve no purpose to exasperate her by contradicting her and reminding her of how much she had once desired what she now made such a show of despising. In any case, the flat was a mere detail; what really mattered was something quite different. "Never mind the flat," I said, trying to control my voice and adopt a conciliating, sensible tone; "it's not the flat I wanted to talk about, but your feeling towards me. You lied to me yesterday when you said, for some reason or other, that you loved me. You lied to me, and that's why I have no further desire to work for the cinema . . . because I did it entirely for you, and if you no longer love me I have no reason for going on with it."

"But what makes you think I lied to you?"

"Nothing and everything. We talked about that yesterday, too, and I don't want to begin all over again. There are things that can't be explained, but which one feels . . . and I feel you no longer love me . . ."

She showed, suddenly, a first impulse of sincerity. "Why do you want to know these things?" she asked unexpectedly, in a sad, tired voice, looking away towards the window: "why? Let it alone . . . it will be better for us both."

"Well then," I persisted, "you admit that I may be right?"

"I admit nothing. I only want to be left in peace. Leave me in peace!" There was a hint of tears in these last words. Then she added: "I'm going now. I want to change my clothes"; and she rose and went off towards the door. But I caught her as she went, seizing her by the wrist. I had made this gesture more than once before: when she had risen, saying she must leave me, and I, as she passed in front of my chair, had taken hold of her by her long, slender wrist. But formerly I had seized hold of her because I felt a sudden desire for her, and she knew it and would stop obediently, awaiting my second gesture, which consisted in embracing her legs and burying my face in her lap, or in pulling her down on to my knees. All this would end in love-making—after a little resistance and a few caresses—just where we found ourselves, in the armchair or on the divan close by. This time, however, my intention was different, and I could not help being aware of it, with some bitterness. She did not resist but remained standing close beside me, looking down at me from her great height. "Really," she said, "what *do* you want, I should like to know?"

"I want the truth."

"You want to insist on making trouble between us—that's what you want!"

"Then you admit that the truth would not please me?"

"I admit nothing."

"But you said it yourself—making trouble between us . . ."

"Oh well, I had to say something. . . . Now let me go!"

She did not struggle, however, nor did she move; she simply waited for me to release her. I felt I should have preferred violent rebellion to this cold, contemptuous patience; and, as though hoping, by a renewal of the old gesture which once had been the prelude to love, to arouse in her a feeling of affection, I let go of her wrist and put my arms around her legs. She was wearing a long, very ample skirt, full of folds; and as I embraced her I felt it shrink and tighten around her fine straight legs, hard and muscular, like the ample sails of a ship round the mast. And then I felt desire for her, in a way that was almost painful because of its suddenness and because of the sense of impotent despair that accompanied it. Looking up at her, I said: "Emilia, what have you against me?"

"I haven't anything at all . . . and now let me go!"

I clasped her legs more tightly with my two arms, pressing my face into her lap. Generally, when I made this gesture, I would feel, after a moment or two, the big hand that I loved so much being laid on my head in a slow, tentative caress. This would be the signal of her emotional response and of her willingness to do my pleasure. But this time her hand remained dangling and inert. This attitude on her part, so different from her former one, smote deep into my heart. I released her, and taking her by the wrist again, cried: "No, you shan't go. . . . You've got to tell me the truth . . . this very minute. . . . You shan't leave the room until you've told me the truth."

She went on looking down at me from above: I could not see her but I seemed to feel her hesitating gaze on my bowed head. At last she said: "Well, you've asked for it. All I wanted was to go on as we are. It's you who've asked for it: it's true, I don't love you now. There's the truth for you!"

It is possible to picture the most disagreeable things and to picture them with the certainty that they are true. But the confirmation of such fancies, or rather, of such certainties, always comes unexpectedly and painfully, just as though one had not pictured anything beforehand. Really and truly I had known all the time that Emilia no longer loved me. But to hear her say it had, nevertheless, a chilling effect upon me. She did not love me now: those words, so often imagined, assumed, when pronounced by her lips, an entirely new significance. They were fact, not fancy, however mixed the latter might have been with certainty. They had a weight, a size, which they had never before had in my mind. I do not remember clearly how I received this declaration. Probably I gave a start, like someone who goes under an icy shower-bath knowing that it is icy, and yet, when he feels it, gives a start just the same, as if he had never known at all. Then I tried to recover myself, to show myself, somehow, reasonable and objective. I said, as gently as I could: "Come here . . . sit down and explain to me why you don't love me."

She obeyed and sat down again, this time on the divan. Then she said, rather irritably: "There's nothing to explain. I don't love you now and that is absolutely all I have to say."

I realized that, the more I sought to show myself reasonable, the more deeply did the thorn of my unspeakable pain sink into my flesh. My face was twisted into a forced smile as I answered: "You must at least admit that you owe me an explanation. Even when one sacks a servant, one explains the reason."

"I don't love you any more: that's all I have to say."

"But why? You did love me, didn't you?"

"Yes, I loved you . . . very much . . . but now I don't any more."

"You loved me very much?"

"Yes, very much; but it's all over now."

"But why? There must be a reason."

"Perhaps there may be . . . but I don't know what it is; I only know that I don't love you."

"Don't repeat it so often," I exclaimed almost in spite of myself, and raising my voice a little.

"It's you who make me repeat it. You refuse to be convinced and so I have to go on repeating it."

"I'm convinced now."

There was silence. Emilia had lit a cigarette and was smoking it with downcast eyes. I was bending forward with my head between my hands. Finally I said: "If *I* tell you the reason—will you recognize it?"

"But I don't know it, myself."

"But if I tell it to you, perhaps you'll recognize it."

"All right then, come on . . . tell me."

"Don't speak to me like that!" I wanted to cry to her, wounded by her curt, indifferent tone. But I restrained myself and, trying to maintain my reasonable air, began: "Do you remember that girl who came here some months ago to type out a script for me . . . that typist? You caught us kissing. It was a stupid weakness on my part. But there was only that one kiss, I swear it; it was the first and the last . . . and I've never seen her since. Now tell me the truth—wasn't it perhaps that kiss that first came between us? Tell me the truth—wasn't that kiss the first thing that made you lose your love for me?"

As I spoke, I watched her carefully. Her first movement was one of surprise, and of consequent denial: it was as if my supposition seemed to her completely absurd. Then, as I saw clearly, a sudden idea made her change expression. She answered slowly: "Well, suppose it *was* that kiss. Now that you know, does it make you feel any better?"

At once I was absolutely certain that it had not been the kiss, as she was now insisting that I should believe. It was quite clear: at first Emilia had been downright astonished at my supposition, so remote was it from the truth; then, a sudden calculation had made her accept it. I could not but think that the true reason of her loss of love must be much more serious than that one kiss which had led to nothing. It was a reason, probably, that she did not wish to reveal because of some remaining regard for me. Emilia was not unkind, as I knew, and did not like hurting anyone. Evidently the real reason would be hurtful to me.

I said gently: "It's not true, it wasn't the kiss."

She was astonished. "Why! But I've just told you it was."

"No, it wasn't the kiss . . . it was something else."

"I don't know what you mean."

"You know perfectly well."

"No, on my word of honor, I don't know."

"And I tell you you do know."

She became impatient, almost like a mother with a child. "Why do you want to know so many things? It's typical of you. . . . Why do you want to pry into everything? What does it matter to you?"

"Because I prefer the truth, whatever it is, to lies. And above all, if you don't tell me the truth, I might imagine anything. . . . I might imagine something really nasty."

She looked at me for a moment in silence, in a strange manner. "What does it matter to you?" she went on then. "You have a clear conscience, haven't you?"

"Yes, certainly I have."

"Then how can the rest matter to you?"

"It's true, then," I persisted. "It really is something nasty."

"I didn't say that. I only said that, if you have a clear conscience, all the rest ought not to matter to you."

"It's true that I have a clear conscience . . . but that doesn't mean anything. Sometimes even one's conscience deceives one."

"But not yours, surely?" she said, with a faint irony that did not, however, escape me, and that seemed to me even more wounding than her indifference.

"Yes, even mine."

"Well, well, I must go," she said suddenly. "Have you anything else to say to me?"

"No, you shan't go until you've told me the truth."

"I've already told you the truth: I don't love you."

What an effect they had upon me, those four words! I turned pale, and implored her, miserably: "I asked you before not to say that again. It hurts too much!"

"It's you who compel me to repeat it. . . . It certainly doesn't give me any pleasure to say it."

"Why do you want to make me believe it's because of that kiss that you've stopped loving me?" I pursued, following the train of my reflections. "A kiss is nothing at all. That girl was a perfectly ordinary little fool and I've never seen her since. You know and understand all that. No, the truth is that you've stopped loving me"—now I was not so much speaking as spelling out my words carefully in an attempt to express my own difficult and obscure intuition—"because something has happened . . . something that has changed . . . s towards me . . . something, in fact, that has . . . nged, first and foremost, the idea you had of me, . . . ently your feelings as well."

. . . be admitted that you're intelligent!" she said, in . . . genuine surprise, almost of praise.

". . . e, then?"

". . . idn't say it was true. I only said you were intelligent."

". . . sought about in my mind, feeling that the truth was, so . . . speak, on the tip of my tongue. "To put it briefly," I insisted, "before a certain thing happened, you thought well of me . . . afterwards, you thought badly . . . and therefore ceased to love me."

"It might possibly have happened like that."

All of a sudden I had a horrible feeling: this reasonable tone of mine, I realized, was false. I was not reasonable, I was suffering, in fact, I was desperate, furious, I was shattered; and why in the world should I keep up a reasonable tone? I don't know what happened to me at that moment. Before I knew what I was doing, I had jumped to my feet, shouting: "Don't imagine I'm here just to keep up a bright conversation!" and had leaped on top of her and seized her by the throat and thrown her back on to the divan and was

yelling into her face: "Tell me the truth . . . tell it once and
for all. Come on!"

Beneath me the big, perfect body that I loved so much
was struggling this way and that, and she had grown red
and swollen in the face; I must have been squeezing her
throat tightly, and I knew that, in my heart, I wanted to kill
her. I kept on saying: "Tell me the truth, once and for all,"
and at the same time I squeezed with redoubled force and
thought: "I'm going to kill her . . . but better dead than my
enemy!" Then I felt her trying to kick me in the belly with
her knee, and indeed she succeeded in doing so, and with
such violence that it took my breath away. This blow hurt
me almost as much as the phrase: "I don't love you"; and it
was in truth the blow of an enemy, an enemy who seeks to
harm his adversary as much as possible. At the same time
my murderous hatred ebbed, I relaxed my grip somewhat, and
she struggled free, giving me a push that almost threw me
off the divan. Then, before I could recover myself, she cried
out in a voice of exasperation: "I despise you . . . that's the
feeling I have for you and that's the reason why I've stopped
loving you. I despise you and you disgust me every time you
touch me. There's the truth for you. . . . I despise you and
you disgust me!"

I was standing up now. My eye, followed at once by my
hand, moved towards a massive glass ashtray that stood on
the table. She certainly thought I intended to ▮▮▮
she uttered a groan of fear and covered her fa▮
arm. But my guardian angel stood by me. I d▮
how I managed to control myself; I put the asht▮
the table and went out of the room.

## C H A P T E R   1 0

As I have already mentioned, Emilia had not ha▮
good education: she had attended only the first elementary
school and then, for a few years, the normal school; then
she had broken off her studies and had learned to typing
and shorthand, and at sixteen was already employed in a
lawyer's office. She came, it is true, of what is called a good
family—that is, of a family which in the past had been in
easy circumstances, having owned property in the neighborhood of Rome. But her grandfather had dissipated his
heritage in unsuccessful commercial speculations, and her
father, up to the day of his death, had been merely a minor
official in the Ministry of Finance. So she had grown up in
poverty, and, as regards her education and manner of thinking, could almost be described as belonging to the working

class; and, like many women of that class, she seemed to have nothing to fall back upon except her common sense, which was so solid as to appear sometimes like stupidity or, to say the least, narrowness of ideas. Yet by virtue solely of this common sense she sometimes succeeded, in a wholly unexpected and, to me, mysterious, manner, in formulating comments and appreciations that were extremely acute; just as, indeed, happens with people of the working class, who are closer to nature than others, and whose consciousness is not obscured by any convention or prejudice. Certain things she said merely because she had thought them over seriously, with sincerity and candor, and indeed her words had the unmistakable ring of truth. But, since she was not aware of her own candor, she felt no complacency about it; thus in a way confirming, by her very modesty, the genuineness of her judgment.

And so, that day, when she cried out: "I despise you," I was immediately convinced that these words, which in the mouth of another woman might have meant nothing, when pronounced by her meant exactly what they said: she really did despise me and now there was nothing more to be done. Even if I had known nothing of Emilia's character, the tone in which she had uttered the phrase would have left me in no doubt: it was the tone of the virgin word that springs directly from the thing itself and pronounced by someone who had perhaps never spoken that word before, and who, urged on by necessity, had fished it up from the ancestral depths of the language, without searching for it, almost involuntarily. So indeed may a peasant, among a number of mutilated, worn-out, dialect expressions, sometimes utter a remark that sparkles with crystal-clear moral wisdom—a remark which in a different mouth might not be surprising, but which, in his, is astonishing and appears almost unbelievable. "I despise you." These three words, I noticed with bitterness, held the same absolutely genuine tone as those other words, so very different, which she had spoken to me the first time she had confessed her love: "I love you very much."

I was so sure of the sincerity and truth of those three words that, once I was alone in my study, I started walking up and down without thinking of anything, my hands trembling, my eyes distraught, not knowing what to do. Emilia's words seemed to be penetrating more deeply every minute into my sensibility, like three thorns, with sharp and increasing pain; but beyond this pain, of which I was acutely conscious, I was incapable of understanding anything. The thing that made me suffer most, of course, was the knowledge that I was not merely not loved but actually despised; and yet, utterly unable as I was to discover any reason at all, even the slightest, for this contempt, I had a violent feeling of injustice and, at the same time, a fear that, in reality, there was no injustice about it, and that the contempt had an objective foundation of which I was myself unaware, though to others it was quite obvious. I had a respectable opinion of myself, mixed with just a dash of pity, as of a man who is not too fortunate, a man upon whom Fate has not smiled as she ought to have done; but not in any way contemptible, quite the contrary. And now, behold, those words of Emilia's were completely upsetting this idea, were making me suspect, for the first time, that I did not know myself or judge myself as I really was, and that I had always flattered myself beyond all truth.

Finally I went into the bathroom and put my head under the tap, and the jet of cold water did me good; my brain had seemed to be red hot, just as though Emilia's words had set fire to it, discovering in it a combustible quality hitherto unknown. I combed my hair, washed my face, retied my tie, then went back into the living-room. But the sight of the table ready laid in the window embrasure aroused in me a feeling of rebellion: it was impossible that we should sit down as we did every day and eat together, in that room which still echoed with the words that had so deeply affected me. At that very moment Emilia opened the door and looked in, her face now recomposed into its usual serene, placid expression. Without looking at her I said: "I don't want to dine at home this evening. . . . Tell the maid we're going out, and then get dressed at once . . . we'll go and dine out somewhere . . ."

She answered, in some surprise: "Why, it's all ready . . . the whole thing will have to be thrown away."

A sudden rage swept over me, and I shouted: "That's enough. Throw away anything you like, but go and get dressed because we're going out." Still I did not look at her, but I heard her murmur: "What a way to behave!" Then she closed the door again.

A few minutes later we left the house. In the narrow street, flanked on both sides by modern buildings like our own, with façades full of balconies and verandas, among all the big, expensive motor-cars, my own small, utilitarian car awaited us—a recent acquisition which, like the flat, had still, to a great extent, to be paid for out of the earnings of future film-scripts. I had only had it a few months, and I still had that feeling of slightly childish vanity which such a possession can at first inspire. But that evening, as we walked towards the car, side by side, not looking at each other, in

silence and not touching each other, I could not help thinking: "This car, like the flat, represents the sacrifice of my
ambitions . . . and that sacrifice has been in vain." And in
truth, just for a moment, I had a sharp sense of the contrast
between the luxurious street in which everything looked new
and expensive, our flat which looked down upon us from the
third floor, the car that awaited us a few yards further on,
and my own unhappiness, which made all these advantages
appear useless and wearisome.

When I had got into the car, I waited until Emilia was
seated and then stretched out my arm to shut the door.
Usually, in making this movement, I brushed against her
knees, or, turning a little, gave her a light, quick kiss on the
cheek. This time, however, almost spontaneously I avoided
touching her. The door closed with a bang and for a moment
we sat motionless and silent. Then Emilia asked: "Where
are we going?" I thought for a few seconds and replied at
random: "Let's go to the Via Appia."

Slightly surprised, she said: "But it's too early for the Via
Appia . . . it'll be cold and there won't be anyone there."

"Never mind . . . *we* shall be there."

She was silent, and I drove off quickly towards the Appian Way. Coming down from our own quarter, we crossed
the center of the city and went out by the Via dei Trionfi
and the Passeggiata Archeologica. We passed the ancient
mossy walls, the gardens and vegetable-plots, the villas hidden in trees along the first part of the Appian Way. Then we
came to the entrance to the Catacombs, lit by two feeble
lamps. Emilia was right; it was still too early in the year
for the Via Appia. In the restaurant with the archaeological
name, when we came into the big sham-rustic room adorned
with amphoras and broken columns, we found nothing but
tables and a quantity of waiters. We were the only customers, and I could not help thinking that, in that chilly deserted room, surrounded by the tiresome solicitude of too
many attendants, we should have no hope of solving the
problem of our relationship—on the contrary. I remembered
that it was in that very restaurant, two years before, at the
time of our deepest love, that we had constantly dined; and
all at once I understood why, amongst so many, I had
chosen it, so dismal at that season of the year, and so forlorn.

The waiter was standing, menu in hand, on one side, and
on the other the wine-waiter was bowing, with the wine-list.
I began ordering our dinner, making suggestions to Emilia,
and bending forward slightly towards her like an attentive,
gallant husband. She kept her eyes lowered and answered
without looking up, in monosyllables: "Yes, no, all right." I

also ordered a bottle of the choicest wine, although Emilia
protested that she did not want to drink anything. "I'll drink
it," I said. The wine-waiter gave me an understanding smile,
and the two waiters went off together.

I do not wish to give a description here of our dinner in
all its details but merely to depict my own state of mind, a
state of mind which was entirely new to me that evening but
which was thenceforth to become normal in my relations
with Emilia. They say that, if we manage to live without too
great an effort, it is entirely owing to the automatism which
makes us unconscious of a great part of our movements. In
order to take one single step, it seems, we displace an infinite
number of muscles, and yet, thanks to this automatism,
we are unaware of it. The same thing happens in our relations with other people. As long as I believed myself to be
loved by Emilia, a kind of happy automatism had presided
over our relations; and only the final completion of any
course of conduct on my part had been illuminated by the
light of consciousness, all the rest remaining in the obscurity
of affectionate and unnoticed habit. But now that the illusion of love had faded, I discovered myself to be conscious
of every one of my actions, even the smallest. I offered her
something to drink, I passed her the salt, I looked at her,
I stopped looking at her: each gesture was accompanied by
a painful, dull, impotent, exasperated consciousness. I felt
myself completely shackled, completely numbed, completely
paralysed; at each act, I found myself wondering: am I doing
right, am I doing wrong? I had, in fact, lost all confidence.
With complete strangers one can always hope to regain it.
But with Emilia, it was an experience of the past, a thing
defunct: I could have no hope whatever.

And so, between us, there was a silence that was only
broken from time to time by some quite unimportant remark:
"Will you have some wine? Will you have some bread? Some
more meat?" I should like to describe the intimate quality of
this silence because it was that evening that it was established for the first time between us, never to leave us again.
It was, then, a silence that was intolerable because perfectly
negative, a silence caused by the suppression of all the things
I wanted to say and felt incapable of saying. To describe
it as a hostile silence would be incorrect. In reality there was
no hostility between us, at least not on my side; merely impotence. I was conscious of wanting to speak, of having many
things to say, and was at the same time conscious that there
could now be no question of words, and that I should now
be incapable of finding the right tone to adopt. With this
conviction in my mind, I remained silent, not with the re-

laxed, serene sensation of one who feels no need to speak, but rather with the constraint of one who is bursting with things to say and is conscious of it, and runs up against this consciousness all the time, as against the iron bars of a prison. But there was a further complication: I felt that this silence, intolerable as it was, was nevertheless, for me, the most favorable condition possible. And that if I broke it, even in the most cautious, the most affectionate manner, I should provoke discussions even more intolerable, if possible, than the silence itself.

But I was not yet accustomed to keeping silent. We ate our first course, and then our second, still without speaking. At the fruit, I was unable to hold out any longer, and I asked: "Why are you so quiet?"

She answered at once: "Because I've nothing to say."

She seemed neither sad nor hostile; and these words, too, held the accent of truth. I went on, in a didactic tone: "A short time ago you said things that would need hours of explanation."

Still in the same sincere tone, she said: "Forget those things. Try and imagine I never said them."

I asked hopefully: "Why should I forget them? I should forget them only if I knew for certain that they are not true . . . if they were just words that escaped you in a moment of anger."

This time she said nothing. And again I hoped. Perhaps it was true: it was as a reaction from my violence that she had said she despised me. Cautiously, I insisted: "Now confess, those horrible things you said to me today were not true . . . and you said them because at that moment you thought you hated me and you wanted to hurt me."

She looked at me and was again silent. I thought I detected—or was I wrong?—a faint glistening of tears in her big dark eyes. Encouraged, I put out my hand and took hers as it lay on the tablecloth, saying: "Emilia . . . they weren't true, then?"

But now she pulled away her hand with unusual violence, drawing back not only her arm but, it seemed to me, her whole body. "They *were* true."

I was struck by her accent of complete, albeit disconsolate, sincerity as she answered. It was as though she were aware that, at that moment, a lie would have put everything to rights again, anyhow for some time, at least in appearance; and clearly, just for a second, she had been tempted to tell such a lie. Then, on reflection, she had rejected the idea. I felt a new and sharper stab of pain, and, bending my head, murmured through my clenched teeth: "But do

you realize there are certain things that can't be said to anyone, just like that, without any justification . . . not to anyone, least of all to your own husband?"

She said nothing; all she did was to gaze at me, with apprehension almost; and indeed, my face must have been distorted with rage. At last she replied: "You asked for it and
I told you."

"But it's up to you to explain."

"How do you mean?"

"You've got to explan why . . . why you despise me."

"That I shall never tell you . . . not even if I were on the
point of death."

I was struck by her unusually resolute tone. But my surprise did not last long. I was filled with a fury which now
permitted no time for reflection. "Tell me," I insisted, and
again I seized her hand, but this time in a far from caressing
manner, "tell me . . . why do you despise me?"

"I've already said I shall never tell you."

"Tell me . . . if not, I shall hurt you." Beside myself with
rage, I twisted her fingers. She looked at me in surprise for a
moment, then screwed up her mouth in pain; and, immediately afterwards, the contempt of which hitherto she had
merely spoken, showed itself clearly in her expression. "Stop
it," she said roughly; "so you want to hurt me now, as well."
I noticed this "as well," in which there appeared to be an
allusion to other severities that I wished to inflict upon her,
and was left breathless. "Stop it . . . aren't you ashamed of
yourself? The waiters are watching us."

"Tell me why you despise me."

"Don't be a fool; leave me alone."

"Tell me why you despise me."

"Ow!" She wrenched her fingers away with a violent jerk
that knocked a tumbler off the table. There was a sound of
broken glass, and she jumped up and walked away towards
the door, saying loudly: "I'm going to wait for you in the
car . . . while you pay the bill."

She went out, and I was left sitting motionless where I
was, humiliated, not so much from shame (it was true, as she
had said, that all those idle waiters had been watching us the
whole time and had not missed a single word or gesture of
our quarrel) as by the strangeness of her behavior towards
me. Never before had she spoken to me in that tone, never
before had she abused me. The words "as well" continued,
moreover, to echo in my ears like a new and unpleasant
enigma that had to be solved, amongst so many others: how
and when had I inflicted those things upon her of which,

with her "as well" she was now complaining? At last I summoned the waiter, paid the bill, and followed her out.

Outside the restaurant, I found that the weather, which all day had been cloudy and uncertain, had turned to a thick drizzle. A little farther on, in the darkness of the open space, I could just see the figure of Emilia standing beside the car: I had locked the doors, and she was waiting there, patiently, in the rain. I said, in a shaky voice: "I'm sorry, I'd forgotten I had locked the car"; and heard her voice, quite quietly, answer: "Never mind . . . it's not raining much." Once again, at those forgiving words, hope of a reconciliation reawakened, crazily, in my heart: how was it possible to be filled with contempt, if one spoke in a voice so quiet, so kindly? I opened the door, got into the car, and she got in beside me. I started the engine, and said to her, in a voice that seemed to me, all of a sudden, strangely hilarious, almost jovial: "Well, Emilia, where would you like to go?"

She answered without turning, looking straight ahead: "I don't know . . . wherever you like."

Without waiting, I drove off. As I said, I now had a kind of jovial, carefree, hilarious feeling; it seemed almost as though, by turning the whole affair into a joke, by substituting lightness for seriousness and, frivolity for passion, I might succeed in solving the problem of my relations with Emilia. I do not know what it was that possessed me at that moment: perhaps desperation, like an over-potent wine, had gone to my head. I said, in an amused, deliberate playful tone: "Let's go wherever luck takes us . . . we'll just see what happens."

I felt absurdly awkward as I said these words; rather like a cripple trying to demonstrate a dance-step. But Emilia did not speak, and I abandoned myself to this new humor of mine, which I imagined to be an inexhaustible stream but which very soon turned out to be no more than a thin and timid trickle. I was now driving along the Via Appia, of whose cypresses and brick ruins and white marble statues and Roman pavement, with its big, irregular paving-stones, I caught a glimpse now and then by the light of the headlamps on the road in front, through the thousand glistening threads of rain. I went straight on for a little and then said, in a tone of false elation: "Let's forget, for once, who we are, and imagine we're two young students looking for a quiet corner, far away from indiscreet eyes, where they can make love in peace."

Still she said nothing, and I, encouraged by her silence, went a short distance farther along the road and then brought the car suddenly to a stop. It was pouring with rain now; the windshield-wipers, going backwards and forwards on the glass, did not move fast enough to sweep away the streams of water. "We're two young students," I said again in an uncertain voice; "I'm called Mario and you're Maria . . . and we've at last found a quiet place though it's rather wet. But inside the car we're all right . . . Give me a kiss." As I said this, with the decisiveness of a drunken man, I put my arm around her shoulders and tried to kiss her.

I don't know what I was hoping for: what had occurred in the restaurant should have made me understand what I ought to expect. At first Emilia tried to withdraw herself, with quite a good grace and in silence, from my embrace; then, when I persisted and, taking her chin in my hand, tried to turn her face towards mine, she thrust me harshly away. "Are you crazy?" she said. "Or are you drunk?"

"No, I'm not drunk," I murmured; "give me a kiss."

"I wouldn't dream of it," she answered with honest indignation, thrusting me away again. After a moment she went on: "And then you wonder that I tell you I despise you . . . when you behave like this . . . after what has happened between us."

"But I love you."

"I don't love *you*."

I felt ridiculous, but in a distressed kind of way, like someone who realizes he has been forced into a position which has the double disadvantage of being both comic and irreparable. But I was not yet disposed to consider myself beaten. "You're going to give me a kiss; if you won't do it for love, I'll make you do it," I muttered in a voice that was meant to be brutal and masculine. And I threw myself upon her.

She said nothing this time, but she opened the door, and I fell forward on to the empty seat. She had jumped out of the car and run away down the road, despite the rain which was now falling very heavily.

I paused for a moment in astonishment, confronted by this empty seat. Then I said to myself: "I'm an idiot," and I too got out of the car.

It was raining really hard, and when I put my foot to the ground I felt myself plunge up to the ankle in a puddle. Exasperated, I called out: "Emilia . . . come on, come back here and don't worry. I won't touch you."

From some point that was indistinguishable in the darkness but not very far off, she answered: "Either you stop it, or I walk back into Rome."

I said, in a voice that trembled: "Come along, I promise anything you wish."

It was still raining heavily; the water was running down

between the collar of my coat and my shirt-collar, wetting the back of my neck in a disagreeable fashion, and I felt it trickling over my forehead and the sides of my head. The headlamps of the car lit up only a small stretch of the road, together with a fragment of ruined Roman brickwork and a tall black cypress, truncated by the darkness; and, strain my eyes as I might, I was unable to see Emilia. Disheartened, I called again: "Emilia. Emilia . . ." and my voice ended on an almost tearful note.

At last she came forward out of the darkness into the beam of the headlamps, and said: "Do you promise you won't touch me?"

"Yes, I promise."

She went over and got into the car, adding: "What sort of a joke is this? I'm soaked through now . . . and my head's dripping. Tomorrow morning I shall have to go to the hair-dresser."

I got into the car too, in silence, and we started off at once. She sneezed, then, a couple of times, very loudly, in a vindictive way, as if to let me see I had made her catch a cold. But I did not take up the challenge: I was driving now as though in a dream. An ugly dream, in which I was really called Riccardo and I had a wife who was called Emilia and I loved her and she did not love me, in fact, she despised me.

## CHAPTER 11

I awoke next morning languid and aching, and with a deep and pervading sense of repugnance for what awaited me that day and the days following, whatever was destined to happen. Emilia was still asleep, in the bedroom; and I lay idle for a long time in the half-darkness, on the divan in the living-room, slowly and disgustedly regaining full consciousness of the reality which sleep had made me forget. Turning things over in my mind, I realized that I had to decide whether I would accept or refuse the *Odyssey* script; I had to know why it was that Emilia despised me; I had to find the way to win back Emilia's affections.

I have said that I was feeling exhausted, languid, inert; and this almost bureaucratic manner of summarizing the three vital questions of my life was, fundamentally, as I immediately realized, nothing more than an attempt to deceive myself with regard to an energy and a lucidity that I was very far from possessing. A general, a politician, a businessman will try, in this way, to get a close hold on the problems he has to solve, to reduce them to clear-cut objects, easily handled and lifeless. But I was not a man of that type; on the contrary.

And, as for the energy and lucidity which I pretended to myself I possessed at that moment, I felt they would fail me completely once I passed from reflection to action.

I was well aware, however, of my insufficiency; and as I lay on my back on the divan with my eyes closed, I became conscious that, as soon as I attempted to formulate a reply to these three questions, my imagination no longer rested on the firm ground of reality but soared away into the vacant heaven of aspiration. Thus in imagination I saw myself doing the *Odyssey* script as though it were nothing at all; reaching an explanation with Emilia and discovering that the whole story of her contempt for me, in appearance so terrible, sprang in reality from a childish misunderstanding; and finally being reconciled with her. But, as I thought of these things, I realized that all I had in view was the happy conclusions which I longed to achieve: between these conclusions and the present position lay a gaping void which I was totally unable to fill—to fill, anyhow, with anything that had even the slightest quality of solidity and coherence. My ambition —to put it briefly—was to solve the problem of my present position in accordance with my highest desires, but I had not the least idea of how I should contrive to do it.

I dropped into a doze, no doubt, and then suddenly awoke once more and caught a glimpse of Emilia sitting at the foot of the divan, in her dressing-gown. The living-room was still in semi-darkness, the shutters being lowered; but on the table, close to the divan, a small lamp was burning. Emilia had come into the room, turned on the light and sat down near me without my noticing it.

Seeing her sitting there at the end of my bed, in a familiar attitude that reminded me of other, very different awakenings in happier times, I had a moment's illusion. Sitting up in bed, I stammered: "Emilia, do you love me?"

She waited a little before answering; then she said: "Listen, I've got to talk to you."

I felt suddenly cold; and I was on the point of answering her that I didn't want to talk about anything, and would she leave me in peace because I wanted to go to sleep. But instead, I asked: "Talk about what?"

"About us two."

"But there's nothing to be said," I replied, trying to overcome a sudden anxiety. "You've ceased to love me, in fact you despise me . . . that's all there is to it."

"No, I wanted to say," she announced slowly, "that I'm going back to my mother's—today. I wanted to tell you before I telephoned. There, now you know."

I had not at all foreseen this declaration, which, after all, considering what had happened the day before, was perfectly logical and to be expected. The idea that Emilia might leave me had never entered my mind, strange though that may seem; I thought that she had already reached the farthest limit of her hardness and cruelty towards me. And yet, here was that limit being passed at one bound, in a fashion that was totally unexpected. Scarcely understanding what she meant, I stammered: "You mean to leave me?"

"Yes."

For a moment I was silent; then, all at once, I felt an urgent need for action, driven on by the very sharpness of the pain that pierced me. I jumped from the divan and went, in pyjamas as I was, to the window, as though I intended to push up the shutters and let in the light; but then I turned back and shouted in a loud voice: "You can't go away like that. I don't want you to go."

"Don't talk like a child," she said in a reasonable manner. "We've got to separate; it's the only thing now for us to do. There's nothing left between us two—at least as far as I'm concerned. It'll be better for us both."

I do not remember at all what I did after she had spoken these words: or rather, I remember only a few sentences, a few movements. As though in the grip of some kind of delirium, I must have said and done things then of which I was not in the least conscious. I believe I went around and around the room with long strides, in my pyjamas, my hair all untidy, at one moment beseeching Emilia not to leave me, at another, explaining my own position, and then simply addressing my remarks to the air, as if I had been alone. The *Odyssey* film-script, the flat, the instalments to be paid, my sacrificed theatrical ambitions, my love for Emilia, Battista, Rheingold, all the aspects of my life and all the people in it were jumbled up in my mouth, in a rapid, incoherent rush of words, like the little pieces of colored glass at the bottom of a kaleidoscope when a violent hand shakes it. But at the same time I felt that this kaleidoscope was nothing but a poor, illusory thing—simply, in fact, a few bits of colored glass with no order or design about them; and now the kaleidoscope was broken, and the pieces of glass lay scattered on the floor, under my eyes. I had at the same time a very precise feeling of abandonment and of fear of being abandoned, but beyond this feeling I could not go; it oppressed me and prevented me not merely from thinking, but almost from breathing. My whole self rebelled violently at the thought of the separation and of the loneliness that would follow; but I realized that, in spite of the sincerity of this feeling of rebellion, I was not speaking convincingly; on the contrary. And indeed every now and then there was a rent in the clouds of alarm and terror that enveloped me, and then I would see Emilia sitting on the divan, still in the same place, and calmly answering me: "Riccardo, do be sensible: it's the only thing for us to do now."

"But I don't *want* you to go," I repeated for the last time, stopping in front of her; "I don't *want* you to."

"Why don't you want me to? Be logical."

I don't know what I said, and then I went to the far end of the room again and thrust my hands into my hair and pulled it. Then I saw that, in the state I was in, I was quite incapable not merely of convincing Emilia but even of expressing myself. I managed, with an effort, to control myself, and I went and sat down on the divan again and, bending forward and taking my head in my hands, asked: "When do you intend to go?"

"Today."

After saying this she rose to her feet and, taking no further notice of me as I sat hunched up with my head in my hands, went out of the room. I had not expected her to do this, just as hitherto I had not expected any of the things she had said and done; and for a moment I was astonished and almost incredulous. Then I looked round the room and felt a strange sensation, chilling in its exactness: the separation had already taken place and my loneliness had already begun. The room was the same as it had been a few minutes earlier, when Emilia was sitting on the divan; and yet, I realized, it was already quite different. It was, I thought, as though it had lost a dimension. The room was no longer the one I had been accustomed to see, knowing that Emilia was there; it was already the one I should be seeing for an unknown length of time, in the knowledge that Emilia was *not* there and never would be there again. There was a deserted look in the air, in the aspect of all the things, everywhere, and, strangely, this look did not go out from me towards the things but seemed to come from the things back towards me. I did not think all this so much as become aware of it in the depths of my dull, aching, dazed sensibility. Then I found I was crying, because I felt a sort of tickling sensation at the corner of my mouth, and, when I put up my finger, found my cheek was wet. I heaved a deep sigh and began to weep openly, violently. In the meantime I had risen and walked out of the room.

In the bedroom, in a light which, after the semi-darkness of the living-room, and being in pyjamas with my face bathed in tears, seemed dazzling and intolerable, Emilia was sitting on the untidy bed, listening at the telephone; and from a single word I knew that she was speaking to her mother. I thought I noticed that her face wore a perplexed, disconcerted expression; and then I sat down too, and, taking my face between my hands, went on sobbing. I did not very well know why I was crying like this: perhaps it was not only because my life was ruined, but because of some more ancient sorrow that had nothing to do with Emilia or with her decision to leave me. In the meantime Emilia was still listening at the telephone. Her mother was evidently making a long and complicated speech; and, even through my tears, I saw a disappointed, angry, bitter expression, swift and dark as the shadow of a cloud over a landscape, pass across her face. Finally she said: "All right, all right, I understand, we won't talk about it any more"; but she was interrupted by another long speech from her mother. This time, however, she had not the patience to listen right to the end and said suddenly: "You've told me that already, all right, I understand, good-bye." Her mother said something more, but Emilia repeated her "good-bye" and hung up the receiver, although her mother's voice was still audible through it. Then she raised her eyes in my direction, but without looking at me, as though dazed. With an instinctive movement I seized her hand, stammering: "Don't go away, please don't . . . don't go."

Children believe that tears have a decisive value as a form of sentimental persuasion; and so, in general, do women and persons of feeble and childish spirit. At that moment—like a child or a woman or other feeble creature—although I was weeping from genuine sorrow, I cherished some kind of hope that my tears would persuade Emilia not to leave me; and this illusion, if it comforted me a little, at the same time aroused in me a feeling almost of hypocrisy. It was just as if I were weeping on purpose, as if I intended to make use of my tears in order to blackmail Emilia. All at once I was ashamed; and, without waiting for Emilia's reply, I rose and left the room.

After a few minutes Emilia followed me. I had had time to recompose myself as best I could, to wipe my eyes, to put on a dressing-gown over my pyjamas. I had sat down in the armchair and was automatically lighting a cigarette which I did not want. She also sat down, and said at once: "Don't worry . . . don't be afraid. I'm not going away." But she said it in a bitter, despairing, apathetic voice. I looked at her: she kept her eyes lowered and appeared to be reflecting; but I noticed that the corners of her mouth were trembling and that her hands were occupied in turning back the edge of her dressing-gown, a gesture that showed she was disturbed and perplexed. Then, in a suddenly exasperated voice, she added: "My mother doesn't want me. She says she has rented my room. She had two already; now she has three and the whole house is full. She says she doesn't believe I'm really in earnest . . . that I ought to think it over. And so I don't know where to go. No one wants me . . . and I shall be compelled to stay with you."

I was struck by this last phrase, so cruel in its sincerity; and I think I gave a violent start, as if I had been stabbed. I could not help exclaiming, in resentment: "Why do you talk to me like that? 'Compelled' . . . What have I done to you? Why do you hate me so?"

Now it was she who was crying, as I perceived, although she was trying not to show it, by hiding part of her face with her hand. Then she shook her head and said: "You didn't want me to go away. Well, I'm staying. You ought to be pleased, oughtn't you?"

I got up from the armchair, sat down beside her on the divan and took her in my arms, although I was conscious, at the first contact, that she withdrew and resisted me. "Certainly I want you to stay," I said, "but not in that way, not 'compelled.' What have I done to you, Emilia, that you speak to me like that?"

"If you like, I'll go away," she answered; "I'll take a room somewhere . . . and you won't have to help me except just for a short time. I'll get a job as a typist again. And as soon as I find work, I shan't ask anything more from you."

"No, no," I cried. "I want you to stay. But, Emilia, not 'compelled' to stay, not 'compelled.'"

"It's not you who compel me," she replied, still weeping, "it's life."

Once again, as I clasped her in my arms, I felt a temptation to ask her why it was that she had ceased to love me, why, in fact, she despised me, and what had happened, what I had done to her. But now, perhaps as a counterpoise to her tears and bewilderment, I had regained, partly, my composure. I said to myself that this was not the moment to ask certain questions; that probably, by such questions, I should gain no ground at all; and that perhaps, in order to get at the truth, I ought to have recourse to different, and less brusque, stratagems. I waited a little, while she went on weeping in silence, her face turned away from me. "Look," I proposed, "let's not have any more discussions or explanations . . . they serve no purpose except to make us hurt each other. There's nothing more I want to know from you, at any rate for the present. But just listen to me for a moment: I have agreed, after all, to do the *Odyssey* script. But Battista wants us to do it somewhere in the Bay of Naples, where most of the exteriors will be taken . . . so we've decided to go to Capri. I'll leave you to yourself, there, I swear; in any case I won't be able to help doing so, as I shall be working all day with the director, and I may or may not see you at meal-times. . . . Capri is an extremely beautiful place, and soon it will be possible to go swimming. You can rest, and bathe, and go for walks; it'll be good for your nerves, and you can think it all over and decide at your leisure what you want to do. Your mother is really right, after all: you ought to think it over. Then, in four or five months' time, you can tell me what you've decided, and then—and not till then—we'll talk about it again."

She kept her head turned sideways all the time, as if to avoid seeing me. Then she asked, in a somewhat comforted tone of voice: "And when should we be going?"

"At once . . . that is, in about ten days . . . as soon as the director comes back from Paris."

I was wondering now, as I held her against me and felt the roundness and softness of her breast against mine, whether I dared take the risk of kissing her. Actually, she was taking no sort of share in our embrace, but merely submitting to it. All the same, I deceived myself into thinking that this passivity was not entirely the result of indifference, and that it contained some element of interest. Then I heard her ask, still in the same comforted yet reluctant tone: "Where shall we stay, in Capri? In an hotel?"

I answered joyfully, thinking to give her pleasure: "No, we shan't go to an hotel . . . hotels are so tiresome. I've something better than an hotel; Battista is lending us his villa. . . . We shall be able to use the villa the whole time I'm working at the script."

I was immediately aware—as I had feared a few days before, when I had too hastily accepted Battista's offer—that Emilia, for some reason of her own, did not like this plan. In fact, she at once freed herself from my embrace and, drawing away to one corner of the divan, repeated: "Battista's villa . . . and you've already accepted?"

"I thought you would be pleased," said I, trying to justify myself; "a villa is far better than an hotel."

"You've already accepted?"

"Yes, I thought I was doing right."

"And we shall be there with the director?"

"No, Rheingold is going to live at the hotel."

"Will Battista come there?"

"Battista?" I replied, vaguely surprised by this question. "I suppose he may come now and then . . . but only for a

short time, a week-end, a day or two . . . just to see how our
work is going."

This time she said nothing: but she fumbled in the pocket
of her dressing-gown, took out her handkerchief and blew
her nose. As she did so, she pushed aside her dressing-gown,
which fell wide open almost up to her waist, uncovering her
belly and her legs. She kept her legs tightly crossed, as if
from modesty, but the white, youthful, plump belly flowed
over on to the crossed, muscular thighs with a generous
innocence that seemed more powerful than any rebuff. Looking at her then, as she seemed to be unconsciously offering
herself, I felt a violent desire, of unparalleled spontaneity,
which for a moment gave me the illusion that I might approach and possess her.

But I knew that, however great my longing might be, I
would not do so; and all I did was to watch her, almost
furtively, while she blew her nose—as though I were afraid
of being discovered in the act of looking at her, and put to
shame. As soon as she had finished, however, she remarked
that I had now reached the point of looking secretly at my
wife's nudity, with the excitement with which one looks at
forbidden things, like a boy peeping through a crack into a
bath house; and with a feeling of violent annoyance I put
out my hand and pulled down the edge of her dressing-
gown over her legs. She did not appear to be aware of my
gesture but, putting her handkerchief back into her pocket,
said in a voice that was now perfectly calm: "I'll come to
Capri, then . . . but on one condition—"

"Don't talk to me of conditions. I don't want to hear anything," I cried, unexpectedly; "all right, we'll go . . . but I
don't want to hear anything . . . and now go away, go away."
There must have been some kind of fury in my voice, for
she immediately got up, as though she were frightened, and
hurriedly left the room.

## CHAPTER 12

The day arrived when we were to leave for Capri.
Battista had decided to accompany us to the island, to do us
the honors of his house, as he himself expressed it; and that
morning, when we came down into the street, we found the
producer's high-powered red motor-car standing beside my
own unpretentious little machine. It was now the beginning
of June, but the weather was still unsettled, cloudy and
windy. Battista, wearing a leather wind-jacket and flannel
trousers, was standing beside the car talking to Rheingold,
who—like a good German, thinking of Italy as the land of

sunshine—had dressed very lightly for the occasion, with a peaked cap of white cloth and a striped linen suit of colonial cut. Emilia and I came out of the house followed by the porter and the maid carrying our suitcases; the other two at once left the car and came to meet us.

"Well, how shall we arrange ourselves?" asked Battista, after we had greeted each other. Then, without waiting for an answer: "I suggest that Signora Molteni comes with me, in my car, and Rheingold with you, Molteni. Then you can begin talking about the film during the journey. . . . Because," he concluded with a smile, but in a serious voice, "the real work begins today . . . and I want to have the script in my hands in two months' time."

I glanced, automatically, at Emilia, and noticed on her face that curious look of disintegration of the features that I had observed on other occasions—the sign, in her, of perplexity and aversion. But I attached no importance to it; nor did I in any way connect this expression with Battista's proposal, which was in any case quite reasonable. "Very good idea," I said, forcing myself to appear cheerful, as the happy circumstance of this trip to the seaside seemed to demand. "Very good idea. . . . Emilia will go with you and Rheingold with me. . . . But I don't promise to talk about the script."

"I'm frightened of going fast," began Emilia, "and you, in that car of yours—you always drive too fast . . ." But Battista, impulsively, took her by the arm, crying: "No need to be frightened with me. Besides, what are you frightened of? I've got my own skin to think about, too"; and as he spoke he almost dragged her off towards his own car. I saw Emilia look at me with a bewildered, questioning air, and wondered whether I ought not to insist on taking her with me. But I thought Battista might take offence; motoring was a passion with him and, to tell the truth, he drove extremely well; and so I again said nothing. Emilia made one more feeble objection: "But I should rather have gone in my husband's car"; and Battista protested, facetiously: "Husband indeed! Why, you spend the whole day with your husband. Come on, or I shall be offended." In the meantime they had reached the car. Battista opened the door, Emilia got in and sat down, Battista was walking round the car to get in, himself, on the other side. . . . Watching them in a rather dreamy way, I gave a start as Rheingold's voice said to me: "Are we ready, then?" I roused myself, got into my own car, and started the engine.

Behind me I heard the roar of Battista's car as it started; then it passed us and went off swiftly down the hill. I had scarcely time to catch a glimpse, through the rear window, of the head and shoulders of Emilia and Battista side by side; then the car turned a corner and vanished.

Battista had suggested that we should talk about the script during our journey. The suggestion was superfluous: when we had traversed the whole length of the city and I had turned into the Formia road at the moderate speed allowed by my small car, Rheingold, who so far had been silent, began: "Now tell me honestly, Molteni, you were afraid, that day in Battista's office, weren't you, that you were going to be forced into making a *kolossal* film?" He stressed the German word with a smile.

"I'm still afraid of it," I answered absent-mindedly, "partly because that's the way things are going at present in the Italian studios."

"Well, you're not to be afraid. We," he said, assuming all at once a hard, authoritative tone, "we are going to make a film that is psychological and only psychological . . . as indeed I said to you that day. I, my dear Molteni, am not accustomed to doing what the producers want, but what *I* want. On the set, it is *I* who am the master, and no one else. Otherwise I don't make the film. Quite simple, isn't it?"

I answered that it was, indeed, quite simple; and I spoke in a tone of sincere pleasure, because this assertion of autonomy made me hope that I would easily come to such terms with Rheingold as would result in the work being less tedious than usual. After a moment's silence, Rheingold resumed: "And now I should like to explain some of my ideas to you. I presume you can drive and listen at the same time?"

"Of course," I said; but at that same moment, as I turned very slightly towards him, a cart drawn by two oxen appeared out of a side road and I had to swerve suddenly. The car heeled over, zig-zagged violently, and I had considerable difficulty in righting it, just in time to avoid a tree, by a narrow margin. Rheingold started to laugh. "One would say *not*," he remarked.

"Don't bother about that," I said, rather annoyed. "It was quite impossible for me to have seen those oxen. Go on: I'm listening."

Rheingold needed no persuading. "You see, Molteni," he went on, "I've agreed to go to Capri . . . and in fact we shall certainly shoot the exteriors of the film in the Bay of Naples. But that will be only the background; for the rest we might as well stay in Rome. The drama of Ulysses, in fact, is not the drama of a sailor, or an explorer, or a war veteran. It is the drama of Everyman. The myth of Ulysses conceals the true story of a certain type of man."

I remarked, at random: "All the Greek myths depict

human dramas—dramas without time or place, eternal."

"Exactly. All the Greek myths, in other words, are figurative allegories of human life. . . . Now, what ought we moderns to do in order to resuscitate such ancient and obscure myths? First of all, to discover the significance which they can have for us of the modern world, and then to fathom that significance as deeply as we can, to interpret it, to illustrate it . . . but in a live, independent way, without allowing ourselves to be crushed by the masterpieces that Greek literature has drawn from these myths. Let us take an example. No doubt you know O'Neill's *Mourning Becomes Electra,* from which the film was also taken?"

"Yes, certainly I know it."

"Well, O'Neill too understood this very simple truth—that the ancient myths have to be interpreted in a modern manner, including the *Oresteia*. But I don't care for *Mourning Becomes Electra*—do you know why? Because O'Neill allowed himself to be intimidated by Aeschylus. He thought, quite rightly, that the Orestes myth could be interpreted psychoanalytically; but, intimidated by the subject, he made too literal a transcription of the myth. Like a good schoolboy writing out an exercise in a book with ruled paper—you can see the lines, Molteni." I heard Rheingold laughing to himself, pleased with his own criticism of O'Neill.

We were driving across the Roman *campagna* now, not far from the sea, between low hills yellow with ripe corn, with an occasional leafy tree here and there. We must be far behind Battista, I thought; the road, as far as the eye could reach, was empty—empty in its long, straight tracts, empty at every bend. At that moment Battista would be driving, far ahead, at sixty miles an hour, perhaps more than thirty miles in front of us. I heard Rheingold's voice begin again: "If O'Neill understood this truth, that the Greek myths must be interpreted in a modern manner, according to the latest psychological discoveries, he ought not to have respected his subject too much, but should have torn it to pieces, turned it inside out, put new life into it. This he did not do, and his *Mourning Becomes Electra* is tedious and cold . . . it's a school exercise."

"I think it's rather fine," I objected.

Rheingold disregarded the interruption and went on: "We've now got to do with the *Odyssey* what O'Neill did not wish, or did not know how, to do with the *Oresteia* . . . that is, open it up, as a body is opened up on the dissecting table, examine its internal mechanism, take it to pieces and then put it together again according to our modern requirements."

I was wondering what Rheingold was driving at. I said,

rather distractedly: "The mechanism of the *Odyssey* is well known: the contrast between the longing for home and family and fatherland, and the innumerable obstacles which stand in the way of a quick return to fatherland and home and family. Probably every prisoner of war, every war veteran who for some reason is detained far away from his own country after the end of a war, is, in his own way, a little Ulysses."

Rheingold gave a laugh which sounded like the clucking of a hen. "I was expecting that: the veteran, the prisoner. No, no, none of that, Molteni. You're going no farther than the externals, the facts. In that way the *Odyssey* film, really does run the risk of being nothing more than a *kolossal* film, an adventure film, as Battista would like it to be. But Battista is the producer and it is right that he should think in that way. Not you, however, Molteni, you who are an intellectual. Molteni, you're intelligent and you must use your brain. Try to use it."

"I *am* using it," I said, rather irritated; "that's exactly what I am doing."

"No, you're not using it. Take a good look and think carefully and observe one fact before all others: the story of Ulysses is the story of Ulysses' relations with his wife."

I said nothing, this time. Rheingold continued: "What is the thing that strikes us most in the *Odyssey*? It is the slowness of Ulysses' return, the fact that he takes ten years to get home . . . and that, during those ten years, in spite of his much-proclaimed love for Penelope, he does, in reality, betray her every time he gets a chance. . . . Homer tells us that Ulysses thought only of Penelope, that the one thing he desired was to be reunited with Penelope . . . but ought we to believe him, Molteni?"

"If we don't believe Homer," I said, more or less jokingly, "I really don't see who we are to believe."

"Why, ourselves, men of the modern world, who know how to see right through the myth. Molteni, after reading and re-reading the *Odyssey* several times, I've come to the conclusion that, really and truly—and of course without realizing it—Ulysses did not *want* to get home, did not *want* to be reunited to Penelope . . . that's my conclusion, Molteni."

I said nothing, and again Rheingold, emboldened by my silence, resumed. "Ulysses, in reality, is a man who is afraid of returning to his wife—and we shall see later why—and, with this fear in his heart, seeks, in his subconscious mind, to create obstacles in his own path. . . . That famous spirit of adventure is really no more than an unconscious desire to slow down his journey, frittering away the time in adventures that delay him and take him out of his way. . . . It is not Scylla and Charybdis, Calypso and the Phaeacians, Polyphemus, Circe and the gods who are opposed to the return of Ulysses; it is Ulysses' own subconscious which, step by step, creates good excuses for him to stay a year here, two years there, and so on."

So this was what Rheingold was driving at—this classic Freudian interpretation of the *Odyssey*. I was only surprised that I had not thought of it before: Rheingold was a German, he had started his career in Berlin, at the time of Freud's first successes, he had spent some time in the United States where psychoanalysis was held in great esteem; it was only natural that he should seek to apply its methods even to that hero who was, *par excellence,* devoid of complexes, Ulysses. I said drily: "Very ingenious. But I still don't see how . . ."

"One moment, Molteni, one moment. It is therefore clear, in the light of my interpretation—which is the only correct one in accordance with the latest discoveries of modern psychology—that the *Odyssey* is merely the inside story of what I may call a conjugal repugnance. This conjugal repugnance is debated and examined at great length by Ulysses, and it is only after ten years of struggle with himself that he finally succeeds in overcoming it and dominating it by accepting precisely the situation that had caused it. In other words, Ulysses, for ten years, invents for himself every possible kind of delay, makes every possible kind of excuse for not returning to the conjugal roof . . . he actually thinks, more than once, of binding himself to another woman. At last, however, he does succeed in gaining command over himself, and he goes home. And this return home of Ulysses amounts precisely to an acceptance of the situation owing to which he went away and did not want to come back."

"What situation?" I asked, genuinely stupid this time. "Didn't Ulysses go away simply in order to take part in the Trojan War?"

"Externals, externals," repeated Rheingold with impatience. "But as to the situation at Ithaca before Ulysses' departure to the war, the suitors and all the rest of it, I will speak about that when I explain the reasons for which Ulysses did not wish to return to Ithaca and was afraid to go back to his wife. In the meantime, however, I should like to stress first one important point: the *Odyssey* is not an extended adventure through geographical space, as Homer would have us believe. It is, on the contrary, the wholly interior drama of Ulysses . . . and everything that happens in it is a symbol of

Ulysses' subconscious. Of course you know your Freud, Molteni?"

"Yes, a little."

"Well, Freud will serve us as a guide through this interior landscape of Ulysses, not Berard with his maps and his philology which explains nothing . . . and, instead of the Mediterranean, we shall explore the mind of Ulysses—or rather, his subconscious."

Vaguely irritated, I said, with perhaps excessive violence: "What's the point of going to Capri, then, for a boudoir drama? We might just as well work in a furnished room in a modern quarter of Rome."

As I spoke, I saw Rheingold throw me a glance of mingled surprise and resentment; he then laughed disagreeably, as though he preferred to make a joke of a discussion that threatened to end badly. "We'd better resume this conversation, calmly, at Capri," he said, and then went on: "You can't drive and discuss the *Odyssey* with me both at the same time, Molteni. Now you had better devote yourself to driving, and I, for my part, will admire this extremely beautiful landscape."

I did not dare contradict him; and for almost an hour we went on in silence. We passed through the region of the ancient Pontine Marshes, with the thick, sluggish water of the canal on our right and the green expanse of the reclaimed plain on our left; we passed through Cisterna; we came to Terracina. After this latter town, the road started to run close beside the sea, being sheltered on its other side by rocky, sun-scorched mountains of moderate height. The sea was not calm; it could be seen beyond the yellow and black dunes, and was of an opaque green, a color that one guessed to be produced by the large quantity of sand stirred up from the bottom by a recent storm. Massive waves rose languidly, and their white water, like soapsuds, invaded the brief stretch of beach. Farther off, the sea was in movement but there were no waves, and the green color changed into an almost violet blue, over which, driven by the wind, appearing and disappearing, white curls of foam ran swiftly. The same capricious, lively disorder reigned in the sky: there were white clouds travelling in all directions; vast blue spaces swept by radiant, blinding light; sea-birds turning and swooping and hovering, as though taking care to follow, with their flight, the gusts and eddies of the wind. I drove with my eyes upon this seascape; and, all of a sudden, as if in reaction against the remorse aroused in me by Rheingold's surprised, offended look when I described his interpretation of the *Odyssey* as a "boudoir drama," there flashed into my mind the thought that, after all, I had not been wrong: upon that bright-colored sea, beneath that luminous sky, along that deserted shore, it would not have been difficult to imagine the black ships of Ulysses outlined between one wave and another, sailing towards the then virgin and unknown lands of the Mediterranean. And Homer had wished to represent a sea just like this, beneath a similar sky, along a similar coast, with characters that resembled this landscape and had about them its ancient simplicity, its agreeable moderation. Everything was here, and there was nothing else. And now Rheingold was wanting to make this bright and luminous world, enlivened by the winds, glowing with sunshine, populated by quick-witted, lively beings, into a kind of dark, visceral recess, bereft of color and form, sunless, airless: the subconscious mind of Ulysses. And so the *Odyssey* was no longer that marvellous adventure, the discovery of the Mediterranean, in humanity's fantastic infancy, but had become the interior drama of a modern man entangled in the contradictions of a psychosis. I said to myself, as a kind of conclusion to these reflections, that, in a sense, I could hardly have happened upon a more unfortunate script: to the usual tendency of the cinema to change everything for the worse which had no need to be changed at all, there was added, in this case, the particular gloom, entirely mechanical and abstract in quality, of psychoanalysis—applied, into the bargain, to a work of art as untrammelled and concrete as the *Odyssey*. We were passing along, at that moment, very close to the sea: beside the road were the green sprays of an exuberant vineyard planted almost in the sand, and beyond it a brief tract of shore, black with debris, upon which the big waves broke heavily from time to time. I pulled up suddenly and said drily: "I simply must stretch my legs."

We got out of the car, and I immediately started off down a path that led through the vineyard to the beach. I explained to Rheingold: "I've been shut up indoors for eight months. . . . I haven't seen the sea since last summer. Let's go down to the beach for a moment."

He followed me in silence; perhaps he was still offended, and still cross with me. The path wound through the vineyard for not much more than fifty yards and then petered out in the sand of the beach. The dull, mechanical sound of the engine had now been replaced by the irregular, echoing roar—to me a delicious sound—of waves piled upon each other and breaking in disorder. I walked a short distance, now going down on to the shimmering wet sand and now withdrawing again, according as the waves advanced or retired; finally I stopped and stood still for a long time on top of a sand-dune, my eyes turned towards the horizon. I felt I had offended Rheingold, that I ought to resume the conversation again in some more courteous manner, and that he was expecting me to do so. So, although it irritated me very much to be forced to interrupt my rapt contemplation of the far-off spaces of the sea, I finally made up my mind. "I'm sorry, Rheingold," I said all at once, "perhaps I didn't express myself very well just now. But, to tell you the truth, your interpretation didn't entirely convince me . . . if you like, I'll tell you why."

He answered at once, solicitously: "Tell me . . . tell me . . . discussion is part of our work, isn't it?"

"Well," I resumed, without looking at him, "I am not entirely convinced, though I'm not saying that the *Odyssey* may not have that significance too. But the distinctive quality of the Homeric poems and, in general, of classical art is to conceal such a significance and a thousand other meanings too, that may occur to us moderns, in a conclusive, and what I may call a profound, form. What I mean is," I added, with sudden, inexplicable irritation, "the beauty of the *Odyssey* consists precisely in this belief in reality as it is and as it presents itself objectively . . . in this same form, in fact, which allows of no analysis or dissection and which is exactly what it is: take it or leave it. In other words," I concluded, still looking not at Rheingold but at the sea, "the world of Homer is a real world. Homer belonged to a civilization which had developed in accordance with, not in antagonism to, nature. . . . That is why Homer believed in the reality of the perceptible world and saw it in a direct way, as he represented it, and that is why we too should accept it as it is, believing in it as Homer believed in it, literally, without going out of our way to look for hidden meanings."

I paused, but my attempt at clarification, far from calming me, had strangely exasperated me, as though it had been an effort that I knew perfectly well to be useless. And almost immediately came Rheingold's reply, accompanied by a burst of laughter, this time triumphant: "Extrovert, extrovert. . . . You, Molteni, like all Mediterranean people, are an extrovert, and you don't understand anyone who is an introvert. But of course there's no harm in that. I am an introvert and you are an extrovert . . . it was precisely for that that I chose you. You, with your extrovert character, will counterbalance my introvert character. Our collaboration will work marvellously well, as you'll see."

I was on the point of answering him; and I think my answer would have been such as to offend him again, for I again felt violently irritated at his pig-headed obtuseness;

when a well-known voice suddenly reached me from behind: "Rheingold, Molteni . . . what are you doing here? Taking the sea air?"

I turned and saw, clear-cut in the strong morning light, the two figures of Battista and Emilia, at the point where the dunes were highest. Battista was coming quickly down towards us, waving his hand in greeting, and Emilia was following more slowly, looking down at the ground. Battista's whole bearing showed a cheerfulness and an assurance even greater than usual; while that of Emilia seemed to me to exude dicontent, perplexity and an indefinable disgust.

Rather surprised, I said at once to Battista: "We thought you were far ahead . . . at Formia, at least, or even farther."

Battista answered, in a self-possessed voice: "We went a long way around. . . . I wanted to show your wife a property of mine near Rome where I'm building a villa . . . then we found a couple of grade crossings closed." He turned towards Rheingold and asked: "Everything all right, Rheingold? Been talking about the *Odyssey?*"

"Everything all right," replied Rheingold in the same telegraphic style, from beneath the peak of his cloth cap. Obviously Battista's arrival annoyed him, and he would have preferred to continue the discussion with me.

"Splendid, that's wonderful"; and Battista took us both confidentially by the arm and moved away, drawing us towards Emilia who had stopped at a little distance along the beach. "And now," he went on, with a gallantry that seemed to me insufferable, "now, fair Signora, it's up to you to decide. Shall we lunch at Naples, or shall we lunch at Formia? You must choose."

Emilia gave a start and said: "You three must choose . . . it's all the same to me."

"No, no, goodness gracious, it's the ladies who have to decide."

"Well then, let's lunch at Naples; I'm not hungry now."

"All right, Naples let it be. Fish soup with *sughillo*. A band playing *O sole mio* . . ." There could be no doubt of Battista's cheerfulness.

"What time does the steamer leave for Capri?" asked Rheingold.

"At half past two. We'd better get on," replied Battista. He left us and went off towards the road.

Rheingold followed and, catching him up, walked beside him. Emilia, on the other hand, remained where she was for a moment, pretending to look at the sea, as though to allow them to go on ahead of us. But, as soon as I came up to her, she took me by the arm and said in a low voice:

"I'm coming in your car now . . . and please don't contradict me."

I was struck by her tone of urgency. "Why, what's happened?"

"Nothing . . . only that Battista drives too fast."

We walked up the path in silence. When we reached the road, near the two stationary cars, Emilia moved in a determined manner towards mine.

"Hi," cried Battista, "isn't the Signora coming with me?"

I turned: Battista was standing beside the open door of his car, in the sun-filled road. Rheingold remained in uncertainty between the two cars, looking at us. Emilia, without raising her voice, said quietly: "I'm going with my husband now. We'll all meet at Naples."

I expected Battista to give in without any more ado. But, to my slight surprise, he came running over to us. "Signora, you're going to be with your husband for two months, at Capri . . . and I," he added in a low voice, so as not to be overheard by the director, "I've had just a bit too much of Rheingold in Rome, and I assure you he's not amusing. Surely your husband doesn't mind you coming with me, do you, Molteni?"

I could not but answer, although it was an effort to me: "No, not at all. But Emilia says you drive too fast."

"I'll go at a snail's pace," promised Battista, facetiously but with warmth. "But I do beg of you not to leave me alone with Rheingold." He lowered his voice again. "If you knew what a bore he is. He talks of nothing but films."

I don't know what came over me at that moment. Perhaps I thought it was not worth while annoying Battista for so frivolous a reason. Without giving myself time to reflect, I said: "Come on Emilia . . . won't you do this to please Battista? . . . He's quite right, anyhow," I added with a smile, "there's nothing you can talk about to Rheingold except films."

"Exactly," confirmed Battista, satisfied. Then he took Emilia by the arm—very high up, right under the armpit—saying: "Come along, fair Signora, don't be unkind. . . . I promise you I'll go at walking pace."

Emilia threw me a glance which, at the time, I was quite unable to account for; then she answered slowly: "Very well, if you say so." She turned with sudden decision, and adding "Let's go, then," walked off with Battista, who still kept a tight grip on her arm, as if he feared she might escape. I was left standing in uncertainty beside my own car, gazing at Emilia and Battista as they moved away. Beside Battista, thickset and shorter than herself, she walked indolently, slowly, with an air of discontent that was yet full of an intense, mysterious sensuality. She seemed to me, at that moment, extremely beautiful; not the middle-class "fair Signora" to whom Battista alluded, in that greedy, metallic voice of his; but truly very beautiful like some creature outside time or place, in harmony with the sparkling sea and the luminous sky against which her figure was outlined. And her beauty had about it a look of subjection, of reluctance, the cause of which I was at a loss to identify. Then, as I looked at her, I was struck by this thought: "Idiot . . . perhaps she wanted to be left alone with you . . . perhaps she wanted to talk to you, to explain things once and for all, to confide in you . . . perhaps she wanted to tell you that she loves you. And you forced her to go off with Battista." This idea brought me a feeling of sharp regret, and I lifted my arm as though to call her. But by now it was too late: she was getting into Battista's car and Battista was getting in beside her and Rheingold was walking towards me. So I got into my car, and Rheingold took the seat beside me. At that same moment Battista's car went past us, grew rapidly smaller in the distance, and disappeared.

Perhaps Rheingold had become aware of the violent ill-humor that overcame me at that moment; for instead of resuming—as I feared he would—our conversation about the *Odyssey*, he pulled his cap down over his eyes, settled down into his seat and was very soon asleep. I drove on in silence, therefore, urging my far from powerful little car to its greatest possible speed; and all the time, in an uncontrollable, frantic manner, my ill-humor increased. The road had turned away from the sea, and was now crossing a prosperous countryside, golden in the sunshine. At any other time I should have rejoiced in these luxuriant trees which, here and there, met over my head, forming a living gallery of rustling leafy branches; in these grey olives scattered, as far as the eye could reach, over the red hillsides; in these orange groves laden with glossy, dark foliage in the midst of which shone the round, golden fruit; in these old, blackened farm buildings guarded by two or three tawny haystacks. But I saw nothing; I drove on and on, and as time passed my wretched ill-humor increased more and more. I did not try to discover the reason for it, which undoubtedly went far beyond simple regret at not having insisted upon taking Emilia with me; even if I had wished to do so, my mind was so obscured by anger that I should have been incapable of it. But, like some kind of uncontrollable nervous convulsion which lasts as long as it is due to last and then by successive phases, gradually dies down and ceases, leaving its

victim all aching and dizzy, so my ill-humor gradually
reached its highest point as we passed through fields and
woods, plains and mountains, then decreased, and finally, as
we came near Naples, vanished altogether. Now we were
going swiftly down the hill towards the sea, in sight of the
blue waters of the bay, amongst pines and magnolias; and I
was feeling dull and torpid—like, an epileptic who has been
shaken, body and soul, by a convulsion of irresistible
violence.

## CHAPTER 13

Battista's villa, as we learned on our arrival in
Capri, was a long way from the main *piazza,* at a lonely
point on the coast in the direction of the Sorrento peninsula.
After we had accompanied Rheingold to his hotel, Battista,
Emilia and I went off towards the villa along a narrow lane.
At first our road took us along the sheltered walk that
runs around the island, halfway up the mountain-side. It
was almost sunset, and only a few people passed, slowly and
in silence, along the brick paved walk in the shadow of the
flowering oleanders or between the walls of the luxuriant
gardens. Now and again, through the foliage of pines and
carobtrees, one caught a glimpse of the distant sea, a sea of
a hard and peerless blue, shot with the glittering, cold rays
of the declining sun. I was walking behind Battista and
Emilia, stopping from time to time to observe the beauties
of the place, and, almost to my surprise, for the first time
after a long period, I felt, if not exactly joyful, at least calm
and composed. We traversed the whole length of the walk;
then we turned off along another, narrower path. Suddenly,
at a bend, the Faraglioni became visible, and I was pleased
to hear Emilia utter a cry of astonishment and admiration; it
was the first time she had been to Capri and so far she had
not opened her mouth. From that height the two great, red
rocks were surprising in their strangeness, lying on the surface of the sea like two meteorites fallen from heaven on to
a mirror. Elated at the sight, I told Emilia that there was a
race of lizards on the Faraglioni that existed nowhere else
in the world—bright blue because they lived between the
blue sky and the blue sea. She listened to my explanation
with curiosity, as though for a moment she had forgotten
her hostility towards me; so that I could not but conceive a
fresh hope of reconciliation, and in my mind the blue lizard,
which I described nestling in the cavities of the two rocks,
suddenly became the symbol of what we ourselves might
become, if we stayed a long time on the island. We too

should be of a pure blue within our hearts, from which the clear calm of our sojourn by the sea would gradually wash away the sooty blackness of gloomy town thoughts—blue and with a blue light within us, like the lizards, like the sea, like the sky, like everything that is bright and gay and pure.

After we had passed the Faraglioni, the path started to wind amongst rocky precipices, and there were no more villas or gardens. At last, on a lonely point, there appeared a long, low, white building with a big terrace jutting out above the sea; this was Battista's villa.

It was not a large villa: apart from a living-room that opened on to the terrace, there were only three other rooms. Battista, who walked in front of us as though to display his pride of ownership, explained that he had never lived in it, and that it was scarcely a year since he had come into possession of it as part payment of a debt. He drew our attention to the way in which he had had all preparations made for our arrival: there were vases of flowers in the living-room; the glossy floor emitted a pungent smell of wax polish; when we looked into the kitchen, we saw the caretaker's wife busy in front of the cooking-stove, preparing our dinner. Battista, who made a special point of displaying all the conveniences of the villa to us, insisted on our examining every nook and corner of it; he carried his politeness even to the extent of opening the cupboards and asking Emilia if there were enough coat-hangers. Then we went back into the living-room. Emilia said she was going to change her clothes, and went out. I should have liked to follow her example; but Battista sat down in an armchair and invited me to do the same, thus preventing me. He lit a cigarette and then, without any preamble, asked, in a wholly unexpected manner: "Well, Molteni, what d'you think of Rheingold?"

I answered, in some astonishment: "Really I don't know. I've seen too little of him to be able to judge. He seems to me a very serious sort of person. He's said to be an extremely good director."

Battista reflected for a moment and then went on: "You see, Molteni, I don't know him at all well either, but I know, more or less, what he thinks and what he wants. . . . In the first place, he's a German, isn't he?—whereas you and I are Italians. Two worlds, two conceptions of life, two different sensibilities."

I said nothing. As usual Battista was taking a roundabout course and keeping away from all material concerns: so I waited to see what he was getting at. "You see, Molteni," he resumed, "I wanted to put you, an Italian, to work beside Rheingold, just because I feel him to be so different from us.

I trust you, Molteni, and before I go away—and I ought to leave here as soon as possible—I want to give you a few words of advice."

"Go on," I remarked coldly.

"I've been watching Rheingold," said Battista, "during our discussions about the film; either he agrees with me or he says nothing . . . but I know too much about people, by this time, to believe in that kind of attitude. You intellectuals, Molteni, all of you, all of you without exception, you think, more or less, that producers are simply business men, and that's all there is to it. Don't deny it, Molteni; that's what you think, and of course Rheingold thinks just the same. Now, up to a point, it's true. Rheingold perhaps thinks that he can fool me by this passive attitude of his, but I'm wide awake, very wide awake, Molteni!"

"The fact of the matter is," I said abruptly, "you don't trust Rheingold?"

"I trust him and I don't trust him. I trust him as a technician, as a professional. I don't trust him as a German, as a man of another world, different from our world. Now—" and Battista put down his cigarette in the ashtray and looked me straight in the eyes—"now, Molteni, let it be quite clear that what I want is a film as much like Homer's *Odyssey* as possible. And what was Homer's intention, with the *Odyssey?* He intended to tell an adventure story which would keep the reader in suspense the whole time . . . a story which would be, so to speak, spectacular. That's what Homer wanted to do. And I want you two to stick faithfully to Homer. Homer put giants, prodigies, storms, witches, monsters into the *Odyssey*—and I want you to put giants, prodigies, storms, witches and monsters into the film . . ."

"But of course we shall put them in!" I said, somewhat surprised.

"Yes, you'll put them in, you'll put them in . . ." cried Battista in sudden, unexpected anger; "perhaps you think I'm a fool, Molteni? I'm not a fool." He had raised his voice and was staring at me with a furious look in his eyes. I was astonished at this sudden rage; and, even more, by the vitality of Battista who, after driving a car all day long and crossing from Naples to Capri, instead of resting when he arrived, as I should have done in his place, still had a desire to discuss Rheingold's intentions. I said, softly: "But what makes you imagine that I think you're a . . . a fool?"

"Your attitude, the attitude of both of you, Molteni."

"Please explain."

Slightly calmer now, Battista took up his cigarette again and went on: "You remember—that day when you me

Rheingold for the first time in my office—you said then that you didn't feel you were cut out for a spectacular film, didn't you?"

"Yes, I think I did."

"And what did Rheingold say to you, to reassure you?"

"I don't quite remember . . ."

"I will refresh your memory. Rheingold told you not to worry . . . he intended to make a psychological film—a film about the conjugal relations of Ulysses and Penelope. Isn't that so?"

Again I was astonished: Battista, under that coarse, animal-like mask, was sharper than I had believed. "Yes," I admitted, "I think he did say something of the kind."

"Now, seeing that the script hasn't yet been started and that nothing has yet been done, it is just as well that I should inform you with the utmost seriousness that, for me, the *Odyssey* is not a matter of the conjugal relations of Ulysses and Penelope."

I said nothing, and Battista, after a pause, went on: "If I wanted to make a film about relations between husband and wife, I should take a modern novel, I should stay in Rome, and I should shoot the film in the bedrooms and drawing-rooms of the Parioli quarter. . . . I shouldn't bother about Homer and the *Odyssey*. Do you see, Molteni?"

"Yes, yes, I see."

"Relations between husbands and wives don't interest me —do you see, Molteni? The *Odyssey* is the story of the adventures of Ulysses on his journey back to Ithaca, and what I want is a film of the adventures of Ulysses . . . and in order that there should be no more doubts on the matter, I want a spectacular film, Molteni—spec-tac-ular—do you see, Molteni?"

"You need have no doubts about it," I said, rather irritated, "you shall have a spectacular film."

Battista threw away his cigarette and, in his normal voice, endorsed what I had said. "I don't doubt it," he said, "seeing that, after all, it's I who pay for it. You must understand that I have said all this to you, Molteni, so as to avoid unpleasant misunderstandings. You begin work tomorrow morning, and I wanted to warn you in time, in your own interest too. I trust you, Molteni, and I want you to be my mouth-piece, so to speak, with Rheingold. You must remind Rheingold, whenever it may become necessary, that the *Odyssey* gave pleasure, and has always given pleasure, because it is a work of poetry . . . and I want that poetry to get over, complete, into the film, exactly as it is!"

I realized that Battista was now really calm again: he was,

in fact, no longer talking about the spectacular film that he
insisted upon our producing, but rather poetry. After a
brief incursion into the earthy depths of box office success,
we had now returned to the airy regions of art and the
spirit. With a painful grimace which was meant to be a smile,
I said: "Have no doubts about it, Battista. You shall have
all Homer's poetry . . . or anyhow all the poetry we're capable of finding in him."

"Splendid, splendid, let's not talk of it any more." Battista
rose from his armchair, stretching himself, looked at his
wrist-watch, said abruptly that he was going to wash before
dinner, and went out. I was left alone.

I also had previously thought of retiring to my room and
getting ready for dinner. But the discussion with Battista
had distracted and excited me, and I started walking up and
down the room, almost without knowing what I was doing.
The truth was that the things Battista had said to me had,
for the first time, given me a glimpse of the difficulty of a
task which I had undertaken rather light-heartedly and thinking only of material advantage: and now I felt that I was
succumbing in advance to the fatigue from which I should
be suffering by the time the script was finished. "Why all
this?" I said to myself; "why should I subject myself to this
disagreeable effort, to the discussions that will doubtless take
place between ourselves and Battista, to say nothing of those
that will crop up between me and Rheingold, to the compromises that are bound to follow, to the bitterness of putting my name to a production that is false and commercial?
Why all this?" My visit to Capri, which had seemed to me
so attractive when I looked down upon the Faraglioni from
the high path a short time before, now appeared as it were
discolored by the dreariness of a thankless and questionable
undertaking—that of reconciling the demands of an honest
man of letters such as myself with the wholly different demands of a producer. I was once again conscious, in a painful manner, that Battista was the master and I the servant,
and that a servant must do anything rather than disobey his
master; that any methods of cunning or flattery by which he
may seek to evade his master's authority are in themselves
more humiliating than complete obedience; that, in brief, by
appending my signature to the contract, I had sold my soul
to a devil who, like all devils, was at the same time both
exacting and mean. Battista had said quite clearly, in a burst
of sincerity: "It's I who pay!" I, certainly, had no need of all
that amount of sincerity to say to myself: "And it's I who am
paid!" This phrase sounded continually in my ears, every
time I turned my mind to the film-script. Suddenly these

thoughts gave me a feeling of suffocation. I felt a strong desire to escape from the very air that Battista breathed. I went over to the french window, opened it and stepped out on to the terrace.

## CHAPTER 14

Night had fallen, by now; and the terrace was gently illuminated by the indirect, but already intense, brilliance which a still invisible moon spread across the sky. A flight of steps led from the terrace to the path that ran round the island. I hesitated a moment, wondering whether to descend these steps and go for a walk, but it was late and the path was too dark. I decided to stay on the terrace. I stood looking over the balustrade and lit a cigarette.

Above me, black and sharp against the clear, starry sky, rose the rocks of the island. Other rocks could be dimly discerned on the precipice below. The silence was profound: if I listened, I could just hear the brief rustling sound of a wave breaking, from time to time, on the pebbly beach in the inlet far below, and then retreating again. Or perhaps I was wrong, and there was no rustling sound but only the breathing of the calm sea swelling and spreading with the movement of the tide. The air was still and windless; raising my eyes toward the horizon I could see, in the distance, the little white light of the Punta Camapanella lighthouse on the mainland, ceaselessly turning, now flashing, now extinguished again, and this light, scarcely perceptible and lost in the vastness of the night, was the only sign of life I could see all around me.

I felt myself growing quickly calmer under the influence of this calm night; and yet I was aware, with complete lucidity, that all the beauty in the world could produce only a fleeting interruption in the sequence of my troubles. And indeed, after I had stood for some time motionless and thinking of nothing, staring in the darkness, my mind, almost against my will, came back to the thought that dominated it, the thought of Emilia; but this time, perhaps as a result of my conversations with Battista and Rheingold and of the place I was in, so similar to places described in Homer's poem, it was strangely mingled and bound up with the thought of the *Odyssey* script. Suddenly, from some unknown spring of memory, there rose into my mind a passage from the last canto of the *Odyssey,* in which Ulysses, in order to prove his true identity, gives a minute description of his marriage bed; and so, at last, Penelope recognizes her husband and turns pale and almost faints, and then, weeping, throws her arms

around his neck and speaks words which I had learned by
heart from having so very often re-read and repeated them
to myself: "Ah, Ulysses, be not angry, thou who in every
event didst always show thyself the wisest of men. The gods
condemned us to misfortune, being unwilling that we should
enjoy the green and flourishing years side by side, and then
see, each of us, the other's hair grow white." Alas, I did not
know Greek; but I was aware that the translation could not
be a truly faithful one, if only because it failed to reproduce
the beautiful naturalness of the Homeric original. Nevertheless I had always taken a singular pleasure in these lines,
because of the feeling that shone through them, even in so
formal an expression; and, as I read them, it had so happened
that I had compared them with Petrarch's lines in the sonnet
that begins:

> *Tranquillo porto avea mostrato amore*

and ends with the triplet:

> *Et ella avrebbe a me forse risposto*
> *Qualche santa parola, sospirando,*
> *Cangiati i volti e l'una e l'altra chioma.*

What had struck me, both in Homer and in Petrarch, was the
feeling of a constant, unshakable love, which nothing could
undermine and nothing could cool, even in old age. Why did
those lines come back now into my mind? I saw that the
recollection arose from my relations with Emilia, so different
from those of Ulysses with Penelope or of Petrarch with
Laura, relations which were in peril not after thirty or forty
years of marriage but after a few months, relations to which
the comforting expectation of ending our lives together was
certainly denied, or of remaining lovers always, as on the
very first day, notwithstanding that "our faces were changed
and the hair of both of us." And I—I who had so ardently
wished that our relations might be such as to justify the hope
of this expectation—was left with a feeling of astonishment
and terror in face of the rupture—to me incomprehensible—
that was preventing my dream from coming true. Why? Almost as though I were seeking a reply from the villa which
in one of its rooms enclosed the person of Emilia, I swung
around towards the window, turning my back on the sea.

I happened to be standing at one corner of the terrace, in
such a way that I could see, albeit slantwise, right into the
living-room, without myself being seen. As I looked up, I
saw that Battista and Emilia were both in the room. Emilia

who was wearing the same low-necked, black evening dress
that she had worn on the occasion of our first meeting with
Battista was standing close beside a little movable bar; and
Battista, bending over the bar, was preparing some drink in
a large crystal glass. I was suddenly struck by something unnatural in Emilia's demeanor—a look of mingled perplexity
and impudence, something between embarrassment and temptation: she stood waiting for Battista to hand her the
glass and in the meantime was looking around her with an
uneasy expression in which I recognized that look of disintegration that was caused in her, by doubt and bewilderment.
Then Battista finished mixing the drinks, carefully filled two
glasses, and held one out to Emilia as he rose; she started, as
though awakening from a fit of deep abstraction, and slowly
put out her hand to take the glass. My eyes were upon her at
the moment as, standing in front of Battista, leaning slightly
backwards, she raised one hand with the glass in it and
supported herself with the other on the back of an armchair;
and I could not help noticing that she seemed, as it were, to be
offering her whole body as she thrust forward her bosom and
her belly beneath the tight, glossy material of her dress. This
gesture of offering herself, however, did not betray itself in
any way in her face, which preserved its usual expression of
uncertainty. Finally, as though to break an embarrassing silence,
she said something, turning her head towards a group of
armchairs at the far end of the room, round the fireplace;
and then, cautiously, so as not to spill her brimming glass, she
walked towards them. And then the thing happened which by
now, in reality, I was expecting; Battista caught up with her
in the middle of the room and put his arm around her waist,
bringing his face close to hers, over her shoulder. She immediately protested, with no severity in her manner, but with
a vivacity that was imploring and perhaps even playful, as,
with her eyes, she indicated the glass which she was now
holding tightly between her fingers, in mid-air. Battista
laughed, shook his head and drew her more closely towards
him, with a movement so abrupt that, as she had feared,
the glass was upset. "Now he's going to kiss her on the
mouth," I thought; but I failed to take into account Battista's
character, Battista's brutality. He did not in fact kiss her, but,
grasping the edge of her dress on her shoulder in his fist,
with a strange, cruel violence, twisted and pulled it roughly
downwards. One of Emilia's shoulders was now completely
bare, and Battista's head was bending over it so that he might
press his mouth against it; and she was standing upright and
still, as though waiting patiently for him to have finished; but
I had time to see that her face and her eyes, even during the

kiss, remained perplexed and uneasy, as before. Then she looked in the direction of the window, and it seemed to me that our eyes met; I saw her make a gesture of disdain and then, holding up the torn shoulder-strap with one hand, leave the room hurriedly. I turned and walked back along the terrace.

My chief sensation at the moment was one of confusion and astonishment, because it seemed to me that what I had seen was in complete contradiction with what I knew and had hitherto thought. Emilia, who no longer loved me and who, in her own words, despised me, was in reality, then, deceiving me with Battista. And so the situation between us was now reversed: from being vaguely in the wrong I had become clearly in the right; after seeing myself despised for no reason, it was I, now, who had full justification for despising; and the whole mystery of Emilia's conduct towards me resolved itself into a perfectly ordinary intrigue. It may be that this first harsh yet logical reflection, dictated largely by my own personal pride, prevented me, at that moment, from being conscious of any pain caused by the discovery of Emilia's unfaithfulness (or what appeared to me to be unfaithfulness). But as I approached the balustrade at the edge of the terrace, feeling irresolute and half-stunned, I became suddenly aware of the pain, and, recoiling to the opposite extreme, was certain that what I had seen was not, could not be, the truth. Certainly, I said to myself, Emilia had let herself be kissed by Battista; but, in some mysterious way, my own guilt did not on that account disappear, nor, as I realized, did I now have the right to despise her in my turn; in fact—why, I did not know —it seemed to me that she still retained this right towards me in spite of the kiss I had seen. And so, really and truly, I was making a mistake: she was not being unfaithful to me; or, at most, her unfaithfulness was merely apparent; and the essential truth of this unfaithfulness still had to be discovered, lying, as it did, right outside mere appearances.

I remembered that she had always shown a determined and, to me, inexplicable, aversion for Battista; and that, no longer ago than that very day, that very morning, she had twice besought me not to leave her alone, during the journey with the producer. How could I reconcile this behavior on her part with the recent kiss? There could be no doubt that this kiss had been the first: Battista, in all probability, had managed to take advantage of a favorable moment which, before this evening, had never occurred. Nothing, therefore, was yet lost; I might still come to know why in the world it was that Emilia had let herself be kissed by Battista; and why, above all, I felt, in an obscure but unmistakable way, that in spite of the kiss our relations were not changed, but that—as before and no less than before—she still had the right to refuse me her love and to despise me.

It may be thought that this was not the moment for such reflections, and that my first and solitary impulse should have been to burst into the sitting-room and reveal my presence to the two lovers. But I had been pondering too long over Emilia's demeanor towards me to give way to a candid, un-prepared outburst of that kind; and furthermore, what mattered most to me was not so much to put Emilia in the wrong as to shed new light upon our relationship. By bursting into the room, I should have precluded, once and for all, every possibility either of getting to know the truth or of winning back Emilia. Instead, I told myself, I must act with all possible reasonableness, with all the prudence and circumspection imposed upon me by circumstances which were at the same time both delicate and ambiguous.

There was another consideration which kept me from crossing the threshold of the living-room, this one, perhaps, of a more selfish kind: I saw that I now had a good reason for throwing over the *Odyssey* script, for ridding myself of a task that disgusted me and returning to my beloved theater. This consideration had the quality of being good for all three of us—for Emilia, for Battista, and for myself. The kiss I had witnessed marked, in reality, the culminating point of the falsity against which my whole life was contending, both in my relations with Emilia and in my work. At last I saw the possibility of clearing away this falsity, once and for all.

All this passed through my mind with the swiftness with which, if a window is suddenly thrown open, a blast of wind rushes into the room, bearing with it leaves and dust and all kinds of rubbish. And just as, if the window is closed again, there is a sudden silence and stillness within the room, so my mind, in the end, became all at once empty and silent, and I found myself standing there in astonishment, staring into the darkness, with no more thought or feeling in me. In this stupified condition, and almost without knowing what I was doing, I left the balustrade and went over to the french window; I opened it and went into the living-room. How long had I remained on the terrace after coming unawares upon Battista embracing Emilia? Longer than I had thought, certainly, for I found Battista and Emilia already seated at table, halfway through dinner. I noticed that Emilia had taken off the dress which Battista had torn and had again put on the one she had worn for the journey; and this detail, for some reason, troubled me deeply, as a particularly cruel and eloquent proof of her infidelity. "We thought you must have gone for a nocturnal swim," said Battista jovially. "Where the devil have you been hiding yourself?"

"I was just outside there," I answered in a low voice. I saw Emilia raise her eyes in my direction, look at me for a moment, and then lower them again; and I was quite sure she had seen me watching their embrace from the terrace, and that she knew that I knew she had seen me.

## CHAPTER 15

Emilia was silent during dinner, but without any visible embarrassment, which surprised me because I thought she ought to be troubled and I had always, hitherto, considered her incapable of dissimulation. Battista, on the other hand, did not conceal his jubilant, victorious state of mind and never stopped talking, uninterruptedly, while at the same time eating with a good appetite and drinking with a freedom that was perhaps excessive. What did Battista talk about, that evening? Many things, but, I noticed, mainly about himself, whether directly or indirectly. The word "I" boomed aggressively from his mouth, with a frequency that irritated me; and I was no less disgusted by the way in which he contrived to make use of even the most far-fetched pretexts to descend by degrees to his own self. I realized, however, that this self-applause was due not so much to simple vanity as to a wholly masculine wish to glorify himself before Emilia, and possibly to humiliate me: he was convinced that he had made a conquest of Emilia, and now, very naturally, was taking pleasure in strutting like a peacock and showing off his most brilliant plumes in front of his victim. I am bound to admit, at this point, that Battista was no fool; and that, even during this display of masculine vanity, he still kept his feet on the ground and said things that were, for the most part, interesting; as when, at the end of dinner, he told us, in a lively manner but also with seriousness of judgment, of his recent trip to America and of a visit he had paid to the studios of Hollywood. But this did not prevent his arrogant, self-centered, indiscreet tone from becoming intolerable to me; and I imagined, somewhat ingenuously, that the same must be true of Emilia, whom I still, for some reason, held to be hostile to him, in spite of what I had seen and knew. But once again I was wrong: Emilia was not hostile to Battista—on the contrary; more than once while he was speaking I seemed to catch in her eyes a look which, if it was not exactly love-sick, at least showed a serious interest and was even, at moments, full of a wondering esteem. This look was as disconcerting and bitter to me as Battista's male vanity

—if not more so; and it recalled to my memory another, similar look; but where I had noticed it, I could not at first remember. Then, suddenly, at the end of dinner, it came back to me: it was the same look—or anyhow, not far different—as the one I had caught, not very long ago, in the eyes of the wife of the film-director Pasetti, when I had had lunch with them at their home. Pasetti—pallid, insignificant, precise— was talking; and his wife gazed at him with spellbound eyes in which could be read, simultaneously, love, awe, admiration and self-surrender. Certainly Emilia had not yet reached that point with Battista, but it seemed to me that her look already held the germ of the feelings that Signora Pasetti cherished for her husband. Battista, in fact, did quite right to show off; Emilia, inexplicably, was already partly subjugated, and would soon be wholly so. At this thought I felt myself transfixed by a feeling of pain even sharper, perhaps than the pain I had felt shortly before, when I had seen them kissing. And I could not prevent the expression on my face from becoming visibly more gloomy. Battista must have noticed this change, for he threw me a penetrating glance and then suddenly asked: "What's the matter, Molteni? Aren't you pleased to be at Capri? Is there something wrong?"

"Why?"

"Because," he said, pouring himself out some wine, "you look gloomy . . . not to say ill-humored."

This was his method of attack: perhaps because he knew that the best way to be on the defensive is to be offensive. I answered with a promptness that surprised me: "I started feeling ill-humored while I was out on the terrace looking at the sea."

He raised his eyebrows and looked at me questioningly but with no sign of agitation. "Oh, really . . . why?"

I looked at Emilia: she did not appear to be worried, either. They were both of them incredibly sure of themselves. Yet Emilia had certainly seen me, and in all probability had told Battista. Suddenly these unpremeditated words issued from my mouth: "Battista, may I talk to you frankly?"

Again I wondered at his imperturbability. "Frankly?" he asked. "But of course! I always like people to talk to me frankly."

"You see," I went on, "when I was looking at the sea, I imagined for a moment that I was here working on my own account. My ambition, as you know, is to write for the theater. And so I thought how this would be the ideal spot, as they say, to devote myself to my work: beauty, silence, peace, my wife with me, nothing to worry about. Then I remembered that I was here, in this place which is so lovely and so favorable in every way, not for *that* purpose, but—I'm sorry, but you wanted me to be frank—in order to spend my time writing a film-script which will certainly be good but which, in fact, really and truly doesn't concern me. I shall give of my very best to Rheingold, and Rheingold will make whatever use of it he likes, and in the end I shall be given a check. And I shall have wasted three or four months of the best and most creative time of my life. I know I shouldn't say such things to you, nor to any other producer . . . but you wanted me to be frank. Now you know why I'm in a bad temper."

Why had I said these things instead of the others that were on the tip of my tongue and that concerned the conduct of Battista towards my wife? I did not know; perhaps owing to a sudden weariness of overstrained nerves; perhaps because in this way I expressed, indirectly, my desperation at Emilia's unfaithfulness which I felt to be somehow connected with the commercial and subordinate character of my work. But, just as Battista and Emilia had remained untroubled by my ominous preamble, so now they failed to show any relief at all at the wretched confession of weakness that had followed it. Battista said seriously: "But I'm sure, Molteni, you'll write a very fine script."

Having started out on the wrong track, I was now committed to it to the bitter end. I answered in a tone of exasperation: "I am afraid I didn't make myself clear. I am a writer for the theater, Battista, not one of the large number of professional writers of film-scripts . . . and this script, however fine, however perfect it is, will be, for me, merely a script . . . a thing—allow me to say frankly—that I do simply in order to earn money. . . . Now at the age of twenty-seven one has what are commonly called ideals—and my ideal is to write for the theater! . . . Why am I unable to do so? Because the world to-day is so constructed that no one can do what he would like to do, and he is forced, instead, to do what others wish him to do. Because the question of money always intrudes—into what we do, into what are, into what we wish to become, into our work, into our highest aspirations, even into our relations with the people we love!"

I realized that I had become over-excited and that my eyes had actually filled with tears. And I was ashamed and in my heart I cursed my excess of feeling which encouraged me to make confidences of this kind to the man who, a few moments earlier, had successfully tried to entice my wife away from me. But Battista was not put out of countenance for so small a matter. "You know, Molteni," he said, "hearing you talk, I seem to see myself again at the time when I was your age."

"Oh, really?" I stammered, disconcerted.

"Yes, I was extremely poor," pursued Battista, helping himself to more wine, "and I also had, as you say, ideals. . . . What those ideals were, I could not now say, and perhaps I did not know even then . . . but I had them nevertheless . . . or perhaps I did not have this or that ideal, but Ideals with a capital I. . . . Then I met a man to whom I owe a very great deal, if only for having taught me certain things." Battista paused a moment, with characteristic, heavy solemnity, and I could not help calling to mind, almost involuntarily, that the man to whom he was alluding was without doubt a certain film producer, forgotten now, but famous in the days of the early Italian cinema, with whom, and under whose orders, Battista had indeed started out upon his prosperous career; a man who, however, as far as I knew, was to be admired for nothing except his capacity for making money. "To that man," Battista went on, "I made more or less the same speech as you've made to me this evening. You know what he answered me? That ideals, until one knows exactly what one wants, are best forgotten and put aside . . . but, as soon as one has planted one's foot on solid ground, then one should remember them, and *that* should become the ideal . . . the first thousand-lire note one earns—*that's* the best ideal! Then, as he said to me, one's ideal develops and becomes a film studio, a theater, films that have been made and that are going to be made—one's every day work, in fact. That's what he said to me . . . and I did as he told me and everything turned out well. But you—you have the great advantage of knowing what your ideal is—to write plays. Well, you *will* write them!"

"I *will* write them?" I could not help asking, feeling doubtful but, at the same time, already somewhat comforted.

"Yes, you will write them," Battista affirmed; "you will write them if you really want to, even if you *are* working for money, even if you *are* making scripts for Triumph Films. D'you want to know what the secret of success is, Molteni?"

"What is it?"

"Get into the queue, in life, just as you get into the queue at the booking-office, at the station. Our moment always comes, if we have patience and don't change queues. Our moment always comes, and the booking-office clerk gives each person his ticket . . . each person according to his merits, of course . . . anyone who is going a long way, and is capable of doing so, may even be given a ticket for Australia. Others who are not going so far are given tickets for shorter journeys—for Capri, possibly!" He laughed, pleased with this ambiguous allusion to our journey, and then added:

"I hope you yourself may receive a ticket for a very far-off destination . . . how about America?"

I looked at Battista, who was smiling at me in a fatherly manner, and then I looked at Emilia and saw that she too was smiling; it was a very faint smile, it is true, but no less sincere on that account—at least so it seemed to me. And I realized once again that Battista, that day, had somehow managed to change her aversion into a feeling that was almost one of liking for him. At this thought I was overwhelmed anew by the sadness that had assailed me when it seemed to me that I detected Signora Pasetti's look in the eyes of Emilia. I said sadness, rather than jealousy: in reality I was extremely tired, owing both to the journey and to the various events of the day, and weariness was intermingled with all my feelings, even the most violent, deadening them and changing them into an impotent, despairing melancholy.

Dinner came to an end in unexpected fashion. After listening sympathetically to Battista, Emilia appeared suddenly to remember me—or rather, to remember by existence—in a manner that once again confirmed my uneasiness. To an insignificant remark from me: "We might go out on the terrace . . . the moon should have risen by now" she replied: "I don't want to go out on the terrace. . . . I'm going to bed. I'm tired"; and without more ado she got up, said good night to us, and went out. Battista did not appear to be surprised at this abrupt departure; in fact—or so it seemed to me—he looked almost pleased at it, as a flattering indication of the havoc he had contrived to create in Emilia's mind. But I felt my uneasiness to be doubled. And although, as I said, I felt exhausted, although I was well aware that it would have been better to postpone all explanations till next day, in the end I could no longer contain myself. With the excuse that I felt sleepy, I too said good night to Battista and left the room.

## CHAPTER 16

My bedroom communicated with Emilia's by means of an inside door. Without any delay I went to this door and knocked. Emilia called to me to come in.

She was sitting on the bed, quite still, in a thoughtful attitude. When she saw me, she at once asked, in a weary, irritable voice: "What more do you want of me?"

"Nothing at all," I answered coldly, for I felt perfectly calm and lucid now, also less tired; "just to wish you good night."

"Or is it that you want to know what I think of the conversation you had this evening with Battista? Well, if you want to know, I'll tell you at once: it was not only inopportune but ridiculous as well."

I took a chair and sat down, then asked: "Why?"

"I don't understand you," she said, annoyed, "really I don't understand you. You set so much store by this script, and then you go and tell the producer that you're working simply to make money, that you don't like the work, that your ideal would be to write for the theater, and so on. But don't you realize that although, out of politeness, he gave in to you this evening, tomorrow he'll think it over, and he'll take good care not to give you any more work? Can't you possibly understand a thing as simple as that?"

So she launched her attack. And although I knew she was doing it in order to conceal other, more important, anxieties from me, I still could not help noticing a certain sincerity in her voice, however painful and humiliating it might be for me. I had promised myself that I would keep calm. But her tone of utter contempt made me flare up in spite of myself. "But it's the truth," I cried all of a sudden; "I don't like this job, I've never liked it. And it's by no means certain that I'm going to do it."

"Of course you're going to do it." Never had she despised me so much as at this moment.

I set my teeth and tried to control myself. "Perhaps I may not do it," I said in a normal voice. "I had intended to do it even as late as this morning . . . but certain things have happened during the course of today which will cause me, in all probability, to announce to Battista, not later than tomorrow, that I am giving it up."

I uttered this sibylline remark deliberately, with a feeling almost of vindictiveness. She had tortured me so much, and now I wanted to torture her by alluding to what I had seen through the window, without, however, speaking of it directly or precisely. She looked at me fixedly, and then asked in a quiet voice: "What things have happened?"

"Plenty of things."

"But what?"

She was insistent: it seemed to me that she sincerely desired me to accuse her, to reprove her for her unfaithfulness. But I continued to be evasive. "They're things to do with the film . . . things between myself and Battista . . . there's no need to mention them."

"Why don't you want to mention them?"

"Because they wouldn't interest you."

"Possibly; but you won't have the courage to give up the job. You'll do it all right."

I could not quite make out whether this remark showed merely the usual contempt, or whether it contained an unspecified hope. I asked, cautiously: "Why do you think so?"

"Because I know you." She paused a moment and then sought to gloss over what she had said. "It's always like that with film-scripts, anyhow. . . . How many times have I known you declare that you wouldn't do this or that job, and then you've done it! The difficulties in scripts always get smoothed out in the end."

"That may be, but this time the difficulty is not in the script."

"Where is it, then?"

"In myself."

"What do you mean by that?"

"Battista kissing you," I should have liked to reply. But I restrained myself: our relationship had never been clarified right down to the bare truth, it had always been carried on by means of allusions. Before we reached the truth, there were so many other things that would have to be said. I bent forward slightly and declared with the greatest seriousness: "Emilia, you already know the reason; as I said at dinner, it's because I'm tired of working for other people and want at last to work for myself."

"And who's preventing you?"

"You," I said emphatically; then, seeing at once that she started to make a gesture of protest: "Not you directly . . . but your presence in my life. . . . Our relations are unfortunately—what they are: don't let's speak of them . . . but all the same you are my wife, and I, as I've told you before, I take on these jobs mainly because of you. If it wasn't for you, I wouldn't accept them. To put it briefly—you know it perfectly well and there's no need for me to repeat it—we have a great many debts, we still have several instalments to pay on the flat, even the car hasn't yet been completely paid for . . . that's why I do these film-scripts. Now, however, I want to make you a suggestion."

"What?"

I imagined myself to be very calm, very lucid, very reasonable; and yet at the same time a faint feeling of uneasiness warned me that there was a certain falsity—a worse than falsity, an absurdity—in my calm, in my lucidity, in my reasonableness. After all, I had seen her in Battista's arms: and that alone was what should have mattered. I went on, nevertheless: "The suggestion I want to make to you is as follows: that you yourself should decide whether I am to do this script or not. I promise you that if you tell me not to do it, I'll go and tell

Battista so, first thing tomorrow morning—and we'll leave Capri by the first boat."

She did not raise her head, but appeared to be meditating. "You're very cunning," she said at last.

"Why?"

"Because, if you regret it afterwards, you'll always be able to say it was my fault!"

"I shan't say anything of the kind . . . considering it's I myself who am asking you to decide."

She was now, obviously, reflecting upon the answer that she should give me. And I saw that her answer would provide an implicit corroboration of her feeling for me, whatever it might be. If she told me to do the script, it would mean that she now despised me to the point of considering that my work could continue, in spite of everything; if her answer, on the other hand, was in the negative, it would imply that she still retained some respect for me and did not want me to be dependent on her lover for my work. And so, after all, I came back again to the usual question: whether she despised me and why she despised me. At last she said: "These are things that one can't allow other people to decide for one!"

"But I'm asking you to decide."

"Then remember you insisted on my deciding," she said all at once, with sudden solemnity.

"Yes, I shall remember."

"Well, I think that, since you've taken on the job, you ought not to give it up. You yourself, in any case, have said that to me many times. Battista might be annoyed and never give you any more work. I think you should certainly do this job."

I thought of that kiss, and said, in an almost hostile manner: "Very well then. But don't tell me later on that you gave me this advice because you'd realized that, really and truly, I wanted to do the job . . . like that day when I had to sign the contract. Let it be quite clear that I *don't* want to do it."

"Ugh, you've exhausted me," she said carelessly, getting up from the bed and going over to the wardrobe. "That's my advice, anyhow . . . but of course you can do what you like . . ."

She had reassumed her tone of contempt, thus confirming my suppositions. And quite suddenly I experienced the same pain that I had felt that first time in Rome, when she had flung her aversion in my face. I could not help exclaiming: "Emilia, why all this? . . . Why are we so hostile to each other?"

She had opened the wardrobe and was looking at herself in

the mirror on the door. She said, in an absent-minded way: "Well, well, it's life, I suppose!"

Her words took my breath away, leaving me rigid and silent. Emilia had never spoken to me in that way, with such indifference and apathy and in so conventional a phrase. I knew I could have reversed the situation again by telling her I had seen her with Battista, as she herself knew perfectly well; that, in asking her to decide for me about the film-script, I had simply wished to put her to the test—which was true; and that, in short, the question between her and me was still the same as ever. But I had not the courage, or rather, the strength, to say these things: I felt utterly tired, and quite unable to start all over again. So, instead, I said, almost timidly: "And what will you do all the time we're in Capri, while I'm working on the film?"

"Nothing special. I'll go for walks . . . and swim, and sun-bathe . . . the same as everyone does."

"All alone?"

"Yes, all alone."

"Won't you be bored, alone?"

"I'm never bored. I've plenty of things to think about!"

"Do you sometimes think about me?"

"Yes, of course I do."

"And what do you think?" I too had risen, and had gone over to her and taken her hand.

"We've talked about that so many times already." She resisted my hold, yet without disengaging her hand.

"Do you still think about me in the same way?"

This time she pulled herself away from me and said brusquely: "Now listen, you'd better go to bed. I know there are certain things you don't like, and indeed it's quite natural. On the other hand, I can only repeat what I've said before. What's the point of talking about them again?"

"But I *do* want to talk about them again."

"Why? I should only have to say again all the things I've already said so many times. I haven't changed my mind just because I've come to Capri: on the contrary."

"What do you mean by 'on the contrary'?"

"When I said 'on the contrary,' " she explained rather confusedly, "I meant that I haven't changed—that's all."

"You still have the same . . . the same feeling about me, in fact? Isn't that so?"

Unexpectedly, and in an almost tearful voice, she protested. "Why do you torment me like this? Do you think it gives me any pleasure to say these things to you? I dislike them more than you do!"

I was moved by the pain which I seemed to detect in her

voice. Taking her hand again, I said: "Anyhow, *I* think a great deal of *you* . . . and I always shall," I added, as though to make her see that I forgave her for her unfaithfulness, which indeed was true, "whatever happens."

She said nothing. She looked away, and seemed to be waiting. But at the same time I felt her trying to disengage her hand from mine, with a sly but persistent and obstinately hostile movement. And so I abruptly bade her good night and left the room. It was with a sharp renewal of pain that I heard the key, almost at once, being turned in the lock.

## CHAPTER 17

Next morning I rose early, and, without taking steps to find out where Battista and Emilia were, left—or rather, made my escape from—the house. After the night's rest, the happenings of the previous day and, above all, my own behavior, appeared in an unpleasant light, as a series of absurdities which had been confronted in an equally absurd fashion; now I wanted to think calmly over what I ought to do, without compromising my own freedom of action by some hurried and irreparable decision. So I left the house, went back over the path I had traversed the evening before, and made my way to the hotel where Rheingold was staying. I inquired for him and was told he was in the garden. I followed; and at the far end of an avenue caught sight of the slender parapet of a summer-house bathed in the brilliant light of the calm, sun-filled sea and sky. A few chairs and a small table were arranged in front of the parapet, and as I appeared someone rose to his feet with a gesture of greeting. It was Rheingold, all dressed up like a naval captain, in a white cap with a gold anchor on it, a blue jacket with gold buttons, and white trousers. On the table was a tray with the remains of breakfast; also a portfolio and writing materials.

Rheingold seemed extremely cheerful. He immediately asked me: "I say, Molteni—what d'you think of a morning like this?"

"I think it's an exquisitely beautiful morning."

"What would you say, Molteni," he went on, taking me by the arm and turning with me towards the parapet, "what would you say to letting our work go hang, hiring a boat and rowing slowly all round the island? Don't you think it would be better, infinitely better?"

I answered him without conviction, thinking in my heart that an excursion of that kind in the company of Rheingold would lose a good deal of its charm. "Yes," I said, "in a sense it would be better."

"You've said it, Molteni!" he exclaimed triumphantly. "In a sense . . . But in what sense? Not in the sense in which *we* understand life. For us life means duty—doesn't it, Molteni? Duty, first and foremost . . . and so, Molteni, to work!" He left the parapet and sat down again at the table; then, leaning towards me and looking into my eyes, he said, with a certain solemnity: "Sit down here, opposite me . . . this morning we'll just talk. I have a great many things to say to you."

I sat down. Rheingold adjusted his cap over his eyes and resumed: "You will remember, Molteni, that I was explaining my interpretation of the *Odyssey* to you during our drive from Rome to Naples . . . but this explanation was interrupted by the appearance of Battista. Then, for the rest of the journey I was asleep, and so the explanation was postponed. You remember, Molteni?"

"Yes, certainly I do."

"You will also remember that I gave you the key to the *Odyssey*—in this way: Ulysses takes ten years to return home because really, in his subconscious mind, he does not *want* to return."

"Yes, indeed."

"I will now reveal to you, then, the reason why, according to my idea, Ulysses does not want to return home," said Rheingold. He paused a moment as if to mark the beginning of the revelation and then, wrinkling his eyebrows and gazing at me with characteristic dictatorial seriousness, he went on: "Ulysses, in his subconscious mind, does not wish to return to Ithaca because in reality his relations with Penelope are unsatisfactory. That's the reason, Molteni. And these relations had been unsatisfactory even before the departure of Ulysses to the war . . . in fact really Ulysses had gone off to the war because he was unhappy at home . . . and he was unhappy at home precisely because of his unsatisfactory relations with his wife!"

Rheingold was silent for a moment, but without ceasing to frown in that half-dictatorial, half-didactic manner; and I took advantage of the pause to turn my chair so that I did not have the sun in my eyes. Then he continued: "If his relations with Penelope had been good, Ulysses would not have gone off to the war. Ulysses was not a swaggerer or a warmonger. Ulysses was a prudent, wise, wary kind of man. If his relations with his wife had been good, Ulysses, simply in order to prove to Menelaus that he supported him, would perhaps just have sent an expeditionary force under the command of some man he trusted . . . instead of which he went off himself, taking advantage of the war to leave home and thus escape from his wife."

"Very logical."

"Very psychological, you mean, Molteni," corrected Rheingold, having noticed, perhaps, a touch of irony in my tone, "very psychological. And remember that everything depends upon psychology; without psychology there is no character, without character there is no story. Now, what is the psychology of Ulysses and Penelope? This is it: Penelope is the traditional feminine figure of archaic, feudal, aristocratic Greece; she is virtuous, noble, proud, religious, a good housewife, a good mother, a good wife. Ulysses, on the other hand, anticipates, in character, the men of a later Greece, the Greece of the sophists and the philosophers. Ulysses is a man without prejudices, and, if necessary, without scruples, subtle, reasonable, intelligent, irreligious, sceptical, sometimes even cynical."

"It seems to me," I protested, "that you're blackening the character of Ulysses. In reality, in the *Odyssey*—"

But he interrupted me impatiently. "We're not going to worry ourselves in the least about the *Odyssey*. Or rather, we're going to interpret, to develop the *Odyssey*. We're making a film, Molteni. The *Odyssey* is already written . . . the film is yet to be made!"

I was silent again, and he resumed: "The reason for the bad relations between Ulysses and Penelope must therefore be sought in the difference between their characters. Before the Trojan War, Ulysses had done something to displease Penelope. What? This is where the suitors come in. In the *Odyssey*, we know that they aspire to the hand of Penelope and in the meantime live extravagantly at Ulysses' expense, in his house. We've got to reverse the situation."

I gazed at him open-mouthed. "Don't you understand?" he asked. "Well, I'll explain it to you at once. As for the suitors, it may perhaps be convenient for us to reduce them to one person, Antinous, for instance. The suitors, then, have been in love with Penelope since before the Trojan War . . . and, being in love, they shower presents upon her, according to Greek custom. Penelope, being proud and dignified, in the antique manner, would like to refuse their presents, would, above all things, like her husband to turn the suitors out. But Ulysses, for some reason that we don't know but that we shall easily find, does not wish to offend the suitors. As a reasonable man, he does not attach much importance to their courting of his wife, since he knows she is faithful; nor does he attribute much significance to their gifts, which perhaps do not really displease him at all. Remember that all Greeks were greedy for presents, Molteni. Naturally Ulysses does not for a moment advise Penelope to yield to the suitors' desires, but merely not to offend them because he does not consider it worth while. Ulysses wants a quiet life, and he hates scandals. Penelope, who was expecting anything rather than this passive attitude on Ulysses' part, is disgusted, almost incredulous. She protests, she rebels . . . but Ulysses is not to be shaken, there seems to him no cause for indignation . . . so he again advises Penelope to accept the presents, to behave kindly—what does it cost her, after all? And Penelope, in the end, follows her husband's advice . . . but at the same time conceives a deep contempt for him . . . She feels she no longer loves him, and tells him so . . . Ulysses then realizes, too late, that, by his prudence, he has destroyed Penelope's love. Ulysses then tries to remedy matters, to win his wife back again, but he is unsuccessful. His life at Ithaca becomes a hell. Finally, in desperation, he seizes the opportunity of the Trojan War to leave home. After seven years the war ends and he puts to sea again to return to Ithaca, but he knows he is awaited at home by a woman who no longer loves him, who, in fact, despises him, and therefore, unconsciously he welcomes any excuse for putting off this unpleasant, this dreaded, return . . . and yet, sooner or later, return he must. But, on his return, the same thing happens to him as happened to the cavalier in the legend of the dragon—do you remember, Molteni? The princess demanded that the cavalier should kill the dragon if he wished to be worthy of her love, so the cavalier killed the dragon and then the princess loved him. In the same way Penelope, at Ulysses' return, after proving that she had been faithful to him, gave him to understand that her faithfulness did not mean love but merely virtue: she would recover her love for him on one, and only one, condition—that he would slay the suitors. Ulysses, as we know, was not in the least bloodthirsty or vindictive; he would perhaps have preferred to dismiss the suitors by gentler means, by persuasion. But this time he made up his mind, knowing, in fact, that upon killing of the suitors depends the esteem of Penelope and consequently her love also. So he kills them. Then, and only then, does Penelope cease to despise him, only then does she love him again. And so Ulysses and Penelope are again in love, after all those years of separation, and they celebrate their true marriage—their 'Bluthochzeit,' their blood-marriage. Well, do you understand, Molteni? Now to sum up! Point one: Penelope despises Ulysses for not having reacted like a man, like a husband, and like a king, to the indiscreet behavior of the suitors. Point two: her contempt causes the departure of Ulysses to the Trojan War. Point three: Ulysses, knowing that he is awaited at home by a woman who despises him, delays his return as long as he can. Point four: in order to regain Penelope's esteem and love, Ulysses slays the suitors. Do you understand, Molteni?"

I said I understood. All this was not very difficult to understand. But now, the feeling of aversion I had had for Rheingold's interpretation from the very beginning sprang up again, stronger than ever, and it made me perplexed and bemused. In the meantime Rheingold was explaining pedantically: "Do you know how I arrived at this key to the whole situation? By means of a simple consideration of the slaughter of the suitors, as it is told in the *Odyssey*. I observed that this slaughter, brutal, ferocious, ruthless as it was, was in absolute contrast to the character of Ulysses as hitherto presented to us: cunning, flexible, subtle, reasonable, cautious . . . and I said to myself: 'Ulysses might very well have politely shown the suitors the door . . . he had the possibility of doing this; being in his own house, and being king, all he had to do was to show himself as such. As he doesn't do it, it is a sign that he has some good reason for not doing it. What reason? Obviously Ulysses wishes to prove that not only is he cunning, flexible, subtle, reasonable, cautious, but also, if necessary, as violent as Ajax, as unreasonable as Achilles, as ruthless as Agamemnon. And to whom does he want to prove this? Obviously to Penelope—and so: eureka!' "

I said nothing. Rheingold's argument was very nicely worked out, and fitted in perfectly with his inclinaiton to transform the *Odyssey* into a psychoanalytical case-history. But, precisely because of that, it gave me a feeling of great repugnance, as though I were confronted with a kind of profanation. In Homer, everything was simple, pure, noble, ingenuous, even the astuteness of Ulysses, poetically contained as it was within the limits of an intellectual superiority. In Rheingold's interpretation, on the other hand, everything was debased to the level of a modern play, full of moralizings and psychologizings. In the meantime Rheingold, extremely pleased with his own exposition, was concluding: "As you see, Molteni, the film's already there, in all its details . . . all we have to do is to write it down."

I broke in, almost violently: "Look here, Rheingold, I don't care for this interpretation of yours at all!"

He opened his eyes very wide, more astonished, one would have said, by my boldness than by my disagreement. "You don't care for it, my dear Molteni? And why don't you care for it?"

I answered with an effort, but with an assurance that grew steadily as I spoke: "I don't care for it because your interpretation implies a complete falsification of the original character of Ulysses. In the *Odyssey* Ulysses is described, certainly, as a man who is subtle, reasonable, astute if you like, but always within the bounds of honor and dignity. He never ceases to be a hero, that is, a brave warrior, a king, an upright husband. Your interpretation—if you will allow me to say so, my dear Rheingold—runs the risk of making him into a man without dignity, without honor, without decency . . . apart from the fact that it's much too far removed from the *Odyssey*."

As I spoke, I saw Rheingold's half-moon smile grow narrower and narrower till it faded away altogether. Then he said, in a harsh tone and putting into his voice a Teutonic accent which he generally managed to conceal: "My dear Molteni, allow me to say that, as usual, you have understood nothing at all!"

"As usual?" I repeated, hurt.

"Yes, as usual," asserted Rheingold; "and I say so at once because—now listen to me carefully, Molteni."

"I'm listening, you can be sure of that."

"I do not wish to make Ulysses, as you seem to imagine, into a man without dignity, or decency, or honor. I merely want to make him into the man who appears in the *Odyssey*. . . . Who is Ulysses in the *Odyssey*, what does he represent? Ulysses in the *Odyssey* is, simply, civilized man, he represents civilization. Amongst all the other heroes who are, to be precise, *non*-civilized men, Ulysses is the only one who *is* civilized. And in what does Ulysses' civilized quality consist? It consists in not having prejudices, in always making use of reason, at all costs, even in questions—as you say—of decency, of dignity, of honor . . . in being intelligent, objective, I would almost say scientific. Naturally," Rheingold went on, "civilization has its inconveniences. It forgets, for instance, very easily, the importance that so-called questions of honor have for people who are not civilized. Penelope is not a civilized woman, she is a woman of tradition. She does not understand reason, she only understands instinct, blood, pride. Now listen carefully, Molteni, and try to understand me. Civilization, to all those who are not civilized, may appear—in fact often does appear—to be corruption, immorality, lack of principles, cynicism. That, for instance, was the complaint that Hitler, a man who was certainly not civilized, had to make against civilization, and he too talked a great deal about honor, but we know now what Hitler was and what honor meant to *him*. In the *Odyssey*—to put it briefly—Penelope represents barbarism and Ulysses civilization. Do you know, Molteni, that you, whom I thought to be civilized like Ulysses, argue just like the barbarian Penelope?"

These last words were uttered with a broad and brilliant smile: obviously Rheingold was extremely well pleased with his bright idea of comparing me to Penelope. But I felt this comparison, for some unknown reason, to be quite particularly distasteful. In fact I believe I turned pale with anger, and I said, in a voice that trembled: "If by civilization you mean that a husband should give a helping hand to the man who is courting his wife, well, my dear Rheingold, in that case I am, and I feel, a barbarian."

This time, however, much to my surprise, Rheingold did not lose his temper. "One moment," he said, raising his hand; "you're not being reasonable this morning, Molteni, just like Penelope. Now let's do this. You go off and have a swim now, and think it over. Then, tomorrow morning, come back here and tell me the result of your reflections—is that all right?"

Disconcerted, I answered: "Yes, that's all right . . . but I doubt if I shall change my mind."

"You go and think it over," repeated Rheingold, rising and holding out his hand.

I, too, rose to my feet. Rheingold added serenely: "I'm sure that tomorrow, when you've thought it over, you'll agree with me."

"I don't think so," I replied. And I walked away, down the path towards the hotel.

## CHAPTER 18

I had not been with Rheingold for more than an hour: the discussion about the *Odyssey* had lasted about that length of time. I had, therefore, the whole day in front of me to "think it over," as he had expressed it, to make up my mind, in fact, as to whether I accepted his interpretation or not. To tell the truth, as soon as I came out of the hotel, my first thought was by no means to meditate over Rheingold's ideas but rather to chase away even the very memory of them and enjoy the beauty of the day. On the other hand I felt that there was something in Rheingold's ideas that went right outside the limits of film production; something I could not define, but which had been revealed to me by my excessively strong reaction. And so, after all, I really should have to "think it over." I recalled that, when I left the villa that morning, I had caught a glimpse of a small, lonely cove down below the house, so I decided to go there: there I should be able to take the director's advice and "think it over"; or, if I preferred, not think about it at all but simply take a swim in the sea.

I took the same path as before, therefore, the path that runs around the island. It was still early, and I met scarcely anyone along the shady track—a few boys whose bare feet, in the surrounding silence, made a soft sound on the brick paving; a couple of little girls who walked along with arms round each other's shoulders, chatting in low voices; two or three old ladies taking their dogs for a walk.

At the lowest point of the path I turned off down the narrow lane that winds along the loneliest and most precipitous part of the island. I walked a little farther and found myself confronted by a fork: a smaller path branched off from the lane, leading to a summer-house perched at the edge of a precipice. I turned into this path and, when I reached the summer-house, looked down. The sea, three hundred feet below, trembled and sparkled in the sun, shifting and changing color according to the wind, blue in one place, almost violet in another, green farther away. From this remote, silent sea the perpendicular rocks of the island seemed to be flying to meet me, to be coming upward in swarms, like arrows, their bare points flashing in the sun. Then, all at once, a kind of suicidal exaltation came over me, and I felt I had no further desire to live; and I said to myself that if at that moment I suddenly launched myself into that luminous immensity I should perhaps die in a manner not altogether unworthy of the better part of myself. Yes, I should be killing myself to attain, in death, the purity which in life I had failed to achieve.

The temptation to suicide was genuine, and perhaps, for a moment, my life was really in danger. Then, almost instinctively, I thought of Emilia, wondering how she would receive the news of my death, and suddenly I said to myself: "You wouldn't be killing yourself because you're tired of life; you're not tired of life. You would be killing yourself for Emilia!" I was disconcerted by this idea, which, almost maliciously, it seemed, robbed my exaltation of all quality of disinterestedness. Then I went on to ask myself: "Because of Emilia or for the sake of Emilia? The distinction is important"; and immediately I answered my own question: "For the sake of Emilia. In order to regain her esteem, even in a posthumous way. In order to leave her with the remorse of having unjustly despised you."

No sooner had I formulated this thought, then—as in a children's puzzle, when a number of disordered pieces are put together to form a single design—the picture of my present situation was, in part, completed by this new idea: "You reacted to Rheingold's theories in that violent manner because in reality it seemed to you that, when he was explaining the relations between Ulysses and Penelope, he was alluding, though he did not know it, to the relations between you and Emilia. When Rheingold spoke of Penelope's contempt for Ulysses, you thought of Emilia's contempt for you. The truth, in short, annoyed you, and it was against the truth that you protested."

The picture was still not complete; but now a few more considerations put the last, final touches to it. "You thought of killing yourself because you're not clear in your own mind. In reality, if you want to regain Emilia's esteem, it's not in the least necessary for you to kill yourself, much less than that will suffice. Rheingold indicated what you ought to do. Ulysses, in order to regain Penelope's love, killed the suitors. In theory, you ought to kill Battista, but we live in a less violent and uncompromising world than that of the *Odyssey*. All you need to do is to throw up the script, break off all relations with Rheingold, and leave again for Rome tomorrow morning. Emilia advised you not to throw up the job because, in reality, she *wants* to despise you and wants you, by your behavior, to confirm her in her contempt. You mustn't take any notice of her advice; you must act, instead, just as—according to Rheingold—Ulysses acted."

This was, in truth, the whole matter: I had examined my situation from beginning to end, ruthlessly and with complete sincerity. It seemed to me clear that there was now no further need to "think it over," as Rheingold had advised; I could go straight back to him and announce what was now my immovable decision. But the next moment I said to myself that, just because there was now no necessity to think it over," I must not do things in a hurry, and so give a wrong impression of rashness and obstinacy. I would go during the afternoon, quite calmly, to Rheingold and tell him what I had decided. When I returned home I would, in the same calm manner, ask Emilia to pack her bags. As for Battista, I decided to say nothing to him; in the morning, when we left, I would leave him a short note, attributing my decision to the fact that my ideas and those of Rheingold were incompatible—which was, indeed, true. Battista was a shrewd man: he would understand, and I should not see him again.

With these thoughts in my mind, and almost without realizing where I was going, I turned into the lane, went along it until I was below the villa, and then started running down a steep, crumbling path towards the little lonely cove of which I had had a glimpse when I came out that morning. I was out of breath when I reached it, and, to recover myself, I stood still for a moment on a rock, looking round. The brief stretch

of stony beach was all surrounded by great irregular masses
of rock which looked as if they had that very moment come
rolling down from the heights above; two rocky promontories
closed it in, rising sheer from the green, transparent water
which was penetrated by rays of sunlight that showed up the
white, pebbly bottom. Then I noticed a black rock, all
crannied and corroded and half submerged in sand and
water, and thought I would go and lie down behind it to be
sheltered from the sun which was already very strong. But
no sooner had I walked round it than I caught sight of Emilia
lying, quite naked, on the beach.

To tell the truth, I did not at once recognize her, for her
face was hidden by a big straw hat; in fact my first inpulse
was to retreat, as I thought I had come upon some unknown
sun-bather. Then my eye fell on the arm which was stretched
out on the pebbles, and, following the arm down to the hand,
I recognized, on the forefinger, a ring in the shape of two
little hardstone acorns set in golden husks which I had given
Emilia some time before as a birthday present.

I was right behind Emilia and saw her foreshortened. She
was naked, as I said, and her clothes were lying beside her
on the sand, a little pile of colored garments; it seemed impossible that they could have covered that large body. The
thing that struck me most, indeed, about Emilia's nudity, from
the very first glance, was not this or that detail, but, in general,
the size and powerfulness of her body. I knew, of course, that
Emilia was no larger than a great many other women; but at
that moment her nudity seemed to me immense, as though the
sea and sky had lent her some of their vastness. As she was
lying flat on her back, her breasts were only vaguely defined
by the slight swelling of the stretched-out muscle, but to my
eyes they seemed very large, both in outline and in volume
and in the rosy circles of the nipples; so did also her hips,
spread out over the sand in strong, comfortable amplitude;
so also her belly, that seemed to gather all the light of the sun
into its circle of flesh; and so her legs, which, lower than the
rest of her body on account of the slope, looked as though
they were being pulled downwards by their weight and by
length. All of a sudden I wondered what could be the source
of this feeling in me, of this sense of largeness and power,
so profound and so disturbing, and then I realized that it
arose from the desire that had been re-awoken in me at this
unexpected moment. It was a desire which, in its immediacy
and urgency, was not so much physical as spiritual, a desire to
be united with her, but not with her body, not inside her
body; rather, through the medium of her body. I was hungry
for her; yet the satisfaction of this hunger did not depend

on me but only on her, on an act of consent on her part that would reach out to meet my hunger. And I felt that she refused me this consent, although naked as she was, she appeared by an illusion of the eye to be offering herself to me.

But I could not remain in indefinite contemplation of this forbidden nakedness. I at last took a step forward and said clearly, amid the surrounding silence: "Emilia!"

She made a rapid, double movement. She threw off her hat, stretched out her hand and snatched a chemise from the pile of clothes, as if to cover herself with it; and at the same time sat up and twisted herself around to look behind her. But when I added: "It's me, Riccardo," she at last saw me, and then she dropped the chemise on the shingle. Meanwhile she remained twisted around in order to see me better. She was afraid first of all, I supposed, that I might be a stranger; but then, seeing that it was I, she judged it no longer necessary to cover herself—as though she were in the presence of someone who actually did not exist. I record this thought, fundamentally absurd though it was, so as to give an exact idea of my state of mind at that moment. It never entered my head that she did not cover herself merely because I was not a stranger but her husband. I was convinced that I no longer existed for her, at any rate from the sexual point of view, and in that ambiguous gesture of hers I naturally recognized a confirmation of my own non-existence. I said in a low voice: "I've been standing here looking at you for at least five minutes . . . do you know, I felt I was seeing you for the first time?"

She said nothing; all she did was to turn a little farther around so as to see me better, at the same time adjusting her dark glasses on her nose with a gesture of indifferent curiosity. I went on: "Do you mind my staying here, or would you rather I went away?"

I saw her considering me; then, with a calm movement, she stretched herself out in the sun again, saying: "Stay if you like, as far as I'm concerned . . . As long as you don't take the sun off me!"

So she really did consider me to be non-existent—nothing but an opaque body that might put itself between the sun and her own, naked body, which, according to my desire, ought on the other hand to have felt itself in relationship with mine and have revealed this relationship in some way, whether by a show of modesty or of alarm. Her indifference disconcerted me in a most painful way; I felt my mouth grow suddenly dry, as though with fear; and I was aware that my face was assuming, against my will, an expression of uneasiness, of bewilderment, of false, distressing assurance. "It's very pleasant here, I said, "I shall take a sunbath too . . ." And, in order to put a good face on it, I sat down at a little distance from her, leaning my back against one of the great lumps of rock.

There followed a very long silence. Endless waves of golden light, gently burning and dazzling, enveloped me, and I could not help half-closing my eyes, with a deep sense of well-being and peace. But I could not pretend to myself that I was there simply for the sun; I felt I could never enjoy it fully unless Emilia loved me. Almost as if I were thinking aloud, I said: "This place seems purposely made for people who love each other."

"Yes, doesn't it!" she echoed, without stirring, from under the straw hat which hid her face.

"Not for us, who no longer love each other!"

This time she said nothing. And I remained with my eyes fixed upon her, feeling, at the sight of her, a return of all the desire that had troubled me shortly before, when I had emerged from between the rocks and seen her for the first time.

Intense feelings have in them the virtue of making us pass from feeling to action in a wholly spontaneous fashion, without the concurrence of the will, almost unconsciously. Without my knowing how it had happened, I found myself no longer sitting apart by myself, with my back against a rock, but kneeling beside Emilia, bending over her with my face held close to hers, while she lay motionless and asleep. I don't know how, but I had already removed the hat that hid her face, and, as I prepared to kiss her, I was looking at her mouth as one sometimes looks at a fruit before putting one's teeth into it. It was a large, very full mouth, and the redness of the lipstick upon it looked parched and cracked as though it had been dried up, not by the sun, but by some interior heat. I said to myself that that mouth had not kissed me for a very long time, and that the savor of the kiss, if it were returned by her as she lay thus between waking and sleeping, would be as intoxicating as that of some old, potent liquor. I think I must have gazed at her mouth for at least a minute; then, gradually, I lowered my lips to hers. But I did not immediately kiss her: I paused for a moment with my lips very close to hers. I felt the light, quiet breath that came from her nostrils; and also, it seemed to me, the warmth of her burning lips. I knew that behind those lips, inside her mouth—like frozen snow preserved in a fold of sun-scorched earth—lay the coolness of her saliva, as surprising, as refreshing as such snow would be. While I was relishing this foretaste, my lips came truly into contact with Emilia's. The touch did not appear to awaken her, nor to surprise her. I pressed my lips against hers, first softly, then more and more strongly; then, seeing that she remained perfectly still, I ventured upon a profounder kiss. This time I felt her mouth slowly opening, as I had hoped—like a shellfish whose valves open at the pulsating movement of some living creature wet with cool sea-water. Slowly, slowly it opened, the lips drawing back over the gums; and at the same time I felt an arm encircling my neck . . .

With a violent jolt, I started and awoke from what must evidently have been a kind of trance induced by the silence and the heat of the sun. In front of me, Emilia was lying on the beach as before; and her face was still hidden by the straw hat. I realized that I had dreamed the kiss, or rather, had actually experienced it in that state of delirious hankering which constantly replaces dreary reality with some more attractive illusion. I had kissed her and she had returned my kiss; but the one who had kissed and the one who had returned the kiss were merely a couple of phantoms evoked by desire and entirely dissociated from our two persons as we lay motionless and apart. I looked at Emilia and wondered suddenly: "Suppose I now tried really to kiss her?" And I answered myself: "No, you won't try . . . you're paralyzed by timidity and by the consciousness of her contempt for you." All at once I said, in a loud voice: "Emilia!"

"What is it?"

"I fell asleep and dreamed I was kissing you."

She said nothing. Frightened by her silence, I was anxious to change the subject, so I went on, at random: "Where's Battista?"

She answered in a quiet voice, from underneath the hat: "I don't know where he is. . . . By the way, he won't be at lunch with us today . . . he's lunching with Rheingold at the beach."

Before I knew what I was saying, I blurted out: "Emilia, I saw you yesterday evening, when Battista kissed you in the living-room!"

"I knew you'd seen me. I saw you too." Her voice was quite normal, though slightly muffled by the brim of the hat.

I was disconcerted by the manner in which she received my disclosure; and also, to some extent, by the way in which I myself had made it. The truth of the matter, I thought, was that the stupefying sunshine and the silence of the sea reduced and neutralized our quarrel in a general feeling of vanity and indifference. However, with a great effort, I went on: "Emilia, you and I must have a talk."

"Not now . . . I want to lie in the sun and be quiet."

"This afternoon, then."

"All right, this afternoon."

I rose to my feet and, without looking back, walked off towards the path that led to the villa.

## CHAPTER 19

At lunch we scarcely spoke. Silence seemed to penetrate inside the villa together with the strong light of noon; the sky and sea that filled the big windows dazzled us and gave us a feeling of remoteness, as though all this blueness were a substantial thing, like a depth of water, and we two were sitting at the bottom of the sea, separated by luminous, fluctuating liquid and unable to speak. Moreover I made it a point of duty not to embark upon the explanation with Emilia until the afternoon, as I myself had proposed. It might be imagined that two people who find themselves sitting face to face with an important argument hanging between them do not think of anything else. But this was certainly not the case with us: I was not thinking at all of Battista's kiss or of our relationship; and I was sure that Emilia was not thinking of them either. There was a sort of continuation of the suspense, of the torpor, of the indifference that had prompted me on the beach that morning to put off all explanations till later.

After lunch, Emilia rose and said she was going to rest, and went out. Left alone, I sat still for a while, looking through the windows at the clear, luminous line of the horizon, where the harder blue of the sea joined the deep blue of the sky. A ship, small and black, was advancing along this line, like a fly on a taut thread, and I followed it with my eyes, thinking, for some reason, of all the things that were going on at that moment on board that ship—sailors polishing brasses or washing the decks; the cook washing dishes in his galley; the officers still, perhaps, sitting at table; and, down in the engine-room, half-naked stokers shovelling coal into the furnaces. It was a small ship, and to me, as I looked at it, it was nothing but a black speck; but from close by it was a large object filled with human beings and human destinies. And, conversely, I thought of the people over there looking from their ship at the coast of Capri; their eyes would perhaps be brought to an unwilling halt by an isolated white spot on the coast, and they would not even suspect that that white spot was the villa and that I was inside it and with me was Emilia and we two did not love each other and Emilia despised me and I did not know how to regain her esteem and her love . . .

I became conscious that I was dozing off, and, with an

abrupt burst of energy, decided to put into effect the first part of my plan: to go and inform Rheingold that I had "thought it over" and that, as a result, I would not be collaborating in the script of the film. This decision had the effect upon me of a bucketful of fresh water. Wide awake now, I jumped to my feet and went out of the house.

Half an hour later, having walked rapidly along the path that ran round the island, I entered the hall of the hotel. I sent in my name and went and sat down in an armchair. I felt that my mind was exceedingly lucid, even though with a feverish and somewhat agitated lucidity. But, judging from my growing sense of relief—my joy, almost—at the thought of what I was about to do, I knew that I had at last set out upon the right road. After a few minutes Rheingold entered the hall and came over to me with a clouded, surprised expression in which wonder at my having called at that hour appeared to be mingled with the suspicion that he was about to hear some unpleasant news. For politeness' sake, I asked him: "Perhaps you were asleep, Rheingold? . . . and I've woken you up?"

"No, no," he assured me, "I wasn't asleep, I never sleep in the afternoon. . . . But come this way, Molteni, let's go into the bar."

I followed him into the bar, which at that hour was deserted. Rheingold, as though anxious to delay the discussion he anticipated, asked me if I would like something to drink—coffee, a liqueur. He made this suggestion with an air of gloom and reserve, like a miser who is forced to provide expensive hospitality against his will. But I knew that the reason was quite a different one: he would have preferred me not to come at all. Anyhow, I refused; and, after a few polite remarks, I embarked without more ado on the main subject. "You may perhaps be surprised," I said, "that I've come back so soon. I had a whole day to consider it. But there seemed no point in waiting till tomorrow. I've thought about it long enough, and I came to tell you the result of my reflections."

"And what is that result?"

"That I cannot collaborate in this film-script . . . in fact, that I am throwing up the job."

Rheingold did not receive this declaration with any surprise: he was evidently expecting it. But he appeared to be thrown into a kind of agitation. He said at once, in a changed voice: "Molteni, you and I must speak plainly."

"It seems to me I have already spoken extremely plainly: I am not going to do the script of the *Odyssey*."

"And why? Please tell me."

"Because I do not agree with your interpretation of the subject."

"In that case," he retorted, quickly and unexpectedly, "you agree with Battista!"

I do not know why I, in my turn, was irritated by this unforeseen accusation. It had not occurred to me that not to be in agreement with Rheingold meant to be in agreement with Battista! I said angrily: "What's Battista got to do with it? I don't agree with Battista either. But I tell you frankly, Rheingold, if I had to choose between the two, I should prefer Battista every time. I'm sorry, Rheingold: as far as I'm concerned, either one does the *Odyssey* of Homer or else one doesn't do it at all."

"A masquerade in technicolor with naked women, King Kong, stomach dances, brassières, cardboard monsters, model sets!"

"I didn't say that: I said the *Odyssey* of Homer!"

"But the *Odyssey* of Homer is *mine*," he said with profound conviction, bending forwards, "it's *mine*, Molteni!"

For some unexplained reason I was conscious, all at once, of a desire to offend Rheingold: his false, ceremonious smile, his real, dictatorial hardness, his psychoanalytical obtuseness, all became at that moment intolerable to me. I said furiously: "No, Homer's *Odyssey* is not yours, Rheingold. And I'll say more, since you force me to it: I find Homer's *Odyssey* altogether enchanting and yours altogether repulsive!"

"Molteni!" This time Rheingold appeared really indignant.

"Yes, to me it's repulsive," I went on, becoming heated now, "this desire of yours to reduce, to debase the Homeric hero just because we're incapable of making him as Homer created him, this operation of systematic degradation is repulsive to me, and I'm not going to take part in it at any price."

"Molteni . . . one moment, Molteni!"

"Have you read James Joyce's *Ulysses?*" I interrupted him angrily; "do you know who Joyce is?"

"I've read everything that concerns the *Odyssey*," replied Rheingold in a deeply offended tone, "but you—"

"Well," I continued passionately, "Joyce also interpreted the *Odyssey* in the modern manner . . . and he went much farther than you do, my dear Rheingold, in the job of modernization—that is, of debasement, of degradation, of profanation. He made Ulysses a cuckold, an onanist, an idler, a capricious, incompetent creature . . . and Penelope a retired whore. Aeolus became a newspaper editor, the descent into the infernal regions the funeral of a boon-companion, Circe a visit to a brothel, and the return to Ithaca the return home at dead of night through the streets of Dublin, with a stop or two on the way to piss in a dark corner. But at least Joyce had the discernment not to bring in the Mediterranean, the sea, the sun, the sky, the unexplored lands of antiquity. He placed the whole story in the muddy streets of a northern city, in taverns and brothels, in bedrooms and lavatories. No sunshine, no sea, no sky . . . everything modern, in other words debased, degraded, reduced to our own miserable stature. But you—you lack Joyce's discretion . . . and therefore I, I repeat, between you and Battista, I prefer Battista, in spite of all his papier mâché. Yes, I prefer Battista. You wanted to know why I don't wish to do this script . . . now you do know!"

I fell back in my armchair, damp with sweat. Rheingold was now looking at me with a hard, serious expression and a deep frown. "You do, in fact, agree with Battista," he said.

"No, I do *not* agree with Battista. I *dis*agree with him."

"On the contrary," said Rheingold suddenly, raising his voice. "You're *not* in disagreement with me, and you *are* in agreement with Battista."

All at once I felt the blood leave my cheeks and knew that I had gone deathly pale. "What do you mean?" I asked in an uneven voice.

Rheingold leant forward and hissed (that is the only word for it) just like a snake when it sees itself threatened: "I mean what I said. Battista came to lunch with me today, and he did not conceal his ideas from me, nor the fact that you share them. You are *not* in disagreement with me, Molteni, and you *are* in agreement with Battista, whatever Battista may desire. To you, art does not matter; all you want is to be paid. That's the truth of it, Molteni . . . all you want is to be paid, at any cost!"

"Rheingold!" I cried suddenly in a loud voice.

"Oh, yes, I understand, my dear sir," he insisted, "and I repeat it to your face: at any cost!"

We were face to face now, breathless, I as white as paper and he scarlet. "Rheingold!" I repeated, still in the same loud, clear voice; but I became aware that it was not so much scorn that was now expressed in my voice as a kind of obscure pain, and that that cry: "Rheingold!" contained a prayer rather than the anger of an offended person who is on the point of passing from verbal to physical violence. Yet at the same time I was conscious of the fact that I was going to hit him. I had no time. Rheingold—strangely, for I thought him an obtuse kind of man—appeared to discern the pain in my voice and, all of a sudden, seemed to check and control himself. He drew back a little and said, in a low, deliberately humble tone: "Excuse me, Molteni. I said things I didn't mean."

I made an agitated gesture, as much as to say "I excuse you," and felt at the same time that my eyes were filling with tears. After a moment's embarrassment Rheingold resumed: "All right, it's understood, then. You won't take part in the script. Have you told Battista yet?"

"No."

"Are you intending to tell him?"

"Please tell him yourself. I don't think I shall see Battista again." I was silent a moment, and then I added: "And tell him also to start looking out for another script-writer. Let it be quite clear, Rheingold."

"What?" he asked in astonishment.

"That I shall not do any script of the *Odyssey* either according to your ideas, or according to Battista's ideas . . . either with you, or with any other director. Do you understand, Rheingold?"

He understood at last, and a light of comprehension came into his eyes. Nevertheless he asked cautiously: "To put it shortly, is it that you don't want to do *my* script, or that you don't want to do this script in any way at all?"

After a moment's reflection, I said: "I've already told you: I don't want to do *your* script. However I quite realize, on the other hand, that if I account for my refusal in that way, I should do you harm in the eyes of Battista. Let's put it like this, then: for you, it's *your* script I don't want to do . . . but, for Battista, let it be understood that I don't want to do the script *whatever* interpretation may be given to the subject. Tell Battista, then, that I don't feel like it, that I'm tired, that my nerves are worn out . . . is that all right?"

Rheingold appeared at once to be much relieved by my suggestion. He insisted, nevertheless: "And will Battista believe it?"

"He'll believe it, don't worry . . . . you'll see, he'll believe it."

A long silence ensued. We both felt embarrassed now; our recent quarrel still hung in the air and neither of us could quite manage to forget it. At last Rheingold said: "Yet, I'm very sorry you're not going to collaborate in this work, Molteni. Perhaps we might have come to an agreement."

"I don't think so."

"Perhaps the differences were not so great, after all."

Feeling perfectly calm now, I said firmly: "No, Rheingold, they were very great indeed. It may be that you're right to see the *Odyssey* in that way, but I'm convinced that, even today, the *Odyssey* could be made as Homer wrote it."

"That's an aspiration on your part, Molteni. You aspire after a world like that of Homer . . . you would like it to be so . . . but unfortunately it isn't!"

I said conciliatingly: "Let's leave it at that, then: I aspire after that sort of world. You, on the other hand, do not!"

"Oh yes, I do, Molteni . . . who doesn't? But when it's a question of making a film, aspirations are not enough."

There was a further silence. I looked at Rheingold and realized that, even though he understood my reasons, he was still not altogether convinced. Suddenly I asked him: "No doubt you know the Ulysses canto in Dante, Rheingold?"

"Yes," he answered, a little surprised at my question, "I know it, but I don't remember it exactly."

"Do you mind if I recite it to you? I know it by heart."

"Please do, if you care to."

I did not know precisely why I wanted to recite this passage from Dante—perhaps, I thought afterwards, because it seemed to me the best way of repeating certain things to Rheingold without running the risk of offending him afresh. While the director was settling himself in his armchair, and his face assuming a submissive expression, I added: "In this canto Dante makes Ulysses relate his own end and that of his companions."

"Yes, I know, Molteni, I know; recite it then."

I concentrated my thoughts for a moment, looking down on the floor, and then began: *"The greater horn of the ancient flame began to shake itself, murmuring, just like a flame that struggles with the wind"*—continuing steadily in a normal voice and, as far as I could, without emphasis. Rheingold, after considering me for a moment, with a frown, from beneath the peak of his cloth cap, turned his eyes in the direction of the sea and sat without moving. I went on with my recitation, speaking slowly and clearly. But at the lines: *" 'O brothers!' I said, 'who through a hundred thousand dangers have reached the West, deny not, to this brief vigil of your sense that remains, experience of the unpeopled world behind the Sun' "*—I felt that my voice, in spite of myself, was trembling with sudden emotion. I considered how there was contained, in those few lines, not merely the idea I had formed of the figure of Ulysses, but also of myself and of my life as it ought to have been and, alas, was not; and I realized that my emotion arose from the clarity and beauty of this idea in comparison with my own actual powerlessness. However I more or less succeeded in controlling the tremor in my voice and went on, without stumbling, to the very last lines: *"Three times it made her whirl round with all the waters; at the fourth, made the poop*

*rise up and prow go down, as pleased Another, till the sea
was closed above us."* The moment I had finished I jumped
to my feet. Rheingold also rose from his armchair.

"Allow me, Molteni," he said at once, hastily, "allow me
to ask you . . . Why did you recite this fragment of Dante
to me? . . . For what purpose? It's very beautiful, of course
—but why?"

"This, Rheingold," I said, "this is the Ulysses I should
have liked to create . . . this is how I see Ulysses . . .
Before leaving you I wanted to confirm it unmistakably . . .
I felt I could do this better by reciting the passage from
Dante than in my own words."

"Better, of course . . . but Dante is Dante: a man of the
Middle Ages . . . You, Molteni, are a modern man."

I did not answer this time, but put out my hand. He
understood, and added: "All the same, Molteni, I shall be
very sorry to do without your collaboration . . . I was already getting accustomed to you."

"Some other time, perhaps," I answered. "I should have
liked to work with you, too, Rheingold."

"But why, then? Why, Molteni . . . ?"

"Fate," I said with a smile, shaking his hand. And I
walked away. He remained standing beside the counter, in
the bar, his arms outstretched as if to repeat: "Why?"

I hurried out of the hotel.

## CHAPTER 20

I returned home as hurriedly as I had come; and
with a feeling of impatience and of pugnacious elation
which prevented me from reflecting calmly over what had
happened. In fact, as I ran along the narrow ribbon of cement under the burning sun, I did not think of anything. The
deadlock in an unbearable situation had already lasted too
long, and now I knew I had broken it; I was aware, too, that in
a short time I should at last know why it was that Emilia
had ceased to love me; but beyond the establishment of
these facts I could not go. Reflection belongs either to the
moment after, or to the moment before, the taking of action.
During the time of action we are guided by reflections already
past and forgotten, which have been transformed in our
minds into passions. I was acting; therefore I was not thinking. I knew that I should think later, when action was over.

When I reached the villa, I ran up the stairs leading to
the terrace and went into the living-room. It was empty, but
a magazine lying open in an armchair, some red-stained
cigarette-stumps in the ash-tray, and the sound of subdued

dance-music coming from the radio indicated to me that Emilia had been there until a few moments before. And then, owing perhaps to the softened, pleasing brilliance of the afternoon light, perhaps to the discreet music, I felt my anger subsiding, though the causes which had inspired it remained firm and clear. I was struck, particularly, by the comfortable, serene, familiar, inhabited look of the room. It looked as if we had been living in the villa for months, and as if Emilia had become accustomed by now to regarding it as her settled abode. The radio, the magazine, the cigarette-stumps, all reminded me, for some reason, of her old love of home, of the pathetic yearning, wholly instinctive and feminine, that she had had for a hearth, a stable resting-place of her own. I saw that, notwithstanding all that had happened, she was preparing for a long stay, and that she was, in reality, pleased to be at Capri, in Battista's house. And now, instead, I was coming to tell her that we had to go away again.

Thoughtfully I went to the door of Emilia's room and opened it. She was not there; but here too I noticed signs of her domestic instincts—the dressing-gown carefully laid out on the armchair, at the foot of the bed, the slippers placed neatly beside it; the numerous small bottles and pots and other accessories of beauty tidily arranged on the dressing-table, in front of the mirror; on the bedside table a single book, an English grammar, the study of which she had embarked upon some time before, and with it an exercise-book, a pencil, and a small bottle; and no trace at all of the many suitcases she had brought from Rome. Almost by instinct I opened the wardrobe: Emilia's dresses—not very many of them—were hanging in a row on coat-hangers; on a shelf were arranged handkerchiefs large and small, belts, ribbons, a few pairs of shoes. Yes, I thought, it did not really matter to Emilia whether she loved me or loved Battista: what mattered more than anything was to have a house of her own, to be able to count upon a long, quiet stay, without worries of any kind.

I left the room and went along a short passage towards the kitchen, which was in a little annex at the back of the house. When I reached the threshold, I heard the voice of Emilia in conversation with the cook. I stopped, automatically, behind the open door and listened for a moment.

Emilia was giving the cook instructions for our dinner that evening, "Signor Molteni," she was saying, "likes plain cooking, without a lot of gravies and sauces—just boiled or roast, in fact. It'll be better for you, you'll have less to do, Agnesina."

"Well, Signora, there's always plenty to do. Even plain cooking isn't as plain as all that. What shall we have this evening, then?"

There was a short pause. Evidently Emilia was reflecting. Then she asked: "Would there still be any fish at this time of day?"

"Yes, if I go to the fishmonger who serves the hotels."

"Well then, buy a nice big fish—two or three pounds, or even more . . . But it must be a good quality fish, without too many bones . . . a *dentice* or, better still, a *spigola* . . . in fact, the best you can get. And I think you'd better bake it . . . or boil it. You know how to make *mayonnaise* sauce, Agnesina?"

"Yes, I do."

"All right . . . then if you boil it, make some *mayonnaise* . . . and then a salad, or some kind of cooked vegetables—carrots or *aubergines* or french beans . . . whatever you can find. And fruit, plenty of fruit. Put the fruit on the ice as soon as you get back from your shopping, so that it will be very cool when it's served."

"And what shall we do about a first course?"

"Oh yes, there's the first course too! Let's have something quite simple for this evening. Buy some ham—but be sure you get the best quality . . . and let's have some figs with it. There *are* figs to be got?"

"Yes, you can get figs."

I don't know why, but while I was listening to this domestic conversation, so quiet, so easily foreseeable, I suddenly remembered the last words I had exchanged with Rheingold. He had said that I aspired after a world like that of the *Odyssey;* and I had agreed with him; and then he had retorted that this aspiration of mine could never be satisfied, that the modern world was not the world of the *Odyssey*. And now I thought: "Yet here is a situation that might have occurred just as well thousands of years ago, in the days of Homer . . . the mistress talking to her serving-maid, giving her instructions for the evening meal." This idea recalled to my mind the lovely afternoon light, radiant but soft, which filled the living-room, and, as though by enchantment, it seemed to me that Battista's villa was the house in Ithaca, and that Emilia was Penelope, in the act of speaking to her servant. Yes, I was right; everything was, or might have been, as it was then; and yet everything was so bitterly different. With an effort, I put my head in at the door and said: "Emilia."

She scarcely turned, asking: "What is it?"

"You know . . . I want to talk to you."

"Go wait in the living-room . . . I'm not finished with Agnesina yet . . . I'll be there in a minute."

I went back into the living-room, sat down in an armchair and waited. I now had a feeling of remorse in anticipation of what I was going to do: Emilia, to all appearances, was expecting to stay a long time at the villa; and I, on the other hand, was about to announce our departure. I remembered, at this point, how she, not so many days before, had made up her mind to leave me; and, comparing her almost desperate attitude that day with her present serene bearing, I thought that after all she must have decided to live with me, even if she did despise me. In other words, she was still, at that time, rebelling against an intolerable situation, whereas now she accepted it. And yet this acceptance was far more offensive to me than any kind of rebellion; it indicated, in her, a decline, a collapse, as though now she despised not only me but herself as well. This idea sufficed to banish the slight feeling of remorse from my mind. Yes indeed, both for my sake and for hers, we had to leave, and I had to announce our departure to her.

I waited a little longer; then Emilia came in, went and turned off the radio and sat down. "You said you wanted to talk to me."

"Have you unpacked?" I asked in return.

"Yes, why?"

"I'm sorry," I said, "but you'll have to pack again. We're going back to Rome tomorrow morning."

She remained quite motionless for a moment, hesitating, as though she had not understood. Then, in a harsh voice, she asked: "What's happened now?"

"What's happened," I replied, rising from my armchair and going over to shut the door that led into the passage, "is that I've decided not to do the script. I'm throwing up the whole thing. And so we're going back to Rome."

She seemed to be really exasperated by this piece of news. Frowning, she inquired: "And why have you decided to refuse this job?"

I answered, drily: "I'm surprised that you should ask. It seems to me that, after what I saw through the window yesterday evening, I could hardly do otherwise."

She at once objected, coldly: "Yesterday evening you were of a different opinion . . . and you'd already seen."

"Yesterday evening I allowed myself to be persuaded by your arguments . . . but afterwards I saw that I ought not to take them into account. I don't know for what reason you advise me to do the script, nor do I wish to know. I only know that it's better for me, and for you too, that I shouldn't do it!"

"Does Battista know?" she asked unexpectedly.

"No, he doesn't," I replied, "but Rheingold does. I've just told him."

"You've made a very great mistake."

"Why?"

"Because," she said, in an uncertain, discontented tone of voice, "we need this money to pay the instalments on the flat. Besides, you yourself have said, over and over again, that to break a contract means cutting yourself off from other jobs. You've made a bad mistake: you shouldn't have done it."

I, in turn, became irritated. "But don't you understand," I cried, "don't you understand that my situation had become intolerable . . . that I cannot go on taking money from the man . . . from the man who is in the process of seducing my wife?"

She said nothing. I went on: "I am refusing the job because it would not be decent for me to accept it, in the present circumstances . . . but I am refusing it also for your sake, on account of you, in order that you may change your opinion about me. You—I don't know why—at present consider me a man capable of accepting a job under such conditions. Well, you're wrong. I'm not that sort of man!"

I saw a hostile, malicious light come into her eyes. "If you're doing it for your own sake, well, I don't know . . . but if you're doing it because of me, you still have time to change your mind. You would be doing a useless thing, I assure you. It would serve no purpose except to damage yourself—that would be all."

"What do you mean?"

"I mean just what I say—that it would serve no purpose."

I felt cold about the temples and knew I was turning pale. "And so—?"

"You tell me first what effect this sacrifice of yours is supposed to have on me."

I realized that the moment of final explanation had arrived. It was she herself who was offering it to me. And all of a sudden I had a feeling of fear. I began, nevertheless: "You said, some time ago, that . . . that you despised me . . . that was what you said. I don't know why you despise me. I only know that people get themselves despised when they do despicable things. Accepting this job, at the present moment, would in fact be a despicable thing . . . and so my decision will prove to you, more than anything, that I am not what you believe me to be—that's all."

She answered promptly in a tone of triumph, pleased, one would have thought, at having at last made me fall into a trap: "On the contrary, your decision won't prove anything to me . . . and that's why I advise you to go back on it."

"What do you mean, it won't prove anything?" I had sat down again and, with an almost automatic gesture, in which my distress was visibly expressed, I put out my hand and took hers as it lay on the arm of the chair. "Emilia, tell me that."

She pulled her hand away awkwardly. "Please leave all that alone . . . in fact . . . please don't touch me, don't try to touch me again. I don't love you and it will never be possible for me to love you again."

I withdrew my hand and said in a resentful voice: "Don't let's talk about our love, never mind that . . . Let's talk instead about your . . . your contempt. Even if I refuse the job you'll go on despising me?"

Suddenly she jumped to her feet, as though seized by a violent impatience. "Yes, certainly I'll go on. And now let me alone."

"But why do you despise me?"

"Because I do," she cried all at once; "because you're made like that, and however hard you try, you can't change yourself."

"But how am I made?"

"I don't know how you're made—*you* ought to know. I only know you're not a man, you don't behave like a man."

I was struck by the contrast between the genuineness, the sincerity of feeling that sounded in her voice and the commonplace, sweeping nature of her words. "But what does it mean to be a *man?*" I demanded, with a rage in which irony was mingled; "don't you realize it means nothing at all?"

"Nonsense—you know perfectly well."

She had gone over to the window now, and her back was turned to me as she spoke. I clasped my head in my hands and gazed at her for a moment in despair. She had turned her back upon me not only physically but also, as it were, with the whole of her mind. She had no wish to explain herself, or perhaps, I suddenly thought, she was unable to do so. Clearly some reason for her contempt existed; but it was not so clear that she was able to indicate it precisely; and so she preferred to attribute her feeling of contempt to some original, innately despicable quality in me, a quality that was motiveless and therefore irremediable. All at once I remembered Rheingold's interpretation of the relationship between Ulysses and Penelope, and a sudden enlightenment made me wonder: "Supposing Emilia had had the impression that during these last months I knew Battista was paying court to her, that I was trying to take advantage of it, and, in fact, that instead of expostulating, I was sanctioning Battista's purposes for my own interest?" The impact of this idea left me breathless; even more so because I now recalled certain ambiguous episodes which might have confirmed her in such a suspicion; among others, my own lateness, the first evening we had gone out with Battista—due, in reality, to a taxi mishap, but which she might have attributed to a clever plan for leaving her alone with him. As if to corroborate my reflections, she suddenly said, without turning around: "A man who is really a man would not, for example, have behaved as you did yesterday evening, after seeing what you saw. But you came to me, as if butter would melt in your mouth, and asked me my opinion, pretending not to have seen anything, in the hope that I would advise you to go on with the script. And I gave you the advice you wanted and you accepted it. Then, today—goodness knows what happened with that German—you come and tell me you're giving up the job for my sake, because I despise you and you don't want me to despise you. But I know you by this time; and I can see that it's not you who've given up the job but he who made you give it up. Anyhow it's too late. I've made up my mind about you, and you can give up all the jobs in the world and I shan't change it. So don't make such a fuss about it now; accept the job and leave me in peace, once and for all."

So here we were, back at the beginning again, I could not help thinking: she despised me but refused to tell me the reason. It was deeply repugnant to me to try to formulate the reason myself, both because the reason itself would inevitably be repugnant to me, and also because, in formulating it, I should feel I was in some way accepting its validity. However I intended to get to the bottom of this question, and there was nothing else to be done. I said, as calmly as I could: "Emilia, you despise me and you won't tell me why . . . perhaps you don't even know, yourself. But I have a right to know, so that I can explain to you that it isn't true, and so that I can justify myself. Now listen: if *I* tell you the reason for your contempt, will you promise me that you'll tell me whether it's true or not?"

She was still standing in front of the window, with her back to me, and for a moment she said nothing. Then, in a tired, irritable voice, she said: "I don't promise anything . . . oh, do leave me alone!"

"The reason is this," I said very slowly, as though I were

spelling it out. "You have imagined, on a basis of deceptive appearances, that I . . . that I knew about Battista, and that, for my own interest, I preferred to close my eyes—that, in fact, I actually tried to push you into his arms . . . isn't that so?" '

I raised my eyes in her direction, as she stood with her back towards me, and awaited her answer. But no answer came; she was gazing at something on the other side of the window-panes, and she did not speak. All at once I felt myself blushing right up to the ears, in sudden shame at what I had said; and I saw that, as I had feared, the actual fact of my having said it could not but be interpreted by her as yet another proof of a valid foundation for her contempt. In desperation, I added hastily: "But if this is true, Emilia, I can swear to you that you're wrong. I never knew anything about Battista until yesterday evening. . . . Of course you're at liberty to believe me or not to believe me . . . but if you don't believe me, it means that you want to be able to despise me at all costs, that you want *not* to be convinced, that you want *not* to be able to justify myself."

Once again she did not speak; and I saw I had hit the mark. Perhaps she really did not know why she despised me, and in any case preferred not to know but to continue looking upon me as a contemptible figure—just like that, without reasons, without any references to my behavior, just as one might happen to have dark hair or blue eyes. I saw also that I had not achieved the effect I desired; but, I thought, innocence does not always succeed in being convincing. Urged on by an impulse beyond control, I felt the necessity of adding a physical argument to my words. I rose and went over to her—she was still standing by the window, looking out—and seized her by the arm, saying: "Emilia, why do you hate me so? . . . Why can't you take things for granted, even for a moment?"

I noticed that she turned her face aside, as if to hide it. But she allowed me to hold her arm; and, when I came close to her, so that my side was touching hers, she did not draw back. Then I grew bolder and put my arm around her waist. At last she turned, and I saw that her whole face was wet with tears. "I shall never forgive you," she cried; "never shall I forgive you for having ruined our love. I loved you so much, and I'd never loved anyone but you . . . and I shall never love anyone else . . . and you've ruined everything because of your character. . . . We might have been so happy together . . . and instead of that, it's all quite impossible now. How can I possibly take things for granted? How can I possibly not dislike you?"

A faint hope was born in me: after all, she was saying that she had loved me, that she had never loved anyone but me. "Now listen," I suggested, seeking to draw her to me, "you go and pack now, and we'll leave tomorrow morning . . . and when we get to Rome I'll explain everything to you . . . and you'll be convinced, I'm sure of that."

This time she freed herself, almost furiously, from my grasp. "I'm not going," she cried. "What's the point of my going back to Rome? I should have to leave the flat, and, since my mother doesn't want me, I should have to go and live in a furnished room and become a typist again. No, I'm not going . . . I'm staying here . . . I need quiet and rest, and I'm staying here . . . You go, if you want to. I'm staying here. Battista told me I could stay as long as I like . . . so I'm staying."

Now I became furious too. "You're going with me," I cried. "Tomorrow morning."

"You poor fool, you're quite wrong; I'm staying here."

"Then I shall stay here too . . . and I shall see to it that Battista turns us out of the house, both of us."

"No, you won't."

"Yes, I shall."

She looked at me for a moment; then, without saying a word, she left the room. The door of her bedroom banged violently; and then I heard the sound of the key being turned in the lock.

## CHAPTER 21

And so I found myself bound by a declaration made in a moment of anger: "I shall stay here." In truth, as I realized after Emilia had left the room, it was impossible for me to stay there any longer: the one person who had to leave was, in fact, myself. I had broken off relations with Rheingold, I had broken off relations with Battista, and now, in all probability, I had broken them off with Emilia too. I had become—to put it briefly—superfluous, and it was up to me to go. But I had cried to Emilia that I intended to stay, and, in my heart, whether as a last hope, or out of pique, I felt I wanted to stay. Such a situation in other circumstances would have been positively ridiculous, but in my desperate state of mind it was deeply distressing; it was like that of a mountaineer who, having reached a particularly dangerous point in his ascent, realizes that he can neither stay where he is, nor go backward nor forward. In a sudden access of anxiety and agitation, I started walking up and down the room, wondering what I ought to do. I knew that I could not sit down to dinner that evening with Emilia and Battista as though nothing had happened; I thought for a moment of going to dine in Capri village and not coming home till late; but I had already been four times that day over the path leading there from the house, each time at a run, each time under a burning sun, and I felt tired and had no desire to face it again. I looked at the clock: it was six. There were still at least two hours before dinner. What should I do? At last I made up my mind: I went to my own room and turned the key in the lock.

I closed the shutters and, in the dark, threw myself on the bed. I was truly tired, and, as soon as I lay down, I felt that my limbs were instinctively seeking the best positions for sleep. At that moment I was grateful to my body, which was wiser than my mind and gave, without effort, its own mute response to the painful question: "What shall I do?" After a few moments I fell into a deep sleep.

I slept for some time, dreamlessly; then I awoke and, from the complete darkness that surrounded me, judged that it must be very late. I got up from the bed, went over to the window and threw it open, and saw that night had indeed fallen. I turned on the light and looked at my watch: it was nine o'clock. I had been asleep for three hours. Dinner, I knew, was at eight, or at latest, half past eight. Again I was faced with the question: what should I do? But now I felt rested, and the question at once found its own confident, light-hearted answer: "I am in the villa, I have no reason to hide myself, I shall present myself at the dinner-table and let come what may." I even felt quite warlike and ready for a quarrel with Battista and, as I had threatened, prepared to act in such a way that he would turn Emilia and me out of the house. Quickly I tidied myself and left the room.

But the living-room was deserted, although the table was laid, in the usual corner. I noticed that it was laid for one person only. Almost immediately, to confirm my growing suspicions, the servant appeared in the doorway to tell me that Battista and Emilia had gone off to dine in the village. If I wished, I could join them at the Restaurant Bellavista. Otherwise I could dine at home; dinner, in fact, had been ready for half an hour.

I saw that Battista and Emilia had also put the question to themselves: what is to be done? And that they had solved the problem with the greatest ease, by going away and leaving me master of the field. This time, however, I felt neither jealousy nor annoyance nor disappointment. It seemed to me, on the contrary—and not without a feeling of sadness—that they had done the only thing they could do, and that I ought to be grateful to them for having avoided an unpleasant encounter. I realized also that this tactic of absence and emptiness was intended to make me go away; and that if they continued to make use of it on the ensuing days, they would undoubtedly succeed in their purpose. But that was a matter for the still uncertain future. I told the servant to serve me, that I would dine at home; and sat down at the table.

I ate little and unwillingly, tasting no more than one slice of ham out of the many that covered the dish, and a small piece of the big fish that Emilia had ordered for the three of us. My dinner was over in a few minutes. I told the servant to go to bed, as I should not need her again. And then I went out on to the terrace.

There were some deck chairs in a corner. I unfolded one and sat down beside the balustrade, facing the dark, invisible sea.

I had promised myself, on my way back to the villa after my meeting with Rheingold, that I would reflect calmly over everything after I had talked with Emilia. At that moment I had realized that I still knew nothing about the reasons for which she had ceased to love me; but it certainly did not enter my head that, even after I had had my explanation with her, I should continue to be ignorant of them. On the contrary, I was sure—albeit without reason—that the explanation would bring about a clarification which would in some way reduce and mitigate an issue in which, hitherto, I had seen only a frightening obscurity; so that, in the end, I should be forced to exclaim: "Is that all? . . . and is it for so unimportant a reason that you refuse to love me any more?"

But, instead of this, things had turned out exactly as I had not expected them to turn out: the explanation had taken place—or at least such explanation as was possible between us two—and I knew just as much as I had known before. Worse still, I had discovered that the reason for Emilia's contempt could quite possibly be established through an examination of our past relations, yet she herself was not disposed to recognize this and wished, in her heart, to go on despising me without a reason, thus depriving me of all possibility of exculpating and justifying myself, and shutting herself off, on her side, from any possible return to esteem and love of me.

I realized, in short, that in Emilia the feeling of contempt had preceded by a long way any justifications for it, either real or imaginary, that I might have provided by my behavior. The contempt had been born out of the daily proximity of our two characters, regardless of any important, recognizable test, in the same way as the purity of a precious metal is established by contact with the touchstone. And indeed, when I had hazarded the theory that her ceasing to love me might have had its origin in a mistaken estimate, on her part, of my demeanor towards Battista, she had neither accepted nor rejected it, but had taken refuge in silence. In reality, I thought suddenly, with a stab of pain, she had considered me, from the start, to be capable of this and of even more; and all she asked was that I, by my theories, should confirm her in her feeling. In other words, in Emilia's attitude towards me there was an appraisement of my worth, an estimate of my character, quite independent of my actions. The latter, it so happened, had appeared to confirm her appraisement and her estimate; but, even without such a confirmation, she would not, in all probability have judged me differently.

And indeed the proof, if there was any need of one, lay in the mysterious strangeness of her conduct. She could, from the very beginning, have dissipated the cruel misunderstanding upon which our love had been wrecked by talking to me, by telling me of it, by opening her heart to me. But she had not done this, because—as I had cried out to her a short time before—she did not really want to be undeceived, she wanted to go on despising me.

Up till now I had been lying in the deck chair. But, in the uncontrollable agitation which these thoughts caused in me, I rose almost automatically and went and stood by the parapet with my hands resting on it. I wanted, perhaps, to calm myself by contemplating the calmness of the night. But, as I held up my burning face to catch a faint puff of air that seemed to breathe from the surface of the sea, I thought suddenly that I did not deserve such relief. And I realized that a man who is despised neither can nor ought to find peace as long as the contempt endures. He may say, like the sinners at the Last Judgment: "Mountains, fall on us, and hills, cover us"; but contempt follows him even into the remotest hiding-place, for it has entered into his spirit and he bears it about with him wherever he may go.

I went back, then, and lay down again in the deck chair, and with a trembling hand lit a cigarette. It seemed to me, however, that, whether I was despicable or not—and I was convinced that I was not—I still retained my intelligence, a quality which even Emilia recognized in me and which was my whole pride and justification. I was bound to think, whatever the object of my thought might be; it was my duty to exercise my intelligence fearlessly in the presence of any kind of mystery. If I abandoned the exercise of my intelligence, there was indeed nothing left to me but the disheartening sense of my own supposed, but unproved, despicableness.

And so I started to think again, in a manner both determined and lucid. In what could it consist, this despicableness of mine? There returned to my mind now, inescapably, the words with which Rheingold, without realizing it, had described my position in relation to Emilia, thinking, instead, to describe that of Ulysses in relation to Penelope: "Ulysses is the civilized man, Penelope the primitive woman." Rheingold, in short, after having, by his strained interpretation of the *Odyssey*, unintentionally precipitated the supreme crisis in my relations with Emilia, then consoled me—rather in the manner of Achilles' spear which first wounded and then healed—by informing me, by means of the same interpretation, that I was not despicable but "civilized." I was aware that this consolation was valid enough, if only I was willing to accept it. I was, in effect, the civilized man who, in a primitive situation—a crime in which honor is concerned—refuses to resort to the knife; the civilized man who prefers to use reason even in face of things that are sacred and considered as such. But no sooner had I shaped it in my own mind than I realized that such an explanation—an "historical" explanation, let us call it—could never satisfy me. Apart from the fact that I was not at all sure that the relationship between Emilia and me really resembled the one the film-director had imagined in the case of Ulysses and Penelope, this explanation, valid, no doubt, in the historical field, was not so in the highly intimate and individual realm of conscience, which is outside time and space. Here it is only our own interior spirit that can dictate laws. History could not justify or absolve me in the sphere proper to itself, which, in the situation in which I found myself, whatever the "historical" reasons for it may have been, was not really the spheres in which I desired to operate and to live.

Why, then, had Emilia ceased to love me? Why did she despise me? And, above all, why did she feel the need to despise me? Suddenly there came back to me the phrase she had used: "Because you're not a man," which had struck me because of its sweeping, commonplace character in contrast with the genuine, frank tone in which it had been pronounced; and it seemed to me that that phrase perhaps contained the key to Emilia's attitude towards me. There was, in fact, in that phrase, a negative indication of Emilia's own ideal image of a man who—to use her own words—*was* a man: that is to say, of what, according to her, I was not and never could be. Yet on the other hand the phrase itself, so sweeping, so slovenly in character, suggested that this ideal image had not arisen in Emilia's mind from any conscious experience of human values, but rather from the conventions of the world in which she had found herself living. In that world, a man "who was a man" was, for instance, assuredly Battista, with his animal-like force and his gross successes. That this was true had been proved to me by the looks almost of admiration that she had directed towards him at table, the day before; and by her having finally surrendered to his desires, even if only out of desperation. In fact Emilia despised me and wished to despise me because, in spite of her genuineness and simplicity, or rather just because of them, she was completely ensnared in the commonplaces of Battista's world; and among these commonplaces was the supposed inability of the poor man to be independent of the rich man, or in other words, to "be a man." I did not know for certain whether Emilia really suspected me of having, out of self-interest, favored Battista's aims; but, if this was true, she must clearly have thought along these lines: "Riccardo depends on Battista, he is paid by Battista, he hopes to get more work from Battista; Battista is paying court to me, therefore Riccardo suggests that I should become Battista's mistress."

I was astonished at not having thought of this before. It was indeed strange that I myself, who had so clearly recognized, in Rheingold's and Battista's interpretations of the *Odyssey*, their two different ways of looking at life, should not have realized that Emilia, in constructing an image of me so different from the truth, had done, fundamentally, the same thing as the producer and the director. The only difference was that Rheingold and Battista had set out to interpret the two imaginary figures of Ulysses and Penelope; whereas Emilia had applied the despicable conventions by which she was dominated to two living creatures, herself and me. Thus, from a mixture of moral straightforwardness and unconscious vulgarity there had sprung, perhaps, the idea—not accepted by Emilia, it is true, but not contradicted by her either—that I had wished to push her into the arms of Battista.

In proof of all this, I said to myself, let us imagine for a moment that Emilia has to choose between the three different interpretations of the *Odyssey*—Rheingold's, Battista's, and mine. She is certainly capable of understanding the commercial motives for which Battista insists upon a spectacular *Odyssey;* she can even approve Rheingold's debasing psychological conception; but, with all her naturalness and straightforwardness, she is certainly quite incapable of achieving the level of my own interpretation, or rather, that of

Homer and Dante. She cannot do this, not only because she is ignorant but also because she does not live in an ideal world but rather in the perfectly real world of people like Battista and Rheingold. Thus the circle closed in. Emilia was at the same time the woman of my dreams and the woman who judged and despised me on the basis of a miserable common-place; Penelope, faithful to her absent husband for ten long years, and the typist, suspecting self-interest where there was none. And, in order to have the Emilia I loved and to bring it about that she judged me for what I was, I should have to carry her away from the world in which she lived and intro-duce her into a world as simple as herself, as genuine as her-self, a world in which money did not count and in which language had retained its integrity, a world—as Rheingold had pointed out to me—after which I could aspire, certainly, but which did not in fact exist.

In the meantime, however, I had to go on living, that is, moving and operating in that same world of Battista's and Rheingold's. What should I do? I felt that in the first place I ought to free myself from the painful sense of inferiority inspired in me by the absurd suspicion of my own innate and, so to speak, natural, despicableness. For, when all was said and done, this—as I have already mentioned—seemed to be the underlying idea in Emilia's attitude towards me, the idea of a baseness which was, so to speak, constitutional, and due not to behavior but to nature. Now I was convinced that no one could be said to be despicable in himself, irre-spective of all outward appearance and all relationship with others. But in order to free myself from my sense of inferi-ority I had also to convince Emilia of this.

I recalled the threefold image of Ulysses which the *Odys-sey* script had held out to me and in which I had discerned three possible modes of existence—Battista's image, Rhein-gold's, and finally my own, which I felt to be the only true one and which, in substance, was that of Homer. Why did Battista, Rheingold and I myself have three so very different conceptions of the figure of Ulysses? Precisely because our lives and our human ideals were different. Battista's image, superficial, vulgar, rhetorical and senseless, resembled the life and the ideals—or rather, the interests—of Battista; Rheingold's, more real, but diminished and degraded, was in accordance with the moral and artistic possibilities of Rhein-gold; and finally mine, without doubt the loftiest yet the most natural, the most poetical yet the most true, was de-rived from my aspiration, impotent perhaps but sincere, after a life that was not tainted and crippled by money or reduced to a purely physiological and material level. In a sense it was comforting to me that the image I preferred should be the best. I had to try to live up to this image, even if I had not been able to turn it to good account in the script, even if it was most improbable that I should be able to turn it to good account in life. Only in this way should I be able to convince Emilia of my reasons and so regain her esteem and her love. And how was I to accomplish this? I saw no other way than that of loving her still more, of proving to her once again, and every time it might be necessary, that my love was pure and disinterested.

I came to the conclusion, however, that for the moment it would not be a good plan to try to force Emilia. I would stay on until the next day and leave by the afternoon boat, without seeking to talk to her or to see her. Later, from Rome, I would write her a long letter, explaining all the many things I had not been able to clear up by word of mouth.

At this point in my thoughts I heard quiet voices coming, apparently, from the path below the terrace, and soon I recognized them as those of Emilia and Battista. Hurriedly I ran back into the house and went and shut myself in my room. But I was not sleepy; moreover it seemed to me it would be too painful for me to stay shut up in that stuffy room while those other two were talking and moving about the villa, all around me. Since I had been suffering from sleeplessness, especially during these last weeks, I had brought with me from Rome a very strong sleeping-medicine, very speedy in its effect. I took a double dose of it and threw myself down again—in real anger, this time—on the bed, fully dressed as I was. I must have fallen asleep almost at once, for I don't think I heard the voices of Battista and Emilia for more than a few minutes.

## CHAPTER 22

It was late when I awoke—judging, at least, by the rays of sunshine which penetrated into the room between the slats of the shutters—and for a moment I lay listening to the profound silence of the place, so different from silence in a town which, even when it is complete, seems always somehow to retain wounds and aches from sounds already past. Then, as I lay motionless on my back, I listened more carefully to this virgin silence, and suddenly it seemed to me that there was something lacking—not just one of those quiet sounds such as that of the electric pump drawing up water into the cistern in the morning or the servant sweeping the floor, which seem to stress the silence and make it more profound, but rather a presence. It was not a silence that was complete yet full of life, but a silence from which something vital had been withdrawn. A silence, I said to myself, finding the right word at last, a silence of abandonment. This word had barely crossed my mind before I had jumped from the bed and gone to the communicating door that led to Emilia's room. I opened it, and the first thing my eyes lit upon was a letter lying on the pillow at the head of the wide, dis-ordered, deserted bed.

It was brief. "Dear Riccardo, Seeing that you do not want to go away, I am going myself. Perhaps I might not have had the courage to go all alone: but I am taking advantage of Battista's departure. Also because I am afraid of being left alone, and Battista's company, after all, seems preferable to solitude. But in Rome I shall leave him and go and live on my own. However, if you hear that I have become Bat-tista's mistress, don't be surprised: I'm not made of iron, and it will mean that I haven't been able to manage it and couldn't stand it. Good-bye. Emilia."

After reading these lines, I sat down at the head of the bed with the letter in my hand and stared straight in front of me. I saw the wide-open window, and, beyond the win-dow-sill, a few pine-trees, and, behind the trunks of the pine-trees, the wall of rock. Then I removed my eyes from the window and looked all round the room: all was in dis-order, but it was an empty, blank disorder; no clothes, no shoes, no toilet articles, nothing but open, or half-open, empty drawers, gaping wardrobes with bare, dangling coat-hangers, vacant chairs. I had often thought recently that Emilia might leave me and I had thought of it as one thinks of some dreaded calamity; and now, here I was in the midst of such a calamity. I had a dull feeling of pain which seemed to start from the very depths of my being; just as an uprooted tree, if it felt pain, would feel it in the roots that held it upright in the ground. I had, in truth, been suddenly uprooted, and my roots, like those of the tree, were up in the air, and the sweet earth, Emilia, who had nourished them with her love, was far away from my roots, and those roots would never again be able to sink themselves in that love and feed upon it but would gradually dry up, and I felt that they were al-ready drying up and it made me suffer unspeakably.

Finally I rose and went back into my room. I felt stunned and distracted, like one who has had a bad fall from a height and who feels a dull pain and knows that this pain will soon burst forth into an acute spasm, and fears this moment but does not know when it will come about. Carefully watching this hidden pain as one watches a wild beast which one fears may leap upon one at any moment and tear one to pieces,

I automatically took my bathing costume, went out of the house, walked along the path that runs round the island and reached the village piazza. There I bought a newspaper, sat down in one of the cafés, and, almost to my own surprise, since it seemed to me that in my situation I would not have been able to think of anything except the situation itself, I read the whole newspaper through, from the first to the last line. In the same sort of way, I reflected, a fly whose head has been torn off by some cruel child seems, for a time, to feel no effect from the mutilation but walks about or cleans its feet until suddenly it collapses and dies. At last midday struck, and the clock in the companile filled the square with the din of its chimes. A bus was on the point of leaving for the Piccola Marina, and I got into it.

Shortly afterwards I was in the open, sun-filled space where, amid a sharp smell of urine, stood the little carriages with their horses, while their drivers sat together in a group, quietly chatting. I went off with a light step down the stairs leading to the beach-houses, and looked down from above upon the short stretch of white shingly beach and the sea lying blue beneath the tranquil sky. Utterly calm was the sea, smooth and glossy as satin right to the horizon, with great, diaphanous current-tracks winding idly over its surface in the dazzling sunlight. I thought it would be good to go out in a boat that afternoon; rowing would be a distraction, and then I should be completely alone, which, on the already frequented beach, would be impossible. When I reached the beach-houses, I called the attendant and asked him to get a boat ready for me. Then I went into one of the houses to undress.

When I came out, I walked barefoot along the little terrace in front of the houses, looking down and taking care not to hurt myself on the roughness of the warped, salt-worn planks. The June sun blazed overhead, enveloping me in its strong light, burning my back. It gave me a sensation of well-being which was in bitter contrast with my mental state of stunned suspense. My eyes still lowered, I went down the steep steps and walked towards the edge of the beach over the scorching stones. It was only when I was a short distance from the edge that I raised my eyes; and then I saw Emilia.

The attendant, a thin, vigorous old man, brown as leather, with a big straw hat pulled down over his eyes, was standing beside the boat which he had already pushed half into the water; Emilia was sitting in the stern, wearing a two-piece costume that I knew well, of a rather faded green. She was sitting with her legs pressed closely together, her arms stretched backwards to support herself, her bare, slender

waist slightly twisted in relation to her hips, in an attitude
that was insecure yet full of feminine grace. Aware of my surprise, she was smiling and looking straight into my eyes, as
much as to say: "I'm here . . . but don't say anything . . .
Pretend you knew I was here."

I obeyed this unspoken advice and, in silence, more dead
than alive, deeply troubled, my heart in a tumult, mechanically took the hand which the attendant held out to me and
jumped into the boat. The attendant came into the water up
to his knees, slipped the oars into the oarlocks and pushed
the boat off. I sat down, took hold of the oars and started
rowing with my head down, in the burning sun, towards
the promontory that enclosed the little bay. I rowed with
energy and in about ten minutes reached the promontory,
still in silence and still without looking at Emilia. I felt a
kind of restraint at the thought of talking to her as long as
the beach, with its huts and its bathers, was still in sight. I
wanted solitude around myself and her, as I had wanted it
in the villa, as I always wanted it when I wished to say certain things to her.

But, as I rowed, I became aware that, in a sudden overflowing of bitterness mingled with a new, strange joy, tears
had started flowing from my eyes. I rowed on and felt my
eyes burning with tears and my face burning each time one of
these tears detached itself from my eyes and slid down my
cheek. When I was opposite the end of the promontory, I
rowed more strongly so as to make headway against the
current, which at that point made the water rough and boisterous. On my right was a small black rock with a jagged
crest sticking up out of the water, on my left the high, rocky
wall of the promontory; I thrust the bow of the boat into
this passage, rowed vigorously through the swirling water and
thus passed the end of the point. The rock, where it plunged
into the sea, was white with salt, and each time the water
ebbed one could see green beards of seaweed, brilliant in the
sun, and here and there a red fruit like a sea tomato. Beyond the promontory appeared a huge amphitheater of fallen
rock, backed by the perpendicular mountain wall, and here
and there, between one mass of rock and the next, little
beaches of white shingle, completely deserted. The sea, too,
was deserted, with neither boats nor bathers; and the water,
in this inlet, was of a thick, oily blue that appeared to indicate great depth. Farther off, other promontories were
outlined one behind the other upon the flat, sun-filled sea,
like the wings of some fantastic natural theater.

I slowed down at last and lifted my face towards Emilia.
And as though she too had been waiting to speak until we

had rounded the promontory, she smiled at me and asked in a gentle voice: "Why are you crying?"

"I'm crying for joy at seeing you," I replied.

"You're glad to see me?"

"Very, very glad . . . I was sure you had gone away . . . but after all you haven't!"

She lowered her eyes and said: "I had made up my mind to go away . . . and I went down to the harbor this morning with Battista . . . Then at the last moment I thought better of it and stayed."

"And what have you been doing all this time?"

"I wandered about down by the harbor . . . I sat in a café . . . Then I went up to the village in the funicular and telephoned to the villa . . . I was told you had gone out . . . Then I thought perhaps you'd gone to the Piccola Marina, so I came here . . . I undressed and waited for you . . . I saw you asking the attendant to get you a boat . . . I was lying in the sun and you passed quite close to me without seeing me . . . Then, while you were undressing, I got into the boat."

For some moments I said nothing. We were now halfway between the promontory we had passed and another point which enclosed the inlet. Beyond that point, I knew, was the Green Grotto, in which, in the first place, it had been my intention to bathe. Finally I asked, in a low voice: "Why didn't you go away with Battista, as you had decided? Why did you stay?"

"Because this morning, on thinking it over, I saw I had been mistaken about you . . . and that the whole thing had been a misunderstanding."

"What was it made you see that?"

"I don't quite know . . . lots of things . . . chiefly, perhaps, the tone of your voice, yesterday evening."

"And are you really convinced now that I've never done all those dreadful things you accused me of?"

"Yes, I *am* convinced."

There still, however, remained one thing that I had to know, perhaps the most important of all. "But you," I said, "you don't think I'm a despicable person do you? . . . even though I haven't done those things . . . despicable because made of despicable stuff . . . Tell me, you don't believe that, Emilia?"

"I've never believed it . . . I thought you'd behave in a certain way, and that's why you lost my esteem . . . But now I know that it's all been a misunderstanding . . . Let's not talk about it any more, if you don't mind."

This time I said nothing, and she was silent too, and I started rowing with greater energy, with an energy that was now redoubled, it seemed to me, by a feeling of joy which gradually, like a rising sun, grew and mounted within me, warming my spirit which till then had been aching and numb. Meanwhile we had reached a point opposite the Green Grotto, and I steered the boat towards the cave, already visible, and appearing to hang, dark and crooked, above an expanse of cold green water. "And you do love me?" I went on.

She hesitated and then answered: "I've always loved you . . . I always shall love you"; but she said it with a kind of sadness that surprised me. "Why," I insisted in alarm, "why do you say that in such a sad way?"

"I don't know . . . perhaps because it would have been better if no misunderstanding had ever come between us and we had always loved one another as we did in the past."

"Yes," I said, "but all that's over now . . . We mustn't think about it any more . . . Now we're going to love each other forever." She appeared to nod her head, but without raising her eyes, and still rather sadly. I stopped rowing for a moment, and, leaning forward, added "We'll go to the Red Grotto now . . . It's a smaller cave and very deep, beyond the Green Grotto . . . There's a little beach at the end of it, in the dark . . . We'll make love there, shall we, Emilia?"

I saw her lift her head and nod her assent, in silence, gazing fixedly at me, with a look of discreet, and even rather bashful, complicity. I started rowing again energetically. We entered the grotto, beneath the great vault of rugged rock upon whose surface water and sunlight threw gay reflections, casting upon it a close net of quivering emerald. Farther on, at the place where the sea penetrated only at intervals, making the vault resound with hollow reverberations, the water was dark, with a few smooth, black rocks emerging from it like the backs of amphibious beasts. Here was the tortuous opening, a narrow passage between two rocks, that led through to the Red Grotto. Emilia was sitting quite still now, looking at me and following each one of my movements with her eyes, in an attitude of sensual but patient docility, like a woman who is ready to give herself and is only awaiting the signal. By thrusting, first with one oar then with other, against the walls of the channel, beneath the stalactite-hung vault, I brought the boat through into the open and then steered it towards the dark mouth of the Red Grotto. "Look out for your head," I said to Emilia; and then, with one stroke of the oars, I propelled the boat over the smooth water into the cave.

The Red Grotto is divided into two parts. The first, like an entrance hall, is separated from the second by a lowering of the vault overhead; beyond this point the cave bends sharply and runs a considerable distance back to the beach at its farthest end. This second part is plunged in almost complete darkness, and one's eyes have to become accustomed to the gloom before one can discern the little subterranean beach, which is strangely colored by the reddish light that gives its name to the grotto. "It's very dark inside the cave," I went on to say, "but we'll be able to see as soon as our eyes get used to it." In the meantime, carried along by the force of my initial stroke, the boat slid along in the darkness, under the low vault of rock; and I saw nothing more. At last I heard the bow strike the beach, thrusting into the gravel with a moist, resonant sound. Then I let go of the oars and, half rising, put out by hand towards the point in the darkness where the stern of the boat should be, saying: "Give me your hand and I'll help you to get out."

No answer came to me. I repeated, in surprise: "Give me your hand, Emilia!" and for the second time leaned forward, holding out my hand. Then, since there was again no reply, I leaned still farther forward and, cautiously, so as not to strike the face of Emilia, I felt about for her in the darkness. But my hand met nothing but empty air, and when I lowered it I felt beneath my fingers, at the spot where they should have encountered Emilia's seated figure, nothing but the smooth wood of the empty seat. My astonishment was mingled with a feeling of terror. "Emilia!" I cried, "Emilia!" The only answer was a thin, icy echo. In the meantime my eyes had become accustomed to the darkness and could at last distinguish, in the thick gloom, the boat with its bow lying on the beach, the beach itself, of fine, black gravel, and the glimmering, dripping vault curving over my head. And then I saw that the boat was completely empty, with no one sitting in the stern, and that the beach was empty too, and that all round me there was no one, and that I was alone.

Looking towards the stern, I said, in astonishment: "Emila!" but this time it was in a low voice. And I repeated again: "Emilia, where are you?"—and at that same moment I understood. Then I got out of the boat and threw myself down on the beach and buried my face in the moist pebbles and I think I fainted, for I remained motionless, almost without feeling, for a time that seemed endless.

Later I rose to my feet, automatically got into the boat again and pushed it out of the cave. At the mouth of the grotto the strong sunlight, reflected off the sea, smote me. I looked at the watch on my wrist and saw that it was two

o'clock in the afternoon. I had been in the cave for more than
an hour. And I remembered that noon was the hour for
ghosts; and I realized that I had been talking and weeping
in the presence of a ghost!

## CHAPTER 23

My return to the beach-houses was slow; every now
and then I stopped rowing and sat still, resting on my oars, my
eyes fixed dreamily upon the blue, shining surface of the sea.
It was clear that I had had a hallucination, of the same kind
as I had had two days before, when Emilia was lying naked
in the sun and I had imagined that I had bent over her and
kissed her, whereas in reality I had not moved nor gone near
her. This time the hallucination had been far more precise
and articulate; but that it was in truth a hallucination and
nothing more no further proof was needed than the conversation I had imagined myself to have had with Emilia's ghost
—a conversation during which I had made Emilia say all the
things I wanted her to say, and assume exactly the attitudes
I wished her to assume. Everything had begun and ended
with myself; the only difference from what usually happens
in such circumstances being that I had not confined myself
to a wishful imagining of what I wanted to happen, but,
from the sheer force of feeling that filled my heart, had
deluded myself into thinking it really had happened. Strange
to say, however, I was not in the least surprised at having
had a hallucination of a kind that was not merely uncommon
but perhaps unique. As though the hallucination were still
continuing, I turned my attention, not so much to the question of its actual possibility, as to its details, reconstructing
them one by one, dwelling with an almost sensual pleasure
upon those which gave me most pleasure and comfort. How
beautiful Emilia had been, sitting in the stern of my boat, no
longer hostile but full of love; how sweet her words; how
disturbing, how violent the feeling I had experienced when
I told her I wanted to make love to her and she had answered me with that faint nod of agreement! Like one who
has had a voluptuous and very vivid dream and who, on
awakening, lingers with relish over all its aspects and sensations, I was, in reality, still caught up in my hallucinations,
believing in it and joyfully reliving it in my memory; and
little did it matter to me that it was a hallucination, seeing
that I was experiencing all the feelings with which one
usually remembers a thing that has really happened.

As I dwelt with inexhaustible pleasure upon the details of
my vision, it suddenly occurred to me to compare once again

the time at which I had left the Piccola Marina in the boat
with the time at which I had come out of the Red Grotto,
and I was again struck with the great length of time that I
must have spent at the far end of the cave, on the little subterranean beach: allowing three quarters of an hour for the
journey from the Piccola Marina to the Grotto, it must have
been more than an hour. As I have already said, I had attributed this length of time to a fainting fit, or at any rate
to some kind of collapse or unconsciousness very like a fainting fit. But now, on re-examining my hallucinations, which
had been so complete and at the same time had corresponded
so obligingly with my most profound desires, I wondered
whether I had not quite simply dreamed the whole thing.
Whether, that is to say, I had not embarked from the bath-
ing-beach alone and without any ghost on board, and whether
I had not penetrated, still alone, into the grotto, and finally
lain down on the little beach and gone to sleep. During my
sleep—if this were so—I had dreamed that I had started
off in the boat with Emilia sitting in the stern, that I had
talked to her and she had answered me, that I had suggested
making love, that we had gone together into the cave. And
then I had also dreamed that I had put out my hand to help
her out of the boat, that I had failed to find her, that I had
been frightened, that I had thought I must have had a ghost
with me on my boat excursion, and that I had finally thrown
myself down on the beach and fainted.

This supposition now seemed to me to be probably true;
but not more than probably. Now that it had been obscured,
sidetracked and confused by my subsequent fancies, it
seemed to me almost impossible to search out the dividing
line between dream and actual reality, a dividing line that
must be located in that moment when I lay down on the
beach. What had really happened at the precise moment
when I lay down on the little beach at the far end of the
cave? Had I fallen asleep and dreamed that I had been with
Emilia, the real Emilia of flesh and blood? Or had I fallen
asleep and dreamed that I had been visited by Emilia's
ghost? Or again, had I fallen asleep and dreamed that I was
asleep and dreaming one or the other of the aforesaid dreams?
Like those Chinese boxes each one of which contains a smaller
one, reality seemed to contain a dream which in its turn
contained a reality which in its turn contained yet another
dream, and so on *ad infinitum*. Thus, again and again, pausing and resting on my oars out at sea, I wondered if I had
dreamed or had had a hallucination, or—more singularly
—if a ghost had indeed appeared to me; and in the end
I came to the conclusion that it was not possible for me to

find out, and that, in all probability, I should never find out.

I rowed on and came at last to the beach-house. I dressed in great haste, went up again to the road, and was in time to board a bus which was on the point of leaving for the piazza. I was in a great hurry now to be home again: somehow, for a reason I could not explain, I felt convinced that when I reached the villa I should perhaps find the key to all these mysteries. I was in a hurry to get there also because I had still to have lunch and pack my bag and then catch the six o'clock boat; and I had wasted time. I left the piazza at once, almost at a run, by the usual path; in twenty minutes' time I was at the villa.

I had no time, as I entered the deserted living-room, to succumb to the sadness of desolation and loneliness. On the already laid table, beside the plate, was a telegram. Unsuspecting but vaguely troubled, I took the yellow envelope and opened it. Battista's name surprised me and, for some reason, seemed to give me a hope of favorable news. But then I read the text: it announced to me, in a few words, that, as the result of a serious accident, Emilia was "dangerously ill."

I realize, at this point, that I have almost nothing more to say. It is useless to describe how I left that same afternoon, how, when I reached Naples, I learned that in reality Emilia had been killed in a motor accident a short distance south of Terracina. Her death had been a strange one. Owing to fatigue and the great heat, she had apparently fallen asleep, with her head down and her chin resting on her chest. Battista, as usual, was driving extremely fast. Suddenly an ox-drawn cart had come out of a side road. Battista had jammed on the brakes; and, after an exchange of abuse with the driver of the cart, had driven on. But Emilia's head was swaying from one side to another, and she had not spoken. Battista had spoken to her, but she had not answered; and, at a bend in the road, she had fallen on top of him. He had stopped the car, and had then discovered that she was dead. The sudden jamming on of the brakes to avoid the cart had caught her body in a moment of complete abandonment, with all the muscles relaxed, as indeed happens during sleep; and the jolt of the suddenly stopped car had caused an abrupt jerk of the neck, fracturing the spinal column outright. She had died without knowing it.

It was extremely hot—a wearisome thing for sorrow, which demands, like joy, that there should be no rivalry in any other feeling. The funeral took place on a day of unrelieved sultriness, beneath a cloudy sky, the air damp and windless. After the funeral, in the evening, I closed the door behind me as I entered our apartment—for ever useless and empty, now—and I understood at last that Emilia, truly, was dead, and that I should never see her again. All the windows in the flat had been opened wide in the hope of increasing even the faintest breath of air, but I felt I was suffocating as I wandered from one room to another, over the polished floors, in the twilight gloom. Meanwhile the brightly lit windows of the adjoining houses, their inhabitants visible inside the rooms, drove me almost to frenzy, their quiet lights reminding me of a world in which people loved without misunderstandings and were loved in return and lived peaceful lives —a world from which it seemed to me that I was for ever shut out. The re-entry into such a world would have meant. for me, an explanation with Emilia, her conviction of my innocence, the creation once again of the miracle of love which, in order to exist, must be kindled not only in our own hearts but in those of others as well. But this was no longer possible, and I felt I should go mad when I thought that perhaps I ought to recognize, in Emilia's death, a last, supreme act of hostility on her part against myself.

But I had to go on living. Next day I took up the suitcase which I had not yet opened, locked the door of the flat with the sensation of closing a grave, and handed the keys to the porter, explaining that I intended to get rid of the apartment as soon as I returned from my holiday. Then I started off again for Capri. Strange to say, I was driven to return there by the hope that, somehow or other, in the same place where she had appeared to me, or elsewhere, Emilia would again show herself to me. And then I would again explain to her why everything had happened, and I would again declare my love, and would again receive her assurance that she understood me and loved me. This hope had a quality of madness about it, and I was aware of this. Never, indeed, was I so near to a kind of reasoned insanity as I was at that time, balanced precariously between a loathing for reality and a longing for hallucination.

Emilia, fortunately, did not reappear to me, either when sleeping or waking. And when I compared the time at which she had appeared with the time at which she had died, I discovered that they did not correspond. Emilia had been still alive at the moment when I thought I had seen her sitting in the stern of the boat; but she was, in all probability, already dead during the time of my unconsciousness on the little beach at the far end of the Red Grotto. So, in death as in life, there was no true conformity. And I should never know whether she had been a ghost or a hallucination, or a dream, or perhaps some other illusion. The ambiguity which had poisoned our relationship in life continued even after her death.

Driven on by longing for her and for places where I had last seen her, I made my way one day to the beach below the villa, where I had come upon her lying naked and had had the illusion that I had kissed her. The beach was deserted; and as I came out through the masses of fallen rock with my eyes raised towards the smiling, blue expanse of the sea, the thought of the *Odyssey* came back into my mind, and of Ulysses and Penelope, and I said to myself that Emilia was now, like Ulysses and Penelope, in those great sea spaces, and was fixed for eternity in the shape in which she had been clothed in life. It depended upon myself, not upon any dream or hallucination to find her again and to continue our earthly conversation with renewed serenity. Only in that way would she be delivered from me, would she be set free from my feelings, would she bend down over me like an image of consolation and beauty. And I decided to write down these memories, in the hope of succeeding in my intention.